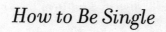

How to Be Single

Also by Liz Tuccillo

He's Just Not That Into You
(cowritten with Greg Behrendt)

How to Be
Single

A NOVEL

Liz Tuccillo

ATRIA BOOKS

New York London Toronto Sydney

ATRIA BOOKS

A Division of Simon & Schuster, Inc.
1230 Avenue of the Americas
New York, NY 10020

First Atria Books hardcover edition June 2008

ATRIA BOOKS and colophon are trademarks of Simon & Schuster, Inc.

For information about special discounts for bulk purchases, please contact Simon & Schuster Special Sales at 1-800-456-6798 or business@simonandschuster.com.

Designed by Jaime Putorti

Manufactured in the United States of America

10   9   8   7   6   5   4   3   2   1

Library of Congress Cataloging-in-Publication Data

Tuccillo, Liz.
  How to be single : a novel / by Liz Tuccillo. -- 1st Atria Books hardcover ed.
      p. cm.
1. Single women—Fiction. 2. Dating (Social customs—Fiction.
3. Self-actualization (Psychology)—Fiction. 4. Chick lit. I. Title.
  PS3620.U284H69 2008
  813'.6—dc22   2008010368

ISBN-13: 978-1-4165-3412-9
ISBN-10:   1-4165-3412-1

*This book is dedicated, as is everything I do,
to my mother, Shirley Tuccillo*

How to Be Single

It's the most annoying question and they just can't help asking you. You'll be asked it at family gatherings, particularly weddings. Men will ask you it on first dates. Therapists will ask you over and over again. And you'll ask yourself it far too often. It's the question that has no good answer, and that never makes anyone feel better. It's the question, that when people stop asking it, makes you feel even worse.

And yet, I can't help but ask. Why are you single? *You seem like an awfully nice person. And very attractive.* I just don't understand it.

But times are changing. In almost every country around the world, the trend is for people to remain single longer and to divorce more easily. As more and more women become economically independent, their need for personal freedom increases, and that often results in not marrying so quickly.

A human being's desire to mate, to pair up, to be part of a couple, will never change. But the way we go about it, how badly we need it, what we are willing to sacrifice for it, most definitely is.

So maybe the question isn't anymore, "Why are you single?" Maybe the question you should be asking yourself is "How are you single?" It's a big new world out there and the rules keep changing.

So, tell me ladies, how's it going?

—Julie Jenson

RULE

1

Make Sure You Have Friends

How Georgia Is Single

"I JUST WANT TO HAVE FUN! NOW THAT I'M SINGLE I JUST WANT TO HAVE FUN! YOU SINGLE PEOPLE ARE ALWAYS HAVING FUN!! *WHEN ARE WE GOING TO GO OUT AND HAVE FUN?!!!*"

She is screaming, *screaming* at me on the phone. "I WANT TO KILL MYSELF, JULIE. I DON'T WANT TO LIVE WITH THIS MUCH PAIN. REALLY. I WANT TO DIE. YOU HAVE TO MAKE ME FEEL LIKE EVERYTHING IS GOING TO BE OKAY! YOU HAVE TO TAKE ME OUT AND REMIND ME THAT I'M YOUNG AND ALIVE AND CAN HAVE LOTS AND LOTS OF FUN! OR GOD KNOWS WHAT I MIGHT DO!!!" Dale, Georgia's husband, had left her for another woman two weeks ago and she was obviously a tad upset.

The call came at 8:45 in the morning. I was at the Starbucks on Forty-fourth and Eighth, balancing a cardboard tray of coffees in one hand, my cell phone and this conversation in the other, my hair in my face, grande mochaccinos tilting toward my left breast, all while paying the nice young twentysomething at the cash register. I'm a multitasker.

I had already been up for four hours. As a publicist for a large New York publishing house, part of my job is to cart our writers around from interview to interview as they promote their books. On this morning I was responsible for thirty-one-year-old writer Jennifer Baldwin. Her book, *How to Keep Your Husband Attracted to You During Pregnancy*, became an instant bestseller. Women all around the country couldn't buy the book fast enough. Because, of course, how to keep your husband attracted to you during your pregnancy should be the main concern for a woman during that very special time in her life. So this week we were making the prestigious morning show rounds. *Today, The View, Regis and Kelly.* WPIX, NBC, and CNN, so far that day, ate it up. How could you not love a segment showing eight-months-pregnant women how to strip for their men? Now the author, her personal publicist, her literary agent, and the agent's assistant were all anxiously waiting for me in the Town Car that was parked outside. I held the lifeline to their caffeine fix.

"Do you really feel like you want to kill yourself, Georgia? Because if you do, I'll call 911 right now and get an ambulance over there." I'd read somewhere that you should take all suicide talk seriously, even though I think all she was really doing was making sure I would take her out drinking.

"FORGET THE AMBULANCE, JULIE, YOU'RE THE ORGANIZER, THE ONE WHO MAKES THINGS HAPPEN—CALL THOSE SINGLE FRIENDS OF YOURS, THE ONES YOU ARE ALWAYS HAVING FUN WITH—AND LET'S GO OUT AND HAVE FUN!"

As I continued my balancing act toward the car, I thought about how tired that thought made me. But I knew Georgia was going through a difficult period and it would probably get much worse before it got better.

It's a tale as old as time. Dale and Georgia had kids, stopped having regular sex, and began fighting. They became distant, and then Dale told Georgia he was in love with a twenty-seven-year-old *whore gutter trash* samba teacher, that he met at Equinox. Call me crazy, but I'm thinking hot sex might have had something to do with this. Also, and I don't want to be disloyal, and I would never even *suggest* Georgia was at fault *in any way* because *Dale is an asshole,* and *we hate him now,* but I can't resist saying, Georgia completely took Dale for granted.

Now, to be fair, I am particularly judgmental about the Married

Women Who Take Their Husbands for Granted Syndrome. When I see a very wet man hold an umbrella out to his wife after he has just walked five blocks to pick up the car and drive it back to the restaurant and she doesn't even say thank you, honestly, it makes me very cranky. So I noticed that Georgia took Dale for granted, particularly when she would talk to him in *that tone*. The tone that you can dress up and call what you want, but the truth is it's plain old-fashioned contempt. The tone is disgust. The tone is impatience. The tone is a vocal eye roll. It is the undeniable proof that marriage is a horribly flawed institution let out in a single "I told you, the popcorn popper is on the shelf *over the refrigerator*." If you were able to fly around the world, collecting the tone as it is let out of all the disgruntled married men's and women's mouths, cart it back to some desert in Nevada, and release it—the earth would literally sink into itself, imploding in sheer global irritation.

Georgia talked to Dale in that tone. And of course that wasn't the only reason for their split. People are irritating and that's what marriage is: good days and bad days. And, really, what do I know? I'm thirty-eight years old and I have been single for six years. (Yes, I said six.) Not celibate, not out of commission, but definitely, fully, officially, here-goes-another-holiday-season-alone single. So in my imaginings, I would always treat my man right. I would never speak harshly to him. I would always let him know that he was desired and respected and my number one priority. And I would always look hot and I'd always be sweet, and if he asked, I would grow a long fishtail and gills and swim with him in the ocean topless.

So now Georgia has gone from semicontented wife and mother to a somewhat suicidal single mother with two children. And she wants to *party*.

Something must happen when you become single again. A self-preservation instinct must kick in that resembles having a complete lobotomy. Because Georgia suddenly has traveled back in time to when she was twenty-eight and now just wants to go out "to some bars, you know, to meet guys," forgetting that we are actually in our late thirties and some of us have been doing that without a break for years now. And frankly, I don't want to go out and meet guys. I don't want to spend an hour using one of the many hot appliances I own to straighten my hair so I can feel

gh to go out drinking. I want to go to bed early so I can
I can make my smoothie and go out and run in the morn-
rathoner. Not in the literal sense; I run only three miles a
ingle person. I know how to pace myself. I am aware of
how long a run it can be. Georgia, of course, wants to line up the babysitters and start sprinting.

"IT'S YOUR OBLIGATION TO HAVE FUN WITH ME! I DON'T KNOW ANY OTHER SINGLE PERSON EXCEPT YOU! YOU HAVE TO GO OUT WITH ME. I WANT TO GO OUT WITH YOUR SINGLE FRIENDS! YOU GUYS ARE ALWAYS GOING OUT!! NOW THAT I'M SINGLE, I WANT TO GO OUT TOO!!!"

She is also forgetting that she is the same woman who would always look at me with such pity when I would talk about my single life and exclaim in one breath "OhmyGodthat'ssosadIwanttodie."

But Georgia would do something that all my other happily married or coupled friends would never even think of doing: she would pick up the phone and organize a dinner party and scrounge up some single men for me to meet. Or she'd go to her pediatrician and ask if he knew any eligible bachelors. She was actively involved in my search for the Good Man, no matter how comfortable and self-satisfied she might have felt herself. And that is a rare and beautiful quality. And that is why on that Friday morning, as I was mopping up coffee from my white shirt, I agreed to call up three of my other single friends and see if they would go out and party with my newly single, slightly hysterical friend.

How Alice Is Single

Georgia is right. We're having so much fun, my single friends and I. Really. Oh my God, being single is hilarious. For instance, let me tell you about the sidesplitting uproariousness that is Alice. For a living, she gets incredibly underpaid to defend the rights of the impoverished people of New York City—against callous judges, ruthless prosecutors, and an overburdened system in general. She has dedicated herself to trying to help the underdog by bucking the system, beating the man, and guarding our Constitution. Oh yeah, and every once in a while she has to defend a rapist or murderer that she knows is guilty and whom she often succeeds in putting back onto the streets. Oops. You win some, you . . . win some.

Alice is a Legal Aid attorney. While the Constitution guarantees the right to a lawyer, it unfortunately can't promise that you'll be defended by Alice. First of all, she is gorgeous. Which, of course, is superficial, who cares. Because those jurors sitting in that drab industrial green jury room with the fluorescent lighting, and that eighty-year-old judge presiding over the general misery of it all, well, they'll take whatever aesthetic pleasure they can find. And when redheaded, sexy Alice talks to you with her deep, soothing voice and her thick, I'm-one-of-the-people-but-much-more-adorable Staten Island–Italian accent, you would drive into Sing Sing and break out every last prisoner, if that's what she asked of you.

She was so startling in her legal acumen and plain old-fashioned charisma that she became the youngest law professor at NYU. By day Alice was saving the world, and by night she was inspiring yuppie born-and-bred law students to forget their dreams of nice Manhattan co-ops and Hampton summer shares to go into Legal Aid law and do something important. She was outrageously successful. She made insubordination and compassion cool again. She got them to actually believe that helping people was more important than making money.

She was a Goddess.

Yeah. I say *was*, because I'm kind of lying. The truth hurts too much. Alice is no longer a Legal Aid attorney.

"Okay, this is the *only* time I believe in the death penalty." Alice, being a fantastic friend, was helping me transport books from my office on Fiftieth Street and Eighth Avenue to a book signing on Seventeenth Street. (The book was *The Idiot's Guide to Being an Idiot* and was, of course, a big hit.)

"The only exception to the rule is any man who goes out with a thirty-three-year-old woman until she's thirty-eight and then discovers he has commitment issues; who gives that woman the impression that he has no problem with marriage and being with her for the rest of her life; who keeps telling her it's going to happen, until finally, one day he tells her that he doesn't think 'marriage is really for him.'" Alice put her fingers in her mouth and let out a whistle that could stop traffic. A cab veered over to pick us up.

"Pop the trunk, please," Alice said, forcefully grabbing a box of the *Idiot* books from my arms and throwing them in the trunk.

"That was shitty," I conceded.

"It was more than shitty. It was criminal. It was a crime against my ovaries. It was a felony against my biological time clock. He stole five of my precious childbearing years from me and that should be considered grand larceny of motherhood and be punishable by hanging." She was ripping each box out of my hands and hurling them now. I thought it best to let her finish this on her own. When she was done, we walked to opposite sides of the cab to get in and she continued talking to me over the cab roof without taking a breath.

"I'm not going to take this lying down. I'm a powerful woman, I'm in control. I can make up for lost time, I can."

"What do you mean?" I asked.

"I'm going to quit my job and start dating." Alice got into her side of the cab and slammed the door.

Confused, I sank into the cab. "I'm sorry, what?"

"Union Square Barnes and Noble," Alice barked to the cabdriver. Then to me, "That's right. I'm going to sign up for every online service, I'm going to send out a mass email to all my friends to set me up with any single guys they know. I'm going to go out every night and I'm going to meet someone fast."

"You're quitting your job *to date*?" I tried to say this with the least amount of horror and judgment in my voice.

"Exactly." She kept nodding her head vigorously, as if I knew just what she was talking about. "I'll keep teaching, I have to make some money. But basically, yeah, it's my new job. You heard me."

So now my dear do-gooder Superwoman, Xena the Warrior Princess, Erin Brockovich, friend Alice, is still spending all her time and energy trying to help the underdog. But this time the underdog is herself: a thirty-eight-year-old single woman in New York City. She's still trying to stick it to "the man." But this time the man is Trevor, who took up all that precious time of hers and has now made her feel old, unlovable, and frightened.

And when Alice is asked what she does with all her newly free time that she once used to help keep young, first-time offenders away from Rikers and imminent horrifying physical abuse, she often goes into this little speech: "Besides the Internet, and the fix-ups, I just make sure I go to everything I get invited to, every conference or luncheon or dinner party. No matter how shitty I feel. Remember when I had that really bad flu? I got out of the house and went to a singles night at New York Theatre Workshop. The night after my hand surgery I took some Percocet and went to that huge benefit for the Central Park Conservancy. You never know what night it will be when you meet the man who's going to change your life. But then I also have hobbies. I purposely do what I love to do, because you know, when you least expect it, that could be when you meet someone."

"When you least expect it?" I asked, during one of Alice's diatribes. "Alice, you have decided to quit your job to dedicate your life to meeting someone. How can you ever, *ever* least expect it?"

"By staying busy. By doing interesting things. I kayak in the Hudson, rock climb at Chelsea Piers, take carpentry classes at Home Depot, which you should totally do with me, by the way, I made an amazing cabinet, and I'm also thinking about taking this sailing course at the South Street Seaport. I'm keeping busy doing things I find interesting, so that I can trick myself into forgetting that I'm really just trying to look for guys. Because you can't look desperate. That's the *worst*."

As she is telling people this, she often comes across as a little deranged, particularly because she's usually chain-popping Tums as she says all this. Her indigestion problems stem, I believe, from a little acid reflux condition called "I'm terrified of being alone."

So, of course, who else would I call first when I needed to go out with a bunch of girlfriends and "have fun" than Alice, who is basically a professional at it now. She now knows all the bartenders, doormen, maître d's, bars, clubs, out-of-the-way places, tourist hangouts, dives, and happening scenes in New York City. And naturally, Alice was ready to go.

"I'm on it," she said. "Don't you worry. We'll make sure tomorrow night, Georgia has the best time of her life."

I hung up the phone, relieved. I knew I could count on Alice, because no matter how Alice's life might have changed, she still loved a good cause.

How Serena Is Single

"It's too smoky, no way."

"You don't even know where we're going."

"I know, but it's going to be too smoky. Every place is too smoky."

"Serena, there's a smoking ban in New York; you can't smoke in bars."

"I know, but it still seems too smoky. And it's always too loud at these places."

We are sitting at the Zen Palate—the only place I have ever met Serena at in the past three years. Serena doesn't like to go out. Serena also doesn't like to eat cheese, gluten, nightshade vegetables, nonorganic vegetables, and pineapple. None of it agrees with her blood type. If you haven't guessed, Serena is very, very thin. She is one of those very pretty, waiflike blond girls you see in yoga classes in every major city across America. She is a vegetarian chef for a New York celebrity family, about whom I'm not allowed to speak due to a confidentiality agreement Serena made me sign so that she wouldn't feel guilty about breaking the confidentiality agreement *she* signed with her employer when she gossiped to me about them. Really. But let's just say for the purposes here, that their names are Robert and Joanna, and their son's name is Kip. And to be honest, Serena doesn't say anything bad about them at all; they treat her really well and seem to appreciate her gentle spirit. But by God, when Madonna comes over for lunch and makes a dig about Serena's cooking, Serena has to be able to tell someone. She's only human.

Serena is also a student of Hinduism. She believes in equanimity in all things. She wants to see divine perfection in all of life, even the fact that she literally hasn't had a date or sex in four years. She sees this as perfection, the world showing her that she needs to work on herself more. For how can you really be a true partner to someone until you are a fully realized human being yourself?

So Serena has worked on herself. She has worked on herself to such an extent that she has actually become a human maze. I pity the man who ever attempts to enter the winding corridors and dead-end tunnels that are her dietary restrictions, meditation schedule, new age workshops, yoga classes, vitamin regimes, and distilled water needs. If she works on herself any more, she will become a shut-in.

Serena is that friend you always see alone; the one whom no one else knows. The one who, if you ever mention her in passing, prompts your other friends to say, "Serena? You have a friend named Serena?" But things weren't always like this. I met Serena in college and she used to be just like everyone else. She was always a tad obsessive-compulsive, but back then it was a quirk and not a lifestyle choice. All through her twenties she would meet guys and go out. And she had a long-term boyfriend for three years as well. Clyde. He was really sweet and was crazy about her, but Serena always knew he wasn't the one. She sort of settled into a nice routine with him—and if you haven't guessed, Serena does enjoy her routines. So we encouraged her not to lead him along—never dreaming that he might be the last real relationship for the rest of her wheat-free life. And after Clyde she still managed to date—not aggressively so, but whenever something came up. But around thirty-five, when she never found anyone who truly interested her, she started focusing on other aspects of her life. Which, to be fair, is what many of the self-help books that I help publicize tell women to do. These books also tell you to love yourself. In fact, if you had to boil every self-help book down to two words, it would be "love yourself." I can't tell you why, but this irritates me immensely.

So Serena started focusing on other things, and thus began the classes and crazy diet stuff. Unlike Alice, at least in terms of dating, Serena decided to go quietly into that good night. It's a slippery slope, the decision just to let go of the dream of love in your life. Because if done well, it can make you relax, enjoy your life, and actually allow your inner light to shine brighter and stronger than ever before. (Yes, I am talking about someone's inner light—we are dealing with Serena right now, after all.) But in my opinion, that strategy, if followed incorrectly or for too long, can make your light go out, slowly, day by day. You can become sexless and cut off. Even though I think it might be extreme to quit your job to start dating, I don't think you can ever just sit back and let love just find you. Love isn't that clever. Love isn't actually all that concerned about you. I think love is out there finding people whose lights are burning so brightly that you could actually see them from the space shuttle. And frankly, somewhere between the high-colonics and the African dance classes, Serena's light went out.

But still, she has a calming effect on me. She is capable of listening to me vent about how much I hate my job, with the patience of Gandhi. Besides the books I have already mentioned, I have helped publicize such tomes as *The Clock Is Ticking! How to Meet and Marry the Man of Your Dreams in Ten Days, How to Know if Your Man Really Loves You,* and the runaway hit *How to Be Lovely* (it's supposedly the secret to all feminine happiness).

I grew up in New Jersey, not so terribly far away, just a bridge or a tunnel from the city of my dreams. I moved here to be a writer, then I thought I might be a documentary filmmaker, then I even took a few courses in anthropology, thinking I might move to Africa and study the Masai warriors or some other almost-extinct tribe. I am fascinated by our species, and loved the idea of reporting on them in some way. But I realized I inherited a strong practical streak from my father. I liked indoor plumbing, and knowing I had health insurance. So I got a job in publishing.

But now, the novelty of being able to afford groceries had definitely lost its initial thrill. And throughout all my complaining, Serena listens quietly.

"Why don't you just quit?"

"And do what? Get another job in publicity? I hate publicity. Or be unemployed? I'm too dependent on a steady paycheck to be that free-spirited."

"Sometimes you have to take a risk."

If *Serena* was thinking I was in a rut, I knew things must be really bad. "Like what?" I asked.

"Like—didn't you always say you wanted to write?"

"Yes. But I don't have a big enough ego to be a writer."

In my professional life, I was a bit stuck. My "voice of reason," so relied on by others, only caused me to talk myself out of pretty much everything. But every Friday, Serena would listen to me bitch about my work frustrations as if it were the first time I was bringing it up.

So I thought, why not? My friends have always been curious about her. Why not try to convince her to go out?

"The chances of any of us going out tomorrow night and meeting the man of our dreams is practically zero. So why bother?" Serena asked as she took another bite of her tempeh burger.

In terms of the facts, Serena has a point. I have been going out at night in the hopes of meeting the one guy that's going to adore me for the rest of my life. Let's say I've been doing this for two or three times a week for, oh, fifteen years. I have met men and dated, but clearly, as of today, not the guy that gets written down in my big book of life as "The One." That adds up to a hell of a lot of nights out *not* meeting the man of my dreams.

I know, I know, we weren't just going out to meet men. We were going out to have fun, to celebrate being single and being sort of young (or at least not yet old) and alive and living in the best city in the world. It's just funny how when you finally do meet someone and begin dating, the first thing you both do is start staying home to snuggle on the couch. Because going out with your friends was simply that much fun.

So I couldn't really argue with Serena. The whole concept of "going out" is somewhat flawed. But I continued my plea. "We're not going out to meet guys. We are just going out to go out. To show Georgia that it's fun to just go out. To be out in the world, eating, drinking, talking, laughing. Sometimes something unexpected happens and sometimes, most of the time, you just go home. But you go out, you know, to *go out*. To see what *might* happen. That's the fun of it."

The argument for the benefits of spontaneity and the unknown was usually not the way to Serena's heart, but for some reason, she agreed.

"Fine. But I don't want it to be anywhere too smoky or too noisy. And make sure they have a vegetable plate on the menu."

How Ruby Is Single

And then, there's Ruby.

It was Saturday, at two in the afternoon, and I had come over to Ruby's apartment to try to recruit her into going out that night—and because I knew she might not have gotten out of bed yet.

Ruby opened the door in her pajamas. Her hair was severely matted, almost in a predreadlocked state of knots.

"Did you get out of bed today?" I asked, worried.

"Yes. Of course. Right now," she said, offended. She proceeded to walk back into her bedroom. Her apartment was impeccably neat. None of your cliché telltale depression signs, such as moldy ice cream cartons, half-eaten doughnuts, or weeks of dirty laundry strewn around. She was a very tidy depressive. It gave me hope.

"How are you feeling today?" I asked, following her into her bedroom.

"Better. When I woke up he wasn't the first thing I thought about." She crawled back into her very fluffy, downy, flowery bed and pulled the covers around her. It looked really comfortable. I was starting to think about taking a nap myself.

"Great!" I said, knowing I was about to hear much more than that. Ruby is an adorable, long-haired brunette, a perfectly curvy, feminine creature of soothing tones and tender words. And Ruby likes to talk about her feelings.

She sat up. "My first thought this morning was 'I feel okay.' You know what I mean—that moment before you remember who you are and what the actual facts of your life are? My first thought, in my gut, in my body, was 'I feel okay.' I haven't felt like that in a long time. Usually, you know, I open my eyes and I already feel like shit. Like in my sleep I was feeling like shit, and waking up was just an extension of that, you know? But this morning, my first thought was 'I feel okay.' As if my body wasn't, you know, housing any more sadness."

"That's awesome," I said, cheerfully. Maybe things aren't as bad as I thought.

"Yeah, well, of course, once I remembered everything, then I started crying and couldn't stop for three hours. But I think it was an improvement, you know? It made me see that I was getting better. Because Ralph can't stay in my memory so strongly, he just can't. Soon I'll wake up and it'll take me three whole minutes to start crying about him. And then fifteen minutes. And then an hour, then a whole day, and then I'll finally be through this, you know?" She looked as if she was going to start crying again.

Ralph was Ruby's cat. He died of kidney failure three months ago. She has been keeping me updated on the physical sensations of her profound depression every day since. This is particularly difficult for me because I have absolutely no idea why anyone would pour all their emotional energy into something that can't even give you a back rub. And not only that, but I feel superior about it. I believe anyone with a pet is actually weaker than I. Because when I ask somebody why they love their pet so much, they invariably say something like, "You just can't believe the amount of unconditional love Beemie gives me." Well, guess what. I don't need unconditional love, how about that? I need conditional love. I need someone who can walk on two legs and form sentences and use tools and remind me that that was the second time in a week that I yelled at a customer service person over the phone when I didn't get my way and *I may want to look into that.* I need to be loved by someone who can fully comprehend that when he sees me get locked out of my apartment three times in one month, that that may very well be the Thing About Me That Is Never Going to Change. And he loves me anyway. Not because it's an unconditional love, but because he actually truly knows me and has decided that my fascinating mind and hot bod are worth perhaps missing a flight or two because I forgot my driver's license at home.

But that's not really the point right now. The point here is that Ruby refuses to step out for a cup of coffee, go shopping, or even take a walk with me, because Ruby is a disaster at handling disappointment. Particularly of the romantic variety. Whatever good times she has with some fellow, it will never be worth the amount of pain and torture she puts herself through when it doesn't work out. The math of it simply doesn't add up. If she dates someone for three weeks, and then they break up, she'll spend the next two months driving herself and everyone around her crazy.

Because I'm an expert on the emotional MRI of Ruby, I can tell you exactly what happens during her descent. She will meet someone, a man, say, as opposed to a feline. She will like him. She will go out with him. Her heart will be full of the possibility and excitement that comes with finally finding someone you actually like who is available, kind, decent, and who seems to like you back.

As I said before, Ruby is attractive; very soft, very feminine. She can be inquisitive and attentive, and a great conversationalist. And when she meets men, they like her for all these reasons. Ruby is actually really good at the dating part of dating, and when she is in a relationship, she is clearly in her element.

However, this is New York, this is life, and this is dating. Things often don't work out. And when they don't, when Ruby gets rejected, for whatever reason it may be, and however the bad news is delivered, a process begins. She is usually fine at the Moment of Disappointment. Like when this guy Nile broke up with her because he wanted to get back together with his ex-girlfriend. At the moment of impact, she is philosophical about it. A burst of sanity and self-esteem washes over her, and she tells me that she knows that it just means he wasn't the one, and she can't take it personally and it's his loss. And then a few hours go by and time will push her further away from that moment of clarity and she will start to slip into the Crazy Pit. Her beloved, whom she once saw at normal size, starts growing larger and larger and larger, and in a matter of hours he becomes the Mount Everest of desirability and she is inconsolable. He was the best thing ever to happen to her. There will never be anyone as good as him ever again. Nile did the most powerful thing he could do to Ruby—he rejected her and now he is EVERYTHING and she is nothing.

I've gotten so used to watching Ruby go through this, that I make a point of being around her during those critical few hours after a rejection, to see if I can stop her at the top of the stairs down to Crazy. Because, let me tell you, once she goes down, there's no telling when she's going to come back up. And she doesn't like to sit there alone. Ruby likes to call up her friends and describe in vivid detail, for hours, what it's like in the basement of broken dreams. The wallpaper, the upholstery, the floor tiles. And there is nothing we can do. We just have to wait it out.

So you can imagine that after a few years of these ups and downs, whenever I get the call from Ruby that she has "met this great guy" or the second date went "really, really well," I'm not necessarily jumping for joy. Because, again, the math is simply not promising. If three weeks can add up to two months of tears, imagine how terrified I am when Ruby celebrates her four-month anniversary with someone. If she ends up breaking up with someone after a few years of living together, well, I don't think at this point there are enough years left in her life to get over him.

Which is why she decided to get Ralph. Ruby was tired of being disappointed. And as long as she kept her windows closed and doors not ajar, Ralph would never leave her. And Ruby would never have to be disappointed again. But Ruby didn't know about feline chronic renal failure.

And now, well, now Ralph was the best cat there ever was. Ralph made her happier than any animal or human could have ever possibly made her and she has no idea how she will ever live without him. She still manages to work. She's got her own business as an executive recruiter, and she has clients who rely on her to get their asses jobs. And thank God for them, because she will always get out of bed to help someone in need of a good nonlateral job placement. But a Saturday afternoon is much different. Ruby isn't budging.

Until I told her about Georgia. How her husband left her for a samba instructor and she's devastated and wants to go out and feel good about life. Then, Ruby understood completely. Ruby understood that there are moments when no matter how badly you feel, it's your duty to get out of the house and help deceive a newly single person into believing that everything is going to be okay. Ruby knew, intuitively, that this was just such a night.

How I'm Single

Let's be honest. I'm not doing it any better. I date, I meet men at parties and at work, or through friends, but things never seem to "work out." I'm not crazy, I don't date crazy men. Things just don't "work out." I look at couples walking down the street and I want to shake them, to beg them to answer my question, "How did you guys figure *that* out?" It has become the Sphinx for me, the eternal mystery. How do two people ever find each other in this city and "work out"?

And what do I do about it? I get upset. I cry. I stop. And then I cheer up and go out and be absolutely charming and have a great time as often as I can. I try to be a good person, a good friend, and a good member of my family. I try to make sure there isn't some unconscious reason why I'm still single. I keep going.

"You're single now because you're too snobby." That's Alice's answer every time the subject comes up. Meanwhile, I don't see her married to the handsome gentleman working at the fruit stand on the corner of Twelfth and Seventh who seems to have taken quite a shine to her. She is basing this judgment on the fact that I refuse to date online. In the good old days, online dating was considered a hideous embarrassment, something that no one would be caught dead admitting to. I loved that time. Now the reaction you will get from people when they hear that you're single and *not* doing some form of online dating is that you *must not really want it that bad.* It has become the bottom line, the litmus test for *how much you're willing to do for love.* As if your Mr. Right is definitely, absolutely guaranteed to be online. He's waiting for you and if you're not willing to spend the 1,500 hours, 39 coffees, 47 dinners, and 432 drinks to meet him, then you *just don't want to meet him badly enough and you deserve to grow old and die alone.*

"I don't think you're really open to love yet. You're not ready." That's Ruby's answer. I'm not even going to dignify it with a response—except to say, I didn't know that finding love had become something equivalent to becoming a Jedi Knight. I didn't know there were years of psychic training, metaphysical trials to endure, and rings of fire to jump through before I could get a date for my cousin's wedding in May. And yet, I know women who are so out of their minds they might as well be barking like dogs, who still find men who adore them, men whom they, in their madness, feel they are in love with. But no matter.

My mother thinks I'm single because I like having my independence. But she rarely weighs in on the subject. She comes from the generation of women who didn't think they had any other option but to get married and have children. There were no other choices for her. So she thinks it's just dandy that I'm single and that I don't have to rely on a man. I don't think my mother and father had a particularly happy marriage and after my father died, she was one of those widows who finally got to come into her own—the classes, the vacations, the bridge and book clubs. When I was still just a girl, she thought she was doing me a great service, giving me this wonderful gift of reminding me that I don't need a man to be happy. I can do anything I want, be anyone I want to be, without a man.

And now . . . I don't have the heart to tell her that I'm not really happy being single, and if you want to be someone's girlfriend or wife, and you happen to be straight, you kind of *do* need a man, *sorry, Mom,* because then I know she'd worry. Mothers do not like to see their children sad. So I steer the conversation away from my love life and she doesn't ask, both of us not wanting to reveal or know about any pesky unhappiness.

"Oh please," Serena—who, among my friends has known me the longest—said. "It's no mystery. You dated bad boys till your mid-thirties, and now that you've finally come to your senses, the good ones are all taken."

Bingo.

My last boyfriend six years ago was the worst one of all. There are some guys you date who are so bad that when you tell the story about them, it reflects just as badly on you as it does on them. His name was Jeremy and we had been dating for two tumultuous years. He decided to break up with me by not showing up to my father's funeral. I never heard from him after that.

Since then, no bad boys. But no great love, either.

Georgia weighed in on this subject of why I'm single on one particularly dark, lonely, regretful night.

"Oh for God's sake, there's no reason. It's just totally fucked. You're kind, you're beautiful, you have the best hair in New York City." (It's really long and curly but never ever frizzy, and when I want to straighten it, it looks just as great. I have to admit, it's my best feature.)

"You're hot, you're smart, you're funny, and you are one of the finest people I know. You are perfect. Stop asking yourself that awful question because there is not one goddamn reason why the sexiest, nicest, most charming man in New York City isn't madly in love with you right now."

And that was why I loved Georgia. And that's how this weekend I ended up spearheading an outing with my mismatched set of friends to make her feel like life was worth living. Because at the end of the day, it's night. And in New York, if it's night there's nightlife, and when there's life, as most optimists will be happy to tell you, there's always hope. And I guess that's a big part of how to be single. Hope. Friends. And making sure you get out of your damn apartment.

RULE

2

Don't Be Crazy, No Matter How You Feel,
Because It Just Makes Us All Look Bad

When you're going out for a night on the town with the main goal being to make a friend stop threatening, however unconvincingly, to commit suicide, you must pick your locations carefully. Alice and I discussed this with the deliberation of generals planning a midnight air assault. The truth is, any night you go out, you must do your research thoroughly. Because a bad night out can be demoralizing even for the fittest of us single women. So you must ask a lot of questions. How many men will there be to how many women? How expensive are the drinks? Is the music good? Is this the right night to be there? You have to take all these factors into consideration, and if need be, use graphs, diagrams, and a couple of well-placed phone calls to come up with the right plan of attack. In this case, the strategy was quite simple: places with tons of men. Because the one idea you don't want anywhere near your newly single friend is the one concept that is so all-pervasive, so oppressive, that it will be the first thought any sensible woman will have when she realizes she is now officially single, and that is of course, *There are no good men left*. And then the next thought would be *I'm going to be alone for the rest of my life*.

Now, the big question of whether there really are no good guys left in New York City is something we could probably debate forever, but for now we will leave the reality of that up to the Census Bureau and the match-making services. What I'm concerned about, for this particular night, is the *perception* that there are tons and tons of handsome single men out there, literally falling out of the skies, out of trees, bumping into you on the street, wanting to have sex with you. So therefore, in Alice's mind, where to have dinner was an easy choice. It had to be a steakhouse, and the biggest one there is. And that would be Peter Luger in Williamsburg, Brooklyn. Now you may wonder what we are doing taking our newly single friend out to Brooklyn. Well, wake up, sleepy—where have you been? Brooklyn is the new Manhattan and Williamsburg is the new Lower East Side and Peter Luger serves so much red meat that you are guaranteed to find heaps of straight men there (or women beefing up for their next weight-lifting com-petition). Either way, that makes the odds pretty good for us, and that's all I'm asking for. At a time like this, the perception of abundance is every-thing, not just with the thirty-eight-ounce steaks, but with the tons of straight men all sitting around large wooden tables in groups of eight and ten, devouring their meat like cavemen.

I don't know if you have ever been responsible for getting people to-gether and deciding where they go for an evening. But if you haven't, let me tell you that it is a surprisingly nerve-racking experience. I say "sur-prisingly," because if you've never been the one in charge, you'll just be wondering why your normally relaxed friend asked you three times if you liked your tortellini. But if you've ever done it, you understand that even the most confident person turns into a jittery, insecure hostess, ob-sessed with every joke, eye roll, and aside made by her companions. And if it doesn't go well, it will be seared into people's minds as the night you took them out and they didn't have fun.

Now, the key to having fun is, of course, a great mix of people. So let me remind you of what we're dealing with here: Georgia, a newly single woman toying with the idea of a nervous breakdown; Ruby, who is still mourning the death of her cat; Serena, the girl in the nondairy wheat-free bubble; and Alice, who God bless her, though she may be working on a gastric ulcer from her dating schedule, is my only hope of getting through this in one piece.

You see, none of them know one another very well. They know each other from my various birthday parties throughout the years, but we are definitely not a gang. I met Alice at a spin class five years ago. I worked with Georgia until she left to raise her kids. Serena's my best friend from college and Ruby and I bonded fifteen years ago at a horrific temp job, then we shared an apartment for three years after that. They are basically strangers to one another. In fact, I could safely say that Alice, Georgia, Serena, and Ruby don't really care for each other that much, for no real reason except that none of them is really any of the others' "types." I always wanted a gaggle of girlfriends, always longed for a posse, my little family of friends, but it just didn't work out that way. It would have been nice if at one job I was able to grab a whole bunch of them, like lobsters in a trap. But meeting a group of women who end up living in the same city, remaining friends, and sharing the most intimate moments of their lives is rare and wonderful and definitely something to pine for, or at least watch on television.

"Oh my God, it's so cold, I should have worn a heavier coat. I hate October. October is the most annoying month because you never know how to dress," said "no-body-fat" Serena.

We had decided to meet on Twenty-third and Eighth, and take a cab to Williamsburg together. Everyone seemed to be fairly upbeat, but I could already tell that Serena, who was so out of her element, was going to be the problem. Not that I wasn't worried about Georgia, too, who was wearing a low-cut shirt and a miniskirt. Georgia is a gorgeous woman who can certainly pull this off. She's a slim five seven, with long, light brown hair and bangs that are just a little too long in that way they're supposed to be so they fall perfectly in front of her eyes. She has naturally bee-stung lips that many women would happily inject themselves for, and before the separation, used to always look effortlessly, carelessly hip. Now, however, it was October. And cold. And I could actually see her ass. We all piled into a cab and were on our way.

As Serena wondered aloud if there was going to be anything vegetarian to eat at this place, and Alice was barking orders at the cabdriver, I had an epiphany as to how this entire night might actually turn out okay. I realized there is a divine spirit looking out for us in this world. Because there's this thing called alcohol. And at that moment, alcohol seemed like such a good idea that I knew there must be a God who loved us enough to invent it.

When we entered Peter Luger Steak House it was just as my alcohol-creating God would have intended it: handsome, clearly employed men as far as the eye could see. The knot in my stomach relaxed. I knew that the first leg of the treasure hunt that is called "Running Around New York City Looking for Fun" was going to be a win for our team.

"Oh my God, I'm a genius," Alice said proudly.

"Yay!" said Georgia.

"I love it here," said Ruby.

"I know there's not going to be one thing here that I can eat," said Serena, as we walked past the multitudes of tables heaped with cooked animal flesh.

It's a funny thing about peer pressure: it works at any age. While we were looking at the menus, Serena ordered a vodka tonic. Now that might not seem like much to you, but it was a momentous occasion in my book. And it came to be simply because my three friends, who didn't know Serena at all, told her she should lighten up. And she got embarrassed. After the past three years of my begging her to try a mojito, it was as simple as that. She still ordered a plate of broccoli rabe for dinner, but you couldn't deny that there was magic in the girl posse and it had already begun.

It's always better when you have a purpose, whether in life or simply for a night out, and for this evening the goal was clear: Georgia needed to flirt with someone recklessly. And here we were, in the land of big steaks and bold moves. So as the red meat and alcohol began to flow, it was time to get into wacky-scheme mode.

Alice decided to approach the table adjacent to us, which, coincidentally, had five men at it.

"Hey guys, we're trying to show our newly single friend a good time and thought it'd be fun to crash your table."

Alice is fearless. Once you've had a few murderers lunge at you from across a table and try to choke you to death, walking up to a group of guys is a piece of cake. And because of Alice, there we were, moving our plates and silverware over to the table next to us and squeezing ourselves in very closely with a bunch of cute men. And Georgia, happily, was getting the lion's share of the attention, like a bride-to-be at her bachelorette party. Nothing like putting your romantic stakes right out on the table to get people hopping, and this time she didn't need to wear the plastic condom veil with matching penis earrings. I looked around the table and this is what I saw:

Georgia giggling like a schoolgirl.

Ruby giggling like a schoolgirl.

Serena giggling like a schoolgirl.

Alice giggling like a schoolgirl.

And, when I gave myself a moment to stop worrying if everyone was having a good time, I was giggling like a schoolgirl, too. And I thought, *My God, we are pathetic creatures. We are lawyers and publicists and businesswomen and mothers with blow-dried hair and lipstick, all just waiting for the sun of male attention to shine down upon us and make us feel alive again.*

They taught us drinking games, we made jokes about their ties. Ruby was talking to a man who seemed particularly enraptured with her and every one of the guys told Georgia that she was hot and she doesn't have a thing to worry about. There was gold in that thar steakhouse.

"Oh my God, that was so much fun!" Georgia said, laughing, as we left the restaurant.

"I can't believe I drank vodka!" Serena said, beaming.

"That guy I was talking to wants to come with us wherever we go next!" Ruby said, giggling. "Where are we going next?!"

Now, the thing about being responsible for people's good time is that the stakes just keep getting higher and higher throughout the night, no matter what has happened the moment before. If dinner was a dud, then boy, you have to make up for it with a kick-ass bar or club to go to next. If dinner was really fun, which in this case it was, then you better not blow it by picking a place that brings the mood down. So I conferred again with my own personal Zagat, Alice. We were sticking with the theme "It's raining men" so Alice made her decision quickly. We headed to "Sports," a fancy sports bar with a clearly unimaginative name on the Upper West Side. Ruby and her new guy, Gary, took one cab and we piled into another. Not the cheapest taxi ride but what's money when there's five drunky girls trying to keep their buzz alive?

When we arrived, I knew immediately that this was a misstep. The problem with sports bars hits you immediately when you walk in: men really are there to watch sports. Because if they really had their sights set on going out to meet women—they wouldn't go to a sports bar. Alice was thinking the same thing.

"We should go to the Flatiron instead."

But Serena had already ordered another vodka and Georgia had walked up to the cutest guy in the place and was trying to talk to him. Unfortunately, there was a big Knicks basketball game on—which I don't understand since it was preseason and the Knicks aren't involved in "big" basketball games anymore. Anyway, Georgia was able to grab his attention during a commercial break and she was using those four minutes to get in as much flirting as possible.

Ruby was talking to Gary, who had clearly fallen in love with her and wanted to be with her forever. But unfortunately for Serena, Alice, and me, we were soon sitting at the bar with our drinks, looking at about twenty screens of various sports that we couldn't give a crap about.

But Alice knew something we didn't.

"Oh my God, there's a foosball table over there!" Alice said, way too excitedly.

"I don't play foosball," Serena said, already grumpy.

"Do you think we should go somewhere else?" I said, ignoring the whole foosball idea.

"No, you don't understand. It is an absolute fact that a group of women cannot play foosball for more than ten minutes without guys coming over to play with them."

"You've spent a lot of time proving this fact?" I said, a little reproachfully. Did I happen to tell you that Alice used to be a lawyer who defended the rights of the poor and disenfranchised, making them feel respected and heard, often at the darkest times of their lives?

"Yes. And I'll prove it to you now."

So we took our drinks and moved over to the foosball table. Alice and I played foosball, while Serena watched the clock. It was exactly three and a half minutes before two guys walked up to us. At four and a half minutes, they challenged us to a game.

Alice scares me, sometimes.

She is, of course, brilliant at foosball, so we kept winning and getting challenged, the foosball suitors lining up to get a piece of our foosball magic. We kept drinking and the giggles started again and the next thing I knew, Serena was eating chicken wings off one of our challengers' plates. A game later, she was licking her hot-sauce-covered fingers and ordering a plate of wings for herself. She was a vegan gone wild. I quickly scanned the room and saw Ruby still chatting with Gary, and Georgia still trying to talk to the cute guy between sports highlights. I had never seen Georgia flirt before; she was already married when I met her. But I could tell from just one look that she was trying too hard. She was talking a little too animatedly, listening a little too earnestly, laughing a little too excitedly. She was trying to compete with the Knicks and, even though they suck, she didn't stand a chance. But instead of cutting her losses, she continued to touch his arm, laugh loudly, and order another drink.

As Alice and I continued to beat these two guys (Bruce and Todd) at foosball, I heard Alice, when asked what she does for a living, say in complete earnestness that she's a "facialist." I looked at her with surprise and she shot me a look of "I'll explain later." I had had my foosball and flirting fill and excused myself, getting Serena to stop shoving poultry in her face long enough to take my place, and I walked over to the bar. On one side I heard Georgia squealing, "Oh my God, I love Audioslave!" (like she knows from Audioslave), and on the other, Ruby was saying to Gary, "I loved Ralph, but I mean, he was just a cat, you know?"

Alice eventually walked over to get a drink. I looked at her, scowling with as much judgment and disappointment as I could muster. Alice took the hint.

"Didn't you hear about that study that came out of England? The smarter you are, the less likely you are of getting married. The dumb girls are getting the guys."

"So you say that you give facials for a living, instead of that you're a lawyer who graduated with top honors from Harvard Law School?"

"Yes, and it works."

"What happens if you start dating one of these guys?"

"I'm just getting them interested by appealing to their basest level. Once I have their interest, I slowly sneak the smart in, but by then they're hooked."

Appalled, I turned around just in time to see Georgia grabbing the cute guy's face and kissing him straight on the lips. Kind of like a crazy person. Cute guy's response: not so excited. He did that sort of laughing, sort of muttering "oh ho ho, you're one wild girl" while trying to politely peel her off him. It was a painful moment for all of us.

Serena ran up to us, her face aglow with hot sauce.

"Bruce and Todd think we should go to Hogs and Heifers."

Serena, who before tonight hadn't been anywhere there wasn't Enya or waterfall sounds playing, thought Hogs & Heifers was a keen idea. I realized she was slightly drunk.

"Cool, I know all the bartenders there," Alice replied.

Ruby and her new boyfriend, Gary, thought it was a great idea, too. Again, the entertainment director in me was concerned. Our evening had degraded from Steaks and Vodka to Beer and Wings to Hogs & Heifers. New York is a big, hip, glamorous city, and there was no need to be ending our night in a touristy, outdated biker bar. I told them this, but alas, the horses had broken out of the barn and were now planning to gallop all the way downtown to Hogs & Heifers with or without me. Ruby came up, excited.

"Gary is going to meet us down there; he just had to go pick up one of his friends. Julie—wouldn't it be an amazing story if Ralph died but I ended up meeting the love of my life right after? Wouldn't that be great? Gary's really cute, right?"

"He is totally cute, Ruby. Totally." And he was. He seemed really nice and into her, and by God, people meet and fall in love every day of the week, so what the heck?

Alice, Georgia, and Serena were already outside hailing cabs with Bruce and Todd. Ruby went outside to join them. I decided to go along. My experience with women not used to drinking or staying out late is that by the time they have the cab ride downtown, they'll be sleepy, slightly nauseous, and ready to go home.

Unfortunately, that was not the case. In their cab going downtown, Todd told Georgia about how Hogs & Heifers is famous for women getting on the bar and dancing, and then somehow taking off their bras. Demi's done it, Julia's done it, Drew's done it. It's the thing to do. At least, that's what Alice told me when I got there, explaining how and why

Georgia had managed to already be on top of the bar swinging her bra around. Ruby was screaming and laughing, Serena was hootin' and hollerin' and the place was going wild. Hogs & Heifers is famous for its "biker redneck" aesthetic. The walls are covered with hundreds of women's tossed-off bras for as far as the eye can see. Wherever there might be a tiny bit of wall space left, there's an American flag or cowboy hat. The bartenders are all women wearing tight denim and even tighter t-shirts and the place is packed. Bruce and Todd had disappeared, but I'm sure they were hootin' and hollerin' from wherever they were. It's so odd how all it takes is a few people dancing on a bar to make people feel as if they're having a hilariously wild night out.

Now, you have to understand why seeing Georgia on top of a bar was disturbing to me. Remember, I met Georgia when she was already married. And Georgia and Dale were not the couple you're going to catch groping each other in the kitchen. So I have never actually seen Georgia get her groove on, so to speak, and it wasn't something I ever really missed seeing. I looked at her on the bar, gyrating and grinding, and I remembered back to a day when I went to the beach with Georgia and her two children, Beth and Gareth. She spent the whole day in the water with them, getting them used to the waves. I helped for a while, playing with them for an hour or two, but she stayed in longer than any adult human being should have to, without a complaint. Then she let them cover her entire body with sand, with only her tired, salty face sticking out. That's the Georgia I remember—Georgia, the wife and mother of two.

But now Georgia was allowing herself to unravel. She was single, she was out, and she wanted to have FUN!

The bar was crowded with lots of guys, many from out of town, some bikers, a couple of cowboys (don't ask me), all sharing the common trait of having a deep respect for women and their struggles on this planet. Just kidding. Serena then got on the bar as well, beer in hand, drinking and dancing. Okay, I'll admit it, that was fun to see. Serena, not only in a bar, but *on* a bar and trying to do a two-step. Alice then got up on the bar, too—my own little White Trash Rockettes. Ruby, however, was now standing by the door, checking her cell phone constantly and looking out onto the street, waiting for Gary. She might as well have been sitting on the windowsill, like her pet cat, Ralph, waiting for her master to arrive.

My stomach began to tighten again at the idea that there might be another impending disappointment in store for Ruby.

The longest country song in the world finally came to an end, and Alice and Serena, as drunk but not completely-out-of-their-minds women do, got off the bar. Georgia, however, stayed, not yet ready to leave the spotlight. A large biker man in his fifties, with a bushy gray beard and long gray hair, helped Serena off the bar. I overheard him ask her if he could buy her a drink.

She said, "Yes, and some ribs would be nice as well." I don't quite understand what happened, but somewhere after her first vodka tonic, Serena's sleeping carnivore awoke, and she turned into a pretty, little werewolf. The biker man told Serena his name was Frankie and he was an art dealer who had just finished a long round of the galleries of Chelsea and came in for a break.

"Wow, that just goes to show you. I would never have guessed you were an art dealer. I know nothing about people, Frank." As she spoke she drunkenly slung her arm over Frank's shoulder. "I've been living a sheltered life. And I know nothing. *Nothing.*"

Alice had also gotten the attention of a few men. I guess their spotlight dance was like a thirty-second dating advertisement. So, there I was again, worrying about my friends and not having any fun on my own. I started wondering if it would be okay for me to leave. I was tired of being Judge McJudgey, and frankly, I was beginning a downward spiral of worry and fear. *What would become of all of us? Would we end up with husbands and children? Would we all stay in New York? What would become of me? Would I just stay at my hateful job, doing work that doesn't satisfy me, being single, alone, trying to make the best of it for the rest of my life? Is this as good as it's going to get? A yuppie biker bar on a Saturday night at 2 A.M.?*

But then a guy came up and started talking to me. And that's all it took to cheer me up. Because, I believe you recall, we are pathetic creatures. He was cute and he picked me to talk to and I was flattered as if I was at my first school dance. I forgot all morose or possibly deep thoughts and just started flirting my ass off.

"So what brings you to this place?" he asked. His name was David and he was in town from Houston with his buddy Tom. I pointed to Georgia, who was still dancing up a storm.

"She just split up with her husband and we're trying to show her a good time."

He looked up at Georgia, and he said, "It looks like you did a good job." As if the universal symbol for having a good time is dancing on a bar swinging your bra around.

He then said, "I split up with my girlfriend two months ago. It was really rough, so I understand what she's going through." Was he really trying to talk seriously with me while "Achy Breaky Heart" was playing and women were taking off their bras on the bar? That's kind of sweet. We sat down at a table, and began to have a lovely conversation, the kind you can have anywhere at any time when you're with someone you really like talking to. I told him about our evening and how worried I was about it, and he immediately began to tease me about being a control freak. I love it when they tease. And he talked about being a little bit bossy since he's the oldest of four, and how much he worries about all his siblings. Cute.

I believe we were talking for an hour, though it could have been five hours or ten minutes. I couldn't tell you. I had stopped worrying, thinking, and judging, and was just trying to have a goddamn nice time.

I finally looked up to see a girl gesturing to Georgia to get off the bar. Yes, Georgia was still on the bar, and for everyone there, the novelty had worn off and they wanted someone else to take advantage of that valuable bartop real estate. I saw Georgia shaking her head as if to say "No fucking way." In fact, I think I heard her actually say that. I walked over to Georgia and saw that Alice was now bartending, because randomly, Alice knows how to bartend and decided to help out. I saw Serena nodding out in a corner with the biker art buyer. He was holding her so she wouldn't fall over and while doing so, had a hand firmly over her right breast. I had no idea where Ruby was. Then a guy from the crowd screamed, "Get your tired old ass off the bar, and give that other girl a chance! She's hotter and younger and you can't dance for shit!" And the entire bar laughed. I turned around to see what asshole said it—and it was David. David whom I was just talking to, David. The cute teaser, David.

Georgia heard this, and I could see the words hit her ears, go into her brain, and wash across her face. She was mortified. And at this moment, the Georgia I used to know would have sort of crumpled off

the bar and run into the bathroom, in tears. But the new Georgia, however humiliated she might have felt, flipped David her middle finger
and refused to give up her spot. The hot girl in question was now pissed
and started grabbing at Georgia's calves to pull her off the bar. A very
large bouncer, perhaps a giant, got to the bar quickly and tried to keep
things calm. And yet Georgia would not get down. She wanted to stay
up there and dance to country music until she goddamn felt like
coming down. She would stay up there until all her pain was gone and
she truly felt attractive and whole and loved again. And if that took her
to next Christmas, by God, I think she planned on being up there until
then.

Now Georgia started dancing even more suggestively than she had
been, like a stripper on speed. It was about as painful a thing to watch as
anything you could imagine. Except for perhaps ten seconds later, when I
looked over to see Serena vomiting on herself. Oh yes. I was about to run
over to her when I saw Georgia try to kick the bouncer, who then pulled
her off the bar. The hot girl took this opportunity to call Georgia a cunt,
and Georgia, now flung over the bouncer's shoulder, managed to seize
the hot girl's hair and tug as hard as she could. The hot girl then slapped
Georgia in the face as the bouncer weaved and turned, trying to get these
women away from each other. He put Georgia down and one of the hot
girl's friends punched her in the arm.

This was when Alice jumped across the bar and started throwing
punches at the hot girl, the hot girl's friends, and anyone else who got in
her way. You can take the girl out of the fight, but you can't take the fight
out of the girl, and until that moment, I had no idea how good Alice was
at actual hand-to-hand combat. Frankly, I was impressed. Not much of a
fighter myself, I ran to Serena.

"Good, you better deal with her. This bitch is fucked up," the biker art
dealer delicately said to me, as he stood up. As if on cue, Serena vomited
on herself again. The only saving grace to all this was that she was out
cold, so she was spared the humiliation of seeing her entire self covered
in half-digested chicken wings and ribs.

"What should I do?" I asked.

"Get her to the emergency room. She might have alcohol poisoning."
He looked at her, disgusted.

Georgia and Alice were still pulling and scratching and swinging. I made my way through the crowd trying to avoid physical injury and managed to scream out to Georgia and Alice that Serena might have to go to the hospital and we had to go. They didn't need to agree with me on this, because they were promptly dragged by the scruffs of their necks by two other very large men, and basically thrown out onto the street. Frank had deposited Serena outside as well. "Jesus, I'm fucking covered in her fucking vomit. Fuck." He shook his head and walked back inside. It was a lovely sight to see: Alice and Georgia scratched and bruised and Serena covered in vomit, all underneath a big neon sign that said "Hogs & Heifers." I realized that I didn't know where Ruby was, but I had a hunch. I went back in and walked through the crowd to the ladies' room. I got there to find, exactly as I suspected, Ruby sitting on the bathroom floor, her pretty heart-shaped face crumpled up in pain, her eye makeup dripping down her face. She was sobbing.

"He didn't show up. Why would he say he was going to show up if he didn't mean it?" I sat down on the floor with her, and put my arm around her.

"How do people do this?" she asked. "How do people keep putting themselves out there when they know they're probably just going to get hurt? How can anyone deal with that much disappointment? It's unnatural. We're not supposed to go through life so exposed. That's why people get married. Because no one is supposed to go through life that vulnerable. No one is supposed to be forced to meet so many strangers who end up making you feel bad!"

I had nothing to say to this. I was in complete agreement with her. "I know. It's brutal, isn't it?"

"But what are we supposed to do? I don't want to be the girl who stays home and cries about her cat. I don't want to be the one that's sitting here now! But what can I do? I liked him and I wanted him to come down to the bar like he said he would and he didn't show up and *I'm so disappointed*!"

I scooped Ruby up and walked outside with her. On the way out, I passed David and kind of shoved him. Hard. Made him spill his drink. I was mad at him—he had humiliated my friend Georgia and ended up not being my husband.

When we got outside, I explained to Ruby what had happened with the fighting and the vomiting. Then Georgia told us Alice had already taken Serena to the hospital. We all hopped in a cab and went to Saint Vincent's.

By the time we got there, Serena's stomach was being pumped, which I have heard is not a pleasant experience by any stretch of the imagination. I was thinking that sounded a little severe until the nurse told me Serena had consumed about seventeen drinks during the course of the evening.

Why hadn't I noticed? I was so busy being happy that she was finally letting her hair down, I didn't even see that she was hazing herself. Alice and Georgia came back from getting treated for their wounds and were covered in bandages like a pair of Roller Derby girls.

Something was terribly, terribly wrong. We were beautiful, accomplished, sexy, intelligent single women and we were disasters. If there was a "How To" book to write, it should be called "How Not to Be Us." We were doing it all wrong, this "being single" business, yet I had no clue as to how to do it better.

As my thoughts were giving way to musings of a better life, I looked over to see two women across from us, very animatedly speaking in French. Both were beautiful, slim, impeccably dressed women in their early forties. One was wearing a brown felt duster with large white stitching on the front side and the other was in a short brown suede coat with fringe. Somehow it worked. I never notice shoes, won't even bother, but a nice thin overcoat that makes you ignore anything else being worn, well, that impresses me. These perfect ladies were obviously disgusted about something. Which is so French. As I tuned in with my two years of college French, I got the gist of it: the health care in the States is *deplorable,* this emergency room is filthy, and America basically sucks. I was now curious as to what brought them here. They looked so elegant, so perfect. What could have possibly gone wrong in their lovely French lives to have them wind up in the emergency room? Did one of their friends OD on contempt?

"Excuse me, is there anything I can do to help?" I tried to appear friendly, but I just felt like being nosy.

The two women stopped talking and stared at me. The one with the fringe coat looked at Ruby and Alice with complete superiority and said, "Our friend sprained her ankle." The other one, darting her eyes around us, decided to get curious as well.

"What brings *you* here?" she said in her adorable French accent. I was thinking about lying when Alice just blurted it out.

"We got into a fight with some girls."

"They made me get off the bar I was dancing on," Georgia said. She stared at them as if to say "and I'm ready for another round." The French women scrunched up their noses as if they'd smelled some bad Brie.

They looked at each other and spoke in French. It was something like, "American women, have no [*something*]. Where are their mothers? Did they not teach them [*something*]?"

I understood everything but that one word. Damn that I didn't keep up with my French studies. Oh, fuck it.

"Excuse me, what does *orgueil* mean?" I asked, a little confrontationally.

The one in the long coat looked me straight in the eye and said, "Pride. You American women have no pride."

Alice and Georgia sat up straight, ready to rumble. Ruby looked like she was going to cry. But I was interested. "Really? Do all French women have pride? Do you all walk around proud and dignified all the time?"

The French women looked at each other and nodded. "Yes, for the most part, we do." And then they moved to another corner of the emergency room. Ouch. Shamed by the cool French ladies.

But I really couldn't argue with them. We were by no means behaving like the strong, independent single women that we were taught we could be. I wondered how we had sunk so low. It's not as if we didn't have role models. We did. We had our Gloria Steinem, Jane Fonda, Mary and Rhoda, and so many more. We have image after image of beautiful single women who lead fun, fulfilling, sexy lives. Yet many of us—I won't say all, I refuse to say all, but many of us—still walk around knowing that we're barely making the best of the untenable situation of not having romantic love in our lives. We have our jobs and our friends and our passions and our churches and our gyms and yet we still can't escape our essential nature of needing to be loved and feel close to another human being. How do we keep going when that's not what life has given to us?

How do we date, having to act as if it's not the be-all and end-all in our lives, while knowing that one great date could change the course of our lives? How do we keep going in the face of all the disappointment and uncertainty? How do we be single and not go crazy?

All I knew was that I was sick and tired of it all. I was sick of the parties and the clothes and the schedules and the taxis and the phone calls and the drinks and the lunches. I was tired of my job. I was tired of doing something that I hated, but being too scared to do anything about it. I was frankly tired of America, with all our indulgences and our myopia. I was stuck and tired.

And suddenly I realized what I wanted to do. I wanted to talk to more single women. I wanted to talk to them all over the world. I wanted to know if anyone out there was doing this single thing any better than we were. After reading all the self-help books that I have, it was ironic—I was still looking for advice.

The next morning I logged on to my computer and spent the day doing research about single women all over the world. I learned about marriage and divorce statistics from New Delhi to Greenland. I even stumbled across the sex practices in Papua New Guinea. (Read about their yam festival, it's fascinating.) The rest of Sunday I walked around Manhattan and thought about what it would be like to leave it all. As I walked downtown along Eighth Avenue, through all the different neighborhoods and communities, crossed to the East Village and saw all the NYU students rushing around with great urgency, then walked past the South Street Seaport and saw the tourists taking their photographs, and made my way to the Hudson River, I thought about what it would feel like to remove myself from this ball of activity and intensity that is New York. By the time I got back to Union Square, and watched all the people selling or buying things at the farmers' market, I had to admit it: If I left town for a little while, Manhattan would really do just fine without me. It would manage.

So on Monday, I walked into my boss's office and pitched her an idea for a book. It would be titled "How to Be Single" and I would travel around the world and see if there is any place in the world where women are better at being single than here. I mean, we might not necessarily have all the answers here in America; we could perhaps be taught a thing or two. I knew the first stop would be France. Those women never want to read our self-help books—they don't give a crap about Bridget Jones—and the French version of *The Bachelor* has yet to be made. Why not start there? My boss, Candace, an extremely unpleasant woman, around sixty, very well respected and quite feared, replied that it was the worst idea she had ever heard.

"'How to Be Single'? Like they need to be good at it because they're going to be single for that long? That's depressing. Nobody wants to be single. That's why you always have to give women the hope that they soon *won't* be single, that the man of their dreams is right around the corner and the horror will soon come to an end. If you want to write a book, write one called 'How *Not* to Be Single.'" She said this without looking up from her computer.

"And, by the way, who cares what they're doing in France or India or Timbuktu for that matter? This is America, and frankly we do know best and I couldn't give a fuck what they're doing in Tanzania."

"Oh," I said. "Then I guess that new statistic that there are officially more single women living in America than married ones means nothing to you?"

She peered at me from over her glasses.

"Continue."

"And that maybe women need a book that's not about how to get a man or keep a man, but how to cope with a state of being that's inherently filled with confliction, emotion, and mystery?"

"I'm still bored," Candace said as she took her glasses off. I continued.

"And that maybe women might want to read a book that helps them deal with something that might be long-term, and not sugarcoat it for them? It's a fact that all over the world women are getting married later in life and getting divorced more easily. Maybe women might be interested in a global perspective on something that's so private. Maybe they would find it comforting."

Candace folded her arms over her chest and thought for a moment.

"Comforting is nice. Comforting sells," she said, finally looking up at me.

"And I'll pay for all my travel expenses," I added. After all these years, I knew what to say to really sell something.

"Well, the idea is certainly getting less unbearable," she said, begrudgingly, as she grabbed a notepad. She wrote down something on the notepad and passed it to me on the desk.

"That would be your advance, if you're interested. Take it or leave it."

I looked at the figure on the piece of paper. It was incredibly low. Not low enough for me to walk out in a huff, but not high enough for me to appear grateful. I accepted the offer.

That evening, I went back to my small one-bedroom apartment, sat on my couch, and looked around. I still lived like I was twenty-five. I had my books, my CDs, my iPod. My computer, my television, my photos. I have no talent for decorating. No personal flair. It was an extremely depressing place. And it was time to go. I got on the phone and cashed in all my stocks, leaving me with a very meager sum of money. I then went on Craigslist and by the time the week was through I had someone subletting my apartment, had a "round-the-world" plane ticket (basically the airline version of a Eurail Pass for the entire world), and I had explained to my mother what I was doing.

"Well, I think that's fantastic. I always thought you needed a break from the nine-to-five. It's time you do something outside the box," is all my incredibly supportive mother had to say. But then she added, "Just don't go anywhere too dangerous. I have no need to hear about you getting blown up in some marketplace."

Then, right before I left, I called up my four dear friends and asked them to please look out for one another. I asked Serena, Ruby, and Georgia to make sure Alice didn't overdose on Tums or dating. I asked Alice, Georgia, and Serena to make sure Ruby got out of the house, and I asked Alice and Ruby to make sure Serena and Georgia didn't leave the house at all. I found out that at least one of those concerns was already taken care of.

"I've decided to become a swami," Serena said, over the phone.

"I'm sorry, what?" was my witty reply.

"I've quit my job and I'm going to renounce all my worldly desires and take a vow of celibacy at my yoga center. The ceremony is next week—can't you postpone your trip to make it? I've invited Georgia, Alice, and Ruby, too."

I lied (yes, I lied to a soon-to-be member of the clergy) and told her I couldn't, I had a big meeting in France with someone about my new, exciting book and I just simply couldn't change my plans. And then I hung up the phone and got ready to get my ass out of New York. Was I going crazy? I wasn't sure. It may have seemed like an insane thing to do at the time, but somehow . . . staying in New York would have been even crazier.

RULE

3

Decide What You Believe In
and Then Behave Accordingly

"Well, I've lined up four women for tonight. They're excited to talk to you."

"They are? You really did that for me?"

"You told me that you wanted to talk to single French women, so I got you single French women."

Steve is my oldest friend in the world. I met him on the first day of my freshman year of high school. He sat behind me in home room. I turned around and told him he looked exactly like Jon Bon Jovi and we have been lifelong friends ever since. We stayed close even when we went to different colleges, and even when Steve moved away to study harpsichord and orchestra conducting in Paris. There were never any romantic notions between us, which never seemed odd to us, and then somewhere during his junior year abroad, Steve realized he was gay. He now lives in Paris, travels the world conducting operas and accompanying singers, and nothing pleases him more than being a wonderful host to his visiting friends and getting junk food—Twinkies, Sno Balls, jelly beans—brought to him from the States.

He took a sip of his coffee and smiled at me. He shaved his head ten years ago when he realized he was going bald, and now he sports a very trendy, I wouldn't say beard, but more like a hair pattern on his face. He has a thin line of hair that follows along his jawline, like an outline of a beard. Somehow the whole effect is quite distinguished— which is crucial when you're a thirty-eight-year-old man who works in opera. I took a bite of the most delicious croissant known to mankind and wondered how I ever thought I wouldn't eat bread while I was in Europe.

"They suggested you meet them at Régine's, which is a great idea."

"What's Régine's?"

"It's this place where hundreds and hundreds of the most beautiful young women in Paris go on Saturday nights starting at eight. To be together and talk."

I was confused. "Hundreds of French women all go to a nightclub to get together and talk? That makes no sense."

"I don't get it, either. But apparently the women have three hours just to be alone, unbothered. They even get a free buffet. After eleven P.M. the men are allowed in. They supposedly line up to get in because they know hundreds of beautiful women are inside. It's a genius marketing idea, really."

"But," I say, my mind already in research mode, "they go just to be together? That's weird."

"We don't have that in the States?" he asked.

"No, women don't need a special night where they get to be alone together. We can do that any day of the week."

After consideration, Steve said, "Well, I don't think French women travel in packs like you girls do in the States. Maybe this is their chance to make new friends."

This was exciting. I'd only been there for a few hours and already I was onto a big cultural difference: *French women like to go out in droves just to be somewhere without men.* I started to think about the ramifications of this. Are French men so aggressive that the women need a place to be away from them? Are French women so antisocial in their daily lives that they need a place to make friends? I couldn't wait to figure it all out.

"It's sweet of these women to agree to talk to me. But I don't know what I'm going to ask them. This is all new. Maybe I can just get them all drunk and see what happens."

"French women don't get drunk," Steve said.

"They don't?" I asked, disappointed.

"They might have a glass of wine or two, but I've never seen a French woman drunk."

"Well, then, difference number two. No drunky French ladies." I took a big sip of café au lait.

"Don't worry. Women are women. Get them all together and eventually they all start talking."

"I sure as hell hope so." I downed the rest of my drink. "Can I take a nap now? Please? Is that breaking the laws of jet lag?"

"You may take a nap now. But only for a few hours."

"Thank you, *mon chéri*, thank you."

And with that, Steve took me to his two-bedroom French flat and put me to bed.

It was a mob scene outside Régine's. What seemed like hundreds of gorgeous young women were all converging on this one nightclub. They were prompt, dressed up, and wanting desperately to get in.

"These women are herding themselves in here just to make new friends? This is insane!" I said to Steve as we got shoved by some six-foot-tall beauty (who I'm sure was *definitely* going to get in).

Just then, we heard a high-pitched voice yell "Steef! Steef!" Charging through the crowd was a short, stocky woman, wearing simple black trousers and a t-shirt. She did not look dressed for a night on the town.

"That's Clara," Steve explained. "She handles all of the business affairs for the Paris opera house. When you told me what you needed, I called her first—she knows everybody."

"*Bonsoir,*" said Clara as she walked up to Steve and kissed him on both his cheeks. Steve introduced us, then leaned his face out to me to kiss, and said, "*Au revoir.*"

"Really? I'm on my own?" I said. I was suddenly overcome with shyness.

"You know the rules, no men allowed . . ." Steve said. And with that we kissed and he was off. Clara then immediately grabbed me and barreled her way to the doorman. She spoke to him forcefully, and got us both into the club.

As we walked down a long set of stairs, and my eyes adjusted to the darkness, I asked, "But what about the other women? How will we find them?"

"I'll get them later. Let's just sit you down at the table."

The club itself seemed to be all red velvet banquettes and pink lighting. And there were women as far as the eye could see, as if I had thrown a bomb into a lake of pretty ladies and these were the ones who had floated to the surface. I was so impressed. I had no idea that French women would fight and haggle and risk possible humiliation with a doorman just to have a precious few hours to be alone with one another. This was a triumph of female kinship. Of course, later they got to meet men. But here it was, eight o'clock, and there was a long line for the buffet table and the banquettes were getting filled up. They had a little roped-off area where some French makeup company was giving free makeovers. This was fantastic. My first day in Paris and I'd already hit on a stereotype-debunking cultural trend: French women needing to be French women together. Maybe this wasn't such a crazy idea after all.

A buff, shirtless waiter in tiny little harem pants walked by with champagne, *free* champagne. Nice touch, love it, fabulous—I helped myself to one as Clara came back with three women: Patrice, Audrey, and Joanne. I stood up to say hello, but Clara shooed me back down and they all came and sat in the banquette. Greetings were exchanged. Patrice was a pretty book editor in her thirties with hair pulled up in an elegant do; Audrey was a very sexy brunette opera singer, with long wild hair and a wraparound dress that showed off her big, lovely—lungs; and Joanne, a jewelry designer, seemed to be about forty-five years old with brown hair in long, cute braids dangling messily down each side of her face. Clara, though not as elegant as the others, was pretty in a farm-girl kind of way. I took out a little hardcover journal I had bought in New York that I thought I would make my notes in. I was trying to appear professional. They looked at me expectantly. It was time I explained myself.

"I'm thirty-eight and single and live in New York. I met these French women in a hospital emergency room, not that that's important, and they seemed to, well, know something that we Americans don't know. About how to be single?" It felt so silly coming out of my mouth, but luckily Joanne piped right in.

"Oh please, we don't have any answers. I mean, c'mon." She dismissed the idea immediately with that superior French accent of hers. The others seemed to agree.

"Really? You don't have anything you can teach me?" I asked. They all shook their heads no again. I decided I should try to dig a little deeper. After all, they were a captive audience.

"For instance, they talked about French women having pride. Does that make sense to you?"

"What do you mean?" Patrice asked.

"Well. Let's say you go out with a guy on a date—"

Patrice stopped me. "We don't go on dates here."

"You don't?"

All the women shook their heads again. No dates.

"Well, what do you go on, then?" I asked, confused.

"We go out, we have a drink, but we don't call this a date. We are just having a drink."

"Yes, but if you like the person, if it's a man you're interested in, isn't it a date?"

The women just shook their heads at me, no.

"But let's say a man you work with asks you to go have a drink, and it's a man you really like. Wouldn't you be a little excited and maybe, let's say, get a little dressed up?" I could see from their expressions that I was already losing them. "And then wouldn't that, in fact, be a date?"

They kept shaking their heads. Clearly *date* was not one of the American words the French co-opted. I was getting nowhere so I changed my tack.

"Okay, what if you've slept with a guy. Someone you liked. And then he doesn't call you. You would feel bad, yes?" The women all shrugged some version of yes.

"So would you ever, in a weak moment, call him and say you wanted to see him again?"

They all started shaking their heads no violently.

"No, never," Audrey said.

"Absolutely not," Patrice said.

"Not really, no," said Joanne.

Clara shook her head also. "No."

"Really?" I said, surprised. "You wouldn't be tempted?"

"No, of course not," said Audrey. "We have our pride."

And they all nodded in agreement.

So there it was again. Pride.

"Well, who taught you about this? This idea of pride?"

"My mother," Clara said.

"Yes, my mother," said Patrice.

"Our world, our culture. It's in the air," said Audrey.

"So a man, a boyfriend, starts pulling away from you, starts calling you less and less, tells you that maybe he's not ready to be in a relationship, what would you do?"

"I wouldn't call him again."

"I would think it's his loss."

"I would not bother with him."

"Even if you really like him?"

"Yes."

"Yes."

"Yes."

"Yes."

I was sitting there staring at four women who were good at accepting rejection—these ladies didn't seem like they were from France, they seemed like they were from Mars.

Elegant Patrice tried to explain it to me. "Julie, you have to understand, it's not that we don't feel things; we do. We fall in love, we get our hearts broken, we're disappointed and sad, but we've been taught that you must always have your pride. Above all."

Again, much nodding in agreement.

"So does that mean you all love yourselves or something?" I blurted out. They all smiled, but this time they differed.

"No," Patrice said.

"Not necessarily," said Audrey. "We've just learned how to hide our insecurities."

"Yes," said Joanne, the beautiful forty-five-year-old with the braids. "I do love myself. Very much."

"Don't you worry about getting older and there not being enough men to go around and all that?"

"No," said Joanne. "There are many men. You just go out, you meet them. All the time."

The other women agreed. And just when I was about to ask where all these men were, a figure passed our banquette dressed like Lawrence of Arabia. As he walked down toward the dance floor, all the women started turning in his direction. The lights on the dance floor started to swirl and Middle Eastern music began to play. Women started to scurry toward the dance floor. Audrey rolled her eyes.

"Ah. The strippers are here." The dance floor was now lined with women standing and watching.

"Strippers?" I asked, surprised. "There's strippers?"

"Didn't Steve tell you? That's why all the women come here at eight. To eat free food and see the strippers."

I was aghast.

"So you mean all this is, is a French Chippendales? Steve made it sound like the women came here to make new friends."

The women all grimaced. "Please," elegant Patrice sniffed. "Who needs to do that?"

So maybe we're not so different after all. We went to the dance floor and checked out the action. I might as well have been at the Hunk-o-Rama in Brooklyn. The two men dancing were taking off their flowing robes until they were in nothing but itty-bitty g-strings. Then they pulled two women out of the audience and sat them on chairs on the dance floor and began dancing and rubbing their *Jean-Pierres* in these women's faces. All the women in the club were screaming and cheering. These women were making friends all right. I couldn't wait to tell Steve. Where had all the cool, detached Parisian attitude gone? It was a good lesson. Sometimes even French women need to strip off their pride and go whoop it up for a night.

About an hour later, we walked upstairs to leave as hordes of men were charging in like bulls out of the pen. Outside was now a mob of men desperately trying to get in.

"This is ingenious. You let in only the most beautiful women, give them free food and drinks, get them loose and crazy with strippers, then send in the men and charge them tons of money. It's diabolical," I said as we walked out of the club, the cool air hitting my face.

"You have to meet the owner, Thomas. He's a bit of a celebrity here. He owns three restaurants and two nightclubs, plus many other venues all over the world. He's very interesting," Clara said, elbowing her way through the crowd. "And he's my brother," she added.

"Your brother?" I asked, surprised.

"How do you think we got in tonight?" Clara asked. I tried not to take that personally. "I know he's here. I just texted him to come out and say hello. He would be good for you to talk to. He has some very interesting theories on the subject." Clara scanned the crowd. "Thomas! *Viens ici!* Over here!"

Now how I remember it is that the crowd began to part in slow motion as a tall, slim man emerged out of the sea of people. He had short, black wavy hair with pale skin and shimmering blue eyes. He looked like royalty. I took one look at him and thought, *Dashing. This is what they mean when they talk about dashing.*

"Thomas, this is the woman I told you about, who is doing research on women and being single," Clara said, politely speaking in English.

"Ah, yes," Thomas said, looking right at me. "So, what did you think of my night here?"

"I think you're an evil genius," I said, smiling. He laughed.

"This is very accurate. An evil genius, yes." He looked at me. "And why are you doing this? Tell me."

"For a book that I'm writing. About single women? About how to be . . . single?" I sounded like an idiot.

"Ah! So much about single women in the States! Relationships, that's much more interesting."

"Um . . . yes, but single women are interesting, too."

"Yes, but sometimes a bit obsessive, don't you think?"

I felt this perfect stranger was insulting me and I didn't really know how to defend myself.

"So what is the problem? Too many single women and no men? Is that it?" He couldn't have made it sound more trite if he had tried.

"Well, yes, I guess that's the main problem, yes. I'm not sure."

He continued on: "But you American women, you idealize marriage so much. Every movie, there's a wedding in it. Or some man is running off a pier or getting in a helicopter to propose to the woman he loves. It's infantile, really."

My eyebrows raised. "As opposed to the French films where everyone is cheating on everyone?"

"That's reality. That's complications. That's life."

"Well, if you don't like it, I guess you can always stop watching bad American films . . ." I responded, quickly.

"But it helps me feel superior," he said, smiling.

"It doesn't seem like you have a problem with that," I said, glaring at him a bit.

Thomas burst out laughing. "Ah, good for you, Miss Single Woman. Good for you!" He then put his hand on my shoulder, apologetically.

"I didn't mean to offend you. I just meant to say, everything is changing. All over the world. It's very difficult to understand what any of it means anymore, single, marriage, any of it. No?"

I didn't know exactly what he was talking about. "I live in America. We don't really know what's going on all over the world."

"Well, then it is perfect that you are taking this trip, isn't it?" he said, his blue eyes sparkling at me. "Have dinner with me. I will explain to you more. I love discussing these things."

Startled, I turned to Clara to see if I had heard him wrong. Clara laughed. "I told you, he has a lot to say on the subject." I didn't know how to respond. Thomas took that as a yes, and I guess it was.

"Come. I'll take you to another club of mine."

We got out of Thomas's car and walked a half a block to a nondescript town house. He pressed the buzzer and a gentleman in a suit and tie answered the door. He greeted Thomas deferentially and ushered us into a dark, elegant room with a long wooden bar and crystal chandelier. Opposite the bar, well-dressed people were seated eating dinner and drinking champagne on black leather banquettes with a golden brass railing separating them from the rest of the room.

"This is your place as well?" I asked, impressed.

"It is."

"Well, this is quite different from men in g-strings and lukewarm tortellini," I joked. We sat down at a little banquette in the corner.

"Yes," Thomas said, smiling as if he had a secret. I wasn't quite sure what was happening; why Thomas had invited me out or what we were doing there. But who really cared? This was a fantastic way to spend my first night in Paris. As the champagne arrived, I dove right in.

"So, was there anything else mildly insulting you wanted to say about American single women? Or were you done?" I was trying to be sassy but cute.

Thomas shook his head and laughed. "I'm sorry if you found me insulting. I will try and behave myself from now on." He looked around the club. "I invited you here to give you a different perspective. To show you that everyone is trying to figure it out. There are no easy answers to any of it."

"Wow. In the few minutes you've known me, I've shown myself to be that ignorant? Thank you for being so concerned with my world perspective."

"We French have to do what we can." Thomas looked me straight in the eyes and smiled. I blushed. I couldn't help it, but I did. He was fantastic.

"For instance, I have an open marriage."

"Excuse me?" I said, trying to sound nonchalant.

"Yes. An open marriage, is how I think you Americans describe it."

"Oh. That's interesting."

"It's one way to go, to deal with this problem."

"What problem?" I asked. The waiter brought us tiny cups of some kind of thick, warm amuse-bouche soup.

"Of boredom, of stagnation, of resentment."

"And you solve that by sleeping with other people?"

"No. We solve that by making no rules for ourselves. By being open to life. When you get married, you tell each other that from that day forward, you will never be allowed to have sex with someone else, to feel passion, to explore a spark, an attraction. You are beginning the murder of a part of your essential nature. The part that keeps you alive."

"But . . . doesn't that make things complicated?"

"Yes, sometimes very much so. But as I said, that is reality. That is life."

"I don't understand. Do you just say, 'Hey, honey, I'm going out to have sex with someone else, see you later . . .'"

"No. We are polite. You must be polite. But for instance, right now I know my wife has a boyfriend. He is not so important to her; she sees him once a week or less. If it truly bothered me, she would be done with him."

"But it doesn't bother you?"

"It is just sex. Just passion. It is life."

I downed my champagne. "It sounds like a little too much life for me. You're giving me a headache." The waiter came and took our orders.

Thomas smiled mischievously. "For example: this club. We have a very nice restaurant. But upstairs, it is a place where people can have sex."

"Um. What?" Thomas poured more champagne into my glass.

"You heard me. It's what you call a sex club—for couples. Everyone must come in with a partner."

"You mean, these people, all around us, are going to go upstairs later and . . . with each other?"

"Most likely, yes." Thomas looked at me. He became quite polite. "I don't want to offend you; I just thought you'd be interested to know."

"No. I'm very interested. I am. I've never had dinner at a sex club before . . ."

Thomas then looked down at his hands, folded at the table. He looked up at me. "If you want to take a tour, I'd be happy to show you around."

I looked straight at Thomas. He shrugged his shoulders. I believed it was a bit of a dare. And I hate backing down from a dare. And besides, it's all in the name of research, right?

I took another gulp of my champagne and set down my glass with purpose. "Sure. Let's go."

We got up. Thomas and I walked toward the bar area. It was only then that I noticed the television at the bar was showing women in lingerie, dancing. Thomas took my hand and walked me toward a dark corner of the room. There I could see a spiral staircase, with a delicate iron railing. He looked at me for a moment and smiled. We began to walk up it, slowly. I have to admit, I was curious. And slightly nervous. When we landed on the second floor, I looked around. I could see it was a long, dark room, but couldn't make out much else. Thomas walked me over to the men's room right by the stairs. Okay, it's a men's room. Then, the women's room. Nice bouquet of flowers by the sink, whatever. And then he opened a door.

"This is the shower room." I peeked in and saw a large tiled room with a single showerhead in the middle of it.

"It fits six." I stood there staring, until he took my shoulders and pointed me toward the other end of the floor. We passed a room with no door, and which had a giant platform bed in it. No one was in there. We began to walk down the center of the long room. It was then that I started hearing, um, noises. The lighting was low, but what I think I saw, and I couldn't testify to this under oath, but what I *think* I saw, was three people on one side of a large platform having sex. The only woman, I believe, was on her back, spread-eagled. On the other side of the room there was a couple having sex against a wall. I put my head down, and tried not to let out a shocked American gasp. At the end of the room, there was another staircase, thankfully, leading down. As I descended, I could hear Thomas laughing behind me.

"You're lucky. Things haven't really started up yet."

"I'm not going to act shocked, no matter how much I am," I said, laughing.

"And that is why I find you so appealing, Miss Tough New Yorker."

As we sat back down, our dinner arrived. I was now very curious. "Now tell me what's so great about that idea," I asked, my elbows firmly on the table, my whole body leaning in.

Thomas shrugged. "It's one way people are trying to keep their marriages exciting."

"By sleeping with other people in front of each other?" I asked a little sarcastically.

Thomas suddenly turned serious, speaking to me as if I were a rude, slightly dim child.

"Julie, have you ever slept with someone for over three years? Over ten years? Over twenty years? Someone you share a bed with every night, have children with, the diapers, the illnesses, the homework, the tantrums, hearing about their bullshit work problems, every day, in and out?"

I was shamed and silenced. I hate the "what's the longest *you've* been in a relationship" card. But he had a point. I felt like a pilgrim. A very immature pilgrim.

"Then, how can you judge?" he said, softening. I drank some more champagne and looked around at all the proper people. I couldn't help but imagine them upstairs without their pearls and silk shirts and wool jackets doing God knows what to one another.

"Isn't this just asking for trouble? Don't you have a lot of divorces that come out of this place?"

"On the contrary. Most of these couples have been coming here for years."

"No pun intended," I said. Thomas gave me a sympathetic smile.

"I thought Paris was supposed to be such a romantic place, and tonight all I'm hearing about is sex."

"No, Julie. You are hearing about people who are trying to keep their love alive. As opposed to you Americans who get fat and stop sleeping with each other, or lie to each other and have affairs with their neighbors."

"You make us sound like one big *Jerry Springer* episode."

"I exaggerate to make a point," he said, smiling. "What I am saying is that marriage is not the only way to go. And a monogamous marriage is not the only way to be married. Everything is moving toward freedom, in whatever form that takes. Being single is going to be just one of many life choices."

"But come on, wouldn't most people agree it's better to be in love and in a relationship than not?"

"Yes, definitely. But how many people do you know that are in a relationship and in love?"

Of course, I've thought about this before. "Not that many."

Thomas folded his hands in front of him, very professorially. "There are only two interesting lives you can lead, in my opinion. You can be in love. That, to me, is very interesting. And you can be single. Also, a *very* interesting life. The rest is bullshit."

I understood exactly what he meant.

"Are you in love with your wife?" I asked, deciding to be nosy.

"Yes, absolutely."

A surprising pang of disappointment hit my chest.

"And we try not to become bored of each other. Because we are in love. And because of that, it's a very interesting life. For instance, the minute you called me an evil genius, I wanted to spend more time with you. Because you seemed funny and interesting and you are beautiful."

I started to sweat a little.

"That doesn't mean I'm not in love with my wife, or that I don't want to be married to her. It just means that I'm a man and I am alive."

I tried to make a joke. "Listen, if you think that kind of talk is going to get me into that jungle gym upstairs you better think again."

Thomas laughed. "No, no, Julie. Tonight, I am just enjoying your company. Entirely." He looked at me, shyly. I could almost swear I saw him blush.

"You know, I think the jet lag is kicking in a little," I blurted out, awkwardly. Thomas nodded.

"Of course, this is your first night in Paris. You must be quite tired."

"Yes. Yes I am."

Thomas pulled up in front of Steve's apartment and turned off the engine. I suddenly got very nervous, not knowing what to expect next from this French fellow. "So, thank you for the ride and the champagne and the sex, I mean you know, the eye-opening . . . you know . . ." I was stammering a little.

Thomas smiled at me, amused at my awkwardness.

"I believe you will be going to the opera on Tuesday and then to the gala? Yes?"

"What? Oh yes, Steve mentioned it. He's conducting."

"Fantastic. I will be there with my wife. I will see you then."

And with that he got out of the car and opened my door for me. Besides the whole showing-me-people-having-a-three-way, he was the perfect gentleman. He kissed me on both cheeks and sent me on my way.

Back in the States

They all got dressed up for the funeral. It was a happy occasion after all. Serena's old self of ego and desire and attachment to this material world was about to die, and Georgia, Alice, and Ruby agreed to all go to the funeral to celebrate. It was ninety minutes out of the city, at an ashram near New Paltz, New York, and Georgia had offered to drive. Ruby was late to meet them at the garage, because she is always late, which immediately irritated both Alice and Georgia, because they are never late and they didn't want to be driving up to New Paltz to watch Serena become a swami in the first place. But they had promised me, and though they weren't about to take a vow of celibacy at the altar of Siva, they did worship at the altar of friendship and keeping promises.

At first, there was an uncomfortable silence in the car. It was nine in the morning, they were all tired and cranky, and none had any idea what they were about to get themselves into. However, if you know anything about women, you know that something about the confinement and intimacy of a car will eventually get even cranky ladies gabbing.

Alice soon began laying out for Georgia her belief system for being single. She verbally drew for Georgia all the maps and diagrams that spelled out the basic tenets of her dating dogma: You have to get out there, you have to get out there, you have to get out there. As they drove up 87, Alice taught Georgia about Nerve.com and Match.com, about not spending too much time emailing these guys, but instead making a date for drinks or coffee, never dinner. She taught Georgia about immediately deleting the guys who use sexual innuendo in the first couple of emails and not feeling bad if she doesn't want to respond to guys she feels are too old, short, or unattractive for her.

As Georgia exited the Thruway, and started driving along tree-lined roads and past farms and cows and goats, Alice told her about rock climbing at Chelsea Piers, about kayaking and trapezing on the West Side Highway. She explained to her about the hottest clubs and bars and what nights you should go where.

Georgia, already on a steady IV of panic and mania, really didn't need any more pumping up. Though it was only an hour and a half in an Acura driving upstate, it could well have been forty-eight hours trapped in a

Motel 6 with a bunch of Scientologists depriving you of sleep, food, and phone calls. By the time they pulled up in front of the Jayananda Meditation Center, Georgia was fully brainwashed on the Gospel according to Alice and she was hooked.

In the backseat, Ruby slept the whole way. She woke up just as Alice pulled in to the gravel driveway.

"Does anyone know what we're actually going to be seeing here?" Ruby asked as they drove past the sign for the center.

"I have no idea," Georgia said.

"I just hope we don't have to do any crazy chanting," Alice added.

They got out of the car and smoothed out their rumpled outfits. Georgia and Ruby were both wearing dresses with stockings and boots, and Alice had opted for a more professional-looking blazer and pants set. As they followed the smattering of people walking down a grassy hill on a little stone path, they saw that they were clearly overdressed. The other guests were wearing flowing shirts and skirts, the men had various displays of facial hair, and the women were mostly sporting unshaven legs. There were a few Indian men in orange robes and sandals. As Georgia, Alice, and Ruby got to the bottom of the hill, they saw where the ceremony was to take place. A few yards away there was an open-air stone temple. It was circular, with marble floors and stone pillars and pictures of various Hindu figures on the walls. People were taking off their shoes and sandals outside the temple. Incense wafted in the air.

"This is really weird," Georgia whispered.

They wrestled their footwear off and walked in. They immediately took on an air of solemnity befitting the occasion. In the middle of the temple was a stone pit, with a small fire quietly burning in it. The "congregation" all began sitting on the floor, cross-legged. These three ladies were not dressed for the lotus position, but they gamely arranged their skirts and pants in some fashion that let them put their pretty asses on the cold rock floor.

An elderly Indian man in orange robes who seemed to be the head swami started reading from a book in Sanskrit. There were two other male swamis flanking him, an older Italian-looking swami and a really hot fortysomething swami. Next to him was an extremely overweight female swami. They stood silently as the head Indian swami kept reading. Eventually, the initiates were brought out. There were five of them: three men and two women. And one of those women was Serena.

Alice, Ruby, and Georgia let out a collective gasp when they saw her. She had shaved off all her hair. All, that is, except for a little belt of hair trailing down her back. Her beautiful blond hair. Gone. Only a skinny little bird of a thing remained. Serena. In an orange sari. When Serena had called Alice the day before to give her directions, she explained to Alice what she was doing. She believed her calling was to spend the rest of her life meditating and being of service, all in the hopes of achieving some kind of spiritual enlightenment. Serena believed she was done with this material world, and was ready to give it all up. Alice hadn't really understood what Serena was talking about, but now, seeing her in the orange robe and no hair, Alice realized Serena was not kidding around. The initiates stood quietly as the swami finished reading a section of the book. Then the hot swami began to speak. He seemed to be the translator, the temple PR person designated to explain to everyone what was going on.

"I want to welcome everyone here today to this funeral. This is the day these students become sannyasins. They will take vows of poverty, of celibacy, of detachment from family, from friends, from all the pleasures in this physical world. This fire represents the funeral pyre . . ."

"He is really hot," Georgia whispered. "What kind of accent do you think that is?"

"I'm not sure," Alice whispered back. "Australian?" Ruby glared at them. They closed their mouths.

". . . where their old selves will be burned away, to make way for their new self as a sannyasin."

And with that, the old Indian swami picked up some scissors that were lying on the ground and as each initiate kneeled before him, he cut off the last remaining strands of their hair and threw it in the fire. After that was done, the five almost-swamis sat down cross-legged on the floor. One by one, the overweight lady swami placed three cones of incense on each of their heads; Serena was the last. Georgia, Alice, and Ruby watched this, perplexed. A girl they had only met on a few occasions, who last time they saw her she was getting her stomach pumped, was now bald and balancing incense on her head. All six of their eyes widened with dismay as they watched the Indian swami light the cones, one by one. The hot swami explained:

"As the cones of incense burn down to their scalps, these five new sannyasins will meditate on their new path of abstinence; the burning cones may form a scar on their heads, creating a permanent symbol of their new commitment to self-denial."

Alice gasped. Ruby raised her eyebrows, and Georgia just rolled her eyes. Serena looked out into the crowd and smiled. She seemed to be almost glowing. Something about the look in her eyes took their collective breath away. Peace. Calm.

Imagine that.

"I invite you to all meditate with our sannyasins for a few moments."

All eyes in the temple closed. But Georgia looked around as everyone began breathing in and out slowly. She started contemplating the idea of the burning off of the self. If Serena could cast off her old self, so could she. She didn't have to be mad at Dale. She didn't have to be humiliated that she recently broke the promise she made to 230 of her closest friends and relatives and broke up with the man she was supposed to love till death do they part. She could let go of the feeling that she was a failure in her marriage, and therefore at life. She could let go of the agony of knowing that someone with whom she had shared intimacies and embarrassments and joy and sex and the birth of two children had found someone else he'd rather be with.

As she sat there, with a tiny rip tearing up the side of her skirt, her inner voice said, *I can let it all go. I don't have to be a bitter, divorced lady. I can do it any way I want. And I want to date young, hot guys.*

Alice meanwhile felt the pangs of her crossed legs cramping up, but she couldn't help but notice how nice it was just to sit still for a moment. Peace. Calm. To breathe. To stop. She closed her eyes.

Yes, her inner voice said. *I've passed my knowledge on to Georgia. She'll make a valiant and loyal student. It's time for me to stop. I'm fucking exhausted.* Alice kept breathing in and out, in and out, slowly, until her inner voice finally said, *It's time for me to marry the next man I meet.*

In Ruby's mind's eye, much to her surprise, she was holding a baby in her arms, surrounded by all her friends and family in a halo of love and acceptance. Her eyes popped open in shock at the sudden image of her motherhood.

"While the sannyasins meditate, feel free to join us in the main house for some curry and chapatis."

After they drove back to the West Village, where Georgia parked her car, Ruby, Georgia, and Alice said their polite good-byes.

In a contemplative mood, Ruby decided to walk to a park and get some fresh air. But she didn't walk to just any park. Bleecker Street Playground is a mere thousand square feet, but it is chock full o' children—running, climbing, digging, screaming, giggling, fighting, feuding children. There were big brightly colored pails and trucks and wheelie things they can sit on and motor with their little children feet. There were mothers and nannies, all shining with the glow of West Village chic. There were a few fathers, all handsome with their salt-and-pepper hair and well-gymed biceps. Ruby stood looking in at it all, her hands on the bars of the fence that protected those inside from molesters and kidnappers. She walked to the entrance, a big metal gate with a big sign that said "Adults not admitted without a child." She ignored this and, trying to feign the look of a beautiful-mother-now-looking-for-her-adorable-child-and-beloved-nanny, walked right in.

She scanned the park. She wasn't quite sure what she was looking for, but she knew this was the place where she was going to find it. She sat down next to two mothers; white, slim, really good highlights in their hair. She was gathering information, soaking it all in: the kids, the moms, the nannies, everything. Suddenly, there was an eruption in the center of the park, near the monkey bars. A four-year-old devil-girl, with long, ringleted brown hair, screamed and beat on a poor defenseless little boy, throwing him down on the concrete and then wailing at the top of her lungs. Her face was red and her eyes were almost rolling in the back of her head, as if she were the injured party. A young woman ran over to the little girl and hugged her. Another woman raced over and picked up the little boy, who was now also wailing. The monster's mother scolded her demon child, but it clearly was not penetrating. This bad seed was already in the Land of Tantrum, screaming and crying and hitting her mother. When the two mothers sitting next to Ruby saw the look of horror on Ruby's face, they just shook their heads, and almost in unison, said two words that would explain everything: "Single mother."

Ruby nodded sympathetically. "That's so sad," she said, egging them on.

"It was a one-night stand. She got pregnant and decided to do it on her own. It was very brave," said the slim woman with the blond highlights.

"But now, even with help from her sister and babysitters, it's a nightmare," said the other slim woman, with the red highlights.

"A nightmare," said the blonde, to emphasize the point. Ruby couldn't stop herself.

"Well, I know I could never do it. Could you?" Ruby said innocently. From the expressions on their faces, she knew the answer, but she decided to keep going. "I mean, could you even imagine doing it on your own?" She tried to appear as casual as possible, but she waited for their answers as if the Lost Ark was about to be opened.

"Never. Not a chance. It's too hard. Too lonely."

"Absolutely. I would kill myself."

Just as Ruby suspected—being a single mother is even more depressing than being single. But what about the joys of motherhood? The intimate relationship between a mother and child? The gratification of raising a human being from birth and putting them out into the world?

"But don't you think it would still be nice to be a mother? Even without a husband?"

"Not worth it. I'd rather die."

The blond-highlight mom spelled it out. "Just imagine doing everything by yourself. Even if you had all the help in the world, at the end of the day it's still just you worrying if they're sick, deciding what school to go to, teaching them how to tie their shoelaces, ride a bike. You're the one who would have to take them sledding, who would have to organize all their playdates, who would have to feed them and put them to bed every night. You would be the one who would have to make sure they got to school on time, make their lunch, deal with their teachers, help them do their homework. You would get the call if your kid was sick in school, or in trouble, or," she said a little more pointedly, "had a reading disability."

"Right, and imagine if you had a really sick kid, like with cancer or something," said the red highlights.

"Oh my God, just the thought of being in the hospital, having to call a friend or a family member to sit with you, alone, being that kind of burden on everyone. If I was single, that image alone would make me wear five condoms every time I had sex."

"Then imagine being a single mother with a teenager."

"Right, you have to discipline them, set boundaries, deal with drugs and dating and sex, *and,* add to that that now they hate you."

"And if you had a girl, imagine going through menopause and seeing your daughter blossom and become sexually desirable just at the moment you're shriveling and drying up and becoming sexually useless."

These ladies were getting really dark now, even for Ruby. She tried to appear unfazed and attempted to interject some optimism into the conversation: "Well, you might not still be a single mother by the time they're teenagers. After all, you could meet someone."

In unison, the two mothers stared at Ruby. "Like you'd ever have the time," the blonde said. And the redhead said, "Who would want you? These men in New York could have anyone they want. Like they're going to pick a woman with a child?"

Ruby's optimism now came out in a whisper. "Well, if a man fell in love with you, he wouldn't care . . . ?"

The two mothers again looked at Ruby, as if she was a simpleton. The blond woman then asked Ruby, "Well, what do you think? Could you do it alone?"

Ruby looked out into the playground at children she considered for the most part to be adorable, well dressed, and well raised. She thought about the playdates and the homework and getting them to bed and the childhood cancer. She thought about how depressed she got just when a guy didn't call her after two dates.

"No. I couldn't. I could never be a single mother."

The mothers nodded in agreement. Here in the children's park in the West Village, three women were in complete agreement about what they believed in: *Being a single mother would really, really suck.*

Ruby walked all the way up Broadway. She was around Seventy-sixth Street when she made peace with the fact that she would never be a single mother. Guess she could check that off her list now. They were right, and they should know—it was too hard. So then the only thing left for her to do was keep dating. But how? It was so depressing. As she walked, she thought about Serena. Serena believed in God and spiritual enlightenment so much that she renounced everything and burned incense on her scalp. That was pretty hard-core. It made Ruby wonder what she believed in. *Should she pack it in, too? Should she just stop dating and start caring about other things?* It was not such an unattractive thought. But as Ruby walked and thought, she realized she wasn't ready for that just yet. She still had a little more fight left in her. And by Ninety-sixth Street, it finally came to her. She needed to get back on the horse, to love again. She needed to not be afraid to get emotionally involved again. She had to dive back in.

It was time to get another cat.

Now she was walking with a purpose; she was going to go back to the animal shelter where she had adopted Ralph. Her time for mourning was over.

The shelter was a two-floor concrete bunker on 122nd Street and Amsterdam, in a neighborhood that was a little dangerous. It didn't make Ruby scared as much as nostalgic for a bygone era. We don't have that many streets left anymore. By the time she got there, Ruby was proud that she was doing something as life-affirming as choosing to love again.

As she opened the door to the shelter, the smell of animals hit her immediately. It was a suffocating smell, one that made you want to walk right back out the door. But Ruby walked to the counter to a young Irish-looking girl with frizzy hair in a barrette on top of her head. The walls were covered with cheerful posters of animals reminding you "To love me is to spay me," or "Give me an $8 ID tag today, save the $300 reward fee later!" The cement walls were covered with paintings of dogs and cats, but really it was of very little use. The place felt like a bomb shelter no matter how many puppies you painted on the walls.

Ruby told the girl that she wanted to adopt a cat and was buzzed through a door that led to a flight of stairs. The stench of animals got stronger as she walked up the steps. As she opened the door to the second floor, the sound of one dog howling filled her ears. It was a sound that cut right through her; a keening that seemed to be coming from the pit of the dog's soul. Its familiarity made Ruby dizzy. *That's the sound I want to make every morning when I wake up,* Ruby thought.

It was macabre walking through that industrial hallway, with that howling—very *One Flew Over the Cuckoo's Nest,* but with dogs. Ruby quickly walked into the narrow room that had the cages of cats. She closed the door and the dog's cries were muffled a bit. She looked at the cats, one by one. They were all cute and soft and slightly lethargic. But she could still hear that damn dog losing it. Ruby stopped at one cat that was exceptionally adorable, almost a kitten with white and gray fur, named "Vanilla." When Ruby stuck her finger in the cage, Vanilla playfully grabbed at it with her paws. That was that—she would adopt Vanilla. She walked out of the room to tell the man at the front desk about her decision. As she walked down the hall, the crazy dog kept baying. Ruby decided she had to take a look at that thing. She opened the door into the cuckoo's nest. She passed what seemed like cage after cage of pit bulls. She finally got to Loud-Mouth. Ruby looked at the description that was taped on her cage: "Kimya Johnson is a four-year-old white pit mix who was adopted out as a puppy. We recently found her as a stray, and we haven't been able to locate her owner. She's a very nice, friendly and snuggly dog, and appears to be housetrained. Well, her former owner's loss will be a new owner's gain. Perhaps that new owner will be you?"

Ruby's heart sank. Getting adopted from the pound only to be brought back again. Talk about abandonment issues. Kimya was standing up, her front paws on the cage, howling her little heart out. She might as well have been clanging the cage door with a tin cup. Just then a young girl of about sixteen walked into the room. She was wearing the brown uniform of a staff member, with a pin that said "Felicia" in blue Magic Marker, and underneath it, "Volunteer."

"She's so loud, right?" she said in a thick Hispanic accent. "That's why nobody wants her. She's so loud."

Ruby looked at Felicia. This was no way for a volunteer to talk. Kimya kept crying.

"She's so cute, though," Ruby said, trying to be kind.

Felicia looked at Kimya and smirked. "Yeah, but she's too loud. That's why I think they're going to put her down tomorrow. She's so loud. Dang."

Ruby quickly looked at Kimya. "Really? Tomorrow?" Her voice squeaked.

Felicia sucked her teeth. "That's what I heard." She shrugged her shoulders.

Ruby was aghast. "Well . . . aren't you supposed to be trying to convince me to take her?"

Felicia looked at Ruby blankly, taking a nice long pause for dramatic effect. "Well, do you want her? 'Cause you can have her if you want her."

When Ruby shot back, "My building doesn't allow dogs," Felicia rolled her eyes, smirked, waved her hands in exasperation, and walked out the door.

Ruby stared at Kimya. For one moment, Kimya got quiet. She looked at Ruby, her black pink eyes pleading for help.

Ruby walked quickly out of the room and down the flight of stairs. She walked up to the girl at the counter.

"I'm sorry I can't adopt Kimya. I'm really sorry. But I really would get kicked out of my building. You have no idea how strict my co-op board is."

The girl at the counter looked at her blankly.

"But I can adopt Vanilla," Ruby said proudly. "And I'd like to volunteer here once a week."

The woman looked surprised. She handed Ruby another form. "Great. Orientation is this Wednesday at seven."

Ruby smiled brightly. "Terrific. Thanks." As she waited for them to get Vanilla, she breathed a sigh of relief. She knew she would be great at convincing people to take unwanted strays. She would save the lives of dozens of dogs and cats. They needed her here.

*   *   *

Georgia went home that night, put on a pair of two-hundred-dollar jeans, a tight-fitting cashmere t-shirt top, and a pair of trendy little motorcycle boots, and off she went to Whole Foods Market to do some grocery shopping.

In the car that day, her new dating guru, Alice, told her that the Whole Foods in Union Square is a great place to meet really cute guys on a Saturday evening. You can sit and watch a cooking demonstration or stop at an organic-wine tasting or just go searching for homemade hummus and the love of your life.

As Georgia wheeled her cart around this high-end supermarket, she noticed that she felt great. It might have had something to do with watching Serena's funeral, because she felt centered. Optimistic. Dale had the kids all weekend, so she was free to just be a single person in the world; a single person who was attractive, fun, smart, and truly excited to be alive. How hot must that be? As she rolled by the organic greens, she realized that she didn't have to believe a single thing that she had ever heard about finding love in New York. There was no reason she had to buy into the belief system that there are no good men left, that the men in New York are all dogs, that every second that ticks by she gets older and less desirable. She didn't have to believe any of that. Because that was not her experience. She met Dale in New York, at Columbia. She was in grad school for journalism and he was a business major. They had been together ever since. So until she had personally experienced that there were no good men anywhere in the world, she would assume the opposite. As she pushed her cart past the overflowing mountain of cheeses, the French ones, the Italian ones, the ones that come in wheels, the ones from goats, she realized she can simply choose to drive around the entire landfill of presumptions and fears associated with dating in New York. Until it happened to her, none of those stories mattered. She was a blank slate, filled with optimism, unfettered with bitterness; and because of that she felt that she had an edge over most of the single women out there. Men were going to pick up on her joie de dating vivre, and it was going to be irresistible.

She made one lap around the whole store, taking her time enjoying the tour of healthy food. She was now standing over a row of organic beets, pondering how desirable she was going to seem to all of mankind, when a tall, slim man came up to her. He asked her if she had ever cooked beet greens. She looked up and smiled. He had curly brown hair, parted in the middle with just enough scruff on his face to look sexy, but not as if he was in a band.

See? she thought to herself. It doesn't have to be so hard. She then sweetly explained to this cute gentleman that she had, in fact, cooked beet greens, and that they are delicious fried with just some oil, garlic, and salt.

"Wow, thanks. I'm trying to cook more, you know? Eat more greens."

"Well, that's great. They're supposed to be very nutritious."

Then this cute man smiled at Georgia, a sort of devilish and sheepish smile combined, and added, "How was that for an opening line? I've been following you ever since the organic chocolate section but I couldn't think of anything smart to say. But then you landed in the beets and I thought, Ah! Beet greens! Now that's a conversation starter!"

Georgia laughed, blushing, and quickly said, "It was perfect. Didn't seem forced at all, very natural, yet charming."

The cute man extended his hand and said, "Hi, my name is Max."

Georgia shook his hand and said, "Georgia, nice to meet you." And after they talked for about twenty minutes, next to the beets, they made a plan to go out to dinner soon. Georgia left Whole Foods, with three yellow peppers for eight dollars and her newfound optimism validated. She thought to herself, *This dating thing is going to be a breeze.*

·   ·   ·

That night, Alice, our Special Forces of dating, was on her next "op." His name was Jim and he was a fix-up, from a friend of a friend who had been forwarded the famous Alice Email. The Alice Email was a mass email, similar to what you'd send out to the public at large when looking for a good cat sitter. The Alice Email, however, was about looking for a good man. She sent it to all her friends, and asked them to send it to all of their friends, a sort of viral marketing manhunt. Because of it, she ended up meeting a lot of men she might never have met. Unfortunately, she wouldn't have wanted to meet most of them, but that hadn't bothered Alice one bit. She had been out there and that was the name of the game. Jim was an electrical engineer from New Jersey. He was thirty-seven, and from his emails, seemed to be intelligent and friendly. They were going to meet at a small bar in Noho where Alice took all her first dates. It's a tiny, dark, Turkish wine bar with beaded velvet lamps and overstuffed couches. If you can't manage to muster some kind of romantic connection in this place, with its dim lighting, and huge goblets of red wine, then it isn't going to happen anywhere.

As Alice walked to the bar, she thought about the countless dates she had been on this year. She thought about all the men she had met, and wondered why none of them had been the guy for her. There had been a few tiny relationships, a couple of affairs, but for the most part none of these men were guys that she wanted to spend time with. She wondered briefly if this numbers game was really working for her. She was certainly meeting a lot of men, but maybe by increasing her odds, all she was doing was increasing the odds of just meeting guys that she wasn't attracted to. Maybe love is so special, so magical, that it has nothing to do with numbers. Maybe it's just destiny and luck. And destiny and luck have no need for odds. Up until that moment, Alice always thought she believed in the odds, in math. But looking back on the past year, it gave her pause. All those men . . . A wave of exhaustion shimmered over her. She shook it off, and put on her prettiest smile, ran her fingers through her hair, and walked into the bar.

Alice looked around and saw a man sitting on one of the sofas and seeming to be waiting for someone. He was approaching cuteness, but was not actually someone you would say was cute; a little too pasty, a little too soft in the face.

She walked up to him and asked, "Are you Jim?" He immediately stood up and put out his hand and smiled a warm, open smile.

"Alice, so nice to meet you."

She could tell immediately that he was a good man.

They began to talk about the things people talk about on first dates: jobs, family, apartments, where they went to school. But as they talked, as is the case with all first dates, only 70 percent of their brains was talking, listening, and responding to what the other was saying. The other 30 percent was wondering, *Do I want to kiss this person? Do I want to have sex with this person? What would my friends think of this person?* Jim asked Alice a lot of questions about herself, in the way that sweet men do when they really like you. As Alice told her stories and laughed at his almost funny jokes, she could tell from the way he looked at her that he found her adorable.

"What do you mean, you have a trick that makes you able to hear yourself snoring?" he asked, already laughing at her very personal admission.

"Seriously, if you can remember, right before the moment you actually wake up, to make sure you don't alter your breathing—like you almost pretend you're still sleeping, but you're actually awake—you can catch yourself snoring."

Jim just looked at Alice, shook his head, and laughed. He was completely smitten with her. Now this wasn't a new event for sexy, redheaded Alice. Men found her adorable all the time. But because of her usual take-no-prisoners approach to dating, if Alice didn't return the sentiment, only 25 percent of her brain was listening to the man, and 75 percent of her brain had paid the check, caught a cab home, and was now watching *Seinfeld* reruns. If she was interested in the guy as well, then Alice would work as hard as she could to be even more adorable while looking as if she was not trying to be anything but herself. But tonight, she was just allowing herself the enjoyment of being admired by someone. And it felt warm. Relaxing. She started getting tingly and buzzed from her second glass of wine, but she was also tipsy off of this new discovery: sometimes it's okay not to try so hard.

Back in France

The scene was fantastic. As I stepped out of my cab, I saw glamorous, well-dressed men and women getting out of taxis or rushing down the street toward the Palais Garnier. I walked up the stairs of the opera house and turned around to look out at the scene. Paris. How clichéd to be impressed. But I was. It's an unbelievable gift to be able to travel. It just is. That there are these gigantic steel machines that manage to lift us into the sky—that seems an impossible achievement in itself. But then to have the time and the finances to take advantage of it. How thrilling. How thrilling to be somewhere different—where every sight and smell seems strange and exotic. Paris, where I'd been so many times before, was still a foreign city to me. The cafés, the bread, the cheese, the men with their ruddy faces and gray mustaches—and the smell. It smells old and earthy. European. I love it.

We were seeing the opera *Lohengrin*, the story of a princess who dreams about a knight in shining armor coming to her rescue, and when he appears, all she has to do is never ask him who he is or where he's come from. Of course, eventually she can't take it, and she asks him, thus losing him forever. Just like a woman.

As I gazed over the whole mise-en-scène I heard a woman's voice call out to me loudly. "Allorah, Julie. Hallo! Hallo!" Audrey and Joanne, all dressed up, were walking up the stairs toward me. Steve had gotten us all tickets together.

Audrey smiled and asked, "How did you enjoy our talk the other night? Was it helpful?"

"Yes, very helpful," I said, as we entered the opera house. "I was surprised how well French women handle rejection."

"Yes, I was thinking about this," Joanne said, as we walked through the lobby.

"I do believe it has something to do with our upbringing. I think in the States, perhaps, it is considered very bad to fail, to be bad at something. Parents never want to tell their child that they aren't fantastic, they never want to see their child lose. But here," Joanne pursed her lips and shrugged her shoulders, "if we are bad at something, our parents tell us we're bad at something; if we fail, we fail. There is no shame about it."

We gave our tickets to the ushers and walked in. Could it be true that if our mothers and our teachers hadn't coddled us so much in our childhood we would be better able to handle rejection?

I was too busy chatting with Audrey and Joanne to really pay attention to where I was. But then the place hit me full on. We were now in the audience of the Palais Garnier, one of the two theaters that house the Opéra National de Paris. It was opulence to the highest degree. Balcony upon balcony, red velvet seating and gold leaf everywhere you looked. The stage was concealed by a red velvet curtain, and over it all there was a chandelier that, according to the program's notes, weighed ten tons. We sat in our seats and I looked around.

As if I hadn't already seen enough beauty, grandeur, and Parisian charm for one evening, Thomas entered the row behind us with the tiniest, most elegant woman I had ever seen. She had long, blond, straight-as-a-sunbeam hair that fell just below her shoulders. She was wearing a powder blue dress one might describe as a "confection"; it poufed out at her waist and made her look as if she should be on top of a jewelry box. I could swear I smelled a waft of her tasteful perfume from where I sat. Thomas smiled and waved. He pointed me out to his wife; I saw him leaning over to her and whispering in her ear. She smiled and waved graciously to me. I suddenly felt like Andre the Giant and wished I had dressed better.

The orchestra began to play and Steve stood up out of the orchestra pit. He bowed to the audience and they applauded madly for him. My dear high school friend began waving his arms around and it seemed the orchestra was doing exactly what he told them to do. It was very impressive. The opera began and we settled in for the story of a princess who could have had it all if she had been able to keep her damn mouth shut.

When the opera was over twenty-seven hours later, or maybe just four, we were ushered to a room behind the backstage area. It was another gold leaf and rococo extravaganza and it was very old-world Parisian and very grand. I watched proudly as Steve was greeted and congratulated by his adoring, well-educated public. Thomas came into my view as I made my way toward a waiter who was passing out champagne. Thomas saw me and walked over. We took our champagne together.

"Where did your wife go?" I asked, casually.

"She decided to go home. Opera gives her a headache." He looked around at the crowded room, and then his eyes landed squarely on me.

"Would you like to take a walk?" Thomas asked, not breaking his gaze.

"Now?" I asked.

"Please. This is so boring. We must get out of here."

"I can't . . . my friend Steve, I'm his date . . . I couldn't."

I pointed to Steve, who at that moment was talking very closely to a fresh-faced young man in his mid-twenties.

"I believe Steve might have another date this evening. But I'll ask his permission." And at that, Thomas grabbed my hand and pulled me over to Steve.

"No, please," I said, feeling his surprisingly rough hand in mine.

As we walked up, Steve looked away from his gentleman friend and saw Thomas standing there holding my hand.

"You must be Thomas," Steve said, slyly.

Thomas registered this comment with a smile.

"Yes, I am, and I was wondering if I could borrow your friend for the evening. It seems she is the only one I want to speak with tonight, and it is such a warm evening for October, I would love to take advantage."

"Of her?" said my asshole friend Steve, smiling.

"No, no, of course not," Thomas said, laughing. "Of the weather. Of the evening."

"Oh. Of course. Of course."

Thomas shook Steve's hand. "You did an extraordinary job tonight. Bravo, Steve, really." He then put his hand on my back and gently guided me toward the door.

As we walked along the Avenue de l'Opéra, I couldn't help but get right to the heart of the matter.

"Your wife is very beautiful."

"Yes, she is."

I didn't really have anything to say after that. I just felt it was important for her to be brought up.

"What does she do? For a living?"

"She owns a lingerie shop in the Eleventh Quarter. Very successful. All the models and actresses go there."

I thought to myself, *Of course she owns a business that celebrates femininity and sexuality. I'm sure she looks perfect in very little clothes.*

Let me get this out of the way as quickly as I can. I'm a woman living in a large city in America who watches television and goes to movies, so, yes, I hate my body. I know how politically incorrect, cliched, unfeminist, and tired that is. But I can't help it. I know I'm not fat, I am a respectable size six, but if I dig just a tiny bit, I have to admit to myself that I'm absolutely sure the reason I don't have a boyfriend is because of my cellulite and my huge thighs. Women are crazy, let's move on.

"Would you like to sit down and have a coffee?" Thomas asked. We were in front of a café with seats available outside.

"Yes, that would be nice."

A waitress handed us plastic menus, the kind with the little photos of croque-monsieurs and steak frites.

"So, tell me, Julie. As a single woman, what is your biggest fear?" I looked up at Thomas, startled.

"Wow, you're not one for small talk, are you?" I laughed, nervously.

"Life is too short and you are too interesting." He slanted his head, giving me his full attention.

"Well, I guess it's obvious. That I won't ever find someone, you know. To love." I looked down at my menu, staring at the photograph of an omelette.

The waitress came over again and Thomas ordered us a bottle of chardonnay.

"But why should you be so worried about finding love? It will happen. It always does, doesn't it?"

"Ummm, yeah. Actually no. It doesn't feel that way to me and my friends. Back home, the statistics are telling us that it's very hard to find a good man, and that it's only going to get harder. It seems a little bit like a crisis." The waiter came with our bottle of wine. Thomas approved it and the waiter poured two glasses.

"Yes, but with anything in life, you must ask yourself, Am I a statistical person? Or a mystical person? To me, it seems one must choose to be mystical, no? How could you bear it any other way?"

Mystical versus statistical—I had never thought about it that way. I looked at Thomas and decided I loved him then and there. Not in the real sense of love. More in the "I'm-in-Paris-and-you're-handsome-and-saying-smart-things-about-life-and-love" love. He was married and I would never sleep with him, but he was definitely my kind of heartthrob. "That's an interesting theory" is all I said.

We drank our wine and talked for another three hours. It was four in the morning when we had visited our last café and walked all the way back to Steve's apartment. I felt rejuvenated and flattered and attractive and smart and funny. As we stopped by Steve's door to say good night, Thomas kissed me on both my cheeks.

Then he smiled mischievously at me. "We should have an affair, Julie. It would be so nice."

I then began to have a prolonged coughing fit that happens when I suddenly feel exceptionally nervous. It also gave me time to think of what to say.

When I was finally done hacking, I said, "Yeah, well, you know, I don't know if I believe that I'll find the love of my life any time soon, and I'm not sure if I believe I'm a mystical person or a statistical person, but I do believe I shouldn't sleep with married men."

Thomas nodded. "I see."

"No matter if their wives approve of it or not. Call me provincial."

"Okay, Miss Julie Provincial," he said, smiling at me. "Tell me, how long will you be here in France?"

It was then that I realized I hadn't made any actual plans about how long I was staying or where I should go next.

As I stood there I wondered, *had Paris taught me enough about how to be single?* I did learn about pride. And something about the different types of marriages that exist. Maybe I had learned all I needed to know for now. Maybe it was time for me to go.

"I don't know. I might go to Rome next."

Thomas's eyes lit up.

"You must! Paris is very nice, yes, but even we French understand— Rome is . . ." He rolled his eyes in reverence. "I am part owner of a café there. You must go. I know many single women there."

"I'm sure you do," I said, sarcastically. I heard how it sounded before I was even finished with the sentence. It sounded so hard, so cynical, so New York.

Thomas looked at me, earnestly and slightly annoyed.

"You know, Julie, if you dislike yourself so much that you think I must be like this with every woman I meet, that's for you and your therapist. But please, don't paint me as some pig. It's not fair."

Properly scolded, I didn't have a sassy retort.

"Please let me know if you need my help with Rome. It will be perfect for you," he said politely. "In fact—I think it's just what you need."

As I watched him walk away, I realized what I believed in for this moment at least: sometimes the princess really should just shut the hell up.

Back in the States

A week after Georgia had given Max her number at Whole Foods, she didn't know whom to turn to. Because I wasn't around, and because they were the only single women she knew, she called up Ruby and Alice, who agreed to meet her at a West Village Mexican restaurant that served five-dollar margaritas.

"I mean, why would a man ask for your number and then never call you?" Georgia asked Ruby and Alice, incredulous. "Please explain this to me."

Ruby and Alice hadn't even had a chance to get their coats off. They stared at Georgia, frozen, not knowing how to answer.

"Really. I didn't come up to talk to *him*, I didn't ask him for *his* number. I was minding my own business. But then he asked for my number, and I got excited. I looked forward to seeing him. Going on a date with him. Does this happen a lot?" Ruby and Alice looked at each other. Ruby couldn't help but ask, "I'm sorry, but have you never dated before?"

A waiter came over and took their drink orders. It was going to be frozen peach margaritas all around.

"I had a steady boyfriend all through college, and then I met Dale at grad school, so, actually no. I never have really dated before. I listened to Julie and all her stories, but I guess I wasn't really paying that much attention, since I was, you know, married." Georgia suddenly looked very guilty. And confused. She looked up at Alice and Ruby, her eyes searching for answers.

"Tell me, are men really that shitty to women in New York?"

Ruby and Alice looked at each other again. They were facing the same dilemma you face when a friend's about to get her wisdom teeth pulled and she asks you how it was when you had it done. Do you tell her the truth and say you spent two weeks in excruciating pain, swollen like a chipmunk, or do you lie, let her find out for herself, and secretly hope it goes better for her?

Ruby sipped her margarita, which was the size of a small car, and thought about it for a moment. She thought about how many days and nights she spent disappointed and crying over some guy. Alice crunched on a greasy, delicious corn chip, and thought about how many men she had dated, of how much time she put into this whole dating venture. In that brief moment, they both thought about what they actually believed about dating and looking for love in New York. Ruby began.

"No . . . no, it's not like all guys are shitty. You can't think that, you mustn't think that. There are really, really great guys out there. It's just that, well, it can be rough out there, and you have to sort of, well, protect yourself, you know? But not protect yourself so much that you seem, brittle. But you have to be careful, you have to take it all very seriously . . . in a sense, but then not at all, you know?"

Georgia looked at Ruby, confused. Ruby realized she was not helping in any way. Alice, because she was a former trial lawyer, was much more comfortable breaking the bad news to Georgia, straight, fast, and with no salt around the rim:

"Listen, Georgia, the truth is some guys in New York really do suck. They're not really out there to meet the woman of their dreams, to settle down and get married. They're out there trying to have sex with as many women as they can, while they keep looking for the next woman who's going to be prettier, hotter, better in bed. Now as for this guy, Max. He could just be going around collecting women's numbers just because it makes him feel like a big man, to know he can get women to give him their number. He could be doing it just for sport."

Georgia listened to Alice in rapt attention.

"And the only protection we have against this is our resilience. Our ability to go back out there and try to meet someone else; to be able to recognize, weed out, fend off, and recover from all the bad guys out there, just to get to the one good guy. That's our only defense."

Georgia took a big gulp of her frozen margarita. "Well, okay. But I don't think these men should be allowed to get away with . . . ow! Brain freeze. Brain freeze!" Georgia's face suddenly scrunched up as she threw her hands to her head. She sat there for a moment until her face relaxed as the sensation passed away. For a moment she looked truly deranged.

"Okay, anyway, I don't think they should be able to get away with it that easily. I think they need to be retrained. If none of us ever tell them how it makes us feel, they'll think that they can keep going around asking for women's numbers and never calling them. But we have to let them know that it's not okay. We have to take back the night!"

At that, Georgia picked up her pocketbook, got out her wallet, took out twenty dollars, and threw it on the table.

"Thank you for all your help. Drinks are on me."

Ruby asked, fearfully, "Where are you going?"

Georgia put on her jacket and got up from the table. "Whole Foods. I'm going to wait for him there until he shows up. And then I'm going to try and be a catalyst for change in New York!"

Georgia stormed out of the restaurant, leaving Ruby and Alice there, alone, not knowing exactly what to say to each other.

Georgia prowled the Whole Foods aisles like a cougar searching for an unsuspecting hiker. There was no reason why Max should be at Whole Foods on this night, at this time, but Georgia was on a mission. She was hoping that the sheer force of her will might conjure him to appear in the organic greens section right this very minute. She walked up and down the aisles thinking about how she would talk to him, calmly, teaching him how his actions affect others, and so making the world a safer dating place for all of womankind. She walked up and down the aisles for two hours. It was now ten o'clock at night. She had memorized every section in the store, and was now starting to become familiar with all the items in each section, when she saw him by the frozen edamame.

He was talking to a young pretty blond girl who was holding an NYU backpack. Another one of his victims. Georgia didn't waste a minute to pounce. She bounded over to Max and stood right in front of him and the cute NYUer.

"Oh, hey—hi. Great to see you here," Max said, perhaps with a touch of discomfort in his voice.

"Hi, Max. I just wanted you to know, that when you take a woman's number, to call her, and then you don't, it can be hurtful. Most women don't just give their number to just anyone. Most women rarely feel that much of a spark to someone they're talking to, to want to take it further. So when they do give you their number, there's sort of an unspoken agreement, or expectation, that you'll actually call—because, just to be clear, you're the one that asked for the number in the first place."

Max now started looking around the store, his eyes darting nervously. The NYU girl looked at Georgia blankly.

"I'm sure you think you can do that because you have been getting away with it. But I'm here to tell you that you actually can't anymore. It's ungentlemanly."

Max just looked at his sneakers and muttered, "Jesus, don't get all psycho on me."

Of course he went straight for the psycho defense. Men always like to go straight to the psycho defense. For that reason alone we should never go psycho on a guy: just so we'll never be proving them right. ANYWAY, Georgia now got a little pissed.

"Oh, of course you're going to call me psycho. Of course. Because most women don't confront men and their bad behavior, because they've already been so beaten down, they're sure it won't make any difference. But this time, I just wanted to enlighten you. That's all."

By this point, people were glancing over at them. The NYU girl wasn't budging; she was enjoying the show. Max was losing his cool.

"Okay fine, psycho, are you done?"

Georgia now got pissed. "LISTEN, DON'T CALL ME A PSYCHO. YOU WILL NOT INVALIDATE MY FEELINGS LIKE THAT."

The NYU girl, who up to this moment had been silent, began to speak.

"Yeah, I don't think you should call her a psycho. She's just telling you how she feels."

"Oh great, another psycho," Max said.

"Don't call me a psycho," the NYU girl then said, a little more loudly.

"Don't call her a psycho," Georgia said, even more loudly than the NYU girl. Luckily for everyone involved—except maybe the highly entertained onlookers—a short Hispanic man in a crisp white shirt came over to break it up.

"I'm sorry, but you're going to have to leave the store right now. You're disturbing the other customers." Georgia looked around. She looked back at Max, haughtily.

"Fine, I'll leave. I think he's gotten the message." Georgia began to walk proudly out of the store, her head held high. She didn't even notice the smirks and the people giggling at her as she stormed out the exit door. But as she walked down the street and looked back into the window of Whole Foods, she couldn't help but notice that the NYU girl was still standing there talking to Max. And that Max was laughing and making that circular motion with his finger at his head that signifies "crazy."

Georgia turned away from the window. She walked down the street, trying to remain prideful, trying to maintain her dignity. She got two more blocks and began to cry. She thought yelling at him was going to make her feel so much better. And it did for that five minutes when she was screaming. But she was still a freshman at being single, and so no matter what she thought she believed, she still had a lot to learn.

RULE

4

Get Carried Away

(Even Though It's Impossible to Know When You Should

and When It's Just Going to End in Disaster)

Alice had always prided herself on how well she knew New York; she could be a tour guide for this grand city from the Bronx to Staten Island because she knew the ins and outs of the place like no other.

But that was before she had a boyfriend. It was only then that she was reminded that there was a whole other New York out there that existed only for couples. In this past year of professional dating, Alice had gained access to the hottest bars, nightclubs, restaurants, and sporting events that the city has to offer. But because she had not had a boyfriend, there had been a whole other side of New York to which she had not been given admittance.

For example, there was the Brooklyn Botanic Garden, where she was with Jim. Okay, so he wasn't really her boyfriend; it had only been two weeks. But after that first date together, she had decided to let him adore her for as long as they both were enjoying it. They had taken the No. 2 train out to Brooklyn together and were now walking through the tropical pavilion and the bonsai museum, holding hands. It was divine.

They stopped at a little lecture being given about the golden ginkgo trees.

A white-haired little woman was talking to a group of people about how you can distinguish a ginkgo from other gymnosperms by its fan-shaped, bi-lobed leaves. Alice started to think back on these past fourteen days with Jim. They had discovered other couple hot spots, such as the Hayden Planetarium on the first Friday of the month (when it stays open late), the Bronx Zoo (who would ever go without a child or a boyfriend?), and the skating rink at Chelsea Piers (Alice had always wanted to go but could never drag anyone with her). And now she was at the Botanic Garden learning about bi-lobeds.

This is just so cute, Alice thought. *Being in a couple is cute.*

The lecture over, they walked down a pathway strewn with leaves. Jim took Alice's hand and a rush of pure joy warmed her. She was aware that it probably wouldn't have mattered if the hand were attached to the arm of Ted Bundy—holding hands felt fucking great. Holding someone's hand meant that you belonged to them. Not in some profound irrevocable way, but for that moment in time, you were attached to someone. As they walked along the path, Jim said, "We should go apple picking next weekend."

"Cute," Alice said, happily.

They walked toward the Japanese garden pond. The air was cool, but not cold, with the bright sun warming everything up. It was a perfect fall day. They sat under a little pagoda looking out onto the pond. For someone who thought she knew everything there was to know about dating, Alice was shocked to discover what an amazing time she could have with someone she wasn't crazy about. She decided to check in with herself again as to why she wasn't falling in love with Jim yet. He was attractive. His manners were impeccable, which, Alice realized as she got older, was an important thing to her. He was fun, and sometimes even a little silly, which she always loved. And she really liked his laugh. And he thought she was hilarious. He moved in a little closer to Alice. She put her head on his chest. Last week, when they had sex for the first time, she was relieved to discover that she kind of enjoyed it.

If she hadn't, that would have been the deal breaker in this crazy scheme. But the sex was nice. Fine. If there was a worry that it wasn't hot enough, there was also that whole other area in human experience cordoned off for couples only: regular sex. The experience of consistently having an intimate, physical connection with someone. Of not having to worry when the proper alignment of mutual attraction, safety, and appropriate circumstances (him not being a jerk, him not being the ex of a friend who's still in love with him, him not being a friend of a friend so if it doesn't go well it's a disaster so you might as well not even try it, etc.) would allow you to have sexual intercourse. There is nothing worse than looking through your datebook and realizing you haven't had sex in over six months and it went by in what seemed like a day. And then the worry that another six months could go by in a blink without your naked flesh getting anywhere near someone else's. Because of Jim, that worry was now out of the equation, and if it wasn't bodice-ripping, chest-heaving sex, that was fine, Alice reasoned—because it was regular. And that more than made up for any heat that might be missing.

Alice noticed two little turtles swimming in the pond. They weren't the kind you raise in a box with a plastic palm tree and feed hamburger meat. These were bigger, hearty things, and they were swimming in the small pond that must have seemed endless to them.

She kept thinking about Jim, about how nice this all was, and how she hoped to God that she would be able to fall in love with him. But she also knew enough to give herself a break. She wouldn't beat herself up just because she wasn't able to fall in love with every nice guy she met. If Jim wasn't going to be the great love of her life, it didn't mean Alice was afraid of commitment, or that she only liked guys who were emotionally unavailable, or any of the nonsense people like to blame you for. If Jim wasn't the one, that was no one's fault, it was just life. But as she sat there and thought about how nice and cute things had been these past two weeks, she desperately hoped that he might do just fine for a very, very long time.

Alice turned to Jim, who was staring out into space. He had been acting a little odd the whole morning; his usual laid-back manner had a tiny little pulse running underneath it. He kept bouncing his right leg up and down, now making the whole bench vibrate. Alice put her hand on his crazy leg, and asked what the matter was.

"I'm just a little nervous, that's all."

"Why?" Alice asked.

"Because I need to talk to you."

Alice's heart started beating faster. Men don't usually say things like that unless it's bad news or . . .

"I just wanted you to know that I'm having a better time with you than I've had with any other human being in my entire life."

Alice's heart started beating even faster and her breath quickened the way it does for everyone on the planet when another human being is about to go through the embarrassment of revealing a large emotion to them.

"And I just want you to know that you're the one for me. And however fast or slow you want to take this, it's fine with me. If you want to get married next week, I would happily do that, and if you want to take it really, really slow I'd do that as well. Not as happily, but I would."

Alice looked directly at Jim. It was hard to imagine him looking more vulnerable than he did at that moment. She glanced back at the pond and saw her two turtles sunning themselves on a rock. She decided to let herself get carried away. "I've been having an amazing time, too. I know we don't know each other very well, but I want to give this a go, too."

Jim let out the breath he'd been holding in for the past three and a half minutes, and smiled.

"Great. That's great."

"I don't really know what to say besides that right now. Is that okay?"

"Yeah, sure, no, that's fine. Great. I'm just glad you didn't punch me in the face and throw me in the pond."

"Now, why would I do that?" Alice said, sweetly. They kissed. She was happy, safe, content. Because sometimes after swimming around and around in a long black lake, it's nice to get to sit on a rock and sun yourself for a while.

On to Rome

It was ten minutes before the flight and I was hyperventilating a bit. Well, actually a lot.

It's odd when you realize suddenly that you have a new crazy thing about yourself. They say you get more fearful and phobic as you get older, but it's still shocking when you realize you have to add on one more thing to your list of Crazy. I had not a care in the world when I boarded the plane. But now, as I sat in my seat and the minutes ticked by, I became increasingly nervous. How *do* airplanes stay up? What does keep them from just crashing into the earth? Wouldn't that be completely terrifying to be conscious all those minutes that the plane is plummeting to earth? What would I be thinking about . . . ? And as the physics of air travel became even more implausible to me and I was convinced I would never make it to Rome alive, I began having what I imagine was a panic attack. I started sweating and breathing heavy. Why now? I have no idea. I'd traveled from New York to Paris without a care in the world. Perhaps a therapist might say I was nervous about venturing out on my own, to a strange city, with no one that I knew meeting me there; that I was planning on doing all this "research" in Rome, but I didn't really know how I was going to start. Maybe it finally hit me that I had quit my job and left my home without really that much of a plan in place. Whatever the reason, I realized: who better to talk to in this moment than my very own guru? Luckily, I got her on the phone.

"Okay, so Julie, close your eyes and breathe from your diaphragm," Serena said in a soothing swami voice. "Imagine a white light emanating right out of your belly button and radiating out into the plane."

I was imagining. "It's a white light of peace and safety and protection and it's filling up the plane and then the sky and then the whole world. And you are completely safe." My breathing started to calm. My heartbeat slowed down. It was working. I opened my eyes. And Thomas was standing right in front of me.

"Well, hello, Miss Provincial. I believe I have the seat next to you."

A jolt of surprise zapped through my body, Serena's hard work ruined in an instant. "Um . . . Serena, I have to call you back."

"Okay, but I've been meaning to tell you. You should go to India. I mean, their spirituality, their culture—everyone says going to India is a really powerful experience."

"Okay, I'll think about that. Thanks."

"No, really. They say life-changing."

"Okay. I'll talk to you later. Bye, and thanks!" I hung up. I looked up at Thomas, who was emanating his own special brand of white light.

"What are you doing here?"

"I decided to go with you. I thought I could do some business there." He made a gesture with his hand, asking me to get up so he could sit next to me. I stood up into the aisle.

"Of course I don't usually fly economy class," Thomas said as he moved into his seat and we sat. "But I decided to make an exception." As he buckled himself in and looked around, he added, "My God, coach. It's such a tragedy."

He saw I was having trouble piecing it all together.

"I got your itinerary from Steve. Plus, I know someone at Alitalia." He smiled at me and squeezed my wrist. I blushed and got out a piece of mint gum and popped it in my mouth. The announcements about the plane taking off began and I tried to hide the sweat and the panting. How mortifying would it be to have my first panic attack in front of Thomas? There's New York Quirky, and then there's New York Crazy. Just because it was starting to dawn on me which one I was, that didn't mean he had to know right off the bat. While he was busy trying to find a comfortable place to put his knees, and the flight attendants were coming around checking our seat belts, I let out a tiny cry. Thomas looked alarmed.

"Sorry. I'm just. Something's happening. I feel a little like I'm dying. Or drowning. Something. Sorry," I whispered.

Thomas leaned closer to me. "Has this ever happened before?" I shook my head no.

"You are having some kind of panic episode, yes?"

I nodded. "Yes. I think so." I clutched the armrests tightly on both sides of me, but accidentally grabbed on to Thomas's arm. I leaned forward and started gasping for air.

"Excuse me, is everything all right?" the flight attendant asked Thomas.

"Yes, of course. She just has a stomachache. She'll be fine." As the flight attendant walked away, Thomas reached into his bag.

"Julie, you must take one of these, right away. Please. It will calm you down."

I threw myself back onto my chair and gasped, "I can't believe you're seeing me like this. This is mortifying."

"We'll worry about that later, but for now, just take this pill and swallow please, quickly."

"What is it?"

"Lexomil. France's Valium. We eat it here like candy."

I swallowed the tiny white pill dry. "Thank you so much," and I took another gasp of air. I started feeling calmer already.

"You'll probably be falling asleep soon." He put his hand on top of mine. "It's a shame, we won't get a chance to talk," he said, his blue eyes twinkling.

You really are close to someone when you sit next to them in coach. It's like you have to actually make an effort not to bump your lips into them.

Soon enough, I fell asleep.

I woke up to Thomas tapping the back of my hand, quite hard, and saying in his sweet French accent, "Julie, Julie, it's time to wake up. Please."

Like deadlifting four-hundred-pound barbells, it took every ounce of my strength to open my eyes. In a haze I saw beautiful Thomas in the aisle, looking unruffled and slightly amused as a flight attendant hovered over him.

"*Signore,* we have to leave the plane. You must get her off." It was then that I saw that the plane was on the ground and the cabin was absolutely empty. I groaned loudly and put my hands to my eyes to somehow shield myself from the humiliation. Why wouldn't they just let me go back to sleep?

Thomas gently guided me out of my seat. I steadied myself, grabbed my purse, and tried to pull myself together as quickly as possible. As we walked past the many, many rows of seats to the door, I asked Thomas, "Just tell me this—was there a drooling situation going on?"

Thomas laughed and said, "Julie, you don't want to know." He steadied me out the door of the plane.

Later that afternoon I awoke in a room at some kind of pensione. I was a little disoriented, so I got up and looked out my window onto a piazza with a huge circular building off to one side—the Pantheon. I had no memory of getting there. Thomas told me later that I had gone through customs and been mistaken for a drug addict, had all my bags searched, and then passed out in the cab with my head in his lap. That Lexomil doesn't kid around.

On the desk I found a note: "I am next door at a café with my friend Lorenzo, please come by when you wake up. Kisses, Thomas." I shakily got into the shower, fixed myself up, and went out to find Thomas.

Next to the hotel was a tiny café, right on the piazza. Thomas was with a man in his early thirties who was speaking animatedly, gesturing wildly. Thomas saw me and stood up, his friend getting up as well.

"How are you feeling, my Sleeping Beauty?" Thomas asked.

"Fine. A little groggy."

"I'll get you a cappuccino immediately." Thomas waved over a waitress and we all sat down.

"This is my friend, Lorenzo. He's heartbroken and telling me all about it."

Lorenzo was a handsome Italian man, with big, tired eyes and long brown hair that he grabbed and pushed back whenever he was exclaiming something, which was often.

"It's awful, Julie, awful. My heart is broken, you don't understand. Crushed. I'm crushed." He pushed back his hair. "I don't want to live, really. I want to throw myself off a building. She just left me. She told me she doesn't love me anymore. Just like that. Tell me, Julie, you're a woman. Tell me. How is this possible? How can a woman love you one minute and destroy you the next? How can she have no feelings for me overnight?"

Luckily my cappuccino came just then, so I could get a little caffeine into my system.

"Um . . . I don't know. Was it really that sudden?"

"It was! Three nights ago, we made love, she told me she loved me. That she wanted to spend the rest of her life with me. That we should have babies together. Then, yesterday she calls me up and tells me she doesn't want to be with me."

"How long were you together?" I asked.

"One year. One beautiful year. We both agreed that we have never been in such a good relationship. How is this possible, Julie, tell me. Just three nights ago she told me she loved me. Just three nights ago. I can't sleep. I can't eat. It's terrible."

I looked at Thomas, wondering what I just stepped into. As if reading my mind, Thomas laughed and said, "Lorenzo's an actor. He's very dramatic."

"*Ma no*, Thomas, c'mon," Lorenzo said, offended. "This is no exaggeration. This is a real tragedy."

"Was your girlfriend an actress as well?"

"No. She's a dancer. You should see her body. The most beautiful body you have ever seen. Perfect breasts. Perfect. And these long legs, like art. Tell me, Julie, tell me. How can this happen?"

Thomas saw the dazed expression on my face and decided to egg him on. "Please, Julie, you must help him."

I was still a little slow from my drug overdose, but I tried to think as quickly as I could.

"Do you think she met someone else?"

"Impossible! We saw each other all the time."

"Are you sure? Because that could be—"

"No. It's not possible. I know all her friends. Her dancing partners, too. No."

"Well, is she psychotic?"

"No. She was perfectly fine. Sane."

"Maybe," I said slowly, "she wasn't really in love with you?" Lorenzo banged his hands on the table.

"*Ma no*—how could that be? How?" He was truly looking for me to explain.

"Well, if she's not seeing anyone else, she isn't psychotic, and she just changed her mind about you, then maybe she wasn't really in love with you. Or maybe she just doesn't know what love means."

This type of American analysis simply didn't compute for Lorenzo. He just shrugged his shoulders and said, "Or maybe she just fell out of love with me."

"Do you think that love is so fleeting that it can just go away? Just like that?"

"Of course I do, Julie. It finds you, like magic, like a miracle, and then it can go just as fast."

"You really think of love as a mysterious emotion that comes and goes like magic?"

"Yes, of course. Of course!"

Thomas said gently, "I believe you would call my friend a romantic."

Lorenzo threw his arms in the air. "What other way is there to live? Julie, don't you believe this, too?"

"Well, no. I guess I don't," I said.

"Tell me, then. What *do* you believe?"

Thomas leaned in. "Now this is getting interesting."

Again, that question. I stalled, sipping my coffee. I have spent a good deal of time in therapy analyzing why I've been attracted to the people I've been attracted to. What "buttons they push" in me that makes me want them in my life. I've spent a good deal of time analyzing why my friends are attracted to the types of men they are attracted to. I've watched them swear that they've met their soulmate, that they've never felt this way before and that it's destiny—and then break up with that soulmate in less time than it takes to get a sofa delivered. I've watched friends—smart, levelheaded friends—get married, and then I've watched in shock as their marriages fell apart. And I've watched absolutely ridiculous couples stay together for ten years and counting.

And I've been so busy looking for love and being frustrated that I can't find it, that I have never really defined it for myself. So I sat at this little café as the sun went down, and pondered.

"I guess I don't really believe in romantic love," I finally said. Thomas raised his eyebrows and Lorenzo looked as if he had just seen a ghost.

"What do you believe in, then?" Thomas asked.

"Well, I believe in attraction. And I believe in passion and the *feeling* of falling in love. But I guess I don't think that that's necessarily real."

Thomas and Lorenzo seemed shocked.

"Why? Because sometimes it doesn't last?" Thomas asked.

"Because *most* times it doesn't last. Because most of the time it's about what you're projecting onto a person, what you want them to be, what you want yourself to be, so many things that have nothing to do with the other person."

"I had no idea," Thomas said. "It seems we have a very big cynic here."

"This is a disaster, truly," Lorenzo said, throwing his hands in the air. "I thought I had it bad."

I laughed. "I know! I didn't know what a cynic I was until this moment, either!"

"But Julie," Thomas asked, concerned, "how can love ever find you if you don't believe in it?"

I looked at them both staring at me with great concern, and then—I burst out crying. Funny how that happens. One moment you're a strong, independent woman talking about love and relationships. And the next moment someone says an arrangement of words that somehow destroys you.

"No! Julie. It was not meant to be—no!" Thomas was horrified. "Please, it was nothing!"

I put my hand over my face. "No, I know, don't feel bad. I don't know why . . . I'm just too . . . please. Don't worry about it. Really." But as I spoke, the tears rolled down my face. There it was again, the question that always seems to pop out of the subtext when I least expect it. *Why are you single? Why don't you have love?* And now, in Rome, one answer: *because you don't believe in it.*

"I'm just going to go to my room," I said, starting to get up.

Thomas grabbed my hand as Lorenzo said loudly, "*Ma no,* Julie, come on! You can't run back into your little room to cry. That's unacceptable." Thomas added, gently, "How are we ever going to be friends if you run and hide every time you have an emotion?" I sat back down.

"I'm sorry. It must be the Lexomil or something."

Thomas smiled. "Yes, I'm sure. You're relaxed. Your defenses are down."

I turned to Lorenzo, embarrassed. "I'm so sorry. I'm not usually like this." He looked at me with admiration.

"Women! They are fantastic. Look at you. You feel, you cry. So fluid. *Che bella! Che bella!*" He waved his arms around and laughed. I burst out laughing as well, and Thomas looked as happy as any man could look.

• • •

After we went to another restaurant for dinner, and I had the best pasta carbonara I've ever tasted, with large strips of bacon in it—not chunks, not bits, but actual *strips* (you wouldn't think it would work but it did)—it was time to go to sleep. Lorenzo went home, and Thomas and I walked back to the hotel, passing piazza after beautiful piazza, the Trevi Fountain, the Spanish Steps. Rome is so old, so beautiful, it's hard to take it all in. When we got to the hotel, Thomas walked to a motorcycle with two helmets locked to it. He got out a key, unlocked them, and handed a helmet to me.

"And now," he said grandly, "you must see Rome by motorcycle."

"When did you get this?"

"It's Lorenzo's. He has a few. He lent it to me while you were asleep."

I don't like motorcycles. Never have. Because here's what—they're really dangerous. And it would be cold. I don't like to be cold. But the thought of explaining that to him and seeming once again like an unspontaneous, unromantic, panicky American, well, it just exhausted me to the core. So I took the helmet and got on the bike. What can I say. When in Rome. . . .

We drove fast, by random Roman ruins and by the Forum. We wound through tiny streets and raced along the main thoroughfare and up a street that led straight to Saint Peter's Square.

There I was, on the back of a dangerous vehicle that was going very fast with a driver who, let's face it, did have a few glasses of wine at dinner. I was cold. I was frightened. And very vulnerable. I imagined the motorcycle crashing, Thomas losing control as we took a turn, our bodies sliding into oncoming traffic. I imagined some official calling my mom and telling her what happened, and her or my brother having to deal with the horror and hassle of getting my body shipped home.

And then, as we rocketed back toward the hotel, we circled around the Colosseum. It struck me: none of these structures are surrounded by walls or gates or plate glass. They stand unprotected, waiting to dazzle us, accepting their vulnerability to any graffiti artist or vandal or terrorist that might want to come around. And I thought to myself, *Well, if this is how I'm going to go, it's a damn good way to go.* And then I wrapped my arms around Thomas a little tighter and tried to drink in every ounce of magnificent Roman splendor.

• • •

When we got back to the hotel, Thomas took off his helmet and helped me take off mine. There's nothing less sexy than wearing a motorcycle helmet, truly. We walked through the lobby and into the elevator. I was suddenly jarred back into the world of dynamics and morality and innu-endo and not knowing where Thomas was sleeping that night. And as if he had read my mind, Thomas said, "My room is on the third floor. I be-lieve yours is on the second, yes?"

I nodded. I had managed to remember my room key and my room number. Thomas pressed the second- and third-floor buttons and the doors closed. When they opened again, Thomas gave me a polite kiss on both my cheeks and said, "Good night, my dear Julie. Sleep well." I walked out of the elevator and down the hall to my room.

Back in the States

Georgia knew exactly what she was supposed to do. Dale was coming over in a few minutes, and she knew the cardinal rule that everyone, no matter how romantically inept, knows: you always try to look extremely hot when you are meeting with an ex. But on this particular morning, Georgia had said "fuck it." She wasn't going to bathe and blow-dry for Dale. Fuck him. She wasn't trying to woo him back. Fuck. Him. He can go live with his underage samba dancer.

Georgia and Dale were meeting to talk about how they would offi-cially share custody of their children. No lawyers, no fighting. Two adults with no agenda except for the well-being of their kids.

When she opened the door, Dale walked in looking, well, hot, unfor-tunately, but fuck him. The first thing he did when he came in was look up and see that the little door of the smoke alarm was open, and the bat-tery gone.

"Jesus, Georgia, you didn't get a battery for the smoke alarm yet?"

"Shit, no, I've been meaning to."

"Well, don't you think that's kind of important?"

"Yes, I do, but I've been kind of busy around here, you know."

He shook his head. "Don't you think that should be high on the list of priorities? A battery for the smoke and carbon monoxide detector in the house our children live in?"

Georgia knew that this could blow up right away into a fight, and that hip, well-educated New Yorkers don't have to have fights with their exes over stupid things. But she didn't care.

"If you'd like, you can turn around right now and go to the hardware store and get a battery for the smoke and carbon monoxide detector that's in the house our children live in. You are welcome to do that if you like."

"I'll do it after we're done talking, okay?"

"Okay. Thanks so much."

They both took a breath. They walked over to the kitchen table and sat down. There was a long silence.

"Can I get you anything? Coffee? Soda?"

"I'll have a glass of water," Dale said, as he got up from his chair. But Georgia was at the refrigerator. This was her house now and Dale knew better than to get up and help himself to a glass of water. As Dale sat back down, she poured a glass of water from the Brita, then walked over and handed it to him. He took a sip. Georgia sat down across from him, her hands folded on the table in front of her. She felt that if she just kept her hands folded in front of her, things couldn't get that out of control.

As it stood, Georgia had full custody of the kids, with Dale seeing them whenever they both agreed to it, and whenever Georgia needed a break. But they knew it was time to set up some rules.

"I was thinking that maybe you could have the kids during the week, and I got them on the weekend."

The sarcasm leaped out before Georgia even had a chance to stop it.

"That sounds great. I get to get them to school and help with their homework and make sure they have dinner and go to bed and *you* get to go out and have fun with them?"

Georgia didn't even know what she was fighting for; it actually sounded like a good arrangement. Let Dale take the kids on the weekend so she could go out and have fun. Dale didn't need the weekends to go out and have fun because he was home with his samba dancer having hot samba sex every night of the week. But she didn't feel like agreeing with him yet. She felt like being pissy, and she felt like getting one thing perfectly clear.

"She can never be with my children. You know that, don't you?"

"Georgia."

"Seriously, if I hear that she was around the kids, I'll go apeshit on you."

"We'll talk about this later," Dale said, his head down, trying to sound neutral.

Georgia's hands were no longer folded. They were now flapping around, helping her make her points.

"What do you mean we'll talk about this later? Like I'm going to change my mind? Like two weeks from now I'm all of a sudden going to be like, 'Hey, can you please bring that Brazilian whore around my children to show them who broke up their mommy and daddy's marriage?'"

"She didn't break up our marriage, Georgia."

Georgia got up, the civility of sitting down to discuss something at the kitchen table now broken.

"Oh, like you would have left on your own with no safety net? Right. You left the minute you knew you had someone else to be with."

Dale didn't wait to respond. "Maybe that's true, but that doesn't mean that our marriage wasn't over long before that."

Georgia was now pacing and her voice had gone up a couple of decibels in volume. "Really? Okay. How long before? How long was our marriage over before you met the samba dancer? A couple months? A year? Two years?" Georgia stopped right in front of Dale, who was still sitting. "How long!?"

There's an expression that if you have to go through hell, the best way is to drive right through it. Dale decided to do just that.

"Five years. It started going bad for me five years ago."

Georgia looked as if she had just been electrocuted.

"You mean right after Beth was born? Then?"

"Yes, if you must know, then. Yes."

Georgia began pacing again. She was a wounded animal now—wild-eyed and unpredictable.

"So you're telling me that for the past five years that we've been living together, you didn't love me anymore?"

"Yes."

Before Georgia was able to stifle it, she let out a little yelp. She tried to swallow it, hoping Dale might have only heard it as a gasp. She walked over to the kitchen counter, shaking. But being a strong, wild animal, Georgia gathered her wits and went right back on the attack.

"Well, bullshit. You're just saying that to make yourself feel better, so you don't have to actually deal with the truth. And the truth is that you got lucky enough to find someone really hot who wanted to fuck you and so you ditched your marriage and your children for it. You're going to tell me that you haven't been in love with me in five years? I say bullshit. You weren't in love with me when Gareth rode his bike for the first time without his training wheels and you picked me up and twirled me around in your arms and kissed me? You weren't in love with me when you got your promotion and I got the kids to write cards that said 'Congratulations, Daddy' and we papered them around the house and had a big dinner for you when you came home?"

"I loved you, but no, I wasn't in love with you anymore. We never had sex, Georgia. Ever. Our marriage was passionless. It was dead."

Georgia was holding on to her hair at the roots, trying somehow to compose herself. Since the breakup of their marriage, there were tears, there was shouting, but they had never had the "face-to-face" talk. This, apparently, was it.

"So that's what this is all about? Hot, sweaty sex? That's not what a marriage is, Dale. That's what an affair is. A marriage is two people building a life together and raising children and sometimes being bored."

"And sometimes having sex, Georgia. WE NEVER HAD SEX."

"THEN WHY DIDN'T YOU TALK ABOUT IT WITH ME?" Georgia shrieked. "WHY DIDN'T YOU TELL ME THAT YOU WANTED MORE SEX? WHY DIDN'T WE GO TO COUNSELING OR GO AWAY FOR A FUCKING WEEKEND? I THOUGHT EVERYTHING WAS FINE."

Dale got up from the table.

"HOW COULD YOU THINK EVERYTHING WAS FINE? WE DIDN'T HAVE SEX. I'M TOO YOUNG NOT TO HAVE SEX, GEOR-GIA. I STILL WANT PASSION AND FIRE AND EXCITEMENT IN MY LIFE."

"FINE. LET'S HAVE SEX. IF THAT'S ALL IT IS LET'S HAVE SEX RIGHT NOW." Georgia stood with her greasy hair and her sweatpants, her arms outstretched. Dale started backing up, shaking his head.

"Georgia, come on."

"What? You don't think it'll be all hot and sweaty right now? You don't think you can find fire and passion with me?" Georgia was sobbing between bursts of fury.

"You don't just want *sex*, Dale, you want *new* sex. If you wanted sex with me, you would have tried to have sex with me. But all you want is new, hot sweaty sex." Georgia was poking him as she spoke, jabbing at his shoulders and his chest.

Dale put his jacket on. "This isn't going anywhere. We were supposed to be talking about the children."

"Yes." Georgia followed him, standing very close. "The children you left because you need to have HOT, SWEATY SEX."

Dale spun around and grabbed Georgia by the shoulders. "I HATE TO TELL YOU THIS, BUT I LOVE MELEA, GEORGIA, AND YOU'RE GOING TO HAVE TO GET USED TO THE IDEA THAT SHE'S GOING TO BE IN MY LIFE FOR A LONG, LONG TIME."

Dale then basically picked Georgia up by her shoulders and moved her out of his way, practically sprinting to the door. Georgia was officially unhinged.

"SHE'S NOT GOING TO GET NEAR MY KIDS, DO YOU HEAR ME??"

She followed him into the hallway, as Dale flew to the staircase, clearly not wanting to wait for the elevator. Georgia shrieked down at him as he raced down the stairs.

"WHAT? AREN'T YOU GOING TO COME BACK WITH BATTERIES FOR THE FUCKING SMOKE DETECTOR THAT YOU'RE SO CONCERNED ABOUT?"

Dale stopped at the bottom landing and looked up at Georgia glaring down at him from three floors above.

"Get it yourself, Georgia." And he slammed the door.

Back in Rome

While Thomas had business meetings, he had thoughtfully arranged little appointments for me to meet with some of his female friends to talk about love and men and relationships. I was here, after all, for research.

Right away, I learned some very important things about these Italian women. First of all, none of them had slept with Thomas. That might not have been the most monumental cultural or anthropological discovery, but it was pretty interesting to me. I never asked outright; all you have to do is ask a woman how she knows someone and you can usually tell from the expression on her face what's up.

The second thing I learned is that they seemed a little shy, which was surprising. In the land of Sophia Loren and . . . actually, there aren't a lot of new Italian actresses who come to mind, which come to think of it, might support my argument . . . I was surprised at how reticent they were in talking about their feelings. Of course it could have just been the women I met, but it was striking. But soon enough, I started noticing another trend.

In their conversations about their relationships, Italian women often mentioned slapping. For example, "Oh, I got so mad that I had to slap him." Or, "I slapped him and then I walked out the door, I was so angry." It seems these timid women weren't so retiring when it came to a little bit of physical abuse. Of course, I only spoke to a few Italian women, and I normally don't like to generalize, but what would stories about a trip around the world be without generalizing? Even so, I don't want to perpetuate a stereotype. But it was of note.

On my third day, I met Cecily. She was just five feet tall, weighed about eighty pounds, and barely spoke above a whisper. And yet in that whisper, she casually let slip that her last boyfriend got her so mad at a party that she slapped him and went home.

"Um, you slapped him right there? At the party?"

"Yes, I was furious. He was talking to this one woman all night long. It looked like he was going to kiss her, they were so close. It was humiliating."

"You're about the fourth woman I've talked to who's mentioned slapping her boyfriend."

Her friend Lena chimed in, "That's because they make us so mad. They don't listen."

We were sitting at a busy café right near the Trevi Fountain. I was eating a chocolate-filled croissant that was covered in powdered sugar.

Cecily tried to explain. "Julie, I'm not proud of this, I don't think I should slap. But I get so upset. I don't know what else to do!"

"I understand, I do," I said, completely lying. Because the truth was, it's something I would never dream of doing. Yes, because I was taught hitting is bad, and that one must learn how to control one's more violent impulses. But also, I could just never imagine the audacity. *Not that I would want to, really.* But still, I've been beaten down to the point where I wouldn't ask a man to put lotion on my back for fear of seeming too needy. So the thought of feeling comfortable landing the palm of my hand across some guy's face was beyond my imagination.

Lena added, "We can't help it. We get so angry, we need to slap."

Cecily understood the expression on my face.

"Do women slap in the United States?"

I didn't want to sound superior, but I didn't want to lie, either.

"Um . . . I'm sure some women do, but it doesn't seem as common as it is here."

Lena then asked, "Have you ever slapped?"

I shook my head, picked at my sugary croissant, and said no. They both took this in, quietly.

After a moment, Cecily asked, "Julie, but certainly a man has made you so angry that you *wanted* to slap him, yes?"

I looked down at my cappuccino. "No."

They both looked at me with pity. I looked back up at them with envy.

"Then you have never been in love," Lena said.

"You might be right."

They both looked at me as if I had revealed the most tragic secret in the world.

"This is a tragedy. You must go out in Rome and fall in love immediately," Cecily said, quite seriously.

"Yes, tonight," Lena said. "You've wasted too much time already."

"Is it that easy? To just walk out your door and decide to fall in love?"

Lena and Cecily just looked at each other and shrugged.

"In Rome, it just might be," Cecily said, smiling.

Lena added, "At least you should try and be open to it. Be open to losing yourself in love."

"Losing myself? I thought that was a bad thing."

Lena shook her head. "No. That's where you American women have it wrong. Trying to be so independent. You have to be willing to lose yourself, to risk everything. Otherwise, it's not really love."

Finally, these shy women had something they wanted to teach me.

Later, when I went to meet Thomas for dinner, I was still rattled. Those women—those timid, passionate, jealous, temperamental women—made me feel so dry inside, so emotionally limited. How does one start believing in love? How do you turn off your brain and everything you've seen and heard in the past twenty years? How do I all of a sudden believe that these crazy large emotions are not just a bunch of hormones and illusions? How do I suddenly believe romantic love is a real, concrete thing and that I'm entitled to it? I was worried that I was starting to think like a self-help book as I walked into a small restaurant on the Piazza di Pietro. Thomas was already there at the bar, a glass of wine in his hand.

The last few days spent with Thomas had been so simple, yet so extraordinary. Innocent, unbroken happiness. There had been dinners and drinks with his friends, and we'd seen a lot of Lorenzo, whose girlfriend had not returned any of his calls, and who was insisting he was ready to be hospitalized. There had been walks and talks and heated debates and lots and lots of laughter. There were more motorcycle rides, and late-night glasses of Prosecco. It's funny how fast you can feel like you're in a couple. It only takes a matter of days before you're thinking "we" instead of "I."

And through all this, he had not made a pass at me once. Not once. For the past four nights, he politely kissed me good night on my cheeks and then went to bed. Not that I wanted him to make a pass. I mean. Not that I would have done anything. I mean. Not that . . . whatever.

As I sat down, I asked him right out, "Have you dated an Italian woman, and did she ever slap you?"

He laughed. "This is what I love about you, Julie—you're not very good with the small talk, either. We share this trait."

All I heard was that he said he loved something about me.

"I have been with a few Italian women, but they never slapped me. I think they know that a French man might slap them back."

"It seems like the Italian men take it in stride."

"I don't know about that. I don't think they like it. But I do hear of it happening quite often."

I shook my head. "Fascinating." I was already getting a little tipsy off my one glass of red wine.

Thomas's cell phone rang. As he listened he began to look concerned.

"Now please, calm down. You will do no such thing. Now stop it. I am coming right over. Yes." I thought it might be his wife, wondering when he was getting his ass back to Paris. Thomas put down the phone.

"It's Lorenzo. He is threatening to throw himself off the balcony of his apartment."

I grabbed my jacket and purse and we were off.

When we got to his apartment, Lorenzo was distraught. He was crying, and it looked like he hadn't slept all night. There were a few broken dishes on the floor.

"She called me today, Thomas. She wasn't angry, she didn't meet anyone else, she just doesn't want to be with me anymore. She told me to stop calling her! It's over! It's really over!"

He grabbed his long floppy brown hair, sat in a chair, and sobbed. Thomas sat on the chair's armrest and tenderly put his hand on Lorenzo's back. Then Lorenzo jumped up and ripped his shirt off, buttons flying, and threw it in a ball on the floor, leaving him in a white t-shirt.

"I'm going to kill myself. Just to show her."

Why he needed to do it in just his t-shirt, I'm not sure, but it got our attention. He ran to the balcony and opened the doors. Thomas ran over to him and grabbed him by the arm, pulling him backward. Lorenzo broke free and went for the window again; Thomas caught him. They both fell to the floor and Lorenzo crawled toward the window while Thomas held on to his leg. Lorenzo tried to kick Thomas with his other leg, around his head and shoulders.

"*Basta*, Lorenzo!"

"Leave me alone, leave me alone!"

"What should I do? Should I call for help?!" I chimed in.

Thomas managed to get on top of Lorenzo. It was a ridiculous sight. Lorenzo was now lying on his back, thrashing around as Thomas sat on his stomach, scolding him loudly. "Please, Lorenzo, this is too much. I won't get up until you calm down. And I mean really calm down. Please."

After a few minutes, Lorenzo's breathing slowed.

"Um, can I get either of you a glass of water?" I asked, with clearly nothing else better to say. They both surprisingly nodded yes. I ran to the kitchen and got two glasses of tap water. Thomas drank his while still on top of Lorenzo, and Lorenzo managed to drink his while still lying on the floor.

Lorenzo tried, or pretended to try, to throw himself out a window over a woman. Was that crazy? Wars have been started, empires jeopardized, over love. Songs are sung, poems are written, all because of love. Historically speaking, it seems to be very real, this feeling. And in this moment, seeing Thomas sitting on Lorenzo, coming to his rescue, it was hard not to think Thomas was perfect. It was hard not to project all my hopes and desires and assumptions right onto him. He was dashing, he was interesting, he was able to comfort a male friend who was crying his heart out without batting an eye. But he was also able to tackle him to the ground like a linebacker. He was a great friend and a fully realized man.

It's so funny, but when it happens, it really does feel like you're physically falling. And I wanted to feel every moment of it, to get lost in it. Why not? Before I knew what I was doing, before I could talk myself out of it, I ran toward Thomas, knelt on the ground next to him, wrapped my arms around him, and gave him a big kiss on the lips. Lorenzo, looking up at us from the ground, started clapping.

"*Brava Americana.* You are beginning to understand a few things."

I stood up quickly. Thomas looked up at me; he was beaming, almost proud.

"I was just trying to, you know, break the tension," I said, backing away from them.

"No! Don't ruin it with excuses. No," Lorenzo said, still on the floor. "It was *bellissima. Si.*"

It might have been bellissima, but I was now embarrassed. Did Lorenzo know Thomas's wife? How many women had he seen throw themselves at Thomas? Did he even want me to kiss him? There was no way to lose myself in love when I had this kind of mind as my compass. I walked to the kitchen and got a glass of water for myself.

I glanced over and saw Thomas look at Lorenzo and speak sternly in Italian. Lorenzo seemed to say something that reassured him. Thomas slowly stood up. Lorenzo slowly got up and sat calmly on his sofa.

Not to take any chances, Thomas gave Lorenzo a dose of the magic Lexomil and after about twenty minutes, Lorenzo was asleep.

We walked back to the hotel, unusually quiet. Finally, Thomas broke the silence.

"So. My dear Julie. I'm very sorry to say this, but I believe I should be getting back. I think Lorenzo will be fine, and I'm finished with my work here."

So that was the response to my dramatic display. He needed to leave town. It served me right. Shame on me for humiliating myself like that. I had made a fool of myself. I knew it—getting carried away did not suit me at all.

"Oh, of course. Yes. That makes sense. Well, thanks! Thanks for everything."

I hoped to sound cheerful, trying to be like a French woman and keep my dignity. Of course this had to end, of course it was going to be over soon. There was no need to get all weepy about it. We were walking by the Colosseum again. It's just crazy, Rome. You'll be walking and chatting and feeling this and that about whatever the hell, and then you'll just turn your head and be like, *Oh hi, two thousand years ago.*

"How long will you stay here?" Thomas asked.

"I'm not sure. I have to decide where to go next." I really had to get better about planning this trip.

We stopped and took a long look at the Colosseum, ancient and glowing.

Thomas turned to look at me. "So tell me, Miss New York. What is going through that busy mind of yours right now?"

"Nothing."

"Oh really? Somehow I have a hard time believing that."

"I just, you know, feel a little stupid, that's all. I mean I kissed you because I thought I should try to get carried away, like everyone is telling me. But it felt dumb. You're married, first of all, and so handsome and charming, you must have . . . I just don't want to look like a silly . . ."

"But tell me, Julie, how did this week feel to you? Tell me that."

I thought for a moment. I didn't really want to tell the truth. I had had a perfect time and I felt like I was falling in love with him. I don't even know what that means, but it's how I felt.

"Stop thinking, Julie, just tell me."

You really shouldn't stand in front of one of the great wonders of the world and lie. Even I could sense that. So I told the truth. What did I have to lose? "It felt fantastic. Like . . . like a miracle. Like hours flew by in seconds and I never ever wanted to leave your side. Everything you said seemed so interesting, so funny. And I just loved looking at you, your face. I loved just being near you. Sitting near you, standing near you. And then when I saw you wrestling Lorenzo, it just made me completely adore you."

Thomas walked up closer to me. "And can you believe that during this week, I felt the exact same way?"

"Well, I never wrestled Lorenzo, so . . ."

Thomas raised his eyebrows. "You know what I mean."

I looked at him, and wanted to say, "No, actually, I can't. Because things like this don't ever happen to me. And I don't think that I'm so great that I can really understand what you would find so captivating about me, so, no, I don't believe it one goddamn bit." But instead, I thought about the hours we'd spent together, the meals and the talks and thoughts shared. It felt very real. And mutual. I thought about the Italian women and their telling me to lose myself in love. I guess people do meet and fall in love or in infatuation without much reason why. It just happens. And all you can rely on is how you feel, because it might not make any sense. You just have to trust the feeling and the moment.

"It's hard for me to believe that, but I guess I can try" is what I ended up saying. And then Thomas put his arms around me and kissed me. In front of the Colosseum with its history and decay and majesty, we kissed. Like two teenagers. Like two people who believed in the wonder of love.

I woke up in Thomas's bed the next morning. I looked over and saw him sleeping soundly. I thought about the night before. How we came back to the hotel and went into his room. How I let myself get carried away. I scanned my mind. How did I feel? Guilty? Yes. Yes, I felt guilty. Even if it was okay with the both of them, he *was* someone else's husband. So, I felt guilty. But did I regret it? No, I did not. Then I felt guilty for not regretting it. How else did I feel? Happy? Yes. Definitely. I felt happy. I had allowed myself to enjoy a moment. I looked over at Thomas and knew that I had felt something, something like falling in love, and it felt real and I hadn't hurt anyone. And that was enough for now. I was ready to leave Rome. I had learned all I needed to learn here.

5

Figure Out the Whole Sex Thing—
When You Want It, How to Get It, Who to Do It With
(Just Make Sure You Have It Every Once in a While; Just My Opinion)

It seemed like a good idea at the time. Georgia and I were in Rio de Janeiro trying on expensive bikinis at a boutique in Ipanema.

Georgia came out of the dressing room to show me hers: a little orange number with white piping and little silver hoops on the hips and right in the middle of her cleavage, holding all the fabric together. Very sixties, very Bond girl. I forgot what an amazing body Georgia has—so had Georgia, it seems, because she was very excited about it.

"Look at me. Look how hot I am. Like she's the only one who's hot? Please. Look how hot I am!" She twirled around and looked at her tight little butt in the mirror and said to the salesgirl, "I'll take it." Then she turned to me, still dressed and clutching a modest two-piece, trembling slightly.

"Now it's your turn."

I believe I told you. I hate my body. And just when I've convinced myself that it's all in my mind, I turn around at the mirror and realize—no, it's all in my butt. Acres and acres of cellulite. In that bikini store, clutching my little two-piece, I felt so debilitated by my cellulite that I should have been given a wheelchair.

Georgia was on a mission. She had called me in Rome to tell me all about her fight with Dale. She was upset and said she needed to get away from it all. That wasn't so surprising, but when she suggested going to the home country of the Other Woman, I was confused. That didn't seem so much like getting away from it all as diving right into it. But I agreed. Her parents had been dying to take care of the kids, so they flew in and she took off.

I used my round-the-world pass to go back to Miami, where I met Georgia, and we flew to Brazil together panic-free. I had heard so much about Rio, about its sexiness, its fun, its danger, I was excited to see it all for myself.

But Georgia had something to prove. It was clear the minute I met her in Miami and we shared a plate of deep-fried stuffed mushrooms at one of those classy airport restaurants.

"What's so great about her? Oooh, she's Brazilian. Oooh, that's so exotic. Well, guess what? I'm a sexy American. That's hot, too." She shoved a forkful of the cheesy mushroom situation in her mouth. "Damn, that's good."

So now Georgia was prancing around in the store like a happy little Creamsicle trying to prove whatever she needed to prove in as little clothing as possible.

So, first off, let me tell you my thing about two-piece bathing suits: they're underwear. Why don't we just admit that? For some reason, when you put sand and water and sun together, you're allowed, even pressured, to go out in public in your underwear. You're expected to expose yourself to friends and family members, sometimes even colleagues, in a way you would never do in any other given moment in time. If Georgia were walking around *this very same store* in her underwear, I would say, "Hey Georgia, put on some clothes. You're walking around in your underwear, that's weird." But because the underwear is orange nylon, it's okay.

I don't want to wear my underwear in public.

My solution has been to wear a cute little bathing suit top with men's surfing trunks. All problem areas covered, even when swimming. The only problem is that I can get away with this for maybe another two years before I overhear some kid at the beach saying, "Who's that weird old lady dressed like a boy?"

As Georgia changed, I explained my philosophy on the bathing suit situation until she cut me off.

"We're in Rio. You're going to wear a bikini on the beach. Go try it on. Seriously. Enough."

Her tone was so perfectly "I'm the mother, do as you're told," I had no choice but to do so. As I was changing behind a curtain, I heard Georgia speaking to the saleswoman, trying her best to cheer me on.

"Women in Rio love their bodies, right? They are proud of their bodies and like showing them off, right?"

"Oh yes," I heard the young saleswoman say. "In Rio we worship our bodies."

I looked at myself in the mirror. I didn't think I would be hanging this sight up on an altar and praying to it any time soon. And then I got really sad. I'm simply too young to hate my body. I'm going to be old in like two minutes, and my body really will be difficult to love. But now, well, it's fine. Why shouldn't I admire it? It's mine and it keeps me healthy and I should accept it, just the way it is. There are people who are sick or disabled and would kill to have a strong, healthy body, and the last thing they're worrying about is their fucking cellulite. It's a show of ungratefulness to my health and mobility and youth to hate my body so much.

And then I turned around. There was so much cellulite on my ass and thighs it made me want to throw up on myself.

"Goddamn it!" I said. "The lighting in here is just as bad as it is in the States. Why do they do that with the overhead lighting? To make us want to kill ourselves instead of buy clothing? I don't get it!"

"Julie, just come out, you're exaggerating."

"No. No way. I'm putting my clothes back on."

"Julie, for Pete's sake, come out. Now," Georgia said in that tone, and by God, it worked again. I walked out and they looked me over.

"You're crazy. You look fantastic. Look at your abs. They're insane."

"Ooh, very nice, miss, very nice," said the saleswoman.

"Oh yeah?" I said, angrily—my need to prove my point overshadowing any vanity I had left. I turned around and showed them the rear view. "Now what do you think?"

Here's the bummer about women: it's so easy to tell when we're lying. Not about the big things; when we're prepared to lie we can be masters. But about small things, like this? God, we're transparent. Georgia's voice immediately went up two octaves.

"Oh please, what are you talking about?"

"Oh, I think you know what I'm talking about."

"You're insane."

"Really, I'm insane? You mean I don't have cellulite from the back of my knees up to the top of my thighs? You mean that's just some crazy 'cellulite hallucination' I've been having for the past five years?"

"It's not as bad as you think. Really."

"See!? I just went from 'fantastic' to 'not as bad as you think.'"

I noticed the salesgirl suddenly went mute. "So, what do you think? I look terrible, right?"

She was silent for a moment. Torn, I realize now, between her job as a bikini saleswoman and her civic duty. She took a deep breath and said, "Maybe you don't need to go on the beach. There are other things to do in Rio."

Georgia gasped loudly. I stood there with my mouth and eyes wide open, speechless. Finally, I got out, "Wha . . . ?"

Georgia jumped right in. "How could you say that?! I thought you said the women in Rio all loved their bodies, worshipped their bodies."

The saleswoman remained calm. "Yes, but these women all work out, they diet, they do liposuction."

"So you can only love your body if you've had liposuction?!" Georgia screamed.

I was seeing stars. I managed to mumble, "So I shouldn't go to the beach because of my cellulite?"

"Or wear a wrap if you do."

"So, you're telling me that my cellulite shouldn't be let out in public."

The young, thin, surely undimpled salesgirl shrugged. "This is just my opinion."

"Oh my God, I think I'm going to faint," I said, seriously.

Georgia was fit to be tied. "That's a horrible thing to say to someone. You should be ashamed of yourself for talking to her that way. You're a

BIKINI SALESWOMAN, for God's sake. Where's your boss? I want to talk to her."

"I am my boss," she said quietly. "I own this store."

Georgia clenched her fists while I watched the room spin in my own cellulite shame spiral.

"Well, fine. We're out of here. We're not going to buy anything in your store. We're not going to give you a dime." Georgia pushed me back in the dressing room.

"Come on, Julie, let's get dressed and go." I got my clothes on quickly and we walked to the door, Georgia still furious. Just as we got to the street, she turned around and went back inside.

"On second thought. No. You can't tell us who's allowed to wear a bikini on the beach and who's not. No one hired you to be Rio's Cellulite Police. Fuck that. I'm going to buy that bikini she was wearing. And she's going to wear it at the beach and she's going to be hot." I tried to protest, because Rio would have to freeze over before I put a bikini on my body. In fact, I wasn't sure if I would ever let anyone see me naked ever again.

Again, the saleswoman just shrugged. "That is fine with me." Georgia looked at me with a that'll-show-her look. "Don't worry, it's my treat." She then looked over at the salesgirl, who was wrapping up my bikini, and said a little more sheepishly, "And I'll take the orange one, too, while you're at it."

Four hundred and eighty-five dollars later—two hundred and forty-two dollars and fifty cents of which will never see the light of day, nor sand nor water—we walked out of the store.

Yep, we really showed her.

So there we were on the beach, right across the road from our hotel in Ipanema. Georgia was in her James Bond swimsuit, and I was in my men's surfing trunks, bikini top, ski pants, and parka. Just kidding. I was still recovering from this morning's shooting, I mean *shopping* spree. As we lay in silence, I could hear the sounds of three women laughing and talking in Portuguese. With my eyes closed, I could pick out the different voices. One was deep-throated and immediately drew me to it. Another was smooth, light, and feminine, and the third was more girlish. The deep-throated one was telling a story and the other women were laughing and chiming in. I opened my eyes, rolled to my side, and looked at them. The woman telling the story was tall and tan, young and lovely . . . Actually, she was tall and black, really black, her skin the color of onyx—she was gorgeous. Her two friends were equally beautiful. One had red curly hair that flowed way past her shoulders, and the other had short jet-black hair in a cute little bob. They looked to be in their late twenties and were all wearing tiny string bikinis. Georgia sat up and saw me watching them.

"I wonder if they like stealing husbands, too."

"Georgia . . ."

"I'm just curious. Why don't you ask them? For your research. Ask them if they like stealing women's husbands."

"Stop it."

The women saw us looking at them. The tall, deep-throated one looked at us a little suspiciously. I decided to be outgoing and introduce myself.

"Hi. We're from New York, and were just listening to you speak Portuguese. It's a beautiful language."

"Oh, New York, I love New York," said the woman with the short black hair.

"It's a wonderful city," I said.

"Yes, I go all the time for work, it's fantastic," said the deep-voiced one.

"Are you here on vacation?" asked the redhead.

"Sort of," I said.

But Georgia, being the good, pushy friend that she is, said, "Actually, my friend Julie is here trying to talk to single women. You all seem so sexy and free-spirited. We wanted to know your secret." She was smiling. I didn't think the ladies noticed any sarcasm in her voice, but I knew it was dripping all over.

They all smiled. The redhead said, "It's not us, it's Rio. It's a very sexy city."

They all agreed.

"Yeah, blame it on Rio," Georgia said. Then she added under her breath, "Or maybe you're just all whores."

"Georgia!" I whispered, glaring at her.

The deep-voiced one said, "We were just talking about that. Last night

I was out and this boy came up to me and said, 'Oh, you are so beautiful, I need to kiss you right now!' And then he did!"

"Now this is not the unusual part. This happens all the time in Rio," said the redhead.

"It does?" I asked.

"Yes. All the time," said the black-haired woman.

"Really?" Georgia said. Now she was interested.

"The funny thing is," continued the deep-voiced one, "that I decided to try it out on this boy Marco, who was so cute. I went up to him and told him that he was so sexy and I had to kiss him right now. He then grabbed me and kissed me for ten minutes!" The other girls started laughing.

"And then she had a *fica*," said the black-haired girl, giggling.

Then the deep-voiced girl said something in Portuguese, seeming to admonish her friend.

"Please, they're from New York."

"What's a fica?" I asked.

The deep-voiced woman sort of pursed her lips to the side and shrugged. "A one-night stand."

"Oh! Great," I said, not knowing what my response should be. But I was trying to bond. "Was it fun?"

"Yes, it was fun. He's from Buenos Aires. So hot."

"Buenos Aires, that's where all the good men are. We never date men from Rio," said Red.

"No, never," said Deep-voiced.

"Why not?" I asked.

"Because they can't commit."

"They are cheaters."

"Wait a minute!" The black-haired lady started laughing.

"Anna is engaged to a boy from Rio. So she doesn't like to hear these things!"

"Not all Rio men are cheaters!" said the black-haired woman, whose name was apparently Anna.

"Well, congratulations," I said. "I'm Julie, by the way, and this is my friend Georgia."

"Ah, like the state!"

"Yes," Georgia said, crisply. "Like the state."

"I'm Flavia," said the deep-throated one, "and this is Caroline," gesturing to the redhead, "and Anna."

Georgia went right in there. "Tell me, Anna. Are you afraid other women are going to try and steal your husband?"

"Georgia!" I shook my head. "Please excuse my friend; she has no manners."

"I'm from New York," she said. "We like to get to the point."

Flavia joked, "No. Women don't steal husbands. Husbands like to stay married forever, and cheat."

"Besides, it's not just the other women we have to worry about so much. It's the prostitutes," said Caroline.

"Prostitutes?"

"Yes, these men love the prostitutes. They all go together. For fun," Caroline said.

"It is a problem really," Anna said. "I worry."

"You worry that your husband is going to go to prostitutes?" Georgia asked.

"Yes. It's very common. Maybe not now, because we're in love. But later. I worry."

Flavia spoke up. "Who cares if he fucks a prostitute? I mean, really. If he sticks his dick in some other woman, who cares? Especially one that he's paid. He's a man, she's a hole. He fucks her. That's what men are like. You're not going to change them."

This is what I love about women. We have no problem just getting into it.

"I don't care. I don't like it," Anna said.

Caroline now joined in. "Anna, please. He's marrying you. He's going to have children with you. He's going to take care of you when you're sick, you're going to take care of him. So what if he goes to a prostitute?"

"If he cheats, I won't leave him, of course. I just don't like it."

Georgia and I looked at each other, surprised.

"If you found out he goes to a prostitute or sleeps with other women, you wouldn't leave him?" Georgia asked.

Anna shook her head. "I don't think so. He's my husband." She began to frown. "But I wouldn't like it."

Georgia and I gaped at each other.

Flavia smiled. "It's very American, this idea of fidelity. I think it's very naïve."

I've heard this before. And I thought about my participation in Thomas's infidelity. A wave of guilt shimmered through my body, and then I just felt sad. I missed him and even though I wished I didn't want him to call, I wished he would call.

Caroline agreed. "Men weren't meant to be faithful. But that's okay; it means we can go out and cheat, too."

Anna looked up at us, sadly. "I try to be realistic about things. I want to be married forever."

Georgia looked at the three of them. I couldn't tell if she was about to start a beach brawl or invite them out for a piña colada. She decided on a new line of questioning.

"So tell me. Are there male prostitutes for women?"

The three women all nodded their heads.

"Yes, definitely," Flavia said. "It's not as common but yes, they have them."

"There are agencies for them," said Caroline.

Georgia's eyes lit up. "Well, at least there's something for the women, too. At least there's an equality in that."

Flavia said, "You two should come out with us tonight. To Lapa. We're going out dancing."

"You'll get to meet Frederico, my fiancé," Anna said. "It will be fun."

"Samba dancing?" I asked, excited.

"Yes, of course, samba," Flavia said.

"Will there be kissing at this place?" Georgia asked.

"Oh, definitely," said Caroline.

"Then we're there!" said Georgia.

You know you're in Rio's Lapa district when you see the large concrete aqueduct towering above you. It was built in 1723 by slaves—a massive structure of archways that once brought water from the Rio Carioca. Now it's the giant doorway to the best party in town. Flavia and her two friends picked us up at our hotel in a minibus. Not very chic, but it seems the minibus is the preferred mode of transportation for rich American tourists when they come to Rio (usually accompanied by an armed body-guard or two). But Flavia borrowed the car from her company, a well-known photography studio. The driver, who we later found out was Anna's brother, Alan, was a tanned, good-natured guy with an easy smile, and not a word to say to anyone. And tonight, this minibus was ready to party. Caroline, Anna, and Flavia were already drinking when we got into the car. They opened the cooler and showed us a big pile of Red Bulls and a bottle of rum. They mixed us drinks and we were on our way.

Twenty minutes later we passed through the aqueduct archway that leads directly onto the main street of Lapa, where all the clubs, bars, and restaurants are. Samba music filled the air, and there were people every-where. It was a giant block party. We parked and walked up the cobble-stone streets. I bought a chocolate bar from a young child selling candy from a box he was carrying, with a strap around his neck. There were a few transvestite prostitutes standing on the corner. Many of the clubs had large windows that allowed you to look inside, often to the sight of bodies bouncing to the rhythmic music. It all felt surreal and a little dangerous. We went into Carioca de Gema, a smallish club packed with people of all ages.

There was a Brazilian woman singing, with two drummers behind her, but no one was dancing yet. We headed to the back room, where we found a table, and Flavia ordered us some food. I began to get the im-pression that she knew everyone in the place. And why shouldn't she? As she walked into the club and kissed everyone hello, Flavia was the star of the show—she was wearing tight denim jeans that perfectly conformed around her round Brazilian butt, and a tan halter top that had tiny beads running all down the sides. Flavia was beautiful, tough, fun-loving, and always ready with the good, hearty laugh. The more I saw her in action, the more I liked her.

When the food came, it was a large plate of dried meat, onions, and what appeared to be sand. Don't ask me how dried meat, onions, and sand could taste so good, but it did. Flavia ordered us caipirinhas, but with vodka in them, not cachaça, the official drink of Brazil. We were under strict orders from Anna's brother, Alan, to stay away from the stuff.

I saw Flavia at a distance, talking to some women who looked at me curiously. I had no idea what she was saying, but I didn't mind. I was too busy shoveling the delicious sand in my mouth and listening to the music and reminding myself that I was, in fact, in Rio, at a nightclub. How cool was that?

Georgia was swaying to the rhythmic beats of the drums. She leaned over and said, "I better get kissed tonight!" A couple in their sixties was standing in front of us, listening to the music. They started doing that crazy thing with their feet, the fast, beautiful, and mysterious step that is samba dancing. It was fantastic. We couldn't take our eyes off them. Flavia came over to us.

"Julie, I have some single women for you who'd like to talk to you about what it's like to be single in Rio."

"Really? Now?" I asked, surprised.

"Yes, I'll bring them over."

For the next hour, my new cultural attaché, Flavia, brought single woman after single woman over to me. I drank and ate sand and meat and listened to the music and heard their stories. I scribbled in my book as fast as I could.

Now, I know that I was just one woman talking to a tiny fraction of the population of women in Rio, but they all seemed to be in agreement about one thing: The men in Rio suck. They don't want to commit and they don't need to. There are beautiful women in bikinis (without any cellulite) everywhere they turn. Who needs to settle down? They are eternal bachelors. Or if they do settle down, they cheat. I'm not saying all men from Rio are like that; I'm just telling you what they told me.

So what is a single woman in Rio to do? They work out a lot. And they travel to São Paulo, where, everyone seemed to agree, the men are more sophisticated, more mature, less childish than the men of Rio.

But they all also agreed that the men of Rio are fantastic kissers and passionate, sexy, skillful lovers. They were all in such vocal agreement about this, that while I was too shy to ask them what made them so good at it, I couldn't help but get very curious. Particularly because all evening there was a tall, dark, and gorgeous man with large, muscular arms standing quietly in the corner staring at me. I was beginning to understand why fica was the first Portuguese word I had learned.

The women also spoke about "husbands," and men they were "married to," and it took me a while to realize that they might not actually be legally married, but were using it as a term to mean a long, serious relationship. I asked Flavia about this later.

"Oh yes, we use it to mean any long relationship, when you live with someone."

It's all pretty confusing. Living with someone can be referred to as "married," but "married to someone" can also mean "I sleep with prostitutes."

Anna's Frederico arrived. Introductions were made and he sweetly apologized to Anna for being late. He was tied up at his popular hang-gliding business near Sugarloaf, a big rock in the middle of the city, well traveled by the tourists.

"Excuse us, we must dance now," Frederico said as he took Anna's hand and led her onto the dance floor. Anna, who had before this been somewhat quiet and soft-spoken, suddenly began to beam. She started moving her feet and shaking her ass and she became instantly the most adorable creature I have ever laid eyes on. And Frederico kept up—working his crazy feet and twirling her around. How could any two people not have great sex if they could dance like that together? This city was awesome.

"I'm going to walk around," Georgia said, and got up from our table. I think all the sweat and sexy dancing was getting to her.

I looked up and saw that Flavia was talking to someone; he was touching her on the arm and leaning in to talk to her. I turned to Caroline, who was sitting next to me.

"Hey, who's the cute guy that Flavia's talking to?"

"That's Marco, the fica from last night. He called today and she told him to meet her here."

"Interesting. The fica calls . . . how often does that happen?"

"Not very often, I think. But sometimes."

"In the States, some people think that if you want them to call again, you shouldn't have a fica first."

Caroline rolled her eyes. "This is your puritan ethics. In Rio, a fica, not a fica, he might call you, he might not—it doesn't matter how you meet."

Flavia and Marco came over to us, and she introduced us all. He had long black hair and lots of stubble. He had a big dopey smile, and a lot of energy.

"Ah, New York! I love New York! I love it!"

That's all he could say to me in English, and he said it to me all night long. To which I would reply "Rio! I love Rio!" It wasn't much, but it was still fun.

I spotted Georgia milling around the crowd. For a moment I didn't understand whom or what she was looking for. She was sort of shuffling around, fluffing her hair, looking a bit lost. I watched her for a little while longer, while she made a loop around the whole bar area, stopping by any cute guy or two. It was then that I realized what she was in search of—she was on a kiss hunt. I wasn't sure if kisses were something that you were supposed to look for, but I did admire her tenacity.

Anna came back to the table without Frederico and stood by the table, dancing in place.

"What the hell are your feet actually doing?" I asked, a little tipsy on my second caipirinha.

"Come, I'll show you." I stood up and she started slowly, moving her feet around, back and forth, heel to toe, toe to heel. I was copying her, getting the hang of it, until she started going a little faster and adding her wiggling ass to the mix. Then she lost me. But I just faked it, bouncing my feet and shaking my butt. I think I more resembled a fish flapping on a sidewalk than a samba dancer, but it got a smile out of the tall, dark drink of cachaça in the corner, so it was worth it. We all continued dancing by our table, the music throbbing, the singers singing in shouts over the drums, whipping the crowd into a sweating, bouncy-feet mass.

Georgia, meanwhile, bumped into Frederico, who was on his way to the men's room. He asked her what she was doing all the way over there, away from her friends.

"I heard people like to kiss a lot in Rio. I'm waiting for someone to try and kiss me."

Frederico smiled. He was extremely handsome: young, tan, with a little beard on his chin and wavy brown hair. With his brown eyes and nice white teeth, he looked like a Latin pop star.

"Well, I'm sure it won't be long. This is Rio after all." And with that he smiled and walked away.

Georgia had learned her lesson; she wasn't going to be the aggressor this time. She had learned from the sports bar that night that the fun wasn't grabbing someone and kissing them. The real rush was someone choosing to kiss *you*. So she kept walking around, wetting her lips and trying to look kissable.

I was still dancing, aware that my man in the corner kept looking over at me. While I continued my stomping, I saw Flavia and Marco walk over to talk to him. She put her arm on his shoulder—of course, Flavia, mayor of Rio, knew him. When Flavia and Marco came back over to us, I asked, "You know that guy?"

Flavia smiled. "Yes, he's an old friend of mine."

"What's he doing in the corner?" I asked.

"He works here, doing security."

I nodded and thought to myself, Hot.

"What—do you like him?" Flavia asked, smiling. We both turned and looked at him, which he immediately noticed. I quickly looked back at Flavia.

"Well . . . he's just . . . sexy, that's all," I said.

"Paulo. He's really sweet, too. He's like a brother to me," Flavia said.

I gave him another look. He saw me and smiled. I smiled back. As I turned around, I felt a sudden pang of something. Guilt. It was the strangest thing. I felt guilty for being attracted to Paulo because I had only recently slept with open-married Thomas. Just thinking about Paulo and smiling at him made me feel slutty. I had recently had sex with a man whom I was kind of crazy about. A man who, let's just be honest, also hadn't called me since, and whom I probably would never see again. But still, I had recently had sex with someone, and it was odd thinking about being attracted to someone else so soon after. I wouldn't have known this was a problem for me, since I don't have this kind of conundrum in New York.

Another reason to travel, is all I have to say about *that.*

Georgia walked back up to us, frustrated, just in time to see Frederico start making out with Anna. Georgia rolled her eyes, jealous and repulsed at the same time. She sat down next to Alan the Silent One.

"Tell me, Alan. Do you go to prostitutes?"

I laughed, surprised, and looked at Alan to see what his response would be. Alan simply smiled, leaned over to Georgia, and gave her a wink.

"Really. Well, I guess it's the quiet ones you always have to look out for," Georgia said, sipping her drink, unfazed. But she wasn't done. "But what if you ever caught Frederico cheating on your sister. Would you kill him?"

Alan looked at Georgia like she was from another planet. Or the United States. He laughed and shook his head. I was now completely engaged in this conversation.

"Really? Why not?" I asked.

Alan took a drink from his beer and said, "We men, we have to stick together."

Georgia raised her eyebrows. "Are you kidding me? Even if it's your sister?" Alan just shrugged and drank from his beer. Georgia looked at him and then at Caroline. "I don't understand. If brothers aren't even looking out for their sisters—then who is?"

Caroline also shrugged. "I guess no one."

Georgia and I stared at each other, depressed. I checked my cell phone and saw that it was 3 A.M. We all agreed it was time to go.

We were at the exit buying CDs of the music we had just heard when I saw Paulo make his way through the crowd. He seemed to be looking for someone. I walked out the door and onto the street. I looked back to see if I could get a last glimpse at him. Just then, he walked out of the club and landed his sights right on me. He walked up to me and put his hand out.

"Hello, my name is Paulo. You are very beautiful." My eyes widened and I started to laugh, looking around to see if Flavia had set this up.

"Well, thank you . . . my name is . . ." and before I had a chance to say another word, Paulo put his velvety lips on mine. Softly, gently, as if he had all the time in the world and had waited his whole life for this moment. When he let me go I blushed and kept my eyes to the ground, not wanting to look up and see who might have seen.

"Give me your cell phone, please," he demanded sweetly. As if in a trance, I took it out of my bag and handed it to him. I kept my eyes directly on his shoes, while he programmed his name and his number into my phone, gave it back to me, and walked away. When I got the nerve to look up, Flavia, Alan, Caroline, Frederico, Anna, and Georgia were all looking at me, laughing and clapping. Even Marco began to laugh.

I walked up, blushing.

"Well, at least one of us got kissed this evening," Georgia said, smiling. And at that, we went back under the aqueduct and to our hotel. The party, at least for tonight, was over.

When I woke up around noon, Georgia was sitting at the little table in our suite, flipping through something, drinking a cup of coffee.

"What are you doing?" I asked groggily, sitting up in bed.

"I'm looking through a portfolio of male prostitutes," Georgia said, calmly.

I rubbed my eyes with my fingertips. I thought I'd try again. "What did you say?" I asked.

"I'm looking through a portfolio of male prostitutes I got from an agency. I had to pay a hundred bucks just to look at it."

"What? What are you talking about?"

Georgia kept flipping pages. "I asked Flavia about it last night, and she gave me the name of an agency. I called them this morning and they sent it over."

"Georgia, you're not really going to have sex with a prostitute."

She looked up. "Why not? Wouldn't it be great to have sex with someone and have absolutely no expectations. You couldn't feel bad about them not calling, because they're a *prostitute*."

"But don't you think it's kind of . . ."

"What, gross?"

"Yeah. Kind of."

"Well, maybe that's something we have to get over. I think it's a great idea, paying for sex. I know a lot of women who really need to have sex. I think it would be good if we could get past the whole gross thing."

"And the whole AIDS thing, and the whole 'aren't they all gay' thing?"

Georgia put her coffee down. "Listen. I don't want to be one of those single women who hasn't had sex in three years. I want the charge of someone on top of me. Kissing me. Holding me. But I don't want to have sex with assholes who pretend they like me when they really don't. I think hiring a prostitute is the way to go."

"But you're paying them. Doesn't that take the fun out of it?"

Georgia shrugged her shoulders. "Maybe." She was still formulating her theory. "That's what I want to find out. Because I think that's how to be single. To try and stay sexually active, at any cost."

"*Literally* at any cost," I couldn't resist adding, still appalled. "It's different for women. The men are going to be penetrating us. It's weird."

"Julie, come look at these guys. They're not gross. They're hot."

I sighed and swung my feet out of the bed, traipsing over to the kitchen table in my flannel boxer shorts and t-shirt. Georgia passed the book to me.

"Well, I thought I'd have bagels for breakfast, but I guess it's going to be stud muffins instead," I quipped.

Georgia wasn't amused. I looked at the photos. There were shots of men in suits, and then the same men with their shirts off. As I flipped through the pages, I had to admit that while they were cheesy, in a hunky, coiffed, and slightly gay kind of way, they weren't terribly gross.

And I could imagine the innocent side to all this. Maybe they were just men who happened to possess an innate talent for pleasuring women, a talent that they'd decided to use for financial gain. Maybe they thought of themselves as sex social workers or *extremely* personal trainers. Perhaps because it was men, we didn't have to see this paid exchange as a kind of victimization. These men on page after page in suits and ties and bathing suits looked like the pleasant male strippers we saw in Paris. Overly built, a little corny, and willing to please. Of course, looking at them in another way, they also looked like they could be your average neighborhood serial killer.

"I guess they don't look so bad," I said.

"I told you. I'm going to do it. If no one kisses me tonight, I'm making the call first thing in the morning. I want to have some kind of physical contact with a man before I leave tomorrow night."

I kept my mouth shut, thinking about how I would have to get someone to kiss her tonight or else. Georgia added, "Flavia invited us to a big party tonight, at some samba school. I told her we'd love to go. She's picking us up at eight."

"Does that mean someone's going to teach us how to samba?" I asked hopefully.

"Well, if they don't, you can always ask my husband's girlfriend,

Melea, when you get home. I bet she has quite a following," Georgia said as she sipped her coffee. "I wonder if it's going to be a whole room full of husband-stealing samba teachers. Wouldn't that be fun?"

She raised her right hand and pushed her hair behind her ear. I had never woken up with Georgia before, and without makeup and with the sun hitting her face, she looked young and so beautiful. At that moment, her future seemed to hold so much possibility for happiness and light. I wished she could have felt it. But I knew, as she thought about Dale and Melea, that I was the only one in the room who could see what was possible for my divorcing, grieving, funny, slightly crazy friend.

Back in the States

Wearing Jim's pajama bottoms and a tank top, Alice stood in Jim's kitchen and poured herself a glass of water, pondering this whole phenomenon of regular sex. As she drank the water, she admitted to herself that there was now a fly in the ointment.

Having sex with someone all the time only works if you are truly excited about them. Then it's just the world's best thing. But if you happen not to be in love with that someone, it might become a problem. The last couple of times Alice and Jim had sex, she realized she was bored. He didn't do anything wrong, he was perfectly good at it all. But she was simply not passionate about him. As she stood at the counter, she thought about how dreary it would be to have passionless sex for the rest of her life.

Alice wanted desperately for it to work out. And Alice is a problem solver; there's not a difficult situation in the world she can't make right. If she knew more about geophysics, she'd beat this whole global warming thing in a heartbeat. As Alice put the glass in the sink, she was convinced that the problem of having passionate sex with Jim just simply couldn't be that hard to solve.

Alice walked down the hallway and into Jim's bedroom. Jim was in bed, reading. He looked up and smiled.

"Hey, baby," he said.

"Hey," Alice said. Even in Jim's pajama bottoms and a tank top, she looked hot and Jim couldn't help but notice. Alice looked at him for a long moment, wondering what passion actually was; what are its ingredients, what are its component parts? When describing someone, people always say, "They're a very passionate person." But what does that mean? Alice walked over to her side of the bed and sat on it, her back to Jim as she thought. *It means they are excitable*, she thought. *They are enthusiastic. They get worked up over things they believe in strongly.* Jim put his hand on her back and stroked it. Alice was excited about being in a relationship, excited about not dating, about feeling secure. She was excited about what a nice man Jim was and how much he seemed to love her. Alice closed her eyes and tried to direct all that excitement to her groin area. After all, emotion is just energy. So she could take that energy and make it sexual. She felt Jim's hand on her back and let her thoughts flow. It's nice to be touched. It's nice to have sex. She turned around to Jim and put her hands on each side of his face and kissed him deeply. She climbed on top of him and pressed her body forcefully against his. He put his hands under her shirt to touch her breasts. She sighed with pleasure.

Alice smiled to herself. She didn't need to be passionate about Jim to have passionate sex. *Because she's a passionate person.* She believes passionately in rights for the underprivileged. She is passionate about being against the death penalty. She is passionate about world peace. She kept kissing Jim deeply as she hugged him tightly. She tilted her body just enough to roll Jim on top of her. She pulled off his t-shirt. She tugged off his boxer shorts. Jim took off her pajama bottoms and put his hand in between her legs. Alice gasped with excitement. She thought about how she was going to have someone do that for the rest of her life. She gasped again, louder. Jim could not have been more excited—he had never seen Alice like this. He was hard, breathing heavily as he entered her. Alice wrapped her legs around his back and tugged at his hair as they kissed—passionately, tongues and teeth and lips, and shallow breaths. Alice was moaning loudly. She loved penises, she loved penises inside her and she was going to love Jim, who grabbed her and lifted her up to him. She was straddling him now, as they sat up and were rocking back and forth. He was kissing her neck and as Alice was moving up and down, a thought flashed across her mind: *how will I ever keep this up?* They kept moving and Alice was groaning, concentrating on coming when another thought flashed across her mind: *this is taking a lot of energy.* Jim kept thrusting and kissing while Alice had the best idea she'd ever had in her entire life. An idea that made her understand how it was all possible, how she could keep this up forever and ever and how it wouldn't have to take so much energy: she could just think about Brad Pitt. It was an obvious choice but she didn't care. She went through his entire oeuvre. She thought about Brad Pitt's slim torso in *Thelma and Louise,* his muscular torso in *Fight Club,* and his really muscular torso in *Troy.* She thought about how he threw Angelina Jolie against a wall in *Mr. and Mrs. Smith.* As she got close to coming, Alice realized she could think about Brad Pitt for the rest of her life. It was a free goddamn country and no one would ever need to know. She could think about Brad Pitt and Johnny Depp and even Tom Cruise—who she knew was weird, but she loved buff torsos, no matter what the torso happened to believe in. When her inner passion wasn't enough, they would always be waiting in the wings. And as she imagined Brad Pitt in gold metal armor jumping through the air in slow motion, she came.

"Oh my God!" Alice screamed. Jim only had two more thrusts in him until he came as well—he had been having a hard time containing himself up to that point, what with all the excitement going on.

"Oh my God," Alice said, catching her breath as a new thought flashed across her mind: *I can do this! I am really going to be able to do this.*

*   *   *

Now, as any dieter knows, the minute you tell yourself that you're not allowed something, that is precisely when you can't stop thinking about it. Serena hadn't had sex in four years and her sex drive, due to lack of attention, had driven far, far away. So the minute she was told she would never be allowed to have sex again, well, that was just the thing to kick-start her lifeless libido.

Serena was now stationed at a yoga center in the East Village. This particular yoga organization had branches all over the world and Serena managed to get stationed in a beautiful brownstone less than two miles from where she used to live. Walking around the East Village with her shaved head and her orange outfits, she was aflame with the most dirty thoughts imaginable. Each morning, as she sat cross-legged on the floor of the meditation room, the scent of incense wafting through the air, her mind raced with thoughts of naked flesh and men on top of her. She had a recurring dream in which she was walking down a New York City street and just kept grabbing men and making out with them as they walked by. She would wake up sweaty and shocked. Serena had just assumed that for her, taking a vow of celibacy was merely a formality. This deluge of pornographic thoughts took her completely off guard.

That is why it was so easy for everything to happen the way it did. One of the jobs given to Serena, now known as Swami Durgananda, was to wake up a little earlier than everyone else and prepare the altar plate. This meant getting up at 5:45, cutting up some fruit or arranging some dates and figs on a platter, and then putting it on the altar as an offering to the Hindu gods before group meditation began at 6:00. And every morning, Swami Swaroopananda, otherwise known as the "hot swami," would be at the kitchen table, reading a book and looking hot. At 5:45 in the morning. Serena wasn't yet sure what the rules of engagement were for swamis at the center, but as she opened the refrigerator to decide what to offer up to the gods, she decided to say something.

"Is this when you normally like to read? Early in the morning?" Serena whispered softly.

He looked up at Serena and smiled. "Yes, it seems like the only time I have to read is at this hour."

"Wow. You actually wake up early to read. That's impressive." She took out a pineapple and put in on the counter. She got out a long knife and started skinning it. He went back to his book. As she chopped up the pineapple she would steal glances at him. For a man of Vishnu he was really built. Was that really just from doing yoga? Were swamis allowed to go to the gym? She didn't think so. His face was hard to describe, but it was the face of a real man. His head wasn't completely shaved—it was more of a very close buzz cut, and it was a look he was made for. He looked like he could maybe have been an army sergeant—tall, with a muscular chest and long, ripped arms. And his orange swami robes, instead of making it all seem silly, made him seem, well, super orange hot.

They would talk only briefly, but Serena didn't need much to fan her flames of desire. Each morning she got up a little earlier just to talk to him. And every morning, he'd be sitting on a stool at the counter, quietly reading, little circular glasses on the tip of his nose.

Tuesday at 5:30 A.M.:

"Good morning, Swami Swaroopananda."

"Good morning, Swami Durgananda."

"How's your book? Are you enjoying it?"

"Yes, it's one of the better ones I've read about Pranayama." He put his book down this time. "By the way, how are you adjusting to your new life?"

Serena made her way to the refrigerator. "It's been surprising, some of the things that come up, you know, when you're trying to calm the mind."

Swami Swaroopananda crossed his arms over his chest and looked at Serena. "Really? Like what?"

Serena felt her face get red and she wondered if, without hair, her entire head would blush as well.

"Oh, just the flotsam and jetsam of a cluttered mind, you know. So, how long have you been a part of this organization?"

And then they began to really talk. He told her that he was from New Zealand (*that's the accent*) and he'd been a swami for eight years. He told her about how his meditation practices had gotten so intense, the experiences he was having were so blissful, that he felt compelled to take the next step and become a renunciate. Serena wanted to know more. While they talked, Serena assembled quite an abundant offering plate.

Wednesday at 5:15 A.M.:

"Good morning, Swami Swaroopananda."

"Good morning, Swami Durgananda. How are you this morning?"

"Very well, swami." Serena started getting out flour and honey and walnuts. She was going to make her famous banana nut bread for the offering this morning. After all, she had to do something with all her time while pretending she wasn't flirting with a man of the cloth, forgetting entirely that she was now a woman of the cloth herself. Besides, she reasoned to herself, what better way to start the day than with the nice aroma of banana bread floating around them while they meditated? And besides, they could have the rest of it for breakfast. She began mashing the bananas in a bowl.

"How is your meditation practice going? You mentioned a lot of thoughts coming up, yesterday. Do you have any questions about the practice itself?"

The only question Serena had now was how she could have sex and still be celibate, but she knew that wasn't something she should say. So she made something up.

"Well, yes, I do, swami. When I meditate, I feel my thoughts slow down; I feel calmer, more at peace, more in touch with a higher power, so that's good. But I don't have any visions. No white lights, no colors swirling in my mind. I'm just meditating, you know?" Serena was now pouring flour and sugar in another bowl. She cracked an egg and started mixing it up by hand.

Swami Swaroopananda closed his book. "That's perfectly normal. There shouldn't be a goal to your meditation; that's the antithesis of the practice. The point is merely to be still. Everyone's experience is going to be different. The last thing you should be hoping for is fireworks when you're meditating."

Serena smiled. She poured the mashed bananas into the batter and stirred them together.

"Now, speaking of fireworks, Swami Durgananda, tell me. Have you been thinking a lot about sex lately?"

Serena looked up from her stirring. She wasn't sure if she had heard right. By his expression, which was serious and unembarrassed, it seemed like this was a normal spiritual question. She turned to the cabinets. While her back was to him, she admitted, "Well, actually, yes. I have been thinking a lot about it. Like not being able to think of anything else, really." She pulled out three loaf pans from a top shelf and brought them to the counter. She tried not to look at Swami Swaroopananda, but couldn't resist. She peeked up and he was smiling at her.

"You shouldn't be ashamed, that's part of the process. Your mind is just reacting to your body's desires. It will quiet down soon enough."

"I hope so. It's just like when I'm fasting. I can't stop reading cookbooks the whole time." She poured the batter into the loaf pans and pushed them one by one into the oven. Serena looked at the clock. It was only 5:30. She had no idea she could make banana bread that fast. There were still thirty minutes before meditation.

"I guess I'll go in and start, you know. Meditating."

Swami Swaroopananda closed his book. "Don't rush off. Why don't you sit for a moment. Let's talk some more. Where are you from?"

Serena smiled and shyly sat on the stool next to Swami Swaroopananda, also known as Swami Swaroop. He looked at Serena closely, and for the next thirty minutes he asked her questions about her family, the jobs she'd had, and what her favorite music used to be. In the basement of this yoga center, the smell of banana bread in the oven, as she sat next to a man wearing a bright orange dress, both of them basically bald, Serena realized she hadn't been on this great a date in years.

By the following Monday, Serena was baking fresh, yeasted, wake-up-early-so-you-can-make-the-dough-let-it-rise-and-punch-it-down-and-then-do-it-all-over-again bread. And he would always be there, sometimes reading, sometimes watching, but always talking to her. By the end of the week, they were mixing and kneading together.

For that past week and a half, Serena couldn't think about anything else but him. The beatific, blissed-out expression on her face, which might have been construed as spiritual awakening, was really just dumb puppy love. All day long, all night long, she thought about seeing him the next morning. And then in the morning, when she was with him, it wasn't so much that she was talking and listening to him as she was *absorbing* him. During meditation and yoga and chanting and working, she was supposed to be trying to become one with God. But instead, each morning as she made the most elaborate altar offering plates in the history of the Jayananda Yoga Center, Serena was becoming at one with Swami Swaroop. The way he said things, the opinions he had, seemed so in tune with how she thought and felt that when the words came out of his mouth and hit her ears it was like they mutated into a warm ooze that spread throughout her brain.

It was joy. For every minute that she was with him, she felt the undeniable sensation of joy. The thought of adding sex to this intense emotion had almost become too much for her to fathom. *Almost* too much for her to fathom. And in the meantime, the entire yoga center was gaining weight, gorging at breakfast on hot bread, walnut loafs, and muffins.

On Thursday, at 4:30 in the morning, as she walked into the kitchen, Serena looked for him, her heart beating fast, worried that for some reason he wouldn't be there. But he was standing by the counter. He smiled shyly at her. Long gone were the formal greetings of "Good morning, Swami Swaroop" and "Good morning, Swami Durga." They had now been replaced by two people who met each other in the morning by beaming wordlessly at each other.

All the kneading and rising and mixing had to lead to something. And on this morning, Swami Swaroop walked up to Serena, took her by the shoulders, looked to make sure no one else was around, and kissed her on the lips. Serena wrapped her arms around his neck and kissed him back, deeply. Now, her eyes closed and her body finally touching his, Serena finally saw the white light, the one everyone talks about, of unity, peace, and divine happiness. Finally.

So Serena still got up at 4:30 in the morning, but the altar plate went back to being a few dried-up grapes and a couple of figs. They had finally figured out what else they could be doing during that time, and they were doing it everywhere they could get away with it: the pantry closet, the furnace room, the basement. If Serena was the kind of girl who could get out of control over a couple of buffalo wings, you can imagine what she was like now that she was having sex with someone she was madly in love with. Eventually, they couldn't wait until the morning, and were recklessly finding places to meet during the day as well. When Swami Swaroop took the center's van to Hunts Point to do grocery shopping, of course he needed help and why not ask Swami Durgananda? So there, too, in the back of the van on the side of a road in some industrial wasteland in the South Bronx they unleashed their forbidden swami love. It may have taken a vow of celibacy to do it, but Serena finally had a sex life. Her dry spell was officially over.

Back in Rio

When they talked about this samba school party, I had an image of a dance school with mirrored walls and ballet barres, and maybe some streamers draped around and some punch in a punch bowl, with instructors available to teach the newcomers samba. But no. Flavia, Alan, Caroline, Anna and Frederico, Georgia, and I drove in the minivan to

one of the poorest neighborhoods, called Estácio, far from the fancy
tourist areas of Ipanema and Leblon. We parked by a massive concrete
structure that looked like it used to be an airport hangar, except that it
was painted blue and white and covered in beautiful graffiti artwork of
stars and beams of light. In big white graffiti letters was the name of the
samba school, G.R.E.S. Estácio de Sá. People were pouring into the
place, and we joined the flood into what can only be described as a
huge high school dance and block party combined. The place was the
size of a football field. Everyone was walking around with plastic cups
of beer, and the floor was already littered with empty cups and cans.
The excitement of knowing I was about to witness something that most
tourists would never get to see already had my heart racing.

But that was nothing compared to what the drums would do to me.
From the moment we entered, the loudest, most vibrant drums I'd ever
heard shook the building, cutting right through my heart. From a raised
set of bleachers about forty drummers were whipping the crowd into a
frenzy.

We made our way up some stairs to a little VIP balcony that looked out
over the entire scene. At the far end of the hangar were two singers on a
raised stage, shouting out joyfully. This was not the crowd of young people
at Lapa, dressed up for a night on the town. These were men in jeans and
t-shirts, shorts and sneakers. There were women wearing some of the tight-
est jeans I have ever seen stretched over a human form, and some skirts
that were so short I wanted to throw a jacket over them and send them to
their rooms without supper. It's true what they say, the Brazilian women do
have the most beautiful butts, and tonight they were all on display. Most
people were sambaing, talking, drinking beer. And there were others
dressed in red and white outfits just milling about. I wasn't quite sure what
this place was, and what we were doing there, but I knew I would never
have gotten to see it if it weren't for our new best friend, Flavia.

"I don't understand: why do you call it a samba school?" I asked
loudly, over the drums.

"Each neighborhood has a school where they drum and do samba.
Each school picks a song that they're going to do at Carnival, and then
they compete with all the others."

"So they're kind of like neighborhood teams?"

"Yes, exactly. This one is my samba school. And in a few minutes they are going to present for the first time the song they'll be competing with at Carnival." Flavia looked down to where the masses of people were and suddenly smiled. "There's Marco!"

Marco looked up and saw Flavia and waved. Flavia turned to me, a tough smirk on her face. "I don't mind that he's here," she said, trying not to seem at all happy. She motioned for him to come up the stairs. "I better go and make sure the bouncers let him up."

I looked over at the drummers and tried to find Anna. This was her samba school, too, and she was going to be drumming with them tonight.

The song they were playing stopped, and the drums began again, slow at first, it seemed, to get everyone's attention. People started to move toward the center of the room, the whole space newly energized. Frederico turned to us and said, "Come, let's go on the dance floor." Georgia, Frederico, Alan, and I made our way down the stairs. The drums were now at full speed and the whole space was pulsating, jumping, in united celebration.

We all began dancing. Well, Frederico and Alan began dancing. Georgia and I sort of wiggled around a bit, trying to shake our asses as best as possible, but the samba is really not a dance you can fake. Then the dancers paraded out. There were dozens of them, and the crowd parted, making a wide lane for them to dance through. They were all wearing their "team" costume: red and white sequins. The women came out first, in tiny red skirts and high, high heels, dancing so fast, their lower bodies moving so rapidly, it seemed that they were vibrating in some kind of sexual ecstasy. Their arms were flying around, their legs were whirling, and their asses were shaking so fast they could have whipped butter.

Following the young gorgeous women, in their tiny skirts and their bikini tops, were the little old ladies. They were also dressed in red and white, but their outfits were knee-length skirts, short-sleeved tops, and hats. They came out in a single line and formed a frame around the young women, or more accurately, a defensive perimeter against any wolves who might come in and devour these beauties whole.

They danced like women who had seen it all. They no longer needed to shake their asses and wave their arms around, though I'm sure they had done their share of that. Now, they more paraded about. I don't know what the rest of their lives were like, and I'd hate to imagine how difficult they were, but I knew that at this moment, they were in the midst of celebration. They were red and white peacocks strutting and prancing for everyone to see, proud of themselves and their neighborhood and their song.

Georgia, Frederico, and Alan had meanwhile gone to get beers. As they were waiting in line, far away from the dance floor, Frederico leaned over to Georgia and said, "You don't need to look for someone to kiss you, beautiful Georgia. I would be happy to make love to you any time you ask."

And at that, engaged Frederico kissed single, horny Georgia, as Anna's dear brother Alan laughed and drank his beer. Frederico was sexy, young, Brazilian, and gorgeous. Georgia's revenge fantasy had been to come to Brazil and steal someone away from his wife. Now Georgia had her chance; Frederico was the male Melea and he wanted her. Georgia, new to dating, still instinctively understood one of the cardinal rules of being single: *We ladies have to have each other's backs.*

So Georgia gently pushed Frederico away and said they should get back to the party. It was then that Georgia answered the question of who was looking out for the women in Rio—and sadly, the answer was her. Then she turned back to Alan and put her finger right in his face. "And you. Shame on you. You're her brother."

We all met up when we rejoined Flavia and Marco on the balcony. The queen and king of the samba school were now dancing down the center of the madness, the man in a crisp white suit and a white hat, the woman in a red gown and a crown. People were swirling flags around them as they danced separately, and then together, hand in hand.

Just then something flew into the air from down below. I didn't see what it was, but Flavia grasped her face and stumbled a few steps backward. Caroline was right there, holding Flavia's arm and asking what happened. On the floor near Flavia was a full can of beer. Someone had thrown it up toward us either in wild abandon or with a more malevolent intent. Either way, Flavia was the one who ended up getting hit in the face. Caroline sat her on a chair, and I watched as tough, deep-throated Flavia scrunched her lips up in a smirk and tried not to cry.

Everyone was trying to figure out what the hell happened, as Flavia's eye started to swell up. Caroline had gone to get her some ice, and Georgia was rubbing her back. Anna was now there, and when she saw what had happened she got down on her knees and started to stroke Flavia's hair. But Flavia just leaned over and picked up the offending can of beer and put it to her eye, to stop the swelling. Marco stood there a little helplessly. This woman, whom he barely knew, was hurt but he wasn't quite sure what to do or what his role should be. So he just sort of paced around, running his fingers through his hair. After the shock wore off, Flavia told everyone that she was fine. Anna suggested it was time to leave, and we piled into the minibus—Georgia, Flavia, Marco, Alan, Anna, Frederico, and myself.

So, considering it was Rio and it was three in the morning, the only reasonable thing to do was go to Pizzaria Guanabara, a local restaurant. As we walked in, I saw grown-up men and women, completely sober and well dressed, all gathered civilly eating pizza as if it were eight at night, some with their children.

We all sat down and talked and tried to make Flavia laugh, while she iced her puffy eye. She was a good sport in the truest sense of the word, not a trace of self-pity. Looking at her, I felt I had learned something else about how to be single: *There are some nights you might have to take a can of beer to the face. That's just the way it is, and it's best not to be a wimp about it.*

Flavia started to fold herself gradually into Marco, leaning into him as he put his arm around her. He had found his place, encouraging her body to nuzzle against his and draping his arm around her, letting her feel protected. She may be the toughest, coolest girl in Rio, but she had been wounded, ambushed. No matter how many girlfriends were around to help at that moment, nothing would beat the feeling of a strong chest against her cheek and muscular arms enveloping her.

Later, when we dropped them off at Flavia's house, Marco helped her out of the van, and put his arm around her sweetly. One more thing about being single: *On the unfortunate night when you're the one who gets the can to the face, you never know who might be there, ready and willing to comfort you.*

When Alan finally dropped us off at the hotel, the only ones left were

Georgia and me. Georgia looked at Alan and said, one last time, "Shame on you."

• • •

"You're having sex with a fellow swami?" Ruby asked, confused. She and Alice had been summoned by Serena to a diner on Twenty-fourth and Eighth, and frankly, they all felt a little embarrassed. Not because of Serena's admission of swami sex, but because Serena looked like one of those Hare Krishna people that you never even see anymore at the airports— and everyone was staring at them.

Ruby added, "Didn't you just take a vow of celibacy?"

"And didn't you have sex before taking your vow, like—never?" Alice asked, not very tactfully.

"I hadn't had sex for four years."

Ruby looked at Serena with great sympathy. Alice kept interrogating the witness.

"So, you have no sex, take a vow of celibacy, and now you're having sex?"

"It's not like that," Serena said, defensively. "I fell in love. I could have fallen in love with someone I met at a coffee shop, or at a class at school— I just happened to fall in love with someone I met being a swami. This is big, it's a once-in-a-lifetime thing."

The ladies didn't know what to say to this. They were still trying to ignore the fact that everyone was staring at Serena.

"Well," Ruby said, "I guess priests and nuns fall in love all the time."

Alice took a sip of her Diet Coke. "And it's not like any of this is real, right? It's kind of a make-believe religion, isn't it? No one is going to tell you that you've sinned and you're going to hell or anything?"

"Hindus don't believe in hell. Just karma."

Alice picked at Ruby's french fries. "So if you break your vows, do you believe that in the next life you would come back as an ant or something?"

"More like a hooker, probably," Serena said, guiltily.

Alice laughed. "It's true, you'd probably come back as a dirty street whore."

Serena wasn't amused. "I called you guys because Julie is gone and I have no one else I can talk to. I made this really big commitment and I think I made the wrong choice."

The ladies sobered up.

Alice asked, "Have you asked him how he feels?"

Serena put her head in her hands. "He feels guilty. He feels terrible."

Ruby jumped in. "Does he want to leave the church? I mean, temple, or whatever you call it?"

"He's not sure. He said this has never happened to him before."

Alice grabbed two french fries and stuffed them in her mouth. "If it really is love, you two should forget everything and go for it. It's love, for God's sake. That's a miracle. Nothing else matters."

"But it doesn't really mean anything. There are lots of people who fall in love and can't make it work. In the Hindu religion they talk a lot about how this whole world, this existence is an illusion. I'd probably fall in love with *anyone* who was the first person I slept with in four years. He's been a swami for eight years. How can I talk to him about this when there's no guarantee it will work out? Falling in love doesn't mean anything."

Alice hoped Serena had a point. She hoped being in love didn't mean anything. She hoped respect and kindness and a little Brad Pitt would win the day for her and Jim. Maybe being in love is just infatuation and passion and no one should make a big life decision based on that.

Ruby thought about all the men she thought she was in love with, with whom she had fantastic sex, and with whom it didn't work out. They all meant nothing to her now. Serena was right. It is an illusion. Before the words got out of Ruby's mouth, Alice had said them.

"Maybe you shouldn't do anything drastic right now. It's still so new, you have no idea what's really going on with you two. You don't want to get ahead of yourself."

Serena nodded her head, relieved. "You're right. You're right. That's a good plan. I should just wait."

They sat in silence, somewhat satisfied that at least this problem could be solved. Ruby took a sip of her coffee and glanced out the window. She saw two thirteen-year-old boys dressed in hip-hop clothes, pointing at Serena and laughing. Ruby looked away quickly, pretending she didn't see a thing.

Back in Rio

The next morning, I woke up to see Georgia lying on her bed, staring at me.

"I'm going to hire a prostitute today."

"And good morning to you."

"Why not? I don't have to be at the airport until eight. I have lots of time."

And with that, she opened the Prostitute Book to a page she had ear-marked and picked up the phone. She dialed without hesitation. In a very businesslike voice, she asked if she could see Mauro at one o'clock that day. She gave the address of the hotel and our room number, agreed to the price of five hundred dollars, and hung up the phone. We sat in silence for a moment.

Then she burst out laughing. "I can't really go through with this, can I? I'm a mother, for Pete's sake."

I breathed a sigh of relief. "No, you can't. I'm glad you've finally come to your senses. Call them back."

And then Georgia gave it a second thought. "No, actually, I think I will do it. I want to know if I could enjoy having sex I've paid for. And besides, we *are* in Rio after all . . ."

I couldn't believe it. Georgia was actually planning on having sex with someone she hired. I was mortified, nervous, irritated, and—I'll admit it—slightly impressed.

At noon, Georgia and I started getting ready for her "date" with Mauro. We had agreed that I would be there when he arrived so we could both check him out before she was left alone with him. I was partially hoping that she would chicken out at some point before he showed up. This did seem a bit insane. But until then, we carefully decided what she should wear. After looking through her suitcase full of sundresses, shorts, high heels, and evening wear, a decision was made: jeans and a t-shirt. For some reason, we didn't want her to seem too eager. I wanted her to wear something that, if for some reason the mission was aborted, she wouldn't feel silly in. I mean, what's worse than sitting alone in your hotel room in some skimpy negligee after you've just sent a male prostitute home without sex? Jeans and a t-shirt felt right to us both. Because after all, isn't that what the five hundred dollars is for? So she could have sex and not have to worry about how she looked?

At one o'clock on the dot, the concierge announced that a Mr. Torres was there to see Georgia. "Thank you. Could you please tell him to come up in five minutes?" Georgia said in a monotone and then hung up the phone. And then we both screamed and started running around the room.

"What do we do? What do we say when he comes in?" I shrieked as I jumped onto the sofa.

"First we have to let him know that you're not staying, that we're not trying to get a two-for-the-price-of-one-type situation."

"How do you say that without it sounding . . . I don't know!"

"This is crazy! Am I crazy? I'm crazy!!" Georgia said, now pacing, trying to compose herself.

"Wine! You need to be drinking! How did we not think of that before?" I was now getting into it—the train was chugging down the track and I was curious to see where it was going to take us.

Georgia raced to the minibar. She uncorked a mini bottle of wine and chugged. She passed it to me. Somehow I needed to get loaded, too.

"What are we going to talk about?" Georgia asked, nervously. "Normally on a first date you ask questions like 'So what do you do for a living?' 'Do you like your job?' 'Where do you live?' But what am I going to say to him?"

I took another swig of the chardonnay. "I don't know. Just talk about Rio, ask him questions about Brazil. Ask him what that stuff is called that we like so much. The stuff that looks like sand."

"Rio and food. Okay."

I finished off the little bottle of wine and then opened another one.

"I'll pour two glasses, one for you and one for him."

"Okay, okay, right, that's a good icebreaker." Georgia got out two glasses. Then she stopped.

"Wait, what if he doesn't drink?"

"A sober prostitute? Do you think?" I said as I poured the wine, my hands shaking.

"You're right, you're right." Georgia put the full glasses on the counter.

"Now we have to have a plan. We need a code word for if one of us gets a bad vibe from him."

"Got it, right," I said, now just pacing. "How about, um, samba dancing. I'll say that we went samba dancing and it was fun."

"No, that's too positive. I'll get confused and think you like him."

"Okay, how about, 'We went samba dancing and it was too hard for us to do.'"

"That's good, samba dancing, bad, means he's bad, got it. Now what if I get a good vibe from him and I want you to leave?" Georgia was now looking at the mirror, fluffing her hair. She turned around and ran into the bathroom. She took out a bottle of Listerine and started to gargle.

"Just be honest. Say, 'Well, Julie, I guess you should be going to that appointment of yours.'"

"Okay, good." Georgia, now back in the room, took a big gulp from her glass of wine. She made a face. "Eew, Listerine and chardonnay, ecch!" She ran and spit it out in the bathroom and rinsed her mouth again.

Then I asked, "But what if you tell me to leave, but I have a bad feeling about him?"

"Then, after I tell you to leave, say, 'Okay, but hey, can I talk to you for a minute about something?' and then we'll go into the hallway and talk." Georgia came back into the room and took another gulp of wine. She made no face this time, and kept gulping.

"Okay, that sounds good." I stopped pacing. "All right. I think we're ready." And as if on cue, there was a knock on the door. Georgia and I froze. Then we ran to each other and excitedly grabbed each other's hands.

"I'll open it," I said, in a burst of courage. I walked over and put my hand on the doorknob. Before I turned it, I looked back at Georgia. We both screamed silently at each other. I turned and opened the door.

Right out of a board game from the seventies, there he was, our Mystery Date. Mauro. I don't know what it is about these Brazilians, but he had a dazzling smile that immediately put you at ease. He could have been a soap star with his small pointed nose and short-cropped hair with a little product in it. He was young, around twenty-seven. Coincidentally, he was wearing jeans and a t-shirt. My first thought was, *Not gay and not a serial killer*. My second thought was to ask, *What's a nice guy like you . . .* But instead I said, "You must be Mauro. Please come in."

He smiled and entered the room. Georgia had a smile plastered on her face so wide I thought her skin might crack. In order to avoid any confusion, I said, "I'm leaving soon. I just wanted to say hi and make sure everything's . . . okay."

Mauro nodded. "Yes, that's fine. Of course."

Georgia walked over holding out a glass of wine. I could see her hands were trembling.

"Would you like a glass of wine?" Her voice seemed much calmer than her hands.

"Yes, that would be nice." He took the glass and said, "Please, sit down, let's relax." We both immediately sat down like obedient puppies. Georgia and I were on the couch, and Mauro sat in an armchair to the right of Georgia. I realized that in the midst of all our nervousness, we had forgotten one important thing: it may have been our first time doing anything like this, but it definitely wasn't his.

"So, how are you enjoying Rio?" he asked, cheerfully. As Georgia talked about the beach and Lapa and whatever else she was saying, I tried to just soak Mauro in. He didn't seem like he hated his job. He didn't seem like he was on drugs or had some big guy wearing furs and a fedora waiting for him downstairs to beat him up and take his money. He seemed perfectly content to be here with us. Maybe he was relieved; Georgia is beautiful, even in a t-shirt and jeans. Maybe he simply liked having sex with women. Why not make money from it? But how does he get it up anyway for all these women? That's not something you can actually fake. What about the really unattractive ones he must meet? Does he have an IV drip of Viagra somewhere? I had so many questions, I couldn't resist.

"So, tell me, Mauro. Do you enjoy this line of work?"

Georgia stared at me, her wide eyes trying to telepathically shut my mouth.

Mauro just smiled. Again, this probably wasn't the first time he'd encountered a nosy lady.

"Yes, very much. It's not easy to make a living in Rio, and I love women," he said, pleasantly. I looked him over again and he still felt safe to me. But there was something about him that seemed vaguely empty. Vacuous.

I pressed on, "Is it difficult for you to have sex with women who are— you know, not . . . attractive?"

Mauro just raised his eyebrows and shook his head. "No woman is unattractive when she is being pleasured."

Granted, it was a line right off the first page of the Male Hookers Manual, but it worked. The next thing I heard was "Julie, don't you have to get to your appointment?" I looked at Georgia, who was now trying to transport me telepathically out the door. Women are really just as easy as men when it comes to sexual arousal. But instead of porn, we just need a man who can lie to us and tell us we're beautiful no matter what.

"Yes, of course, I really do have to go." I got up from my chair, and so did Mauro. He was trained well. "It was so nice meeting you." I got my purse and put on a little jacket and walked to the door. I turned back to look at Georgia. She wiggled her fingers at me in a wave and grinned. I knew she was going to be all right. Perhaps better than all right.

I decided to take a walk on the beach to kill some time. From the sand, I looked out at the two shapely green mountains jutting out of the ocean, the mountains that many have compared to the shape of a Brazilian woman's buttocks.

I couldn't escape it. Even the mountains had a better ass than me.

As I walked along the beach, I thought about Thomas, about our time together. Maybe I had imagined it all, the connection, the romance. As I walked past the women in their string bikinis with their asses hanging out, I tried to see if there was any cellulite to be found. Not so far.

As I walked looking at all the perfect, smooth bodies, I wondered if the reason Thomas hadn't called me was because of my cellulite. He must have slept with me because he felt some connection, but then later on, when he thought back on the horrors that he had seen and touched, he came to his senses. I sat down in the sand and wondered when it ends. When do I get to feel like I'm great just the way I am? It's just too much to ask me to love myself on my own. Heterosexual women need men to tell them they're beautiful and sexy and fantastic; we just do. Because every day the world is telling us that we're not beautiful enough, not skinny enough, not rich enough. It's too much to expect us to be able to feel good about it all with just a few affirmations and a couple of candles. But as I started to get sucked into a vacuum of self-pity and despair, I remembered something: that guy Paulo had given me his phone number.

I had almost forgotten this delightful piece of information, but like someone clutching at a life preserver, I grabbed my phone and looked up his number. I dialed. I couldn't help myself. It was, after all, Rio. And Thomas had never called me.

Then I remembered that Paulo didn't speak English. I decided to text him, so if he happened to be around someone who knew English, they could help him out. I typed into my phone, "Hi, Paulo. Would you like to see me today?" Then I shut my phone and wondered how things were going with Georgia.

Were we disgusting? Sleeping with prostitutes, sleeping with married men, having one-night stands. Was this any way to be single? Before I could really ponder this any further, my phone beeped, telling me I had a text. It was Paulo. He said he could meet me at my hotel in ten minutes. As Thomas would say, "You must say yes to life." And one of the best things about being single is that you get to say yes to life *as often as you feel like it.*

I raced back to the hotel and used my credit card to get an extra room. Thank God, they had one room available. I texted Paulo my new room number and he came right over. When I opened the door, his eyes were sparkling.

"Hi, Paulo!" I said, not knowing how much he could understand. But before I could say anything else, he had wrapped his arms behind my back and kissed me. His tongue was soft as a feather and touched mine slowly and gently. We stood there, suspended together in time by our lips and our tongues. It was as if all his concentration was going into these kisses, making sure his tongue never made a wrong move. We stood in the middle of the room for about fifteen minutes, kissing. He was the best kisser I had ever had the privilege of laying lips on.

Then he wrapped his arms around my waist and picked me up. He was lifting and kissing me, and it made me feel tiny. Delicate. He put me back down, and he started kissing my neck, softly. He touched my head, my hair, massaging my shoulder as he kissed. Then he gently turned me around, lifting up my hair and kissing the back of my neck, keeping our bodies close. His hands ran slowly over my breasts, down to my waist and under my t-shirt. I turned my head back to him and he leaned in and kissed me, all the while caressing my breasts with his hand. His left hand was now slowly moving down my leg, over my thigh. He slipped his hand under my long, loose skirt, and gently guided it up. Our breathing was getting faster and I let out a gasp as his hand found its way between my legs. My right hand was on the desk, balancing myself as he pressed his body against mine. He raised my left leg onto the chair by the desk. My left arm was behind me, running over his ass, his thighs. I could feel his hardness pressed right on the small of my back. He was running his fingers between my legs, searching, exploring. I was breathing very heavily now. He took both hands and slowly pulled my skirt and underwear down my legs. I stepped out of them as he pulled my t-shirt over my head. Then he took his own shirt off. I could feel his warm, smooth skin against mine. I wanted to turn around and rub my hands all over his chest, throw my arms around his waist, and look into his face, but I didn't dare move.

And then, as if this man weren't genius enough, he took his hand and reached into the back pocket of his shorts, and pulled out a condom. My mind was already dreading the moment when we would have to pull away from each other, someone mumbling something to the effect of "Do you have a . . . ?" "Shouldn't we get a . . . ?" But I was spared. Paulo was a gentleman and an amateur porn star and he pulled out the condom, unwrapped it, and put it on.

I imagine there are women who are really good at the whole condom transfer situation; the unwrapping and uncoiling and putting it on their waiting man. But not me. Since about age thirty-five, condoms represented to me the grave possibility of a lost erection. I don't know if it was the men I was with or something about me, but there were so many lost opportunities once the condoms came out that they began to terrify me. After a certain number of these mishaps, I just refused to go near them. I would use them, of course, but my hands would not get anywhere near one. It was going to be the man's problem. He would have only himself to blame for his lost erection. ANYWAY, Paulo had his erection, his condom, and his groove on and he gracefully slipped himself inside me. His head was next to mine, his arms, his shoulders, his biceps were all around me, enveloping me. He whispered into my ear, "You are so beautiful." He kissed my ear. Then, his tongue slowly licked my earlobe and moved its way around, his hot breath tickling me. He was a one-man band, this fellow, as his right hand was again between my legs, hitting just the right spot, his tongue was giving me goosebumps down my neck, and he was also inside me, moving and thrusting gently, perfectly. All while standing up, thank you very much. I felt like I was in a three-way with every sensitive, sexual area being touched or kissed, but this lovely man was doing it all by himself. I was making loudish noises that I've never heard come out of me before. He didn't miss a beat as my body twisted and arched and I orgasmed. I turned around to face him and kissed him deeply on the mouth. He picked me up and carried me to the armchair, where he sat down with me on top of him, still inside me. I wanted to give him an award. He put his hands on my hips and set the rhythm. Now it was my turn to do some work, and I moved with his guidance, willing my thighs to stay strong—a charley horse would be so impolite right now. I watched his eyes close, his concentration now all going to his pleasure. But then he looked up and pulled me toward him, kissing me, his hands in my hair. We moved together, with my arms around his neck, kissing and panting, until suddenly he grabbed the arms of the chair, pulled my legs around him tight, and stood up. He walked me over to the bed and put me down. For a moment I got paranoid. Was I not doing it right? Had I gotten the rhythm wrong? Sometimes, on top, it's hard to get in the right . . . I pushed that thought away as his body pressed down on me, my legs wrapped around his torso. His eyes opened once in a while to look into mine and he would smile and kiss me. He was on his own now, knowing exactly how to move to make himself come. Which he did, in Portuguese, saying, "Meu Deus, meu Deus!"

He rolled on his side, and I rolled over to face him. We kissed softly, our arms and legs curled around each other. After twenty minutes of this, he whispered in my ear, "I must go now." And about three minutes after that he was dressed and kissing me good-bye. He said to me softly, "I like you," and then he was history. I lay back on the bed to think about how I felt about all this, but I didn't have much time to ponder because Georgia called on my cell phone. It was safe to return to our room. *Well, weren't we the swingers*, I thought to myself.

When I got back, the bed was thankfully made and there were no visible signs of sex anywhere. Georgia was packed and ready to go to the airport.

"Hey, Julie," she said, not giving anything away.

"Hey," I said as I sat on the couch. I decided not to be coy. "Well, how was it?!"

Georgia sat in the armchair and thought about it for a good two minutes. "I have to say, it's really not bad to pay for sex."

Georgia didn't look any different. I realize that's a strange thing to notice, as if paying for sex would somehow be immediately traceable on one's appearance. If that were the case, there'd be a lot more wives filing for divorce all across America. *Anyway*, I waited for her answer.

"It was a good thing. A very good thing."

"Well, tell me about it!!"

"Okay, okay." Georgia was being very serious, as if she were an astronaut describing what it was like to walk on the moon. "He was amazing in bed. Like, truly a professional. He was able to stay hard a really long time, he was really strong and threw me all around the room—in a good way—and it was really satisfying."

"So, it was good," I said. "It was a good thing. Are you happy you did it?"

Georgia thought again. "Yes. I am. I mean, it was physically perfectly satisfying." She got up from her armchair and walked over to a mirror by the desk. She grabbed a lipstick from the desk and started applying it.

"And . . . ?"

"And . . . that's it. It was completely physically satisfying. If I have a complaint, I'd say it was a little cold. Not cold like harsh, or unfeeling. Cold, like . . ."

"Like you were having sex with a prostitute."

Georgia started to laugh. "Exactly. Like I was having sex with a prostitute."

Just then the phone rang. Georgia's taxi was here. "But you know what?" Georgia said. "'Completely physically satisfied' is not a bad way to leave a room."

I smiled. It was not a bad way at all.

It was time for Georgia to go. I walked her to the taxi and gave her a big hug. I thought about how nice it would be just to get in the car with her and go home. But I resisted. She handed me a piece of paper.

"This is the number of my cousin Rachel in Australia. She's really fun and knows everyone there."

"What? Australia?"

"It's just a thought."

"You have family in Sydney, Australia? That's kind of far away."

"I know, but don't you have that pass thingy?"

"Yeah, but that seems too far. I don't want to have an anxiety attack and run out of Lexomil, and then be flipping out over the South Pacific."

"Here." Georgia handed me a little plastic bag with some pills in it. "Take some of my Xanax. Just to supplement the Lexomil. They're amazing."

"But I'll be flying alone. That's a really long trip."

"But once you get there, you'll know my cousin Rachel. She'll help you with everything you need."

I looked down at the little Baggie. I definitely had enough medication for the trip. "Well, I read there was a man drought there. It *would* be a good place to go for my research."

Georgia looked at me with that look, and spoke to me with that tone. "Julie. Go."

I immediately obeyed.

RULE

6

Make Peace with the Statistics Because There Really Isn't Anything We Can Do About Them (Or Is There?)

I always assumed that we live in a world where, if one wanted to go from Rio de Janeiro, Brazil, to Sydney, Australia, one would just hop on a plane, perhaps have a little stopover in, say, New Zealand, and then be on one's merry way. But when I got my itinerary printed out at the front desk of the hotel, it read like an issue of *National Geographic*. Flying from Rio, I'd have a layover four and a half hours later in Santiago, Chile. That sounded cute. I would then take a five-hour flight from Chile to Hanga Roa. Where is Hanga Roa, you ask? It's the "capital" of Easter Island. Where is Easter Island? It's off the coast of Chile, in the South Pacific. The natives call it Rapa Nui, population three thousand, and it's famous for the mysterious giant sculptures of scary stone men that line the coast. It's supposed to be a lovely place to visit, with snorkeling, horseback riding, mystical ruins, and spectacular hiking and views. But I would only be spending an hour at the airport, waiting for my connection to Papeete, Tahiti. Getting to Tahiti would take another five hours, with me arriving at 11:30 at night. And then after waiting in Papeete till three in the morning, I would take the eight-hour flight to Sydney.

I handled most of my 22.5 hours of air travel masterfully, mixing my drugs like a skilled pharmacist. I took Tylenol PM to Chile, then again to Easter Island. I popped a Lexomil to Tahiti and a Xanax to Sydney. It was genius.

This time it wasn't *during* my flight that I started breathing heavily, sweating, and becoming dizzy. The drugs worked quite well for that. No, this time it was in the various airports where I almost lost my mind.

I had decided to start reading about this supposed "man drought" plaguing Australia and New Zealand during my layovers at the various airports. So I printed out all the articles I could find online and read them. In airport bars and waiting areas throughout the South Pacific, I got the bad news: that a thirty-two-year-old New Zealand woman had as much chance in 2004 of finding a male partner her own age as an eighty-two-year-old woman did; that there are five women to every man in Sydney, Australia. Then there was the British report that stated that for every sixteen-point rise in a woman's IQ, there is a 40 percent drop in her likelihood of marriage, not to mention the oft-quoted advice given to Australian women in their twenties to "tag and bag" their men before they hit thirty, because after that it's anyone's guess if you'll ever be able to meet a guy, let alone get him to commit.

By the time I was headed to Papeete, I no longer was panicking about plunging through the clouds, spiraling down to my death, those last few minutes turning into an eternity and so giving me time to realize that these would be my last minutes on earth, that I would never again see my friends, my family, that I would never fall in love and have children, that my life was about to be over. No, that no longer worried me. It was now scary enough just reading about being a single woman over thirty-five. As I got on my flight to Sydney and popped the Xanax, I was confounded. Whatever happened to the idea that there was a goddamn lid for every pot? People have to stop saying that shit. Because here's what—the statistics are telling us that there definitely is *not* a lid for every pot. It sounds like a lot of the lids have left the kitchen to go find better pots elsewhere, or maybe to meet younger, prettier pots. Whatever the reason—it seems like there are a lot of big empty pots hanging out in the kitchen these days.

The Xanax was trying to take hold as my mind was racing, obsessing, worrying. What's going to happen to all these women? If there isn't a guarantee that there's a pea for every pod, then what are these women supposed to believe? That they might not ever fall in love, get married, have a conventional family? Or do some of them realize that they'll have to settle: not everyone gets to have love in their life, so they should just make the best of it? And what are they supposed to think about the idea of never ever having someone in their life whom they really love, who loves them back, deeply and passionately? And when I say "they," I mean "we." And when I say "we," I really mean "me."

So my question is, How sad are we supposed to think this is? On the one hand, we are told by movies and love songs, and our own personal experiences at times, that a life without love is a tragedy; it's one of the worst fates imaginable. On the other hand, we're also told that we're not supposed to need a man in our lives. That we're vital, fantastic people who are fabulous the way we are. So which is it? Is it a tragedy if we never have the love we're all still searching for, or is that an old-fashioned, antifeminist notion? Or has love been completely overrated? Maybe not overrated, but *oversimplified*. Maybe we should stop watching films and listening to music that makes it seem like people are falling in love and living happily ever after as often as they buy chewing gum. They should tell us that it's more like winning the lottery. Lots of people play, but very few actually win. Depending on which study you look at, 43 to 51 percent of all American marriages end in divorce. In fact, the average American will spend more years *unmarried* during their adult years if they live past the age of seventy. And a new census study shows that married couples who head households have officially become a slight minority.

The lights inside the plane were now being shut off. I love that about night flights. The flight attendants turn into camp counselors and decide when it's "lights out," subtly forcing an entire cabin of grown-ups to go to sleep. But I couldn't. Even with the Xanax, I was obsessing over the idea of statistics in general. What were we supposed to do with these hateful things? I mean, any woman living in New York City can tell you about the little statistic from 1986, when *Newsweek* told us that if you were over forty and living in New York you were more likely to get hit by a terrorist attack than get married. But then, lo and behold, twenty years later, after many forty-plus women moved to Vermont, or married guys they didn't love, or spent thousands of dollars on Marianne Williamson courses or plastic surgery, or just woke up every morning in sheer terror because of that damn statistic, *Newsweek* published an article saying, basically, "Ooops! We were wrong! Sorry. You guys actually have a fine chance of getting married. Everyone, go about your business now, carry on."

But here are my statistics. One: every man I know, see, or hear about, poor, boring, bald, fat, arrogant, or whatever, unless he's actually a shut-in, can get a girlfriend whenever he wants. And two: I know dozens of smart, funny, gorgeous, sane, financially stable, professionally fulfilled, fascinating, fit women in New York in their mid-thirties to mid-forties who are single. And not just single like "in between boyfriends" but single for years. When I hear of a couple breaking up, I know that the man will be in his next relationship much sooner than the woman.

I took out my trusty vinyl sleep mask and put it on. Because I knew it looked really good on me. Just kidding. I was trying to shut my brain off. Because here's the other thing. This little monologue I've been doing? It's been performed for many years. Not just by me, but by many women before me, women my mother's age, and perhaps even before that. And the complaint remains the same: *There are not enough good men out there.* So what does one do? How do you be single when the statistics (and reality) are telling you that you are doomed?

I arrived at the hotel tired and cranky; after more than twenty-four hours of traveling I just needed to get to bed. As the bellhop got my suitcases out of the cab, I turned and looked into the distance.

Even in my haze of drugs and sleep deprivation, I couldn't help but be a little dumbstruck at the sight of the Sydney Opera House, jutting out into the harbor like a little miracle. I really don't have much of a passion for architecture in general, but seeing it up close, I was surprised at how breathtaking I found it. I had never before seen a building that seemed to be such an organic extension of a city's natural landscape. Apparently the architect, Jorn Utzon, designed the roof to look like a "ship at full sail." And that's what I saw—the Sydney Opera House setting sail right before my eyes.

My hotel was right on the wharf, and even though all I wanted to do was go to bed, I had to stand there, as my suitcases were taken into the hotel, just to soak it all in. As I did, I became sure that, statistics be damned, I was going to have a great time in Sydney. The ride from the airport had been pleasant, the weather warm and the sun shining. Sydney seemed modern, yet quaint, English yet Pan-Asian. The gloom and doom I felt on the plane had lifted. I had overindulged in statistics and they had made me sick. The reality of Sydney was a different situation altogether.

As I entered my room, the good news was that it was really great-looking, with a view of the water and lots of space. The bad news was that there was someone already sleeping in one of my double beds. I let out a little gasp and froze in my tracks. Assuming I had barged into someone else's room, I slowly backed up, trying to get out before I woke the person up. Then I heard a sound I would be able to recognize anywhere: Alice's sleep-breathing. It wasn't really a snore, it was much more delicate than that. It was like a loud purr. I knew it from trips we took to the Bahamas and New Orleans. I walked closer to the bed and saw I was right: it was Alice, sound asleep. I didn't know how she got there, but there she was. I lay down on the other bed and passed out.

When we woke up, Alice explained that Georgia had called her from the airport in Rio to tell her what a good time she had. Alice, who's a little competitive and never likes to miss a party, asked Georgia where I was going next and decided to join me. Now, I wasn't sure what was going on with Jim at this moment, but I didn't think it was a good sign that Alice, in the middle of a new relationship, decided she just *had* to go halfway around the world. So, being a friend, I had to ask.

"So, tell me about this Jim guy, how's it going?"

Alice bobbed her head and sort of half smiled. "He's great. Really nice. I mean, oh my God, so nice." Alice quickly got out of bed. "Should we go get something to eat? I'm starving."

That night, we met Georgia's cousin Rachel for a drink at the hotel bar. We were sitting at a table outside, overlooking the harbor. The water was sparkling and the wind was balmy and that darn opera house was showing off again. It was heavenly.

Rachel was a thirty-year-old Australian girl-about-town. She was bubbly and upbeat, with long curly blond hair. She worked as a publicist for a very successful family-run company that owned many restaurants and hotels all throughout Sydney. She talked really fast and sort of through her nose, as people with Australian accents sometimes do. We were drinking a lovely Australian rosé, and she was telling us all about the night to come.

"It's going to be an absolutely brilliant party, it is. This man, whose birthday it is, he's really rich. His family made their money in cattle. It's a big deal that we're getting to go. My friend Leo got us the invites. Isn't it absolutely brilliant?"

"Yes, we're so excited," I said, politely.

"And the guys in Sydney are just gorgeous, they *are*."

"But what about this man drought?" I asked. "Is it true?"

Rachel nodded her head vigorously. "It does seem like the men have the pick of the litter. That's why I'm never going to leave my boyfriend. No matter how much of a tosser he is."

"Is he not nice to you?" I asked, guessing at the meaning of *tosser*.

"Not at all. But he's absolutely *yummy*."

When we got to the party, it was already in full swing. The most beautiful men and women in Sydney were there, all in their Saturday-night coolest. The women were in cute little tops and jeans or flowing dresses, with their hair all fluffy and flipped, their lips glossy and pink. The men looked slick in their jackets and jeans and groomed hair. The folks in Sydney knew how to dress for the occasion—it could be called "casual-fabulous." The private club seemed to be going for a Paris opera house aesthetic, all in red velvet, gold leaf, and murals.

As we made our way to the bar, a tall man with black hair that had a lot of product in it came over to us. Rachel told us that this was our host, Clark. He kissed Rachel on the cheek.

"So these must be the ladies from New York?"

"Yes, this is Julie and Alice."

He looked at me. "Are you the one interviewing single women all over the world?"

"Yes, I guess I am," I said, a little embarrassed.

"Brilliant," he said. "Can I get you three some Sammy's? That's what everyone's drinking tonight."

"Perfect," Rachel said, and he leaned over to order.

"What's a Sammy?" Alice asked Rachel.

"A Semillon. It's a local white wine. It's not big in the States, but it's everywhere in Australia."

Clark brought the wine over.

"Would you like me to introduce you to some single ladies that you might like to talk to?"

"Sure," I said, taking my little journal out of my bag.

Alice took my wrist. "No, not right now," she said. "It's time for Julie to talk to some single men." She then led me toward a crowd of men. Then she added, "Man drought my ass. Statistics don't mean anything. I'll prove it."

Soon enough, Alice had made friends with a group of four young men, all in business suits. She had the whole group in rapt attention as she started telling how she once got a judge to let a drug dealer go because of a lack of evidence, and the drug dealer promptly offered to thank her by giving her an ounce of blow. They were enthralled and impressed.

"That's awesome, really," one of the exceptionally handsome men said.

"It's impressive, to be so young and so accomplished," another said.

Jim back home must have been doing something good for Alice, because at that moment she didn't feel the need to lie or minimize herself in any way. She felt good enough about herself to just blurt out the truth. "Well, I'm not that young. I'm thirty-eight."

All the blokes looked incredulous. The exceptionally handsome one said, "I thought you were around thirty-two!"

"I reckoned you were about thirty," the shorter, stockier one said. Their two mates murmured in agreement.

"No. Thirty-eight." And then Alice had to drag me into it. "Julie here is thirty-eight, too."

Now, let's be honest, the only correct response from any man at that moment would be a gigantic display of disbelief, which they all thankfully made.

I always feel so guilty at how pleased I am when someone thinks I look much younger than I am. As if it's such a disgrace to just look your age. Every time I say "thank you" when someone says I look much younger than I am, I always think, *We both just acknowledged that it's terrible for a woman to be old.*

"Wow, you both look great for your age," the short, stocky one said. Somehow, just by the detached way he said that, I suddenly felt ancient. The music started to get louder and people were begining to dance. Suddenly, two of the men seemed to have somewhere else in the room they urgently needed to be. The exceptionally handsome blond man wasn't going to get away that easily. Alice asked him to dance. He said okay, and then, the shorter, stockier man and I stood there and stared at each other until I asked him if he wanted to dance. He politely said yes.

Alice and I got on the dance floor with these two men. Now, I don't want to brag, but Alice and I know how to dance. We don't go crazy on the dance floor, nothing embarrassing, mind you, we're just two girls who have a little bit of rhythm. "Groove Is in the Heart" was playing, and who doesn't love to dance to that? Alice and I were boogying away, shaking our hips and moving our feet, clapping our hands a bit, but the men were just shuffling their feet a little. Okay, they're not dancers, that's fine. But it immediately put a damper on the boogying vibe. I started to shake my hips a little less, move my feet a little slower. Alice, on the other hand, kept at it, dancing closer to the handsome guy, putting her hand on his hip for a moment, then taking it away and swirling around. She wasn't making a fool of herself by any means. She was just out there having fun. But Handsome Guy didn't seem to want to play along. I was still having fun because I love the song, but it was hard not to notice that Short-Stocky Guy was looking above my head as he danced with me, not making eye contact with me at all. Now, here's what I love about dancing: it's a time when you can feel free and sexy and flirty with someone you might not necessarily even be interested in. Like kissing in Rio, it's a great way to rev up your sexy engine without having to actually sleep with someone you don't want to.

So I was looking at Short-Stocky Guy, smiling, trying to be friendly and flirty. He had very closely cropped hair and a big round, ruddy face.

He smiled back at me, briefly, and he went back to sort of staring four feet over my head. It was pretty disconcerting. So when the song ended I was planning on just getting off the dance floor and away from Stocky Guy. But then "Hey Ya" by Outkast came on, and I really, *really* love to dance to that. So I kept dancing, not giving Stocky Guy a chance to slip away.

As I was bouncing up and down, I made a moment of eye contact with Stocky Guy and smiled. He just sort of ignored me and again turned his attention to four feet above my head. In that split second I knew exactly what was going on: *He did not find me even remotely sexually attractive.* Of course I've felt that before, on dates, in conversations, but never on the dance floor doing my sexy moves. A wave of humiliation came over me.

"You're reading too much into it," Alice said later as we waited for our Sammy's at the bar. "He didn't like to dance. I had the same experience with my guy. That's why he just swayed back and forth to the music. You don't see me taking it personally."

"Alice, he stared above my head the whole time. ABOVE MY HEAD." I was practically shrieking.

We drank our wine, which was delicious. The music was still really great for dancing.

"Let's go dance by ourselves," Alice suggested. "Fuck these guys."

I looked around at all the beautiful people. This was my first night in Sydney and I was damned if I was going to have a bad time because of some Above-the-Head-Starer. We set our wine down and headed out to the dance floor.

I was still on a roll. Yelling over the music, I said, "I'm telling you, if I was on fire, that guy wouldn't have gone near me to put it out."

Alice yelled back, "I'm telling you, Julie. Some guys just don't like to dance! It has *nothing* to do with you."

Just then, my eyes glanced past Alice. There was the short-stocky-above-my-head guy doing the cabbage patch with a twenty-two-year-old blond pixie. He was perspiring, he was dancing so hard. From the expression on my face, Alice turned around and saw him. She turned back to me, speechless. Then, at the same time, we looked to our left and saw Exceptionally Handsome Guy grinding a woman on the dance floor. He had his hands on her hips and his pelvis was thrust close into hers. He must have met her about three and a half minutes ago. His hands moved toward the side of her face and he kissed her. They stopped dancing and they just began making out on the dance floor. Alice saw this. And this is another reason why I love Alice. She knows when to admit defeat. She leaned in to me and said, "Let's get the fuck out of here."

Back in the States

The cutest thing about Georgia's date was that he was nervous. Shy. This was Sam's first date since his divorce four months ago and he seemed like a boy at his high school prom. They had been set up by Alice, who knew Sam from her days in Legal Aid. Now that she and Jim were "exclusive," Alice had a lot of extra time and energy to dedicate to finding other people boyfriends.

They were at an out-of-the-way little restaurant on a block Georgia had never heard of, Tudor Place, which was slightly elevated above the rest of the neighborhood. This allowed for a 360-degree view of New York at night, with one side featuring the United Nations building looming above like a giant. Georgia was entranced. The restaurant was all candles and drapery, which made the room feel as if you were in some sheik's love tent. Sam took charge and ordered a bottle of wine for them, which impressed Georgia immediately. Dale knew a lot about wine and she had to admit, it was something she always liked about him. Actually, it was something she always liked about *them*. Before the kids, they would take wine-tasting classes at the local wine store and once even went to Sonoma for a wine-tasting vacation.

Tonight Sam ordered a lovely Shiraz, and then he began his adorable, completely winning confession.

"This is my first date since my divorce, and I'm really, really nervous. I tried on three different shirts before I left the house." He was smiling, his eyes looking at his hands, which were drumming nervously on the table.

Georgia liked him already. An honest, vulnerable man who knew about wine.

"Well, you look perfect."

And he did. He was a tall beanpole of a man, with beautiful sleek brown hair, that came down just past his ears. He looked a little like James Taylor, if James Taylor still had hair.

"Thank you." Sam looked up at Georgia, and then back down at his hands.

"Alice told me that you were really beautiful and smart, so I knew the pressure was on." Sam now looked straight at Georgia. "I just didn't know how beautiful you actually were going to be." He nervously pushed his hair back away from his face. "Thanks for agreeing to have dinner with me. I really appreciate it."

Georgia laughed. "I'm not doing it as a favor. You sounded nice on the phone and Alice said you were great."

Sam laughed, embarrassed. "Right. I guess I shouldn't sound so pathetic, right? It's just, going through a divorce, and the unhappy years of a marriage, well, it kind of undermines your confidence, you know?"

Georgia nodded slowly and said, "Oh yes. I know."

But what she was really thinking, while she looked at him, was, Guileless. He was completely without guile or pretense. He was a grown-up, openhearted man who told her she was beautiful and practically blushed. She wanted to dart him, cage him, and bring him back to her place, where she could keep him to herself, unspoiled by the outside world. As they ate their dinner, she learned that he was from the Midwest, which perhaps explained a lot. His manners were impeccable. He was kind to the waitress but he also had a dry sense of humor that amused Georgia to no end. Best of all, when he spoke of his ex-wife, it was clear that it pained him to say anything bad about her; it was well into the conversation before Georgia got out of him that his wife had cheated on him. Many times. They talked and talked, sharing their personal stories about their marriages and how they ended, and besides being completely smitten, Georgia was totally impressed. Somehow this man managed to make being a beleaguered, cuckolded, mistreated husband—hot. He was noble and kind and funny with just enough self-awareness of the absurdity of it all to be utterly charming about his disastrous wreck of a marriage and fifteen lost years. They finished dinner and ordered another bottle of wine. They drank that and were both officially a little drunk. He waited while Georgia got in her cab and kissed her good night. And then, with complete sincerity, Sam told her he had had a great time and would love to see her again. They made a date for exactly a week later, which seemed like a long time away to Georgia, but she knew he was new to this whole dating thing, so she didn't want to push. Georgia went upstairs to her apartment, paid the babysitter, and went to bed, happy. There was hope now and hope's name was Sam.

Back in Australia

I got up early the next morning to search for more statistics. I couldn't get enough of them. While I was surfing the Web for "man drought," there was one writer whose articles kept coming up. Her name was Fiona Crenshaw from Tasmania (a small island off the coast of southern Australia) and she wrote articles for the single ladies of Australia. She did it with cheeky Australian humor, but was adamant that no matter how bad the drought, the ladies must remember that they're *Goddesses,* that they mustn't settle, and must stay positive. She gave one woman the earth-shattering advice that—get this—*she has to love herself.* Isn't that novel? Apparently, as long as you love yourself the men are going to start lining up in droves.

This irritated me immensely. I sat on my bed, listening to Alice purr, and felt furious. Here's a woman who was reciting the statistics in her columns, but telling the ladies to love themselves and "stay positive" anyway. If there were a starving village, with no food in sight, no one in their right mind would tell the village that all they had to do was love themselves and think positively and food would show up. But love has a mystical quality about it that makes us feel we can ignore the cold hard facts—one of them being that there aren't enough men out there.

Luckily, I didn't have to think about this for long, because our hostess, Rachel, called to brighten my day.

"My friend, Will, wants to take you out on his boat today. Can you two make it? It seems like it's going to be a super day for that."

"Really? He wants to take us out on his boat?"

"Yes, he's a businessman, so he loves doing all this networking rubbish."

"But he knows that Alice and I aren't necessarily . . ."

"Oh please, you're writing a book about dating. Who doesn't love that? He's going to bring some of his mates on board so you can get the male perspective on it."

"Well, that's awfully nice . . ." I wasn't used to all this generosity. I'm a New Yorker and we're all too busy to be that accommodating to anyone.

"See you at two at the hotel. The boat will pick you up right there." And she hung up.

His boat was a Donzi—a speedboat that looked very expensive and went very fast. We were rocketing around the harbor, our skin getting pushed back on our faces as the wind hit us, our hair getting knotted and gnarled. Will showed us where Russell Crowe lived (good going, Russell) and he pointed out the building that Rupert Murdoch owned. He also had brought along two of his mates, John and Freddie. They were in their early thirties, handsome, and, from what I could gather, extremely rich. John was the first swarthy man I had seen in Sydney, looking almost Italian. Freddie was a member of the family that Rachel worked for. In his own right, Freddie owned or partly owned five or six restaurants or hotels in downtown Sydney alone. He reminded me a bit of Lance Armstrong: tall, slim, confident, and kind of an asshole. He had narrow eyes and the ability never to crack a smile or look at you directly. I took one look at these handsome, rich gentlemen who live in the middle of a man drought and saw them as one thing and one thing only: *kids in a candy store.*

So that was the attitude I took when Will finally slowed the boat down and I was able to sit down for a chat with these blokes. Will poured us all champagne, and Rachel had brought some tiny "nibbles"—itsy-bitsy pieces of black bread with salmon and crème fraîche on top. They were delicious. I asked the men if any of them had girlfriends. They said they didn't. I asked them if it was because there were too many options, and they all just laughed and shrugged. Well, Freddie didn't laugh because he was too cool to laugh.

"So that means yes," I said.

They all just shrugged again, sheepishly. But John tried to explain.

"It's not like that. I want to settle down, I do. To fall in love. But I just haven't met the right girl yet."

"But don't you think that you might be having a hard time meeting the right girl because you're never quite sure if there's another right girl coming right after her?"

Will spoke up this time. "No, when you fall in love, it just hits you, doesn't it? You just know. There could be five hundred supermodels and you wouldn't give a toss."

The others agreed. I really had only one question that I had wanted answered. It was about the damn statistics.

"What does it feel like? To not have to worry about finding someone to love?"

John looked at me, surprised. "What do you mean? I worry. I'm not sure."

Will agreed. "I work all the time. When do I have time to meet anyone?"

John added, "Just because there's lots of women around doesn't mean I'm guaranteed to meet someone I can fall in love with."

Will poured himself a little more champagne. "In fact, it can be more depressing really, meeting all these women, and none of them being 'the one.'"

There was no way Will was going to get me to feel bad for him because there were too many women. I pressed on. "So you're saying it's just as hard for you to find love here in Sydney as it is for the women?"

The two men nodded. Freddie was just staring out into the ocean, stone-faced. I didn't let it drop.

"But wouldn't you have to agree that the odds of you falling in love are better, simply because you're meeting more people who might be 'the one' than the women are? Don't you think that has to help your odds?"

John said, "I don't think it works that way."

Will said, "All it takes is one."

These men had an entirely different way of viewing the statistics than I did. Apparently, to these men it doesn't matter if there are a lot of fish in the sea. Finding the one fish to love for the rest of your life is difficult no matter where you swim.

Alice continued the interrogation.

"So have any of you ever been in love?"

They all nodded their heads. Will began. "When I was a teenager I was in love. I got my heart crushed. I had a girlfriend when I was nineteen who just trampled me."

John agreed. "I treated my girlfriends well when I was young. I brought them flowers, wrote them love poems."

Will laughed and John went on, embarrassed. "I couldn't help it, I was a romantic! I had a girlfriend when I was twenty-one whom I would have married. I was head over heels for her. But she broke up with me because she said I was getting too serious."

I wondered where this woman was now. I hoped she wasn't single and living in Sydney.

Alice looked at Lance Armstrong. "So, Freddie. You've been awfully quiet."

Freddie just looked at Alice and shrugged. "It was the same for me. I got crushed when I was younger. But I figured it out. Until a woman is around thirty, thirty-two, she has all the power. We hit on them, we fight over them, we chase after them. Then, around thirty-two, thirty-three, it all shifts. We get the power and they're the ones fighting and chasing after us. I think it's just payback. For all the shit they put us through when we were younger."

The other men looked at Freddie, not really disagreeing, but not wanting to start trouble. Alice narrowed her eyes, shifted in her seat, and calmly took a sip of her champagne. I dove in.

"Would any of you consider going out with an older woman? Someone in her late thirties or even forty?"

"I prefer the strategy of 'divide your age and add four,' if you know what I mean," Freddie said, not really joking. The other guys laughed.

I did the math. That meant that they all wanted to date nineteen- or twenty-year-olds. I was considering jumping off the boat right then and there.

Freddie added knowledgeably, "We don't meet single older women when we're out, because there aren't any."

Alice quickly said, "Excuse me?"

In a cool, slow tone, as if talking to two imbeciles, Freddie explained, "There aren't women that age out at my clubs and restaurants because they're all married."

I had to step in now. "Are you telling me that you think all the women over, like, thirty-eight are married? That's why they're not at your clubs?"

"Yeah. Of course." The other guys agreed.

Alice, confused, said, "You're saying there are literally no single women in Sydney who are over, say, thirty-eight?"

Freddie nodded his head confidently. "Yes."

I stared at him for a minute and then cleared my throat. "Do you realize that the statistics, with which I'm quite familiar, don't support that at all?"

Freddie shrugged. "I own half the bars and restaurants in this town. Who are you going to believe, the statistics or me?"

I was unable to stop talking. "Do you think, Freddie, that the reason you think there aren't any women over the age of thirty-eight who are single is perhaps that you're just not noticing them? That they might be invisible to you?"

Freddie just shrugged. "Maybe." Alice and I looked at each other. This was the biggest confession we had gotten out of any of these blokes all day.

"Well, you two don't have anything to worry about for years, so what's the fuss?" Will asked. "How old are you ladies? Thirty-one, thirty-two?"

Even here, on this boat with these men, it made me feel good to hear that. Damn me to hell. This time, Alice didn't feel the need to correct him.

That night, Alice may have blow-dried her hair and put on her heels and mascara, but she might as well have been wearing khakis, hiking boots, a safari hat, and carrying a rifle. She was out to track down where all the women over thirty-five were.

We went to one of Freddie's places, wittily called "Freddie's World." It was a cavernous space with a huge circular bar in the middle and throngs of people mingling about. And there seemed to be no man drought here.

"You fan out to our right, I'll go left. We'll meet up by the archway up ahead."

I went right, my eyes peeled for any woman with light lines on her forehead and creases stretching from the bottom of her nose to the corners of her mouth. All I saw were baby-faced cuties, with under-thirty radiant skin. I got to the archway as Alice came up.

"I went up to two women who I thought might be over thirty-five. They told me they were twenty-seven. One of them almost punched me and the other one left to go cry in the bathroom." Alice looked around again. "Otherwise, I came up with nothing."

"Let's go to one of his restaurants," I said. "I mean, women over thirty-five still have to eat, don't they?"

We walked a few blocks and found Freddie's Fish, a very trendy sushi restaurant that wrapped around the whole corner, with high windows to show all the beautiful people eating rice and raw fish inside. Luckily, we were seated at a table in the middle of things. The table next to us was empty, but by the time our sake had arrived, four women, all of whom had forehead creases and expensive handbags, sat down next to us. Jackpot.

After they ordered, we tried to look at them and smile every once in a while, to appear friendly. Alice hid our low-sodium soy sauce in her bag so she could ask, in her thickest Staten Island accent, to borrow theirs. They took the bait.

"Are you from New York?"

"Yes. Yes, we are," Alice said. "My friend Julie is writing a book about being single all over the world. Sort of a self-help book with a world view."

The women were interested. One of them asked, "So, you've come to Sydney to do research?"

"Yes, I have."

"What have you found?" asked another.

"Well, I haven't learned anything yet, but I have some questions," I said, shyly.

The four women leaned toward Alice and me. They were all very pretty. One of them smiled and said, "Okay. Shoot."

Alice jumped in. "Where do you women go out to meet men? Bars?"

"No, no," said one. "I never go to bars."

"Never," said another one.

The third one said, "I go out sometimes with a few of my other friends and it's usually pretty depressing."

"The men our age, they act like we're invisible."

Alice banged her fist on the table. "I knew it! Do you go to any of Freddie Wells's clubs?"

"It's hard to avoid them," the fourth one said. "But I've pretty much stopped. I'm thirty-seven and I started feeling completely over-the-hill."

Everyone else agreed. "Now we just go out to dinner."

"Or if it's a function for work."

"Otherwise, I just stay home."

Maybe Freddie was right after all. Maybe this was the Town of Lost Women, where ladies over a certain age are forced to stay home and watch television. I looked at these beautiful, vital, stylish women talking as if they were ready to play shuffleboard and get cataract surgery.

I had to ask: "Do you ever think about moving? Somewhere where there are more men?"

"Or where they have bars for people over twenty-five?" Alice added.

One of them said, "I was thinking of moving to Rome."

"Yes, Europe. There I think the men will fuck you when you're fifty," another one said, hopefully.

The other women seemed heartened by this concept. I thought this might be correct. Maybe that could be another bestselling self-help book: *Places Where Men Will Fuck You When You're Fifty.*

"But really. How could we? Just pack up and leave our home because our love lives are so bad? That seems ridiculous," one of the women said.

As we sat eating our edamame and drinking our sake, I thought about me and my friends. Our love lives could be considered disasters. But I would never dream of suggesting any of us leave New York to find a man. Or would I? Shouldn't we all be taking these statistics a little more seriously? We finished our sushi, and being appropriate women in our late thirties in Sydney, we went home and went to bed.

Back in the States

Georgia's week was filled with two quick, witty emails from Sam, a brief phone conversation, and even a text saying "gr8t talking to u!" The text struck Georgia as a bit out of character for the sweetly unhip Sam she met a week ago, but she didn't give it more than a passing thought. She was just relieved that she had a romantic prospect—no matter how far-flung. This thin strand of hope can get you through a lot of days of making your children's lunches alone, and going to bed alone and imagining your husband having sex with a young, nubile dancer with sinewy thighs. Georgia had a prospect, and even when Sam emailed her, asking if they could push back their date a couple of days because something "came up," she didn't even notice. All she cared about was that he didn't cancel on her, that he was still a prospect.

They met at a bar in Brooklyn. Sam suggested it since it was close to his apartment. Georgia didn't mind. Why shouldn't she be the one to travel? Living in Brooklyn, he must be on the subway all the time. He had to wake up in the morning for work, and had had to travel farther the last time they met. It only seemed fair. But when Georgia walked in, she was surprised at how young the crowd seemed; it felt like your standard college pub.

And the minute she saw Sam, Georgia could tell something was different. He looked literally flush with . . . something. Confidence. That's what it was. He seemed much more confident than just a week and a half ago. She let that observation pass and kept focused on the task at hand: being delightful.

"You don't mind if we just sit at the bar, do you?" Sam asked, casually, *confidently*.

"No, no, of course not, that's fine."

Sam pointed toward one lone stool at the corner of the bar. "Here, why don't you sit there?"

Georgia was a little confused. "Oh. Okay, well . . . don't you want to . . . ?"

"No. I've been sitting all day; it'll be good for me to stand for a bit." Georgia sat down dutifully on the stool and looked at Sam as he leaned against the bar.

"What can I get you? They have great Guinness here."

Georgia couldn't help but notice the demotion: from restaurant to bar, banquette to stool, wine to beer.

"That would be great," Georgia said. Sam gave the bartender their order and turned back to Georgia, smiling. The smile that last week was sheepish and tentative was now radiant. He was wearing the same kind of clothes, but they looked different on him now. Trendy. They chatted pleasantly, he standing, while Georgia sat. Georgia had not been dating enough to know why this felt incredibly awkward. Why shouldn't he stand if he wanted to? It's a free country.

"So, how have you been since we last saw each other?" Georgia asked, casually, sipping at her Guinness.

"Great. Really great."

"That's wonderful. So what's been going on that's so 'really great'?"

"You know. I'm just getting out there, you know. Meeting people, finding out who I am without Claire. Spreading my wings. It's exhilarating."

"Exhilarating. Wow. That's great. Exhilarating. Well, you can't beat exhilarating, can you?"

"No. You can't beat exhilarating!" Georgia thought about her life since getting a divorce from Dale. Well, she did sleep with a Brazilian prostitute. She guessed that could be considered exhilarating.

Sam took a big gulp of beer and wiped his lips with his sleeve. Georgia looked at him, not knowing if she wanted to know more, but unable to stop herself.

"So. What makes things so exhilarating?"

"Well, it's really fascinating, actually. I've been meeting all these women, you know?"

Georgia raised her eyebrows. Sam explained himself.

"Well, both of us, we're going out, we're meeting people, you know? We're getting back in the game, seeing where we fit in the whole scheme of things, right?"

Georgia nodded politely. "Yes. Exactly."

"So I'll admit. I've been doing some online dating this week. Like every night of the week. I just decided to just jump in headfirst. Whoosh!" Sam made a big diving motion and then a big splash with his hands.

"Whoosh!" Georgia mimicked, agreeably.

"And it's amazing what I learned. I mean, my wife didn't sleep with me for years. So I guess I assumed it was because I was actually physically repellent. But now I've been dating, and women want to see me again. They don't mind that I have two kids or only make sixty thousand bucks a year. They want to see me again!"

Georgia gave him the response he wanted. "That's great, Sam! Good for you!"

Sam leaned in and grabbed Georgia's arm. "The truth is, all my life, I never got the girls. I was the nice guy who all the girls said they just 'liked as a friend.' And then they would go out with the assholes. Well, guess what? Those girls are now unmarried women in their thirties and forties and me, the nice guy with a decent job? I might as well be Jesus Christ himself."

Georgia felt her stomach turn. A complete flip-flop as the words "Jesus Christ himself" came out of Sam's mouth. She leaned against the bar, trying to remain calm. She knew that this was probably the truth, but so far no one had spelled it out so unrepentantly. In New York, in terms of dating, nice guys over forty do in fact finish first. They are as miraculous as loaves and fishes falling out of the sky. Georgia felt herself flushing, with tears forming at the rims of her eyes. "You know, I'm not feeling very well."

Sam immediately became concerned. "What? Really? I'm so sorry. Can I get you anything? Water?"

The thing was, Sam really was a nice guy—which is exactly why he was such a deadly dating agent in New York.

"No, that's okay. I think I'm just going to get a cab and go home, if you don't mind. I'm so sorry." But in fact, Georgia wasn't that sorry. Sam had so many dates lined up he probably would be relieved to have a night off. She now understood the whole standing-up-at-the-bar thing. He had been dating so much his ass hurt. Or maybe he knew he was going to have to dash to his next date that evening and didn't want a stool to slow him down. Georgia got up. Sam helped her put on her jacket, walked her outside, and waved down a cab.

"Will you be okay?"

Georgia looked at him, a dull pain filling up her entire body. "Don't you worry. I'm fine. I think I ate something bad at lunch. It's been bothering me all day."

Sam opened the cab door and Georgia climbed in. "Okay, I'll call you in twenty minutes to make sure you got home safe. Is that all right?"

"Yes, of course. Thanks," Georgia mumbled. She turned her head so he wouldn't see that she was now crying, her sadness washing over her. Georgia had just learned another important lesson about being single. You might be out there dating to meet the love of your life, but the other person might be just wanting to eat a nice steak on a Saturday night—or just trying to "dive in." She felt humiliated. How could she have thought it was going to be so simple? A nice guy meeting her, liking her, and wanting to be with her. This was New York, and she felt the statistics were now spitting in her face.

Being true to his word, Sam did call exactly twenty minutes later to see how she was. He really was nice. What an asshole.

*   *   *

Two hours into her first shift as an animal shelter volunteer, Ruby watched as they took three dogs to their deaths. They didn't necessarily say that was what was happening, but she could tell. A man in a white coat would take the dog out of the cage and leave the room with it. The dog would never come back. Ruby was horrified. She knew that was what they did here, that was their policy, but she had no idea that it happened so often. It felt so random, so cruel. As the third dog was being taken out of its cage, Ruby stopped the young man.

"Excuse me, sir?"

The young man looked up at Ruby, with the door opened.

"Could you please tell me—how do you choose?"

The young man closed the cage door, almost as if he didn't want the dog to hear.

"You mean, who we . . . take?"

Ruby nodded.

This was obviously an uncomfortable subject. He cleared his voice. "We decide by their adoptability, so we take into account their age, their health—and their temperament."

Ruby shook her head. "Temperament?"

The young man nodded.

"So, the crankier the dog, the more chance that he'll get put down?"

The man nodded. He clearly wasn't happy about it, either. He smiled at Ruby politely, and then opened the cage door again. He took out Tucker, a German shepherd mix. He didn't make a peep, but he did look skinny; sickly. Ruby was now fighting back tears.

"May I hold Tucker, please? Just for a moment?"

The young man looked at Ruby. He studied her face and ascertained that he didn't have a nutcase on his hands. He led Tucker out of the cage and walked him over to Ruby. Ruby kneeled down and gave Tucker a big hug. She petted him and whispered in his ear how much she loved him. She didn't cry, she didn't make a scene. She just eventually stood up and let him go.

As she did, the strangest thought came across her mind, a thought she wasn't necessarily proud to have: She was glad that she decided to volunteer at this shelter. And not because she felt she could do good here; not because she felt the animals needed her. No. *If I can do this and not lose my shit,* she thought to herself, *I'll be able to do anything—and that includes dating again.*

Eventually, this became the routine. Ruby became the Sister Mary Prejean of the animal shelter. She would make sure that the last face they saw before they met their maker was a face of love. So whenever Ruby worked, which was once a week, on Thursday evenings, if there was a dog that was about to be put down, that young man, Bennett, would walk the dog over to Ruby. She would then administer his or her last rites, which was a big, big hug and lots of long, whispered affection. Then they were walked into the room, where they were given their injections and put to sleep.

• • •

Meanwhile, Serena was meeting her man everywhere: in broom closets, pantry rooms, and even in the ladies' room of Integral Foods on Thirteenth Street.

The one thing they never risked doing was meeting in one of their rooms. That's the first place one looks for you if they need you, and there was no good way she could explain sneaking out of Swami Swaroop's closed bedroom. But every other enclosed space was fair game. If the purpose of becoming a swami was to help her feel a powerful, all-encompassing love that made her tap into God's transcendent spirit, then those crazy sannyasin vows completely did the trick.

While she sat meditating on this particular morning, after already having a brief tête-à-tête with Swami Swaroop in the basement bathroom, her thoughts replayed the whole scenario: her ass on the sink, he in front of her, then both of them on the closed toilet seat, then them against the wall. These were definitely "extraneous thoughts" that the meditation leader would be wanting her to clear from her mind. But as hard as she tried, Serena couldn't. Because she was in love. And because this was her first time, she was struck by how perfectly apt those words were: *in love*. Serena loved this man so much that she felt as if she were floating in a bubble. A bubble of love. That she was existing, every moment of every hour, *in* love. And it was, ironically, the most spiritual experience she'd ever had. No yoga class, no meditation course, no ten-day juice fast had ever gotten her as close to the exultation she felt as this brand-spanking-new sensation of being in love.

During this meditation, she let herself say all the things she wanted to say to herself. "*This is what everyone has been talking about. All the love songs and the poems and the films. This is what life is all about. Being in love. Loving someone. Having someone love you.*" And as she let her breath go in and out, slowly, she went even a step further. "*I had no understanding of what it meant to be alive. Without love in your life, it is meaningless.*" There. She said it. And she meant it. How could she ever, *ever*, go back to living in the world without this feeling? This is everything, this is life, this is truth, this is God. Luckily, she didn't have to live without it. Because Swami Swaroop wasn't going anywhere. Oddly, she still called him Swami Swaroop. At their most intimate moments, she might say, "Oh, Swamiji," but that's as civilian as it ever got. And Mr. Oh Swamiji seemed to be existing in the same bubble of love, always wanting to be with her, touch her, talk to her. Sneaking a glance, a smile, a touch. He even gave her a gift, a secret sign that she was his: a tiny black string. He tied it around her ankle and told her that every time he saw it, he would know that they were bound together. To Serena, this proved that he was in love as well, and she was content to let things float on as they were.

The only thing that slightly diminished the joy of this cosmic commingling of souls was the fact that she had not yet expressed the enormity of her emotions to anyone. With my traveling, we kept trading phone calls, and she hadn't spoken to Ruby, Georgia, or Alice in a while. She certainly hadn't said any of this to Swami Swaroop. And it was starting to get to her. This joy was lodged inside her, warming her, uplifting her, but it also needed to be let out. It needed to be put into the world, as a truth, as a reality, so she could soar even higher than she already was. So that the love had a place to go, out of her heart, and into the world.

It was her turn to teach the first yoga class of the day. It was early, at seven thirty, and made up of just six very dedicated women and one man. She was guiding them through their Pranayama, their breathing exercises, telling them to inhale through the right nostril, pinch the other one closed with their left thumb, and reverse the process. As they moved through this chakra-stimulating process, Serena made a decision. She was going to tell Swami Swaroopananda how she felt. Serena felt it was disrespectful to the universe, to God, not to acknowledge the blessing that had been bestowed upon her.

This particular yoga center was very old-school. This was not cardio yoga or yoga done in a room the temperature of Hell. This was good old-fashioned yoga, and now they were doing their leg lifts. "Left leg up, and down. Right leg up, and down." As she spoke, her mind wandered. She planned how she was going to talk to him. She decided she would break the cardinal rule and go into Swami Swaroop's bedroom after class. She would gently and sweetly just tell him what they both already knew and felt. She would describe the depth of her emotions, not to ask for any decisions or commitments, but just wanting a release from the secret. It should be a celebration, this feeling, and she needed to be able to celebrate it, even if only between the two of them. Just then, as she looked out onto her class and all the legs that were being raised in the air, she saw something that made her gasp. It sounded something like this: "Now both legs, up, and down . . . up, and . . . kahhh!"

Of the twelve raised female legs in the yoga class, four of them were sporting little black strings around the ankle.

Serena immediately tried to control her breathing—she was a swami and yoga teacher after all. She recovered enough to say, "Excuse me. Now both legs up, and down, up and down."

She searched her mind for an explanation. Maybe it was some kind of new trend that Britney Spears or some other celebrity created to honor some disease. Wait! Don't the people who are into Kabbalah wear little strings? These women were all Kabbalists. That's the answer. She got through the class, peacefully and with equanimity. She comforted herself with the knowledge that these women all changed in the same dressing room before and after class—surely they would have noticed the strings. Swami Swaroop knew she taught these women yoga, he knew she was bound to see their ankles during a leg raise or shoulder stand. What kind of man would give all the women he slept with a black string? No. There was some other explanation and she was in love and she was still going to tell him how she felt.

Right after class, Serena looked in the different yoga rooms and offices to see if he was around, but didn't see him anywhere. She went to his room and heard the familiar sound of Swami Swaroop's heavy breathing, doing his morning Pranayama. She walked in without knocking.

The first thing she saw was the black string. On the ankle of Prema, the nineteen-year-old intern who worked in their tiny bookstore/boutique. That string was raised high above Prema's head. Swami Swaroop was on top of her on the bed, thrusting and Pranayamaing away. He looked up and saw Serena staring at him. With incredible equanimity, her breath slow and steady, even as her heart was racing and her hands were shaking, Serena quietly shut the door, making sure she didn't disturb anyone at the center.

She then walked lightly down the stairs to the basement and slipped into the dressing room. There were three women left there—three whom she saw with strings on their ankles. They all looked like they were just about to leave.

"Hi, Swamiji," said the thin twenty-two-year-old girl with the light brown hair and the long brown hairy armpits. She was putting her coat on. "That was a great class."

"Yeah, really great," said the thirty-five-year-old blond-haired woman. She was now wearing a business suit and putting on her lipstick in the mirror.

"Thanks, I was just . . . was there a sweatshirt in here? Someone called and said they left it."

The ladies, including a fifty-something woman with an outrageously hot buff body, all started helpfully looking. Serena didn't know exactly what she wanted to do or say, but she knew she had to do or say something.

"Wow. That's so funny. I noticed in class you all have black strings around your ankles. Are you all into Kabbalah?"

The women looked at one another and smiled mischievously.

"I think that's a red string," the hairy-armpits girl said.

They all started giggling. The fifty-something politely said, "Actually, we belong to a different kind of cult."

"Really?"

The women looked at one another, not saying another word. They all started collecting their bags and getting ready to scurry out of there as quickly as possible. The blond business-suit lady opened the door to the dressing room, about to make her exit.

Before she realized it, Serena had kicked the door shut and was keeping it closed, her right foot flat against it. The black string on Serena's right ankle was now completely in view. The women's eyes got wide at the sight of it. The hairy-armpitted girl was incredulous. She pointed at Serena.

"But . . . you're a *swami*," she said, outraged.

"So is Swami Swaroopananda!" Serena shouted back. "I don't get it! You all knew about each other and didn't care? Did he hit on you all at once and you guys decided to go for it as a group?"

The buff woman spoke, calmly. "Swami Swaroop came on to me about six months ago, actually, in this very dressing room."

Been there, done that, thought Serena, as the twenty-two-year-old at the same time giggled, "Been there, done that!"

"Anyway," the buff hottie continued, "when he gave me the string, I thought it was sweet. Soon enough I saw Gina had one," she said as she gestured to the blonde, "and so did Ricki," as she gestured to the armpit.

"I didn't care because I'm married; it's just for fun. We talked about it one day in the dressing room and we had a big laugh."

"He's so hot," Ricki said, "we were happy to share."

"Share? Hot? He's a swami?!"

The blonde smiled naughtily. "His spirituality, the forbidden nature of it. It's very hot. But you must know that. You're a swami, too, so that's doubly taboo."

"Doubly taboo. Yeah. That's super hot," said Ricki, who was now less incredulous and more jealous.

The women all looked at Serena enviously and it seemed for a moment that they wished that they had shaved their heads and been sworn to celibacy and orange clothes just to get the added naughtiness of it all.

"So, you're all basically his harem, is that what you're saying?" Serena asked, outraged.

The women all kind of smiled. The blonde shrugged. "Guess you're a part of it now, too."

Serena shook her head furiously. She reached down and grabbed the string around her ankle and pulled. And pulled some more. It wouldn't budge. It's amazing how durable a piece of string can be sometimes. She pulled a few more times until it seemed that she might start cutting through skin. Then she scanned the room, desperately looking for a sharp object. Nothing.

"Does anyone have a fucking key?" Serena the Swami shrieked.

The blonde quickly handed over her house keys. Serena took them, using a single key to start sawing away at her ankle string. The women watched, a little alarmed, as Serena tried to emancipate herself.

"Here's what I'm not a part of. Anyone's fucking harem. This is fuck-ing *bullshit*." And as she said *bullshit,* the string broke. Serena turned and immediately stormed out, leaving the women standing there.

She ran back up the stairs to Swami Swaroopananda's bedroom, but it was empty. Serena remembered that he taught a meditation class at that time.

Oh, fuck it, she thought. And she raced back down the stairs to the Kali Room and opened the door. Three women and two men were breathing in and out; Swami Swaroopananda was now in class leading them in an "om." Serena walked in and threw the piece of string at him. It fell right in front of her, invisible, with the result that she looked more like she had just angrily pawed at the air. Swami Swaroopananda opened his eyes and Serena saw that at that moment, underneath the powerful spirituality that he might be always emanating, there was also a slight twinge of fear. She picked up the string and threw it at him again. It again fell right in front of her. Swami Swaroopananda blinked.

"I loved you. Did you know that? *I loved you.*"

Swami Swaroop got up to somehow stop the impending train wreck. But Serena turned and stormed out of that room as well. She ran all the way back up the stairs to Swami Swaroopananda's room again. She walked in and opened up his closet, taking out every single orange thing in it. She then raced down a flight of stairs to her own room, now taking all her own orange clothes and adding them to the pile. The heap of orange clothing was towering about three feet over her head, and she wasn't able to see very well, but Serena managed to carry it all down and out the front door, down the brick steps, and then dump it all on the sidewalk. Swami Premananda, the heavyset swami, had followed her out of the building.

"Swami Durgananda, please, you're creating bad karma for yourself. You are attaching too closely to your ego."

"Kiss my orange ass," Serena said.

By this point, Swami Swaroop and his students were outside on the stoop looking at Serena.

Serena looked up at Swami Swaroop and said, "Yeah, right, you burned up your desires for God." She then looked at the center's van parked right next to her. There was a "clergy" sign on the dashboard. It had taken the Jayananda Center a long time to get the city to agree to give them clergy status, and it helped them immensely with parking in New York. As her last act of defiance, Serena reached in the half-open window, scraping her arm and almost dislocating her elbow as she grabbed the sign, pulled it out, and ripped it to pieces in front of her little audience on the stoop.

"If you're a member of the clergy so is Howard Fucking Stern," Serena said as she ripped and ripped and ripped. She then started to stomp on the orange pile of clothes as if trying to put out a fire.

So, this was how Serena's career as a swami came to a spectacular end. The students and Swami Swaroop went inside, and Swami Premananda asked Serena to immediately pack her things and go before she had to call the police. Serena was only too happy to oblige.

Back in Australia

That night, the jet lag was at it again. At four in the morning, I got up and reread one of Fiona's columns in the *Hobart News*. In this piece, she was telling a woman to mentally spoon herself—she needed to wrap her self-love around herself every night before she went to bed. I wanted to kill this woman.

She had an email address where one could contact her, and since it was four in the morning and I was an angry and bitter woman, I decided to write. It went something like this:

"Don't you think it's a little irresponsible of you to tell women that all they have to do is love themselves and be optimistic and love will find them? What if they live somewhere where there are literally no men? What if they are older or overweight or unattractive? All they have to do is love themselves and be confident and filled with joy and someone will appear to love them? Really? Can you guarantee that? Can we call you when we're eighty years old and tell you how it worked out for us? And if you were wrong, can we come and punch you in the face?"

I didn't send that one. I sent this one.

"Don't you think it's a little irresponsible of you to tell women that all they have to do is love themselves and be optimistic and love will find them? What if they live somewhere where there are literally no men? Do you really think the statistics, the reality of it all, means nothing? That we can all, if we shine brightly enough, not be one of the statistics?" I then went on to explain that I was writing a book about single women, and I was single myself, and this was of great interest to me.

I finally got to bed around six. When I woke up at ten, Alice had left a note that she was at the free breakfast downstairs. I got up and checked my email to see if Ms. Fiona had anything to say for herself. She had.

"Julie, I'd like to talk to you in person, if you fancy. It's a much better way to explain myself. Could you take a little day trip to Tasmania so we can chat?"

Well, that was awfully civilized. I wondered if she did that for every disgruntled reader. Maybe she was one of those people pleasers, always trying to make sure no one was mad at her. Or maybe it's because I mentioned that I was from New York and I was writing a book. That seemed to be opening up a lot of doors for me.

I went down to breakfast. Alice was there, with a large pot of coffee next to her, making an awful face.

"I just tried Vegemite. I've been looking at it now for days, and I thought it might be time to try it. Jesus, that stuff tastes like ass." She took a big gulp of water and then added, "Yeasty ass."

I poured myself a cup of coffee. "Alice, how would you like to go to Tasmania with me today?"

"That's a real place?" she asked seriously. Again, Americans, not so great with the geography.

"Yes, it's a real place. I want to go talk to a woman there who writes about dating in Australia. She's really, like . . . cheerful."

Alice looked at me. "Cheerful? About dating in Australia?" She put down her piece of toast dramatically. "This I've got to see."

Back in the States

Georgia decided not to take things lying down. She was still new to dating, so she felt that somehow she would be able, with the sheer force of her will and clever strategy, to win. So she came up with a plan. The first step was to call up Sam and see if he could fit a dinner at her place into his busy dating schedule. She knew that he was a good guy, so if necessary she would appeal to his good manners. She picked up the phone, ready to leave a message. But he picked up.

"Hey, Georgia, how are you? Are you feeling better?"

"Oh. Hi, Sam. I am. I'm so sorry about the other night. I was wondering if I could make it up to you."

"Oh, there's no need . . ."

"Well, I want to. I was wondering if you'd like to come over for dinner some night when the kids are with their father."

"Sure, that would be great. I actually had plans this Saturday night that fell through. Would you be free then?"

"That would be great. How about eight o'clock?"

"Great."

Georgia smiled, satisfied, and gave him her address.

Saturday night came and everything was going according to plan. Georgia was making her famous Chicken Riesling for dinner, and the smell of the chicken, cream, and herbs was permeating the apartment. She also had hundreds of dollars' worth of flowers bought by Dale's credit card, placed in conspicuous places all around the apartment. Note cards from the person who had supposedly sent the flowers were placed perfectly casually near each bouquet, along with remnants of some ribbons and paper in which they had arrived. She had the Shiraz breathing and she looked gorgeous. Everything was perfect. The doorbell rang and Sam was there, holding a tiny bouquet of flowers.

"Hi!" From his expression Georgia knew what he was thinking: she was prettier than he remembered.

"Wow. You look great!"

"Thanks." Georgia ushered him in the door. He gave her his tiny bundle of six roses, just as he noticed the huge bouquets of flowers that seemed to be everywhere.

"Wow, I guess you must like flowers," Sam said, sort of awkwardly, looking around. For a moment Georgia saw a little bit of the insecurity she had seen on their first date. Her plan was already working; she had caught her enemy off guard. Georgia acted out an "embarrassed fluster" with the ease of Julia Roberts.

"Oh, those . . . it's a long . . . guys . . . you know, sometimes they get, you know . . . overenthusiastic. They're nice though, aren't they?"

"They're beautiful."

"But yours are beautiful, too, oh my God. Beautiful. Let me put them in water."

Georgia took Sam's minuscule bouquet and put the six sad roses in a vase. She couldn't have predicted he would have brought her flowers; that was just a little gift from the heavens.

"So how have you been? Good? Busy, I'm sure," Georgia asked as she put the roses out on the counter.

"Yes. Definitely busy. But it's nice to be here."

"I'm so glad you're here. It's hard making plans with so much going on for the both of us. It's amazing this was even able to happen. Please, have a seat."

Georgia motioned to the stool by the counter of her beautiful open kitchen. He sat down as commanded and she gave him a glass of Shiraz. This time he would be the one sitting while she was standing. While she put the finishing touches on the meal, they laughed as she told stories of disastrous meals she had made in her day. So far, a great date.

Then Sam told a story about one of his kids. It was rather involved, about a parent of one of the kids on his son's Little League team. It was an amusing story, and he was telling it confidently. Georgia was laughing when the phone rang. Like clockwork.

"I'll let it go to voice mail. Keep going, please."

"So the man went crazy, screaming and yelling, and he had this ice cream in his hand . . ." Just then, a desperate male voice came out of Georgia's answering machine.

"Hey, Georgia, this is Hal. Just wanted to let you know I had a great time last night. I hope I'll get to see you again soon. How about Wednesday? Are you free Wednesday? I can't stop thinking about—"

Georgia "raced" over to the machine. "I'm so sorry, it's . . . I thought I'd turned down the machine . . ." She adjusted the phone, then turned to Sam, an actual blush on her cheeks. "I'm sorry. Continue, please."

Sam just looked at her, a little surprised.

"Wow. He's got it bad."

"No, it's just, we went to this play that was really funny and it just was a great . . . never mind . . . it's not—please, what happened with the ice cream?"

Sam stood up from his stool and leaned on the counter, him on one side of it, her on the other. Suddenly, the counter seemed like a big desk and he was on a job interview. Or an audition.

Sam laughed nervously. "Right. So anyway, the coach told him that if he didn't calm down, he was going to kick his kid off the team for good.

The guy took the ice-cream cone and just flung it right at the coach, like a two-year-old. Then his kid just ran over to him and said . . ."

Just then the answering machine picked up and another man's voice was heard, deep and commanding—the voice of a CIA operative or president of the United States.

"Hey. Georgia, this is Jordan. I really enjoyed our having drinks the other night and I was hoping I could see—" Georgia feigned surprise and irritation at herself.

"I'm so sorry, I must have turned the ringer off instead of the machine, this is so rude . . ." She went to the phone and fiddled with some more buttons.

"It's off now. It's completely off," Georgia said sheepishly. "I'm *so* sorry."

"It's fine. No problem," Sam said. Georgia noticed that Sam was truly flustered at this point. He didn't even comment on this particular man's message, and Georgia chose not to explain it. She thought it was best to let the other man's desire hang in the air.

"So what did his kid say?" she asked sweetly.

Sam looked at Georgia and then back down at the counter. "Nothing. It was nothing."

"Well, dinner's ready anyway."

They began eating, but everything was different. For one thing, Sam was now really looking at her. Women spend so much time wondering how the men they're with feel about them; they'll analyze emails, replay phone messages. But the simple fact is that all you have to do is watch how he looks at you. If he looks at you as if he doesn't want to take his eyes off you for fear that you might disappear, then you are with a man who really likes you. And now, that was how Sam was looking at Georgia. At the pub he barely made eye contact. Now he was staring at her, hard.

Georgia had pulled off a feat that Wall Street brokers and economists would be in awe of. In just one hour, she had raised her stock by manufacturing "demand" out of thin air, and it looked like there might be a bidding war. She made herself seem to be the one thing that everything in our culture wants her to believe she is not: valuable. And all it took was a couple of hundred dollars' worth of flowers and phone calls from the gay couple down the hall. She watched Sam try to impress her with his jokes, nervously running his fingers through his hair. She smiled to herself when he touched her arm to make a point or she felt his eyes follow her as she went to get more wine. At the end of the date he only stopped kissing her when Georgia told him it was time to go.

Now, you may ask, did Georgia feel badly that it was all a lie? That she had to create an entire reality in order to feel good about herself? Did she feel badly that none of this was true? That she actually sent herself flowers to get some midwestern cornhead's attention? No. All she felt in this moment was proud. She saw reality and she refused to kid herself about it. With clearheadedness and foresight, she'd understood the power shift that had occurred with Sam and his new view of the world and then did something about it. She made herself into a "catch" and she felt that someone should give her a medal for it. Women are fucked, the numbers are against them, time is against them, and if their only recourse is to completely fabricate a personal life in order to jump up a notch in the brutal dating pecking order, then that's just fine.

Sam called her the next day. His voice sounded nervous, probably wondering if hot, sought-after Georgia would even take his call.

"Hey, Georgia. It's Sam."

"Hi, Sam!" Georgia said, warmly. "How are you?"

"Great, great," Sam said, trying to sound cheerful, but not too eager. "Listen, I just wanted to let you know that I had a really great time last night and I was hoping I could see you again soon."

Georgia had already decided what she was going to do when this call came (which she knew it would). "Listen, Sam, I had a great time, too. But I just got off the phone with Hal, and we've decided to see each other exclusively."

Sam cleared his throat. "Oh. Okay. Wow. Well, I'm really disappointed, I'm not going to lie, but I appreciate you telling me."

She knew her decision was a risky one. She had cut off the only dating prospect she had. And, as I've made clear, we love the dating prospects. But at the end of the day, Georgia wanted to be with someone who didn't have anything to prove to himself, who didn't need to play the field, and didn't need competition to notice how valuable Georgia was. Besides, flowers are really expensive.

• • •

Unfortunately, Serena had let go of her apartment, something no one in New York should ever do, whether for a relocation, a marriage, or a baby. Only if you're dead, then maybe you can give it up. Even then, try not to.

But Serena did. So now she was hairless and homeless. As I had sublet my apartment, and Serena didn't have money for a hotel, she didn't really know what to do. So she called up the one person who would understand the depression into which she was about to plunge. She called Ruby and asked if she could crash at her house. Ruby, being Ruby, immediately agreed.

When I heard what happened, via a text message, I thought it might be best to do a conference call. I even asked Georgia to come by to make sure the two of them were going to be okay together. I worry sometimes.

Alice and I were still in Sydney, packing to take our trip to Tasmania. Ruby was sitting at her dining room table with Serena and Georgia. They were all on speakerphone and I shouted my disbelief.

"A guy who's not supposed to be having sex with anyone was having sex with at least five different women!?"

"Who were all more than happy to share him. THEY WERE ALL MORE THAN HAPPY TO SHARE HIM," Serena shouted back.

Georgia just shook her head. "Wow. Now celibate guys are having harems. It's the end of the world."

"Maybe they should just start euthanizing us all," Ruby said, almost to herself.

Everyone gasped, even me, on the phone.

"What?!" I said, hoping that my connection had made me misunderstand.

"I mean it," Ruby said matter-of-factly. "Just like with the dogs. Maybe the mayor's office should just start killing off all women who are ill-tempered, not in perfect health, have bad teeth, or whatever. To give the good candidates a better chance at finding a suitable home."

We were all stunned into silence. Clearly things at the animal shelter had started to get to Ruby.

Serena finally asked, "You're the one I've decided to live with to cheer me up?"

Georgia said, "Ruby, I don't know you very well, so please forgive me if this comes out wrong, but if you don't pick up the phone and quit that volunteer job right this minute I will have to punch you in the face."

"Seriously, Ruby, that was the worst thing I have ever heard anyone say in my entire life," I added.

Georgia started to laugh. "I can't believe you actually said that."

Serena started to giggle. "You actually suggested that the city start *gassing* us."

Ruby threw her head down on the table and started laughing, starting to see how far she'd fallen. "Oh my God, and I still kind of believe it. I'm losing my mind!"

Alice and I were in our hotel in Australia, listening to them all scream with laughter.

Georgia took out her cell phone. "Gimme the number. Of the shelter. Now."

Ruby did as she was told. Georgia dialed her cell phone and handed the phone to Ruby. Ruby began to speak.

"Hello? This is Ruby Carson. I'm a volunteer there. I wanted to let you know that I won't be coming in again. It's very bad for my mental health, thank you." She quickly hung up as Ruby and Georgia burst into applause.

"I couldn't hear—did Ruby just quit her volunteer job?" I asked from the other side of the world.

"Yes. Yes, she did," Georgia said. "Now we just have to get Serena a job and our mission for tonight will be accomplished."

"Can you go back to your old job? With the movie star?" Alice asked.

Serena shrugged. "I'm sure they hired someone else."

I piped in on my end. "But Serena, from everything you told me about them, they sounded really nice. You seemed to really like them."

"It's true," Serena said into the phone. "I've actually missed them a little. Joanna really was sweet to me. And Robert was really fun to be around."

Georgia got out her phone. "Call them and find out. What's their number?"

Serena hesitated.

"Please, I'm not going to sell it to *People* magazine. I'm just trying to get you a job."

Serena gave Georgia the number. Georgia dialed and handed the phone to Serena.

"Hello, Joanna? This is Serena." Everyone watched as Serena listened to the voice on the other end. Serena's eyes began to light up.

"Well, actually, it's funny you ask. It didn't really work out for me at the yoga center. So I was wondering if you were . . . really? Oh. Wow. Great. Yeah, I'll come by tomorrow and we can talk about it. Okay. See you then."

Serena closed Georgia's phone, looking puzzled. "They don't have anyone."

Georgia clapped and said, "That's amazing!"

"Yeah," Serena said. "But I don't know . . . she sort of sounded sad."

"What?" I said, the sound having dipped out for a minute.

Serena leaned into the phone and said again, louder, "*She sounded sad.*"

Back to Australia

The flight to Tasmania was only an hour and a half long. I imagined it would be an island wilderness with kangaroos hopping around, and aboriginal tribespeople greeting us with their didgeridoos. But Hobart, the capital of Tasmania, is quite civilized. It's a quaint, colonial-feeling town on a picturesque harbor. Short sandstone buildings line the streets, renovated into pubs and shops. Sadly, I even saw a Subway sandwich shop there.

I had emailed Fiona before we left Sydney, telling her that we'd be coming. She kindly offered to meet us at the local pub to talk. I was still suspecting she had an agenda—being a New Yorker, I had to assume she couldn't be doing this just to be nice.

I have to admit, my mood was not very good. It's one thing to read the lousy statistics, it's another to watch them played out with above-the-head-staring men, women who feel over the hill at thirty-five, and young men who are dividing by two and adding four. In New

York, there's not much difference between the way a twenty-five-year-old behaves and a thirty-five-year-old. In New York, if you're pushing forty, you can be so busy having a good time it doesn't even faze you when you get an invitation to your twentieth high school reunion. But in Sydney, my bubble of self-delusion officially burst. For the first time in my life, I felt old.

We met at a harborside Irish pub with a long wooden bar and a giant sign that said "Fishmonger."

As soon as we walked in, we heard, "Now these must be my New York girls!" A woman walked toward us with her arms outstretched and a big smile on her face. She was exactly as I imagined, with a round, open face and pale Britishy skin. She had thin, light brown hair that was pulled back in a ponytail. She was absolutely pleasant to look at—appealing, innocuous, and a bit bland. She looked us over. "Why you're absolutely gorgeous!" I immediately felt guilty for thinking she looked bland. She ushered us to the bar. "Come on now, if you're here in Hobart, you're going to have to have a pint. Have you tried the James Boag's?"

"No," I said. "I don't really drink beer."

"Me neither," Alice said.

"But you must try just a bit. You're at the docks. We can't have you sipping wine down here, now can we?" Both Alice and I were thinking, *Why yes, yes you can,* when Fiona went to the bar and ordered beers for us. She waited until they came, paid for them, and gave them to us.

"Now tell me, do you think I'm an absolute idiot for the things I write? Are you here to tell me off? Come on, let's have it then." She was so warm and open, I didn't have the heart to get all combative with her.

"I didn't come here to yell at you, it's just . . ."

"I seem too much all sunshine and lollies, is that it?"

"It's just that you telling women to love themselves and they'll find love seems, I don't know . . ."

"Like a lie," Alice jumped in to say. "It's statistically impossible. Even if we all started marrying gay men, the numbers still wouldn't work out."

Fiona took the criticism in stride. "The statistics are very compelling. Did you hear that someone suggested we give our blokes tax incentives just to stay in Australia? What kind of rubbish is that? They already think they're God's gifts, the men here." Fiona waved at some women walking into the bar. "Katie! Jane! We're over here!" She looked back at Alice and me. "Just try and get a man to take you out on a proper date; it's like trying to make a koala run." Katie and Jane came over and Fiona kissed them both on the cheeks and introduced us all.

"I'm just telling them dating in Tasmania doesn't exist."

Jane and Katie nodded knowingly.

"Well, what do you do instead?" Alice asked, curious.

Fiona took a gulp of beer and laughed. "Well, we go down to the pub, get drunk, fall on top of each other, and hope for the best. It's a frightful situation, really."

We all laughed. Fiona kept waving and kissing people hello. She greeted each person with something flattering, and with each person she really seemed to mean it.

I realized that we were in the presence of one of those people God has blessed with an abundance of serotonin and a joyful disposition. You know. A happy person.

"And it's true. I do tell my readers that if you just love your life and are filled with that, then you're going to be irresistible—and the men are just going to come out of the woodwork."

I couldn't help but become insistent. "But that's simply not true. I know dozens of single women who are fantastic and ready and charming and shining and they can't find boyfriends."

"And they're not too picky. They don't have unrealistic expectations," Alice chimed in. She knew a loophole when she saw one.

It was starting to get crowded and the music was up loud, so Fiona practically shouted at us. "Yet!"

"What?" I asked.

"They haven't found boyfriends *yet*. It's not over for them, is it?"

"No. But, that's their reality now."

"And tomorrow everything could change. That's what I think about. Tomorrow everything could change!" As if on cue, a guy in a t-shirt and long cargo shorts walked over to Fiona and said hello to her. She greeted him warmly and kissed him on the cheek. "This is Errol. We fell on each other last summer and were together for three whole weeks, isn't that right?" Errol smiled sheepishly. She playfully pinched his ear. "He was a real wanker to me. Weren't you, Errol?"

"I was an asshole. It's true." Then he walked away.

"So tell me, Julie. What do you think I should tell people? What do you think we should believe?" Fiona asked, good-naturedly.

There it is, that question again. What do I believe in? I looked around the bar. It was a sea of men and women, predominantly women. And the women looked as if they were trying a lot harder than the men.

"That maybe life isn't fair," I said. "That just as not everyone is guaranteed to win the lottery or have perfect health or get along with their family, not everyone is guaranteed to have someone love them." I was on a roll now. "Maybe then we can start a new way to think about life. One that doesn't make it so tragic if love happens to be the thing you end up not getting."

Fiona thought about it for a moment. "I'm sorry, ladies. If I told my readers that, I'd be responsible for the first mass suicide in the history of Australia. There would be hundreds of girls floating facedown in the Tasman Sea."

Alice and I looked at each other. It did sound pretty dark, even to us. "Besides, I think it goes against human nature," Fiona said. "We all want to love and be loved. That's just the way it is."

"Is that human nature, or is that Hollywood?" Alice asked.

A band started to play on a tiny stage set up in the back of the room. They were a lively Irish band, and soon the dance floor was full of drunken white people jumping up and down.

I thought out loud. "Maybe our true human nature is to be in a community. That's the only thing that seems to endure. Much more than marriage, that's for sure."

Fiona got very serious. She stood up and placed a hand on each of our shoulders, looking squarely at us. "I have to say this, and I really mean it from the bottom of my heart. You both are gorgeous women. You are smart and funny and hot. To think that you would end up with no love in your lives is absolutely bullcrap. It's just not possible. You two are goddesses. I know you don't want to believe me, but it's true. Beautiful, sexy goddesses. And you shouldn't consider, even for a moment, that you won't have as much happiness in your life as you can possibly stand." With that, Fiona turned to get another beer.

My eyes started to water up. Alice turned to me, her eyes a little teary as well. She was good, this one.

The music and the dancing became even more raucous and Alice grabbed my hand and dragged me onto the dance floor to jump up and down. Fiona came with us, along with about ten of her closest girlfriends. I watched her, laughing and twirling and singing along to some lyrics I couldn't understand. No matter what I say, no matter how smart I am, I could clearly see that Fiona was happier than me. She had inoculated herself against the poison of the statistics that had weighed me down all week. As I watched the sweat start forming on her cheeks, and her face lit up with laughter, I had to admit it. She was one of those people that everyone wants to be around, and at the end of the day, people who are positive and optimistic are simply more attractive than people who are negative and pessimistic. Alice put her arm around me and pretended to sing a song that we couldn't understand the words to. "Fly into my flah flah baby baba ba . . . yeah." Fiona was dancing with Errol and Jane and Katie, making them laugh by trying to do a hip-hop step. Alice said loudly into my ear, "I like her. She's cool."

A handsome, rugged-looking guy then walked onto the dance floor, making his way through the crowd and right toward Fiona. When she saw him, she threw her arms around him and he gave her a big kiss on the lips. They spoke for a few moments together, their arms wrapped around each other. He went up to the bar, and Fiona saw the curious expressions on our faces and came up to us to explain.

"We just met a few weeks ago. His name is George. I'm absolutely mad about him. He's lived in Hobart his entire life, but we'd never laid eyes on each other till last month. Isn't that the strangest thing?"

Alice and I just looked at her, confused. "Were you not going to tell us about him?" I asked, amused.

Fiona just shrugged, laughing. "Don't you hate those women who think they know everything just because they managed to meet a nice guy? I'd rather die than have you think I was her!"

I looked at Fiona, impressed. She had the ultimate weapon in her arsenal, and she didn't use it. She purposely chose not to play the "well, look how well it worked for me" card. She wanted to make sure I didn't feel that my point of view was any less valid than hers just because she had a boyfriend and I didn't. This truly made her a goddess, and taught me another important rule: *When you finally do fall in love, don't you dare be smug about it.*

In our taxi back to the Hobart airport, I couldn't stop thinking about Fiona. It would be dishonest if I didn't admit that she had been right, in a sense. She shone her light so brightly that a man did actually appear out of the woodwork of Hobart for her. Did that mean I believed that that would happen to everyone who behaved like her? No. Did I suddenly think everyone is guaranteed love in this life? No. Did it make me think that you should ignore the statistics and just make sure you're absolutely adorable? No.

But here's what I did learn from Fiona and Australia about statistics and being single: *One hundred percent of all human beings need hope to get by. And if any statistic takes that away from you, then it's not worth knowing.*

And take trips as often as possible to places where you know there will be lots of men.

Hey, there's nothing wrong with trying to help your odds.

It was time for Alice to get back to New York. In our hotel room in Sydney, as I watched Alice pack, I became filled with homesickness. I missed my bed, my friends, my city. Also, Sydney had rattled me. The farther I got from Fiona and her glow, the less hopeful and optimistic I became. I made a decision.

"I'm going home. I'm going to go home and back to my job and work off my advance and be done with this. I can't do this anymore."

Alice sat on the bed, deciding what she should say.

"I'm sorry you're feeling this way. But I think this has been good for you. You've always been so responsible, you've always had a desk job. It's good for you to not know what's going to happen next."

To me, it was excruciating. I felt unbearably lonely.

"I feel just so . . . frightened."

Alice nodded. "Me, too. But I don't think it's time for you to go home. I just don't."

As I walked Alice to her cab, she asked, "Why don't you go to India? Everyone seems to have some kind of spiritual awakening there."

"Serena said the same thing. I'll think about it."

As the cab pulled away, Alice called out, "Keep going, Julie! You're not done yet!"

I watched her drive away, and was again filled with an unbearable loneliness. *Why was I putting myself through this? And why hadn't Thomas ever called me?* Now this wasn't a new thought; I had thought it every day since Italy, because as I might have mentioned before, I am a pathetic creature and when we women have a connection with someone, geez, it's hard to let it go. The good news is, I never called him. Thank God. Thank God. Because here's a rule I've learned about how to be single, a rule I learned the hard way and didn't have to travel around the world to find: *Don't call him, don't call him, don't call him.* And then, just when you think you have the perfect excuse to call him, *don't call him.* Right now, I was seriously considering calling him.

Just then, the phone rang. I answered it and a man with a French accent was speaking to me.

"Is this Julie?" he asked.

"Yes, it is," I said, not believing what I thought I was hearing.

"It is Thomas." My heart immediately began racing.

"Oh. Wow. Thomas. Wow. How are you?"

"I am well. Where are you? Singapore? Timbuktu?"

"I'm in Sydney."

"Australia? That's perfect. Bali is very close."

"Bali?" I repeated, shifting my weight from one foot to the other nervously.

"Yes. I have some business I need to do there. Why don't you meet me?"

My heart skipped a beat. "I don't know about that . . ."

Then Thomas's voice became much more serious. "Julie. I made a promise to myself. If I could go three days without thinking about you, without wanting to pick up the phone to ask when I could see you again, then I would never call you. I wasn't able to go one day."

It was a shocking thing to hear someone say. Especially in Sydney, where my self-esteem had taken a beating, where my light was on its last watt.

"Julie. Please don't make me beg. Meet me in Bali."

I looked around Sydney Harbor and thought about statistics. What were the odds that a handsome French man would want to see me in Bali? What were the odds that it would ever happen again? And what about the wife?

So I asked, "But what about your wife?"

"She knows I'm going to Bali, but the rest, she doesn't ask."

I said yes. Because on the rare occasion that the odds happen to be in your favor, how can you say no?

RULE

7

Admit That Sometimes You Feel Desperate (I Won't Tell a Soul)

When Alice arrived back in New York, she was a changed woman. Sydney had done something to her. She was scared. Although she was impressed with Fiona, it didn't stay with her long. As she thought back on the past six months of dating and Australia and the man who didn't want to dance with her, she had to admit to herself: it's hell out there. She had made the best of it, she had given it her Alice-who-can-do-anything all, but the thought of ever having to date again was too much for her to bear. She was so relieved to be with Jim that it almost bordered on delirium. Was she in love with him? No. Was this the man of her dreams? Absolutely not. But she appreciated him to the point that it was almost like being in love, almost like he was the man of her dreams.

And so Alice, redheaded, Staten Island superhero Alice, was ready to settle. Never in court, not a chance, but now, in her life. She saw a flash of a vision of her future without Jim and it truly scared her.

She was walking down Prince Street, thinking all these things, as she headed to meet Jim for the first time since she had gotten home from Sydney. She turned the corner and there he was, in the window of a nice little dive bar, the only one still left in Soho. He was on time, of course. He saw Alice through the window and smiled and waved. She smiled and waved back, picking up her pace so that by the time she was inside she was at a gallop. She threw her arms around him and kissed him hard on the lips. He laughed, surprised, and wrapped his arms around her.

When they finally broke apart, Alice looked at him with utmost seriousness. "Let's get married," she whispered. Jim pulled away, putting his hands on her hips and looking directly in her eyes.

"Are you serious?" His voice was slightly breathy from shock and excitement.

"Absolutely," Alice said, smiling and laughing. She hugged Jim as if she would never let go. Jim picked her up, right there in the bar, and twirled her around as she laughed and buried her head in his neck.

So what if it wasn't exactly how she imagined it would be? Sure, there was no knee and ring and proposal, and she was the one who had asked. But he did scoop her up in his arms and let her know that he felt like the luckiest guy on earth.

As she laughed and twirled she thought to herself, *I really do love Jim. I do.*

On the Way to Bali

I was on the plane from Tokyo to Denpasar, Bali, when it happened. I had been in a nice, sound Lexomil sleep when I suddenly woke up. I was seated on the aisle. The shade on the window on my row had not been closed, so I was able to look out at the utter blackness. Something about all that blackness, that abyss right when I woke up, started my heart beating. Fast. I started breathing heavy, my chest suddenly heaving up and down. I was gasping for air as though I was being strangled. My neighbor, a pudgy Asian man in his twenties, was asleep, his little blue blanket tucked around his chin, his head resting against the black window. The poor thing had no idea there was a crazy lady next to him. I looked around. Everyone was pretty much asleep. I assumed it would really freak them out to wake up to the sound of an American woman screaming at the top of her lungs. I leaned over, propping my elbows on my thighs, and held my head in my hands and tried to breathe. But it felt like there was blackness all around, about to swallow me up whole. Tears formed in my eyes and I desperately tried to hold them back.

Of course, I didn't want to cry because I didn't want to disturb my fellow passengers, alarm the flight attendants, embarrass myself, or otherwise cause a scene. But there was a much more pressing and vainer reason why I didn't want to start tearing up. When I cry, even if it's one drop, my eyes puff up like two Jiffy Pop containers and the circles under my eyes become instantaneously jet-black and loop down practically to my chin. My main concern was that I was meeting Thomas at the airport in Denpasar, and I wanted to look pretty. There, I said it.

I wondered if there was a way to cry without making a sound or producing tears. I tried it for a few seconds, contorting my face in this crazy silent sob while blinking rapidly so as not to let any water well up. I can't even imagine what I looked like. Of course since I was in the middle of a panic attack and had no control over myself, this didn't work. I started to cry. I was crying because I was having a panic attack, and I was also crying because I knew I was going to look hideous now. We only had thirty minutes left on the flight and were going to have to belt ourselves in soon for the descent. I decided to go to the bathroom, where at least I could go crazy in private. I managed to gain control of myself enough to walk down the aisle, past all the men, women, teenagers, children, and babies, sleeping. I walked as fast as I could to the bathroom and went in. I sat on the toilet and released an immediate sob and then kept going. I tried to do this as quietly as I could; I had enough self-protection remaining that I didn't want an international incident. I started rocking back and forth on the toilet seat, my arms wrapped around myself like a disturbed little child. I grabbed at my hair. I crumpled farther in to myself. At some point I looked in the mirror and saw my hundred-year-old turtle face. I cried even harder. I felt lost, suspended in the air, in darkness. I didn't know where I was going or what I was doing—with Thomas, with love, with my life. I felt catastrophe was imminent.

I splashed some cold water on my face. It never helps. Ever. Why do people tell you to do that? They announced that we had to get into our seats for landing, so I stood at the sink and willed myself to calm down. I closed my eyes and focused on slowly getting my breathing back to normal. I started to relax. In a minute I was completely fine, as if nothing had happened. I walked to my seat and sat down quietly in my chair. I looked over at the cozily sleeping neighbor and felt victorious. Yes, I had an attack, but this time, no one noticed. I was able to contain it to the bathroom. I knew I looked like hell, and no amount of makeup was going to change that. But for now, this was good enough.

In situations like this, when you're seeing someone you haven't seen in a while, and the stakes are maybe a little high, and there's a nervousness and a feeling of not knowing what to expect, I think the first second you lay eyes on them is everything. That's the moment when you realize exactly how you feel about that person, and how your time together is going to go. I was now at baggage claim. I glanced at the clock on the wall. It was midnight. There were a lot of tired tourists waiting for their bags, and a lot of drivers milling about, hoping to catch a fare.

Then I saw him.

He was standing a little bit away from everyone else. He was wearing a brown t-shirt and jeans, and he was waving at me, his blue eyes sparkling. He was smiling, but not too broadly, just enough for me to know that he was delighted to see me. In a flash I was running up to him and hugging him. He wrapped his arms around me and held me, kissing my head. There we were, holding each other, kissing and smiling. We must have looked like the greatest of lovers.

He took my face in his hands and looked at me. "Now, tell me. How was your flight?"

I looked him straight in the eyes and I lied. "It was great. I didn't have any problems."

He examined my face and said, "Really? You look like you've been crying." I broke away from him and just sort of looked down at my feet. I lied again, saying, "No. It was fine, really. I'm just tired."

Thomas looked at me closely and smiled. "Okay, I'll pretend I believe you. Now let's get out of here!"

We got to our hotel at around two in the morning. A porter took us down a little stone pathway. When he opened the door to our accommodations, I couldn't help but gasp.

Thomas had reserved a huge villa for us, twice the size of my apartment. The walls were all glowing in light brown wood and the bamboo ceiling above seemed to go on forever, coming to a point high above our heads. There were marble floors and a king-size bed, which faced a private balcony. One side of the villa was all windows, looking out over endless rice paddies. Even at night, the view was stupendous.

"This is . . . this is so beautiful. I can't believe it!" I stammered. No one had ever taken me somewhere so beautiful. No one could ever afford to take me somewhere so beautiful. I turned to Thomas and just stared at him in wonder. He took me in his arms and kissed me.

Now how do I describe what happened next? Okay, let's just say that sometimes in life, after years of just coasting along, trying to make the best of a bad situation, keeping your chin up, sometimes the heavens give you a reward, a tiny little prize for all your hard work. Life gives you a brief taste of how simply glorious it all can be. You don't know how long it's going to last and you don't really care, because you know at that moment you have stumbled upon a little pond of bliss and you're not going to take a minute worrying about when you have to get out of the water.

What I mean to say is that for the next eight days, we didn't leave the hotel. We barely left the room, but if we did, it was only to have a meal. I can't even remember the last time that happened to me. The truth is, I don't have boyfriends that often. I have dates, I have flings, I have "situations." But I don't have men, one after the other, whom I cart around as my boyfriend, and then break up with for some reason or another and say later to my friends "What was I thinking?" Unfortunately, I always know what I'm thinking, and they do, too. So no one is really able to kid themselves for too long, and things pretty much end quickly and relatively painlessly. *Anyway*, all this is my way of saying that it had been a long time since I had spent a lot of time, day in and day out, with one man. It had been a long time since there was anyone with whom I wanted to spend a lot of time and who wanted to spend a lot of time with me. Someone I wanted to wake up with, have sex with, talk with, eat with, have more sex with, etc. It was sad that it felt so unusual. It made me realize how, when you're single, you really do get used to a lack of that kind of intimacy in your life. *Anyway*, what I am trying to say is that the week was unbroken happiness for me.

During that time, Thomas made nine phone calls, six about business, and three to his wife. He would always leave the room when he was talking to her, so I didn't know if she asked him when he was coming home or how he might have answered her. While he spoke with her, I would sit on the bed feeling a bit ashamed and deeply uncomfortable. I couldn't help wondering what kind of marriage they had. He was in every way a supremely intelligent man, one who did not suffer bullshit and valued honesty. But when it came to his marriage, was it real? If your spouse can go off with someone else on a whim, how can you think you really have a marriage? Or was I just minimizing his marriage in order not to feel like a dirty slut?

Eventually, I couldn't help myself—I asked him if his wife was wondering when he was coming home. He told me that they had an agreement—they could disappear for two weeks in a row, but no longer, no questions asked. Then, it was time to come home.

It was an interesting little arrangement, and now at least I knew when our time was up. I no longer had to wonder when our little honeymoon was going to be over. Two weeks, then "Selamat tinggal," as they say in Balinese.

On one of these days, while Thomas was making his calls, I was on the phone with my mother, just letting her know that I was safe and healthy. As I was getting off the phone with her, I heard my cell phone beep with another call coming in. I took it. The voice on the other end was distinct, superior, cold. It was Candace, my publisher, calling me from New York. A tiny jolt shot through me. I sat up a little straighter.

"Hello, Julie, this is Candace. I was just checking in to see how the work was going."

"Oh. Hi. Hello, Candace. Um. The work is going great. Really. I'm learning so much, it's amazing."

"Well, that's nice to hear. I was worried that you hadn't just taken off with some Italian and was spending all our money vacationing in *Capistrano*," she said with a perfect Italian accent.

"No, no, of course not. I'm working very hard. Very hard." At that moment I looked around and Thomas was in just a towel, heading to the little wading pool just outside our bedroom. I began to perspire a bit.

"Well, good. I realize the decision was made somewhat impetuously by me, but we did give you a check, and you did sign a contract, so I just want to make clear that we expect you to honor that."

"Of course," I said. Thomas then plunged into the pool, making a huge splashing sound. I put the phone close to my chest to try to muffle the sound. "I am happy to honor that. I'm gathering so much information, it's going to be an amazing book."

I made a few more assurances to her about how hard I was working, how many women I was talking to, and then I got off the phone with her as quickly as I could. I then tried to put the conversation out of my mind just as fast. I mean, I was on *vacation*, for God's sake.

So eventually, on our eighth day in Bali, we decided to venture outside our hotel and take walks. We strolled down Monkey Road and looked at some of the local art galleries. At one little café we sat and shared a plate of *ayam jeruk:* fresh chicken sautéed with garlic and coconut milk, the local specialty. As we sat staring into each other's eyes and smiling (I was glad to be far from home, so no one saw this moronic kind of behavior), a couple pulled up on a motorcycle. He was a young man, around twenty-five, and she was an older woman in her fifties. They put their helmets on the bike and sat down near us, talking and holding hands. Then she leaned over and kissed him. I stopped staring at Thomas and started staring at them.

Thomas watched me watch them, and smiled.

"Ah, the anthropologist has a new subject." I looked away from them. I had no idea how obvious I was.

"Well, it is interesting, no?"

Thomas looked at them. "Tell me, what do you see?"

I glanced at them quickly. The woman was attractive, but not young-looking. She was in the full bloom of her middle age, with a thick midsection, untoned arms, and gray hair swept up on her head with bobby pins. The boy was beautiful. His black hair was parted in the middle and came down a little past his ears, in a bob. He had a delicate face, but thick eyebrows and big brown eyes that gave him a sense of intensity. He had a skinny body, but even so, it seemed muscular, taut.

"A man taking advantage of a woman," I said.

"Ah. So you see a desperate woman being tricked by a young man."

"Maybe."

"That's very interesting. I see a woman taking advantage of a man."

"Really?" I asked.

"Maybe. It might be that she is here to have a very good time, but she might be making the boy think that she loves him; that she's going to take care of him forever. Then she will go back home to London or Sydney or Detroit, satisfied, but he will be left here. Alone."

"Like the men usually do."

"Yes, like the men usually do."

I pondered this for a moment.

"Isn't it sad we assume it has to be one or the other?"

"What do you mean?"

"We both immediately assumed, because of the age difference, that one of them must be taking advantage of the other."

"Well, yes, of course, Julie. I mean, we're not idiots, are we?"

I laughed at that declaration, and Thomas put his hand over mine. He looked me right in the eyes, gleefully. "Your laugh! Your smile. It's all quite addictive, really."

I looked down at the table. I tried hard not to feel anything.

We walked to the center of Ubud, to the famous temple of Puri Saren Agung, to see a performance of a traditional dance called Legong. As we strolled past cafés and trinket shops, Thomas brought up the couple again.

"You know, Bali is quite famous for this type of situation. Women go here, in droves, for this."

"They do?"

Thomas nodded. "Not usually in Ubud, but in Kutu. That's where they all meet."

"Where's Kutu?"

"It's on the beach, near the airport. It's a very touristy town, with everyone trying to sell you things. That's where all the Balinese gigolos go to meet the women."

"That makes me sad."

"Why?"

"Because I wish the women didn't feel like they had to come here to get someone to have sex with them. It's so . . . desperate."

"Ah yes, and there is nothing more sad than a desperate woman, cor-rect?"

"Well, it's sad when anyone is feeling desperate . . . but yes, it does feel a little tragic."

Then we walked in silence. All I knew about Bali was that it was an island flourishing with the arts, and there was no word in the Balinese culture for "artist," because art was something done by all so there was no need for any delineation. And the people made this art—danced, painted, played music—all in honor of the Hindu gods and their temples. That's what I knew about Bali. Not that it was a place to bang Bali boys.

"Speaking of Kutu, I think we might need to leave here and go to Kutu tomorrow, if you don't mind. It's time I did a little business." He stopped on the road. "Even though this has been absolutely wonderful." As he put his hand on my cheek and kissed me, I got a little queasy; I wasn't used to all this pleasure. I told him I'd be happy to do whatever he needed. Then, suddenly insecure, I wondered if he was hoping to get away without me.

"I mean, unless you were thinking that you wanted to go alone. I mean, I don't want to assume . . ."

He put his arms around me and whispered in my ear, "Shut up, Julie, you are annoying me," and kissed me again.

We walked through a large courtyard and saw that the performance was already taking place. The audience was sitting in a horseshoe on the ground, and the performers were entering from one of the courtyard's gates. It was all women in colorful blue and gold saris with large gold headdresses, their eyes accented with thin eyeliner. The choreography was so precise that everything down to the hand gestures and the fan movements was performed in perfect unison. I noticed that the couple from the restaurant was there as well. I tried to see if she looked like she was in love with him. They weren't making any physical contact at the moment so I tried to glean clues about who might have the upper hand by watching how they looked at each other as they watched the perfor-mance. It was hard to tell. I looked back up at the dancers. As I listened to the live gamelan music that accompanied them, I noticed that even these dancers' eye movements were choreographed. Every look, to the left, to the right, up or down, was planned. I looked at Thomas. His eyes were sparkling with interest and wonder at all that was going on. I could tell it was all being absorbed into that brilliant brain of his, then getting swirled around with all the knowledge from his French education and mixing in with his overall perceptiveness and wisdom, so that eventually he would say something about this experience that would be utterly fascinating to me. Thinking about leaving Ubud, and then Bali soon, I realized that soon this whole affair would be over. He would go home to more love, more sex, more intimacy, and more companionship. I would go to my next adventure alone. It was clear who had the upper hand in this relationship.

After the dance ceremony, as we walked out of the gate that led us out to the road, I saw the couple again, kissing on the street a few feet away.

When they finally broke apart, the woman smiled at me and said in a thick Australian accent, "Didn't we see you two at the café today?"

Of course she was Australian. She got smart and actually did move somewhere where the men would fuck you when you're fifty.

I said we were indeed at the café that day, and introductions were made. Her name was Sarah and her companion was Made (pronounced MAH-day). She told us that she'd been living in Bali for six months and was thinking about moving there permanently.

"Are you two on your honeymoon?" she asked us.

"No, this is just a vacation for us," Thomas said.

"Oh, it's just you two look so much in love. I couldn't help but notice when we were at the café." I wondered if that's a main pastime among couples—looking at other couples, trying to find out how happy they are.

"Well, thank you," Thomas said. "We are." He looked at me, his blue eyes now full of mischief.

"Won't you two have dinner with us now? It would be so nice to talk to Westerners and hear what's going on in the rest of the world. They do have CNN here, but I still feel isolated sometimes."

I really didn't want to spend our last night in Ubud with another couple, but I didn't know how to say no. Thomas at least tried.

"I think tonight is not very good for us. We're leaving for Kutu tomorrow . . ." Thomas said, relying on his usual charm.

"Please, I'm desperate for some Western companionship," Sarah said, interrupting. "Let's have an early dinner so you can have the rest of the night to yourselves. Let's go to the Lotus Café. It's beautiful there." We didn't seem to be able to refuse. "We'd love to," I said.

As we all walked down the road, Thomas and I were a few feet ahead of them. I let the silence settle between us, before I turned to him and said, "In love, huh?" And he said, "Yes. In love."

We arrived at the Lotus Café, and were seated at what seemed to be the best seats in the house, right by a pond lit up by tiny lights that showed off the ancient trees that framed it; small gargoyles lining the pond spouted water from their mouths. Towering over us from the far side of the pond was a dazzling temple, the Pura Taman Kemuda Saraswati. It was so exotic, very *Lara Croft: Tomb Raider,* but still austere. It was impossible not to be humbled by it. Thomas ordered a bottle of wine for us and we began to get acquainted. We sat down, Sarah next to me, Made next to Thomas. We were all seated perfectly to be able to look across at our beloveds.

"How long have you two been here?" Sarah asked.

"It's been a week," I said.

"How marvelous. Did you get to see the cremation ceremony two days ago? That was a spectacular sight."

Thomas and I both smiled and shook our heads.

"Did you go to the Monkey Forest? I love monkeys. I find them to be so amusing."

I shook my head, embarrassed. "No, we really didn't get to that."

"What about that trek up to Mount Batur? No?"

We both shook our heads again. Thomas leveled with her. "We didn't really leave our hotel. It's quite a romantic spot."

"Ah." She smiled knowingly. "I understand completely." She looked at Made lovingly. "Bali is an exceptional place to fall in love." Thomas took my hand from across the table and said, "It is."

"There's something about the scenery, obviously, but also just the Balinese culture, their dedication to art and beauty and worship. It is very . . . sweeping." Sarah brushed a strand of hair away from Made's eyes. "It's impossible not to be taken in by it all."

Made finally spoke. "Yes, that's Bali. It is an island dedicated to all kinds of love. Love of God, love of dance, of music, of family, and . . . romantic love."

Sarah reached her hand across the table. He held it in both his hands and kissed it sweetly. What's the crime in that?

Nothing, except it was still, for me, hard to ignore the fact that she was old enough to be his mother. Now to be fair, I feel the same way when I see a much older man with a younger woman. One time I saw Billy Joel on the street with his young wife and I thought, *He should be paying her college tuition, not having sex with her.*

But who was I to be judging Billy Joel? Or Sarah and Made. If they're all happy, so be it.

By our second bottle of wine, we had covered a myriad of subjects. Made talked about the Balinese lifestyle, of families living in a compound; the parents, children, the children's wives and families, all living in individual houses connected by a central courtyard. Made also explained a bit about Hinduism, about death and their belief that life is a cycle of life, death, and reincarnation until your soul has reached the pinnacle of enlightenment, of Samadhi.

Sarah was now reaching the pinnacle of her inebriation, and was beginning to lean on Made, putting her head every now and then on his shoulder like a teenager. A pair of Brits sitting at the next table couldn't stop looking at the two of them. Sarah was less reserved about her feelings on the situation. She talked a little too loudly.

"I know what they're thinking. They're thinking that because of my age, Made is just using me. But he doesn't ask for anything. Not a thing."

I nodded at her reassuringly.

Sarah took a sip of wine. "We met on the beach at Kutu. He came up to me and said I was the most beautiful woman he's ever seen. Of course I knew that was rubbish, but it was still very sweet."

Sarah must have picked up something from my expression, even though I was trying desperately to look supportive.

"It's not what you think. He sat down in the sand with me and we just talked and talked. For hours. It was lovely."

"That sounds so romantic," I said, encouragingly. Sarah was now getting more insistent and a little loud. She started tapping her finger on the table to make her point.

"He's never asked me for a thing. I mean it. I bought him his motorcycle because I wanted to. I gave money to his family because I love Made and I wanted to help. They're very poor. He lives with me and I pay for things for us, because I can, because it's my pleasure. But he never asked me. Never! He works at a boutique just down the road. Every day. He has an amazing work ethic." She stared drunkenly and directly at the British couple and repeated it loudly. "An amazing work ethic." The couple looked at her and then toward each other. The man waved down a waiter and asked for their check.

"It's getting late. Maybe we should get going," I said as I shifted in my chair uncomfortably.

Sarah just scowled a little and curled her arms around Made. "He loves me better than any man I've ever known. And I just get so sick of it sometimes. All the looks."

Made kissed her on the forehead. "Some people. They don't understand what we share. It's okay, my love."

"Yeah, well, all those people are assholes," she said, now loud enough for the whole restaurant to hear. "Assholes." Then she looked at me.

"Besides, Julie, show me one relationship that is truly equal—show me one couple that are both feeling exactly the same things for each other at exactly the same time. You show me that, Julie. Show me *now*!"

The whole restaurant was now looking at us. I didn't really want to answer.

"Exactly. It doesn't exist," Sarah said, banging her fist on the table. "*It doesn't exist*. So what if I give him and his family money? So what? He loves me. That's all anyone needs to know. *He loves me*."

The bill came and Thomas paid it faster than I've ever seen anyone pay a check, and we made a quick exit.

As we walked down the road, I felt a little shaky. I walked faster. I couldn't get away from them quickly enough. To me, she truly was a desperate woman. Desperate for the world to see them as a true couple. And desperate not to allow herself to see that the man who has loved her better than any man she has ever known is doing it as a part-time job. *In my opinion*.

This past week had been a miracle; I had been so happy that I prayed to the gods, Hindu and otherwise, for it to never end. When I thought about going back to my life of concrete sidewalks and appointments and lunches and unemployment, of dates and parties, it took everything in me not to start shrieking. If Thomas had asked me to stay there with him for the rest of my life, never live near my family or friends again, just stay there and build a life with him in Bali, I would have said *yes yes yes* in a heartbeat. It's like he had opened up this little trap door in my heart, one that was covered all those years by a bookcase and rugs, and he unleashed more need in me than I ever thought I possessed. All I wanted to do at that moment was fling myself at his feet and beg him to never ever leave me.

Instead, I just kept walking. Fast.

We went back to our little villa and immediately collapsed into our lush canopied bed. We wrapped our arms around each other and started kissing, our bodies pressed tightly against each other.

Back in the States

It's never a good thing when both people in the relationship are depressed. It's extremely helpful always to have one person capable of comforting and bucking up the other at any given moment. Serena and Ruby weren't in what you might consider a classic intimate relationship, but Serena was sleeping on Ruby's sofa, and both of them were having a hard time getting out of bed. This particular morning, Serena woke up and for a moment had completely forgotten her quick stint as a swami—until she sleepily ran her fingers through her long blond hair and realized that it wasn't there anymore. Then, she started to cry.

Ruby was in the other room having a nightmare about the last pit bull that she'd hugged before he was taken away. His big brown eyes looked so . . . unsuspecting. She woke up, sobbing into her pillow. If someone had slipped into Ruby's apartment they would have been able to hear them both in a muffled fugue of sorrow.

Finally, Ruby stopped crying, realizing she was awake. As she lay collecting her thoughts, she heard Serena's quiet sobs from the living room. She was confused as to what to do. All she knew about Serena was that she had decided to shave her head and join a yogi convent after getting her stomach pumped for alcohol and chicken wings. She wasn't sure exactly how well she wanted to get to know Serena. But Serena was crying in Ruby's home.

So Ruby got up out of bed. She was wearing flannel pajamas with pictures of tiny dogs on them. She put on her fuzzy white slippers and walked out of her bedroom and down the hall. Vanilla was in the hallway, rubbing up against Ruby's leg. Serena heard Ruby walking toward her and quickly clammed up. There's nothing worse than a stranger seeing you cry. If there's one single reason to live without roommates it's that you can cry in private. Serena pretended she was asleep, hoping Ruby would go away. But Ruby stood by the pullout bed. She waited a moment, then whispered.

"Serena, are you okay?"

Serena moved around a bit. "Oh, yeah," she said, fake-groggily. "I'm fine."

"If you need anything, let me know, okay?"

"Okay. Sure." Ruby then padded down the hallway and got back into her bed. As she pulled the comforter over her head, she thought, *This is what my home has become. Sad Girl Land.* Then Ruby started daydreaming. Which is something she did a lot. In fact, during her darkest times, it's the thing that always managed to keep her going. Daydreaming of a better life. On this particular day, for some reason, she began to daydream about what her morning would be like if she had a small child in her home. She wouldn't have time to stay in her fluffy bed with her downy pillows. She would have gotten up already to fix breakfast and make up the lunch box and get her child dressed and ready for school. Instead of that idea exhausting her, it made her smile. Ruby realized she couldn't wait for the day when she didn't have the time to think about herself. It was then that she realized this really was such a day. Serena may not have been seven, but she was in need. She was depressed and crying, and if Ruby remembered correctly, Serena was meeting with her old boss in about an hour. This morning, Ruby could be of help. She threw off her comforter, jumped out of bed, and padded back down the hall. Serena was no longer crying, but she was in a fetal position, her arms cradling her head, covering her eyes, breathing softly.

"Serena. Can I get you anything? Some tea or coffee? Maybe an egg or something?"

Serena just shook her head into her arms. Ruby stood there, not knowing exactly what should happen next. She thought about what mothers do in this type of situation. They wouldn't take no for an answer. That's what they would do. They would go make something even after the person had refused all help or comfort. So Ruby turned back around and went into the kitchen. She poured some water into her teakettle, turned a burner on, and set the kettle down. She then opened up her cabinet and perused. She assumed Serena was a tea drinker, being the yogi she was. Ruby remembered that she had bought a box of green tea once, in her one attempt to start drinking it for its amazing antioxidant attributes, even though no one had ever successfully explained to her what an antioxidant was. She reached deep into the shelf and pulled out the green tea and, when the kettle whistled, made Serena a cup. Ruby opened a little container of Fage (a thick, tasty Greek yogurt) and got a spoon. She walked back to Serena, deciding to push the intimacy a bit by sitting right on the bed. She touched Serena's arm.

"Would you like a cup of green tea? It's right here."

No answer. Ruby's instincts were kicking in and she knew to just wait. After a moment, Serena slowly pushed herself up and leaned against the back of the sofa bed. Ruby thought that, with her shaved little head and her puffy eyes, Serena looked an awful lot like a baby ostrich.

"Thanks, Ruby. I appreciate it," Serena said weakly. She took the green tea and sipped it. Hallelujah. Ruby felt her heart swell with maternal pride. "Do you want to talk about it?" asked Ruby.

Serena looked down into her tea and didn't speak. "I just had no idea how nice it felt to be in love." The corner of Serena's lips started turning down and tears formed in her eyes. "It made me so stupid."

Ruby took Serena's hand and just softly said, "I'm so sorry, sweetie."

Serena continued. "And then it wasn't even real. It was all a fake. So how could I have even been in love if it was all a lie? Was I so desperate to be in love that I just made it all up?"

Ruby truly didn't know what to say. But she tried to be helpful. "Maybe this was just a rehearsal. Maybe you needed this one to open you up to be in love with someone who's worthy."

Serena glanced at the container in Ruby's hand.

"What is that?"

"It's Greek yogurt with honey. Really thick and yummy. Want to try?"

Serena nodded subtly. Ruby dipped the spoon into the yogurt and held it out for Serena to take. But instead, Serena leaned in and opened her mouth, as if holding the spoon would take more energy than she had. Ruby placed the spoon in Serena's mouth. Serena smiled. "That's good."

"Don't you have a meeting soon?" Ruby asked gently.

Serena nodded slowly. She took a deep breath. "I guess I should get up."

But before Serena swung her legs out of the bed to get up, she looked at Ruby.

"Thank you, Ruby."

Ruby smiled. She was good at this.

After Serena left, Ruby started thinking that maybe there was a way around this whole single-motherhood issue. She realized that maybe she didn't have to do it alone. There were many ways to get a father into this situation. As she walked down the street to her office, which was conveniently just blocks away, she started thinking about who could possibly knock her up. It came to her instantly. Her friends Dennis and Gary. They were her friends with the most stable relationship she knew of. They had been together three years and lived in a beautiful loft on Eighteenth Street in Chelsea. Ruby lived on the Upper West Side—but she would be happy to move to Chelsea so they could share parenting duties. She thought she remembered them talking about having children one day. She couldn't believe she didn't think of it before. They were the two most nurturing people she'd ever met. Often, one person in a couple is the really sweet one, and the other is more the "bad cop" kind. But with Dennis and Gary, they are both so caring that when you go to their house you feel like you've entered a magical bed and breakfast where everything is soft and cozy and your every need is taken care of. Ruby met Gary when he lived next door to her five years ago, and they've been close ever since. When Dennis came along, he and Ruby liked each other immediately. They got together fairly often, one big happy family. Ruby started playing it out in her mind. She would have primary custody of the baby, but they could be around as much as they wanted. And best of all, she wouldn't have just one dad for her kid, she'd have two. She would have the freedom to go out and still have a life, because Dennis and Gary would be there to take the child. Maybe they could even find apartments in the same building.

Ruby wondered exactly how this would all happen. Whose actual sperm would it be? Gary or Dennis? They're both deeply good-looking, both ridiculously fit. Dennis is a little more stocky than Gary. But Gary has terrible eyesight. But Dennis is starting to lose his hair. But Gary was her friend first; maybe it would be better if it was Dennis's child, so he wouldn't feel left out. She had read somewhere that sometimes male couples mix the sperm together and play a semen version of Russian roulette. Ruby could see it all. The child in a BabyBjörn carrier, dressed all in pink. Or blue. Ruby carrying the blue or pink baby around, as it gurgled and babbled. The blue or pink baby walking around the apartment, she and Dennis and Gary clapping and laughing. And then maybe she'd meet someone. And that someone would think she's so cool with her crazy, modern clan and he'd fit right in. Maybe he'd have kids of his own and they'd be this kooky progressive mixed family. She loved the idea so much she couldn't wait another moment. She pulled out her cell phone and made a date to see Dennis and Gary for lunch.

On the day of the lunch, Ruby had decided to dress "maternally." She wore a loose-fitting peasant blouse, loose pants, and a cute pair of flats. The way the blouse fit, she almost looked pregnant already and that was exactly the plan: Let Dennis and Gary see what it would be like if she was already carrying their child. How soft and womanly and maternal she could be. Unfortunately, she wasn't sure how soft anyone would seem amid the clamor of hipsters eating salads and burgers, yelling over the throbbing music.

They told her to meet them at Cafeteria, which, upon arrival, Ruby realized was a misstep. Cafeteria is possibly the noisiest restaurant in New York City. With the combination of the loud techno music and the din of the diners it was like trying to have lunch in the middle of a rave.

Ruby was nervous; she had never had this kind of conversation before. She had never even asked a guy out; she didn't believe in it and never had to resort to it. Now, she wasn't just going to propose marriage, but rather something that you could never take back. It would be a decision that would bond them together for the rest of their lives. More than that, she was about to have the nerve to ask these uber-caregivers if they thought she was good enough to be the mother of their child.

They arrived. Gary was wearing a suede jacket, impeccable, perfect, and Dennis was in a black cashmere turtleneck with a down vest over it. Very Lands' End adorable. They sat down, obviously pleased to see her.

"It's so great to see you, Ruby," Dennis said, grabbing Ruby's hand and giving it a squeeze. Ruby relaxed immediately. These men were going to think she was a good mother. They knew her good qualities better than anyone else. That she's patient, gentle, calm. So what if they had also been witnesses to a few bouts of her bone-crushing disappointment? No one is perfect. She suddenly remembered Gary once coming over and taking her for a drive in her pajamas. She had been despondent over one guy or another. He told her to get in his car "or else," and they drove all the way up to Bear Mountain and back. Ruby, in her pajamas and parka, was so touched that it shook her out of her depression and she was able to move on. Now she regretted that Gary had ever seen that side of her. He might use that touching moment against her. She silently cursed herself for not always being perfectly cheerful around her close friend. What if he thought she was too mentally unstable to be the mother of his or Dennis's baby?

She decided to just blurt it out. "I want you to inseminate me."

Ruby put her hands on the table to steady herself.

Gary turned to Dennis and said, "I told you so."

Ruby looked at them. "What?"

Gary simply shrugged. "I just had a hunch."

Ruby began her pitch. "You know how responsible I am. I never miss a deadline, no matter how depressed I am or upset I am. Not that I would be depressed or anything, because the reason why I was depressed before was because of guys, you know, giving them so much power over my life. But when I'm a mother, I could never be that depressed about some guy or anything because I would be having a higher calling. I would be a mother."

Dennis and Gary looked at each other. They looked back at Ruby, each with a different expression of uncomfortable pity in his eyes. Dennis leaned over and touched Ruby's arm.

"I'm sorry. We just gave our semen to Veronica and Lea."

Ruby sat there for a moment, taking in this new information. Then she thought, *Who the hell are Veronica and Lea?* She had never even heard of Veronica and Lea.

"Who are Veronica and Lea?" Ruby asked, a little too much outrage in her voice.

Gary answered. "They're our friends that we met doing volunteer work at the soup kitchen near our house. A lesbian couple. They're really nice."

"New friends? You gave new friends your semen over me?" Ruby said, softly but with a trembling in her voice.

"We didn't know you wanted it!"

"But you could have asked! Before you gave your semen over to strangers you should have thought for just a minute of which one of your good friends might want your semen first!" Ruby's voice was raised just a bit, but in the cacophony of talking and techno, no one even noticed. "You should have been more considerate!"

This time, Dennis spoke. "Honey, the last time we talked to you, your cat had just died and you hadn't gotten out of bed in three days."

"We came over and washed your hair for you, remember?" Dennis added.

Ruby cringed. She knew it. While they were being nice and nurturing, they had been making little mental notes on her fitness for motherhood. She felt betrayed. She made up her own new rule about how to be single: *Never let anyone see you at your worst. Because someday you might want that person's sperm or to date their brother, so you can't ever let them see you crazy or sad or ugly.* That's what she would tell me to put in my damn book the minute she had the chance. She immediately calmed down.

"I was depressed. But a lot has happened since then. I went and helped kill dogs at the shelter uptown to toughen up and now I'm ready to have a child."

Gary and Dennis looked at her, confused. Dennis went in first.

"You helped kill dogs at that awful shelter up in Harlem?"

"Yes. Okay. That's not the point." Then Ruby, being a businesswoman, decided to start negotiating. "The point is, I don't think there's anything wrong with your lesbian offspring having a half sibling in New York City somewhere. We'll arrange playdates. It'll be fun!"

"Ruby, I don't think—"

The waiter came over to take their orders. He didn't get the chance.

Ruby raised her voice even louder. "It's because I'm single, is that it? You'd rather give your semen to a couple even if they're lesbians, than one single straight woman. I get it now. Single discrimination. Fine." The waiter quietly excused himself from the table.

Ruby started to get up, but Gary grabbed her arm and sat her back down. "Honey, we're so sorry, we are."

Ruby leaned back in her chair. "I'm sorry. I didn't mean to overreact. I'm just disappointed."

"We know, sweetie," Dennis said, softly. "After we see how this goes, maybe we'd consider having another."

"Never mind. I understand." But Ruby wasn't really sure if she understood. She didn't know if the real reason they didn't ask her first was that it didn't cross their minds, or because they thought she would be a terrible mother. She didn't know if they really would consider her in a year or two, if things went well with the first child. She didn't know anything, except that she wanted to retain whatever dignity she might have left.

"I should have asked sooner," she said, trying to smile. Then the waiter came over and took their orders.

By the time she got back to her office, she had decided that this time she wasn't going to give in to her disappointment. Theirs was not the only semen in the sea. There were lots of possible fathers out there for her to choose from. And as she was walking into the elevator, she had another brilliant prospect: her gay friend Craig. A former theatrical lighting designer, he'd made a career change a few years before and now drove around selling rare and gourmet mushrooms to the high-end restaurants in the city. He was single and made a decent living, but his sperm couldn't possibly be as sought-after as the highly cultivated and high-income sperm of Dennis and Gary. She decided to give him a call. But this time she laid it all right out there from the beginning.

"Hi, Craig, this is Ruby. Can we get together and talk about you possibly being the father of my child? How about we meet at Monsoon, at, say, eight tonight? Give me a call."

When Craig called back, Ruby let it go to voice mail. He agreed to meet her.

At 8:15 Ruby walked into Monsoon, a low-key Vietnamese chain restaurant with great food and unpretentious décor. This time she had decided to have him sitting there waiting for her—it put her in the power position. She sauntered in, wearing an extremely expensive top from Catherine Malandrino and high heels. Not knowing what his reaction would be to this big question, Ruby decided she should at least try to look wealthy. Even though she desperately wanted something from him, she was going to make sure she had something, too. She sat down. Before she had a chance even to say hello, Craig blurted it out.

"I'm HIV positive, Ruby. I never told you."

Ruby's stomach flipped. She hadn't even entertained this as a possibility, mainly because she assumed he would have told her if he was. So she just assumed he wasn't. She realized now that that was naïve of her. She was also flummoxed as to what the appropriate reaction was. Being HIV positive today means something so different than it used to. Does she say she's sorry? Does she ask how he is? How his T cells are? What kind of cocktail he's on?

"I'm sorry to hear that. Are you . . . ?"

"I'm fine, I've been on drugs for years, no side effects. I'm going to live to be a hundred."

"I'm so glad," Ruby said, relieved. "Do you want to talk about it?"

"No, I'm okay, I just thought you should know, now, because of . . . everything."

Ruby nodded. They both got quiet. She thought about this news for a few minutes. Then she came back to thinking about how badly she wanted this child. She had known Craig since college—longer than she'd known Gary. He was an incredibly sweet person, and loyal and kind and consistent. He would be a great father.

"You know, I heard you can do a wash now," Ruby said.

"What?"

"You know, an HIV wash. On your sperm. Before you inseminate someone. They can clean your sperm of the HIV before you inject it in them and everyone is fine."

Craig fidgeted in his chair. "Really?"

"Yeah. I read about it in the *Times* science section, a year ago I think. I think you might have to go to Italy or somewhere to do it, but it can be done." Ruby didn't want to seem too pushy, but at the same time, she was determined.

"Oh." Craig paused, sipping nervously at his tea.

"I know you might be worried about how it could affect me and my health, but I could do research . . ."

Craig put down his tea. "I know about the wash."

Ruby brightened up. "Oh, you do? So, does it seem doable? Is it something you might be interested in—"

Craig interrupted. "Ruby, I don't want to hurt your feelings and I didn't think you'd suggest the wash . . ."

Ruby looked at Craig, confused. "I don't understand."

"My friend Leslie already asked if she could do the wash. She's forty-one and she—"

Ruby pushed her chair out and slammed her hands on the table. She began to speak without thinking.

"No no no no, I don't want to hear it. I thought I was being generous by being willing to do the wash. I had no idea you were *fielding offers* from women who were willing to do it."

"I was surprised, too. But Leslie liked that I went to Brown and was tall," Craig said sheepishly.

"Who is this Leslie person anyway?" Ruby's hands were flapping in the air, gesturing at no one in particular.

"She's my Pilates instructor."

Ruby pushed her chair back into the table and leaned over to Craig. "Your *Pilates instructor?*"

Craig looked at her helplessly. "Ruby, if you had asked me first I would have been happy to . . ."

Just then, the waitress came over. "Do you know what you'd like to order?"

Ruby stood, her coat still on. "Yes. I would like a little, healthy baby girl or boy, ten fingers and toes, with one responsible, kind, coparenting partner on the side. I mean really, is that so much to ask?"

The waitress gave Ruby the death stare, which signified "I'm not going to acknowledge you until you say something not crazy."

Ruby took a breath. "No, thank you. I'm not hungry." She then turned to Craig. "I'm so glad you're okay, and I'm so happy that you're going to be a father one day. But I think I'm just going to go home now if that's okay with you?" Craig nodded as Ruby quickly stood up. She leaned down and gave Craig a big kiss on the cheek, turned, and walked out the door.

Back in Bali

Our hotel in Kutu was another obscenely luxurious villa, this one with its own little backyard and private swimming pool overlooking the ocean. I know. Insane. Thomas had gone to a business meeting an hour ago. The bad news was, I missed him terribly. This was the first time we had been apart in over a week and it was horrible. I'd become completely emotionally dependent on him. I was never a possessive girlfriend, even in my teens and twenties, but if I could have sewn a pocket into my skin and tucked Thomas inside me, I would have. I didn't want him to ever leave my side.

It took all my energy to fight the urge to stay in that hotel room and refuse to leave it for the rest of my born days. But Thomas had told me Kutu was a big surfer beach, so I decided to go watch the surfers; finally I might not look so out of place in my surfing trunks. But I was also curious if I was going to see some gigolos waiting to tell some lady that she was the most beautiful woman they had ever seen. And I wondered if the beach would be full of older women waiting for their day to be Made.

The beach was dotted with surfers, all waiting for the next wave. The beach wasn't crowded yet, and as far as I could tell, there were no gigolos or women waiting to be gigoloed.

As I sat in one of the chairs provided by the hotel, a young Balinese man came up to me with a big plastic bag.

"Excuse me, miss, would you like one? Very cheap."

He pulled from his bag something that looked like a Rolex watch—

I'm going to go out on a limb and say I don't think it was real. I shook my head.

"But look, they are so nice, very cheap. Buy one."

Being a New Yorker, I know how to get my point across. I shook my head forcefully, and said loudly, "No thank you." He got the message, picked up his bag, and walked away.

The surfers had found a wave and I watched them doing their best to ride it. They made it look so easy, most of them keeping their balance until the wave deposited them gently on the shore.

My thoughts quickly drifted back to Thomas and the fact that he was going to be going home in less than a week. Back to Paris, to his wife. It started to dawn on me that in only a few days, I might never see him again.

I began to think again about what a great deal this had been for him. A nice little vacation he must be having from the monotony of marriage. And he could go home guilt free, because he had been completely honest with me about his open marriage, and his wife didn't seem to mind. He had a perfect arrangement. I was starting to get pissed off.

Just then, an older Balinese woman came up to me and asked if I wanted my hair braided. I said no, forcefully, with one very big shake of my head. She moved on.

It also began to dawn on me that I might not be the only woman Thomas had done this with. I know, sometimes I'm a little slow. I realized that this might be where he takes all his lady friends. In fact, he might've known he was going to Bali and made sure he had a girlfriend lined up for the trip. Who knows? All I knew for certain was that I had bought it all, every last romantic bit of it, like a tourist snapping up a fake Rolex.

A man came by with an armload of t-shirts. But before he could speak, I barked "No!" and he scurried away.

I then had the thought that no woman in my situation should ever allow herself to have. I started to imagine Thomas telling me that he wanted to leave his wife for me. I imagined him with tears in his eyes, begging me to be with him, he loved me too much, he couldn't bear living without me.

I shook my head, trying to dislodge this dangerous thought as quickly as possible. It was going to be terrible saying good-bye. I wondered if there was a way to just guilt him into staying with me. If there was a way I could seem as pathetic and vulnerable as possible and just cry and plead with him to stay. I've seen it work on the soaps.

A young Balinese man came up and sat down on the chair right next to me.

"Excuse me, miss, but you are the most beautiful woman I have ever seen on this beach. I had to come over and tell you that."

And at that, I said, very loudly, *"Okay, that's fucking it."* I stood up from my chair, grabbed my towel, hat, and beach bag. He jumped at my little outburst, but I have no idea what he did next, because I walked away from him quickly without ever looking back.

I can tell you that at that moment, I had never felt so completely, literally, utterly, whatever, insulted in my life. He actually mistook me for a woman who was desperate and lonely enough to believe his line of bullshit.

As I walked back to our little villa of lies, it occurred to me that maybe this Balinese boy had read my mind. Maybe he sensed that I was a woman at that moment scheming on how to make myself so pitiable that a man might be guilted into staying with me.

Maybe that kid knew *exactly* whom he was talking to.

As I stomped down the stone path, I realized that it had to stop. I desperately loved Thomas, I wanted desperately to have someone in my life, and in New York I had been desperately lonely. But as I got close to the door of the villa, I also decided that this was fantastic. This was going to be my saving grace. I was a desperate woman. Good. Now that I knew this about myself I could be on guard for it. It wasn't going to ambush me suddenly and force me to do something embarrassing. Not me. Because the truth is, there's absolutely nothing wrong with feeling desperate—*it's just that under no circumstances are you ever allowed to act it.*

I started throwing all my things into my suitcase: my clothes, my toiletries, everything. As I was running around the room grabbing up my things, Thomas walked in with a big smile on his face.

"Julie, I've missed you—" He saw my suitcase on the bed and looked immediately distressed.

"But, what are you doing?" he said, panicked.

"You're going home soon anyway, back to your wife and your life. It's better I leave now, before things get . . ."

I stopped. It was very important for me not to cry. "I just want to leave, now."

Thomas sat on the bed. He put his head down, thinking. I kept running around the room, looking to see if I had missed anything. When Thomas finally looked up, he had tears in his eyes. My first thought, because I'm from New York and fucked up, was that he was faking it.

"I spent this entire meeting thinking of you, Julie. I couldn't keep you out of my mind. I missed you so much."

I stayed firm. It was easy for him to have all these romantic notions, with his nice, big Paris safety net. I spoke to him a little coldly.

"You've been through this before, I imagine, so you understand. This was going to end in a few days anyway, so it's just ending a little sooner. That's all." I zipped up my suitcase. This time I had a plan. "I'm going to go to China. It's really interesting, I read that there are so many more men there than women, due to the policies involving—"

Thomas stood up, grabbed me and kissed me.

"Yes, Julie, I admit it, I've been through this before. But this feels so very different. Please, please, let me go with you wherever you are going next, please. China, Zimbabwe, wherever. I can't leave you, I can't. Say you'll let me stay with you, please. I beg of you." He pulled me close to him, his hand around my head, clutching at my hair, desperately.

Back in the States

I'm going to try to be brief with this because it's upsetting, but I'm not sure if I'll be able to because I need you to have all the details. The details are important.

Ever since the Sam incident, Georgia had actually been feeling pretty good about things. There's nothing like deciding not to see a perfectly good man to make a girl feel a little up on herself. She had been going on some dates with a few men she met online, none of them really for her, but not disasters, either. Dale had been taking the kids as often as Georgia asked, and she also had a long list of reliable babysitters. She might not have been paying as much attention to her kids as she should have, but she was feeling optimistic. So there had been some improvement.

She met Bryan at a parent-teacher conference at school. They were both waiting out in the hall, on those tiny chairs, and they struck up a conversation. His son was six and in the same class as Georgia's daughter. He was of average height, with a thin face and bright cheeks—he looked Scottish. He had been divorced for three years. They got on the subject of their respective marriages and breakups, bonding over the toll it takes on everyone involved. By the time Bryan was called in to speak to the teacher, he had asked Georgia if he could call her. Which he did. That night. Two days later, they went out. They had dinner and he walked her to her building and they kissed and kissed in front of her house and he said he had had a great time and asked if he could see her again. He called her the next day, to tell her what a nice time he had had and to make plans. They made a date for two nights later. This time she went to his house (his son was with his mother) and he cooked her a delicious pot roast and they ate and talked and he was very sweet and they made out on his bed, very tenderly—but not without passion. He called her the next day and asked her when he could see her again. She told him she was free Tuesday or Thursday and he said, "Well, Thursday feels too far from now, so how about Tuesday?" Well, how about that. Let me say it to you again, because Georgia repeated it to me, over and over again, long distance, in the ensuing Many Long Days of Bryan. He had said "When can I see you again?" And Georgia had said "Tuesday or Thursday" and he had said "Well, *Thursday feels too far from now, so how about Tuesday?*" Got it? Okay. This kind of insanely consistent, straightforward, I-am-incredibly-excited-to-have-met-you-but-not-so-much-that-it's-unbelievable behavior went on for the next week and a half. They spoke on the phone nearly every day, and all things pointed to one thing only: "game on." This was something real with a consistent, affectionate man who had not, in anything he said or did or mumbled or joked about, revealed himself to be anything other than a man who was ready and excited to enter into a relationship with Georgia. No red flags, no vague or direct warnings, no "I just need to let you know" conversations. Again, Georgia had the feeling you have when things are finally clicking. Suddenly, it's easy. Suddenly, you didn't know what the fuss was all about. She became a little smug, and thought to herself yet again, *I knew it wouldn't be that hard to find a great man.*

And then they slept together.

It was a Saturday night, and Georgia had to get home to her sitter. There had been enough affection and tenderness to cushion her post-coital exit, so she didn't feel like a complete slut when she had to leave. She went home, paid the sitter, and went to bed, happy and secure. She had done everything right. They had laid the groundwork of friendship and established a rhythm of dates and calls that obviously suited them both. So when she woke up Sunday, as her eyes popped open, her first thought was Bryan. She remembered the sex. She still actually *felt* the sex. And a big, easy smile came across her face.

It would be safe to say that Georgia had been fairly impatient with her two children ever since Dale left. For some women, having their children during a time like that would give them a sense of comfort—of still belonging to something. But for Georgia, the day-to-day tedium of raising her children only served to underscore whatever misery and loneliness she was experiencing at that moment. So when Beth screamed for Georgia to hail a cab because she didn't feel like walking the half a block back to the apartment, well, maybe Georgia hadn't exhibited the same kind of patience she did when she had had a husband.

But this Sunday she woke up smiling, with nothing but patience and adoration for her two young children. She got them up, got them dressed, made them breakfast, and took them for a walk along Riverside Drive. Beth was on her bike, Gareth was on his scooter. She barely looked at her phone because there was no need to. She was dating a nice man whom she had just slept with for the first time, and she would be talking to him sometime today as she usually did.

So when Georgia saw that it was four o'clock in the afternoon, she didn't even flinch. He was probably busy with his son. "He probably doesn't want to call when he can't really talk," Georgia said to herself. She took her kids for an early dinner at their favorite Chinese restaurant and went home.

But by eight o'clock, when Beth came out of her room and asked for her third glass of water, Georgia snapped. "What did I tell you, Beth?! No more water. Go back into your room." Beth started to whine. "I SAID GO BACK INTO YOUR ROOM!"

Bryan hadn't called. Georgia turned on the television. She started having the tiny stirrings, the first whisper of a feeling, but it was there: panic. And when panic starts to creep in, even on tiptoe, a woman's mind goes on overdrive. At least Georgia's mind did. It may have seemed that she was watching television but in reality she was summoning all the creative powers she could muster to keep that rumbling of panic at bay. Sometimes after an intense sexual experience a man might need to take a step back, just as a cooldown, to compose himself emotionally. Maybe he was really busy. Maybe something happened to his son. Maybe he's not feeling well. There are so many reasons why he might not have called.

I'm not going to be one of those women who go crazy just because a guy didn't call, Georgia thought to herself. *It's not a big deal. He'll call tomorrow.* "I SAID GO BACK TO YOUR ROOM," Georgia screamed at Gareth when he appeared in the hallway. Georgia tried to put it out of her mind, but the dread wouldn't really leave her. Wisely, she went to bed. Tomorrow was another day. And tomorrow he would call.

When Georgia's alarm clock rang at six thirty the next morning, the first feeling that hit her was excitement. *Yay! Bryan is going to call me today!* She wondered how long she would have to wait. Georgia tried to put it out of her mind. She got up and looked at what she could make the kids for breakfast. She sighed. It all felt like drudgery. She took out eggs and bread and got to work. The kids woke up and first Beth didn't want eggs and then she didn't want the oatmeal that Georgia made, and then she wouldn't eat the toast because Gareth touched it for a second. Which is when Georgia told Beth that there are many children that don't get a choice of what to eat for breakfast and she better eat what's on her goddamn plate or she'll go to school hungry. Which is when Beth threw a piece of toast at Georgia and stomped angrily into her room.

After that it was an all-out brawl to get them to school. Screaming, tears, names were called. And that was just from Georgia. *Ha ha.* At school she looked around for Bryan, but he wasn't there. She walked back home, exhausted, and checked the clock. It was nine. Nine o'clock. *What is he doing right now?* Georgia wondered. *What is he doing right now that is more important than calling me?* She decided to get productive. It was time for her to look for a job. Ever since the divorce, she had been putting that off, wanting to punish Dale with her financial needs. But now it was time to move on. She knew that that is what a smart, empowered woman would do.

It was then that she had the most comforting, peaceful thought she had ever had in her entire life.

She could call him.

Oh my God! She could call him! She loved it. Now, she knew that it was always better to not call the guy, but this was different. This was killing her. This was not empowering—waiting by the phone for some guy to call. This was not in any way what she called women's lib. She was going to call him. But Georgia did know enough to get a second opinion. Unfortunately, she ended up getting a second opinion from Ruby because she couldn't get me on the phone (I was with Thomas in Bali, I'm sorry!) and Alice didn't pick up when Georgia called. If Georgia had spoken with either Alice or me, we would have said, "Don't call, don't call, don't call."

In my book there are many reasons why you shouldn't call, but the main one is that it's the only way to find out what his intentions really are. You need to know how long he can go without talking to you, unencumbered by your meddlesome phone calls, emails, or texts. If you call, you are contaminating the evidence. But we weren't available and Georgia called Ruby, and Ruby is all heart, all emotion, and you could basically get her to say anything you wanted her to.

Georgia quickly explained the situation to Ruby, then asked, "So, there's nothing wrong with calling him, right? I mean, there's no rule saying that I can't call him, is there?"

Ruby shook her head as she clicked on the NYU Medical Center website. She was searching the Net for information about artificial insemination. "I don't think there's a rule, per se, but I have a feeling there's a strong suggestion out there not to call."

"I know. But I can't get any work done. It's driving me crazy! I just need to know what's going on!"

Ruby didn't know Georgia well, but she could tell when someone was becoming mildly hysterical. Then Georgia pulled out the real trump card, the defense for calling, which only highly experienced daters can argue against.

"But maybe something happened to him," Georgia pointed out. "What if something has happened to him and I'm sitting here with my pride instead of treating him like any other friend who I was expecting to hear from and didn't? I would be worried and I would call him."

It seemed like a completely logical argument. (Why-oh-why didn't Alice and I pick up our phones?)

"You're right. If he was just a friend of yours, which he is, you would call him and find out what's up."

"Exactly!" Georgia said happily. "I have the right to treat him just as I would any friend."

She hung up on Ruby and started dialing Bryan's phone as quickly as she could get her fingers to move.

Like someone who has just taken a shot of migraine medicine, Georgia was ecstatic that her pain was going to be alleviated momentarily. As she dialed, she felt proactive. Strong. There's nothing worse than feeling powerless over your own life. Or helpless over some guy.

Now if she had spoken to me or Alice, we would have both said something like "He's not your friend. Sex changes everything. That's the sad truth of it. *Assume he's fine.* Assume his life is exactly the same as it was the last time you saw him. And if you find out later that his son was bitten by a rare South American bee and Bryan had spent the past few days sleeping in the highly-contagious-disease section of Mount Sinai Hospital, well, send him a nice email and apologize." But we were not there for Georgia. So instead, she gleefully dialed.

She left a message. She knew there was a very good possibility she'd get his voice mail, and she was ready.

"Hey, Bryan, this is Georgia. Just calling to say hi! Hope you're well." And then Georgia hung up, almost proudly. *Well. That took care of that.* She let out a triumphant sigh. The worry, the dread, the panic, whatever you want to call it, had been lifted. She knew immediately she had done the right thing and she felt like a superwoman.

For exactly forty-seven seconds.

Then an awful realization hit her and gave her a feeling of doom unlike anything she had experienced. It dawned on her that she was now just waiting for him to call *again*. All she had done was give herself the briefest pause from the agony of waiting for him to call her. And now she was back to waiting—*but it was far, far worse. Because now she had actually called him.* Now if he didn't call, he would not be simply taking his time calling her after having slept with her, he would be actually *not returning her call.* She had doubled the misery.

So now, to speed things up a bit: The rest of the day went by. Bryan didn't call. And Georgia literally had to take to her bed. The kids were picked up by a sitter who stayed and made dinner for them. Georgia was still lying in bed at nine o'clock, when the church bells rang, the doves sang, the clouds parted, and the angels played their harps.

Because he called. He called, he called, he called. Georgia doesn't know when, in all her born days, she had felt such deliverance. They chatted. And laughed. The knot in her stomach went away. Oh my God, she didn't know what she was so worried about. Women can get so crazy sometimes! They talked for about twenty-five minutes (of course Georgia was keeping track) before Georgia started to wrap up the conversation. Right when they were about to hang up, finally, Bryan started to make plans.

"So. We should get together soon."

"Yeah. That would be great," Georgia said, two days of stress and worry releasing from her body.

"I'll call you this week and we'll make plans," Bryan said.

"Oh-h-h. Okay," Georgia stammered, confused. She hung up the phone and her first thought was, *What the fuck? Why did he have to call her to make a plan when they were already on the phone now?*

Now she began the next phase of the disassembling of a dream. She became obsessed with figuring out what she had done wrong. What had she done that made him go from "No, Thursday is too far away" to "I'll call you this week and we'll make plans"?

So Georgia waited again. Tuesday, Wednesday, Thursday. She tried to put it out of her mind. She got herself a couple of job interviews. She met up with Alice and they did some shopping. She tried to yell at her kids less. The shameless devil on her shoulder was telling her that if she wanted to see Bryan so badly, she should call him. That there's nothing wrong with a woman asking a man out; it's the twenty-first century, for goodness sake. But on Friday, just as she was about to pick up the phone, a stay of execution was granted. And he called and asked her out for

Tuesday night. Tuesday night? Well, okay. He must have known that you shouldn't ask a woman out for the weekend on a Friday night; that's not polite. And she guessed she could ask Dale to take the kids.

So they went out on Tuesday night. Georgia remembered why she liked him so much. Every once in a while the nagging thought would enter her head, What would have happened if I had never called him last Monday? Would he have ever called me? But she put it out of her mind as quickly as it came in. They went back to his house. They had sex. And Georgia got another shot of the love/sex drug that would make her obsess about him for the next four days, during which all he did was text her once to say, "Hey, let's get together soon!" But this time she did not call him. She was resolute. More than needing to see him, to have sex, and to be validated, much more than all of that she needed to know how long he could go without seeing her. Now, that required strength, stamina, and emotional fortitude on a level that had never been asked of her before, not even in childbirth. And the only way she was able to muster this Herculean restraint was to call and torture Ruby and Alice. (And me, when she could get me on the phone.) The conversations went something like this:

Georgia to Ruby: "But I just don't understand. If he didn't want to go out with me, why wouldn't he just stop asking me out? But if he does like me, why doesn't he like me as much as he did in the beginning?" Ruby would have no good answer, because really, how do you answer that?

Georgia to Alice: "Maybe he's never going to call me again. I mean, he said he was going to call me but he didn't say when. Is it so hard to make a plan for the future? Even a tentative one? What does that mean when you don't want to make a next date while you're still on your current one? Is he that busy? Does it feel like too much pressure?" And Alice, a girl after my own heart, just kept saying, *Don't call him, don't call him, don't call him.*

I guess it would be fair to say that Georgia, whose sanity was really not that fully present to begin with, had now officially completely lost it.

There are some people who have catastrophic results when alcohol and their blood mix together. One could say the same thing for Georgia when it came to mixing her disposition with longing. Some people can suffer through it; some people can overcome it and move on. Georgia was felled by it. Like an aborigine with a bottle of Wild Turkey, Georgia spiraled out of control. She took to her bed again. She would get the kids to school, come back, put on her pajamas, and go back to bed. It seemed like the best way to have the time go by as quickly as possible until he called. If he called. And, in Georgia's defense, she was always able to get back up and pick the kids up from school, bring them home, and make them a snack. And then she would take to the sofa. It was as if someone had squeezed all the air out of Georgia, and now she was the carcass of a balloon, broken and lifeless, lying on the sofa, popped. Okay, maybe it wasn't just Bryan. Maybe it was the culmination of the trauma of divorce, of missing Dale more than she wanted to admit, of becoming a single mother, of having jumped in too quickly to the brutal world of dating. Or maybe it really was that she was desperate for Bryan to call. Who knows. The love drug she had ingested turned out to be toxic and she was slowly being poisoned to death.

Finally, he called. At nine o'clock. Wednesday night. Bryan told her that he was at a little coffee shop across the street from her. Were the kids with her or could she come out?

The kids were indeed with her. So that's what she should have said. But she wasn't in her right mind. She needed to see him in person and find out what happened. What did she do wrong? She needed to know so she wouldn't make the same mistake again. She didn't want to confront him; she just wanted the quiet, possibly brutal truth. So she said that the kids were with her, but her sister was there, so she could run out for a few minutes.

I know! But you have to understand; Beth never, *never* under any circumstances ever gets up in the middle of the night. She could drive you to your wits' end before she goes to bed, but once she is asleep, a bulldozer ripping through her bedroom wall wouldn't wake her. And as for Gareth, it was the same. Also, he was old enough that if for some reason he did wake up, he could read the note that she would leave him, reading "Back in FIVE minutes! Don't be scared!" She knew that what she was doing was dicey. But she was desperate to get this over with. So she wrote the note and ran out of the apartment, down the stairs, and across the street to the coffee shop. Bryan was sitting by the large window, and when he saw her walking across the street, he started waving with a big smile on his face.

Georgia sat down and tried to be casual. She knew it was all about not seeming like a hysterical woman. She must not cry. She must not have Trembly Voice. Can't have Trembly Voice when talking to a man about Things. You must have Casual Lighthearted Voice.

"Can I get you a coffee, or is it too late?" Bryan asked, politely. Georgia just shook her head, too busy trying to slow her breathing and quiet the pounding in her chest to speak. "I'm sorry to call you at the last minute. I was just grabbing a cup of coffee and thought I'd take a shot you were free."

Georgia finally spoke. "I'm so glad you called. I've been meaning to ask you something." So far, so good. No trembly voice. "I was just wondering, it's not a big deal, but it did cross my mind, that you don't seem that"—Georgia added a casual shrug and wave of her hand—"excited about me anymore. And that's okay, but I was just wondering if I had done something wrong. Because it seemed like you were excited about me, and now you're kind of . . . not." Bryan caught this gentle lob of emotional vulnerability with utter grace and chivalry.

"Oh, Georgia, I'm so sorry you feel that way. Of course you didn't do anything wrong. Of course not. I think you're fantastic. I didn't know it felt like that. I'm so sorry. I just got busy with school and . . . it's only been a few weeks, right? So I guess I thought we were just taking it slow . . . ?" Georgia looked at him. It made perfect sense. It had only been a few weeks. He was really busy with school. He thought they were just taking things slow. For a moment, she felt like a jerk. Why did she get so worked up over this? He didn't do anything wrong. He was just being *responsible. Levelheaded. Grown-up.* But then she remembered something. She remembered "Tuesday Thursday." This was that guy. When she met him he wasn't Taking It Slow Guy. He was Tuesday Thursday Guy. And once a girl knows what it feels like to be dating Tuesday Thursday Guy, no matter how much she wants to pretend she believes that he's busy or taking it slow, she can never forget that that same man thought that Wednesday, cruel, relentless Wednesday, and Thursday, that nasty, interminable Thursday, were far too long to go without seeing her.

She tried to imagine now what she had been hoping he was going to

say in this moment. "I'm so sorry, Georgia, you're right, thank you for reminding me that I'm in love with you. From now on I will see you twice a
week and call you every evening to wish you a good night." Or, "Well,
now that you mention it, Georgia, what happened is that because of my
recent divorce, I equate sex with commitment, and from the minute I
penetrated you I knew I needed to keep you at arm's length because ultimately I'm never going to be able to love you and deep down I knew that
already." Whatever closure she was trying to find, Georgia realized it
wasn't going to be discovered at the Adonis Coffee Shop. And her two
children were upstairs without adult supervision.

"You're right. Of course. We're taking it slow. Absolutely. It never
hurts to just check in, right?" Bryan nodded agreeably. She looked at her
watch. She had been there exactly four minutes.

"You know, I should get back. I have a feeling my sister wants to get
home."

"Sure, okay, that sounds fine," Bryan said. "I'll give you a call soon."

"Definitely," Georgia said. Very casually.

She walked away from the coffee shop with a nice, relaxed stride because she knew Bryan would be watching her. But the minute she was
inside her building she bounded up the four flights of stairs and into her
apartment. No fire. No dead bodies. She walked quickly to her children's
rooms. Beth was sound asleep. She breathed a huge sigh of relief and
walked down the short hall and peeked into Gareth's room.

That's when time seemed to stop.

Gareth wasn't there. She raced to her room and was relieved to see
him sitting on her bed, frightened but perfectly fine. It was what he said
next that truly terrified Georgia.

"I called Daddy."

Georgia took a deep breath, in a gasp. "What? Why did you do that?"

"I was frightened. You weren't here. I didn't know where you were."

"But didn't you see my note? I left it on the pillow next to you! I said I
was going to be right back."

He shook his head, his little-boy fear turning into large droplets of
tears practically jumping off his face.

"I didn't see it!" he wailed. "I didn't see it!"

Georgia grabbed him and held him tightly. She rocked him and kissed his head and tried to do whatever she could think of to make up to him for the last four minutes. She stayed there for what was probably ten minutes, possibly less, when she heard Dale burst in. Georgia put Gareth down and tried to head him off at the pass, running into the living room so he could see that she was home and everything was okay.

"I'm here, I'm here!" Georgia whispered emphathically. "Everything is fine."

But Dale was not going to be placated so easily.

"Where the fuck were you? Are you out of your mind?"

Georgia took a few steps back. This was bad. Very bad.

"Seriously, Georgia, where the fuck were you?"

Georgia was dumbstruck; his fury and her blatant guilt left her with no words to use in her defense. "I . . . I . . . It was an emergency."

"An emergency? What kind of emergency could make you leave your kids alone? *That's* the fucking emergency."

It was then that Georgia started to cry. She didn't want to, she couldn't help it, but she did.

"I'm . . . sorry . . . it was just . . ."

"Was it some guy?" Dale walked toward her, menacingly. "Did you leave the house for some fucking guy?"

Georgia heard the way it sounded, heard her insanity in Dale's accusation. And she just cried harder.

"I'm sorry. Please. It won't happen again."

"Damn right it won't happen again. I'm taking the kids, Georgia."

Georgia immediately stopped crying, as if instinctively she knew that her full faculties were needed for this attack.

"What?"

"I'm hiring a lawyer. I want full custody. This is bullshit."

Georgia let out a scream, but it also came out as "WHAT?"

"You heard me. It's over. The dropping them off with me whenever you have a hot date. The yelling at them all the time. The teachers say they look dirty, they're acting out at school. You obviously would rather be single and go out and get laid, so now's your chance."

Georgia stammered. "You can't do that . . . you can't."

Dale started to leave, but he turned back to point right at her. "You should be happy. You'll get to go out every fucking night of the week if you want to. Don't try to fight it, Georgia, send me a thank-you card in-stead." And with that he walked out of the house. If he had looked to his left before he did, he would have seen Beth and Gareth standing in the doorway, having heard everything.

Georgia sat down at the kitchen table and started to let out a sob. She realized she had just endangered her children and now her own mother-hood because of her desperation—the desperation that she had no idea how deeply she felt until it was too late.

RULE

8

There's Really So Few People Who Have It All So Try Not to Bother with That Whole Envy Thing

On the plane from Singapore to Beijing, it felt as if Thomas and I were on the lam. Every moment we spent together now felt almost criminal; it was an act of rebellion against the agreement he and his wife had for their marriage. They were allowed to leave each other and their marriage for up to two weeks at a time. Now, he wanted more. It was like choosing to escape from a Club Med.

When he called his wife from our hotel room in Bali to tell her that he was going to be away a while longer, I had left the room. The whole thing really wasn't pretty. No matter how I tried to rationalize it, I was participating in something that was probably causing someone else anguish. I wasn't sure of this, because, as I said, I had left the room. When I returned, I couldn't help but ask him how it went.

Thomas, looking very serious, just said, "She wasn't happy."

I didn't ask anything else.

So, now, going to Beijing, it all felt a little illicit, a tiny bit dirty, and somewhat dangerous. So of course some panic was to be expected. Right before we got on the plane I had taken a full Lexomil. But still, as we got up into the air, I began to feel a tightening in my chest. I'm not sure if Thomas was trying to distract me from a panic attack or if he was just trying to distract himself from his domestic concerns—but he decided to play the part of my research assistant on this trip. He had heard about my phone call from Candace, so I think he was also slightly concerned I wasn't getting enough work done. He began filling me in on what he had learned.

"This is a very interesting thing, I think, to find out about this woman drought. I think we must get to the bottom of this." He glanced over at me, slightly worried. "The Lexomil should start working soon."

There was a group of fifteen people, all together, chatting excitedly a few rows ahead of us. There seemed to be four couples and seven women traveling alone, all Americans. They were swapping photos and sharing stories. There were two others who appeared to be their guides. As I tried to slow down my breath and take my mind off my oncoming terror, I eavesdropped on their conversations.

I looked over at Thomas and whispered, "They're going to China to adopt children." I nodded my head toward the group. Thomas looked up at them. I stared at the women who appeared to be without partners. They seemed so excited, as if they had won the lottery and were going to pick up their winnings.

"It's amazing, isn't it? They're choosing to be single mothers. I think it's very brave," I said as my body started to relax.

Thomas looked at the women, and then back at me. "Do you want to have children, Julie?"

I tensed up again. "Well. I don't know. I think if I met the right person I would. I don't know if I could ever do it alone."

The truth is, ever since I met Thomas I had been thinking about children. It was such a cliché, but it was true. I had met someone I loved and suddenly I was imagining having his children. I was embarrassed at how quickly I became so predictable. Of course, it was not a fantasy that ever got very far, since I quickly reminded myself that my beloved was already married. But it had engendered such startling new images in me: Thomas with me at the birth, us lying together in bed with a baby, or clapping at the child's first step. The idea of a man and a woman falling in love and raising a child together did right now seem like kind of a genius idea.

Thomas nodded. "You would make a very good mother." He put his hand on my cheek. He kept it there a long time, and just gazed at me. I wanted to ask him if he wanted children. What his plans were for the future, for a family. He would make a fantastic father. But I reminded myself that none of those plans would include me. So I broke away and closed my eyes. I started feeling a little sleepy.

Thomas decided to get some investigating done before everyone started sleeping or watching movies. There was a woman who I guessed was in her thirties who was sitting across the aisle from us. She appeared to be Chinese and did not have a wedding band on. Thomas leaned over to her and smiled.

"Excuse me, do you speak English?"

The woman looked up from the book she was reading.

"Forgive me for asking such a question, but my friend here has been traveling the world talking to women about what it's like to be single in their culture. She's going to Beijing now to talk to Chinese women. I was wondering if you might have any knowledge of this subject."

The woman glanced over at me. I tried to put on the most trustworthy face I could, no matter how groggy I was. She was quite pretty, and looked sweet; possibly a little shy. I wondered if she would be offended at this brazen question.

"I do, yes. I'm single and I live in Beijing."

Thomas turned to me, as if to give me a little nudge.

"Hi, my name is Julie." I leaned over Thomas and extended my hand to her. She shook it.

"My name is Tammy. Nice to meet you. What is it that you would like to know?"

"Well, there have been reports in the news, that because of the one-child policy of the eighties, and all the girls that have been adopted, that there is now a woman drought in China, and the men are having a hard time dating."

Tammy laughed and shook her head. "Maybe in the countryside, yes, but not in the cities, not at all."

"Really?" Thomas asked.

"Really. The men have it so good in Beijing. They can date as much as they want, and when they do settle down, they often have mistresses. The rich ones at least."

Even with my Lexomil, I started to get depressed. "Seriously?"

Tammy just nodded her head, amused. "Yes, unfortunately. Your theory is not correct at all."

I leaned back on my chair. This was not what I had wanted to hear. I whispered to Thomas.

"So we're going all the way to China to find out that the men here have a hard time committing and like to cheat?"

Thomas laughed. "This is not good news—for us, or for the Chinese women."

I leaned over Thomas again to talk to Tammy. This would be my last attempt at conversation before I passed out. "So what do you do about this?"

Tammy shrugged. "I never date Chinese men. I think they're awful."

"Never?"

"I haven't had a Chinese boyfriend since I was a teenager. I only date foreigners. Australian, German, American. But never Chinese. Never."

Thomas was interested as well. "So tell me, where do you meet these men?"

"I work for an American company, so my last boyfriend I met at the office. But there's also a bar I like to go to, Brown's, where there are a lot of expats."

"Brown's?" Thomas repeated. "Like the color?"

She nodded. "Yes, it's in the Chaoyang District. It's a lot of fun."

Thomas looked at me. "So, to Brown's tonight? Yes?"

"Yes," I mumbled, and then fell asleep.

When we got out of the cab at our hotel in Beijing, it was quite a scene. We were staying at one of the nicer places in the center of the city. In front of us, some very fancy woman had gotten out of her big black car and twenty to thirty photographers snapped away as she walked into the lobby. We walked inside, right behind her, where there were another dozen important-looking people waiting to greet her officially. Then they whisked her away into an elevator, for what I assumed would be some kind of press conference. When we finally were allowed to walk up to the reception desk, I asked who the woman was.

"The vice president of Spain."

This, it seems, was the perfect introduction to Beijing. Things were happening here, from the high-rises being built everywhere you turned your head, to the influx of businesses trying to get a piece of this growing global power, to the vice president of Spain stopping by for a visit. This was the new China. And Thomas and I had a very important job to do. I had to go to a bar tonight and talk to women about dating.

It was a little sad. Our first night in Beijing and we were having beers at an English pub and eating buffalo chicken wings. There was a DJ who was playing "Get Right with Me" by Jennifer Lopez and the place was packed with foreigners of all shapes and sizes. I heard German, British English, Australian English, American English. There were some Italians in the bunch and a couple of French people. And yes, some Chinese as well. The crowd seemed to be mainly in their thirties, and everyone was having a good time dancing, talking, and flirting.

Thomas was still taking his job as assistant cultural observer seriously, and soon enough he was talking to some German men at the bar. I let him go it alone, thinking he might be able to get more information out of them than I could.

A young woman, around twenty-five, came up to me and handed me her business card. Her name was Wei and her card said she was a "tourist consultant."

"Hello, my name is Wei. Where are you from?"

"New York," I said loudly, trying to be heard over the music.

"I love New York," Wei said, laughing. "I love New York so much!" She laughed even louder. She had long black hair that went straight down her back and she was wearing a short black skirt and tall black suede boots. She couldn't have been cuter.

"Do you know that show *Sex and the City*? I love it so much!" Again, with much laughter. "Me? I am Samantha. That's who I am!"

I raised my eyebrows, understanding exactly what that meant, but not knowing exactly how to respond. "Oh, wow. That's great. So you must be having fun being single."

She laughed again. "Yes. I love being single. I love it. I am so happy not to have to be married and having babies. I love my freedom!" She laughed again and pointed to her card that I was now holding.

"If you need any help while you're in Beijing, anything, you let me know. I work for a travel agent. We help people with everything they need."

"Thank you, that's very nice of you." But not wanting her to leave just yet, I added, "So, are you here for business tonight, or just to meet a nice expat boy?"

Wei laughed again loudly. "Both! You are so smart!"

I laughed with her, trying to be polite, and asked, "So, are you not so interested in Chinese men?"

Now Wei stopped laughing. Her eyebrows furrowed and she pursed her lips.

"Chinese men are boring. All they care about is money. They don't know how to communicate. They don't know how to be romantic." Then she shook her head in disgust. "No, only Western men. They are much more fun."

Wei looked over and saw a tall blond man that she knew. She started waving and laughing. "Ben! Ben!" She turned to me. "What do you do in New York?"

"Well, I was a book publicist, but now I'm sort of . . ."

"Really? I am writing a book about my crazy life in Beijing. Just like New York!"

"Wow, that's great," I said enthusiastically.

"I must go, but I'll come back, okay?"

"Yes, of course."

Wei ran up to the guy named Ben and gave him a big laughing hug.

Just then, Thomas came back. "Julie, I have been working very hard for you. We have much to discuss." He pulled up two available bar stools and we sat.

"I spoke to two German men who said they were here to meet Chinese women."

I smiled, enjoying his enthusiasm about this subject. "Really? What else?"

"They said that they like Chinese women more because they are more devoted than Western women. With their German women, they said, it's too much about power and negotiation. But with Chinese women, they let them be men, they don't try and change them."

My eyebrows rose again. Thomas shrugged. "I'm just telling you what they told me."

"Well, this really is perfect then. Western men are here to meet Chinese women, and Chinese women are here to meet Western men."

"Yes," Thomas said, narrowing his eyes. "I'm very upset I didn't think of this idea. There is a lot of money to be made in this."

Just then, Wei came back over.

"We are all going to Suzie Wong's next. It's much fun. You must come." She then burst out laughing.

They say that to understand the Chinese people, you have to understand their language. So at Suzie Wong's, as Thomas and I sipped our Long Island iced teas in a little side room that we shared with two Chinese businessmen, Jin and Dong, we were given a lesson in Mandarin.

Jin broke it down for us. First of all, there are four different tones in the Mandarin language. So for each word, it may have four different meanings depending on how you say it, sometimes more. For instance, the word *ma,* said in a straight, flat tone, means "mother." But said in a tone that sort of dips slightly and then comes back up, it means "troublesome." When you say *ma* with a deeper dip, almost as if you are disapproving of something, it means "horse." When you say it sharply, it means "to curse." Now add to this that you have two different ways of learning the language, either with pinyin, which is when it is spelled out in Roman letters, or in the original Chinese characters. All forty thousand of them. These two men told us that in school it takes most Chinese people—who, by the way, *speak Chinese*—four to six years to actually learn the language.

So. The next time you want to make fun of some Chinese person's inability to speak English, just keep in mind that that person, even if he or she is just a short-order cook at your local Chinese restaurant, can kick your ass at one of the hardest languages in the world. And think of this: when it takes that much discipline and determination simply to speak your own language, you could easily end up with a work ethic that just might help you take over the world. *I'm just saying.*

After two rounds of Long Island iced teas, I was able to move them from Mandarin to the language of love.

"So tell me, is it true because of China's recent history, that there aren't enough women for the men?"

The two men started laughing immediately. Jin said, "No, where did you hear that?"

I thought for a moment. "Um, I think the *New York Times*? And maybe *60 Minutes*?"

Dong shook his head. "Maybe in the country, but here? This is not true at all. This is a very good time to be a single man in Beijing. A very good time."

Jin nodded in agreement. "It's not difficult to find women to date. But frankly, I prefer Western women."

I perked up a bit at that. "Really? Why?"

"The Chinese women have become very materialistic. All they care about is how much money the man makes."

I turned and looked at Dong. "Do you agree?"

Dong nodded. "I had a girlfriend who when we broke up after two years, asked me to pay her seventy thousand yuan."

"For what?" I asked, confused.

Dong shrugged. "I don't know. For her time?"

"Were you the one that ended it?" Thomas interjected. "Was she angry?"

Dong hit his hand to the table, his voice raised. "This is what was so crazy. She broke up with me!" He shook his head at the memory of it. "Western women, they're better. More independent. Less materialistic."

In terms of dating and China, it seems the grass is always greener on the other side of the world.

After the full effects of our drinks took hold, Thomas and I made our way down to the dance floor. There were some Westerners here and there, but this was a place where trendy locals came to mingle.

Wei was on the dance floor with a few of her beautiful, chic friends. She saw me and waved us over.

"These are my friends, Yu and Miao. They want to talk to you about being single here in Beijing."

"Wow, great," I said loudly over the music. "What do you want to tell me?"

Yu's English wasn't that great, but she made her point. "We are so lucky, to be able to be free. To be independent. To travel, to work. I love it so much!"

Her other friend, Miao, agreed. "I can have sex with whoever I want. It's very exciting to me!"

Just then I saw Thomas take out his cell phone, which must have been vibrating in his pocket. He looked at the number and his expression became quite serious. He made a motion to me that he was going outside to take the call.

We all started dancing to Shakira's "Hips Don't Lie." I was jealous of these women, in a way. They were experiencing the joy of newfound independence. The world had opened up for them only a few years ago, and now they had options, from what shoes to buy to what kind of man to sleep with. I wish I could see singlehood in that way again, with that kind of excitement and delight. I looked at all these made-up, miniskirted, and writhing cuties and I was envious. They were young, they were single, and they were having the time of their lives.

After a few songs, Thomas was still nowhere to be seen. I excused myself and walked outside. Thomas was leaning against the wall of the neighboring building, still on the phone, talking intimately, emotionally. My stomach tied into a little knot. Again, my French was limited, but I knew that there was some kind of negotiation going on. There was arguing and explaining and cajoling.

I knew she was calling him right now and demanding that he come back home. And I knew that she knew he would ultimately listen to her—because he was hers. I was just borrowing him and everyone knew that.

"Okay. Je comprends. Oui." He hung up.

I decided to just be brave and say it first.

"You can leave tomorrow if you need to. I don't want to keep you . . ."

Thomas wrapped his arms around me. "But I don't want to leave you; this is the problem." He kissed me on the forehead. He gently said, "She is threatening to come here and drag me back home." I must have looked quite alarmed, because he added, "I've never done this before. She understands this is different."

I said quickly, "Well, then you have to go home. That's it." I felt myself get choked up but I swallowed hard and continued. "This has been very nice, but you're married. *You're married.*" I took a quick, deep breath to control myself. It worked. I looked up at him, calmly. "We knew it had to end. So. This is it. It's okay. It's been fantastic. It will be a beautiful memory." I then looked down at the sidewalk and took another deep breath. I was proud, I didn't fall apart. Thomas nodded.

Thomas wrapped his arms around me again. "So, in three days I must go back to France." It was now official. There was a bottom line.

"This agreement my wife and I had, it has worked very well up to now. Very well."

I buried my head into his chest.

"You are a very exciting woman, Julie. So funny, so filled with life. I had no idea this would happen."

He kissed me on my forehead. "But that is life, I guess. This is what happens when you keep yourself open." He tightened his grip around me. "I am very sorry for all this drama."

We stood there for what seemed like forever. He was going to go back to her. This would be just another story in their crazy life together. She would win. Of course she would win; she should win, she is his wife, his history, his promise to the world.

"I love you very much, Julie. I hope you know that."

It was merely a consolation prize, that admission, but it was nice to hear anyway. We went back to our hotel and lay on the bed together, our arms wrapped around each other until we went to sleep. It was too sad to do much else.

Back in the States

Serena had always, deep down—and maybe not so deep down—resented them all. Let me phrase that better. It wasn't resentment; that's too strong a word. It was a little touch of envy. It's the hazard of any job where one is being paid to take care of someone who is wealthy enough to hire someone to take care of them. At first Serena chalked it up to being in such proximity to wealth. And it wasn't ostentatious, wasteful, stomach-turning wealth. Theirs was something much, much more enviable. For the three years that Serena was the cook to a famous movie star, his lovely former-model wife, and their one young son, Serena got to see firsthand that money does indeed buy happiness. Don't let anyone tell you differently, because the equation is simple: Money buys you the freedom to do more of the things you want to do, and less of the things you don't want to do. Thus, you are spending more of your time happy, less of your time unhappy. Therefore, money buys happiness.

Then let's just talk about where money can let you live in New York while you are spending more of your time being happy. You can live in a five-thousand-square-foot loft on West Street off Franklin, in Tribeca. The entire back wall of your huge loft can have windows facing the Hudson, so when you walk into the apartment you feel as if you've just boarded an ocean liner.

Money also made everyone look good. The wife, Joanna, was gorgeous and fit, Robert was gorgeous and fit, and their son, Kip, was adorable mainly due to winning the genetic lottery, but he also wore perfect cute boy outfits that made him look even more adorable than his DNA already did.

Since Serena had gone back to work for them, she would sometimes look at Joanna jetting off to some board meeting for some charity, going to the gym, taking her son to the park, or just sitting next to Robert on the couch reading the paper with him, and Serena couldn't help but just be envious. Joanna's DNA made her beautiful, which allowed her to be a model, which allowed her to meet Robert, who of course fell in love with her, and which then gave her this extraordinarily blessed life.

And when Serena was able to stop noticing all the important, profound things she could be jealous of, she could then move on to the more superficial things. And for Serena, that meant literally their things. They had the most amazing kitchen: a Viking stove, a Sub-Zero refrigerator, an overhanging pot rack, an entire cabinet just for their accompanying lids. Serena was able to go out and buy every type of olive oil infusion you could imagine: rosemary-infused olive oil, basil-infused olive oil, roasted-garlic-infused olive oil. And then there was the forty-five-dollar bottle of balsamic vinaigrette. And the appliances. The gorgeous Kitchen-Aid mixer. The ice-cream maker. The panini-maker. It was Disneyland for cooks. Her favorite part of the kitchen was the long, narrow column of shelves that housed all the CDs in the house, as well as a CD player and an iPod and speakers. Because you must have music when you cook and dine. Money = happiness, see?

Now the truly wonderful part of this story is that this very fortunate, wealthy, happy family happened to love Serena. Because for all the people who could have worked for them, learned their habits and their little eccentricities, and have been around when their son was misbehaving and they didn't feel like being charming parents, Serena was the one you'd want to be there pretending to be invisible.

And she's a damn fine cook. They say the turnover for private cooks is two years, because every chef, no matter how hard they try, has a style of cooking that after two years people naturally get tired of. So when Serena quit her job with them and went to the yoga center, she had already outlived her shelf life by a year. That's because Serena could cook anything. And one of her favorite things was to find a new recipe and try it out for fun. And one of this family's favorite things to do was to eat the new recipes that Serena made. And she had no idea how much they appreciated her. When Serena told Joanna she was leaving, Joanna was gracious and wished her good luck and hoped she would be happy. Serena had no idea that after she walked out of their apartment, Robert laughed and said, "Well. I guess I won't be having another decent meal in this house ever again."

When Serena began working for them the second time, something was different. She realized that there were a lot of things she really liked about this family that she didn't even notice until they were missing. For one thing: Robert. He was actually an enormously likable, down-to-earth guy who might lumber around the kitchen in a spare moment and start joking with Serena.

"What are we having for dinner, See?" he'd ask. "See" was his nickname for her. Serena assumed it was less an endearment and more because he was a movie star, and don't all movie stars like to call people by nicknames?

"Chicken with a mustard sauce and broccoli rabe," Serena might say, which is when he would invariably make a face and say, "That's disgusting, I won't eat that, you're fired." Like clockwork. It's not very funny the first thirty times it's done, but by the thirty-fifth, well, it makes things kind of feel like home.

It's not that Robert was no longer there; he was. But he seemed different. More subdued. Joanna seemed a little distracted, and everything Serena did for them, from organizing the pantry to giving the pots and pans a good cleaning, was met with such an enormous amount of gratitude that it confused her. She knew something was going on, but she didn't ask, because as I mentioned before, the main job of a household employee is to go as unnoticed as possible.

But one day, while Serena was preparing broiled salmon and a big green salad for lunch, Joanna and Robert walked into the loft after being out at an appointment. Robert smiled and clapped his big hand on Serena's shoulder.

"How ya doing, Eagle?" he said. That became his new nickname for Serena the first day she walked into their home with her new head of no hair. Robert put his hand on Serena's scalp and told her she looked like an eagle. As in bald. But this time, he could barely get out a smile when he said it. He just walked away down to his bedroom. Joanna looked like she was about to cry, or explode, or collapse onto the floor. She smiled a tight smile and tried to remain professional. She cleared her throat and began to talk.

"I know this is a complete change in what you're used to, and I know this is absolutely not in your area of expertise, but I was wondering if from now on, if you would be interested in starting to cook a raw food diet for us."

Serena was startled. A raw food diet is incredibly complicated and time-consuming and she had no experience with it whatsoever.

"I know it's an extreme diet, but there'll be a doctor consulting with you on a daily basis, and we have all the cookbooks you'll need, and a list of things for you to shop for." Joanna took a deep breath. Her voice was trembling a bit. "Would you be willing to try? I know you can make that awful food taste delicious for us," she added, trying to make a joke.

Serena said of course, she would go shopping that very day and start tomorrow. There was no need to say anything more. In this loft with the views of the Hudson and the KitchenAid mixer and the CDs in the kitchen, Serena began to understand that the charming, handsome, down-to-earth man of the house was very sick. And no one in this house could possibly be happy. At all.

*   *   *

Ruby had run out of gay men to get her pregnant, but she still couldn't shake the whole baby thing. She knew she could adopt, but ever since she thought of having someone impregnate her, she couldn't help but want a baby of her own.

Which is how it came to be that Alice, only one week later, was coming over and sticking a needle in Ruby's ass.

Okay, maybe I need to explain. Ruby decided to look into artificial insemination with a donated sperm. She picked her donor father—Ivy League, Jewish, tall—and got the ball rolling. A blood test showed her hormone levels needed a little boost, but with the right drugs she could get pregnant on the first try. Of course, she could also end up with quintuplets, but Ruby wasn't going to worry about that. What she did worry about was that there was no way she could stick a needle in her own ass for two weeks. She tried it at the doctor's office and couldn't even stick a grapefruit. The thought of actually piercing her own flesh made her sick. No matter how much she wanted to get pregnant and hold a squealing baby of her very own, she would never be able to stick a needle in her own butt.

Her first thought was Serena, who was still living with Ruby until she found her own place. Serena had been looking in Park Slope, Brooklyn, for an apartment because she found out the hard way how high the rents in Manhattan had gotten. (Never give up your New York apartment, never give up your New York apartment, never give up your New York apartment.) It looked like she would find something soon and Ruby wasn't worried; on the few occasions that they were actually in the apartment at the same time, she enjoyed Serena's company.

Ruby walked into the living room, where Serena was sitting, reading. Ruby didn't know exactly how to broach the subject, so she just started talking.

"So. You know how I mentioned that I was thinking of maybe having a baby on my own?"

Serena put down her book and nodded. This didn't seem like it was going to be one of their casual roommate we-happen-to-be-in-the-kitchen-at-the-same-time conversations.

"Well," Ruby continued, "I've decided that I'm going to get the hormone shots first, to help my odds. And, I think it might be really hard to stick myself with a needle. You know?"

Serena nodded. She hoped this wasn't going where she thought it was going, but if it was, she thought it would be polite not to make Ruby have to spell it out for her.

"So do you want me to do it for you?"

Ruby breathed a sigh of relief. She loved Serena at that moment for not making her spell it out.

"Well. I know that that might possibly be the weirdest request known to mankind, but yes. How weird is that?"

"It's not weird, not at all," Serena lied. "I'd be happy to do it," Serena lied again.

"I know it's kind of a big thing to ask."

"Actually, I think if you asked me to carry your child, that would be a bigger deal."

"Well, that's true." Ruby took a beat. "We would start tomorrow. Is that okay?"

Serena was surprised. She had no idea they were talking about something that would happen *tomorrow.*

"Like, in the morning?"

"Yes. Before you go to work?"

"Okay. Fine."

"Great. Okay. Well, thanks."

And yes. It was the weirdest conversation Serena had ever had.

But in the morning it got even more awkward. There was Ruby in the bathroom leaning over the sink, her underwear slid down her butt, her butt cheek exposed, all white and vulnerable. She was imploring Serena to stick it in her ass, just do it, just do it! But Serena couldn't. She stared at Ruby's white flesh, and then at the needle in her hand, and she started to get dizzy. She looked at Ruby's reflection in the mirror.

"I can't do it," Serena said, slightly hysterical.

"You can't?" Ruby said, sweetly, but concerned.

"No. I thought I could. But I can't. I can't stick you with this. It's freaking me out."

Ruby was gentle. "That's okay, honey. If everyone was good at sticking people with needles we wouldn't have a nursing shortage, right?"

Serena felt awful. Here she was, a virtual stranger, living rent free in Ruby's apartment. The least Serena could do was stick a needle in her ass. But she couldn't do it. She was mortified. Ruby stood there with her ass literally hanging out, concerned. In order not to go off this very important schedule, she had to start the shots today.

"You really can't do it? Just today?"

Serena knew how important it was.

"Okay. I'll try. I will."

Serena took the needle, put her hand on Ruby's butt cheek, took a deep breath, and . . . still couldn't do it.

"Why don't I call Alice?"

Ruby perked up.

"Alice? That's a really good idea. I bet you she could do this without blinking an eye. Do you think she's going to think it's weird?"

"Maybe. But who cares. I'll call her and explain."

Ruby breathed a huge sigh of relief.

Two hours later, she breathed another as Alice injected the follicle-stimulating hormone drug known as Repronex into Ruby's ass.

Ruby didn't know how to ask, but she really needed Alice to give her the shot every day for the next two weeks. But there was Serena, who had no trouble speaking up because it wasn't her favor and it wasn't her ass and Alice wasn't actually her friend.

"So. We'll see you tomorrow, same time, same ass?" Serena said, her attempt at being casual.

Alice turned around and looked at them, surprised. "Oh. Do you . . ."

". . . and for the next twelve days after that?"

"You mean like every morning?"

Ruby nodded, mortified.

"Okay. Sure," was Alice's immediate reaction.

Ruby was actually oozing gratitude from every pore when she said, "Thank you, Alice. Thank you so much."

Alice flicked her hand, shooing away the moment, and said, "Please. It's nothing." And she walked out the door.

During the next week, Alice came over every morning and gave Ruby a shot.

It was then that Ruby was reminded that everything comes at a price.

Alice was now in full wedding planning mode. And like every bride that has come before her, it was all she could talk about. Every day, while she was shooting Ruby's ass full of hormones so Ruby could use a stranger's sperm to become a single mother, Alice would rattle off the latest developments on flower arrangements or what color linens she decided to use.

"Jim's mom is really into peonies, but *my* mom loves hydrangea, which you really can't have in a bouquet, because they're ginormous. So, I'm thinking of maybe hydrangea for the tables and then peonies for my bouquet."

"That sounds like a good compromise," Ruby said, bent over the bathroom sink. "I love both."

"I know, but the florist of course has his own whole idea on what it should be that does not include hydrangea or peonies." Alice stuck the needle into Ruby's ass. "I brought croissants today—do you want?"

So every day, Ruby would stand there in the bathroom with her pants down listening to all of Alice's wedding conundrums and stories and she was plain jealous. *Jealous.* Alice was Ruby's age, but she was going to get married and then get pregnant and then have children running around the playground. She was going to have a family with a mommy and a daddy. And Ruby wasn't. Alice was picking out a wedding dress. Ruby's breasts were starting to swell from the hormone injections. But Alice was doing her an enormous favor, so Ruby had to bend over and take it.

Alice started bringing over pastries and bagels for Serena and Ruby. They would sit and chat every morning before Ruby and Serena had to go to work. Alice, not being completely unfeeling, also asked them what was going on in their lives. Ruby noticed that Alice seemed to really enjoy her time with them, and soon her visits stretched from ten minutes to a half hour, to an hour. And even though Alice was annoying with her wedding talk, she was funny to listen to and, Ruby realized, good company.

Over the following weekend, Alice met Jim over at his sister Lisa and brother-in-law Michael's house for brunch. They all got started talking about the upcoming wedding, and Lisa and Michael started talking excitedly about their fond memories of their own honeymoon. Soon enough, Michael had carted out his Mac and started giving Alice and Jim a little slide show.

As they started digging into their scrambled eggs and bagels, Michael clicked on their first photo: the two of them at the beginning of the Inca Trail in Peru. They were beaming newlyweds, with Michael's arm around Lisa and her head bent in, almost leaning on Michael's shoulder. Lisa no longer needed to face the world straight on, with her head erect and her posture strong. She was in love and could smile and lean. They were up in the mountains, with the clouds seemingly only three feet above them.

"We were so far up, it was like we were walking on air," Lisa said, it all coming back to her.

"We were . . ." Michael said, putting his arm around Lisa and giving her a kiss on the lips. "Remember?" Lisa smiled and kissed him back. She then turned to Alice.

"I'm so glad you and Jim have found each other. Some people might think you guys are going too fast, but I just think when you know, you know, right?"

"Yes, it's totally true." Alice nodded, a knot tightening in her chest. Click.

"This is when we finally got to Machu Picchu. Isn't it amazing?" Michael said. He grabbed Lisa's hand and gave it a squeeze. Click.

"This is the temple of the sun. They say it was built for the astronomers of the village," Lisa said. She squeezed Michael's hand back. Click.

"This is what they call the Jail. They think they held prisoners there," Michael said, the photo showing the couple kissing, surrounded by tall rock walls. Click.

"This is the hotel at the base of Machu Picchu. It's not fancy but the view is unbelievable," Lisa gushed.

"We spent an extra day there and didn't even leave the room," Michael said, with his eyebrows raised. Lisa giggled and hit Michael in the arm.

"Michael, Alice and Jim don't need to hear that."

"Sorry, guys!" Michael laughed. "The trip was just so great. I hope you guys have just as much fun on your honeymoon, wherever you go."

Alice hoped so, too. Click.

"Michael, no!"

"What? Just a few."

"Please, we don't need to bore Alice," Jim said, laughing.

Michael couldn't resist, and decided to show Alice a few of their wedding photos. The one on the screen now was of them outside the church, kissing. Michael and Lisa fell silent, almost worshipful. Alice could have sworn that she heard them sigh in unison, in a reverie of unified bliss.

Then Lisa said the thing that took the knot in Alice's chest and twisted it into a stabbing pain. "It was the happiest day of my life."

Alice had come for brunch, but she ended up being treated to a pictorial study of love; the kind of love she always wished she would have, and the kind she knew she would never feel with Jim. Her wedding day would not be the happiest day of her life. She would never look at Jim the way Lisa looked at Michael. No matter how she rationalized it, no matter how she spun it, that was the truth. If she married Jim, she was never going to have that. She watched the photos click by of them dancing at the reception, of them cutting the wedding cake. She knew in her wedding photos she and Jim could look just as happy as they did. At their wedding, no one would suspect a thing. But she would know.

As Alice and Jim left the building and walked down the street, it was only now that she truly understood what it meant to settle. She wasn't just making the decision, "You know what, by golly, this is good enough." She was saying, *This is the level of happiness I'm willing to stop at. Forever.*

The next day, Alice brought over cheese Danish because she knew it was Ruby's favorite, to celebrate the last shot of the series. This time, however, after the injection, when they were sitting at the kitchen table, there were no swatches or magazine tear sheets or photos of flower arrangements to look at.

"I really hope you get pregnant, Ruby. I really do," Alice said, quietly, as she picked at her Danish.

"Thank you. I've gotten really excited at the idea," Ruby nodded shyly.

"It's really nice for you to have done this, Alice. I'm sorry I was such a wimp," Serena added.

"It's no problem. You asked, and I thought, Why not give it a shot?" Alice said, laughing. Ruby and Serena sort of laughed and groaned at the same time. "Besides, I think it's really brave what you're doing, Ruby. Really brave. You're going after something you really want. It's amazing."

Ruby was feeling such goodwill in the air that she felt sincerely inclined to say, "So, you haven't given us the daily update on your wedding plans!" Alice nodded.

After walking for many hours yesterday, Alice had come to a major decision. She couldn't ignore the fact that she was, in fact, settling. She also couldn't ignore the fact that her wedding day would not be the happiest day of her life. She knew that she was a strong, clever, stubborn woman—and could do whatever she set her mind to do. That night she went over to Jim's apartment. She talked it all out with him, and even though he was deeply disappointed, he knew it was what Alice wanted. And in the end, all he wanted was Alice's happiness.

"We've decided to elope," Alice said. She managed to then dodge everyone's reactions by taking a big wedge of Danish and shoving it in her face.

Ruby and Serena did indeed react—it was the last thing they were expecting Alice to say. "It just got to be too much." Ruby and Serena just nodded, pretending they understood what Alice meant.

"Every couple always threatens to do it. I think it's great that you are," Ruby contributed.

"I'm really psyched. We're going to go to Iceland next month and get married there. Just us," Alice said. Ruby and Serena sat there, at a slight loss for words.

Finally, Ruby just said, "Iceland?"

Alice nodded. "It's supposed to be really gorgeous there. And with all the darkness now, I think it's going to be really romantic."

Alice just kept chewing and not looking them in the eyes—now it was her ass hanging out there in the wind. She changed the subject quickly and they made plans to meet up soon for lunch. Then, she was gone.

As soon as the door closed, Ruby turned to Serena. "Does she look like someone who's madly in love and excited about getting married?"

Serena gave Ruby a look. "She's going to Iceland so she can get married *in the dark.* So no, no she doesn't."

Ruby, who had just spent the past two weeks seething with envy over Alice and all that she had, was now worried about her. Maybe Alice didn't have everything that Ruby wanted. But instead of that making Ruby feel good, it just made her sad. "Maybe it's time to call Julie."

Not to Put Pressure on You, But Start Thinking About the Whole Motherhood Thing

(You Really Don't Have Forever)

The next morning, I woke up to see Thomas walking into the room. For a moment a shudder went through me—I realized exactly how much I was going to miss him. There he was: his humor, his intellect, his good nature, all in one beautiful package. It was all going to be ending soon and I would be devastated. I tried to put those thoughts quickly out of my head.

"Where have you been?" I said, sleepily.

Thomas's blue eyes were bright with excitement. "I have been doing some investigating for you. There is a park we must go to today. It will be perfect for your research!"

After a typical Chinese breakfast consisting of a rice congee—a watery rice porridge that can have meat or fish thrown in it—we took a cab to Zhongshan Park. Thomas had practiced saying the name of the park during the entire breakfast, but in the end I had to show the cabdriver the paper that our concierge gave us, spelled out in the Mandarin characters. As I said, Mandarin isn't something to be taken lightly.

Thomas wouldn't tell me what this trip was all about, so my curiosity was piqued. As we got out of the cab and walked into the park, Thomas finally explained.

"I read about this online—parents come to this park to make matches for their unmarried children. Every Thursday and Saturday afternoon."

"Really? You mean it's sort of like horse trading but with people?"

Thomas shrugged and took my hand. "Let's find out."

In the park we saw a few dozen people standing around a fountain. Some were sitting silently, some were chatting. But all of them were holding a big white sign to their chests. It was all in Chinese, but Thomas's research had paid off.

"They're holding up facts about their son or daughter. How old, how tall, what type of education."

These older Chinese parents meant business. Some would start talking to others, to see if there could be a match. Sometimes they would show one another photos of their children that they had been hiding from view. It seemed like a somber process, with people talking very seriously with one another, and looking at us Westerners with great suspicion. Many of the parents were just sitting there staring into space, with the photo or information of their son or daughter hanging from their necks.

I don't think these older Chinese people would be telling me how happy they were that their sons and daughters had so many options available to them, and how delighted they were that their thirty-six-year-old daughter was still unmarried. These parents were so dismayed over their children's love lives that they had literally taken to the streets. In a country with a notable distaste for public gatherings, these people were out there with signs on their chests, trying to get their children married off. These parents were experiencing the ramifications of their children's independence. It was hard not to find it depressing.

I tried to look on the bright side of things.

"Maybe we should think it's sweet. How concerned they are. And what harm does it do?"

"Or you could think of it another way," Thomas said. "Because of the one-child rule, they only have one child to care for them as they get older. Maybe they think it's better for their own well-being to have their children married off."

I shook my head. "That is so dark."

Thomas smiled and took my hand. "I know how you like the theories. I was just offering mine."

We had decided to take a little tour of Houhai, a beautiful little neighborhood that has some of the last remaining courtyard houses, or *hutongs*. These little gray structures, some attached by a courtyard, all connected by little alleyways, were once the typical domicile for most of the people in Beijing, but now were being torn down to make way for high-rises. But in Houhai, the little shops and food stands in the hutongs themselves had now become a main tourist attraction. This neighborhood just might be spared in Beijing's new development craze.

We stopped to have some lunch at one of the little "restaurants" in the middle of the hutong. It was a dirty, tiny place that basically served only dumplings and noodles. The jars of chili pepper paste that were on the table looked as if they hadn't been wiped down in years, and flies were buzzing all around. The two people working there spoke absolutely no English. In a world where it's getting harder and harder to find anyone who can't speak English or doesn't know where the nearest Starbucks is, this was a comfort. We were in the middle of something authentic, even if the only reason it was kept authentic was for the tourists. Something about it all made me get emotional. We sat there sharing a plate of noodles with vegetables, and a plate of boiled dumplings. After a few moments in silence, I spoke.

"I want you to know that this was good for me," I said, trying to sound philosophical, yet casual.

Thomas looked at me, not saying a word.

"It gives me hope, that there's love out there, there's possibility. You shouldn't feel badly about any of it. I understood your situation."

Thomas put down his chopsticks.

"My dear Julie, I don't feel sorry for you. I know you will be fine. This is what is so difficult for me."

He smiled and took my hand. I didn't want to cry in front of him, since I knew my French counterpart would have much more pride. I asked the woman who served us our dumplings where the bathroom was.

"WC?"

She pointed to outside on the street.

I was confused. I said it again. "WC?" She nodded and spoke to me in Chinese and again pointed outside. I stood up and looked out the door. A few yards away some women were walking out a doorway.

"Wish me luck," I said to Thomas and walked out the door.

In Beijing, as I soon found out, they enjoy "squatter" toilets. Even in some of the upscale establishments, they had not yet found the need for a good old Western toilet. This was something I was prepared for, having been to Rome and not being all that squeamish about these things. But walking into this public "WC" I actually experienced a bathroom situation that I not only had never encountered, but had never even heard existed.

First of all, as I walked toward this public facility, the stench was incredible. I had to stop breathing through my nose while I was still on the street outside. I considered just turning back, but I really did have to pee. I walked into the entryway and took a few steps in. I looked around. I was in one large room, no doors, no walls; just about eight squatting toilets altogether with Chinese women squatting on them. The only thing that separated each squatter was a little metal partition, only about two feet high, in between each one. So it sort of gave the feel of being in a squatting pen.

I walked in and saw this and I was actually shocked. This, for a New Yorker, is not an easy thing to be. I was shocked by simply seeing four or five Chinese women squatting and peeing together, and then I was shocked with the quick realization that I was expected to do the same.

A few of the women looked up at me and I had a strange moment of some new kind of pride. I didn't want to be a wimp about things right now. This is my life, I am in the hutongs, and this is how they pee.

I walked to one of the squatters, unbuttoned my pants, and squatted. I looked up and found I was face-to-face with an old Chinese woman who was in the squatter right across from me, only about a foot away. If we spoke the same language we could have had a nice little chat. Instead, she farted, and I looked down and finished peeing.

So I had gone from a kiss at the Colosseum to falling in love in Bali to a squatters' pen in Beijing. It was all quite clear to me. My grand affair was indeed coming to an end. There was nothing I was going to be able to do about it except get through it as quickly and with as much dignity as possible. I took out a crumpled tissue I had brought with me and dried myself off.

When we got back to our hotel, there was a message on our phone from our new best friend, Wei, inviting us to a party at this restaurant and bar called Lan.

"It's going to be so much fun! So exciting!" And then she let out her long, loud laugh.

Thomas and I got dressed up and walked to the bar, which happened to be across the street from our hotel. When the elevator opened up, we were immediately ushered into one of the more impressive spaces I had ever seen. We had to pass through the massive nightclub-restaurant to get to where our party was. The whole place was done up in melodramatic elegance, as if it were a king's palace, with velvet drapes and huge chandeliers in what seemed to be thousands of square feet. There were different restaurant spaces, bar areas, and lounges, all designed to create a different opulent mood.

We walked to the end of the restaurant where the party was taking place. We could hear the din of people talking and laughing. As we got closer, we saw that it was another beautiful crowd of Chinese hipsters, everyone fabulously attired and drinking. The minute we walked in we saw Wei.

"Oh my God, it's so good to see you, my friends!" She ran over to us in a tiny white and black sequined minidress and gave us a big kiss on our cheeks. She pushed us over to the bar and then ran off to say hello to someone else. As Thomas ordered us wine, I turned to see Tammy, the woman we had met on the airplane, standing with a martini in her hand. We looked at each other, surprised—trying to remember how we knew each other.

"Oh! Hi, I met you on the plane," I said.

"Yes, that's right. Hello."

"Hi."

Thomas came over to me with our glasses of wine.

"So tell me, how do you like Beijing? Are you learning a lot about single women here?" Tammy asked, pleasantly.

"I am, actually. Thank you. It's a very exciting time to be here."

"Yes, it is," Tammy said. "There have been so many changes, so fast—it's been very interesting to see it all."

"Really? What kind of changes?" I asked, curious.

"Well, it's only been in the past ten years that we had supermarkets. Before that, I wasn't able to touch my groceries."

"I'm sorry, what did you say?" Thomas asked.

"It wasn't until only a few years ago that we had grocery stores where we could actually take our groceries off a shelf and look at them before we bought them. Before that they were all behind the counter."

For some reason the idea of not being able to touch your groceries was fascinating to me.

"So now you're free to be single, to get divorced, to touch groceries—everything's different."

"Yes, we have so much freedom now. Not like our mothers did."

"So tell me—do women here ever think about becoming single mothers? Is that something that's done?" I asked casually.

Tammy took a bite of a spring roll and said quite matter-of-factly, "No."

Thomas and I looked at each other. It was such a definite answer. So black-and-white.

"Really? Never?"

"No. Never. It's not possible."

"But what do you mean?"

"It's not possible."

I took a pause, not wanting to push. And then I just repeated, "But what do you mean?"

"Each child is registered at birth. With this registration, they are given access to health care and other services. A child born out of wedlock is not given a registration. It's not recognized by the government. It does not exist."

Thomas and I stared at her for a moment.

"So, tell me, Tammy, what does a single Chinese woman do if she gets pregnant?" Thomas asked.

"She has an abortion," Tammy said, as if it were the most obvious answer in the world.

"What about adoption? Can't a single woman adopt one of these Chinese babies in the orphanages?" I was shocked by this new piece of information.

"No. It's not possible," Tammy said again, with complete seriousness.

"But why not? There's so many of them."

Tammy just shrugged. "Don't you see? If you let a single Chinese woman adopt, you would be allowing them to be single mothers. It would be almost the same as letting them have their own children. This will never happen. Or maybe it will happen, but not for many years."

It then began to dawn on me that all these women that were out and about in Beijing enjoying their freedom, refusing to settle, working hard on their careers, had one very big difference to us Western women. They didn't get to have a Plan B. We get to date the wrong men and have our little affairs and in the end, we still know that our motherhood isn't ultimately at stake. Many of us don't want to be single mothers, many of us will not choose it even if it's our only option, but it's still an option.

These ladies, who now get to choose from three different kinds of shampoos, don't have the option to be a mother even if they haven't found the right man. Their singleness came at a price much higher than I realized.

"So, if you're thirty-seven or thirty-eight and you want to be a mother, what do you do?" I asked.

Tammy shrugged again. "You marry the next man you meet."

She must have detected the sad look on my face. "It happens all the time."

Suddenly those parents in the park didn't seem so crazy to me.

The two gentlemen we met the night before at Suzie Wong's came in, Jin and Dong. I introduced them to Tammy. Even though Tammy made it clear that she didn't enjoy Chinese men, for a moment I had hoped that she and Jin would hit it off. They talked for a while, as Thomas and I made conversation with Dong. Eventually, Dong and Jin went to the bar to get some drinks. I decided to play matchmaker.

"I know you don't like Chinese men, but Jin seemed nice, no? I thought you two might hit it off."

Tammy looked over at Jin, who was the Chinese equivalent of the nice stable guy in the States who sells insurance or becomes a dentist, except a little more handsome and able to speak more languages.

"Please," she said, rolling her eyes. "If I wanted to marry *that* guy, I could have been married a long time ago."

I went to the bar and got myself another drink.

The next day, our last together, we decided to walk from our hotel to the Forbidden City, the main tourist destination of Beijing. Thomas took my hand as we walked down the street. It was rush hour, with cars whizzing by, and crowds of cyclists going to work. Many of the cyclists were wearing masks over their faces, to protect them from the intense pollution there—another result of Beijing's growing economy. Thomas stopped me and gave me a long kiss. It felt sad, like the beginning of good-bye.

At first glance, the Forbidden City isn't all that impressive. All you see from the outside is a long red wall with a picture of Mao Tse-tung that hangs over it all. It looks a little drab, I'm not going to lie. But once you get inside, it all changes. You are in the largest palace still standing in the entire world. What seems like miles and miles of walkways lead to the various temples and halls that all the great emperors used from the Ming dynasty on. The halls all have grand and majestic names that I couldn't help but find amusing: the Gate of Heavenly Purity, the Palace of Supreme Harmony, the Hall of Mental Cultivation, the Hall of Lasting Brightness. Even the modern antilittering signs to the tourists were filled with melodrama: "A Single Act of Carelessness Leads to the Eternal Loss of Beauty."

Thomas and I chose to do the audio tour, which was quite stressful at first. Both of us were wearing headphones and carrying around a little GPS device and trying to understand where we were supposed to look and what we were actually looking at, based on what the guide in our ears was saying.

"Is yours on yet?" I asked Thomas.

"Yes, mine is saying something about musical instruments—do you not have that?" he asked.

"No. I don't have anything . . ."

"Well, maybe you should try . . ."

"Shh . . . it's coming on. Wait, are we in the right place? Are we in the Hall of Supreme Harmony? Where's the statue of the lion? What's she talking about?"

That sort of thing. But eventually we got into a nice rhythm and we were able to walk around with the little guide in our ears that knew exactly where we were at all times, and what we needed to know. It was perfect. Thomas and I were together, holding hands, experiencing the grandeur of the largest palace in the world, and we didn't have to talk to each other about anything.

Near the end of the tour, as I was looking at one of the little temples, I glanced over to see Thomas taking out his cell phone. The light was flashing. He took off his headphones and started talking on his phone. Again, he looked fairly animated. I chose to turn away. I listened intently to my audio guide, who sounded a bit like Vanessa Redgrave. In fact, I think it *was* Vanessa Redgrave. As I was looking at the Palace of Heavenly Purity, Vanessa was telling me about how the emperor hid the name of his successor, whom only he could choose, under a plaque that said "Justice and Honor." At the same time he carried a duplicate copy in a pouch around his neck, so that if he died suddenly, there could be no high court shenanigans. As I was listening to this tale of palace intrigue, I glanced over at Thomas. He had shut the phone and had started pacing, nervously. I took off my headphones.

"What's the matter?" I asked.

Thomas ran his hands through his black wavy hair. He didn't answer.

"Ça c'est incroyable," he muttered in French.

"What?" I asked, now a little worried.

Thomas didn't answer. He just kept shaking his head.

"She's here. In Beijing."

"Who's here . . . ?" I asked, hoping I didn't understand what he had just said.

"Dominique, she's here."

It was then that I realized I didn't even know her name. I had purposely pushed her so out of the realm of my reality that I didn't even know what people called her.

"Your wife?" I asked, alarmed.

Thomas nodded. His face was getting a little red.

"She came to Beijing?" I asked, trying not to shriek.

Thomas nodded again, tugging at his hair.

"She didn't believe I would ever come home. So she's come here to get me."

I stood there, standing on the tiny steps that lead to the Palace of Heavenly Purity. There were now throngs of tourists, mostly Chinese, shoving past me.

"Where is she now?"

Thomas crossed his arms over his chest. Then he started biting his thumb. He put his hands down by his sides.

"She's across the street, in Tiananmen Square. She's coming here, now."

"How can she be across the street—how did she . . . ?"

Thomas looked at me, astonished. "I don't know. I think she just got here and told the taxi to take her to Tiananmen Square, and then she called me."

I looked at him, incredulous. "Well, what should I do . . . where should I . . . ?"

I looked around, like an empress trying to find her route of escape from the advancing army.

"Let's just take you out the back entrance and then I'll go talk to her."

"Okay," I said, my heart beating rapidly. "Okay."

We walked quickly through the Imperial Garden (it looked lovely from what I could tell) and were about to walk through the doorway that said "exit here." I turned to Thomas to tell him that I would go back to the hotel, and he could call me there—or, I don't know what, really—when I saw him looking over my head. His expression was fixed, but his eyes looked like someone had just pushed a fire alarm. I turned around, and saw this beautiful, tiny blond woman in a long cashmere coat and fashionable heels walking toward us fast. Her hair was in a high ponytail, and it bounced behind her as she stormed toward us. She had entered the gates of the Forbidden City and was about to confront us both in the Imperial Garden. What better place for a wife to confront her husband and his concubine?

Thomas is an outstandingly cool and elegant man, but even he, at this moment, looked as if his head was about to explode all over the cypress trees.

"What should I . . . what . . . ?" I stammered.

I wanted to flee, to run the three miles back to the front gate and through the streets of Beijing to the hotel and jump under the covers and hide. In two more seconds it would be too late for that.

Dominique charged up to Thomas, yelling at him in French. Then she looked over at me with utter disgust, and started to yell some more. I could make out some of the things that she said, about the years they'd been together, how much she loved him. I kept hearing that over and over again, "Est-ce que tu sais à quel point je t'aime?" ("Do you know how much I love you?") She kept pointing at me and yelling. Even if my French wasn't perfectly accurate, I got the gist of it: Why would you throw away everything we have for her, for this woman, for this whore, for this nobody. Why is she so special? She's nothing. We have a life together, she doesn't mean anything to you. Thomas wasn't defending me, but how could he? He was just trying to calm her down. Throughout all this, I have to admit, she looked beautiful—and dignified. I was amazed; she flew all the way around the world to rip him out of the arms of another woman, and she looked gorgeous and chic the whole time she was doing it. The Chinese tourists were staring, confused and a little surprised, but they kept on moving. With over a billion people in their country they didn't have the time or the space to really give a shit about anything.

I was taking a few steps backward, when Dominique just put her hands on Thomas's chest and pushed him back, hard. Now the tears were falling down her face. Thomas looked truly surprised, as if he'd never seen his wife this upset before. I turned around to go when I heard her scream out "Je suis enceinte" in French.

I wasn't sure, but I thought she'd just said, "I'm pregnant." And judging from the look on Thomas's face, that's exactly what she said.

I lowered my head and, without a word, escorted myself out of the Forbidden City. I was officially dethroned.

In one of the Chinese travel books I had bought at the airport, I read that there's a common saying to sum up the total regime of Mao Tse-tung: It had been "70 percent good and 30 percent bad." I liked that. I think percentages are a good way to sum up most things in a person's life. As I walked back to my hotel, I tried to trace my steps backward, to remember all I had done to land me now on the Street of Great Humiliation and Sorrow. I had been trying to say yes to life and play by someone else's rules and experience love and romance and go for it. Was that so wrong?

In Bali it seemed like a really great idea. Now, on West Chang An Avenue, maybe it was more accurate to say it was a 70 percent bad idea and a 30 percent good one. All I knew for sure was that I had made a French woman cry on the street, that I was called a whore, and that the man I was in love with was about to go off and start a family with his wife. As he should. I was mortified and ashamed. I had done it again. I had gone and dated a bad boy. Maybe a boy who was only 20 percent bad and 80 percent good, but a bad boy nonetheless. So besides experiencing the shame of the public humiliation and the guilt at my own behavior, now I got to add to it the realization that I was still making the same damn mistakes.

"Don't come home," Serena said. I had called her at six in the morning her time. "You can't just run home because of a man; that's insane."

"Well, what am I supposed to do?" I asked, sobbing on the phone. "I don't want to travel anymore. I'm sick of it . . ." My voice trailed off as I wept.

"Go to India!" Serena said. "I know of an ashram right outside of Mumbai. It's a great place to just go and heal. You'll feel better there— you'll see. India is an amazing place to give you perspective."

"I don't know . . ." I couldn't imagine taking another plane all the way to India. I just wanted to get back to New York, with my bed and my apartment and all the sights and smells that I'm used to. Then I realized I had to give my subletter two weeks' notice. So I wouldn't be able to go back to my apartment now even if I wanted to.

"Think about it. Don't make any big decision just yet. Give it a few hours."

"But he's going to have to come back here. I don't want to see him."

"He's not going to come back there for a while, trust me. Just take an hour or two to calm down and think."

I hung up the phone and sat on the bed. I didn't know what to do. I hated the idea of going back to New York because of a broken heart— that seemed so weak. I put my head down on the pillow, exhausted.

I woke up to the sound of the hotel phone ringing in my ear. I practically jumped to the ceiling at the sound of it. I sat up in bed and stared at it as it rang and rang. I wasn't quite sure how long I had slept. An hour? Three days? I didn't think it could be Thomas, he would call me on my cell, but I wasn't sure. I let it go to voice mail. When I went to check the messages it was Wei.

"Julie! I am having a big karaoke party right now in your hotel for some big Chinese businessmen. I'm in lounge on eighteenth floor! You and your boyfriend have to come!" And then, of course, she laughed.

The party never stopped for that one. It really irritated me. Besides calling Thomas my boyfriend, how could she be partying away as if she didn't have a care in the world? Didn't she know her days were numbered? That someday she's going to be pushing forty or fifty and she might not find everything as funny as she does now? That she might end up a single, childless woman alone in a country that considers itself communist but expects you to pretty much take care of yourself? I wasn't sure if she knew this, but for some reason—let's blame the jet lag and/or the fact that Thomas was absolutely gone from my life, *gone*—I decided it was my job to let Wei know the truth about being single.

I jammed on the little terry cloth slippers the hotel provided, grabbed my plastic hotel key card, and went out the door. I walked briskly to the elevator and got in. There were two nice-looking midwestern men in the elevator. They chatted to each other, but both of them at some point glanced down at my feet. I guess they'd never seen anyone walk around a hotel in their slippers before. I got out on the eighteenth floor, and so did they. I followed them into a large room just opposite the elevator, called "The Executive Suite." For this night it had been transformed into a karaoke lounge, with a disco ball in the middle and a large video screen. There were lots of young women prancing around in their designer outfits, and lots of Chinese and Western businessmen drinking and chatting with the girls.

Wei was standing on a little stage that had been set up, singing a song in Chinese while the karaoke machine displayed the words on the screen, along with a video of a Chinese man and woman walking along a babbling brook. I don't know what she was singing about but—wait a minute—could she be singing about—I don't know—love? Do you think? Just as she was finishing up her song and everyone started clapping, I stormed up on the little stage and stood right next to her. I looked out on this sea of twenty-something Chinese girl cuteness and men in suits going along for the ride. I grabbed the mike out of Wei's hands.

"I just want you ladies to know that you should think very carefully about what you're doing," I said loudly into the microphone. Everyone stopped talking to stare at the crazy lady. Wei just looked at me. She cupped her hand over her mouth, covering a smile.

"You think you have all the time in the world, you think that it's so fun to be so free and independent. You think you have all these options, but you don't really. You're not always going to be surrounded by men. You're not always going to be young. You're going to get older and know more about what you want and you won't be willing to settle and you're going to look around and there will be even *fewer* men for you to choose from. And you're not only going to be single, but you're going to be child-less as well. So you should understand there are consequences to what you're doing now. *Very serious consequences!*"

No one said a word. Clearly, they all thought I was a lunatic. I handed the mike back to Wei. She kept her hand over her mouth and laughed.

"Oh, Julie, you're so funny! You are so funny!"

Back in the States

It was the day Ruby was to be inseminated and she didn't have anyone to accompany her. And, really, what could be more depressing than that? By this point Ruby was bloated. Fat. Her breasts felt as swollen as if she were already pregnant. She imagined someone pricking her with a needle and having the water just come gushing out of her, and bringing her back to her normal size again. She had also been really emotional for the past three days, which she attributed to the hormones, but, really, let's face it, it could also be because she was about to be ejaculated into by a syringe and then possibly spend the next nine months pregnant and alone. I'm just saying.

Her good friend Sonia was supposed to be her plus-one to the ejacu-lation, but she canceled at the last minute because her daughter was sick. Ruby didn't want to call Serena because Serena had told her what was going on at her job and she didn't want to bother her. She called Alice, but she didn't pick up. Ruby would have asked her gay male friends but she was still mad at them. The only person left was Georgia. They really didn't know each other very well, and Ruby thought Georgia was a little crazy, but maybe it would be better to go with a crazy person than no one at all? She wasn't sure.

But then, Ruby considered the alternative—getting in a cab, going to the clinic, lying on a table, getting shot full of semen, hailing a cab home. Alone. So she picked up the phone and called Georgia. Alice had told her about the daily shots so she wasn't taken completely by surprise and she said yes immediately. Georgia was desperate to have something to do besides think about the upcoming custody fight with Dale and the visit with the court-appointed social worker that was happening later that day. The kids were at school, as opposed to at home, unattended, and she was free to think about someone else's life for a change.

When Ruby got to the clinic, Georgia was already outside. Ruby relaxed. It was nice to have someone there for her, waiting for her.

"Hey Ruby," Georgia said, sweetly. "How are you feeling?"

Ruby just smiled and said, "Fat. Nervous."

"This is really exciting," Georgia said as they were about to walk through the revolving doors. "You might become a mother today."

"I know. Isn't that weird?" Ruby replied, putting her hand on the revolving door and pushing it.

Georgia followed right behind Ruby and said, "You know what? *It's all weird.*"

The waiting room was mercifully quiet. There were only two women there, both pregnant—which seemed like a good sign to Ruby. Ruby signed in and she and Georgia sat down to wait.

"I think it's fantastic that you're doing this. Being a mother is one of the most wonderful experiences in the world. Really," Georgia said.

Ruby smiled. She was happy to hear that right now.

"You'll never really be able to understand it until it happens to you, but it's like this awesome responsibility is given to you—to take care of another human being on this planet. That little person becomes everything to you." Georgia seemed to be lost in thought. "It's incredibly sweet."

Ruby looked at Georgia. For once, she seemed soft. Vulnerable. Gentle. Not crazy.

"So, you're going to do it as a single mother. What does it matter?"

Georgia added. "We all end up getting divorced and becoming single mothers anyway. You're just starting out that way."

Ruby thought that was a little bleak, but perhaps Georgia was just trying to make her feel better about being single. Ruby glanced over at the magazine rack filled with *Woman's Day* and *Redbook* and *People*. Georgia continued her pep talk. "It's a fuck of a lot better for the kid this way."

Now Ruby wondered where this was going.

"At least with you they won't be subjected to an asshole father who wants to go to court to prove that you're an unfit mother. At least there won't be that."

"What?" Ruby said, taken off guard.

"Oh. Yeah. That's what's going on right now. Can you believe it?"

Ruby never let her gaze stray from Georgia, so as not to reveal in any way the thought crossing her mind, which was "*Well, actually . . .*"

Georgia took a breath. She picked up a *Parents* magazine and started to flip through it. "But today is not about me. It's about you. And my point is that you shouldn't feel badly about this. Why deprive yourself of having children just because you don't want to be a single mother? By the time we're fifty, everyone we know is going to be a single mother." She stopped to look at a photo of the "Five-Minute Brownie."

"The problem with single mothers is we're all competing for the same men—the ones who are willing to date women with kids. I mean, how many of those guys are there in New York? How can we all possibly find one?"

Ruby had the impulse to put her hand over Georgia's mouth and not take it off until her name was called. Instead, she leaned back in her chair, closed her eyes, and sighed. Maybe it wasn't a good idea to have invited Georgia to her insemination party after all.

"Ruby Carson?" a nurse called out, and Ruby stood up immediately. Georgia sat up and squeezed Ruby's hand.

"Do you want me to go in with you?"

The image flashed through her mind of Georgia sitting there while some doctor or nurse put a syringe of semen in her woo-woo.

"No, that's okay, you can stay here, I'll be fine."

"Okay. But if Julie was here, she'd be in there with you, so I just wanted you to know that I would."

"Thank you. I appreciate it. I think it's really fast. I'll be fine."

"Okay," Georgia said, a little relieved. "Have fun!"

Ruby was undressed and sitting on the examining table. She felt like a little girl, her feet dangling down, clutching at her paper robe. She remembered her first gynecological exam. She was thirteen, and was brought by her mother right when she got her first period. She sat there, just like now, waiting, not knowing what to expect, but understanding that it was a rite of passage, one that would usher her into a whole new chapter of her life, as a woman. The only difference then was that her mother was with her; her mother who now lived in Boston; her mother who raised her as a single mother, by the way; a mother who was always extremely depressed. Her father left them when she was eight, and her mother never remarried.

She closed her eyes and tried to think fertile thoughts. But all she could see was her mother sitting at the kitchen table, smoking, staring out into space. She thought of her mother coming home late at night from work, carrying the groceries. She thought of the three of them at the kitchen table—Ruby, her brother Dean, and her mom—quietly eating together. Her mother, too tired, too depressed to talk, her brother and she trying to lighten things up, with mashed-potato fights, with milk coming out of their noses. She remembered her mother's anger; then often, her mother's tears.

"Don't you know how hard I work? Don't you understand how tired I am?" she shouted once as she got up and grabbed a sponge and walked over to the wall to attack a big gob of mashed potato. Ruby remembered that they laughed at her in that moment. She seemed like just a grotesque caricature, not a real person. It seemed funny to them at the time, their mother with all that crazy emotion. Of course at that moment, at the sight of her children's smirks and giggles, Ruby's mother broke down and cried.

"I can't take it anymore! I can't!" she said as she threw the sponge in the sink, letting out a series of sobs as she leaned against the kitchen counter, her back to her two children. "Burn the whole house down if you want to," she screamed as she raced out of the room.

Ruby remembers the feeling she had in the pit of her stomach in that moment. She didn't know what it was at the time, but as she got older, she found herself recognizing that feeling over and over again. She had it when she saw a blind person, all alone, tapping along a busy Manhattan street, or once when she saw an old woman fall down on the ice. It was pity. At ten years old, she was giggling at her mother because she didn't know how else to process the sick feeling in her gut of feeling sorry for her own mother. As she became a teenager, as she saw her mother have a string of boyfriends, all in differing shades of lame, she processed the pity in a whole new way: she hated her. Not like this is the most unique story ever told, but for Ruby's last two years of high school, she stopped speaking to her mother. Yes, they didn't get along, yes, they fought about things like curfew and outfits and boyfriends, but more importantly, Ruby just couldn't stand pitying her anymore. So the less she engaged with her in any way, the less Ruby had to feel that queasy, awful feeling in the pit of her stomach.

Now here Ruby was, feeling her naked body sticking to the sanitary paper covering the table, and waiting to be inseminated by a doctor. Why? Because when the music stopped and everyone had grabbed their men, she was left standing alone. The race was run and she had lost it. *She had lost.* That was the only way she could see it as she sat there, naked and alone, waiting.

Maybe if I had been there it would have been different. Maybe I would have joked with her and said the right thing and made her feel that what she was about to do was the beginning of a life that, though hard at times, would be rewarding beyond measure. There would be life and joy and children and laughter. But I wasn't there, and I didn't say anything genius, and Ruby started to slide down into that hole like so many times before.

In the middle of her slide, Doctor Gilardi came in. He was in his early sixties, with a distinguished head of white hair and skin that had the kind of tan that came from entitled living. Ruby chose him because he was handsome and gentle and she felt that, as the man inseminating her, he would in some way be the father of her child.

"So," he said with a smile. "Are you ready to go?"

Ruby tried to be chipper. "Yep. Knock me up, Doc!"

Doctor Gilardi smiled. "I'm just going to examine you one last time, and then the nurse will come in with the specimen."

Ruby nodded and lay back, put her feet in the stirrups, and opened her legs. The doctor wheeled a chair over and sat down, ready to take a look.

Lying there, Ruby felt that old feeling again. She wondered if it was called "pity" because it was always felt in the pit of your stomach. It didn't matter how the word was made, all she knew was that she felt it now, for herself. There in the paper robe and the fluorescent lighting and the absence of any man anywhere in the world who loved her, she was pitiful. She thought about all the men she had dated and spent too much time grieving over. There was Charlie and Brett and Lyle and Ethan. Just guys. Guys it didn't work out with, for whom Ruby had cried and cried. She knew they weren't jerking off into a cup right now so some surrogate mother could have their children. She was sure they all had girlfriends or wives or whatever the hell they wanted to have. And there she was, about to be a lonely, sexless, depressed single mother.

The nurse came in carrying a big cooler. She opened it up and the smoke of the dry ice came billowing out. Out of it she took a canister that looked like a large silver thermos. This was filled with Ruby's children.

"Here it is," the nurse said, sweetly. Doctor Gilardi stood up and took it from her. He looked at Ruby.

"Everything looks fine. Are you ready?" A million thoughts came to Ruby at this moment. About going home afterward to her empty apartment. About taking a pregnancy test and finding out she was pregnant. About not having a man there with her, who would be ecstatic about the news. About being in the delivery room with her friends, her family, but no man. But the one thought that truly made her cringe in pity was the memory of her mother crying, talking to some friend on the phone. "I can't take it," Ruby remembered her mother saying through her tears. "It's just too much for me. It's too much. I don't know how I'm going to do this, I don't!" And then her mother crumpled into a chair, sobbing.

Ruby shot up, yanking her feet out of the stirrups.

"No, I'm not ready. I'm not ready at all." And she turned to the side and hopped off the table. She held her robe together as she said, "I'm so sorry to waste your time, I'm so sorry to waste all that good sperm, and I'm really, *really* sorry that I just wasted over seven thousand dollars, but I have to go."

. . .

It was eleven thirty in the morning. Georgia opened her refrigerator door for the twelfth time in five minutes and stared inside. She had milk. And eggs. And bread and vegetables and fruit and little cheese sticks and fruit juice boxes and pudding cups. She had some cooked macaroni and cheese in some Tupperware, as well as some pieces of fried chicken wrapped up in plastic. She thought this would be a very homey touch, showing that she had cooked a nice meal the night before—what said "good mother" more than some leftover mac and cheese and fried chicken?

She did not have a good attitude about this interview. It was a mother-fucking humiliating motherfucking interview with some bullshit social worker or psychologist or whoever who was going to come into *her* home, and look into *her* refrigerator and ask *her* questions about how she was raising *her* kids. And then this woman, this bitch, this do-gooder, "I'm so noble" *busybody* was going to decide whether she would be allowed to keep *her* children. Georgia slammed the door of the refrigerator.

She thought that perhaps she should get into a better mood before the social worker came.

She paced around her apartment. "This is serious," she said, to herself. "This is as serious as it gets." She tried to breathe. In and out. In and out. She started thinking about bad mothers. The mothers she saw on the streets, screaming at their kids, slapping their kids, calling their kids names like "stupid" and even "you little asshole." She thought about all the stories she had read in the paper about women who had burned their children with cigarettes, or abandoned them for three days, or let them starve to death. She stopped pacing and looked around her lovely apartment in the West Village. *There's no way they're going to take my children away from me. I'm their mother, for God's sake.* Then she thought about crazy-ass Michael Jackson and his diabolical Neverland and his dangling his child out a window as he greeted his fans. *And he got to keep his children*, Georgia thought to herself as she walked to the bathroom. She opened the door to the medicine cabinet and looked around at the Band-Aids, baby aspirin, real aspirin, bandages. Was there anything she didn't have in her medicine cabinet that was going to make her seem unfit? She couldn't believe Dale had the nerve to call her an unfit mother. Okay—So, fine. She left the house once with the children unsupervised. Georgia closed the medicine cabinet and looked in the mirror. That *was* really, really bad. But doesn't every parent once in their fucking parenting life do something really, really negligent? Was she the only one in the whole world that's made a mistake? Georgia stared at her face in the mirror. Okay, so it was over a guy. That was also really bad. It was. She had spiraled and lost her bearings and she went a little nutso. Okay—so, fine. She didn't dangle anyone over a fucking balcony.

She walked out into the living room and looked around. Were there any sharp objects around, any dangerously jutting corners on the furniture that could make her seem like an unfit fucking interior decorator? Georgia, still burning with rage, walked into the kitchen and looked into the pantry. Ah, the pantry. What's better than a big pantry? This almost relaxed her, the corn muffin mix and the chocolate chips and the vanilla extract and the flour and the coconut flakes. Her mother had once told her that every home should have the ingredients to make toll house cookies at all times. She never forgot it. *Now does that seem like the thinking of a motherfucking unfit mother?* Too angry. Much too angry. She was trying to just breathe when the doorbell rang. Georgia wanted to burst out crying. But she didn't. She took a breath and walked calmly to the door. She breathed again, but as she put her hand on the doorknob she couldn't help but think, *Dale will burn in fucking hell for this.*

She opened the door with a smile. Standing there was a short man with a gray ponytail and mustache. She knew his type immediately. Liberal do-gooder social worker throwback to the sixties. He smiled benignly. Georgia smiled benignly back. She hated him. How would he know what a good mother was? He was a man, just like Dale, and he could just kiss her ass.

"Please come in," Georgia said sweetly and waved him in. He walked in and quickly looked around the apartment. Georgia's eyes moved with his. She could see what he saw: a clean, privileged, well-cared-for home.

"My name is Mark. Mark Levine."

"So good to meet you, Mark." *So good to have you come into my fucking house and judge me.* "Can I get you anything to drink? I have coffee or

tea, grape juice, orange juice, pear juice, grapefruit juice, tap water, bottled water, sparkling water, Gatorade . . ."

"A glass of water would be fine, thank you," he said.

Georgia went in the kitchen and opened the door to the refrigerator
wide, revealing its maternally full contents. She saw him notice it, and
she smiled to herself as she pulled out the Brita pitcher and filled up two
glasses. "Why don't we talk in the living room, Mark?"

"That would be fine."

They walked to the living room and sat down. Georgia wondered if
she should put coasters down on the coffee table—would that make her
seem like a good mother because she had an attention to detail, or a bad
mother because she was too anal? She decided for the coasters. She sat
back and sipped her water and looked at Mark Levine.

"I know this must be a particularly difficult time for you," Mark said,
gently. "I'll try to be as sensitive as possible, even though I'm going to be
asking you some personal questions."

"Ask away," Georgia said, cheerfully. *Asshole.*

"Well, to start, it's always good for us to inquire about your relationship with your ex-husband. How you feel about him and how you talk to
your children about him."

*My relationship with him is great. That's why you're sitting in my fuck-
ing apartment deciding whether my children should be allowed to live
with me.*

"Well, considering the situation, I think we're getting along remarkably well. I encourage him to see the children. I was, and still am, perfectly ready to work out some kind of official custody arrangement with
him."

Mark looked at his notes. "He mentioned that you had some problems with his new girlfriend."

Georgia's stomach did a tiny little flip as she took a sip of her water.
"Well, yes, she is quite young, and he did just meet her." She looked up at
Mark Levine with wide, innocent eyes. "Wouldn't any mother have con-
cerns?"

Mark Levine nodded his head. He checked his notes again and then
gently said, "He mentioned that you called her a 'whore'? 'Gutter trash'?"

Georgia looked him dead in the eyes. *So this is how it's going to be, asshole.* "Have you ever gone through a divorce, Mr. Levine?" Georgia asked, as neutrally and as calmly as possible.

"Yes, unfortunately, I have."

"So then you understand there is a period, a small regrettable period, when emotions are heightened? When we might do or say things that we regret later?"

"Of course," Mark Levine said with an obligatory tight little smile. He continued to look down at his notes. Georgia imagined drilling a hole in his forehead.

"And these feelings, possibly of resentment toward his new girlfriend, did you make your children aware of them in any way?"

Georgia answered this one quickly. "Of course not. Even the most . . . I don't know . . . unsophisticated parent knows by now that you should never *ever* bad-mouth your spouse or his friends in front of the children."

"Of course," Mark Levine said delicately. He took a breath. "So when your husband said that Beth had called his girlfriend a 'cheap Brazilian whore,' would you say that . . ." Mark Levine paused, not really knowing how to finish that question or if he really needed to.

"That's an absolute lie," Georgia said, lying. "This just goes to show what lengths my ex-husband will go to in order to portray me as some kind of vindictive, out-of-control monster." Georgia got up from the sofa and just stood with her hands on her hips, then off her hips, then on again. "Do I look like the kind of woman who would call another woman a 'cheap whore' in front of my four-year-old daughter?"

Mark Levine looked up at her and didn't say anything.

And then it began. She started talking.

"Not that it's not painful, mind you, to find out your husband of twelve years has decided to leave your marriage and break up your home and start seeing a woman almost fifteen years younger than him. A woman whom he wants to introduce to your children, to go to the park with them, maybe go get Chinese food in Chinatown, maybe all go see a movie, like one big happy *family.*" Georgia was now pacing around the apartment, in front of Mark Levine sitting on the sofa, behind Mark Levine sitting on the sofa.

"Like it's completely appropriate to live with your wife and children one day, and then the next being like 'Hey, kids, I want you to meet my new girlfriend.' Does that seem appropriate to you? *I,* meanwhile, am just trying to go on a few dates, just trying to find a decent man of an appropriate age who *one day,* a long, long time from now, when my children are healed and well and strong, I *might* bring home to meet them. Yet, I am the one that gets criticized. Judged. Now tell me, Mr. Levine, is that fair?"

Again, Mark Levine said nary a peep.

"Truly, Mr. Levine, does my husband's behavior seem like that of a man who is sensitive and understanding of the needs of his children? Or does he seem like a man who is perhaps in a sex-induced haze because he's getting fucked three times a night by some Brazilian *whore.*" Georgia stopped dead in her tracks. Mark Levine put down his pen and looked up at Georgia, expressionless.

"I . . . I mean . . . shit. Shit. Fuck." Georgia realized how she sounded. "I mean, I mean . . ." Georgia sat back down on the couch and shut up for a minute, tears welling in her eyes. She looked up at Mark Levine.

"You have to understand. This is an incredibly stressful thing. To have you come in here, and ask me questions . . . it's very upsetting. And then you put the word *whore* into my head. I mean, you used the word *whore* first, you put it in my head and then I was upset and then, pop!"—Georgia made a gesture with her hands by her head to signify, well, a pop!—"it came out of my mouth!"

Mark Levine closed his notebook.

"I completely understand. This must be a very difficult time for you." It was clear from Mark Levine's body language that he had seen enough and was about to get up and go.

"Yes, it is. I hope you understand that. We're talking about my children. About whether my children are going to get to live with me. What's more important than that? What could be more stressful than that?"

Mark Levine, again, left the question unanswered. He stood up to go. Georgia had nothing left to say. She had run out of rope to hang herself with.

"I think it's best if I come back another time. The next time I'll talk with you and your children together. Is that okay?"

Georgia stayed motionless on the sofa. "That would be fine, thank you."

Mark Levine let himself out.

After about a good ten minutes of Georgia staring out into space, frozen, unable to cry or scream, she stood up. Without thinking, she walked to the kitchen and opened the refrigerator door. She stood staring at the milk and the bread and the eggs and the fruit and the vegetables and the sparkling water and the chicken and the mac and cheese for a very long time. She closed the refrigerator, leaned against the door, and began to cry.

• • •

Serena was doing everything by the book. She had begun pureeing vegetables, making salads, and getting recipes for things like hemp pesto and zucchini "pasta." She was not cooking anything over 110 degrees. She was making sure every single vegetable was organic and then scrubbed within an inch of its raw life.

Serena, as I mentioned before, knew that part of her normal job description was to be as unobtrusive a presence as possible in their home. But now she was trying to be invisible. This family, with whatever hardships they were going through, at least deserved some privacy. This seemed to be exactly what Joanna and Robert wanted and fortunately, they seemed to be getting it. The press didn't have a clue what was going on. There were no friends, no family traipsing in and out. Their loft was a solemn yet tranquil oasis. So Serena attempted to be the invisible sprite floating on the outskirts of their suffering. She wanted to feed them, nourish them, keep them going, perhaps without them even remembering she was there. She would try to bear no witness, leave no footprints. Instead, she attempted to put all her "presence" into the food. Some of her yoga training remained, and she began preparing the food as if doing a meditation. She began visualizing her healthy life force pouring into the food; she pictured all her healing energy radiating out of her fingers and imbuing the raw food with magical curative powers. In her own small way, with her zucchi-getti and her sunflower seed patties, Serena was trying desperately, quietly, to save Robert's life.

But as far as Serena could tell, none of it was working. From her perspective, all the medical equipment that started getting wheeled in clanged and banged like a death knell and the beautiful loft now looked like a hospital ward. From what Serena could tell, as she drifted like a ghost in and out of their home, Robert was going in for chemo once a week and it seemed to be making him incredibly sick. Any other normal person going through this would be in the hospital right now, but because of who he was and how much money he had, they had managed to bring the hospital to him.

And at eight o'clock every morning, Serena would use the key they gave her and let herself in. Joanna would invariably walk out of her bedroom and greet Serena with a bright "Good morning!" Serena would smile and meet her with as cheerful a "Good morning" as she could muster, and then she would cast her eyes down and walk to the kitchen and get to work. They both had it down to a science. Serena would prepare lunch and dinner and snacks for Robert and Joanna (who was also on the raw diet to support Robert) and then a different dinner for Kip. She would stay all day in the kitchen, which was a big open one that everyone had to walk past to get anywhere, but Serena always kept her eyes down, never acknowledging that anything was even happening for her to see.

But that day, around two thirty in the afternoon, as Serena was moving her hands over some broccoli sprouts, praying over them, meditating on them, Joanna walked up to her, looking ashen, her voice shaky.

"I'm sorry, Serena, I would normally never ask you this, but Robert's having a hard time breathing. The nurse is on her way, but I don't think I should leave now to pick up Kip. I know it's not your job, but I was wondering if you could pick him up from school? Just this once?"

"Of course, I can go. Of course," Serena said, immediately taking off her apron. "It's Tenth Street, right?"

"Yes. He comes out the front door usually right at three. But if he sees you, he might . . . he might get nervous, so if you could . . ."

"I'll make sure he knows everything is okay, and you just got busy."

"Thank you. Thank you so much, Serena," Joanna said, closing her eyes in relief.

Serena took this opportunity to actually look at Joanna straight in the face, which she almost never did. She was a beautiful woman, the kind with naturally jet black hair and white, porcelain skin. She had just a few absolutely adorable freckles dotting her nose. She also looked very tired. Serena quickly got on her coat and left.

As she walked over to the school, Serena thought about having to make conversation with Kip. She really didn't understand eight-year-old boys and would have to say she didn't really even like them all that much. Every seven- to thirteen-year-old boy Serena had ever come into contact with had seemed to be a maze of uncommunicativeness and superhero obsessions and video games. Really, who could care less, except their mothers, whose job it was to blast through that crap with maternal goodness and feminine tenderness so they could rest easy knowing they weren't raising the next generation of hazing frat boys and date rapists.

Kip was no different. He was all Xbox and Club Penguin and boredom. He was impenetrable and somewhat spoiled and Serena was always more than happy to be invisible around him and he was more than happy not to notice that she even existed. Especially now with her crazy short hair. The only person in the whole world who could get him to light up, giggle, act silly, and talk nonstop was his father. When he wasn't working, Robert would pick Kip up after school, and they would burst through the door, sounding like they were in the middle of an outraged debate, both refusing to back down from their impassioned positions. It might be about who they thought it would be better to be, Flash or Batman, or which they would rather eat, dirt or sand. They might take off their shoes and try to settle the argument by seeing who could slide the farthest in just his socks. Robert would tickle Kip and reduce this stoic pre-man to fits of squirmy laughter.

Now, Serena was standing in front of the school practicing the casual, cheerful, but not too cheerful expression on her face that she would have when Kip first saw her. An expression that immediately showed him, before his stomach could leap anywhere near his heart, that everything was fine, there was no emergency, and this was just a pesky little deviation from an otherwise normal day. The doors opened and teachers and children started streaming out of the school. Kip took one look at Serena and his eyes grew wide, his normally impenetrable face filled with fear. Serena got to him as quickly as possible to allay his fears.

"Your mom's busy but everything's fine. She just got tied up with a few things."

Serena hoped to God that she wasn't lying. She knew there were probably a million reasons why his breathing was labored and was sure the nurse was there right now taking care of it. Even though Robert was sick, even though things looked very bad, still, from her narrow perspective she couldn't imagine Robert would actually die. Movie stars don't die of cancer. Name one young, handsome movie star who died of cancer. None. They just don't.

"Let's go home and you can see for yourself," she said as she put her arm gently on his shoulder.

As they turned the corner at Watts Street, they both saw the ambulance at the same time. Serena instinctively went to put her hand on Kip's shoulder but he was already running. They were only half a block away and Serena could see Joanna coming out of the building next to a stretcher. Serena began to run, too, to catch up with Kip. Her greatest fear as she watched the stretcher come out was that there would be a sheet covering his head. *Please make it not covering his head.* As she got closer, she saw Robert on the stretcher with an oxygen mask on his face. Alive. Joanna was crying as she walked quickly behind the EMS workers. She looked up and saw Kip. She tried to return her face to that of a cheerful mother, but she couldn't. Kip was now right by her, crying, too.

"What happened?" Kip screamed, his voice childish and raw.

"Daddy was having a hard time breathing," Joanna said, the one sentence she was able to get out calmly before she started to sob again. Serena didn't want to intrude, but she went to Joanna and put her arm around her. Joanna then turned and buried her face into Serena's shoulder. She began to sob deeply.

Serena looked over at Kip. He was staring at his mother with enormous confusion and terror in his eyes. He turned away the minute he saw Serena look at him.

Joanna quickly picked her head up and looked at Kip as well. She wiped her eyes and went over to him. She crouched down to talk to him.

"I have to go in the ambulance with Daddy . . ." she began to say. Kip didn't let her finish her sentence; he just started screaming.

"No! No!" he wailed, as he stomped his feet and flailed his arms around.

It was then that Serena noticed something out of the corner of her eye. She looked up and saw it and it started moving before she had even a moment to think about it.

The "it" was not an object, it was Steven Sergati. Steven Sergati was a man who proved that sometimes you can indeed absolutely judge a book by its cover, because he looked like a weasel. Or a rat. His long, slicked-back black hair slid down his back, ending in a long little rodent tail. His pointy eyes hid behind a pair of five-dollar glasses, bought cheap because they had gotten broken so often. His four front teeth jutted out into a little point that would be perfect for gnawing on phone wire, which he had probably done at some point in his life for some nefarious reason. He was the most beaten-up, sued, spit-upon snake of a cockroach of a paparazzo in all of New York City. You weren't a VIP bouncer in New York City if you hadn't given, at some point, Steven Sergati a beat-down. Preferably in some alleyway where no one saw you do it. This man was infamous for disrupting film shoots, breaking into buildings, frightening young actresses, and stalking one particular celebrity for so long and so relentlessly that the celebrity had to get a restraining order against him. He had been seen screaming at a young television star as she walked down a lovely tree-lined New York street with her newborn, shouting that she had a fat ass and no one was going to want to fuck her anymore—just so he could get a photo of her being a new mom and scowling like Medea.

Serena recognized him from a news article Robert had shown her about him last year. Robert had his own grudge against Steve, since he had picked Robert and Joanna to stalk for a period when Kip was two. But six-four Robert, a former college football player who had just finished playing an action hero, was not someone who was going to wait for a judge. And there happen to be a few little alleyways on this one strip of Tribeca. So Robert was one of a group of celebrities, which included Sean Penn, Bruce Willis, and George Clooney who had been known to issue Steve a beat-down of their own. That was the only restraining order Mr. Sergati needed and he left them alone after that.

But there he was. He had been waiting for the right moment, when he knew his enemy was vulnerable, to stage his next attack. Joanna was about to get into an ambulance with her dying husband as their son Kip, his face red and contorted, was stomping his feet and shrieking in full view of the snapping camera. Even Serena, who was not media savvy in the least, knew that a photograph of Robert's son wailing as Robert was whisked away in an ambulance would fetch a great deal of cash.

Before she knew what she was doing, she placed Kip behind the ambulance out of view and marched across the street. Not a march, really, more like a stride that sped up as she got closer to him—the way a lioness would move just before she caught an antelope and tore its rear legs off.

Steve, who was used to this sort of thing, stood up straight, raised both his hands in the air, and said, "I'm not doing anything illegal. You can't stop me!"

The only good thing about Steve Sergati was that he was painfully skinny. So it was easy for Serena to shove him down, grab his camera, and then smash it on the ground, but not before she got the digital card out of it.

"I'm going to call the cops!" Steve shrieked, in his high-pitched rat squeak. "I'm going to sue you, you bitch! You can't do that to me! I know everyone! Everyone."

Then Serena, the former swami, leaned down and got right in his face, her nose practically touching his.

"Listen, motherfucker," Serena growled in a voice that was no longer hers, "I own a gun. And if you come anywhere near this family ever again I swear to God I will blow your fucking head off." And then Serena stood up and just looked down on him lying on the ground and added, "Please. Try me."

Across the street, Joanna and Kip were looking at her as if they'd just seen a ghost. But, in fact, it was the exact opposite. For at that moment, Serena was no longer circling on the outskirts of their lives like a mist. She had plunged right into the middle of it all. She walked back across the street to the stunned Joanna. Right now there was other business to attend to.

"I haven't had time to call anyone . . ." Joanna stammered. "Do you mind staying with Kip until . . ."

"I'll stay as long as you need me. Please don't worry."

Joanna looked at Kip. "I'll call you the minute I get there, okay, sport?"

Kip nodded. The doors of the ambulance closed, and Joanna and

Robert were whisked away. Serena turned to Kip, this distraught eight-year-old male creature, and didn't know what to say to him. He took care of that for her.

Kip watched as Steve Sergati got up and rambled shakily away. Then the boy looked up at Serena, his big eyes filled with awe.

"Wow. You kicked that guy's *ass*." This was the first time in all the three years that she knew him that Kip had actually spoken to her directly.

Serena smiled. "Yeah, I guess I did." And then Serena, the superhero, took Kip back upstairs.

. . .

The afternoon after her canceled insemination, Ruby decided to go visit her mother in suburban Boston. Every now and again, a girl just needs her mommy.

On the train north, Ruby tried to figure out why she was going. What did she want to get from her mother? As the train rode through Connecticut, and she looked out at all the little houses with their covered-up pools, and their doghouses and their plastic jungle gyms, she decided that she needed to know if her mother really was as miserable back then as Ruby remembered her to be. Maybe it wasn't such hell raising her and her brother. Maybe her mother wasn't as unhappy as Ruby's childish memories made her out to be.

She rang her mother's doorbell. She lived on a quiet little street in Somerville. No one answered. She rang again, surprised—Ruby had called and told her she was coming. She walked down the driveway, around to the back of the house. Shelley was in the back raking leaves. She was now sixty-eight years old, with dyed light brown hair, which had streaks of gray in it and was cut in a short, curly little bob. She had Ruby's body—round, voluptuous, but with the added weight that comes from deciding to grow old gracefully rather than spending every spare moment at the gym. Unseen, Ruby watched her mother for a moment; she looked hearty. Comfortable in her own skin. She wondered how happy she was these days. Her mother looked up.

"Ruby!" she said, coming over and giving her daughter a big hug. "It's so wonderful to see you!"

Of course it is, because you're my mother and I'm your daughter and all mothers are always happy to see their children. There must be a reason for that.

"You look great, Ma," Ruby said, meaning it.

"So do you! So do you! Let's go inside!"

After Ruby showered and changed, she walked into the kitchen, where her mother had the tea ready. "I made some cinnamon toast, too! Just like the old times!" Ruby smiled, thinking that was such a nostalgic thing to do. Every time it snowed, there would always be cinnamon toast waiting for Ruby when she came inside. It was her mother's little tradition, one that was passed down from her own mother. The tea for them was an adult tradition, one that they shared down to the idiosyncratic detail. They both liked weak American tea—Lipton will do just fine, thank you very much—and when together, like today, they knew implicitly that they would share a tea bag between them. She sat down at the table.

"Tell me all about New York. What's going on?"

Some people have sophisticated mothers, ones they can talk to about their abstract thoughts and who can tell them where to go to buy the one bra they're looking for.

That was not Shelley, which never bothered Ruby a bit. Because what you got instead of someone who might have seen that documentary about Sudanese refugees was a mother who reacted to everything you did with complete wonder and glee. You got someone who wanted to hear everything about Manhattan and your business and your life because it was all still so exciting to her.

"Well, a new restaurant opened in the Village," Ruby said, "but no one can get in because it's always filled with the owner's friends. It's pissing everyone off."

"Really? That's so interesting. Are there a lot of celebrities there all the time?"

"Every night."

Ruby's mom just shook her head. "That's not right."

Ruby smiled. "It's not." She sipped her tea and picked up a piece of cinnamon toast. She took a bite.

"Mom. I've been wondering. About what it was like for you."

"What it was like how, dear?"

"Well, you know, as a single mother."

Shelley rolled her eyes. "Oh, it was hell. It was awful. I had a miserable time."

"Were you lonely?"

"Honey, I was so lonely that I thought about killing myself on a number of occasions. I'm not joking. It was horrible, it really was." Shelley sipped her tea. "So who is the owner of this restaurant? Is he famous, too?"

"Yeah, sort of. He runs a magazine." Ruby tried to get her mom back on track. "So, it really was just as awful an experience for you as I remember?"

"Oh, I'm sure it was worse than you remember. It was the worst time in my life," she said, with a little laugh.

Ruby took another sip of her weak tea and burst out crying. She put her elbows on the table and her head in her hands. "I'm sorry, Mom." Ruby looked up at her mother. "I'm sorry you were so unhappy. I'm so sorry."

Ruby's mom put a hand on Ruby's arm and leaned in close, smiling. "But don't you see? I'm fine now. I'm happy. I have friends and my garden and I go out all the time."

Ruby started to sob even harder. "It's too laaaaate! You needed to be happy back then! So I could think it was okay to be a single mom! It's too late!"

Shelley looked at Ruby, trying to take this in. She didn't feel attacked, just terribly sad. She touched Ruby's shoulder. "But honey, you're not like me, you're nothing like me! If you want to be a single mother, you won't be like me at all!"

Ruby leaped out of her chair, with tears streaming down her face, her voice choked and trembling. "But I'm just like you. I like tea and I'm depressed and I stay in bed and I cry a lot and I'm really, really lonely."

Ruby's mother got up and put her hands on Ruby's shoulders. "Well, if you're so much like me, then do what I did. Get yourself to a doctor and get yourself on a nice antidepressant. Lexapro worked for me."

Ruby looked at her mother, surprised.

"What?"

"I've been on an antidepressant for the past year. It's changed my life."

"You . . . what?" Ruby stammered, still trying to process this news.

"There's no reason for you to be walking around depressed. There's no good reason whatsoever. You should get a prescription, too."

Ruby sat down at the kitchen table again. It was shocking. Even after the countless nights spent crying, the days of not being able to get out of bed, Ruby had never even considered taking an antidepressant. It hadn't even crossed her mind. And yet here in the suburbs, her unsophisticated mother had beaten her to it.

She spent the rest of the day sitting at her mother's kitchen, crying. She told her about the fertility drugs, about not being able to go through with it, about how she remembered how miserable her mom was, and how it made her leave the doctor's office. It was Shelley's turn to start crying.

"I'm sorry. I'm so sorry, I should have tried harder to hide how unhappy I was, I'm so sorry."

Ruby continued to cry as well, saying, "It's not your fault. How could you have hidden that? You did your best, I know that. I do."

"Yes, but I wish someone had told me . . ."

"What?"

"That it was also my job, besides feeding you and getting you dressed, and making sure you did your homework, it was also my job to somehow make myself happy. For you. So you could see that. I'm so sorry."

Ruby reached over and held her mother's hand. "There's no way you could have done it all. There's no way." Then she and her mom sat there the rest of the day, talking and holding hands, making each other feel better and sipping their Lipton tea.

. . .

Georgia's children were staring at Mark Levine. Mark Levine was smiling a wide, closed-lipped smile, as if he had just caught something in his mouth that he didn't want to let out, but wanted to make sure everyone knew he was happy.

"So," he began. "How are you two today?"

Beth and Gareth looked at him blankly. Georgia had some sort of satisfaction at this. Her kids instinctively knew he was an asshole and that they shouldn't talk to him. His lips went back to their closed smile. He tried again.

"I'm here because your mother and dad want me to find out how you two are doing now that your dad isn't living here anymore."

Silence.

"For instance, I heard that one night you were left all alone, isn't that right? And were you scared?"

Georgia looked down at her hands. She felt beads of sweat popping up on her forehead. She had never before realized how much energy it could take to *not* kill someone.

Again, silence. Blessed, hostile, sullen, child silence.

Mark Levine looked at Georgia. "Maybe it would be best if I spoke to them on my own?"

Georgia looked at him, startled. "But . . . I didn't know that you're allowed to . . ."

"We are absolutely allowed to question the children without you in the room. For your protection, I have a tape recorder so it's not just my word you'll have to take."

Georgia, of course, wanted to protest, but considering how the last meeting went, she decided to restrain herself.

"Of course you can. I'll just go into my bedroom and shut the door."

"Thank you," Mark Levine said. "This shouldn't take too long."

Georgia stood up and looked at her children. Her children who were now her judge, jury, and executioner. Her moody, fibbing, childish, adorable, bratty, unpredictable children who were now going to have every word they said written down as if they were the Dalai Lama. Georgia glanced at Gareth. *Last week he had an imaginary friend who was a giant tarantula. Yeah, talk to them about who they want to live with. Motherfucker.*

"Now you talk to Mr. Levine, okay? Tell the truth and answer all his questions. We both want you to just say how you feel, okay?"

She then walked slowly and confidently back to her bedroom. When she got to her room she closed the door and threw herself on her bed, buried her face in a pillow, and let out as loud a scream as she dared. After a moment, she sat up and stared into space.

Georgia wondered how she had gotten here; to a place where a court might rule that she was an unfit mother. She thought about her marriage. Images started flashing before her eyes of the fight she had with Dale on the street once about how he never picked up the mail. She thought about how she would snap at him in the morning, because he always dumped coffee grounds on the counter—and there's nothing she hated more than having to wipe up coffee grounds and then wrestle them off the sponge. She thought about how stupid she thought he was for never knowing how to use the microwave, or how angry he would get when the paper wasn't delivered correctly, but would never bother to call and complain about it. She wondered when she started disliking him so much, and when she became so unrestrained in making him aware of that. It must have been after the kids came. She heard that was common in marriages. Why was that? After they are done procreating, do women subconsciously decide the man has fulfilled his duty, and so they let him know in big and small ways that they have no use for him any longer? Why would she feel that way? It was not like she wanted to be a single mother. It was not that she wanted to go out and date again.

She thought about Sam and buying herself all those flowers. She thought about dancing on top of the bar and the man telling her to get off because he wanted a hotter girl to get on. She thought about chasing the guy down at Whole Foods. It was all coming in flashes, each image more humiliating than the next. And of course, she thought about the Bryan frenzy that caused her to feel the need to run out of the house, leaving her two children alone.

She realized then that she really had gone crazy. And she had no one to blame but herself. In the marriage, she felt entitled to have unbridled irritation for Dale at any time, with any provocation. Then, being left by Dale made her feel entitled to act without any restraint whatsoever. Somehow she had lost control of herself, and now she had lost control over her own motherhood. She sat wondering what her kids could possibly be saying about her. She remembered when she was called to the school after Gareth had hit another boy. She came and talked to the principal while Gareth sat on a bench in the hall outside, nervous and ashamed. *Well, the tables have certainly turned, haven't they?*

After about twenty-five minutes, which was an eternity, Georgia decided to peek her head out and see what was going on. *I am their mother, after all.*

"Just making sure everything is all right!" Georgia said, with her body in the bedroom, her head leaning out into the hallway.

Everyone was where they were before, the two kids on one sofa facing Mark Levine on the other. No one seemed particularly traumatized, no one seemed particularly angry at her.

"We're actually done, perfect timing," Mark Levine said.

There was nothing in his demeanor to suggest that anything particularly earth-shattering or indicting had been said. He gave Georgia his usual tight smile, said good-bye to the children, and left.

Georgia looked at her children. They didn't seem upset or angry. But still, she wanted very badly to ask them to act out the entire twenty-five-minute interview. But instead, Georgia did something she hadn't done in a very long time; *she showed restraint.* Georgia walked into the living room and up to Beth and Gareth and sat down next to them. She gently asked, "Are you guys okay?" They both nodded. She looked at them carefully, to see if there was anything that needed to be done. "Do either of you have any questions?" They didn't say anything. They looked okay; unharmed.

"Okay, then. Who wants a snack?"

10

*Remember That Sometimes There Are More
Important Things Than You and Your Lousy Love Life
AND
Get Your Friends More Involved in Helping You
with Your Lousy Love Life*

Basically, I cried all the way to India. And by this point, I didn't care who saw me. The man next to me asked if he could change his seat (which he was able to do) and two flight attendants asked me if I needed anything.

When I arrived, a friend of a friend of a friend of Serena's from the yoga center, a woman named Amrita, was going to meet me. I had no idea what would make this perfect stranger be willing to do this, but I was very grateful. I didn't have the will to be adventurous and strong. I had an image of India of lepers begging on the streets and cows running rampant. But I also read *Time Out Mumbai* between crying jags on the plane, and I couldn't imagine that a city where they had a *Time Out* review of performance art would also have cows and begging children. So, I didn't know what to expect.

As I walked into the airport, the first thing I thought was that it didn't look very different than any other airport I had been to, just less modern. It had the white walls and floors, fluorescent lighting, signs telling you where to go. But after I got my bags and walked outside, I knew I was in India. There was chaos everywhere. Men standing next to their dilapidated taxis were calling loudly to passengers coming out of the airport. Cars were jammed up against one another, honking and trying to get out of the parking lot. The air was thick and hot. There was an odd, unidentifiable odor everywhere.

If I weren't meeting Serena's extended friend, I might have had a nervous breakdown right there. But as soon as I walked out, a beautiful woman with long, thick black hair, and wearing jeans and a loose-fitting cotton tunic, came up to me. "Excuse me, are you Julie?"

"Yes I am. You must be Amrita."

"I am. Welcome to Mumbai."

We got into her little car and she took off. It was dark, so it was difficult for me to really see out the window. But I thought I could make out makeshift huts and lean-tos on the sides of the road, and people sleeping out on the street, but I wasn't sure. I was hoping I was mistaken.

Amrita cheerfully asked me about my project.

"I heard you're writing a book about single women all over the world."

I cringed. It was really the last thing I wanted to talk about. I straightened her out.

"I'm here just to find comfort. I've heard it's such a spiritual place."

Amrita nodded, silently. Well, she didn't really nod. She had this odd little habit of bobbling her head in a way that made you not really sure if she was saying "yes" or "no." She also had a habit of honking an enormous amount while she was driving, a habit most of the other drivers shared with her.

As Amrita tapped on her horn, she said, "Most of the yoga ashrams are outside of Mumbai. Were you planning on going to one of those?"

"Yes, my friend Serena suggested one."

She kept driving and honking. I squinted out the window and saw a young couple zip by on a moped. The woman was wearing a sari and it flapped in the wind as she rode sidesaddle.

Amrita spoke again. "I think this idea of how to be single is a very good one. There are many decisions we have to make when we're single. Very important ones."

She furrowed her thick, black eyebrows. She seemed to have something on her mind. I couldn't help but ask . . .

"What decisions do you have to make?"

Amrita shrugged. "I'm thirty-five. My family is pressuring me to get married. I have been dating, hoping for a love marriage. But . . ."

She looked like she was about to cry. Here's the last thing I felt like hearing about: someone else's lousy love life. But I took a deep breath and listened.

"The last man I dated had no money. I paid for everything. Dinners, movies, even trips. My family thought I was crazy. They said he was using me. One time, we went shopping, and he asked me to buy him a sweater. And I did! Then he broke up with me, just like that."

Tears started to fall down her cheeks. I felt like Angela Lansbury in *Murder, She Wrote*. Every time she went anywhere, even on vacation, the poor old gal stumbled across a murder. Everywhere I went, relationship dramas seemed to unfold.

"He said I was too independent, too focused on my career." The tears kept falling. She kept driving and honking. I nodded, trying to be sympathetic.

"Yeah, well, it seems like he didn't mind your career when it could buy him a sweater."

Amrita bobbled her head vigorously. "Exactly. I think I dated him so long because my family hated him. I thought they were being racist, because we're Brahmins, and he's Vaishya. But now I see they were right."

I looked out the window again and saw what appeared to be an entire family on a moped. A father, mother, son, and daughter all squeezed in together. I blinked. Yep, that's what I saw.

I was extremely tired. I was so grateful to Amrita for allowing me not to have to take a cab from the airport, but I really just wanted her to shut up.

"So now, I am letting my family find him. They have been looking on the matrimonial sites and have picked out some men for me. Their horoscopes look good, and so I'm going to start meeting them."

Okay, that woke me up. Matrimonial sites? Horoscopes? As we drove into the city through narrow streets, she told me about the popularity of the matrimonial sites, which are just like dating sites but for the specific purpose of arranging marriages. She told me that often it's the family that puts the son or daughter's photo up.

"Well, that's kind of great, sparing the actual people the embarrassment and hassle of doing it themselves."

Amrita's eyebrows rose. "But that's not why they do it. They do it because it's understood that parents know better who would be a good match for their children than the children themselves." I thought of my own romantic decisions. This idea was beginning to make sense to me.

She also explained the important role the horoscope played in matchmaking, all about the planets and moons and birth time—I got the impression that it wasn't the same kind of astrology that the *New York Post* employed to tell me what kind of day I was going to have.

"If the astrology is not a good match, I won't even meet the man." I was definitely not in the West Village anymore.

We parked near where I would be staying, a modest "economy" hotel in South Mumbai. As Amrita helped me roll my luggage down the street, I realized that these single Indian women have something that we American women don't really have: a backup plan. They can go out into the world, discarding their families' outdated views on marriage to look for love on their own—and if it doesn't work out, their moms and dads and aunts and uncles and cousins and sisters-in-law are more than happy to swoop in and get things cracking.

"Would you like to meet my sister tomorrow? She decided on an arranged marriage, and she's very happy."

I looked at Amrita, surprised. I was planning on spending the day crying and then maybe figuring out how to get to the ashram Serena recommended. I was over the whole "research" aspect of this trip and was looking forward to just doing shoulder stands and drinking mango lassis.

"I think it might be good research for your book." I didn't know how to tell her that I'd rather gnaw off my arm and beat myself over the head with it until I passed out than go talk to a happily married couple about how in love they are. So instead, I said, "I'd love to."

"Good. I'll pick you up at noon? Is that okay?" I agreed and checked in.

My room was small, with two double beds, a television, and a desk. It was no marble-covered Bali bungalow, but then we're not in Bali anymore, are we? Or China. We're in India. And I still didn't quite understand what that meant.

The next day, I was back in the car with Amrita. The difference between driving with her then, as opposed to the previous evening, was the difference, well, between night and day. As we spoke about her sister Ananda, it was difficult for me not to notice the poverty now fully visible outside my window. On the highways, you could see crumbled and dirty buildings that seemed more like bunkers than places to live. But going into the town where we were supposed to be meeting her sister, I saw the images that one might see taken by any photojournalist in any third world country: the naked children on the street walking next to what had to be raw sewage. Children, not in school, but playing on heaps of rubble. Older children banging on pieces of tin scraps, as some kind of menial job. And mothers walking around, barefoot, in and out of their little makeshift huts, right on the side of the road. When our car came to a stop, a little girl banged on my window. She had a dirty face and big black vacant eyes, and she kept putting her fingers to her mouth, in a gesture that seemed to be her way of saying she was begging for money for food. Amrita saw me look at her.

"Don't give these children money. It's all organized crime. They have to give the money to someone who is in charge of this neighborhood. They go to you because you're white and they think you'll feel bad for them."

I looked at the girl as she kept putting her fingers to her lips. Well, I did feel bad for her, actually. Was I really supposed to just drive by without doing anything? Yes, I was. And we did. As we drove through this village, right by the ocean, I decided I didn't want to become the cliché. I didn't want to be one of those tourists who go to India and then come back and tell people with that tone of overwrought pity in their voice, "Oh, India, the poverty there, it's just *unimaginable*." This wasn't my country, this wasn't my problem, and I don't know a damn thing about anything.

We drove up a road and into a high-rise building with a wraparound parking lot. Over to the side there was a lawn area, green and lush with trees and bushes and benches. This seemed like a fancy place to live, by Mumbai standards, even though the building, no matter how high-end, seemed to be covered in a thin layer of soot. But come to think of it, that could be said of all Mumbai.

The few things I felt I knew about India before coming here was that one must never, *ever*, drink the water. This was such a serious issue that I read you shouldn't even brush your teeth with the stuff, and as much as possible, turn your face away from it when you were showering.

But here I was, sitting in front of this woman, a woman who had allowed me into her home, who was about to talk to me about her marriage just to help me with my book, who was now holding out a glass of water for me to take.

"You must be thirsty; it's very hot today."

I took the glass and watched her watch me not drink from it. Not wanting her to think that I thought her water, and thereby her home, was dirty, I took a sip.

"Thank you. I appreciate it." I imagined the germs and the parasites now swimming down my throat and into my intestines.

"Amrita told me that you are writing a book about love and being single all over the world?" Ananda asked.

I nodded my head politely. "I am. It's been a very interesting experience."

Ananda and Amrita sat on a sofa together, with me in the armchair across from them. One of Ananda's daughters, around five years old, came and sat on her lap. She had short black hair with a little pink plastic clip pushing her bangs back.

"So, Amrita said that you decided to go with an arranged marriage, instead of a love match?"

Ananda nodded her head. She seemed excited to speak. "Yes. I had just finished my master's in psychology. I wasn't sure what I was going to do next, but I was thinking about going to get my doctorate. I had been dating on my own, like Amrita."

I looked at the two of them. I had found Amrita to be very attractive, but now seeing her with her sister, I saw that Ananda was probably the one who was considered the prettiest. She was more petite than her sister, and her delicate features made her seem a bit more regal.

"I wasn't like Amrita. When my parents would tell us every now and then that they had a boy they wanted us to meet, Amrita would always refuse." She put a hand on Amrita's shoulder. "I would at least humor them."

Amrita shrugged her shoulders, a bit regretfully, it seemed to me. She jumped in to help with the story. "So one day, my parents said they wanted her to meet someone. So this man came with his family to our home. The families talked for a bit . . ."

"And then we went on the terrace to chat. He seemed nice. After twenty minutes he asked what I thought. I said, 'Okay, why not?' So we came downstairs and told our parents that we would get married."

They both started laughing at the memory of it. Ananda continued. "My parents were shocked. You should have seen their faces. They thought this was going to be another boy I just sent away."

Amrita added, "When she called me and told me, I thought she was playing a joke on me. It took her a half hour just to convince me that she was serious . . ."

I was so confused. "But . . . I don't understand . . . was it love at first sight? Were you just tired of dating?"

Ananda shrugged. "I don't know. He seemed nice."

I looked at her, with her five-year-old snuggled beside her. I didn't know how to ask this politely, but here I was and there they were, so . . .

"And so . . . it worked out? You're happy?"

"Yes!"

Amrita decided to elaborate for her sister. "She's very happy. He's a very good man. It's one of the reasons I'm letting my parents help now. Because it worked so well for her. I always thought it was just a fluke, that she just got lucky. But now, I don't know. Maybe my parents and the horoscopes do know best. Maybe if I meet someone whom I have no expectations about whatsoever, there's more of a chance it will work out."

Ananda smiled. "Tonight, she's meeting two men, one after the other. It's different than when my parents got married. Amrita would never be forced to marry someone she didn't want to marry. We get to decide."

I thought about all the women I knew in New York and around the world, who might want to rethink the whole idea of letting people get involved in their love lives. Maybe one way to deal with looking for your mate after a certain age is to put an APB out on him. Maybe it was time to notify the authorities, set up roadblocks, and send out a search party.

"How long did you date before you married?" I asked.

"Two months," Ananda said. "We saw each other once or twice a week."

At this point, it seemed like just as valid a way of doing things as dating someone for five years and then finding out he can't commit. Or going to Bali with a married man and pretending he's not married. It's so crazy it just might work.

Amrita drove me back to the hotel. Through the slums and the huts and the sewage and the shoeless children. Again Amrita noticed my discomfort at it all. She tried to make me feel better. "They're not unhappy, these people, you know?"

I looked at her, not sure what she could possibly mean.

"This is what they know, this is their lives. They're happy. They don't have the same expectations as you or I."

I looked out my window and saw a toddler, a gorgeous tan child, about two years old, standing by the street in the dirt in front of his little "hut." He was adorable in a little pair of pink shorts and a white t-shirt. Finally, a sweet sight. And just as I was taking in this adorable sight, a waterfall of pee gushed down his legs, completely soaking his shorts and forming a puddle right around his bare feet. I watched him as he just stood there, unfazed. My stomach immediately tied up in a knot. It was clear he was not going to be cleaned up any time soon. And at that, the car moved on.

After I wished Amrita good luck with her two dates that night, I went to my room and took a shower and then went to sleep.

After my nap, I decided to get dressed up and go to a trendy restaurant suggested by *Time Out Mumbai* called Indigo, right down the block. As I walked in, I saw what must be considered the beautiful people of Mumbai. The men were in jackets and jeans and pressed shirts; the women in dresses and heels. I think I even spied a few gay Indian men, which somehow comforted me and made me feel at home. I took the stairs to the top floor, which opened up onto a roof-garden restaurant with an enclosed lounge area off to the side.

I went into the lounge and straight to the bar. I ordered a white wine and I sat down near three done-up Indian ladies in their thirties who were all smoking and drinking and talking very loudly in English. As the bartender served me my drink, I remembered an image from the drive back to the hotel: an Indian family who lived outside under a highway; three of the children were running around in the dirt, playing, while the mother sat there with their belongings in a little circle around her. Then my mind flashed to the little boy peeing on himself. I shook my head, trying to dislodge the image.

"I was just remembering a little boy I saw today. On the street. It was very upsetting."

The bartender nodded. "You know, these people. They're not un-happy."

That old chestnut again. "You mean they like living in the dirt and banging on tin for a living?"

"It's what they know. It's their life. Yes, they're happy."

I sipped my wine and nodded at him politely. Clearly, I just didn't get it.

To the right of me, these three women were discussing something of the utmost importance. And, being me, I decided to start more assertive eavesdropping. It seemed that one of them was having problems with someone she was dating. He didn't want to see her as much as she wanted to see him. She was telling her friends that she liked him, so it seemed crazy just to break up with him, but at the same time she hated not getting to see him. She was very agitated, waving her arms around, running her fingers through her hair. Her friends were trying to help, asking questions and giving suggestions.

I almost fell asleep right there at the bar. I mean, really. I didn't come all the way to Asia, by way of Europe, South America, and Australia, just to hear this shit. Congratulations, Mumbai ladies. I'm so happy that you have worked hard for your independence and your singleness. You've gone against tradition and your family and you are going out and getting jobs and living in your own apartments and having drinks at bars and taking men home with you. Now that you aren't being forced to marry men you don't love and have children you don't want, this is how you are rewarded: you get to sit in bars just like the rest of the women all over the world and complain about some guy not liking you enough. Welcome to the party. Isn't it fun?!

If I were being ambitious and inquisitive I would have asked them if they would ever go back to the way it was. I would have asked them if they would ever consider marrying someone their parents set them up with when they were a bit older. I should have asked them if they felt it's worth it to refuse to settle, even though it might mean they stay single for a long, long time. But I didn't because I couldn't care less about them and their stupid dating problems. I just cared about me and my stupid dating problems. I paid for my drink and left the lounge. I walked down the stairs—and with each step downward, so went my mood.

As I headed back to my hotel, I was deeply depressed. I decided that I felt cheated. *Great, that's all I was given. A couple of weeks of love. That was it for me. And now I have to go back out there and look for it again. But this time he has to be someone whom I like just as much as Thomas, but is also completely available to me. Yeah. That's going to happen soon.*

The next morning I decided to stay in bed. You can do that when you're all the way across the world and you're depressed and there's no one that's calling trying to cheer you up. I stayed in bed until one in the afternoon. I hadn't done that since I was a teenager and it felt great. Then the phone rang and it was Amrita. I asked her how her fix-ups went last night.

"Well, they really weren't my type. But they were nice. My mother and father have two more for me tonight."

"Wow, they've been busy," I said, trying to seem interested. Which I wasn't. I pulled the covers to my chin and tucked myself tight into my bed.

"Yes, they have. It will be very interesting to see who comes tonight," she said, brightly.

I rolled over to my right side, while moving the phone to my left ear. "You sound a little excited about this."

Amrita laughed. "I have to say, I am. It's really nice to have someone else worrying about my love life for a while. It's a great relief, actually."

I thought about this idea for a moment and I liked it: handing the crisis that is your singlehood over to other people and make it *their* problem. I wondered how I could stay in India, get adopted into a family, and make them take care of all this shit for me.

"Anyway, I was wondering if you wanted to come tonight to watch. For your book."

I rolled onto my back and rested my arm on my forehead. "Well, actually. I was planning on going to that ashram today at some point . . ."

"You can do that tomorrow. Tonight you'll get to see me meet these men. It will be like those reality shows you Americans enjoy so much. Very voyeuristic."

"But isn't this a private thing between families?"

"Yes, but no matter. I'll tell them you're visiting from New York, and had nowhere else to go. It'll be fine."

As it was already one in the afternoon and I hadn't gotten out of bed, I realized the odds of me finding my way to this ashram today were slim. So I agreed to go. After all, it would be great research for my *book*.

Just then the hotel phone rang again. It was Alice. I had sent her my travel info because that's what one does when they don't have a husband or a boyfriend looking out for them. Can you tell? I was a little bitter.

"Julie, hey, how are you?"

She sounded distressed, so I lied. "I'm good, how are you?"

I heard Alice take a deep breath. Then, "I don't think I can go through with this, you know? The marriage. Iceland. I don't think I can."

"Why not?" I asked, even though I knew the reason.

"Because I'm not in love with Jim. I love him, I'm so fond of him, but I'm not in love with him. I'm not."

Now, this is the part of the story where the best friend tells her *of course you shouldn't marry a man you don't love. Of course you shouldn't settle. Of course there will be someone better out there for you.* But I was in Mumbai, for God's sake. I couldn't be held responsible for what I did or said.

"Alice, listen to me. *Listen to me.* You marry him, do you understand me? *Marry him.*"

There was a long silence on the other end.

"Really?"

"Yes, really. This whole falling-in-love thing is bullshit, it's an illusion, it doesn't mean anything, and it doesn't last. Are you and Jim compatible?"

"Yes."

"Do you two respect each other? Do you like to take care of each other?"

"Yes."

"Then *marry him*. We have been brainwashed to have these high expectations. Marry him and love him and make a family and have a good life. The rest is just a lie."

"Really?"

"Yes, really. Go through with it. You'll regret it later if you don't."

And with that I hung up the phone and went back to sleep for a while.

Amrita picked me up at my hotel to bring me to her parents' house. She was dressed in a long, gold Indian tunic, over a thin pair of black cotton pants. She was wearing red lipstick and a little mascara. She looked quite beautiful.

"I could have taken a cab. You shouldn't have to worry about driving me on a night when you might be meeting your husband," I joked.

Amrita shook her head. "The cabdrivers will rip you off if you don't know where you're going."

And then we were at it again—driving through frickin' Mumbai. Getting another glimpse of its house of horrors. At one point, we stopped at a red light, and I heard a loud crack on the window of my car. I looked over and saw a young girl at my window. She had banged her head against it to get my attention. She was around seven years old and was holding a baby in her arms. Then she took one of her hands and brought it up to her mouth, over and over again. I looked over at Amrita, my mouth open, tears forming in my eyes. She was unmoved. She drove on.

After a few moments in silence, I tried to form a question, anything to try and understand things. I asked her, "Do these children go to school?"

Amrita bobbled her head. "Some do, but most don't. These people are mostly Muslims, so they don't really believe in education. They want their children to start businesses."

"You mean like selling peanuts on the street?" I asked, a little sarcastically. I really wasn't getting it.

Amrita nodded her head. "Yes, like that." We drove the rest of the way in silence.

We arrived at another large high-rise, this one so tall and pristine it looked like it had been built and painted the day before. We drove past tennis courts and an outdoor swimming pool. In the lobby, a uniformed man waited to let us in.

Amrita's parents politely greeted me at the door and invited me in. Amrita's mother, Mrs. Ramani, was dressed in a traditional blue and white sari, with a long-sleeved cotton t-shirt underneath it. Mr. Ramani wore simple trousers and a button-down shirt. There were also three other older women sitting in the living room, with another older man. They were introduced to me as Amrita's grandmother, uncle, and two aunts. I was invited to sit down on a sofa next to Amrita's grandmother. Amrita's mother brought me a glass of water. Like hell I was going to offend anyone right now, so I took a nice sip and set it down on the coaster next to me.

Amrita sat down and they all started speaking in Hindi, and from what I could tell from the gestures, one of the aunts was complimenting Amrita on how she looked. Then the father started talking for a bit, and everyone was listening very intently.

"He's telling us about the first man that I'm going to meet. He's an engineer who works for the city, something to do with the gas and the oil lines. Our horoscopes are very compatible, and he has no problem with the fact that I work."

"And her age. He does not need a young wife," her father added.

Everyone nodded their heads gratefully.

"He lived in the States for two years. He's very modern," Amrita's father told me.

I felt extremely awkward being there, in the middle of all this. I didn't know where I should be when the man and his family arrived.

"Would you like me to go outside or to another room when they come . . . ?"

Amrita's mother looked at her husband. The husband thought for a moment. In that moment's pause, I jumped in with "You know, when the family gets here, I'll just go outside and get some air. So you can have your privacy."

The mother and father looked at each other. The father bobbled in agreement. "You can go in the other room with Amrita, while we talk."

The doorbell rang and Amrita's mother went to the door. Amrita nervously waved for me to get up and we scurried into a nearby bedroom like two teenage girls.

We waited there, sitting on the bed cross-legged.

"What are they talking about?" I asked.

"The parents have to make sure they like each other. This is very important. They both must feel we come from good families."

"And what makes a family seem like a good family?"

"Well, first, these men are all from the Brahmin caste, like my family, so that already is very helpful."

"Does the caste system really matter anymore?"

"Not as much as before, but with things like marriages it does."

"Really?" I thought the whole system was long gone.

"In a way, yes. The Brahmins, my caste, were the priests and teachers, the intellectuals. Then you have the people who were the farmers. Then the people who were the laborers. It's very similar to your country, with the blue-collar and the white-collar workers, but here it comes from a long tradition, and we've given them names."

"But what about the untouchables. Is that what those people are? The ones on the street?" I asked Amrita.

"Yes."

"So they are born poor and they're going to die poor, with no hope of advancing themselves?"

Amrita bobbled her head. "The government is starting to help them, but this is what they know."

I didn't want to get into a political argument with her while she was backstage before her big date, but still, it was a hard topic for me to comprehend. Amrita could sense my disapproval.

"You tourists, you come to Mumbai and you see the poverty and you take your photographs. You go home and you think you've seen Mumbai. But that's not all Mumbai is. That's not all that India is." She sounded defensive. I thought I should change the subject.

"So, what else do the families talk about together?"

"They want to know if the father has a good job, if the other siblings are responsible and have good jobs. Mostly, they want to know if they are all well educated. That's very important."

After an hour, Mrs. Ramani knocked and walked in.

"You can meet him now," she said, with a timid smile on her face. "His family is very nice."

Amrita looked at me, gave a little shrug of "here goes nothing," and walked out the door. I sat back on her childhood bed. I was exhausted. I sat there for a few minutes staring at the wall in front of me. Just as I started to drift off, the door opened again and Mrs. Ramani came in.

"His family has left. She is going out for a walk with him. Come out and sit with us."

I quickly jumped up, trying not to look as if I had just fallen asleep in their home.

"Thank you. That would be nice."

I sat down on the sofa. Amrita's family was still all assembled. We were just awkwardly staring at one another, so I decided to jump right in with my so-called "research."

"I find it interesting how important a role astrology plays in marriages here in India."

Mr. Ramani bobbled his head emphatically. "It is everything. We saw matches online, from very good families, from our community, with good jobs. But the horoscopes were not compatible. So it could not be."

Mrs. Ramani bobbled in agreement.

"We don't have that in America. It's a very odd concept to me," I said.

Mr. Ramani got up and started to walk around the living room, explaining it all to me like a schoolteacher.

"It's very simple. A marriage must be composed of three things: you must be emotionally compatible, intellectually compatible, and physically compatible. If you don't have all three, a marriage will not work."

I was surprised by the "physically compatible" part. I had assumed that the sex life of the couple was the least of anyone's concerns.

"Relationships start out very fast, with a burst, a lot of attraction, but it does not last. This is because they were not compatible. The horoscopes can tell you if they will be truly compatible. Who can predict that? Not the couple. Not the family. But the horoscope can."

As he was talking, I became more and more intrigued. If this was true, then it meant that these people had figured out years ago something that still perplexed us stupid Americans. How do you know if your relationship will last? If you were to go solely by the incredibly low divorce rate in India (1 percent), one could assume that they might be on to something. Of course, there are many more factors at work, such as how different their expectations are when they go into a marriage, as opposed to ours. I decided to continue my probing.

"If you don't mind me asking, where does romance come into this?"

Mr. Ramani kept pacing around the room. What appeared at first to be his enthusiasm for teaching me about Indian culture now seemed to me to be nothing more than a case of nerves. It dawned on me, as I watched him yank his hands in and out of his pockets and walk around the room, that he was simply a nervous father waiting for his daughter to come home from her date.

"Romance. What is romance? Romance means nothing," he said, as his lips curled upward in distaste.

Mrs. Ramani seemed to agree. "This is a very Western idea. With Indian marriages, you don't think about romance. You think about taking care of each other. I take care of him," she said as she pointed toward Mr. Ramani, "and he takes care of me." She put her hand to her heart. I smiled agreeably. The image of Thomas taking care of me when I was having my panic attack on the plane quickly flashed in my mind. It felt like a tear through my flesh.

Mr. Ramani continued. "These men you see, who try to be romantic. They say 'Honey baby this, honey baby that.' If he can say 'honey baby' to you, that means he can say 'honey baby' to the next girl. These words don't mean anything."

I thought about Thomas. How he called me "my darling." Until his other darling came halfway across the world to take *her* darling back.

Mr. Ramani glanced at the clock. Amrita had been gone almost an hour.

Mrs. Ramani asked, "So, how old are you?"

"I'm thirty-eight."

"And you aren't married?" The two aunts perked up at this question, looking at me and waiting for my answer.

"No, no, I'm not." My glass of water was still on the coffee table and I nervously took a sip.

The grandmother seemed to understand what I had just said, but she spoke Hindi to Amrita's father. He translated the question she had for me. "Why are you still unmarried?" Ah, *that* question again. I considered which response I should use this time. After a few seconds, I just went with the obvious. "I guess I haven't met the right guy yet," I said.

Mr. Ramani translated, and the grandmother looked at me sadly. One of the aunts spoke up in English. "Isn't your family looking for someone for you?"

They all looked at me intently. I shook my head. "No, we really don't do that in the States. We don't get our families involved like that."

"But don't they want you to get married?" Mrs. Ramani asked, the un-mistakable tone of worry having crept into her voice.

I am much more comfortable when I do the inquiring. I took another sip of water. "They do, very much. But I guess they think I'm happy the way I am."

Now the uncle spoke up. "This cannot be," he said. "The human being is designed for many things. Loneliness is not one of them."

I swallowed hard. I tried to nod in agreement. My stomach tightened into a little knot again.

Mrs. Ramani leaned into me, and said, as a statement of fact, "We are not meant to go through this life alone."

I tried to force out a smile, but the blood started draining out of my face. I looked at all of them staring at me. And, being the good emotional wreck that I was, tears started rolling down my face.

"May I use your bathroom?" I asked, my voice shaky. Everyone looked at one another, not sure what to do.

Mrs. Ramani stood up. "Yes, yes, of course, please come with me."

I sobbed for a few moments in the Ramanis' toilet, as quietly as I could. After about five minutes, I heard Amrita's voice and what sounded like a lot of commotion. Bored with my own drama, I blew my nose, splashed water on my face (which, may I remind you, *never works*), and went out. Just as I got to the living room, Mr. Ramani turned to me smiling, and said, "We have a match! They are going to be married!"

Amrita was beaming. His parents were smiling and hugging their son. Her now-betrothed, a tall man with very thick black hair combed away from his face, and a thick black mustache, looked like he was about to start dancing a jig. I just stood there with puffy eyes watching the whole scene unfold before me like a Merchant-Ivory film.

When the hugging and kissing started to slow down, Amrita came over to me. She took my hand and walked a few feet away from everyone else. "He was so nice. We just talked and talked. We have so much in common. He's really funny and smart! I'm so lucky! I can't believe I'm going to get married!" She hugged me, laughing. "I would never have met this man on my own. Ever!"

I couldn't help but marvel at the speed of all this. In New York, if you like the guy a lot—you go on a second date. Here, you plan the engagement ceremony. But if you consider how truly miraculous it is to meet anyone you want to go on a second date with, maybe they have the right idea. Maybe wanting to go on a second date with someone is proof that you might as well just get engaged, give it a shot, and nail that shit down.

Mr. Ramani had taken out a bottle of champagne that he was saving for just this occasion, and Amrita's mother was handing out glasses. Both families were absolutely ecstatic. The reason was obvious: these two lost souls who were floating around for years, unmoored, loose strands in the fabric of society, who were not designed for loneliness, had now found their place. They were now a couple within two families, that would start their own family. In this one decision, in this one hour, they had given themselves a place in the world, neatly carved out, ready to go.

Besides the fact that I was intruding on an extremely private moment, I also realized that if I didn't get away from all this matrimonial glee I was going to hurl myself out a window. I asked Amrita to call me a cab, and I left as soon as I could.

And then another car ride. Luckily it was again night, so most of the children who were normally playing and begging in the streets were now sleeping on blankets or cots along the side of the road with their families. It was bedtime in Mumbai. Still, there were some older children out, and as we came to a stoplight, one little girl, her right arm amputated below her elbow, used the truncated limb to bang on the window, her left hand putting fingers to her mouth.

The cabdriver looked at the girl and back at me. "Don't give them money. It's all an act. It's all organized crime."

I looked out the window. That was a really great act she had going

there, impersonating a poor child from India who had only half a right
arm.

"Why doesn't the government help them? Why are they being left on
the streets?"

The cabdriver just bobbled his head. The perfect answer for what is
I'm sure a complicated question. The little girl was still banging the car
with her stump.

For just a moment, I imagined what this must look like. Me, this
white American woman, all dressed up, staring at this child, and refusing
to open the window, refusing to help. I looked at the child, this dirty girl
with matted, long black hair. This was her place in the world. This was
her caste. She lived on the streets and she probably would do so her entire
life.

"Fuck that," I said quite loudly, and I opened my purse and took out
my wallet. I opened the car window and I gave her five dollars. And I did
that very same thing to the next four children who came begging to the
car during that drive. The cabdriver shook his head in disapproval, and
in my mind, I told him that he could kiss my ass. Because here's what. I
hate to be a cliché, but the poverty in Mumbai is really appalling. The
quality of life for these people is nightmarish. The fact that no one seems
to care was even more outrageous. I was the American tourist who could
only see Mumbai for its poverty. I was the American tourist who would
go back to New York and say, "Mumbai, oh my God, the poverty. *It's
awful.*" That would be me. Guilty as charged.

By the time I got to the hotel, my stomach was feeling a bit upset. But
ever since I arrived in Mumbai, due to the spicy food, the air that smells
like burning rubber, and the overall misery, my stomach had been in a
general state of displeasure anyway. So I didn't think much of it. I walked
into the hotel elevator and breathed a sigh of relief. I'm telling you, those
car rides in Mumbai could suck the light out of the sun.

As I rode the elevator to my room, the images of those children
popped into my head again. They wouldn't go away. It was like a horror
movie that played in a loop, that I was unable to turn off.

I took a shower, hoping that would somehow soothe my stomach and
clean off the car ride. I thought about how concerned these families were
for one another, concerned with getting everyone married off, making a

family, becoming part of the larger society. And here were these people, these families, just outside on the street, who would never be allowed into this society for the entirety of their lives. And these other families, the families in the houses and apartment complexes with the champagne and the education, these families didn't care one bit about those others.

As the water hit my face, I tried to tell myself that this is such a complicated issue, something that I couldn't begin to understand in just a few days. But all I could think of was the emptiness in those children's eyes. Their robotic waves as I drove on, as if they were merely shells of flesh, impersonating children.

By the time I got out of the shower, I felt nauseous. I went to the bathroom and discovered I had diarrhea. And that, folks, was the rest of my night: bathroom runs and sweating, all the while having images of small dark figures sleeping on the streets, standing in their huts, begging for food. I was sick and alone in Mumbai.

I slept till noon the next day. Then, I stayed there. I couldn't bear the thought of going outside one more time. I needed a Time Out Mumbai.

Then I thought about Amrita's mother. She was right. We aren't meant to go through life alone. It is against our human nature. Single people should be pitied. We are living with a glaring deficiency in our lives. We are being denied love. And let's face it, it's kind of true, all you need is love. I have everything but that, and my life feels very empty.

I realized how pathetic I sounded, even to myself. But I didn't care. For me, when I am feeling sorry for myself, which is often, I like to just really indulge in it, to really push myself to feel as badly as I can. Call the cops if you want to shut it down; otherwise this pity party is going to go on all night.

But here I was, in India. Where literally the streets were teeming with people in the worst cases of need. Children with no homes, no food, no clothes, no *hands*. Could I really sit there and cry because I didn't have a boyfriend?

I hoped the answer was no, but I wasn't sure. I got on some clothes and went down to the tiny concierge desk. There was a beautiful woman with thick dark eyeliner working the desk. My hair was disheveled and my eyes were puffy. I can't imagine what she must have thought of me.

"Excuse me," I asked, my voice rough from not having spoken all day. "I was wondering if you knew of any organization I could volunteer for. You know, to help."

The woman at the desk looked very confused. This was not the sort of request she was used to.

"I'm sorry, what do you mean?"

"I'm just wondering, if I could spend a few days helping, you know, the people here. On the streets."

I assume she thought I was a madwoman. She smiled politely and said, "Just one moment, I'll ask my colleague." There was a door that led to some back room, it seemed, and she disappeared behind it, for ten minutes. Finally, she came back.

"I'm sorry, but we really don't have any kind of recommendations like that for you. I'm sorry."

"Really, there's no place I could go to just volunteer for a bit?" I asked again.

The woman bobbled her head. "I'm sorry, no. It's not possible."

Just then, a young woman who worked at the front desk, around twenty, interrupted.

"Excuse me, are you interested in volunteering somewhere?"

I nodded and said, "Yes."

Her eyes lit up. "Three of my friends and I get together on Saturday nights and we go to the outdoor festivals. We buy food for the kids who are standing around and we take them on the rides. We're going to-night."

"Can I join you?"

She bobbled her head. "Of course, I will meet you here in the lobby at six. You can come in my car."

I almost smiled. "Thank you so much."

"It's no problem." And then she stuck out her hand. "I'm Hamida, by the way."

"It's nice to meet you. I'm Julie."

"It's nice to meet you, Julie."

That night, I stood in a sea of what seemed to be the entire population of India. We were at an outdoor festival for some important Muslim Baba (spiritual leader) in Mumbai. There were crowds of teenagers, there were families, there were couples, all shouting and laughing. There were about a half dozen big Ferris wheels, all lit up, which made the entire scene feel like one big dusty circus. Indian music came out of the loudspeakers, as well as a man's voice talking nonstop in Hindi. It was absolute chaos.

I was standing with Hamida and her friends Jaya and Kavita, who were sisters. They were both very modern-looking young women, with nice jeans and cute designer tops. Jaya and Kavita were born in London and their father was a businessman who had come back here for work. Never having seen that kind of poverty before coming to Mumbai, they were appalled. They had met Hamida at the fancy private school in Mumbai that they attended, and they all decided to do something to help.

So this was what they did. They would go to fairs and find children who were running around unescorted or who were out begging for money, and offer to take them on rides and buy them food. It wasn't much, but it was something.

Of course, since I was there, the white lady, it was like bees to honey. In a matter of moments, five children came up to me altogether, with their hands to their lips. I looked at Hamida and her friends, waiting for them to take charge. Hamida started speaking to them in Hindi. They suddenly got very quiet, as if they didn't understand what she was saying and were slightly afraid.

"This happens all the time," Jaya whispered to me. "They're confused. They never heard of someone asking if they want to go on the rides."

Hamida kept talking to them, pointing to the stands of food and the Ferris wheels.

The children seemed truly puzzled. Kavita started talking to them as well. I could tell it was difficult to get them to switch gears from beggars to children—like someone asking a puppet to realize it's actually a little boy. Finally, after much cajoling, the women were able to walk the children over to a stand that was selling ice cream. They bought all the children ice cream and gave them the cones one by one. The children started licking away at them happily. Soon enough, they were smiling, and we were able to get them on a Ferris wheel. We piled them on it, making sure there was an adult with each group of kids. As the Ferris wheel turned round and round, the children began smiling and laughing. They pointed out to the horizon, amazed at what they could see up there. They screamed and waved at each other from the different seats they were on.

We did a variation of that for the entire night with as many kids as we could find. We ran around with them, bought them some real food and treats, and took them on a few other rides. I didn't speak any Hindi, obviously, but I was able to do some funny dances and make some funny faces that cracked them up. It was exhausting, I must admit. I looked at these three young Indian women and felt enormous admiration for them. They had figured out how to go straight to the heart of the matter. They spent their Saturday nights not with their boyfriends, at parties, or at bars, but at these noisy, dirty fairs, breathing life back into a few children if only for a few hours.

When I got back into my room, I collapsed on the bed, covered in dirt and ice cream. As I thought about the night and the children, I was filled with a lightness. I had helped some children. I was not a selfish person, but a kind one. I wasn't a pathetic crybaby but a noble mother to the world . . . But then, like having a scab that you just have to pick at, my mind started drifting toward the image of Thomas and his wife summering in the countryside with their baby crawling on the green grass; them opening presents on Christmas; them lying in bed all together, on a lazy Sunday morning. I tried to push them away, force them out of my mind. I began to pace, to clear my thoughts, and I happened to glance back at the full-length mirror with the overhead lighting. I saw the cellulite covering my upper thighs. I looked down and swore I saw the first signs of cellulite on my knees.

I couldn't help it. I'm sorry. I started to cry. And yes, I wasn't crying because of those poor little children, I was crying because my heart was broken and I now had knee cellulite.

This was certainly not my proudest moment.

Back in the States

Alice was in her bedroom, with the suitcase out on her bed, already packed for Iceland. They weren't leaving for three days but she was ready to go. It hadn't been that stressful a task, packing, as she assumed they were going to be in the dark the whole time, so it really didn't matter what she wore. But just as in finding a husband, Alice doesn't like to wait until the last minute.

She had spent some time picking out just the right dress for the big day. She found it last week with Jim's sister, Lisa. She had settled on a "winter white" skirt and jacket set, woolen, with the sleeves of the jacket and the hem of the skirt trimmed in mink. It wasn't politically correct, but it was cute, very *Doctor Zhivago*. She made a mental note to donate money to PETA after the honeymoon.

It was nine o'clock in the morning and she didn't have a damn thing left to do. She didn't have to go give Ruby her shot. Obviously, she didn't have to meet with any wedding planners or florists or deejays anymore, because there was no wedding. Alice had spun it to Jim (and Jim had subsequently spun it to his family) that she realized getting married was an incredibly intimate event, and she wanted to share it with just Jim. And that it always was Alice's dream to get married in Iceland—which it wasn't, so just add that lie to her guilty list along with the dead minks. The only way they got away with this plan, among all the families, was by promising to have some big party when they got back from their honeymoon.

So now Alice was sitting on her bed with not one thing to do that entire day. She wasn't being a lawyer, she wasn't being a bride-to-be, she wasn't even being a friend. She reminded herself to call Ruby in a few days to check in about the news. She wondered how to make that phone call: *Hey Ruby, I was just wondering—are you pregnant?* She then realized it was one of those situations where it's better not to ask. The news would get to you when it wanted to. She went into the kitchen and poured herself a cup of coffee and thought about how similar that was to dating. She couldn't bear the fake-casual phone calls the day after a big date.

"Hey Alice, it's Mom, I'm just sitting here vacuuming, and I was just wondering how it went last night . . . ?"

"Hey, Al, it's Bob. Didn't you tell me you had a big date last night? How did it go?"

"Hey, Al, it's me, how'd it go with Hedge Fund Guy? Tell me everything."

As Alice sat and sipped her second cup of coffee she let a feeling of relief wash over her. Those days were over. No more phone calls. Now she had the time to think about Ruby and be one of those annoying people, calling, saying, *Hey Ruby, are you pregnant?*

Unfortunately, Alice's mind did have the time to think about the real current event—her marriage to Jim. She had the impulse to actually squeeze the sides of her temples together to somehow push whatever integrity or bravery she had left in her psyche out into some kind of action. But it never came. Because all she ever thought about was how she never wanted to go out on another date. She knew it was weak. She knew she was settling and she tried to care. She tried to feel guilty about that, as opposed to the minks. But instead, all she kept remembering were all those dates and all those phone calls and she knew that she wasn't going anywhere.

But she did decide to call Ruby anyway, and ask her how it all went. When she picked up the phone, Ruby answered and told her everything. How she had left at the last minute; how she saw her mother and realized she was from a long line of depressed women; how she was now *really* depressed. She also told Alice how she hadn't seen Serena in days. Alice was worried. She was worried for Ruby, and she was worried for Serena. Finally, she had something else to think about.

· · ·

Mark Levine was sitting at the head of a conference table. Dale and Georgia were sitting across from each other, on opposite sides of Mark Levine. Georgia, of course, was a nervous wreck. She had no idea what the children had said to Mark Levine, and consequently, she had no idea what Mark Levine was going to say to them. If he recommended something that they didn't agree with, she would have to hire a lawyer and spend enormous amounts of money and end up in court. But she was ready to do that if need be. She wasn't going to let squirrelly Mark Levine be the final word about where her children should live if she didn't want it to be.

Georgia looked over at Dale. He looked odd, a bit disheveled. He hadn't shaved for the big day. He managed to throw on a blazer, but didn't bother to put on a tie. *Finally,* Georgia thought to herself. *It's finally hitting him. What he's done to me. What he's done to his family.*

Mark Levine had just opened their file. Georgia and Dale sat there in silence; Dale had his hands in front of him on the table, picking at a cuticle.

"So. As you know, I've had a chance to speak to both of you, individually, as well as speaking to your children. It's my recommendation that—"

But before Mark Levine could finish, Dale interrupted.

"I think the children should stay with Georgia," Dale said, with his eyes still on his cuticle.

Georgia, startled, looked at Dale and then looked quickly back at Mark Levine. Did she hear correctly? She had to make sure.

"What?" Georgia said.

Dale now looked up at both Georgia and Mark Levine. "She's a really good mother. She's just been going through a hard time. So, she made a mistake. I don't think she would do it again. Would you?"

"No. Never."

Mark Levine took off his glasses and rubbed his eyes. He looked at Dale. "Are you sure about this?"

Dale nodded, his head pointing down again toward the table. Georgia thought she noticed his eyes welling up with tears. She decided to engage him in conversation so she could see for sure.

"Really, Dale, you're positive?" Georgia asked. She didn't really care if he was sure, she just wanted to see if he was crying. Dale looked up at Georgia for a split second and mumbled, "Yes. I'm sure." He was, indeed, all teary. Dale quickly looked down again. Georgia felt a wave of all sorts of emotions well up inside. She felt sorry for him, how sad he looked, gratitude for his change of heart, regret for how everything turned out, and when it all mixed together like that in this one giant surge, it felt exactly like love.

"Well, I believe I can agree to that," Mark Levine said. "I was going to recommend—"

"Do we really need to know?" Georgia interrupted quickly. "I mean, if we're in agreement. Do we need to know what you were going to recommend?"

Mark Levine pursed his lips, and said politely, "No, I guess you don't. But I do feel it's my duty to encourage you to find a way to manage your anger. It's absolutely unacceptable to ever show your children anything but a supportive, cooperative relationship between you and your ex-husband."

"I absolutely agree, Mr. Levine. Thank you."

"Do you want to talk about visitation rights?" Mark Levine said to Dale.

"Can I have them every other weekend?" Dale said. "And dinner once a week?"

Georgia nodded, and said, "Of course, and if you want to see them more often than that, I'm sure we can figure something out."

Dale almost smiled and then looked down again.

Mark Levine got up from the table. "Well, I'm glad this ended so amicably. I'll have them draw up the papers." Mark Levine began to exit the room and cast a look backward, at Georgia and Dale still sitting there. "Will you two be all right in here?" Georgia and Dale gave various facial assurances that they would not in fact start choking each other the minute he walked out of the room.

The door closed behind him and Dale put his head in his hands, his elbows on the table. Georgia leaned over and touched his elbow. Dale was truly crying now. The only time she had seen Dale cry like that was at his mother's funeral. At that time, she found it profoundly sweet. She remembered she had stood there, rubbing his back as he cried in the parking lot of the funeral home. She felt an overwhelming love for him at that moment; an understanding that this is what a husband and wife go through together, births and deaths and tears, and she had been touched and proud that she was able to be there for him. Similarly, today, she felt a deep love for Dale. In that little conference room, she understood that history is something not to be underestimated, and even if the present was gone, a shared history must be respected and, she would go so far as to say, cherished. As she touched Dale's elbow, trying again to comfort him during a moment of intense grief, she knew that he must be having a similar experience. The weight of the dissolution of their shared history and the fracturing of their family was finally being felt. And although she felt great tenderness for Dale at this moment, she also felt vindicated. Finally, there was reflection. Finally, there was regret. Finally, there was gravitas.

"She left me," Dale suddenly blurted out, as he lifted up his face and flashed his big wet soppy tears to Georgia. She thought, hoped, prayed she hadn't heard him correctly.

"Excuse me?" Georgia asked, with a little of her old contemptuous tone sneaking into her voice.

"She left me, Georgia. Melea left me." Dale grabbed Georgia's arm and squeezed it as he turned his head away from her. "She said she didn't want to date a man who had children. It was too complicated."

Georgia took a breath and asked him, calmly, "Is that why you didn't fight for the kids? Because you had wanted to raise them with her?"

Dale, in his vulnerable state, was too weak to lie or even avoid.

"I thought she'd be a great stepmom."

There were a lot of things that Georgia felt entitled to do or say in this moment. She could have screamed at Dale that he had merely seen his children as props in his imaginary dream life with Melea. She could have screamed that he should be thinking about the dissolution of their twelve-year marriage, that by their failure they had now added their children to the statistics of children of divorce. That, because of what was going on right this very minute, there might be psychological repercussions for their children that they might not see until years from now. And that he didn't seem to be noticing any of this, because he was too busy crying over some Brazilian whore—yes, in her mind she could call her a whore, fuck Mark Levine—whom he'd known for just a few months.

But Georgia knew that now was not the time to think about Dale or their lousy love lives. Dale was busy enough thinking about Dale. Now was the time to think about her two gorgeous children of divorce, and how she could make their lives filled with as much joy and stability and discipline and fun as possible. That's what it was time for. That was all she was entitled to—that and only that.

．　．　．

Oftentimes, morning brings better news. The sun rises, people are rested, and the brightness of the day helps things look less bleak. But there are those horrific times in a person's life when things are so bad that the morning just brings a fresh hell of pain, or a new sobbing realization of the doom that has befallen you. For Serena and Kip, that's how this morning began. Kip was sprawled out on the couch, his head still in Serena's lap, when he woke up crying. Then he stood up suddenly and screamed, "I want to talk to my mother! I want to talk to my mother!"

"I'll call her right now," Serena said, jumping up and grabbing the phone. It was six in the morning. She could only imagine what Joanna had been through that night. Kip stood there, tense, breathing heavily, his eyes watery, as Serena dialed the phone.

"Joanna? It's Serena. Kip wants to talk to you." Serena passed the phone to Kip. He took the phone slowly, as if it might blow up in his face.

Kip listened, quietly. Serena had no idea what Joanna was saying to him. Was Robert all right? "Uh-huh," Kip said. "That's really great, Mom." And he hung up the phone.

Serena stood there and looked at Kip.

"Dad's coming back home," Kip said, relieved, and went back to the sofa and sprawled on his stomach. He picked up the remote and started watching a movie Robert starred in where he played a cowboy looking for his lost son.

Robert is coming home? Is that good news or bad news? Serena had no idea. She just started doing the only thing she knew how to do in this situation.

"I'll make you an omelette and some bacon—does that sound okay?" she called out to Kip.

"Yep, thank you, See," Kip said, staring at the television. Serena quietly went to work.

At nine, Joanna called Serena and filled her in on the details. His breathing had not improved and he had been put on a ventilator, which definitely was not good news. Joanna told her that Robert's mother and brother were flying in from Montana, and Joanna's parents were flying in from Chicago. She hoped Serena wouldn't mind letting them in. Serena didn't. She just wanted to be of help; anything she could do was fine by her.

The phones began to go crazy. Joanna had started making calls at the hospital and when people couldn't get her on her cell, they started calling the house. Close friends, acquaintances, colleagues, agents, managers, were all calling. Unfortunately, news had gotten out to the press as well, and photographers started to camp out in front of the building. Flowers began arriving; food, too.

By noon, Joanna's parents had arrived. They were an unassuming elderly midwestern couple, both short and gray and cute, wheeling in their little suitcases and taking off their coats. Kip met them at the door and they must have both stood taking turns hugging him for about fifteen minutes. Eventually, they looked up and saw Serena.

"Hi, I'm Ginnie," Joanna's mother said as she stretched out her hand. "Joanna has told us so much about you, Serena."

Serena shook her hand. "I'm just glad I could help."

"Oh, you've been much more than that," Joanna's father said as he stretched out his hand. "I'm Bud."

"Now," Ginnie said. "What can we do to help?"

Serena saw that these were two sturdy people who dealt with grief and hardship with good old-fashioned hard work. So Serena had Ginnie do laundry. She asked Bud to be in charge of the buzzer. In the meantime, Serena kept cooking nonstop and answering the phone. Kip kept watching the movie over and over again, comatose, mummified.

At two o'clock, Joanna called from the ambulance and told them they'd be home in five minutes. Everything was ready. Their bedroom was spotless, thanks to Ginnie's polishing and vacuuming. There was food to last them for days. And the throngs of photographers outside were under control because Bud got fed up and called the cops, so now there was a police presence outside. Go, Bud.

No one knew exactly what to expect. They all just sat around, waiting until Joanna and Robert came home.

Theirs was an industrial-size elevator, one that opened up directly into their loft. When they finally arrived, a whole new reality entered the home. Robert was on a stretcher rolled in by two paramedics. There were two women dressed in white scrubs who followed, as well as one man in green scrubs who was apparently the doctor. Joanna came out in the middle of the crowd. She was stoic, pale, and looked much older than she had when she left the house twenty-four hours earlier. They all filed toward Robert and Joanna's bedroom. Robert was unconscious, and no longer had a breathing tube down his throat. There was only one IV in him now, rolled along by one of the nurses as they all walked away.

They've brought him home to die. Serena finally allowed herself to think it. She wasn't the only one. Kip began to wail the moment he saw his father rolled out.

"Is he going to wake up? WHEN IS HE GOING TO WAKE UP, MOMMY?"

Joanna went over to hold him but he ran away.

"NO! NO!" Kip ran into his room and shut the door.

At two thirty, Robert's mother arrived from Montana. She was a frail woman, in jeans and a turtleneck. Her little feet were in New Balance sneakers and her thin hair was in a light brown, tight little perm. She obviously had had a long, sad flight, and seemed to be reserving every ounce of energy she had left for her son. When she walked in, she kissed Joanna hello, nodded to everyone else, and went into Robert's room.

By five o'clock, friends had started to arrive. Not just friends, but intimates. The inner circle. The inner, inner, inner circle. It was about twenty people; twenty lovely people who were all, every last one of them, deeply appropriate, speaking quietly, somber but not morbid, occasionally joking and idly chatting, but never without sensitivity.

Serena did crowd control, not with the guests, but with all the food they brought with them. With each person that came, a cake or a bottle of booze or a platter of something was given. Serena unwrapped everything she could, found places to store the rest, and began operating as if she were suddenly the hostess of an impromptu party. She ordered in paper goods, set up a buffet table, and by seven o'clock had set up a full bar.

By nine, Serena had put soft jazz music on the stereo (jazz was Robert's favorite) and it didn't look as if anyone was going anywhere. Serena had not witnessed anything like this before and she was struck by the weight and depth of what she was experiencing.

Moreover, this was no normal group of people—there were recognizable actors and actresses, a newscaster, and a writer who had won an Oscar for best screenplay. Serena began to understand that what she was witnessing was primal. This was a tribe, these show biz folks; one of their own had fallen and so they gathered. Because that is what human beings have done at times of grief since the dawn of man. They gather. They hold one another, they cry, they eat.

As the hours went by, they all continued to talk and drink and then suddenly, someone would start crying, and then someone else would start crying, and everyone's eyes would become moist, and the mood would suddenly be grim and quiet. Men would weep openly, women would just stand with each other, hugging. These people were show people who weren't embarrassed by their emotion, but they weren't show-offs, either.

Every time Joanna would come out of the bedroom, everyone would quiet a bit, waiting. Joanna would look at one of the guests and say, "Would you like to go in and see Robert now?" They would nod, silently, put down their drink, and walk away toward the bedroom. Even as she was living through the nightmarish event of watching her husband die, she was still taking care of the needs of others. She was slowly letting everyone pay their last respects. Clearly, it must not be long.

Throughout all this, Kip hid in his room. There was one young actor, Billy, who had just made his first romantic comedy and was about to become a huge star, and Kip allowed him to come in and play video games together. But that was it.

Joanna walked into the kitchen, where Serena was, to put down a glass of water she had just finished. "I know he must hate this." Serena turned to look at her.

"Having all these people around, in his home, talking and laughing, when his dad is—" Joanna stopped herself. "But later, he'll remember. He'll remember all the love, all the people who were here because they loved his father."

Joanna put her face in her hands and began to cry. Serena walked around the kitchen counter and put her arm around her. At the moment of touch, Joanna quickly stood up and composed herself. "I'm fine. Really. I'm going to go back in." She turned to walk away and then she turned back, with a start.

"Oh my God, Serena. All this time, you've been here—is this okay?

Do you have to be somewhere? I . . . I haven't even had a moment to ask you if you need to go, or—"

"I'm fine. I don't have to be anywhere. Please, don't worry about me again, please."

"Thank you."

As Joanna walked away, Serena realized that she truly had nowhere else to be at that moment. There was no one in the world who needed her as much as these people did right now. There was no boyfriend, no child. She had called Ruby and told her what was going on so she wouldn't worry, but that was it. In a room where it seemed people were practically fused together in their grief and love, no one wanting to leave Robert, no one wanting to leave each other, Serena felt weightless. Untethered. And if it weren't for this group who needed right now to be fed and cared for, Serena felt like she might just float up and away into the sky.

The doctor kept coming and going from the apartment, stopping in every few hours to check on Robert. His name was Doctor Grovner, but everyone called him Henry. He was a family friend of Joanna and Robert's who happened to be an oncologist, which is why Robert was allowed to go home and get the fantastic care he was being given. At eleven thirty that night, the doctor arrived again and went directly in to Robert. At midnight, everyone in the living room heard Robert's mother crying in the bedroom, with Joanna saying, "It's going to be okay, it's all going to be okay."

Doctor Grovner came out. Everyone was already quiet. Anxious. Tearful. He said quietly, "It won't be long now." Billy, who was now back in the living room, began to sob, and Joanna's mother went over and patted his hand gently. Another woman just dashed into a bathroom, where she was heard wailing. Another beautiful woman, someone Serena recognized from starring opposite Robert in one of his movies, just started rocking back and forth. Joanna came out next. She smiled and went directly to the kitchen, where Serena was. She was carrying a washcloth and went to the sink to dampen it. She wrung out the excess water. Serena had been filling up an ice bucket with ice, when Joanna came over. Joanna came up to Serena and said, gently, "You don't need to, please don't feel you have to, but if you want, you're welcome to come in and say good-bye."

Serena burst out crying. She put her hand immediately to her eyes and turned away from Joanna, embarrassed. She quickly wiped the tears away and turned back to Joanna and smiled. "I'd like that."

Serena walked into the bedroom. It was dark. There were two windows that looked out onto the Hudson, the lights from New Jersey twinkling in the distance. The room was otherwise lit only by candlelight, everything designed for the maximum amount of peace. Robert's mother was sitting in a chair by his bed, holding his hand, her eyes closed. The nurse was in the back of the room, almost invisible in the shadows. Joanna sat down in the chair on the other side of Robert and stared at him. Kip was not there. Robert no longer had his breathing tube in him, and his breathing was very light. He was pale, thin, unrecognizable. The first word that popped into Serena's mind was *outrageous*. It felt outrageous that Robert, strong, virile Robert, Robert sliding around the floor in his socks and punching Serena in the arm and teasing his wife mercilessly, was now lying in this bed, looking like that. It was an outrageous indignity for him. A man who deserved nothing but to lead a long, loved, and loving life, with friends and a marriage to a woman that he adored and a child that he should see go to college and fall in love and get married. Not like this. Not thin and pale and with grieving friends gathered outside his door.

Joanna looked at her husband. Whatever the thought or memory or emotion it was that passed through her mind, it was the one that broke her. She lowered her head on the bed and began to sob, her back heaving up and down as she gasped for air in between her cries. It was pure grief that Serena was witnessing; undiluted, unself-conscious suffering from the deepest part of a person's being.

In a flash, Serena understood everything. She understood about life and tribes and weight and connections and friendship and death and love. She understood everything she ever needed to know about what it means to actually *participate* in the experience of being human. She knew in that instant, more than she had ever known anything in her entire life, that life is about risking it all and loving passionately and engaging in the world in a way she had not done in all her regimented, disciplined, pleasure-denying life. She had begun to feel it with Swami Swaroop, but after that debacle, she promised she would never put herself through that again. She assumed she just would go through the rest of her life alone, unharmed. But in that room, in that moment, in the most dark, grotesque, cruel light imaginable, Serena saw what she would be missing. She kept her eyes on the sobbing Joanna. She would never be able to explain it sufficiently to anyone, but it was then that Serena knew, more surely than she had ever known anything, that it was time for her to join the party—the ugly, magnificent, cruel, sublime, heartbreaking party.

11

Believe in Miracles

A few hours after Robert passed away, Serena called Ruby and told her. It was impossible to hide the news from the press, so his death was all over the television and radio anyway. Ruby called Alice and Alice called Georgia.

Serena had gone out just to get some fresh air. People were still filing in and out of the house, now to visit Joanna and Kip, to pay their respects. It looked like she was probably going to be there for a while, so Serena decided to go outside for a quick break. There were crowds and news vans and reporters, but Serena was able to walk through them unnoticed. She kept her eyes down and kept walking past the police barricade. When she finally looked up she saw Alice, Georgia, and Ruby, all looking at her with a collective look of care and concern, and she burst out crying. They all rushed up to her and put their arms around her. She stood there, crying and holding on to them, all the emotion of the past days just pouring out of her. They huddled around her, shielding her from any busybodies, as she wept, her shoulders heaving, the sobs erupting out of her. When she finally looked up, her face red and wet, she looked into their faces. Ruby, Alice, and Georgia were not her good friends; in fact, they were merely acquaintances. Yet here they were.

"I can't believe you all came. Thank you . . . thank you," she said, her voice still jagged with sobs.

Alice put her arm around Serena's shoulders. "We wanted to come."

Georgia said, "We're here for you. So don't you worry."

Ruby added, "Do you want to take a walk?"

Serena nodded. They headed down to the river and sat on a bench facing out over the water. New Jersey was on the other side, with its new buildings going up and the giant Colgate clock telling them the wrong time.

Serena said, "She loved him so much. He really was the love of her life. I can't imagine what she's going through. I can't."

The other women nodded. They hadn't a clue, either.

Ruby shook her head. "It's hard to imagine ever meeting the love of my life, but then to lose him? And so young?"

Georgia thought about Dale and their life together. *Had he been the love of her life?* At one point, yes, she guessed he was. But not now. So maybe he didn't count. Now she had to hope there was a man out there who was the real love of her life. "I hope she feels lucky. To have had so much love in her life."

Serena nodded. "I think she does." She blew her nose on a tissue Alice had given her. "I think so."

Alice spent the whole taxi ride home thinking about that term—*the love of your life.* She thought about Joanna and how different she must have thought things were going to be for her. And, of course, Alice thought about how she was about to take a flight to Iceland to marry someone who wasn't the love of her life.

When she got home she walked into her bedroom. She looked at her suitcase on the bed, packed and ready to go. Their airplane tickets were on her bureau. Jim was about to come over for dinner. Alice sat on her bed. What does it mean, anyway, "the love of your life"? She wished Serena had never said those words. Now she couldn't get them out of her head. She glanced at her fabulous winter white fur wedding suit. She thought about how, when you introduce your husband to people here in

America, there is the assumption that he is the love of your life. That you fell in love with him and decided to get married. It might not be true, but that's what you're led to believe. Now, if you lived in India or China or who knows where, people might not assume that. They might just assume your families arranged it or you married for convenience or whatnot. But here, in America, when you talk about your husband, the assumption is that at some point in your life you were in love with him enough to marry him. Alice wondered if she would be okay with living that kind of lie, knowing she did not marry the love of her life. She had hoped that in the weeks leading up to Iceland she would magically fall head over heels in love with Jim. But it didn't happen. She was always mildly bored with him, and then guilty for feeling that bored. So she would give him more of her attention, she would try to find him as engaging as she possibly could. But in the end, he wasn't the love of her life and he never would be. At best, he would be the man of whom she was very fond and to whom she was very, very grateful.

The love of her life, the love of her life. As Alice took a shower, she realized it came down once again to one thing: What did she believe in? In other words, what kind of life did she want to live? Did she really think the love of her life was out there? Did she think it was wise to go back out into the wilds of being single just in the hopes of finding him? What was she holding out for? As she toweled herself off, she realized that she didn't want to be the girl who refused to settle. She didn't want to be the girl who believed that life is short and it's better to be single and looking for "the love of your life" than to just give up and settle. She didn't want to be that girl. She thought that girl was stupid. Naïve. Alice liked being practical; she was a lawyer, so she preferred to be realistic. Waiting and searching for the love of your life was *exhausting*. It might even be delusional. Again, yes, she knew that some people win the love lottery and get to fall in love with someone who is also mad about them, and their life together is harmonious and filled with love. But she didn't want to be the girl who stubbornly held out for what might never come.

She sat back down on her bed, wrapped in a little towel, and she began to cry. She started sobbing; she hugged her legs as she put her head on her knees and rocked and wept.

She realized she *was* that girl.

That girl who, at thirty-eight, couldn't give up the dream that she would meet a man who made her heart soar and that they would share a life together. She cried knowing it meant that she had to worry about whether she was ever going to start a family, that she would be thrust back into a world where nothing was guaranteed and all she really had was hope. She knew it meant that she would be single again.

When Jim came over, Alice was dressed but hadn't stopped crying. He walked in, rolling his big suitcase. Alice told him right away.

"You deserve someone who knows you're the love of her life," she said, sobbing. She then began to tell him, in a torrent of words and tears and apologies, that she couldn't marry him—not in Iceland, not here, not ever.

Now his eyes filled up with tears. "But you're the love of *my* life. Doesn't that mean anything?"

Alice shook her head. "I don't think I can be the love of your life if you're not the love of mine."

Jim paced around the room. They talked and talked. He got angry. Alice apologized over and over again. And in the end, he understood. He forgave her and wished her the best. He left Alice in her living room crying, devastated. From her point of view she seemed to be much worse off than he was. She looked at him as he walked out the door, shaken, heartbroken, and she felt tremendous guilt. But she also knew that he would fall in love again. He would meet someone and get married and have children and be very happy. As for herself, Alice wasn't so sure. So she lay down on the couch and cried some more.

When I called Alice the next morning and found out what happened, I was relieved. What was I thinking, encouraging Alice to marry Jim? Who exactly did I think I was, giving her advice about anything, let alone marrying someone she didn't love? But Alice still sounded more depressed than I had ever heard her. I thought about coming home and being with her. But then I had a better idea.

"Why don't I meet you in Iceland? Use your ticket."

"What do you mean, spend my honeymoon with you?" Alice asked, not making it sound so fun.

"Well, yeah, Iceland is supposed to be amazing. I've always wanted to go." It's true, everyone I know who's been there has said it was fantastic. I didn't remember exactly *why* they said it was so great, but no matter. "I think you need to get away for a bit."

"Yeah, but maybe not to the place where I was going to spend my honeymoon."

"Please, it's Iceland in the middle of the winter, not Maui. You'll be able to forget that part of it." And then I added, "I promise. Come on, let's do it, it will be fun."

At the Mumbai airport, I walked into the ladies' bathroom. There was an elderly woman in there, wearing a worn purple sari with white flowers, and her eyes were haunted, just like so many other eyes I saw while I was there. I thought she was functioning as a bathroom attendant, but I wasn't quite sure. As I came out, she handed me a paper towel that I was quite capable of getting for myself. Then she put her fingers to her mouth. This city was relentless. She could have been my grandmother. And she was in the bathroom of the Mumbai airport begging for money. I gave her all the rupees I had. Then I did the only thing I knew how to do at the time. I took two Lexomil and hoped for the best.

I woke up, groggy, as the pilot was telling us to get ready for our descent—the Lexomil had gone the distance. We must thank God for these small blessings in life.

The funeral for Robert was held two days after he passed away. Joanna decided that she and Kip were going to go back with her parents for a week or two, just to get away from the press and the chaos and the memories. She gave Serena two paid weeks off—which Serena had absolutely no idea what to do with. So when Alice called her to check up on her, and told her that her marriage was off and that she was meeting me in Iceland, Serena quickly jumped on board.

"Could I come, too? I mean, I know . . . it's your honeymoon . . . I was just thinking . . ."

"Of course, you can come—of course," was Alice's immediate response. "I'm not sure what kind of food they have there, if it's really hospitable for vegetarians, but . . ."

"Oh, fuck that," Serena said. "Everything in moderation, right?"

Alice smiled. "That's right."

In the meantime, Ruby had never really recovered from opting out of the insemination. She was sliding again, thinking about what she had lost, what a mistake that was. She thought about the idea of taking anti-depressants, like her mother, but couldn't imagine it. A depressed single woman taking antidepressants—that sounded so *depressing*.

But she was trying very hard to fight the slide. She was on the floor of her bedroom doing sit-ups, trying to get her endorphins going. After meeting with Serena, and hearing about Joanna and Robert, she was re-minded just how short life is and how you shouldn't be wasting any of it crying over regret and things that could have been. But nevertheless, as she was doing her crunches, she was thinking about how that sperm might have made a baby and how cute he or she would have been. Serena popped her head in the room and mentioned that she had just spoken to Alice and she was going to Iceland with them. Ruby stopped crunching.

"I've always wanted to go to Iceland! Reykjavik is supposed to be amazing! Can I come, too?" Ruby said, excited. Serena looked surprised.

"Um, I would think so . . . you might want to call . . . ?"

"I'll call Alice to make sure." And with that Ruby hopped on the phone.

After their meeting with Serena, Georgia had also gone home thinking about the love of her life. She wondered if it was a cop-out to think maybe her children could be the loves of her life. She knew that they weren't a replacement for a man or an intimate relationship—but it was love. They were two people whom she loved more than anything else in the world. Two little people who, for as long as any of them were alive, would always be her children. And this coming weekend, they were going to be with Dale. And now that she wasn't spending all her time hating Dale and chasing after men, she literally had nothing to do but be lonely. So when Alice called her up and told her that Serena, Ruby, and I were joining her in Iceland for her honeymoon that would never be, well, she decided to whip out that credit card and climb on board, too.

I think you can tell a lot about a place by the ride from the airport. I'm always a little disappointed if there's no sense of foreignness about it. There's nothing like flying twenty hours just to look out your car window and see the same old telephone wires and concrete. But the drive from the airport in Reykjavik to the heart of the city was through a landscape that I had never before seen or even heard about. The only way to describe it was lunar; imagine landing on the moon, which happens to be covered in a lovely green moss, then discovering that it's inhabited by lots of really good-looking blond people.

Now as I arrived on this moon, I couldn't have been feeling more sorry for myself. I was still humiliated by what happened in China, and still traumatized by Mumbai. I wanted to be somewhere as far away from there as possible. Reykjavik seemed like it was going to be just the place.

When I got to the hotel, I was exhausted. It was a tall, corporate-looking skyscraper, owned by Icelandair—not very quaint for Iceland or a honeymoon choice. I checked into Alice's suite. She would be arriving in the morning, so I would have the room to myself for the night. The room Alice booked was spacious—with a living room and kitchenette and king-size bed. But it was more suited for a busy executive than amorous newlyweds. I imagined Alice getting married in the dark, then coming back to this minimalist room to have cold executive sex, and I got ashamed all over again. *Why had I encouraged her to go through with the marriage? Who do I think I am anyway? I have no business calling myself a friend, and certainly no business writing a book about anything.*

At 7 A.M. I was woken up by my four friends barreling into the room. It was still pitch-black out and I was a bit disoriented, particularly from seeing my normally disparate friends all arriving in one bunch, in Iceland. It took me a minute to get my bearings.

"Thank God I booked this room for last night. You should see the mobs of tourists in the lobby. It was ghastly," Alice said as she took off her parka.

"It's true, there's just dozens of poor slobs who just got off some red-eye flight, nodding off on the sofas, waiting for check-in," Georgia said as she sat on the bed.

"Which is at, like, three," Ruby added, exploring the minibar. Then she turned around and stared at me. "I'm so glad to see you! It's been so long!"

I sat up, leaning on the copious pillows, and crossed my legs. "It's so good to see you! I missed you all so much." Serena leaned over and gave me a good, long hug. It felt like she might just burst out crying right there, but she let go and got up.

"I have to pee," she said, sniffling.

Alice looked around. "So this was where I was going to spend my honeymoon, huh? I guess I didn't research that very well, did I?"

"Why don't we go downstairs and have some breakfast and then go to the Blue Lagoon?" I said, brightly, seeing that things in this room could turn morose very quickly.

"What's the Blue Lagoon?" Ruby asked.

"It's a natural thermal pool—a big tourist spot, but the locals go, too. I read about it on the plane."

Alice added, "Jim and I were going to go there the day after our wedding."

"Well, let's go," Georgia said. "We can sleep later!"

They went downstairs to the buffet while I changed. As I was putting on my jeans, my cell phone rang. It was an "unknown" number so I assumed it was from the States. When I picked up, I heard Thomas's voice.

"Hello, Julie? It's me."

Don't you dare say "it's me" when you call. As if we're still intimate. I wanted to throw up.

"Please, leave me alone," is all I managed to get out.

"I'm sorry, Julie, I am. I just needed to tell you again how sorry I am. This all was very difficult."

"I don't really want to talk to you right now. I'm sorry. It's too sad for me." I closed my phone. I leaned against the desk for a moment. If I let myself cry again, I would never get out of this hotel room. So I took a breath and went down to breakfast.

Alice, being Alice, had rented a car at the airport, and had directions to the Blue Lagoon ready. So we all piled in and drove the forty-five minutes out there. It was still dark out, so it was difficult to see where we actually were. But as we got closer, it appeared as if we were driving to a big hole in the ground puffing with smoke. We got out of the car and marched through the turnstile and into the locker rooms, where we put on our bathing suits and showered. We walked right out into the pool.

It was freezing, so we quickly got into the water, which was warm and soothing. There was soft sand under our feet. We walked around for a bit, crouching so that the warm water covered our whole bodies. We settled into a little corner where steam was gushing out of the crevices of some rocks. It created a little shower for us while we soaked. The view was stupendous. The sun was rising so the sky was filled with pinks and blues. There was a geothermal power plant next to the lagoon, and while it spoiled the view a bit, it also puffed out clouds of steam that spilled over the mountains. We definitely weren't in America anymore, and I wasn't quite sure if we were even still on planet Earth.

As I sat there taking in this otherworldly beauty, Georgia was having an entirely different experience.

"Here's the thing with hot springs—the water's so cloudy, there's no way to tell how clean it is." I didn't know how to answer her. I was too relaxed to worry.

Alice reassured her. "I read all about it. The water gets pumped out regularly, so it's always being cleaned."

Georgia looked around. "Good, because I'm sure people come here with all sorts of skin problems that they're hoping to get cured. It could be really gross in here."

Serena looked at Georgia. "Why don't you just try and enjoy the water? It feels so good."

Georgia nodded. It was Saturday, and tourists and locals alike were starting to wade in. Two women sat near us. One blond, the other with darkish red hair. They both were in their early forties and very tall and beautiful. They were speaking what seemed to be Icelandic.

"Excuse me," Georgia called to the women. "Do you know if the water here is clean?"

The women looked at Georgia. I was worried that this might appear to be a rude question, but the women didn't seem to mind. They also didn't flinch at her assumption that they understood and spoke English. Yes, we're Americans.

"Yes, it's clean," the blond women said, in a thick Nordic accent. "I come here all the time."

The other one shrugged. "I don't like it as much, swimming with all these people, but I think it's clean."

Georgia smiled at them sweetly. "Thank you so much. I appreciate it." Georgia crouched down even lower in the water and let it come up over her neck.

Alice looked around. "It's so strange to be here. Tonight would have been my wedding night . . ."

I tried to keep her level. "But you must know you did the right thing, don't you?"

Alice shook her head. "I don't know that. I don't know that at all. What if he was my last chance? What if I'm never going to have another boyfriend again, let alone another husband?"

Again, no one knew what to say. How could anyone predict the future? We were all trying to heal our battle scars here in the Blue Lagoon, and no one had a lot of optimism to share.

Georgia spoke first. "All you need to know is that you tried very hard to go through with it, and you couldn't. That's your answer. You didn't have a choice."

Alice nodded as if she understood. But then her face crumpled into tears. "But why couldn't I? What's wrong with me? What am I holding out for?" I waded over and put my arm around her.

Serena had been fairly quiet since we got here, but now spoke up. "Our time is so precious. You're holding out for someone who you really want to spend all your time with. Otherwise, there's no point to it."

Alice wasn't so sure. "Maybe there is a point to it. Just so you don't have to be so alone."

And at that, I burst out crying. I had been holding it in since my phone call with Thomas and it just came out right then and there. "We're so fucked. We are. We're screwed. We're this generation of women who are just as lonely as any other, but we're just unwilling to settle or compromise to get ourselves out of it. So we're all just waiting for the fucking needle-in-a-haystack guy who we're going to love, who's going to happen to love us, who we're going to meet just at the time when we're both available and living in the same city." Tears were now streaming down my face. "We're totally fucked."

Ruby burst out crying as well. "Oh my God, you're right. You're absolutely right."

Serena had tears streaming down her face, too. Georgia looked at all of us whimpering and tried to lighten things up. "This is not the kind of honeymoon I expected."

We tried to laugh, but we were still crying too hard. The two women who were sitting near us were looking at us, concerned and puzzled. They were talking to each other in Icelandic, while they both looked over at us. We were making a spectacle of ourselves, all the way on the top of the world, and people were noticing. Georgia looked over and for some reason felt the need to explain.

"We're just all going through a very hard time right now. That's all."

If I had to guess, I think it must have been fairly shocking to see such an outpouring of emotion, here in the relaxing geothermal hot springs, amid a sea of reserved Scandinavians and happy tourists.

"Do you need any help?" the redhead asked.

Georgia just shook her head. "No, we'll all be fine, um, someday, hopefully soon."

The blonde couldn't help but inquire further. "What is the matter? May I ask?"

Georgia looked at us all. She pointed at each of us, one by one. "Alice just called off her wedding, Julie had an affair that went very badly, Serena watched someone die, I almost got my children taken away from me, and Ruby is clinically depressed."

The two women nodded, looking sorry that they had asked, and went back to talking among themselves. They looked so rugged, these women, with their strong jawlines and their dark eyes. They turned to the rocks and started rubbing them, taking the mud from the rocks and putting it on their faces. They leaned back and let the steam and mud work its magic.

Georgia looked at them, impressed. "Wow, these ladies know their lagoons."

We stayed in the pool for another hour. We didn't necessarily come here to be healed from a skin disease or get a natural lava facial, but we definitely needed a good cry, and that we did.

When we were back in the locker area, the two women whom we were sitting near walked in and glanced around at us. We were all taking off our bathing suits. I was in my bikini top and surfer shorts. From the looks of the two women, and from my own common sense, I realized that here in Reykjavik, far away from vanity and supermodels and plastic surgeons, I looked like a clown in crazy balloon pants.

Georgia seemed to be fascinated by these two women and couldn't stop staring at them. Finally as they were putting their coats on to go back into the wintry day, Georgia spoke to them again.

"Excuse me, I was just wondering if you could tell us a good place to eat tonight in Reykjavik?"

The blond woman nodded. "There is a very nice place, Silfur, at the Hotel Borg. We are eating there tonight with some friends. It's a little expensive, but has very good *fis*." I assumed this meant "fish" but I didn't want to interrupt.

The other woman added, "There's also a place called Maru, very nice sushi, and Restaurant Lækjarbrekka is more casual, but very good food."

Georgia nodded her head gratefully at them. "Okay, thank you so much!" They walked out, saying polite good-byes to all of us.

"I don't know what it is, I just love those two ladies," Georgia said. We all put on our coats, and our gloves and hats and scarves, and braced ourselves. It was time to leave the lovely, warm amniotic sac of the Blue Lagoon, where we got to feel sorry for ourselves and everyone else we knew, and venture back out into the cold winter air.

After we took naps, we all dressed for dinner in our Nordic finest— turtlenecks and down vests and sturdy winter boots. It wasn't snowing, but it was windy and cold, around ten degrees Fahrenheit. The ladies gathered in my room; everyone was doing her best to make sure there wasn't any downtime on Alice's wedding night. We drank some white wine in the room and tried to keep things light.

"Thank God we didn't go to Finland. I heard Finnish men's penises look like logs of Roquefort cheese," Georgia said.

We all shrieked in our own different ways.

Ruby was appalled. "What?"

"My girlfriend told me that. That they looked, well, marbleized."

"Oh for God's sake, how am I going to ever get that image out of my mind tonight?" Alice asked, almost spitting up her drink.

"Well, here's to us not going to Helsinki for your honeymoon," Serena said, raising her glass of white wine and smiling.

We stood around in the hotel room laughing. Alice was having a good time and we were all getting a little tipsy.

We took two cabs to the restaurant. We chose the restaurant Silfur, basically because we knew those two women were going to be there and Georgia wanted to stalk them. We walked in, and immediately realized we were underdressed; this restaurant was bathed in art-deco elegance, and we looked as if we were going to dinner in an igloo. A trendy igloo, but an igloo nonetheless. We took our seats and immediately ordered white wine. All the waitresses in the restaurant were blond and beautiful. They suggested we order the fis, particularly the lobster. As we were look- ing at the menu, with all the crazy, crazy Icelandic words on it (chicken breast is, phonetically, "koo-kinkablinka"), the two ladies from the Blue Lagoon walked in with two men and two other women. I saw them see us and look at each other. I nodded toward the door and Georgia turned. The waiter was seating them at the table next to us and Georgia waved. "Hi! We decided to take your suggestion and come here!"

The blond woman smiled politely. "I'm so glad. I know you're going to like it." She then put out her hand and said, "I'm Sigrud. This is my boy- friend, Palli. And these are my two friends Dröfn and Hulda." Dröfn was a woman in her late twenties with long white-blond hair and a huge mouth with big white teeth. Hulda was in her late forties, with blond hair in a close pixie cut, a pierced nose with a tiny little stud in it, and large hoop earrings dangling down from her round, pretty face. The redhead from the lagoon introduced herself as well. "I'm Rakel, and this is my husband, Karl." Even if I hadn't had a few glasses of wine in me, I wouldn't have had the foggiest idea how to pronounce all their names.

We introduced ourselves. Georgia explained to the others, "We met at the Blue Lagoon today. We're from New York and we were all a little de- pressed."

Karl nodded. There was something about his demeanor that immedi- ately broadcast a kind heart and good humor. "Yes, well, Rakel kind of mentioned it." The whole group started smiling. "Why are you so sad? You're in Reykjavík now; this is where you come to have a good time."

Ruby joined in. "Well, that's what we're trying to do now. We're out to have a good time!"

Karl looked at us all and said, "Come, you must sit with us. We'll all eat together."

We all looked at one another. They were a big group as it was, and so were we—it seemed like a very burdensome idea. Rakel and Sigrud joined in immediately, though.

"Join us. We'll have some fun," Rakel said.

Sigrud added, "We don't have any friends from New York; come."

Georgia didn't need to be asked twice, and soon enough we were all crammed into a large circular table for ten, even though we were eleven. Soon the white wine (or "veet veen," as they called it) was flowing and we were regaling them with our tales of woe. Somehow it all seemed quite hilarious when we told it to these folks: Ruby's stint at the animal shelter, my China calamity, Georgia's domestic nightmare. Hilarious. The only thing that could never be spun as comic was Robert, and Serena didn't bring it up.

Karl egged us on. "So Julie, tell me about this book you're writing."

I groaned loudly. "I'm not writing it anymore. I'm going home and giving the money back to the publisher. I hate my book. I don't know what I was thinking."

Serena spoke up. "It's a book about what it's like for women to be single in all different cultures."

One of their friends spoke up, "That sounds very interesting. Don't you want to talk to Icelandic women?"

"Actually, I don't want to talk to any women anywhere, ever again, about this subject."

Georgia tried to explain. "She's just a little burned out. I'm sure it would be really helpful for Julie to talk to Icelandic women."

Somehow, Georgia steered the conversation to her two new favorite people, Sigrud and Rakel, asking them about their men. Rakel and Karl didn't get married until after their two children were eight and ten years old. Sigrud had two children with a man named Jon, whom she only married after their two children were four and seven, but now she was with Palli. Dröfn and Hulda both had children, were single, never married, and no one seemed to give a damn about any of it.

I refused to find any of this interesting. My irritating friends, however, were eating it up.

"So you're telling me that you're married, not married, single mother, not single mother, none of it really matters to anyone here?" Ruby asked, interested.

They all sort of just shrugged and said, "No."

Georgia was also intrigued. "So, you don't worry that a man will be put off by you having a child?"

Dröfn seemed actually offended by the idea, looking at Georgia as if it was the first time she'd ever heard of such an idea. "How could that be? If he loved me, he would have to love my children."

Georgia just nodded her head, like *Well, yes, of course I knew that.*

Rakel added, "You have to understand, most women here have children. Many are single mothers. We had a president who was a single mother."

Sigrud added, "If the men here didn't want to date single mothers, they really wouldn't be dating very often."

The table of Icelandic people laughed and agreed.

I just wanted to talk about Björk and if the people in Iceland think she's weird. Anything but this.

Serena now was getting into the act. "It doesn't sound like the church or religion plays a big part in things around here."

Again, the table nodded. "Iceland is mostly Lutheran. The church is run by the state. But no one goes. It's just tradition."

"This is so interesting. It's like we landed on a crazy planet untouched by the church or religion, whose people are guided instead by their own natural, instinctual morality. It's fascinating," Alice said, excited. I had to admit it. Even I was starting to get a little intrigued by these odd people.

They were all going out afterward to see their friends play in a band at a big nightclub in town called NASA. We were invited along, thankfully. We were all growing very attached to them and didn't really feel like leaving them just yet.

We walked into a large nightclub, just like any you might find in the States, packed with tons of people dancing and drinking. The band was playing a jolly mix of Irish and Icelandic music that just made you want to jump around with drunken joy. I had no idea what these men were singing about, but they seemed to be damn happy about it. The Icelanders walked straight to a little VIP area by the stage, and we followed right along. There were tables all ready for them—their friend from the band had arranged it. It was the perfect way to spend Alice's wedding night. Karl bought us all a round of shots—something called Black Death—and we all drank up, except for Serena, who apparently was pacing herself.

I looked out over the crowd. Hulda sat next to me and said, "The problem we have here, is that the men are very lazy. They don't know how to make the first move, so the women have become very aggressive. So then, the men now never have to make the first move. It's a terrible circle."

I nodded. Just as she said that I saw a gorgeous blond woman, in her late twenties, grab the man she was dancing with and start kissing him.

Hulda continued. "This is the other problem. Everyone here sleeps with each other right away. No dating like you do in the States."

It seemed to be another fica situation.

"Do the women mind if the men don't call them afterward?" She had drawn me into the conversation, damn her.

Hulda shrugged. "Sometimes yes, sometimes no. Icelandic women are very strong. We're Vikings, remember?" Then she added, "Besides, if we want to see them again, we can always call them."

She made it sound so easy.

The band started playing "The Devil Went Down to Georgia." We decided this was our cue to get out on the dance floor and start jumping up and down. We did this for hours. We danced and we drank and we met more and more Icelandic men and women—each one seemingly more free-spirited than the last. And the men were handsome and nice, but they are not the story of Iceland. To me, the story of Iceland is the women. The strong, beautiful, Viking women.

Eventually, we went back to our little area and stood by a railing looking over the crowd. Georgia surveyed the situation. "Well, if all these women are mothers, there must be an awful lot of babysitters in Reykjavik."

Alice looked out on the sea of people. "If anyone would have told me that I would be thirty-eight and single and childless and going to Iceland after I called off my wedding, I would never have believed them." I didn't like where this conversation was headed.

"I know. I really didn't expect my life would end up like this, either,"

Georgia said. "I'm divorced. I'm a divorcée. My parents are divorced. I thought it was the last thing that was ever going to happen to me."

Ruby threw in her two cents. "When I was little I didn't think I would be thirty-seven and crying all the time."

And Serena added, "I thought I would have so much more in my life. I thought I would have so much more *life* in my life."

"What's going to become of us?" Ruby asked.

I looked at us all, one big sinking ship about to go down. I got an idea. It seemed brilliant at the time but I was also drinking something called Black Death.

"We need to go somewhere," I shouted to them. "Tonight was supposed to be Alice's wedding night. We need to do something to mark it. We need to do a ritual."

Alice's eyes lit up a bit. "What kind of ritual?"

"I'm not sure yet. It's still in formation." I walked over to Sigrud and Rakel. I now had the notion that I wanted to drive my friends to a beautiful place in the middle of nature. Rakel suggested Eyrabakki, a sleepy little town right on the water. They asked me what I was going to do and I told them I wanted to perform a healing ritual for all of us. They thought it was a funny idea and agreed to join us, and Hulda and Dröfn agreed to come as well. On my way out I grabbed a huge stack of cocktail napkins. When we got out of the club, it was four in the morning. Rakel and Dröfn drove because they were the only sober ones who knew where we were going. Suddenly I had become the Icelandic den mother of the bunch. We all piled into cars and took off.

About twenty minutes later, we had arrived in Eyrabakki. It couldn't have felt more desolate. There was a small street that ran down the center of it, with rocks and water on one side and tiny unlit cottages on the other. It looked as if you could walk from one end of the town to the other in five minutes. We parked our cars in front of what seemed like the town supermarket and started walking toward the rocks. The wind was whipping through the air now, making it feel like it was many degrees below zero.

As we walked onto the rocks, Sigrud said, "It's a shame that you needed water for your ritual. There are other places much more magical. We could have gone where the elves are."

Alice, Ruby, Serena, Georgia, and I turned and looked at her. "Excuse me?" I asked. "Did you say elves?"

Sigrud nodded. "Yes, of course. But they live more inland."

Serena jumped in. "You believe in elves?"

Rakel nodded, very seriously. "Yes, of course."

I looked at them and said, "Elves? As in . . . elves?"

Hulda nodded as well. "Yes. Elves."

Georgia looked intrigued. "Well, have you ever seen them?"

Hulda shook her head. "I haven't, but my aunt has."

Dröfn said, "There is a famous story of these men trying to build a new road very close to here. Everything kept going wrong, the weather, the machinery would break down, all sorts of things. Then they brought in a psychic, who told them that it was because of the elves. They were on sacred elf land. The men moved their construction just a few miles away, and they didn't have a problem again."

I turned to Sigrud. I tried to be polite, but I still needed to get to the bottom of the elf situation.

"Well, what do they look like?"

Sigrud shrugged and, as matter-of-factly as if she were talking about what she had for dinner, said, "Some are small, some are tall, some wear funny hats."

Ruby laughed; she couldn't help herself. "Funny hats?"

Rakel laughed, too, understanding how it sounded. "Yes, and they live in houses, but we just can't see them."

I just shook my head and laughed. "You don't believe in marriage or God or religion. But you believe in elves?"

They all smiled and laughed. Sigrud giggled. "Yes."

"Well." Serena laughed. "That proves it. Everyone needs something to believe in."

We all walked toward the water. It was cold as hell and my initial enthusiasm about this wacky scheme was beginning to wane. I realized that we all could be asleep right now in our beds, if it weren't for me and my crazy ideas. We gathered at the water's edge. Everyone looked at me, expectantly. I decided it was time to start.

"Okay. So. I decided that we need to acknowledge in some kind of way what we're all feeling."

Everyone was quiet. Then Ruby said, "What are we all feeling?"

"I think we're feeling that there are a lot of things we're not going to be anymore. We're not going to be young brides. We're not going to be young mothers. We might not even get a husband and a home and two little children that we've borne ourselves. That doesn't mean that we won't get a husband, or children. But this is to acknowledge that it's not going to happen the way we thought it might. The way we hoped it would."

Georgia looked at me. "Wow, Julie, way to harsh my mellow." My American friends laughed. I don't think the Icelandic ladies understood.

I passed out the cocktail napkins I stole from the nightclub to Serena, Ruby, Georgia, and Alice. I didn't want to impose this ritual on my Icelandic sisters.

"Okay. So. I don't have pens or pencils, so I want you to instead put your disappointment into this napkin. I want you to imagine what you thought your life was going to look like now and I want you to put that in the napkin."

I closed my eyes and thought about what I imagined it was going to look like. I had a very specific expectation of what it was going to be. I never dreamed of marriage and children and always dreamed I would live a glamorous life in New York doing fun things with my fun, exciting friends. I knew that I would watch all my friends get married and have children before me—and then, at the last minute, just at the last minute, which, in my mind, *was last year,* my guy would show up, and he would, against my protestations and despite my cynical nature, sweep me off my feet and make me a wife and mother. That's how I pictured it would go. I was going to be the last entry, but I *would* get in. I never imagined that it might not happen. I put that all into my napkin.

Alice thought about her old boyfriend, Trevor. How she had planned on spending the rest of her life with him. She had imagined having a few children with him and growing old with him. She remembered all the holidays they had shared, all the ornaments they had collected at Christmas, and how she thought they were going to keep collecting them for years to come. She remembered how he had told her that he didn't want to marry her, and she told him that she thought it was time he moved out.

Ruby thought how she had imagined her happy life of love with every single man she had ever dated or spoken to in the past ten years. She saw all their faces fly past her, she remembered all the different lives she had envisioned. She was going to be the doctor's wife to Len. She was going to be emotionally supportive to Rich with his fledgling contracting business. She was going to move to D.C. to be with that lobbyist, what's-his-name. All the disappointments kept scrolling through her mind. She imagined putting them all in the napkin. She liked this ritual. *Because that is what all these men were. Nothing more than a fantasy. A notion left in a bar napkin.* She wondered how she could have ever given any of them so much power.

Georgia thought about Beth's college graduation. She imagined her and Dale sitting there in the hot sun, holding hands, with Gareth sitting next to them, along with all the respective grandparents. When Beth got up to get her diploma, Dale and Georgia would clap and cheer the loudest, then look at each other and kiss—their pride for Beth and love of each other all mixing together as they hugged and kissed some more. Georgia started to cry a little at this image, this image that she hadn't allowed herself to think of in such a long time. Now, here, as the cold wind whipped around, and the sun was nowhere in sight, she felt the loss of that deeply. And tears fell down her face.

Serena realized that she had no image whatsoever of what was going to happen to her. In her perfect yogi way, she had managed to let die any expectations of what her life was supposed to be like. She had no preconceived notions to let go of. She was empty of images of what she thought her life was supposed to look like. She realized that maybe it was time to get some. For her, it was about *starting* to imagine the life she wanted. She put her blank future into the napkin.

I took out a lighter I had borrowed from Karl and went around the circle, setting fire to our napkins, one by one. As they burned quickly, I said, "It's done. We won't have those lives. They're gone." One by one we dropped the napkins on the ground as the fire got close to our fingers.

"Now we're free."

All the women looked at me. Ruby asked first, "Free to do what?"

"Free to move on. Without bitterness. Those lives don't exist. Now we have to go on and live the ones we have."

Everyone was quiet. I don't think anyone had ever seen me so, well, sincere before. I looked at Sigrud, Rakel, and Hulda. They looked surprisingly respectful and solemn. I looked at them and wondered what they were thinking.

"Do any of you have anything you want to say?"

Rakel spoke up. "Congratulations, you all have just discovered your inner Viking."

We American ladies looked at each other, pleased.

We all got back to the hotel, had breakfast, then packed. Our whirlwind weekend was over. It was time to go home. Yes. It was time for me to go home. I was done with this all. Had I learned anything? Yes, I think so. Was I glad to have met Thomas? I would have to wait a little more time to find that out.

As we were heading to the airport, we were all quiet, we were sleep-deprived, hungover, and cranky, trying to hydrate ourselves with bottles of water we took from our hotel room. Alice, who was driving, decided to make a big announcement.

"Well, I just want you to know that I believe in elves."

We all looked at her and smiled, sleepily. Only Ruby had the energy to respond.

"You do? Really?"

"Yes. I do. I believe in elves. I mean, look at this crazy place. Doesn't it just seem like there have to be elves here?"

The rest of us were too tired to reply.

But I thought about this for a minute. We do all need something to believe in, so why not elves? *Or love?*

"Well, if Alice can believe in invisible people who wear funny hats, then I can believe in love. I will believe, from today on, that it's possible to find a person that you can live with and love for your whole life, who loves you back, and it's not just some psychological delusion."

Alice looked at me and began to clap. "Now we're talking," she said. I smiled. Georgia looked at us all and said, "And if Alice can believe in invisible people that mess around with poor construction workers, then I will believe that I can meet a man who not only loves me, but loves my children as well."

Serena nodded her head. "And if Alice can believe in elves and Julie can believe in love and Georgia can believe in love a second time around, I'm going to believe that Joanna and Kip are going to get through this. And someday they're going to be happy again."

"And what about you?" I asked.

"I believe that I'm going to find out how to be happy, too. Yes, me, too," Serena said.

Ruby smiled and raised her bottle of water in the air. "And I'm going to believe that we're all going to be happy. We're all going to get exactly what we want and be just fine." She took a sip of her water. "And Lexapro. I'm going to believe in that, too."

So, in a country of Viking pagans, we all found something to believe in. But I was still inspired.

"Well then," I said, "I'm going to take it one step further. If you all believe that we're all going to find love and be happy, then I'm going to believe in miracles—because that's what it's going to take for all this to really come true." Everyone laughed, but I said it with complete sincerity.

"Here, here," Alice said, raising her bottle of water. "To elves and miracles. Let's believe in them both. I mean, why not?"

We all clapped and raised our bottles in the air and agreed. "Why not?"

The plane was rolling down the runway. I was sitting on the aisle and Serena had the window seat. In front of us were Ruby and Georgia and across the aisle from me was Alice. The plane was now rattling, the sound of the wind was all around us as we started to pick up speed. It was then that I realized that with all the fogginess of being hungover and sleep-deprived, and chatting with my friends, I had forgotten to take any drugs before we took off. Besides that, I had forgotten to even bring them with me in my carry-on. I gripped the arms of my seat as the plane rattled into the air.

"I can't believe I forgot my drugs. I'm such an idiot."

Serena looked at me, my face slowly turning white. She put her hand on my arm and whispered to me. "It's going to be okay, remember? We're all going to be okay." The plane was now ascending, climbing into the air quietly. I nodded. "Right. Right. We're all going to be okay." I loosened my grip a bit.

Soon, we were in the air. Serena started reading to me from *People* magazine, and every once in a while Alice would interject with some gossip she had heard about this or that celebrity. I knew what they were trying to do—they were trying to keep me entertained so I wouldn't start shrieking. It worked. For five and a half hours, no panic. Not a drop of sweat, not a gasp, nothing. I was just like any other sane passenger on this plane. I have no idea why, but maybe it was being with my friends, not feeling so alone. Or maybe it was because of the ritual we did in Iceland, where I allowed myself to let go of all my expectations about my life—maybe it included my expectation that I was going to plunge to my death. Or maybe I knew deep down that we were all going to be okay. And in the far-off chance that we weren't, that we were all going to go down in a giant ball of flames—there was nothing I or my panic was going to do to change that. I let go of everything and just flew home.

But whatever the reason, my panic was gone.

Back in the States

Two weeks later, we all got together to hear about Alice's new job back in Legal Aid. We went to Spice restaurant in Manhattan and sat in a big booth downstairs in the VIP area, thanks to, of course, Alice. She told us all about the first case she was working on, a young kid who was accused of breaking parole but had been set up by one of his friends. She was full of conviction and passion and was excited to tell us all about it. We ordered some wine for the table, but Ruby declined. She was on a new medication, and she wasn't allowed to drink alcohol with it. And she confessed: it was an antidepressant. We all broke out into applause.

"Well, thank the frickin' lord," Alice said.

"What took you so long," Georgia said. "I might be going to take a trip to Mr. Psychiatrist any day myself."

"That's so amazing, Ruby. I know that was a hard decision for you!" Serena said. She had moved out of Ruby's the week before, having finally found an apartment in Park Slope.

"How do you feel?" I asked Ruby. She smiled happily.

"I feel kind of great. I have to say. Not like insanely happy or anything, just not so depressed. It just gives me a shelf. So I never really sink so low."

"That's fantastic," I added. And then Georgia looked at me and said, "So what are you going to do about your book?"

I grimaced and said, "I don't know yet. My publisher doesn't know I'm home, but she did just email me wondering how it was going. I don't know what to tell her."

All the ladies looked at me, slightly concerned that I was throwing my new career down the toilet.

"But don't you think you learned so much? From meeting all those women all over the world?"

I thought about it, as I took a stab at a piece of duck on my plate.

"I'm not sure."

After that, we went to a bar on an enclosed roof of one of the trendy hotels in the neighborhood. There was a deejay, but it wasn't crowded yet. We all piled our bags and our coats in a corner and got on the dance floor as fast as we could.

So there we all were, back in action. This time there would be no brawling, no stomach pumping, no chicken wings, no hogs, no heifers. We were all just out, opening ourselves up yet again, for one more night of adventure and fun and possibility.

The song "Baby Got Back" came on. Now, this is as fun a song to dance to as there is. We all started dancing our hearts out and shaking our "backs" and trying to sing along to the song and failing miserably at it.

I looked around at all my beautiful friends, dancing with each other. In these past two weeks I couldn't help but notice how these women all now called each other on their own, without me having anything to do with it. At dinner they teased each other and got annoyed with each other and knew exactly what was going on in each other's lives, like old friends. As Serena, Alice, Ruby, and Georgia all were laughing and shimmying and whooping it up on the dance floor, it hit me: I had finally gotten what I always dreamed of. While I was on the far side of the world, a girl posse was being born. And now here it was, fully formed, dancing up a storm in New York City.

I wondered again how I could sum up what I had learned from the amazing women all over the world. One thought kept creeping into my head—but I kept pushing it away. On the dance floor, with the music going and me feeling just the carefree abandon of being out with a bunch of my girlfriends, I was mortified even to think it. But I did feel it. I'm horrified even to type the words out now. But it hit me, hard—I am so loath to admit it. Shit. Goddamn it.

I think we are going to have to love ourselves. Fuck.

I know. *I know.* But at least let me just say, I don't mean we have to "love ourselves" in a take-a-bubble-bath-every-night kind of way. Not "love yourself" like "take yourself out to dinner once a week." I think we have to love ourselves fiercely. Like a lioness protecting her cub. Like we are about to be attacked at any moment by a marauding gang of thugs who are out to make us feel bad about ourselves. I think we have to love ourselves as passionately as the Romans love, with joy and enthusiasm and entitlement. I think we have to love ourselves with the pride and dignity of any French woman. We have to love ourselves as if we are seventy-year-old Brazilian women dressed all in red and white parading around in the middle of a block party. Or as if we just got hit with a can of beer in our face and we have to come to our own rescue. We have to aggressively love ourselves. We practically have to stalk ourselves, that's how much energy we need to put into this. We really do have to discover our inner Viking and wear our shining armor and love ourselves as bravely as we ever thought possible. So yes, I guess we fucking do have to love ourselves. I'm *sorry.*

Just as I was thinking all this, a cute guy with hair down to his shoulders walked up on the dance floor and started dancing/talking to Serena. He was wearing weird red baggy pants.

As they danced with each other, I heard Serena ask him, "Excuse me, but are your pants hemp?"

He nodded and leaned over and said to her, "As much as I can, I try not to wear anything that hurts the planet."

Serena nodded, intrigued. "What's a guy like you doing in a club like this?"

The guy smiled at her. "Hey, I may wear hemp but I still love to dance!" And just like that, he put his arm about Serena's back and swirled her around the room. She was laughing and blushing. For a moment as she passed by me, she gave me a look as if to say, "What are the odds of *this*?"

After dancing a bit, Alice, Georgia, Ruby, and I eventually sat down at a little table. We had a 180-degree view of the New York skyline, with the Empire State Building lit up in white and blue. Serena was now at another table, talking to the hemp lad. He seemed to be fully smitten by her, and they were laughing and chatting like two old friends.

"So . . . do you think we're witnessing a small miracle right in front of our eyes?" Alice teased.

I smiled at the thought. "You never know."

I looked around the club at all the beautiful women that were dancing, flirting, talking to men, talking to their friends. They were all out, trying to or having a good time, looking their stylish, unique, sassy best. I thought again about my travels. It could have gotten me discouraged meeting all those single women all over the world, all with their own struggles, their own needs and hopes and expectations. Instead, it comforted me. Because the one thing that I can keep with me, hold it like a tiny love note in one of my pockets, is that no matter what I've learned, or how I might feel about my single status on any given day, there is one thing I am clear about now. I am definitely not alone in this.

I am definitely not alone.

And you know what else? Miracles happen every day.

Acknowledgments

There are many, many people who helped me research this book, particularly the women and men I interviewed all over the world, and all my "hosts" who got me access to those people. The list of all of them by name might be as long as the book itself. But I am deeply indebted to all those people, particularly all those women, who took time out of their busy lives to talk to me about love and dating, with great honesty and great humor. It truly was a once-in-a-lifetime experience and I am humbled, grateful, and in awe of all of them. I thank them all from the bottom of my heart.

Specifically, I would like to mention a few people in each country who were invaluable to my research.

In Iceland, I need to thank Dröfn and Rakel for organizing the amazing meeting of the women of Reykjavík; as well as Brynja, Rakel, and Palli for their friendship, always.

In Brazil, my hero Bianca Costa, along with Tekka and Caroline of Copacabana films. Thank you to Matt Hanover from Yahoo. And Cindy Chupack for her brilliant mind that I wish I could have as my own.

In Europe, my camera crew Aaron, Tony, and James for making us laugh all the way through Paris and Rome. In Paris, my two fixers, Laure Watrin and Charlotte Sector. In Rome, Veronica Aneris and Monica De Berardinis (and John Melfi for always being there to help, in any country he can). For Dana Segal, for a friendly face during a chaotic time. To Gabriele and Domenico for inspiring me always, not just in Rome. In Denmark, Thomas Sonne Johansen and Per Dissing, thank you for being there for me on the last, coldest leg of my Europe trip.

In Mumbai, India—Hamida Parker, Aparna Pujar, Jim Cunningham, Monica Gupta, thank you all for helping us navigate a very difficult-to-navigate city. You were generous hosts to us.

In Sydney, Australia—Karen Lawson, thank you for your endless enthusiasm, humor, and boundless energy. Thank you, George Moskos, for your additional help with the blokes, and your good humor about it all, and a thank-you to Bernard Salt, for giving me so much of his time for a long, hilariously depressing interview. And a special thanks to Genevieve Read, now Genevieve Morton, whom I've never met, but inspired me so.

In Beijing, I must thank two ladies, Chen Chang and Stephanie Giambruno, for all their help making Beijing one of the most memorable trips of my life. And for Chang, for her bravely honest insights. I'd like to thank Han Bing for his additional help and Nicole Wachs for being the best companion an aunt could ever ask for.

And overall, my research and this book would not have been possible if it wasn't for Margie Gilmore and her relentless, tireless persistence, and Deanna Brown for her faith in us both. Margie, thank you again for giving me the world.

In the U.S., I need to thank the people who were there when this was just a germ of an idea and were ready to help. Mark Van Wye, Andrea Ciannavei, Shakti Warwick—and Garo Yellin, for that night when he figured it all out for me.

During the writing of this book, thank you Craig Carlisle, Kathleen Dennehy, and my savior Kate Brown.

And then to those without whom I would be nothing: Andy Barzvi for being the pushiest, most delightful agent a girl could ever ask for, it's all her fault, every last bit of it; my editor Greer Hendricks—I'm still trying to figure out what great thing I did to deserve her; and to my publisher Judith M. Curr, I'm still learning how lucky I am that she's in charge.

Thank you to my sushi and story ladies for being ready and willing to go way beyond the call of duty. Thank you to Marc Korman and Julien Thuan on whom I rely for everything. Thank you to John Carhart for all his hard work and good humor, even when he hates me. A special big international thank-you to Nadia Dajani, for taking this journey with me and being a witness to it all—and I mean all of it. The world would not have been so much fun without you. A special thank-you to Michael Patrick King, because he started it all, and will get a special thank-you always. And to all my friends and family, whose encouragement irritated me so, thank you for your patience with me. I am nothing without you.

PENGUIN BOOKS

NOT QUITE THE DIPLOMAT

Chris Patten is one of Britain's most respected political figures. After reading Modern History at Balliol College, Oxford, he began his career in politics when he joined the Conservative Research Department in 1966. He was elected as MP for Bath in 1979, a seat he held until April 1992. After ministerial posts at the departments of Education, Environment and the Foreign & Commonwealth Office, he was appointed Chairman of the Conservative Party in 1990. He was made Governor of Hong Kong in 1992, a position he held until 1997 when he oversaw the return of Hong Kong to China. In September 1999 he was appointed European Commissioner for External Relations, and on leaving office in Brussels in 2004 was made a life peer.

Lord Patten is Chancellor of Newcastle and Oxford universities and now spends much of his time campaigning for increased funding for higher education. He is the author of *The Tory Case* (1983) and the international bestseller *East and West* (1998), which described his experiences in Hong Kong. He lives in Barnes with his wife Lavender; they have three daughters.

CHRIS PATTEN

Not Quite the Diplomat
Home Truths about World Affairs

PENGUIN BOOKS

PENGUIN BOOKS

Published by the Penguin Group
Penguin Books Ltd, 80 Strand, London WC2R ORL, England
Penguin Group (USA) Inc., 375 Hudson Street, New York, New York 10014, USA
Penguin Group (Canada), 90 Eglinton Avenue East, Suite 700, Toronto, Ontario, Canada M4P 2Y3
(a division of Pearson Penguin Canada Inc.)
Penguin Ireland, 25 St Stephen's Green, Dublin 2, Ireland
(a division of Penguin Books Ltd)
Penguin Group (Australia), 250 Camberwell Road, Camberwell, Victoria 3124, Australia
(a division of Pearson Australia Group Pty Ltd)
Penguin Books India Pvt Ltd, 11 Community Centre, Panchsheel Park, New Delhi – 110 017, India
Penguin Group (NZ), cnr Airborne and Rosedale Roads, Albany, Auckland 1310, New Zealand
(a division of Pearson New Zealand Ltd)
Penguin Books (South Africa) (Pty) Ltd, 24 Sturdee Avenue, Rosebank, Johannesburg 2196, South Africa

Penguin Books Ltd, Registered Offices: 80 Strand, London WC2R ORL, England

www.penguin.com

First published by Allen Lane 2005
Published with revisions in Penguin Books 2006

1

Typeset by Rowland Phototypesetting Ltd, Bury St Edmunds, Suffolk
Printed in England by Clays Ltd, St Ives plc

ISBN-13: 978-0-141-02144-7
ISBN-10: 0-141-02144-6

For my growing family

Contents

List of Illustrations

(Photographic acknowledgedments are given in parentheses)

Acknowledgements

I had a first-class team of officials in my private office – or *cabinet* in Brussels-speak – when I was a European Commissioner from 1999 to 2004. For almost four years, it was led by Anthony Cary, for the last one and a bit by Patrick Child. They were respectively the best that Britain's Foreign Office and Treasury could have provided. The whole team contributed to my education and therefore to this book, and Anthony Teasdale who works in the European Parliament helped me to understand its beguiling mysteries. They were all friends and with Lavender and my daughters kept me sane and (usually) quite cheerful. The book represents my own prejudices as refined and occasionally recast by this amiable and accomplished life-support unit, for whom I was not perhaps quite the Commissioner expected. I hope it does not blight any careers.

Once again, I owe a huge debt of gratitude to my agent, Michael Sissons, and to my editor, Stuart Proffitt. I hope that this book will not be as exciting an adventure for Stuart and me as the last one turned out to be.

I can only type with one finger and my writing is tiny and wickedly crabbed. The book would not exist without patient deciphering by my wife, my daughters, Alice and Laura, Dame Shirley Oxenbury and Penny Rankin. Their reward will come in heaven. My eldest daughter, Kate Meikle, should be grateful that she was in Rome while the runes were being read.

I

Now We are Sixty

. . . I cannot deny my past to which myself is wed;
The woven figure cannot undo its thread.

'Valediction', Louis MacNeice

A few months before starting to write this book, I celebrated my sixtieth birthday. Along with all the sympathetic cards, I received information through the post about my entitlement to a winter fuel allowance and an application form for a 'free travel' bus and train pass. I guess these are prized examples of the famed European social model, cradle to (almost) grave, the need for whose comprehensive overhaul is an urgent consequence of Europe's long-term demographic changes and of its inadequate recent efforts to reinvigorate its economy. Social solidarity requires growth to pay for it, and growth requires workers to create it.

European assumptions about welfarism need to be reviewed; so do the opinions, with which citizens of my generation have grown to adulthood and aged into retirement, about the way our world works and is made both prosperous and secure. The old clichés of international governance and alliance – the Atlantic partnership, European integration, shared Western values – have given way in the blink of an eye to another set of clichés – shifting tectonic plates, the Union that hit the buffers, the Republic that became an empire. Nothing in politics is forever except, it seems, Britain's existential hunt for its own identity: to lose ourselves in Europe or to discover our post-imperial role as America's spear carrier – or at least its interpreter and apologist to the world's wimps. Meanwhile, the great if perennially crisis-wracked European project – a union of free-trading democracies – strikes out in directions unimagined by those who first created it around Franco-German reconciliation. And Washington's leaders of the Free World (as we used to call our alliance against Soviet tyranny and Communist advance) seem keen to close the chapter, which they above all others have written, and which described, regulated and sustained so much of the life of our planet for half a century. If the Western Front has fundamentally changed, or been broken by events and cultural disjuncture, what international configuration will emerge during the short interval of years before the rise of China and India reshapes the world's power politics?

I have lived my life as a pretty enthusiastic citizen of America's undeclared empire, which chose deliberately not to impose an emperor on its denizens: a touch, that, of political genius. I was born the month before the D-Day landings brought American boots and blood to French soil for the second time in under thirty years. My father was not one of that military host. He was serving in Palestine with the Royal Air Force, leaving behind his pregnant wife and my older sister. My mother had made her wartime home in her parents' cathedral city, Exeter, until much of it was flattened in an air raid. She went north to live on the Lancashire coast beyond Blackpool in a seaside house owned by my father's brother-in-law, a prosperous wholesale vegetable merchant. There I was born in the modest comfort of a home bought, with appropriate symmetry, from the proceeds of imported Irish potatoes, whose terrible dearth had driven my father's forebears from Ireland to Lancashire in the previous century.

My wife's father was less fortunate than mine. A Cambridge athlete from the generation after the young men remembered in *Chariots of Fire*, he hurdled in the 1936 Berlin Olympics, briefly made a career with Imperial Chemical Industries (ICI) and then joined the Seaforth Highlanders at the outbreak of war. He fought through north Africa and Sicily, went to Normandy in time for the fight across the *bocage* and was killed just after the Allied breakout at Falaise, shortly before my wife's birth. The list of the war dead at his Cambridge college, Pembroke, contains German names as well as British, Dominion and American. Other college memorials at Oxford and Cambridge tell the same story. We brought young men together at our eminent universities to learn about the values of Western civilization, and then they returned to their homes and were required in due course to kill one another – from Newman's 'umbrageous groves' to trenches and tanks and the war graves of Europe, like the one near Caen where Major John Thornton, the Seaforth Highlander, lies.

The American boys who came from high corn and blue grass, from tenement block and front porch, to help save Europe once again from the bloody results of rampant nationalism, were led by men who believed that the young of their nation should not be required a third time to cross the Atlantic to rescue the old world. Europe's cemeteries contained too many of their own young heroes already. So it was scarcely surprising that American leaders, policy makers and diplomats were such enthusiastic supporters of the efforts to prevent another European civil war through a unique pooling of sovereignty between France, Germany and four other countries, initially achieved by bringing together the industries that fed modern conflict – coal and steel. European integration was an American geo-strategic objective from the very start, and for Washington it was desirable that Britain should be part of the enterprise. Our American friends did not share our own opinion that Britain could sit benignly, patronizingly, apart from the construction of a new Europe as the cherished friend and valued partner of the superpower, the leader of its own worldwide Empire turned Commonwealth, the sagacious well-wisher to our Continental neighbours in their quaint endeavours. Whatever the gallantry of our recent history, whatever the majesty of Churchill's prose, Britain was no longer a top dog, even though we could still lay claim to invitations to the top table.

I grew up during the years when Churchill still growled Britain's past glories, but when his war time lieutenants, Eden and Macmillan, were confronted in their different ways with the reality of Britain's decline. Discharged from the RAF, my father had gone to London, building on the pre-war contacts he had made as a professional musician, to become a popular music publisher, working in Tin Pan Alley. We lived in semi-detached suburban West London, an environment about which I have a passingly Proustian sensitivity. The suburban front-garden smell, to which Michael Frayn alludes at the beginning of his novel *Spies*, I was able to identify immediately – privet! I spring from that world of privet hedges, mock-Tudor, cherry blossom, and well-polished family cars, embalmed between London's arterial roads and its Underground lines, the world in full bloom at the polar extremes of the Central line from Hainault to West Ruislip. My older sister and I were brought up in the sort of loving, comfortable home that should entitle a writer these days to sue for deprivation of literary royalties – no story here of abuse and hardship. My parents were not very political. Indeed, I suspect that my mother would have thought it vaguely indecent and certainly uncomfortable to get involved in a deep – let alone rowdy – discussion of either politics or religion. She had converted to Catholicism, with what insights of faith I know not, in order to marry my father. We were what is called 'practising' Catholics: Mass every Sunday, fish every Friday, convent school for my sister, Benedictines for fortunate me. I can still repeat most of the responses to the Latin Mass from my years in the Guild of St Stephen as an altar boy for the local, always Irish, clergy; the smell of the communion wine on their breath in the early mornings; and in one sad case the whiff of something a little stronger.

The first international event I recall, courtesy of the *Daily Express*, was the gallantry of the 'Glorious Gloucesters' in the Korean War; of much greater consequence was the Suez debacle in 1956. My father had only recently taken me aside, with much embarrassment all round, to give me a little booklet explaining, improbably, how I might in the future play my part in reproducing the species. He told me for a second time that he wanted to say a word to me privately. I was not to tell my mother or sister. What he had to say would only worry them. Events in the Middle East looked very dangerous. The British and French invasion of Egypt could trigger another much larger war. The weapons now available in the world were more terrible than any he had seen used in the last war. I might have to be prepared to behave with a maturity beyond my years – taking responsibility, for example, for my mother and sister. We returned gravely and discreetly to the two other members of the family, unaware as they were of the gathering shadows apprehended by my father. Fortunately, President Eisenhower pulled the plug on this crazy Middle Eastern adventure before it went too far, partly because of his proper concern about its impact on opinion in the Arab world. Anthony Eden went to the Caribbean, and then to a manor house in Wiltshire; Harold Macmillan ('first in, first out' in Harold Wilson's words) went to Downing Street; I went back to cricket and Conan Doyle.

Our house was not very bookish. There were book club editions of Nevil Shute, L. P. Hartley and Nicholas Montserrat, Thor Heyerdahl's Kon-Tiki adventures, books on Second World War heroes and heroics – escapes, dam-busting, navigating cruel seas. Above all there was Damon Runyon and S. J. Perelman – a mark, I think, of how comfortably and naturally we accommodated ourselves to America's cultural imperium. My father's job probably made this inevitable. Before skiffle and the Mersey Sound, most of the popular music he published was from the other side of the Atlantic – the hit tunes of Johnny Ray, Frankie Laine, Guy Mitchell. One of his first big successes was the latter's 'She Wears Red Feathers and a Hoolah-Hoolah Skirt'. My parents' taste was rather better than this. Our 78s featured Frank Sinatra, Ella Fitzgerald, big-band jazz – the music of a country that we instinctively admired and respected, glamorous, generous, gee-whiz. We were Americaphiles. How could we be anything else? All that seemed savviest and sassiest, wittiest and wisest, came from across the Atlantic. Weekly cinema visits confirmed our instincts. From one suburban film palace to another – 'Don't be disappointed if we can't get in,' my father would say on each of our visits – we followed the cultural trail blazed by Hollywood. It was a nice surprise to discover when I went to Oxford University that other countries had been making films too.

We not only loved America and most things American, without ever having been there. We were also – despite reading Lord Beaverbrook's daily newspaper – more than comfortable with our Continental neighbours. My own mother, unlike most of my friends', used garlic when she cooked, and sometimes shopped at an Italian delicatessen in Soho, demonstrating that it was possible to purchase olive oil without going to a chemist's shop. We went to restaurants whose exotic connections with the Mediterranean were advertised by the wicker-covered Chianti bottles that served as lamps. We sometimes drank wine at meals. My sister – five years older than me – left her convent school for the French lycée, and went to Strasbourg to work for the Council of Europe for her first job, and for her second to Rome with the United Nations. We sometimes holidayed abroad, forsaking beach cricket in Devon for beach cricket (to the surprise of the locals) in Brittany. On our first foreign holiday we drove France's *pavé* roads to Luxembourg in my father's Lanchester. Visiting Paris on the way home I locked myself in the lavatory at the Weppler Hotel, an event which left me timorous about the locks in hotel bathrooms throughout my childhood.

These holidays and my father's occasional business trips to Radio Luxembourg – the pirate radio station that brought pop music and the football pools forecasts of Keynsham's Horace Batchelor to the crystal sets of Britain's youth – instilled in him a huge admiration for the recuperative skills of the French and the Germans. He tended to judge the economic ascent of France almost entirely in terms of the smoothness of the motoring, as the infrastructure of *l'Hexagone* benefited from post-war recovery. His admiration for Germany's revival was boundless. By nature a generous and kind man, he spoke more frequently of the spectacular rise of Germany from her wartime legacy of starvation and rubble than of the years he had lost, and the friends too, fighting her. Like Harold Macmillan, though he would not have known it, he regarded Germany's triumphant economic progress as a knock-down argument for joining her and others in what was then called the Common Market.

I first heard the case for this put with stunning eloquence when I went up to Balliol College, Oxford, in 1962. It was the college of Harold Macmillan, who resigned from the premiership at the beginning of my second academic year, but came in the following calendar year to address his fellow college members as the university's chancellor. It was the best speech I have ever heard, and I was pleased to hear variants of it, complete with the same thespian gestures and pauses, on several occasions during the following twenty years. The Edwardian drawl, the hooded eyes, the Donald Wolfit excess, the hand movements that followed rather than accompanied the thought just delivered, the magnificent studied put-downs, the mixture of plump archaism with demotic metaphor – all these complemented a simple argument that I have always found totally convincing, though today there is a great deal more that can be added to it. Macmillan began by evoking the long, hot summer of 1914; described the talented friends who had left Oxford with him that year for the Golgotha of Picardy; recounted their experiences as (in Sassoon's words) 'citizens of death's grey land'; counted off those who had never returned; recalled the memorials from the Menin Gate to the great arch at Thiepval, which were forgotten as we drifted into another terrible war; pointed to the historic decisions taken at Messina and in Rome to prevent the slaughter of a third generation on our continent; and said that one day we too must be part of this adventure, whatever the present whim of an old general to whom we had in the past given so much. Know-all young cynics choked back the tears and then stood to cheer, recognizing perhaps that to speak like this of the fire, you have first to pass through it.

In my first year at Oxford, President Kennedy had skilfully defused the Cuban missile crisis, while my left-wing friends marched to the Martyrs' Memorial to denounce Yankee imperialism. In my second year, Kennedy was shot. There is famously a handful of public events in all our lives, imprinted forever on our memories. Those of us who are old enough all know where we were when we first heard of Kennedy's assassination, as we remember the circumstances on 11 September 2001, when we learned about or watched on television the atrocities in New York and Washington. During the evening of 22 November 1963, I was at a party given in college by one of my history dons when two or three hard-left students burst into the room to tell us gleefully what had happened in Dallas. For them it was almost a cause of celebration that such a popular American president should be cut down to make way for a man who could not possibly charm the world in the same way. It was the moment of my university years when I felt most outraged and most political.

Politics did not then feature much in my life. I acted, wrote revues, played rugby and cricket, and allowed myself to be stretched intellectually rather less than the elastic would actually have permitted. In so far as I had any political views, they were pretty much bang in the middle. I liked and admired Macmillan, Macleod and Butler, thought Douglas-Home's selection as Tory leader was absurd, and was attracted by Harold Wilson's look of modernity until he got into office and we saw him in depressing action. My parents had been gentle, undemonstrative Conservatives, who voted the right way at every election but otherwise seemed largely untouched by political sentiment. That is probably as far as I would have travelled politically myself had it not been for the good fortune of winning my first ever visit to America.

An old member of the college, William Coolidge – a wealthy Boston Brahmin – had established a fund at Balliol as one of his many philanthropic benefactions, to enable a group of those who had just taken their final examinations to cross the Atlantic each year and travel around the USA. I guess that part of the intention was not simply to broaden our horizons but to invest in the creation of future Americaphiles. In most cases, including mine, that was certainly the result. The scholarship in those days was gold-plated. We crossed to New York on the *France*, drinking cocktails, watching films and failing to pick up American beauties who all seemed to dance like Cyd Charisse. Then we flew up to spend a few days with Mr Coolidge – Bill, as we were encouraged to call him – on his Massachusetts estate where the paintings were even finer than the wine. We were kitted out at the Harvard Coop – lightweight suits and slacks, burgundy loafers, Oxford cotton shirts with button-down collars – given a Hertz credit card and a thousand dollars in traveller's cheques; presented with a list of Coolidge's friends and old Balliol men who had agreed to put us up as we travelled the country; and then sent off in pairs to cross and recross America, taking either the northern or southern route.

I drove off in a Dodge Dart for Ohio, Illinois and all points westward with my friend Edward Mortimer (who was to become a distinguished foreign correspondent, commentator and author, and director of communications at the UN). It was my happy experience then and on many subsequent visits to be received everywhere with kindness and generosity. As Charles Dickens said, after his second visit to the United States: 'Wherever I have been, in the smallest places equally with the largest, I have been received with unsurpassable politeness, delicacy, sweet temper, hospitality and consideration.' Americans are exquisite hosts. 'Thank you for visiting with us,' they would say, as we were fêted from Chicago to Billings, Montana, from Salt Lake City to San

Francisco and Los Angeles. We were in southern California at the time of the Watts riots, and drove (probably foolishly) through this grim Los Angeles suburb a day or two after most of the violence had subsided. Travelling back east through Las Vegas (where we watched a historically questionable, nude showgirl tableau of the French Revolution), the Grand Canyon, Santa Fe and New Orleans, we had another brush with contemporary history in Alabama. We were driving a hire car with a Pennsylvania number plate and were taken for civil rights workers in a small town where brave young campaigners from northern campuses had recently been murdered. Our host on that part of the trip, a courtly newspaper editor, came to our rescue explaining that we were English – 'They're just like us over there,' he said to a bunch of Alabama rednecks, a comparison for which we were grateful at the time.

Back in New York, with some weeks of the scholarship still to run if we wished, Edward chose to return to Oxford to sit and, as it turned out, win the annual examination to become a Fellow of All Souls, Oxford's ancient graduate college. What should I do on my own? Bill Coolidge had a bright idea. A rich friend of his was helping to raise money for the mayoral campaign in the city of the Republican Congressman from the silk-stocking district, John Lindsay. It was suggested that I should stay in his friend's apartment (on 5th and 69th) and help on the campaign, which had its headquarters at the Roosevelt Hotel.

I turned up for duty and was assigned as an assistant to a wonderfully smart young Texan lawyer – Yale and Balliol – who was responsible on the campaign for research, particularly regarding the record of Lindsay's opponents. Sherwin Goldman was a joy to work for – witty, civilized, generous and smart as a whip. He took me in hand, giving me a crash course in New York, its politics and its cultural delights. Thanks to Sherwin, who went on to run the New York City Opera Company, I got to the Met and to see several Balanchine ballets. I was also introduced to the (for me) mostly static mysteries of American football, and had my first pastrami on rye at the Carnegie Deli on 7th Avenue.

It was Sherwin, more than anyone else, who infected me with politics, a virus that I have never subsequently managed to remove from my bloodstream. I was given my head and allowed to focus in particular on the past and present pronouncements of the Conservative candidate in the campaign, William Buckley. 'Conservative', in this case, meant well to the right of the moderate Republican, Lindsay. Buckley was a sort of cult Conservative – mannered, funny, well read. He liked to tease and shock, raping and pillaging political correctness in fluently written books and articles. He had worked hard to earn Gore Vidal's sobriquet 'Hitler without the charm'. It was a joy to mine his obiter dicta for nonsense and contradiction. I doubt whether much of my material was ever used. Buckley was not really a serious candidate in any sense, commenting memorably when asked what would be the first thing he would do were he to win the mayoralty of that difficult city: 'Demand a recount.' His main danger to us was that he might siphon off the right-wing Republican votes that Lindsay would need to beat his uncharismatic, diminutive Democrat opponent. Nevertheless, I was made to feel a crucial cog in the campaign, was given plenty of access to Lindsay himself, and became a sort of mascot – a young novelty Englishman, complete with nice manners, a funny accent and odd vocabulary. A smoker in those days, I recall the first time, like the character in a Bateman cartoon, that I asked for a fag.

John Lindsay was a great candidate – 'Supercalifragelisticexpialidocious', as the advertisement on Times Square put it. He was tall, handsome and stylish. He spoke well, looked a dream on television and appeared to enjoy the vulgarities of political campaigning – gladhanding, eating pizzas and hugging New York. I suspect he was probably a better candidate than he was a mayor, though there cannot have been many tougher jobs in those days than running that big, dangerous, glamorous, bankrupt city. He did win, sweeping the Democrats from City Hall, and thus ended for me a glorious fall in New York – golden days, exciting times. In mid-November, I embarked on the old *Queen Elizabeth* and spent four days throwing up as we crossed the stormy Atlantic.

So I came to politics by this odd if glamorous route, joining the young men and women – mostly career politicians from Oxbridge – in the Conservative Research Department in what I thought would be a fill-in job before taking up a graduate traineeship with the BBC.

'Fill-in' became permanent, to the surprise of the BBC and of all my friends. It was the first fateful decision of my life; and the rest is history, of a sort.

Since that first visit to the United States I have returned again and again, as a tourist and holidaymaker, as a lecturer, as a young Member of Parliament, as a minister, as a colonial governor, as a European commissioner, and nowadays as a university chancellor. In a tribute to Roy Jenkins, my predecessor as Oxford's chancellor, Arthur Schlesinger noted that 'few British politicians in the nineteenth and early twentieth centuries . . . showed much interest in the United States, or knew much about American history or institutions'. It was only after the Second World War that British politicians like Jenkins, with easier travel by jet, started to go to America in force to find out what it was really like. For my political generation, it would have been inconceivable not to be a regular visitor: there was so much in America that one needed to understand, and in due course there was so much business to do. My only two prolonged visits came, first, when I had just become an MP and, second, when I became a Cabinet Minister. I spent about a month in the summer of 1980, mostly in Washington, as a guest of the State Department, where I made a number of political friends including the moderate Republican Congressman Jim Leach who, were I to require a double (like Saddam Hussein), would do nicely. We have become even more interchangeable as life has broadened us both. In 1989, as the newly appointed Environment Secretary in Margaret Thatcher's last Cabinet, I spent a month at Berkeley, the visit arranged by a close friend, Professor Nelson Polsby, possessor of one of the sharpest minds and certainly the sharpest tongue in North America. We took our holiday there, swapping our Westminster flat and Wiltshire cottage for a funky, clapboard house just off the gourmet strip in Berkeley. There was a loom in the front room, and mind-clearing, life-changing works by Indian mystics and gurus in the bookcases. It was meant to be a working holiday. I had to give a few lectures and seminars to justify the trip. The routine was hardly demanding but it was certainly bracing. Politicians need an occasional intellectual rub-down, and Nelson and his colleagues used a loofah.

*

As a specifically British minister and public servant, my contacts with America, with its political classes and policy makers, have centred on two issues, about which I shall have more to say later in this book. My first ministerial job was as Parliamentary Secretary in the Northern Ireland Office under Jim Prior and Douglas Hurd. Since then my career has been intermittently entangled with the affairs of the Province and the attempts to promote political reconciliation on our archipelago, most recently as Chairman of the Independent Commission on Policing in Northern Ireland, set up under the Belfast Agreement of 1998. As a moderate and as a Catholic, I was often despatched to America to take part in conferences on the divided politics of the North and to lobby about security issues. In the first category of events, I would find myself alongside moderate spokesmen for Dublin's position (like Peter Sutherland and Mary Robinson) sharing platforms with Nationalist, Republican and Unionist leaders from the North. I used to think it educational for audiences from Boston to Los Angeles to observe the Northern Irish politicians telling audiences how culturally different they were from their political foes as they appeared with every passing row more and more similar. Peter, Mary and I would occasionally get in a word ourselves, the moderates from either shore of the Irish Sea.

Talking to American audiences in those days, and particularly lobbying on Capitol Hill, amounted to a crash course in American exceptionalism. This reflects the central role that America has played as an actor rather than a disinterested observer in so many of the dramas of the Irish story – the famine, the plague ships, the formation of the Fenians, and gunrunning in the cause of liberation and anti-colonialism. The attitude of many Americans is more naïve than hypocritical; they fail to realize how subjective is the neat division of the world into evil terrorists and noble freedom fighters. For me to use the word 'terrorism' in the context of Northern Ireland during those visits was to risk a rumpus. Friends of mine had been killed by the Irish Republican Army (IRA). I had no sympathy for the use of violence for political ends: I thought it wicked. I was pleased to have the chance to argue from time to time that it was (to put at it at its mildest) 'unhelpful' that the IRA could raise money pretty openly in American cities, where they would also spend it on acquiring weapons.

For those fighting Irish terrorism, America was in this sense arguably a much bigger problem than, say, Libya. If terrorism simply divided 'us' from 'them', then in this case America was with 'them'.

I never got anywhere with my arguments. I conceded, of course, many of the grievances of Irish history: I was, after all, a British citizen because of the greatest of them all. I argued against Unionist intransigence, which has again and again searched for ways of extracting defeat from the jaws of victory, ensuring that each time the Unionist leaders are driven by reality to negotiate, they have to do so from a weaker position than the last time they were at the table. I accepted that to accomplish our security objectives there would have to be a political settlement, though this stuck in the craw of all who thought terrorist slaughter evil. In other contexts than Irish politics this sort of political realism would have been called by my American interlocutors 'rewarding violence'. But nothing changed. The collecting tins continued to be passed around; the weapons were purchased; and Irish Republican leaders who had killed and maimed were regularly welcomed to the White House – until the McCartney sisters came along – from which had rung out in recent years so many absolutist sermons about the wickedness of terrorism.

Chairing the policing commission on Northern Ireland, I made several visits to the USA with members of my team. We received much help on technical policing issues from local police chiefs, many of whom are from the Irish diaspora. We also discovered how much tougher were the rules of engagement for Northern Ireland's police officers, when faced with public order violence, than for most American forces. We were comprehensively grilled by American civil liberties organizations and by politicians about past policing practices and the steps we intended to take to make sure that the reformed and reorganized police service in Northern Ireland gave a proper and transparent priority to human rights. I regarded interrogation on these issues as wholly reasonable, and regarded our ability to satisfy these American expert concerns as one of the benchmarks for the success of our report. For me, this experience has cast an interesting light on Abu Ghraib, Guantánamo Bay and other related matters.

The second issue, which brought me sharply into contact with

American attitudes and policies, also concerned human rights, this time in Hong Kong. I have written elsewhere of my efforts as the last governor of Hong Kong to deliver on at least some of the promises made to its citizens about democracy, the rule of law and civil liberties. The support that I got in these endeavours was at best mixed. The British Government was fine, though you did not need a higher degree in reading body language to recognize that there were parts of Whitehall that believed I was several sandwiches short of a picnic. The British business community was at best nervously polite about me, but mostly hostile. The media, on the other hand, were pretty friendly. European opinion was curious about the whole fuss, by and large taking the view that this was a bit of last-minute British grandstanding. France, in particular, was not going to let anything interfere with the aims of its commercial diplomacy in China. For the most consistent, intelligent and outspoken support, I could look only to the USA. President Clinton, the State Department and politicians from both parties were regularly and openly helpful. American non-governmental organizations, lawyers' groups and human rights lobbyists batted for us; the media too. Above all, the local American business community was intelligently forthright about the importance of respecting and retaining the protection of Hong Kong's liberties through the rule of law, strong institutions and our first limited essays at democratic accountability. Again and again, they made the connection between economic liberty and political liberty, between Hong Kong's economic success and its way of life as a free society. It was good to have some friends who believed so uninhibitedly in the same things as I did – and were prepared to say so.

In the early stages of my political life, I was little involved in European affairs. Of course, the issue of Britain's membership of the Common Market – or European Community, as we came to describe it – squatted in the middle of national politics, seeping poison into the main parties. Only the Liberals, metamorphosed by Labour's upheavals of the 1980s (partly provoked by Europe) into Liberal Democrats, remained ever faithful to the European project, while periodically benefiting from its unpopularity through the support of electors who regarded their votes as a way of registering a protest against the other parties rather than as an endorsement of the whims and fancies of Liberalism's high command.

Others with whom I worked in the Conservative Party had long been involved in various pro-European organizations, arguing the case for Britain's European destiny in language often as extreme as that of their opponents within the party. But the opposition was definitely in the minority, usually regarded as slightly cranky as well as 'unhelpful', a dreadful thing to be in mainstream Tory circles. The Conservative Party usually liked to follow its leader and it liked to be liked. The leadership was pro-European, so the loyal thing to be was pro-Europe. Moreover, bright young party members touched by the sort of ambitions that help drive our political system and government, would naturally wish to reflect the attitudes and vision of their elders. Were you more likely to be chosen for a plum parliamentary constituency by declaring your belief in Britain's membership of a club she could aspire to lead (while naturally preserving the 'special relationship' with America), or by doubting the geo-strategic wisdom of Macmillan, Douglas-Home, Heath and all the rest? It was no contest. You also had the comfort of knowing that most newspapers would applaud your pro-European views and excoriate any heresy. Several newspapers, which were then more uncritically pro-European than I have ever been, have in the intervening years totally changed their tune, perhaps – as they claim – because Europe has been transformed into a different enterprise, or perhaps because their proprietors and editors have changed or have switched their views.

There will be time later to examine just how much the European project has altered, and to consider whether there is any truth in the argument that we were sold a pup, signing up to one thing while getting quite another. What the proponents of this argument usually mean is that what we agreed to was a free-trade area but that we have found ourselves trapped in a federalist union well on the way to becoming a superstate. Odd, really, for us to join what was allegedly no more than a free-trade area, when we were already part of one, called exactly that – the European Free Trade Area (EFTA) – an organization that manifestly failed to meet our economic or political aims. The European Community that we joined expressed in those days more explicitly federalist ambitions than are usually heard today except in one or two odd corners of Europe's chancelleries and parliaments. The federalist model exists in its most potent, albeit fictitious, form in London newspaper offices.

In 1975, shortly after I had become Director of the Conservative Research Department, we fought the referendum campaign purportedly to determine whether the cosmetic changes negotiated by Harold Wilson in our terms of membership were sufficient to allow us to confirm our place in the Community. As has been the case with Britain's two other European referendum commitments, this one was a result of government weakness. Wilson wanted to hold his party together, split as it was over Europe. The successful campaign achieved this in the short term, but short meant short. Throughout the early 1980s Labour tore itself to shreds over the subject, provoking the departure from its ranks of some of its most attractive figures as well as the establishment of the Social Democratic Party, and ensuring that it was unelectable until Neil Kinnock and then Tony Blair put it back together again. Labour's turmoil in the 1980s presaged that in the Conservative Party a decade later.

The referendum campaign was the first time I had worked closely with Margaret Thatcher, who had only recently been elected leader of the party in a surging peasants' revolt against the incumbent, Edward Heath. As the party's leading European, he was brought huffily out of the tent to which he had retreated to lick his wounds (a process that took many years), to play a prominent part in the all-party Yes campaign. Thatcher was for once wisely happy to play second fiddle. But it was not because of any hesitation about the cause. She made some good pro-European speeches, which I helped to draft, and never tried by word or gesture to put any distance between herself and Heath and his co-campaigners.

One of those on the other side of the argument was my wife Lavender's uncle, Sir Derek Walker-Smith, who later became a life peer, taking the name of his Hertfordshire constituency, Broxbourne. Derek Walker-Smith was a distinguished Conservative parliamentarian and a successful barrister. He had entered the House of Commons after the war, chaired the backbenchers' 1922 Committee and been appointed Minister of Health by Harold Macmillan. He was never happy about the decision to sue for terms to join the European

Community. His argument was principled and, as I shall argue later, the core of the case that has to be answered one way or the other, once and for all, if Britain is ever to come to terms with its place in Europe. For Derek, the great struggles in British history had been to establish and safeguard the sovereignty of Parliament. The law was made at Westminster, and interpreted and administered by the courts and judges of the land. By signing the Treaty of Rome we were conceding the supremacy of another law-making body – the European Council and Parliament – and accepting that European courts and judges should have overriding authority in the maintenance of the rule of law in Britain. This represented a rupture in our history. It changed fundamentally the way we were governed, the way free men and women chose to run their own affairs – and could they then be as free as they once had been? Were we not surrendering cherished liberties?

Derek Walker-Smith put his case for many years with the skill of a top-class courtroom advocate. The clauses of each sentence were locked in place with a jeweller's skill; the very rotundity of his prose caused gentle amusement. I once heard him declare, 'When I hear the words "economic and monetary union", I am able without undue strain or difficulty to contain my enthusiasm within the bounds of public decorum.' They don't, as my father would have said, make them like that these days. Walker-Smith fought the good fight at Westminster and he took it to the European Parliament where he became, in his later years, the chairman of its legal affairs committee. He was obsessive about his arguments in the sense that he did not give up putting them. But he did not allow this passion to subsume all other considerations: the Conservative Party's political prospects, the national interest, the obligation on responsible politicians to eschew mindless populism, moderation in all things. He did not set out to wreck the Conservative Party with whose leaders he had disagreed, and since the die had been cast believed that the role he should play was to make the best of what had been decided. This was the national interest, and he served it in the European Parliament and in organizations of European lawyers.

As a minister, my first experience of working in Brussels came as a member of the Council of Development Ministers; indeed I was plunged into chairing it since my promotion to the Overseas Development Administration coincided with the periodic six-month British presidency of the Community. Our main task and achievement was the reform of Europe's policy of food aid, preventing the dumping of surpluses on poor, developing countries in ways that threatened their ability to sustain indigenous agricultural production. I was also caught up in lengthy renegotiation of the Lomé Convention, which had brought Europe and most of its former colonies together in a contractual trade and cooperation agreement that had first come into force in 1976. I co-chaired with a smart finance minister from Senegal the subcommittee that determined the amount of aid that would lubricate the deal and found myself locked into what has become a familiar position down the years, between the rhetoric of heads of government and the more down-to-earth preoccupations of their finance ministers.

After three years in that job I was moved in 1989 to the Environment Department, a lumbering Whitehall giant that covered a range of sensitive issues from planning, housing, urban regeneration and water privatization to local government, local tax and national and international environmental protection. Environmental issues had shot up the political agenda, with a surge of support for Green candidates in the elections that year for the European Parliament. It was thought that the department needed a friendlier face after the stewardship of my predecessor Nicholas Ridley, whose many qualities did not include public geniality.

Ridley was close to Margaret Thatcher, and a strong believer in markets. In private and in public he was stridently (and for him, in due course, fatally) critical of the European enterprise. He was by no means a safe politician, so while the Prime Minister was happy to comfort herself from time to time with his prejudices, she probably recognized that his ability to self-detonate made it necessary to keep him at a safe distance. Like Norman Tebbit, he did however have a licence to snarl. Michael Heseltine, Ridley's predecessor as Environment Secretary, had taken a particularly active interest in the economic and social renewal of Liverpool after the riots there in 1981. The Archbishop and Bishop in the city, heads respectively of the Catholic and Anglican dioceses, were particularly grateful for his leadership.

When Ridley moved into the office, he showed no interest in the city whatsoever, and after some months, the religious leaders asked if they could go and see him. The meeting was worse than frosty. Mr Heseltine, they noted, had regarded himself as the Minister with Special Responsibility for Liverpool. Did he, Nick Ridley, feel the same? Well, he drawled, he was responsible for protecting the natterjack toad, for combating pollution and for the discharge of sewage sludge, so he supposed he could add Liverpool to his list. Hearts and minds did not meet.

My difficulties in Europe as Environment Secretary were exacerbated by Ridley, who had been moved to the Department of Trade and Industry. At the time, the European Commission was trying to raise standards of environmental protection with the enthusiastic support of most of the northern member states. The Italian commissioner responsible, Carlo Ripa di Meana, whose wife's testimony concerning his performance in bed earned him a certain notoriety and the tag (for reasons into which I have never indelicately enquired) 'the orgasm of Utrecht', was putting Britain under a lot of pressure – ironically, given that our readiness to implement whatever was agreed almost certainly exceeded that of the country he knew best. A complication was that we were in the throes of privatizing the water industry – a policy regarded at the time by most of the public as a crime against nature and quite possibly a sin against the Holy Ghost. A condition of the sale of the water companies was for us to make clear to prospective shareholders and investors what health standards would be expected of them and how much additional investment would be required in order to meet these standards. My attempts to hold the line in Europe on politically defensible positions were constantly undermined by Ridley. We would argue a position in Cabinet or a Cabinet committee, but just before the meeting in Brussels Ridley would pop up the backstairs in Downing Street to convince Thatcher that we were being too feeble with the wretched Europeans and should harden our line. I would get new, sometimes incoherent, instructions giving me less elbow room to negotiate a settlement. I remember in particular being cornered during negotiations over the dumping of sewage sludge in the North Sea. This is not the easiest practice to defend, particularly in the face of assault from our marine neighbours, or indeed from indignant British holidaymakers. (I recall the saying: 'You cannot swim off Blackpool beach any longer; you can only go through the motions.') My hands were tied by a last-minute intervention from Downing Street in response to Ridley's private lobbying. I endured an uncomfortable meeting before managing to secure slightly more flexible negotiating instructions. Looking back, it is fair to say that European membership has driven up our environmental standards, especially in relation to air and water quality.

On environmental issues, Thatcher was not always a backmarker. She was an early convert to the case that our climate was being changed by fossil fuel emissions and the destruction of tropical rain-forests. She understood earlier than most others the arguments about the greenhouse effect, and enthusiastically backed my efforts in Europe and at an international conference held in London in 1990 to strengthen the Montreal Protocol's restrictions on the use of halons and chlorofluorocarbons (CFCs). Perhaps by that stage in her premiership, it helped that the main pressure for these changes did not come through European directives.

Conventional wisdom holds that Europe brought Margaret Thatcher down. In this case, I believe that conventional wisdom is correct, though what happened was both more subtle and more complicated than that – or so it seemed to me as the minister responsible for implementing the policy that drained away most of Thatcher's public support: the poll tax. Entangled in a Downing Street duel with her Chancellor of the Exchequer Nigel Lawson, as well as her Foreign Secretary Geoffrey Howe, over whether 'her' pound should shadow the Deutschmark or even join the Exchange Rate Mechanism (ERM), the Prime Minister allowed her attention to be diverted from what she normally did best – ascertaining the impact of any and every policy on Conservative voters: homeowners and ratepayers. The Conservatives had been committed since mid-1974 to reform of the local tax system, domestic rates. Ministers had run through almost every option without picking a winner before a collection of very clever minds hit upon a woefully foolish scheme. Charity deters me from setting out the roll of honour of the poll tax's authors. Initially this tax had the dubious virtue of simplicity. Everyone would pay an equal contribution to the cost of local services, reflecting not ability to pay (except at extremes of poverty) but the distributed expenditure of local councils. The poll tax, or Community Charge as it was never called save by government spokesmen, was railroaded through the Cabinet against the heavy resistance of Lawson and the Treasury. To his credit, his political judgement was absolutely correct; to his discredit he then did everything in his power to ensure that its introduction was disastrous, beginning with a financial settlement for local councils in 1989–90 that was bound to bring far higher bills for local taxpayers.

I was transferred from Overseas Development – where I had been happily removed most of the time from domestic politics – to the Environment Department in time to take responsibility for the first year's operation of the poll tax. This was what in rugby football is called a hospital pass. It did not take long for me to realize just how calamitous the new tax was likely to be. On the whole, domestic rating had weighed proportionately least heavily on middle-income families in mid-price properties in averagely prosperous areas. This is a pretty good way of describing floating voters in marginal constituencies. These were the families who were really clobbered by the new system, which also doubled at a stroke the number of direct taxpayers in the country. Shortly after I moved to the Environment Department's bleak slab blocks (now demolished) in Marsham Street, I commissioned a study of what would actually happen to people's bills in a selection of constituencies in the first year of the tax's operation. Predictably, the poll tax homed in like a heat-seeking missile on floating voters in marginal seats. I went to see Margaret Thatcher with the figures, and with a complicated and expensive but manageable scheme to cap the losses people would suffer in moving from the old tax to the new. Lawson was furious, dressed me down and complained to Thatcher – not unreasonably – that my scheme would scupper the alleged merit of the original, which linked umbilically councils' spending plans with the demands placed on taxpayers. Thatcher did not really focus on the political storm that was inevitably going to hit us. She was distracted; her mind was elsewhere, plotting the next move to thwart Lawson and Howe, Kohl, Mitterrand and Andreotti. Our scheme for partial salvation died the death of a thousand cuts and caveats in Cabinet committees. A policy only slightly less unpopular than the Black Death was unleashed on the land, and Conservative Members of Parliament muttered darkly about what it would do to them and whether, for their part, they could do anything about it and its authors.

The feud with Lawson and Howe was only settled by their sequential departures from the Cabinet, securing in the process the deservedly rapid rise of John Major. But with each ministerial resignation came more bad blood, more turbulence in the parliamentary party. It is politically incontinent to lose senior figures like this, raging into the night. More troublesome still, Thatcher appeared to cross the line between forceful European diplomacy and obsessive hysteria. The voice went up; the support went down. The last act, to whose consequences I shall return, mixed the maudlin and the genuinely tragic. She left the stage with one last magnificent performance in the House of Commons, shouting defiance into the teeth of the gale.

As the Conservative Party Chairman under Major's premiership, I played only a small role in the successful attempts to tear the fangs out of the poll tax and to re-establish a more normal relationship with our European partners. I went with the Prime Minister to Bonn when he spoke at the Konrad Adenauer Foundation (the Christian Democrats' think tank), memorably pledging that Britain would resume its position at the heart of Europe. Since my days at the Conservative Research Department I had enjoyed a close relationship with German Christian Democrats, and admired their role in the reconstruction of German democracy – in working out a philosophy that combined market economics and social responsibility – and now in the reunification of Germany. I said as much in an interview with *Marxism Today*'s highly intelligent editor Martin Jacques, and was dubbed a closet Christian Democrat by the *Daily Telegraph* and others, a label to which I do not object despite my strong reservations about the vacuity of much of the last century's Catholic social teaching.

I had established a good rapport with Chancellor Kohl, in every sense one of the political giants of the last fifty years, and this helped secure an objective born more of political common sense than of philosophical conviction. British Conservatives in the European Parliament formed a group on their own, alongside but outside the main centre-right grouping dominated by Christian Democrats. This meant that Conservatives were less influential in the Parliament than they could otherwise have been. There were differences in national party programmes but these hardly seemed to raise insurmountable obstacles. With the strong approval and support of Members of the European Parliament (MEPs), the Prime Minister, Foreign Secretary and Chief Whip, I set about completing the negotiations for British associate membership of the larger group, a process that had begun under Thatcher's premiership. It involved some bizarre outings – explaining to obscure Christian Democrat politicians that the Conservative Party had been around for some time, perhaps a couple of centuries longer than their own parties, and was not a populist rump – and having especially taxing encounters with several Italian politicians whom the judicial authorities were shortly and permanently to remove from the scene. Eventually we got what we wanted, a modest success, though one which causes apoplexy in some parts of today's Conservative Party.

The principal triumph for European policy was John Major's negotiation of the Maastricht Treaty in 1991. This was an exemplary combination of party management and European diplomacy. Major handled his Cabinet and parliamentary colleagues with great skill, keeping his ministers informed about and involved in working out all the bottom lines. He concluded the negotiations to general satisfaction across the board. Returning to Cabinet with the job well done, he received tributes all round, led warmly by the Home Secretary Kenneth Baker. So successful politically was the operation, that Europe was hardly mentioned throughout the general election campaign that shortly followed, even by those who were to become such virulent critics of the Maastricht Treaty in the next parliament. This was an assembly from which the electors of Bath, alas, excluded me, thus securing for all practical purposes my exit from full-time, mainstream British politics.

After five years in Hong Kong, trying to manage Britain's exit from empire with as much dignity and decency as was possible in the circumstances, I returned home, chaired the policing commission in Northern Ireland, and went to Brussels in 1999 as one of Britain's two European commissioners, with responsibility for external relations. Much of this book is infused with my experience in that job, working in the boiler room of the efforts to create a common European foreign and security policy, and in the course of that work dealing with the world's only superpower, the Not-So-United States of America.

The preceding autobiographical pages – the nearest I shall ever get to writing my memoirs – will explain, I hope, the way in which I came to hold the opinions I took with me to Brussels, the intellectual baggage that I unpacked in 1999 in my flat overlooking the Parc du Cinquantenaire. I came to the job in the European Commission as someone who loved and admired America, and who believed – without a disproportionate sense of romance – that Britain had taken historically the right decision about joining the European Union, but thought as well that the politics of Britain's membership and the success of Europe itself were in the first case confused and in the second hampered by the gap between rhetoric and reality. I have some sympathy for the 'Cleopatra's nose' view of history. People *do* make a difference to the playing out of events, so perhaps the (to be polite) pretty uninspiring present generation of European leaders bears some of the responsibility for today's muddle. This is particularly true in the two countries around which the whole sovereignty-sharing enterprise was formed, France and Germany. Each country faces a complex existential question, to which I shall shortly turn. Maybe, given our own psychodrama in Britain, we should be understanding about the difficulty their leaders have in answering this question. What is clear is that so long as France, Germany and Britain are confused about their own roles in Europe, so long will Europe be mixed up too.

There have always been two French visions of Europe. General de Gaulle believed in a Europe of nation states led by France and Germany, with the latter paying for its past by accepting the primacy of the French national interest on matters of major substance. Harold Macmillan said of de Gaulle, 'He speaks of Europe but he means France.' The tradition lives on. The other French conception of Europe was Jean Monnet's; his was a Europe in which the nation state submerged itself in a greater continent-wide, or at least western Europe-wide, enterprise. Nation states were old hat. It is difficult to straddle both positions intellectually and politically without the risk of serious rupture. The French political class was able to do so for so long without too much discomfort because France was running the show, dominating the Brussels bureaucracy, standing guard over some of its sacrosanct programmes, such as the Common Agricultural Policy (the CAP), and providing both the language and the culture of decision-making. *Autres temps, autres moeurs.* In some ways I was always surprised that France had made so little fuss (at least until the treaty referendum campaign) about the transformation of the European Union, largely as a result of its successful enlargement to twenty-five states, but also as a result of profound changes in other countries, most notably Germany. So long as France does not really know what sort of Europe it wants, so long as it tries from time to time to turn the clock back almost whimsically to a golden age of French superior distinctiveness, so long as its politicians led by President Chirac remain trapped in an ignorant and impoverishing hostility to the policies required to create jobs and compete successfully in the world, it will punch significantly below its weight and Europe will be all the poorer.

France's problems were manifested by four events in 2005 that ran the gamut from bungling political incompetence through tragedy to high farce. First, President Chirac determined to hold a referendum on the EU's constitutional treaty in order to embarrass his political opponents, whom he surmised correctly would be divided over the issue, and to corner the British by showing that France could lead the debate about Europe's future. France gave the treaty and the President a big thumbs down, expediting the departure of the French premier Raffarin (he had been 'Raffarindumed', to borrow a tabloid joke) and leaving the President's administration dead in the water until the next presidential poll in 2007. Second, later in the year, Paris's working-class suburbs exploded in riots, which rapidly spread to other parts of the country from Strasbourg to Toulouse. Muslim youths, mostly of North African origin, burned cars and looted shops. There had been similar riots elsewhere in Europe before, for example in the north of England. The violence in France seemed more a consequence of economic than cultural or religious alienation. Unemployment in France, a direct result of some aspects of the lauded social model of the country, hovers around ten per cent. But for unskilled school leavers called Pierre, it rises to over twenty per cent; for those called

Ishmael, it stands at above forty per cent. Third, President Chirac managed, at the December European Summit, to defend successfully the deal he had brokered with Chancellor Schröder in 2002 to hold spending on the Common Agricultural Policy to over forty per cent of the Union's budget until 2003. (Under this policy, the largest one per cent of French farms receives more subsidies than the total amount that goes to the smallest forty per cent.) One consequence of the failure to reform this policy radically was that the European Union found itself blamed for the near failure of the trade liberalisation talks under the aegis of the WTO in Hong Kong at the end of the year. Fourth, in a surrealist display of protectionism, the French government, led by a self-described 'vigilant and mobilised' President, intervened first to prevent the rumoured takeover of the yoghurt manufacturer Danone by Pepsi Co, and then to publish a decree blocking foreign takeovers of designated industries allegedly linked to national security. Where yoghurt led the way in defending France's way of life, Taittinger champagne (saved from a Belgian takeover) and casinos (protected by the new decree) followed. As a result, will globalised manufacturing and service industries grant France exceptional status, reining in competitive forces as they beat in vain against the yeasty defences of the Danone line? Demonstrating the treachery of the British government in this manly struggle against the twenty-first century, Whitehall – unvigilant and immobile – lifted not a finger to prevent the takeover by the French company Pernod Ricard of the British-based Allied Domecq. Is nothing sacred in John Bull's island these days? After all, Allied Domecq manufactured Ballantine's whisky and Beefeater gin.

There are occasional manifestations of the French trying to hold a line badly frayed by events, with which I have some sympathy. One concerned me very directly. During the behind-the-arras discussions about the choice of a new President of the Commission to succeed Romano Prodi in 2004, my own name was canvassed with some enthusiasm on both the right and the left of the political spectrum. My most prominent supporter was in fact French, the former President Giscard d'Estaing, who had recently presided over the convention that drafted a European constitution. In the margins of a meeting of European foreign ministers, Pierre de Boissieu came to see me. De

Boissieu is France's senior bureaucrat in Brussels – cynical, manipulative, clever. He is the sort of Frenchman whom we British need to exist so that we can recall occasionally how wonderfully generous we were to sign the Entente Cordiale. 'Well,' de Boissieu said, 'I have been to the Elysée and I have a message for you. "They" think you're very good, but "they" can't accept you as president.' The reasons adduced were clear – Britain was outside the Eurozone and outside the Schengen area (for immigration and asylum policy). He was very civil about it; the French had been surprised at how comfortable they had often found it to work with me; they thought I was independent-minded. But there it was. 'Let's be clear,' I said, 'you can't accept a British president.' In response, I got a wintry smile. It is worth recalling that Margaret Thatcher had twice accepted (1985 and 1989) a French candidate, Jacques Delors, and I suspect that in 2004 Mr Blair could probably have been persuaded to support the talented French Socialist Trade Commissioner Pascal Lamy (now sensibly chosen to run the World Trade Organization).

At the European Council in Edinburgh (the heads of state or government summit) under the British presidency in 1992, my friend Tristan Garel-Jones, then Minister for Europe, was discussing Britain's hesitations about committing herself to European monetary union with Germany's Chancellor Kohl. He mentioned worries about loss of sovereignty. Kohl responded by saying that his own political purpose had always and everywhere been to submerge German sovereignty in a wider and broader European sovereignty. I know myself how strongly he felt that. He had been brought up near the historic borders of France and Germany, land that had been fought over again and again. He had seen the terrible aftermath of the Second World War. He wanted to end division and warfare in Europe. More than that, he believed that the emergence of an economically powerful, reunited Germany would only be tolerable to her neighbours if she subsumed herself in Europe, if Germany's national interest was clearly no more and no less than Europe's interest. To reinforce the point, Germany should be prepared to pay the lion's share for Europe's policies, subsidizing the farmers and the poorer regions throughout the Union. Germany had to show that it had slayed its demons by paying for the welfare of its neighbours.

Germany no longer has anything to prove. It is a stable, successful democracy. That has been one of the great political stories of the last fifty years. It continues to pay over the odds for the rest of Europe while also footing the continuing huge bill for reunification. The Kohl case for Europe – essentially no more war and limited German power – is still valid but cannot possibly have the same resonance for today's generation of political leaders. So what sort of EU does Germany want? Does it want to see more sovereignty shared? Hardly. In practice, it fights increasingly against the liberal economic policies coming out of Brussels, which it fears will dismantle the last remnants of economic corporatism that formed the least attractive part of its post-war political settlement. It resists interference with the autonomous prerogatives of its regional states. No one speaks more clearly than Germany about subsidiarity, which is Brussels-speak for taking decisions at the lowest appropriate level. Where does Germany stand as Britain and France bicker about how we should handle our relations with America? Her heart is with Paris, and her head usually with London. Perhaps all this will become clearer with the too-long-delayed departure of Chancellor Schröder after Germany's indecisive election in autumn 2005, and the arrival at the head of a grand coalition of Social and Christian Democrats of Angela Merkel, a protégé of former Chancellor Kohl and, like him, a hugely underestimated political leader.

With France and Germany prominent advocates of the idea, the EU has expressed the ambition to make more of an effective political contribution on the world stage. It wants its member states to act and speak where possible in concert, the impact of the whole being thought to be greater than what can be achieved by individual countries. Much of this book will revolve around this question and particularly its effect on our relationship with America, our past saviour and increasingly confusing partner and friend.

It is confusing not least because it sometimes seems as though the United States is heading off in a totally different direction to the one it successfully taught us, its transatlantic cousins, to take. After the First World War, President Woodrow Wilson tried to establish a network of international agreements, rules and institutions that would compromise traditional views of national sovereignty and curtail the brutal excesses of nationalism. Wilson's world order was scuppered by Washington politics and European mistakes. After the Second World War, Wilsonism was again on parade; and this time America made it stick – the Marshall Plan, the North Atlantic Treaty Organization (NATO), the Treaty of Rome – obliging European nation states to turn their backs on nineteenth-century assumptions about national governance and international relations. This was the only way we could be saved not only from the menace of Soviet Communism but also from our own worst, most distinctive and destructive instincts. European integration was in a sense the price we had to pay for America's protection. It was America who taught us to share sovereignty, both on our own continent and beyond. We are all Wilsonians now.

But is America? Cut through all the arguments about Iraq, the Middle East, Iran and Afghanistan, the role of the United Nations, global democracy, proliferation of terrible munitions, terrorism, and environmental hazard. Is not the real thing we need to know simply this – does America still believe in the world she created, and encouraged and led the rest of us (to our vast benefit) to accept? Has the great republic which ruled our hearts and destinies with such accomplished imperial ease, partly because she eschewed the prerogatives of the emperor, now risked her safety and her standing by today claiming for herself imperial rights? Augustus and the wisest of his successors preserved their inheritance, and guarded the boundaries of Rome's empire by exercising restraint; Edward Gibbon's great history tells what happened when later emperors forgot that lesson. So under American tutelage, we in Europe turned our backs on the bellicose, nationalist politics of the nineteenth and early twentieth centuries, and through our new modes of cooperation – imperfect, sometimes clumsy, even vainglorious – are now bent on coping with the problems of the twenty-first.

Meanwhile, America seems intent on going back to the politics of the century we were previously urged to abandon. Back to gunslinging Teddy Roosevelt . . . with precision-guided missiles. Is that past to be all our futures, or can we even now, by greater European exertion, help to avoid it and save our great friend from herself? Can we help preserve the republic's mostly benign empire? Can we convince the USA, with the geo-strategic importance we benefited from in the age of Soviet threat now a subject for the history books, that Europe still counts for something, and is still worth heeding?

Sometimes historical change comes slowly, creeping up imperceptibly until you suddenly realize you are living in a new country or a new age. At other times, change arrives with dramatic speed. One moment this world, the next another – cards swept from the table. William Waldegrave, another friend of mine, and a minister in the Foreign Office, was visiting Berlin in early 1989. While he was there the East German border guards behaved badly, breaking all the established conventions, and picked up a young man who thought he had swum to safety across a boundary canal, only to be arrested by the guards as he scrambled up the bank on West Berlin's side. Waldegrave protested vehemently and publicly. Local advisers told him he had overstepped the mark; there were ways of handling these matters, customary practices that respected the sensitivities of East Germany. East Berlin and its Communist authorities needed subtler handling. Within months, there were no East Berlin authorities, because there was no wall dividing East from West, no East Berlin, no East Germany. All gone, with no respect for those delicate sensitivities, all swept away into history's voluminous waste bin.

Will the world we have grown up in change as rapidly as that? Do we have time to shape events to our own transatlantic satisfaction before whatever is left of the Western Front is itself challenged by the rise of India and China? And what will Britain make of all this and contribute to it? Will we still be trying to work out who we are and what we want to be as the world moves on? Will we remain trapped in the past while others make the future? Time to look again at the dreams of the old lion, and to see whether we in Britain, to borrow a thought of Alan Bennett's, can really make a policy out of the Last Night of the Proms.

2

Not Tuppence for the Rest

The nations, not so blest as thee,
Must, in their turns, to tyrants fall:
Whilst thou shalt flourish great and free,
The dread and envy of them all.

'Rule, Britannia!', James Thompson

When Mr Blair's press office announced that I was to become the second British member of the European Commission in Brussels – joining Neil Kinnock there – the *Daily Telegraph*, bidding me a tear-free farewell, opined editorially that I was 'turning my back on the British way of life'. The writer packed into one curious insult much that explains the long-running psychodrama of Britain's relationship with the continent just off whose north-western shores our shared islands remain situated, despite efforts to give them a little shove (at least emotionally) towards mid-ocean. We are encouraged to believe by one of Britain's foremost and most obsessive Europhobes, Christopher Booker, that there is only a small number of plots that are used, albeit in various guises, in all storytelling. It would certainly be correct to conclude that the geo-strategic soap opera in which Britain has been engaged now for over fifty years contains not only the same plots, appearing over and over again, but much the same dialogue and even many of the same characters. This is not a storyline that includes many surprises.

The *Daily Telegraph*'s adieu begs a very large question that needs to be defined – what exactly *is* the British way of life? At which point consensus goes up in smoke and we run the risk of provoking a row likely to break through those bounds of public decorum of which Derek Walker-Smith spoke so eloquently. However we approach that question, the way in which it is raised cuts to the heart of the problem of making Britain comfortable with a European role. It touches a raw nerve of xenophobia. We hear the distant wail of air raid sirens in the night and catch a whiff of the garlic breath of duplicity and cowardice. Those things we hold dear, those icons that help define us – warm pints of beer, pounds of our own bangers, the Queen's head on her realm's coin and paper notes, parliamentary democracy encased in Barry's and Pugin's Westminster gothic – are under attack by an insidious alien foe. All this is happening because the God-fearing taxpayers of Britain have had the wool pulled over their eyes, by a self-serving and invariably unelected elite. So, 'turning our back' on our own heritage, the high and mighty take the Eurostar to Brussels to sell the nation's birthright for a mess of euros, all in the name of a political enterprise to which the British electorate has never given its approval, having in the past been hoodwinked into signing on for a quite different political journey.

Some self-styled Eurosceptics will protest that presenting the argument about national identity and attitudes to Europe in these terms caricatures what can often be a perfectly sensible and moderate critique of the way the EU operates and the direction it has taken. There is some truth in this. The problem is that the term 'Eurosceptic' covers all manner of positions; it is stretched elastically from those who criticize aspects of policy or of EU management, while remaining more or less enthusiastic supporters of membership, to those who hate the whole enterprise and want to get out. Some Eurosceptics want the EU to make course corrections that could be both practical and acceptable to many other countries. For example, they (sensibly) wish to see a radical overhaul of the Common Agricultural Policy. Others agree with most of what the EU does but dislike a particular policy and do not wish to be part of it. For example, I think it is perfectly possible to be an enthusiastic supporter of a positive British role in Europe, while opposing our membership of the Eurozone. Maybe there is, in the medium and long term, a price to be paid for self-exclusion, economic and political, but there is also what the former British diplomat Sir Percy Craddock might have called a 'colourable' case for this attitude. Moreover, even those who would have supported British membership of the Eurozone in the last few years would be hard pressed to find a good word for the domestic policies pursued within it by the governments of its three largest economies, Germany, France and Italy.

The supporters of British EU membership who define themselves as sceptics, partly because they doubt the wisdom of mindless enthusiasm about any human organization and refuse to suspend their rational faculties regarding the one based in Brussels, will have found much in the referendum results in France and the Netherlands in 2005 to convince them that their lack of gung-ho enthusiasm has been justified. They could recognize the EU's achievements, political and economic – from the single market to enlargement to the construction of a model of regional cooperation that provided an example to the world of how to work together to meet common threats and seize common opportunities. They could also note that the EU was not a superstate in the making but a construction of nation states, sometimes banging uneasily against one another and defining goals too often in a language spoken almost exclusively by politicians who wish to sound visionary but invariably sound distantly bombastic. They might also think that the crisis discerned by a departing limousine-load of European politicians led by Chirac and Schröder was in fact a heaven- or more accurately electorate-sent opportunity to review old assumptions, redefine purposes and trim ambitions without seeking to wreck the whole enterprise or turn it into something less than it was, a mechanism for sharing sovereignty in agreed areas of national and international life.

There are three other groups of Eurosceptics, whose views ascend the scales from wishful thinking to amnesia to hostility bordering on xenophobia. First there are those who advocate an approach to Europe in which Britain picks and chooses which policies it wants to embrace; negotiates acceptable exits from the ones it dislikes; and in the process shows the other member states the sort of Europe to which they would really like to belong, if only they could come to appreciate that *we* know what is best for them. The assumption behind this approach is that other European countries need us far more than we need them, and that if only we spoke firmly enough to them they would fall obediently into line. This is pretty much the position that the Conservative Party has embraced officially in opposition. It would have been completely undeliverable if the party had ever got out of opposition. Charity suggests that it is naïve rather than dishonest, but whichever it is, it has provided much of the percussion of the Conservative Party's thunder on Europe.

The resounding No votes in the referendums embolden some of these Conservative critics to claim a victory for their own approach. Was it not now clear that British Euroscepticism was on the march right across Europe? Were we not witnessing European voters, stumbling like the prisoners' chorus in *Fidelio* into the light, recognizing – the fools, not to have understood that we had known what they wanted all along – that the Europe project had gone too far, that Europe should become something quite different. Quite different, though quite what exactly is rarely spelled out. These Eurosceptics could take comfort at least from one thing: the votes showed that the nation state lives and flourishes. For all the horror stories about the creation of a country called Europe, here were two countries within Europe voting the same way for different reasons.

There is a second group of Eurosceptics that includes a fair sprinkling of those who used to be passionate supporters of membership. They argue, for instance, that recent developments in the EU involve the wholly unacceptable subordination of our own parliament to European institutions. But as we shall see later, it has always been the case that European legislation, once we were members of the club, 'shall be recognised and available in law and be enforced, allowed and followed accordingly'. It is difficult to believe that any moderately well-informed supporter of membership failed to understand this thirty years ago. Edward Heath had made the point explicitly, for example, in the parliamentary debate after Harold Wilson had announced his review of the case for membership in 1966:

Those who say that the British people must realize what is involved in this are absolutely right. There is a pooling of sovereignty. Member countries of the Community have deliberately undertaken this to achieve their object-ives, and, because they believe that the objectives are worth that degree of surrender of sovereignty, they have done it quite deliberately . . . When we surrender some sovereignty, we shall have a share in the sovereignty of the Community as a whole, and of other members of it. It is not just, as is sometimes thought, an abandonment of sovereignty to other countries; it is a sharing of other people's sovereignty as well as a pooling of our own.

Moreover, the issue was at the heart of the No campaign publicity in the 1975 referendum campaign. The rejected Constitutional Treaty made no fundamental change to the role of our parliament and courts that had not been hard fact for more than half my lifetime.

The last group sometimes masquerades as one of the others. These are the people who claim to be sceptics, but are really phobic about Europe. They do not want adjustment of Britain's relationship with Europe, but changes so fundamental as to destroy the Union in any shape acceptable to its existing members. Failing such changes, they want complete withdrawal – indeed they usually want this with or without any debate about change. They sometimes canvass the Norwegian or Swiss options, 'ourselves (more or less) alone', to which I shall return in the next chapter.

While there are, as I have said, different shadings between these various allegedly sceptical positions, the portmanteau expression usually incorporates at least some policies and attitudes that would be unsustainable as a responsible set of policies for managing our relations with Europe in a way that serves our national interest. What also entitles the critic of Euroscepticism to assume the worst rather than the best about those who wear this badge is that the growth in their numbers is largely associated with the success of the EU's most hostile opponents in boiling the whole European debate down to the question of national identity and what they perceive to be a threat to bury it. Sophistication and modulation, nuance and understatement, have not been prominent in the language of the EU's detractors. They cannot regularly call up the heavy artillery, pounding European positions with some of the most high-explosive political charges, and then complain that they are being traduced as extremist.

No wonder that there is bemusement and confusion in parts of the citizenry. Flying back from Tokyo to Brussels a few years ago, I was confronted head-on by the fundamental question that continues to curdle Britain's relationship with our European partners. My visit to Japan had itself been revealing. I had gone there just after the eruption of a media controversy at home about whether Britain's absence from the Eurozone would have any damaging impact on the enthusiasm of Asians to invest in our country. Most of the British press had pooh-poohed the idea. At my first meeting with the Japanese Prime Minister Mr Koizumi in his democratically shabby office, I embarked on a long overview of the satisfactory state of European relations with his country. As I finished my remarks, Mr Koizumi (barely containing his impatience) came directly to the point. 'When,' he asked, 'is Britain going to enter the Eurozone?' And so it continued, at meeting after meeting, from the Finance Minister to the Foreign Minister to the Trade Minister to the Nippon Keidanren (Japan's industrial federation). If Japanese investors were unfazed by our determination to sit out the first years of economic and monetary union, their representatives showed a curious way of expressing this insouciance.

Reflecting on this in my British Airways lounger at 40,000 feet, as dawn broke over the frozen Russian tundra below, my reverie was interrupted by a charming stewardess who set about laying my table for breakfast. 'Do you mind, Mr Patten, if I ask you a personal question?' Wondering what was coming next, I nervously welcomed the enquiry. 'Do you think,' she said, 'that Britain will ever actually join Europe?'

We could forget all the high-minded and low-minded politics of decades, throw the dust sheets over the conference tables, pack the visionary waffle back into the lexicons. Would we ever *actually* (a word redolent with aspiration harboured but ambition thwarted) join Europe? Who indeed could tell? The question reminds us that it is a subject for therapists as well as political scientists. It has divided parties, consumed the most promising political careers in flames, enfeebled and even destroyed governments, helped to vulgarize and demean parts of our media, distorted the debate about Britain's world role and purpose, and corroded our ability to pursue our national interest. It continues to provoke a collective nervous breakdown in the political classes. Every government eventually appears to succumb to the same virus (with only our most recent one avoiding its worst effects, at least so far). It is as though a higher destiny had ordained that we can only have a relationship with Europe that inevitably becomes fractious and irritating, a relationship that before long has otherwise perfectly serious politicians going through a pantomime of foot-stamping, finger-wagging and name-calling. While we can absolve Mr Blair from this criticism, his Chancellor of the Exchequer does his best to hold fast to the great British tradition. Two terrible wars and a long peace marked the last century on our continent. We in Britain ended it as we began it – troubled, confused, divided about our relationship with our neighbours.

The generally accepted wisdom of modern historians, such as Linda Colley and Norman Davies, is that the whole notion of Britishness and the British way of life, which we are urged to defend against Continental combines and machinations, is a construct. What the English call the Act of Union (and the Scottish, the Treaty of Union), which bound the constituent nations of the British Isles together in the culturally diverse state of the United Kingdom in 1707, had to be underpinned by giving its citizens, and a little later in the century their German monarchs, a previously absent common identity. Britishness was constructed around the Crown-in-Parliament, the Protestant succession, the mighty empire that it assembled initially haphazardly though later with diligence, duty and sanctimoniousness, the naval might that helped secure its commerce and preserve its power, and the capitalism of the Industrial Revolution whose greatest moralist, Adam Smith, came (as Margaret Thatcher would frequently remark) from Scotland – paradoxically the principal socialist holdout against her own revolution. Time corroded these elements of the state's identity kit. The monarchy retained, mostly in a rather passive way, the affections of a majority. But it lost some of the magic and majesty on display at the 1953 coronation, well described by David Cannadine as 'a cavalcade of impotence'. Shortly after that, there was a further sense of the closing of an awesome chapter in our history at the state funeral of Winston Churchill, who is still commonly regarded as the repository and progenitor of our grandest notions of who we are. Protestantism as a state religion for understandable reasons rather lost its nerve, and together with the other Christian churches lost much of its flock to consumerism and other arid faiths. The British

Empire's sway over palm and pine was swept away, with our American friends doing what they could to speed the historical process. The attempt to replace it in the nation's affections with the Commonwealth came limply to nothing. Technological change and the economic development of other countries, primarily in east Asia, closed down industries and wrecked the communities that depended on them. The British identity needed fuel of a different sort in its tank.

Which vision of ourselves were we to draw on? There are competing notions, which perhaps cancel each other out, leaving the field to one overwhelming recent historical experience, less myth than the falsehoods that sustain nationhood in so many countries. My own preferred idea of identity rests heavily on George Orwell's observation that above all we are gentle people. I fear that this land of revolver-free policemen, polite bus conductors, and those old maids on their bicycles, made famous by John Major, as they peddled through the early morning mists to Holy Communion, was only part of the picture even when Orwell drew it. He also noted our bad teeth, British grime, intemperate boozing and foul language. One of Aden's last British governors, Sir Richard Turnbull, mourning the end of the British Empire, told Denis Healey that when it finally sank beneath the waves of history, it would leave behind it only two monuments: one was the game of Association Football, the other was the expression 'Fuck off'.

For me, the gentleness dies hard. I remember a visit to Africa when I was Britain's Development Minister in the late 1980s. We were flying from Cairo to Nairobi. Our plane developed a fault and we had to make an unscheduled landing at Addis Ababa where we were delayed for several hours. We telephoned the British Embassy but the ambassador was travelling up country. We decided in his absence that we would pass the time by visiting the office of the British Council, that admirable organization established to promote the image and cultural values of the United Kingdom in the rest of the world. Arriving at the small block where the office and its library were housed, we were surprised to see a queue stretching down the street and round the corner. Young Ethiopians were waiting patiently in the sun to borrow or return books or to look at well-thumbed editions of British newspapers and weeklies. One young man showed me the book on great

British explorers that he had just read – Livingstone, Shackleton, Scott. He had been especially impressed by Scott. Here was the stuff of high-patriotic romance – a young Ethiopian as moved as we in Britain have been by an archetypal British hero.

It surely says something about us that so many of our heroes, the emblems of our national community, were fallen but magnificent failures. One of the first poems I learned as a boy was Charles Wolfe's verses about the burial of Sir John Moore, the heroic Peninsular war general, at Corunna. I know of course how the poem begins:

> Not a drum was heard, not a funeral note,
> As his corse to the rampart we hurried . . .

But I had forgotten the last lines until, attending in the driving rain an official commemoration in Corunna itself of Moore's contribution to the struggle for Spanish independence against Napoleon's France, a better educated friend reminded me of them:

> Slowly and sadly we laid him down,
> From the field of his fame fresh and gory;
> We carved not a line, and we raised not a stone,
> But we left him alone with his glory!

Left alone in his own glory in a shroud woven from the snow, Scott was a similar hero whose last expedition was rightly included in a recent book of British greats – from Chaucer to fish and chips, from trial by jury to Welsh male voice choirs, from the Proms to the reading of the Saturday afternoon football results. It was hailed – 'Great Scott!' – as a part of British mythology epitomizing in Fergus Fleming's words 'a host of national traditions including monumental understatement (remember Captain Oates' last words "I am just going outside and may be some time"); the struggle against overwhelming odds; the adulation (however perverse) of amateurism; support for the underdog'. Thirty-two years after Scott's death, sixteen years after the end of the First World War, at an event in Cambridge to mark the opening of the eponymous Polar Research Institute that memorializes the explorer, Stanley Baldwin noted that Scott's life and his diaries had been a source of great comfort to the young men whose short lives had ended in the mud and blood of the Flanders trenches. Just as patriotism was not enough, neither – Baldwin argued – was success. Play the game. Winning is not everything. Keep faith with your best selves and your own ideals. Run your own course and possess your own soul. Does all this sound a little quaint, a bit like a headmaster's prize-day speech at a minor public school? Does this gentle, principled heroism have any resonance in today's debate about identity?

One thing is for sure. We are still shaped, all of us, by our history, imprisoned some would say, even though we know so little of it. It is a rather narrow and limited historical memory of our 'finest hour' in the last war: one great dramatic moment of sustained courage so uplifting that, horrendous though some of its aspects were, we were swept along by it, our morale raised so that when we gave up our lives, we did so for 'King and Country'.

The myths of much earlier history are largely forgotten. When I was a Member of Parliament, I enjoyed the paintings in St Stephen's Hall, installed in the 1920s, which told the Whiggish story of Britain's freedom. The tale unfolds from Alfred the Great to the Act of Union, with a pleasing attendant imperial theme: Henry VII presents John Cabot with a charter to find new lands and Queen Elizabeth approves Sir Walter Raleigh's voyage to America. The measured progress in building the greatest empire the world had ever seen, around the core of the oldest parliamentary democracy, is everywhere celebrated in the Palace of Westminster. The individual stories, in each panel or engraving or stained-glass window, may stir old schoolroom memories in the minds of some of the public who throng Parliament's halls. Whether or not they really remember Cabot, or can place in order the Tudor monarchs, the British can understand one clear message – we are the freest, the boldest, the oldest, the best. And the one thing we do all remember, confirms that. We won the war.

Michael Naumann, the German culture minister, caused a furious row in 1999 when he remarked: 'England is obsessed with the war. It is the only nation in the world that has decided to make the Second World War a sort of spiritual core of its national self, understanding and pride.' Exaggerated though this may be – certainly it is not so prevalent an attitude as the right-wing press would like it to be – it does contain a few nuggets of truth. There was an enormous amount to be proud of in the way we stood, for almost two years, alone. Yet there are other things in recent years of which we can also be proud, but which barely get a second thought. We wound up our empire with, on the whole, exemplary skill and more honour than might have been anticipated. We established a welfare democracy that worked pretty well for decades. By and large, we conducted political debate with restraint. We created the best public broadcasting service in the world. We fought Irish Republican terrorism without trampling too heavily over civil liberties. We did not entirely forget the public virtues celebrated by Michael Oakeshott: civility, courage, clubbability. Perhaps it was understandable that another great achievement did not get a look-in. We managed decline without violence or too much self-pity. From one of the 'Big Three' at the end of the war, or more accurately one of the 'Big Two-and-a-Half', we slipped to – what? A top-rank, second-division country? I suppose so, at least on a good day, though as *The Times* pointed out as long ago as 1963 in the context of the European debate, there was no divine right by which we could stay at the head of the second division.

Other European countries found it a little easier, perhaps more convenient and occasionally necessary to forget the past, or at least to reinvent it. But as Jean Monnet noted in his memoirs, 'Britain had not been conquered . . . she felt no need to exorcise the past.' We had not only been invincible; for almost two years we had stood alone – alone against most of the rest of our own continent. Some took comfort from this. At least, alone, we knew where we were. King George VI told his mother how much happier he was 'now that we have no allies to be polite to and pamper'. This was a little like whistling past the cemetery. The years 1940 and 1941 were a hard and worrying time. 'The PM,' Sir John Colville (Churchill's principal private secretary) records in his diary in September 1940, 'seems rather more apprehensive than I had realised about the possibility of invasion in the immediate future and he keeps on ringing up the Admiralty and asking about the weather in the Channel.' The Home Guard waited on the white clifftops; the Spitfires cut trails of vapour in the sky above Kent and Sussex; Mother Russia stirred in the east – and we survived by the skin of our teeth.

The bare essentials of the story are true; we did stand on our own, fortified by little more than courage, protected by little more than the bravery of fighter pilots in their teens (or barely out of them), and by the English Channel. But there is plenty of room for myth to round off the jagged edges of the tableau. Would we all have fought on the beaches, and then contested every inch of chalk from the North Foreland to Dungeness as the German forces landed on Blighty's shore? Arguments in the British War Cabinet in May 1940 about the possibility of negotiating an end to hostilities with Germany remind us that even in the cordite atmosphere of warfare there were those arguing for compromise with evil. Since Churchill not only made our history but also wrote it, no hint of another side of the British character clouds the glorious picture. More important was the Left's rewriting of the history of the 1930s and their part in it. For Michael Foot and others the war and its early catastrophes were the result of the treason of our ruling classes, appeasers who refused to arm our threatened nation – treacherous toffs, Wodehousian in their manners and Nazi in their sympathies. The Londonderry House set was indeed pretty ghastly; many of its members were anti-Semitic. They feared that their own patrician interests were threatened by democracy and the lower orders, and could be best protected by a bit of no-nonsense, jack-booted discipline. Yet the Left's view of history ignores the fact that one reason why appeasement flourished in the 1930s is because it was popular and was indeed their own policy; the national gov-ernment's foreign policy was supported by about 70 per cent of the public until Munich, and could still command a majority in opinion polls thereafter. As for Foot's Labour Party, even after it had aban-doned pacifism with the election of Clement Attlee as leader in 1935, it still voted against rearmament on ten different occasions between then and the outbreak of war. The leaders of the working class were every bit as much to blame for Britain's lack of preparation, and for the shameful encouragement of German aggression, as were the partygoers at Cliveden.

Others perpetuate their own national myths, sometimes from ignor-ance, sometimes from political convenience, sometimes from neces-sary design. I lose count of the number of times I have heard American presidents date the beginning of the Second World War from the attack on Pearl Harbor. They forget the Poles, for example, who had already died by the ten thousand. America-centric history is more excusable than the French rewriting of the past that has been necessary to create 'a certain idea of France' (to adapt General de Gaulle's phrase). The conception of '*La France résistante*', of a nation united in brave underground opposition to German occupation, is (even if one stretches Francophilia to breaking point) more than exaggeration. The fiftieth anniversary of D-Day brought with it a poll in *Le Figaro*, which showed that 90 per cent of French people thought that the Free French forces had played a major part in the liberation of 1944–45; another poll in *Le Monde* indicated that half the country thought the Resistance had done quite as much as the Allies to win the war. A remarkable number of post-war French politicians rather rapidly acquired glamorous war records or shed all evidence of more question- able ones. Thus is national history made everywhere. The real stuff of history, appearing occasionally through the mists of convenient fic- tion, rankles and hurts. 'I may be cynical,' Harold Macmillan wrote in his diary, 'but I fear it's true – if Hitler had danced in London we'd have had no trouble with de Gaulle.'

At the end of the war, Germany and much of the rest of Europe was flattened. The British publisher Victor Gollancz's *In Darkest Germany* described a country on the edge of starvation, at the heart of a continent roamed by ragged throngs of displaced people searching for a home. Britain, though exhausted by war, began the years of peace in incomparably better shape than her defeated or liberated neighbours. In 1947 Britain exported as much as France, Germany, Italy, Benelux, Norway and Denmark combined. In the 1940s the franc was a pretty worthless currency, and the year after the end of hostilities France's national income was what it had been in 1938. Germany and Italy were in even worse shape. If not 'To the victor belong the spoils', at least victorious Britain had a big start on her neighbours as they settled to the task of post-war reconstruction. What was this world to be like, and how were its alliances and partnerships to be configured?

Just as Winston Churchill has left his indelible print on the defining moment of our recollected history, and therefore on our sense of national identity, so too his words even more than his actions pro- vide the prism through which we have sought to argue and define our role in the modern world. It should be regarded as absurd to debate where we should be and where we should go at the outset of the twenty-first century through competing forensic analysis of the writing and speeches of a politician born in 1874. Churchill is fought over by pro- and anti-Europeans, each side seeking to enlist his testimony in history's dock. Truth to tell, as a witness he does not really suit anyone's arguments, though the fact that such efforts are made to shoehorn him into today's political debate is an important reminder of why that argument is so sterile and debilitating.

'Dear Winston', as Margaret Thatcher used to call him with pro-prietary devotion, must reach near the top of the very short list of authentic British national heroes. An unsurpassed wartime leader, he was in many ways larger than life. The story that he painted over a mouse on a Rubens (which hangs at the top of the stairs at Chequers) because he judged it too small for the composition, is classic Churchill chutzpah: audacious, theatrical, supremely confident in his own judge-ment and ability, and splendidly unreasonable. He deserves recog-nition not only as statesman, leader and historian, but as a political visionary. He was not always right. He got India badly wrong and opposed votes for women long after he should have seen the inevita-bility of this change, even if he could not accept the case for it. But for all that, he had great swoops of intuition about the future, which were frequently right. He often saw in events more than others could discern. He was never afraid to think big: looking abroad to discover what the future might hold, and then mobilizing intellectual and political support to meet the challenge. He was a lone voice proph-esying the future in the 1930s, foreseeing the coming war with Hitler. In Fulton, Missouri, in 1946, by contrast, he was heeded. He described how an Iron Curtain had descended across the continent – and his phrase defined an era. That speech was entitled not 'The Iron Curtain', but 'The Sinews of Peace'. Churchill was not a Cassandra, predicting the worst, but a statesman striving for the best, confident that a new war could be prevented if the free world banded together to deter aggression.

As a half-American internationalist, it is not surprising that Churchill recognized the importance of the transatlantic alliance, working tirelessly and brilliantly to bring America into the war until the Japanese did the job for him. Yet he was always clear-sighted. He accepted that American's aims would not always coincide with Britain's. This became clear after the war – with America's determination to hasten the end of the British Empire, with Suez, and with Britain's decision to develop her own nuclear weapons.

One might have expected Churchill's American affections. It is more surprising that he took such a long view of Europe. He wrote as early as 1930 about a 'United States of Europe', and his call for partnership between France and Germany in his speech in Zurich in 1946 was remarkable. But he remained ambiguous about Britain's own role. We were '*with* Europe, but not *of* it . . . linked but not comprised . . . interested and associated, but not absorbed'. He advocated federalism. But he saw it as something for the Continent, proceeding with Britain's benign support. Britain, for its part, played in a different, bigger league. Churchill imagined three interlocking circles or rings: of empire (the British Commonwealth), Europe, and Britain's transatlantic affinities. He bestrode all three – the 'Lord of the Rings'. It is hardly surprising that Churchill failed to see how quickly Britain's power would diminish after the end of the war; how rapidly her empire would fade to a memory; and what a small political role the Commonwealth would come to assume. What *is* remarkable, given Churchill's reputation as a patriot – indeed his magnificent life and character came close to defining patriotism – is that he saw the case for sharing sovereignty many years before that idea entered the political mainstream: a point that I will develop in the next chapter.

Churchill's enthusiasm for creating new political structures in Europe exceeded that of most of his British contemporaries, and he was certainly more positive than they were about the creation of the European Coal and Steel Community (ECSC) in 1952. This was greeted with horror by Whitehall's establishment, with civil servants and politicians alike angry that Britain had been in the dark while it was planned, dismissive of its operational potential, and horrified at the idea of having to sell anything like it to the public. Herbert Morrison declared memorably: 'We can't do it. The Durham miners will never wear it.' Restored to office in 1951, after an election in which Europe's preoccupations hardly featured, Churchill's attention strayed from the implementation of the grand visions he had offered in the immediate post-war years. He was focused on Cold War sum-mitry and on demonstrating his physical fitness for the rigours of office. Elsewhere in his administration, Eden and Butler exemplified the prevailing dismissal of European integrationist pretensions; their attitude made *de haut en bas* seem like a demotic expression coined in the English language. This became more pronounced as the six founding states of the putative European Union negotiated their way towards agreement on the Treaty of Rome, with first Eden's and then Macmillan's governments curling their lip at the whole doomed enterprise or, somewhat contradictorily, conspiring to wreck it.

Believers in the alleged British tradition of wise and disinterested civil service advice would not come up with many scraps of supporting evidence from a trawl through the official papers of the period. But some did see clearly what was coming, expressing the sort of opinions that normally, in Britain, earn the description 'unsound' for their authors. As early as 1949, Sir Henry Tizard, chief scientific adviser at the Ministry of Defence, set out the true nature of Britain's position with withering accuracy: 'We persist in regarding ourselves as a Great Power capable of everything and only temporarily handicapped by economic difficulties. We are not a Great Power and never will be again. We are a great nation, but if we continue to behave like a Great Power we shall soon cease to be a great nation.' His argument was dismissed. As is so often the case in politics, it was the emperor who was the last to notice that he was in the buff.

Even relative British economic success in the 1950s, triggered by the post-war bonfire of controls, failed to generate a sense that the country was fast equipping itself for the modern world. In John Osborne's 1957 play *The Entertainer*, the comedian Archie Rice advised the audience: 'Don't clap too hard . . . it's a very old building.' As that decade rolled into the next, not only did the building seem pretty decrepit – with its caretakers the butt of the young satirists of the age – but the economy began to slow, and we came to realize that the derided Common Market was catching us up and even perhaps leaving us behind. We had set up a loose free trade area of our own – the European Free Trade Association (EFTA) – made up of Britain plus the six neighbours who traded most with us (supplying much of our food). But EFTA was no match for the dynamic economy of the six Common Market countries. The relative importance of the Common Market and our Dominion partners, Australia and New Zealand, as a source of imports and a market for exports shifted substantially in favour of the former during the decade before we sued for membership terms. Britain was literally 'at sixes and sevens' in its European policy. With America's encouragement, and with a clear recognition that what he was doing could split the Conservative Party as surely as Peel had torn it asunder over free trade in the nineteenth century, Macmillan took the plunge.

Thus, we embarked on courtship, rejection, betrothal and the sort of marriage that brings complaints about the noise level from the neighbours and much employment for social workers, marriage guidance counsellors and family mediators. The initial application, famously rejected by President de Gaulle in 1963, was squeezed reluctantly out of a nation that felt bewildered by the sense that we had won the war but somehow lost the peace. Who did these people think they were to sit in judgement on our claims to join their club in our own time and on our own terms? These were the same countries that we had vanquished or saved, and now we had to go cap in hand to them. Since we were manifestly better than they were, how come this odd role reversal? Exactly the same attitudes and prejudices have been predominant for the past forty years, not least in the way the British Government has presented every negotiation and every European development. The basic assumption is that no substantial initiative Europe proposes is ever going to work. Even our more balanced and moderate political leaders, such as John Major, can get sucked into this syndrome, as happened with Major's colourful denunciation of the prospects for economic and monetary union. We politicians announce that, were Europe's initiatives ever to come to anything, the result would end democratic life in 'this scepter'd isle' as we know it, castrating our freedoms and shackling our economy. When we negotiate a compromise, we announce that we have won hands down and that the amended changes that have now been agreed barely amount to a row of beans. In the recent negotiations on the proposed Constitutional Treaty, British ministers scampered under heavy media fire from the announcement of red lines that, like First World War trenches, we said we would defend to the death, to protestations that the whole business was about as significant as discussing the London telephone directory. In attack we are diplomatic lions; in occasional and necessary retreat we are chartered accountants, claiming that nothing significant has been surrendered – just the odd decimal point adjusted in the bottom line. No wonder the British public is confused.

The equally bemused continent with which we have to deal is still regarded with suspicion as a pretty dangerous place by many Britons. During the war years, the hand of God helped to repel the Nazi hordes – an understandable identification of our lonely battle with the defence of Christian civilization. We had long felt that even if God was not actually a British passport holder, He had a particular affinity for the people of these isles. We never seemed to notice that the Germans had already laid claim to Him, even inscribing 'GOTT MIT UNS' on their soldiers' belt buckles. This squabble over God's favour inspired J. C. Squire's 1915 poem:

> God heard the embattled nations sing and shout,
> 'Gott strafe England!' and 'God save the King!'
> God this, God that, and God the other thing.
> 'Good God,' said God. 'I've got my work cut out!'

But we British believed ourselves to be a chosen people almost as clearly as many Americans have believed themselves to be. Until recent years, this Divine British Patriot was pretty clearly Protestant. As a Catholic politician, I can honestly say that I have never been aware of discrimination, though certainly back in the 1950s Catholics were regarded as just a little exotic, like Freemasons with incense and our very own dead tongue mumbo-jumbo. But the identification of the EU with the Catholic Church and Catholic political and social teaching has always made it a harder sell in Britain than it might otherwise have been. Alf Garnet's view of history did, after all, reflect a widespread view. 'God told Henry to ignore the Pope and to build His . . . kingdom on earth here in England.' And it was from then on that England began 'to win the world and rule it for its own good'. Pope Pius XII's wartime prevarications over Nazi wickedness could not have endeared European Catholicism to the British, and there has always been a sense that Catholic countries are a bit unreliable when it comes to supporting democracy. Archbishop Temple's concern expressed in a letter in 1943, that an authoritarian organization of religion was always bound to find itself drawn to authoritarian politics, caught the mood. Catholic social policy has also caused anxiety, mixing (as it often does) wafflingly well-meaning and incompatible aims with a *dirigiste* instinct increasingly out of sympathy with the times. The lilies of the field 'toil not, neither do they spin', so one should not be too dismissive of attempts to turn the New Testament parables and homilies into policy wonkery. But there is no question that this brand of Christian Democracy is not very marketable in Britain.

Germany and France can be even tougher to hawk. 'I tries 'ard,' Ernest Bevin told the commander of the British occupation forces in Germany after the war, 'but I 'ates the Germans.' And when was that sense of Germanophobia mined to exhaustion? 'France surrenders. We're in the Finals' read the wartime newspaper hoarding, and the joke continues to today. It is much funnier if you are not a German. John Cleese's goose-step; the *Daily Mail* on the morning of the 1966 World Cup Final, 'If Germany beat us at Wembley this afternoon at our national sport, we can always point out to them that we have recently beaten them at theirs'; the *Sun* newspaper's successful campaign to prevent German soldiers from taking part in VE-day anniversary celebrations in London, 'The Sun Bans the Hun'. After sixty years, all these echoes of wartime start to seem less reflections of pride than unhealthy obsessions, unhealthy because we need to make new history, not live with our memories and trophies. To be blunt, if France after all her humiliations at Germany's hands can move on – at least with regard to her neighbour across the Rhine – why can't we?

There is a more serious side to all this. In 1945 A. J. P. Taylor produced *The Course of German History*, commissioned during the war years to explain 'The German Problem' to a British audience. What exactly *was* the problem? Taylor sets it out clearly in the first paragraph of the book:

The history of the Germans is a history of extremes. It contains everything except moderation, and in the course of a thousand years the Germans have experienced everything except normality. They have dominated Europe, and they have been the hopeless victims of the domination of others . . . Only the normal person, not particularly good, not particularly bad, healthy, sane, moderate – he has never set his stamp on German history ... Nothing is normal in German history except violent oscillations.

However accurate his historical judgement, Taylor's predictive powers have been proved wrong. History does not always repeat itself, but British policy has sometimes been dominated by the contrary point of view. Germany was governed after the war by a succession of very 'normal' people – 'not particularly good, not particularly bad, healthy, sane, moderate' – and their country became a triumph for the healing powers of democracy and socially responsible market economics. They coped with their history with a mixture of brave honesty and calculated amnesia. The fall of the Berlin Wall – one of the defining moments in our post-war world – and the subsequent reunification of Germany were handled brilliantly by Chancellor Kohl and his colleagues. Retrospective criticism of the generosity of the terms with which West Germany welcomed East Germany to a single nationhood seems to me absurd. You cannot reunite a family on the basis of two different notions of law, welfare and commerce. What should have been regarded as a moment for celebration by British politicians, whose country in the 1940s had helped to set Germany on her successful way, was regarded by some as a cause for gloomy foreboding. Could we stop reunification? How could we deal with its worrying consequences?

Though public opinion in Britain seemed from the opinion polls gratifyingly supportive of allowing the Germans to sort out their own future, Prime Minister Thatcher tried hard herself to derail this historic project with brief initial support from President Mitterrand. Her behaviour was diplomatically crass and morally wrong. Even the truth was bent to try to prove her *Sun*-headline instincts about Germany correct. The leaked record of a seminar at Chequers, held with a small group of historians to help inform her about a subject on which her prejudices were unshakeable, was drafted to reflect her own views rather than theirs. While his remarks probably came close to reflecting her private opinion, Nicholas Ridley, who had begun his political career (like Enoch Powell) as a European federalist, stepped over the line of diplomatic acceptability when he allowed himself to be quoted as saying that the European Union was 'a German racket designed to take over the whole of Europe ... I'm not against giving up sovereignty in principle, but not to this lot. You might as well give it to Adolf Hitler, frankly ... I'm not sure I wouldn't rather have the shelters and the chance to fight back than simply being taken over by economics.' Almost fifty years after the war's end it was back to fighting them on the beaches and the landing grounds, in the streets and in the hills. It was difficult to believe that we were talking about one of our most important friends and allies who, to her credit, simply turned the other cheek – perhaps not long-sufferingly or with pain so much as with growing contempt and pity, which is worse.

Francophobia has a long pedigree in Britain – the stuff of war, envy, slights, commercial competition. It has invariably gone hand in hand with quiet admiration – for the French quality of life, for intellectual achievement and even, in some quarters, for the reverence shown for the State and its institutions. There are also a few closet British Bonapartists, admiring the longevity of centralized institutions, like the education system. (I must say, that is not my own taste; it jars against my preference for the clutter of liberalism.) We make great efforts to overcome the natural elbowing and barging that come inevitably when two very opinionated peoples share the same neighbourhood. We signed the Entente Cordiale in 1904, only six years after the Fashoda Incident in Sudan had almost provoked a full-scale war between the two countries, and we make our regular obeisance to it. During the centenary celebrations of it in Britain, I spoke at two meetings – one with President Chirac, the other with one of his predecessors Valéry Giscard d'Estaing. Giscard spoke of fly-fishing and P. G. Wodehouse, the upper-class Frenchman's admiration for a Britain of well-cut tweed and worldly-wise understatement. President Chirac's message was different. Seated in the hall of Rhodes House in Oxford, the sun streaming through the high windows on to the symbols of empire in Sir Herbert Baker's best effort at Cotswold colonial, President Chirac counted off in his beautifully modulated French all the contemporary links between the two countries – the French working in Britain, the British in France, the exports and imports, the investments and the sporting contacts. It was the real world of

Arsène Wenger and the second homes of Brits in Gascony and the Dordogne. The President noted how many of the villages near his own home in the mountainous Corrèze were being saved by British residents restoring the old houses they had bought and putting life back into villages and hamlets. I recall still the sight of the British Harrier pilot in the first Gulf War, reading a copy of one of Peter Mayle's awful books about life in Provence while waiting to take off. It was the British dream – a little slice of paradise in the French countryside, even if the natives did not all say 'zis' and 'zat' like Mr Mayle's characters.

So we ask for Weetabix and Marmite in the *épiceries* of the Lot, bring home local cheeses that run all over the car, but still assume the worst of our French neighbours whenever we get the chance. This is the country with which we generously came close to merging our destiny in the darkest days of defeat in the last war, as Churchill himself proposed. So why do we still distrust the French? It is largely, I think, because their rather tiresome exceptionalism cuts across our own bumptious certainty of our good intentions. How could anyone imagine that we are not doing our own best, in everyone else's best interests? Since Britain and France are in addition – even allowing for German global commercialism – the only two European countries with worldwide political and economic interests (some perhaps more illusory than real), there is a large stage on which we can discover each other's perfidy. This is unlikely to change. While the French government was clearly correct in its assessment of the case made for the invasion of Iraq and was equally correct about the likely results, and while it was both absurd and dishonest for the British government to lay the blame for the failure of the United Nations Security Council resolution on President Chirac, I am more frequently in the camp that criticizes French policy, for example over NATO. Yet I remain a Francophile like so many of my fellow citizens, and as a former Lord Chancellor, Elwyn Jones, put it, would regard a year without a stay in France as disappointing as a day without sunshine.

So whether it is with France or Germany that we compare Britain, let alone any of the other EU member states, we regard ourselves as fundamentally different from them – different and ultimately superior. Margaret Thatcher conceded in her famous Bruges speech in 1988 that links with Europe had been 'the dominant factor in our history', but she and many others still looked back 'to a golden age that never was' (to borrow a phrase from John Major). Golden and gloriously insular, 'this blessed plot' (the punning title of Hugo Young's masterly book on Britain and Europe, which he had once thought of calling 'this sceptic isle') had a longer and deeper tradition of liberty, parliamentary democracy and the law than our European neighbours; we had twice saved them in thirty years; we were outward looking, independent-spirited and entrepreneurial. And it took a deep sense of magnanimity on our part to forgive them for being, well, foreign. As Flanders and Swann sang:

> The English, the English, the English are best,
> I wouldn't give tuppence for all of the rest.

We have in recent years – principally through the dour oratory of Britain's Chancellor of the Exchequer Gordon Brown – trumpeted our economic superiority. Badly performing European economies are compared with peerless Britain. From time to time I have concluded that the only halfway adequate response to these comparisons between a golden period in Britain and the grim problems that allegedly crowd in on the Eurozone economies is to send food parcels. British productivity levels are behind those in most Eurozone countries, and the gap between our own and those of France, for example, has been growing. Several of them trade a substantially larger share of their gross domestic product than we do, and the Eurozone has been running a trade surplus against a trade deficit in the UK. British household debt and consumption have run ahead of European figures, which would not invariably be regarded as a sign of economic good health. Britain has done much better in recent years thanks, as economic historians note, to Gordon Brown not squandering the legacy of the Major and Clarke years. He deserves credit for that. We do have in Britain a good macroeconomic policy framework and more liberalized markets, and have been able as a result to catch up and overtake some other European economies. This does not justify what Britain's present European Commissioner Peter Mandelson called 'gloating'. Turning from overall economic performance to look at what it pays for, it would strain public credulity to claim that Britain's public services are superior to those in most other parts of Europe. Perhaps we have a few lessons to learn from them.

I return to the basic question – what sort of people do we think we are? Our identification of ourselves as British has undoubtedly weakened as the Scottish and Welsh have asserted their own identities, and as they have become more suspicious of what they regard as English attempts to define Britishness in our own terms. It is interesting that Margaret Thatcher's assertion that she was involved in a battle royal to protect the British way of life was accompanied by a remorseless weakening of the Conservative Party's position in Scotland, leading to its obliteration there in the 1990s.

We in Britain – all the combines of our British state, separately and together – have a great history. We are the heirs to a great intellectual, political and literary tradition. No thanks to successive governments, we have fine universities, the second-best tertiary education system in the world. Our armed forces are as effectively professional as they are overstretched. We speak and write what has become the world's most used and most popular language. All that, and much more, is true. We count for something in the world and, whether through the BBC World Service or the British Council, or our aid programmes, or our trading instincts, or our diplomatic services, we make ourselves felt. To recycle an old saw, we punch above our weight. So, as James Bond says to Tiger Tanaka in *You Only Live Twice*: 'England may have been bled pretty thin by a couple of world wars [note the use of 'England'], our welfare-state politics may have made us expect too much for free, and the liberation of our colonies may have gone too fast, but we still climb Everest and beat plenty of the world at plenty of sports and win Nobel Prizes ... There's nothing wrong with the British people.' The sentiments, for all their period charm, are not wholly misplaced, and we have at least continued to win Nobel Prizes – over forty in the last forty years alone, with Trinity College, Cambridge, winning more than France.

Where we get into trouble is when we give the impression, in the words of Noël Coward (admittedly writing a lyric about 'the pillars of London society'), that 'Nature selected us/protected us', and that we are 'Firmly convinced our position is really unique'. Others have had, as we have noted, to escape from the traumas of their own history. Understandably, we do not feel the need to do that. But we should not be trapped by our history in a cocoon of claustrophobic self-regard. We cannot live happily ever after within the covers of Arthur Bryant's *History of Britain and the British People*, the citizens of 'freedom's own island', forever 'set in a silver sea'.

Consider only the most quantifiable of the relevant comparisons. What do the economic figures tell us? Our GDP is now fractionally ahead of that of France. Fine. But Germany's is now more than a third greater than ours, Japan's more than twice our size, the United States almost seven times. No great surprise, perhaps – we are getting used to that. Looking to the future, however, we would do well to notice that China's economy is now outstripping our own and that India, once the jewel in our crown, will before long do the same. It is no counsel of despair to observe that Thatcher's and Blair's Britain weighs in globally below Churchill's and Macmillan's of the 1950s and 1960s, and that their Britain was relatively less strong than Neville Chamberlain's. We are middleweight not heavyweight, and need to think through the implications of that.

Two arguments that are directly relevant to such an analysis will be dealt with in the next two chapters. First, there is the issue of national sovereignty, a matter which has fuelled the debate in the Conservative Party even if it does not entirely explain that party's flirtation with political suicide. Second, there is the debate about whether our destiny lies primarily with America, or whether we should throw in our lot enthusiastically with our Continental neighbours. This is the issue that has rewritten Mr Blair's role in history and left us bruised and bleeding in what Winston Churchill once called 'the thankless deserts of Mesopotamia', protesting our good faith and honour before a sceptical world.

The condition of our domestic written media does not make it easy to conduct these debates sensibly. There is little point in farmers grumbling about the weather, or politicians about the media; apart from other considerations, such an attitude leads towards illiberal solutions. But it is true that what was once a predominantly pro-European press has turned about, mainly because of changes in editorship and, above all, ownership. It is also true that several of our newspapers are strongly, even rabidly, nationalist about every issue except the ownership of the media. Unlike many other countries, we do not regard holding our national passport as being a precondition for owning our national newspapers and broadcasters. Set all that on one side. We should not put too much blame on editors and proprietors for the public mood. The main blame lies with politicians. For too long, our politicians have been as weak as our journalists and proprietors have been strong. Political leaders have kowtowed to proprietors who are not, contrary to their own opinion, the primary makers of the terms of political trade. 'It's the *Sun* wot won it' was a commonly held view after the Conservative upset victory in 1992, a reference to that Murdoch newspaper's support for John Major in the election. However, the research I commissioned as Conservative Party Chairman at the time indicated that the majority of its readers throughout the campaign thought it a left-leaning and left-supporting paper.

Politicians should not run scared of newspapers, their owners and their headline writers. It is bad for the press, which gets too big for its boots, and bad for the parliamentary system of government, as we saw when Mr Blair buckled to media pressure for a referendum on the European Constitutional Treaty. Referendums are, of course, populist devices that (certainly in Britain) undermine parliamentary democracy. We should debate Europe and the issues that are raised by our membership of the EU at general elections. If these questions – like the euro and the Constitutional Treaty – are as vital as people say, they should determine who governs us. But they have twice now been pushed away into promised referendum campaigns, locked up where they cannot do too much harm. If we want a better and more constructive debate on Britain's relationship with Europe, then politicians will have to show more courage. I now turn to some of the political consequences of a failure of political nerve, and to the results of running before the wind.

3

National Sovereignty and the Descent of Conservatism

'I've got a sort of idea,' said Pooh at last,
'but I don't suppose it's a very good one.'
'I don't suppose it is either,' said Eeyore.

The House at Pooh Corner, A. A. Milne

The Conservative Party got an idea into its head in the 1990s. It was an idea that helped to wreck its prospects, delivering Britain into the hands of a Labour government shorn of principled strategic direction but rich in personal rivalry. The idea was to reverse the international posture it had first warmly embraced thirty years before when it had become a pro-European party. Labour had flip-flopped on the issue: against under Gaitskell; more or less for under Wilson; split and then against under Foot; increasingly for again under Kinnock, Smith and then Blair. When in government and electorally successful, Labour had supported membership of the European Union. There was surely a lesson for Conservatives in this. Instead, some Conservatives worked assiduously to saddle their party with a policy – or, more accurately, an attitude – whose attributes do not obviously include electoral success, unless I suppose you take the bleak view that Conservatism's predicament would be even more dire without the European albatross wrapped around its neck.

In the Conservative Party, as in other political formations, it is not necessary to have an intellectual basis for a policy, for a prevailing sentiment or for a political squawk. Indeed, Conservatives have rather prided themselves on being wise if slow-witted, as opposed to clever and silly. Lord Salisbury's criticism of Iain Macleod as being too clever by half reflects this distaste for intellectualism, though it does scant justice to a tradition that embraces David Hume, Edmund Burke (in whose writings, as Coleridge observed, can be found 'the germs of almost all political truths') and Michael Oakeshott. But in the case of Europe, it was not deemed sufficient to have sniffed out error almost accidentally, to have stumbled on it in a belated journey back to first principles and deepest roots. There had to be a reason – an intellectual argument – for the historic change of course. Conservatives woke up to discover that Britain's sovereignty had been pilfered in the night, as surely as though bits had been removed by vandals from the Albert Memorial. Sovereignty, our ability to rule ourselves, had been seized and had to be restored.

This discovery swept through large swathes of the party while I was far from the scene. The Conservative Party was re-elected in 1992 during a recession, with the negative equity borne by too many home-owners an additional impediment to victory. Under John Major, Con-servatives nevertheless polled more votes than any party in British political history before or since – half a million more than Tony Blair won in Labour's 1997 landslide, and a third of a million more than Margaret Thatcher in 1987. We led Labour in our share of the vote by over 7 per cent. Unfortunately, this large plurality did not bring with it an equivalent harvest of seats. John Major's overall majority was only twenty-one, and as I have already noted it did not include me. I went to Hong Kong, leaving behind a party that had enthusiasti-cally endorsed the Treaty of Maastricht, warmly embraced it in its manifesto, and hardly mentioned Europe during the whole election campaign.

Observing the Conservative Party's subsequent suicidal flirtation with sovereignty from the distant Chinese coast was pretty surreal. Sovereignty was a rum concept to think about in Hong Kong. We were there in the last significant redoubt of empire under the sovereign authority of the Queen in Parliament, although we could not say as much to the Chinese. What was for us land in part ceded for all time, and in part leased for ninety-nine years, was for them territory snatched by imperialists from a dynasty whose feebleness enabled the robbery to be endorsed in unequal (that is, unacceptable if not downright illegal) treaties. We held Hong Kong because they allowed us to do so. Not even the gallantry of a small garrison of Gurkhas and Black Watch was expected to be able to hold off the ranks of the People's Liberation Army, were they to drive south from Guangdong into the New Territories, striking towards the governor's country mansion at Fanling and its encircling golf courses. The only bunkers in this colony were full of sand.

So sensitive was this issue of sovereignty that the Joint Declaration of 1984, which set out the terms of Hong Kong's return to China, delicately sidestepped the question of its location. Was it here? Was it there? Where could it possibly be? We simply could not say. Nor could we give any credibility to the idea that even in a colony there could be citizens who might in some way share in the sovereignty that was exercised in someone or other's name by their governor. Even Hong Kong's senior civil servants, let alone her politicians, had to be kept at one remove from those negotiating the transfer of power on behalf of the British Government. For the British, then, there was no doubt about de jure sovereignty (even if we had to keep quiet about it), while the Chinese conceded de facto sovereignty until such time as suited them – and what suited them, when they were pressed for an answer, was 1997.

I was exposed to other questions of sovereignty during my governorship. I remember in particular a couple of hedge-fund assaults on the peg that joined the Hong Kong dollar to the American. This was an important foundation of the colony's stability during the years of transition. I did not want Hong Kong to be cast adrift on high seas, blown this way and that by financial gales. But avoiding that fate itself exposed us to occasional turbulence. With billions in traded currency crashing across the exchanges at the click of computers in London, Frankfurt and New York, I sometimes questioned what it meant to be sovereign in global markets where technology has speeded and amplified every economic activity.

Hong Kong survived and made it successfully through the transition to Chinese sovereignty from whatever it was that had existed before. My family packed our bags. We embarked on the royal yacht *Britannia*, and sailed through a storm of fireworks out of the harbour into the South China Sea. We joined the largest fleet assembled by Britain east of Suez since the closure of the naval base in Singapore in the 1960s. For the last time, a royal yacht – literally, since the Prince of Wales was on board – sailed majestically through the fleet. (*Britannia* was shortly to be decommissioned – the Government thought it was too expensive to refurbish the vessel, and anyway wanted to get on with building the Millennium Dome.) We cruised on, accompanied by dolphins, flying fish and seventeen ships of the line, to Manila where we were greeted by a 21-gun salute from the Philippine navy (using, we were told afterwards, live rounds). We flew back to London, prosaically ending the British Empire in the queue for a taxi at Heathrow's Terminal Three. I was back home after five years to a political landscape totally transformed by New Labour's political sorcery and the Conservative Party's stupidity. Expressing my consternation at the prevailing scene in an early conversation with a young Conservative MP, he told me that I had lost the plot. Clearly I had, and at the same time the Conservative Party, which has always been my political home, had written itself out of the script. The great benefit of the old plot, unlike the new one, was that it usually seemed to end happily for Conservatives, an outcome too often regarded these days as a secondary consideration.

What had happened to the Conservative Party? Conspiracy and mutiny had been followed by division, division by fratricidal conflict, conflict by defeat, defeat by the imposition of a new orthodoxy, followed by more defeats. It is not the first time that the Conservative Party has torn itself to pieces in this sort of way. But in the past, the biggest splits were either over issues that touched real financial interests, or over rival and coherent visions of Britain's place in the world. When Conservatives were divided over Peel's repeal of the Corn Laws in the mid-1840s, the country gentlemen who opposed him at least had the excuse of defending their pockets. They had more time subsequently for country pursuits, spending all but five of the next thirty years out of office. In the early years of the last century, Tariff Reform split the Conservative Party into three. Its proponents saw it at the heart of a great scheme for imperial unity and industrial survival. Where is the real interest threatened in the case of our membership of the EU? Where is the coherent alternative conception of Britain's role that can be compared with present policies – a conception that can be examined, debated, argued over, preferred, rejected? All that we can really get our teeth into is the accusation that our sovereignty is being whittled away – indeed the whittling may have reduced it already to dust. What on earth does all this mean?

Sovereignty is a notoriously slippery idea. In feudal times, the position was clear enough. Sovereignty rested with God. Royal or baronial critics of this would have done well to reflect on the meeting they would have sooner or later with their Maker, who would sit in final and unappealable judgement on them, sending some to a fate whose torments were explicitly detailed on the walls of every church. For Aquinas in the thirteenth century, human law was derived – by reason or revelation – from divine law. Valid law could not be created by an act of will.

Later, following successful assaults on ultramontanism by a scattering of kings and princes, God was good enough to delegate. Following the Act of Supremacy in 1534, sovereignty in Britain, for example, resided with the King-in-Parliament, a point that King James I sought to dispute. In a speech to Parliament in 1610, he said: 'The state of monarchy is the supremest thing upon earth; for Kings are not only God's lieutenants . . . but even by God himself they are called gods.' This theory of absolute monarchy never recovered from the blow that struck off Charles I's head. The Bill of Rights in 1689 asserted that it was illegal for the king to pretend the 'power of suspending of laws, or the execution of laws . . . without consent of Parliament'. While the monarch could refuse consent or dismiss a government, parliament was in effect sovereign. And that sovereignty was no longer an expression of the will of God, but the will of the people.

As Geoffrey Howe argued in a seminal lecture at the London School of Economics in 1990, well before Conservatism's present troubles, sovereignty is customarily defined in three ways. There is, first, the notion of 'parliamentary sovereignty' according to which the UK parliament has untrammelled authority recognized by the courts to make or amend any law. This has always seemed to me pretty farfetched since it recognizes no geographical boundary nor constitutional limit. Could this sovereign parliament – at least outside wartime – abolish our courts or scrap general elections? Second, there is the notion of 'a sovereign authority', which appears to cover, unhelpfully if uncontentiously, all who are involved in the exercise of supreme authority by the State – monarch, parliament, courts, people. Third, there is what Howe called 'state sovereignty', which he defined as the 'notion that a country has the unique right to control its own destiny, and that its sovereignty is infringed if any other country or outside pressure exercises an unauthorised influence on its affairs'. Under this definition, the Soviet Union's sovereignty, for example, was clearly curtailed by the agreement in the Helsinki Final Act in 1975 to allow other countries to assert their concerns about human rights within its borders.

Howe's central proposition was that legalistic notions of sovereignty do not capture its real practical meaning. After all, what do the concepts that he accurately set out really portend? What do we learn from the statement, for example, that 'Parliament is sovereign'? Sovereign to do what exactly? To safeguard the quality of the air we breathe, and of the 'azure main' around our 'scepter'd isle'? To roll back protectionist measures in our American markets? To prevent the nation going to war in Iraq for reasons that were at best spurious and at worst fraudulent? To hold the Cabinet, let alone the Prime Minister to account? What makes the concept of sovereignty such a difficult one is the confusion between sovereignty de jure – the supreme legal authority (often defined in ways that defy fifty years of our political history) – and sovereignty de facto – the ability to induce men and women to take a desired course of action and to deal with the problems that beset every nation state at the only level on which they can be overcome.

Hotspur understood the difference. In Shakespeare's *Henry IV, Part I*, Glendower says to him, 'I can call spirits from the vasty deep.' 'Why,' replies Hotspur, 'so can I, or so can any man; But will they come when you do call for them?' My favourite example from history comes later and in another country. In 1793, French Jacobins egged on by Robespierre turned violently against the more moderate Girondins, urging the arrest of that faction's leaders and wheeling cannons up to the Convention's door to underline their sovereign Rosseauian rights of participatory democracy. The President of the Convention, asserting his own sovereign legislative authority, sent a message to the armed sans-culottes outside the building urging them to end their intimidation of the elect within. The commander of the mob sent back a simple response. 'Tell your fucking President that he and his Assembly can go fuck themselves, and if within one hour the Twenty-Two are not delivered, we will blow them all up.' The deputies tried to escape, but every exit was blocked. So they returned to the chamber and exercised their sovereign legislative authority to arrest their colleagues.

The reluctance in Britain to confront this difference between the notional and the real betrays perhaps some of our illusions about our own importance in the world, and this in turn finds its symbols in our romantic view of how we are governed. Unlike all other European countries, we have no written constitution, and so we today deride any attempts to spell out in detailed treaty language the way in which sovereignty is to be shared within the EU. When the Constitutional Treaty was still alive and – rather gently – kicking, many argued that we should not for the first time in our history be saddled with a constitution. We needed no such Continental device. We were free men and women with arrangements for self-government that had grown from the first Saxon acorn like a great oak. While we praise Westminster, parliamentary sovereignty, our independent judiciary and our own brand of civil society, what do we actually put up with? We have an electoral system riddled with unfairness; a bicameral legislative structure that the government reorganizes at regular intervals on the back of an envelope; courts whose judges are attacked by the executive because it does not care for the way they seek to protect our liberties; an executive that displays under both Labour and Conservative leadership the attributes of what Lord Hailsham once memorably called an 'elective dictatorship'; local government gutted by manic centralism (a process in which I played an ignoble part); a quangocracy that spirits responsibility away from those elected to exercise it; and a populist endorsement of referendums that undermine such authority as Parliament has left to it. Are these really the sacrosanct instruments of self-rule that need to be preserved and protected against Continental assault – if such an assault is even taking place?

Maybe the argument made more sense forty or fifty years ago when we confronted for the first time the consequences of membership of the European club. Supporters of membership owned up to what it meant; they did not mislead but they certainly cannot be accused of exaggerating the constitutional impact. In public, the Lord Chancellor of the day, Lord Kilmuir, told the House of Lords that both courts and Parliament would be operating in a new world, with the former obliged to defer to the European Court on matters covered in the Treaty of Rome. This meant a greater loss of sovereignty than had previously been involved in joining NATO or the United Nations. It was contractual and would represent 'an unprecedented step'. Privately, he went much further in a letter to the government's chief negotiator, Edward Heath. The constitutional objections were 'serious', though not in his view 'conclusive'. But we would see the transfer of Parliament's 'substantive powers of legislating over the whole of a very important field'. He concluded: 'I am sure it would be a great mistake to underestimate the force of the objections ... But these objections ought to be brought out into the open now because, if we attempt to gloss over them at this stage, those who are opposed to the whole idea of joining the Community will certainly seize on them with more damaging effect later on.' The real charge against supporters of entry is not that they covered up what was involved – remember Edward Heath's remarks in 1966 quoted earlier – but that they did not enthusiastically take up this wise advice, partly I imagine because they too were imprisoned in a sentimental delusion about our pluperfect system of self-rule.

From the outset the Community, now the Union, has had the power to make laws that are binding on the citizens of all its member states. This has always been hotly debated and strongly contested. Derek Walker-Smith argued that British citizens would lose part of their birthright, including 'real things, deeply felt, instinctively understood and traditionally cherished by the British people'. Hugh Gaitskell spoke for many before and since when he asserted in 1962 that membership 'meant the end of Britain as an independent state. The end of a thousand years of history.' This is an argument we often hear these days. But it is plainly not new. It has always been there. What *is* new, however, is that many who opposed Gaitskell's views at the time have come around to echoing them despite the intervening forty years of history, which demonstrates that Britain remains

Britain. Gaitskell would surely have recoiled from the embrace of his xenophobic disciples today.

The 1967 White Paper on European membership asserted that: 'The constitutional innovation would lie in the acceptance in advance as part of the law of the UK of provisions to be made in the future by instruments issued by Community institutions – a situation for which there is no precedent in this country.' Four years later, explaining the content of our negotiations for membership, another White Paper stated more coyly that there would not be 'any erosion of essential national sovereignty'. This begged several questions. The word 'essential', of course, lays claim to weasel status. Above all, it ducks the issue of the virtual and the real – de jure and de facto. Yes, we were to give up notional authority in some areas to gain real power elsewhere. One important strand in British reluctance to join in the early moves in the 1940s and 1950s to establish the European Community had been the wish to preserve national sovereignty. It was all very well for the rest of Europe to combine forces and to develop supranational institutions – indeed it was probably a good thing. But Britain should remain 'master of her fate and captain of her soul'. Licentious foreigners could engage in increasingly 'federastic' practices. But we should preserve our virginity. By standing back at that time, by seeking to preserve de jure sovereignty, did we maximize our de facto sovereignty – our influence over our own destiny? Plainly not. Because we stayed out, we allowed the Community to take shape without us, and according to principles some of which were alien to us. Once it became clear that we had no future as a serious European player outside the political and economic construction that was to dominate the Continent in the second half of the twentieth century, it was too late. We knocked at the door. We were rebuffed by de Gaulle. We had to sue for entry. We got in on terms that were much less favourable than those that could have been agreed more than fifteen years before.

Similar things could be said of the debate in France at the time of Maastricht in 1991. Opponents demanded 'l'indépendence de la politique monétaire' – or de jure sovereignty. But the franc fort already belonged to the deutschmark zone. So de facto sovereignty could be maximized by accepting the single currency. The Bundesbank, quite rightly, takes account only of German interests. But the French have a seat on the European Central Bank, which has to take account of their interests too. This, indeed, is the logic of the whole European project. Its nations, by sharing de jure sovereignty, gain de facto sovereignty, or far greater mastery of their destiny.

This is the process described in the 1971 White Paper as 'a sharing and an enlargement of individual national sovereignty in the general interest'. It leads ineluctably to the process described by Lord Denning as being 'like an incoming tide. It flows into the estuaries and up the rivers. It cannot be held back. Parliament has decreed that the Treaty is henceforward to be part of our law.' Geoffrey Howe pointed out that this metaphor assumed a 'kind of irreducible dry land' of matters solely concerning Britain. So it does. Community law applies when we have willed it to apply by accepting that our interests are best served through common policies commonly applied.

Why does this often seem so intrusive? The reason is a simple one. If we are, for instance, to make a single market work then we need to remove all the obstacles, and that involves detailed legislative inter- vention. So the reason why ministers spend twenty-odd years consider- ing, for example, a lawnmower noise directive is that regulation of such noise is precisely the sort of issue that can be misused as a non-tariff barrier. What else might I discover, with a modicum of exaggeration, if as a British lawnmower manufacturer I want to sell my product to France? Doubtless I will find that my lawnmower breaches scores of French regulations. Perhaps the paint contains a forbidden ingredient, or is the wrong green. Maybe the engine is too loud, and there are safety concerns. So each machine will have to be tested in Perpignan. Moreover, I will have to change the anti-clockwise cutting motions of the blade because this contravenes an ancient French right to clockwise cutting. All this may sound absurd – unless you are a lawnmower manufacturer keen to sell his product. (As I considered whether this example might be deemed a little far-fetched, I heard a radio report of complaints by British caravanners that Euro- pean legislation does not cover the material used to make the sofas in European motorhomes.)

So you need laws – laws that Britain, which has stood aside from Continental practices for centuries, glorying in our differences, now has to obey. Laws that every member state has to obey. What happens each time you agree to such a law, from environmental pollution to the regulation of financial services? If you treat sovereignty as some mystical absolute, a birthright (to follow Walker-Smith) of every Briton, handed down through the generations like a sacred flame, invisible and unalterable, then every European issue has to be resolved by answering one simple question. Does the proposal on the table require the citizens of Britain to surrender any more of their birthright? In this conception the country is giving itself away, piece by piece, 'drifting ever closer to its own destruction' (to quote from a Conservative pamphlet in 2000).

The Conservative leader who gave this drift to destruction its greatest momentum was Margaret Thatcher, who argued for, negotiated and in 1986–7 secured the legislative passage of the Single European Act (SEA). If you define sovereignty in the salami-slicing way described above – here a slice of birthright, there a slice of birthright – then this SEA resembles hacking more than slicing. We surrendered hunks of parliamentary sovereignty. It was all in an excellent cause, and followed the wise insight offered by the same Margaret Thatcher in a speech during the 1975 referendum campaign: 'Almost every major nation has been obliged by the pressures of the post-war world to pool significant areas of sovereignty so as to create more effective political units.' In this case, we were trying to achieve a principal national objective, turning a customs union into a genuine single market.

Only a small minority in the Conservative Party battled away in the birthright's cause. The legislative enactment of the SEA, for example, was driven through Parliament against scant opposition. The party as a whole still bore the stamp of Churchill's wisdom. In the parliamentary debate on the original plan for a European Coal and Steel Community operating under a supranational authority, the old hero had said: 'We are asked in a challenging way: "Are you prepared to part with any degree of national sovereignty in any circumstances for the sake of a larger synthesis?" The Conservative and Liberal Parties say, without hesitation, that we are prepared to consider, and if convinced to accept, the abrogation of national sovereignty, provided that we are satisfied with the conditions and safeguards . . . [we] declare that national sovereignty is not inviolable, and that it may be resolutely diminished for the sake of all men in all the lands finding their way home together.' And so said (nearly) all of us in the Conservative Party, until something happened at a time that made serial acts of folly even more difficult to fathom.

The figure and views of Margaret Thatcher infuse every part of the European debate in the Conservative Party and in Britain. She was a towering figure about whom it is virtually impossible to find a neutral opinion. She is loved or hated, extravagantly adored or wildly scorned. She changed much of what she touched, not content to survive in office but determined to leave an impression and an impact – though the word 'make' may be more accurate than 'leave' since I do not believe she thought much about being followed, about political life post-Thatcher. As Denis Healey once observed, she was not a tree under whose shadowing branches much else was encouraged to grow.

Personally kind and remarkably and agreeably uncensorious about personal conduct – like many women, she was not surprised by the frailty of men – she was nevertheless a political bruiser, who under-stood the importance of an element of fear in political leadership. Her habit of summing up the conclusions of meetings at the outset required small acts of political courage if she was to be deflected from her preferred political course; courage plus as much or more knowledge about the issue under discussion as she invariably possessed herself, until exhaustion in her later years took its toll of her enthusiasm for reading briefs. Different colleagues pursued their own ways of trying to deal with her in her 'force of nature' mode. Peter Carrington made it clear to her in private that he was not prepared to be shouted at in meetings. She took the point. Geoffrey Howe opted for patient and, on his side at least, quiet debate. Watching him courteously approaching again and again her intellectual mangle was a little like seeing a pained country solicitor with a difficult and aggressive client.

Margaret Thatcher's career demonstrates many things. It shows the importance of ideas in politics. She was never satisfied to fight political wars over the terrain inherited from the social democracy of previous years. She wanted to shift, and to a considerable extent succeeded in shifting, the political battlefield to the right – where she would comfortably argue for lower taxes, less regulation, increased privatization and a curb on abusive union power. There is not really a settled political philosophy called 'Thatcherism'; the 'ism' is the aggregate of what she did. Privatizing the railways was described as a 'Thatcherite' policy. But I doubt whether she would have pursued it – too messy and likely to be too unpopular. She favoured big ideas, but invariably (until near the end) pursued them pretty cautiously, carefully testing and preparing the ground. She declined, for example, to do battle with the miners until she had in place all the pieces necessary for success.

Big ideas were accompanied by a simple and clear narrative. Like Ronald Reagan, she understood that most people have little interest in politics and scant knowledge of what individual politicians stand for. She managed to weave together, as neo-Marxists have pointed out, a compelling story – at least outside Scotland and Wales – in which her instinctive feel for some of the issues of national identity helped to sell the case for a leaner, smaller state. Her idea of a state in which homeowners and small businesses were encouraged, taxes were cut and enterprise unleashed, public spending was slashed (oddly, more in rhetoric than reality) and the armed forces and the police were held in the highest esteem, was the political expression of a nation of sturdy individualists, law-abiding, God-fearing, commonsensical, making two and two equal four, grumpy about nannying from Westminster, patriotic, prepared wearily from time to time to put aside the ploughshares and take up the sword to save our untrustworthy neighbours from themselves. Among the scraps of paper in her handbag containing a few lines of wisdom from a variety of sages, you would usually have found something from Rudyard Kipling, perhaps 'The Glory of the Garden' or 'Norman and Saxon':

> The Saxon is not like us Normans. His manners are not so polite.
> But he never means anything serious till he talks about justice and
>   right.
> When he stands like an ox in the furrow with his sullen set eyes on
>   your own,
> And grumbles, 'This isn't fair dealing,' my son, leave the Saxon alone.

This was Thatcher's narrative, and though she appeared to know little history, she had a real feel for at least one simple version of the story of our island home.

Margaret Thatcher was also a lucky politician. True, successful politicians to some extent make their own luck. Whether it was her own intervention in the Conservative leadership election of 1975 and her handbagging of her male opponents, or Tony Blair's expert garrotting of Gordon Brown in a North London restaurant in 1994, there are moments when, if they are to succeed, politicians have to seize the moment. But like Blair, she was fortunate in her opponents whom she trapped rabbit-like in the headlights of her bandwagon as surely as, in due course, did he. In the 1980s the Labour Party was divided – over Europe, over defence, over how socialist it wished to be. It was infiltrated by extremists, whose relentless assiduity drove many traditional activists out of politics altogether. Several of its most popular leaders abandoned the party to start another, a fetal New Labour. Margaret Thatcher made the most of the disarray. When John Major faced his own first election as party leader, he confronted an opposition brought back from the dead by Neil Kinnock, an electoral system quite sharply tilted against the Conservatives, and the beginning of tactical voting between Labour and the Liberal Democrats in marginal seats. It makes his triumph all the more remarkable, explaining also why his victory secured only a small parliamentary majority. Major was not as favoured a political leader as his predecessor.

Thatcher would have been sensible to have ridden her luck for two terms and then made way for a successor. But few political leaders are wise enough – think of Mr Blair – to set themselves, as José María Aznar did in Spain, a two-term limit. As political shelf life shortens, with the increasing dazzle of publicity on leaders taking its toll on their attractiveness after an ever-shorter span, they should take a cue from the theatre and learn to leave the stage while the audience is still clapping.

The Conservative philosopher Michael Oakeshott favoured continuity, disliked ideology, regarded politics as a secondary activity, and approved of a harmonious sense of community. Those of us who rather agree with him inevitably found Margaret Thatcher a shock.

To be fair, that is what Britain needed at the time, and it is why my own view of her, overall, is positive. What would continuity and consensus have meant in 1979? The task of British governments had become the management of decline, which Jim Callaghan undertook with benign competence until he was derailed by one of the principal causes of that decline, irresponsible trade union behaviour. Britain had become virtually ungovernable. Through the 1970s, the trade unions made governments and brought them down. It was a period characterized by the pursuit of an elusive 'social contract' between government and unions, under which governments undertook to deliver gifts that should never have been offered to the unions, in return for the unions making commitments that they never intended to keep. The country needed a good shaking, and being a conservative society with a very small 'c', probably also required a leader prepared to go way out in front of what had previously been deemed the consensus, and shout very loudly. The country responded by taking a few initially hesitant steps in Thatcher's direction. It is interesting that she got a serious hearing from many of the influential and intelligent liberal commentators of the day. Peter Jenkins had mapped Britain's decline, and found that what had been relative could easily become absolute unless we made fundamental changes. Hugo Young disapproved mightily of Thatcher's shrill nationalism but gave her the credit for being serious and principled. So she generally was. While her government's initial policies arguably squeezed the overall economy and even some competitive industries too hard (the concurrent tripling of world oil prices seemed to be disregarded as the policies constructed in opposition were implemented more toughly in government), a combination of tax cuts, public spending restraint, privatization of state-owned industries, union reform and deregulation of markets, turned the economy around. There was no economic miracle but the foundations were laid for an improved economic performance and for some advance in competitiveness, despite increases in productivity still less impressive than those of our neighbours.

Much more importantly, we had a government that could govern again, and we rescued from the broom cupboard all sorts of ideas about markets, tax, incentives and competition, which had been consigned there by political fashion for too long. While Tony Blair was still a young Labour candidate, hugging to his bosom Clause 4 of the Labour Party's constitution (committing it to nationalization) and wearing a Campaign for Nuclear Disarmament badge on his lapel, Thatcher was making it possible for a Labour leader who finished up with the views he today espouses to run his party and to govern the country. Her principles blazed the trail for his (mostly) skilled opportunism.

By and large, Thatcher was surely 'a good thing' (to use the terminology of Sellars and Yeatman in *1066 and All That*). I disagreed with her from time to time, publicly and privately. She got quite a lot wrong. She had no feel for institutional pluralism, took a sledgehammer to local government and ignored the growing financial difficulties of our great universities. She could not see the point of the British Council and disliked the BBC, particularly its marvellous World Service, which attracted the wrath of some of her foreign friends, like Kenya's Daniel arap Moi. She had no feel for Scotland, defining her sense of Britishness in terms so English as to infuriate electors north of the border, whose aspirations for a measure of self-government she spurned. She was equally truculent about the sensitivities of Irish nationalism, though she did reluctantly sign the Hillsborough agreement in 1985, which pointed the way to an eventual political deal in Northern Ireland more than a decade later. Despite all this, I liked her personally and admired her politically, and took comfortably in my stride her occasional joshing about my 'wetness'. She was always much more agreeable than most of her unofficial court, which with one or two exceptions (Gordon Reece and Ronnie Miller, for example) acted as a sycophantic echo chamber for her more extreme views.

The subject of Europe had not featured much in Thatcher's speeches in opposition. She attacked the referendum on Europe in her maiden parliamentary speech as party leader, spoke in support of a Yes vote in the campaign, and occasionally called for greater European solidarity, not least in the face of the continued belligerent existence of the Soviet empire. In government, to the discomfort of colleagues and the disdain of other European leaders, she hurled herself into the debate over Britain's budgetary rebate with undiplomatic passion and focused fury. She got most of what she wanted, which may or may not have been more than she could have been achieved using greater tact and guile. She accepted the greatest strides forwards that had yet been taken in political and economic integration with the Single European Act. She got on surprisingly well with France's socialist President Mitterrand, and badly with Germany's Christian Democrat Chancellor Kohl. Other leaders came and went. She was not a federalist and wished to explore every argument for further integration before accepting it. But an increasing number of Europe's other leaders were only federalists or integrationalists (if at all) on occasional Sundays; they went to church from time to time but few, as it were, believed in God. The bad luck all round was that her most nationalist sentiments came to the fore at the moment when the tide of integration washed further up the beach than ever before or since. Like Canute, she scolded the waves, and her acolytes do to this day, even though they have long since ceased to advance.

The speech that Margaret Thatcher made in Bruges in September 1988 is rightly seen as a watershed. Incensed by the evidence that an activist European Commission President, and a socialist to boot, was determined to press for a 'social Europe' alongside the 'economic Europe' achieved through the single market, concerned that others were moving with remarkable concord towards the creation of an economic and monetary union to underpin that single market, she determined to give the Continentals an uncensored piece of her mind. It was particularly telling because for the first time Thatcher criticized, not the policies that came out of Brussels, but the institutional structure that produced them. It was, in her argument, potentially hostile to British interests. This destroyed at a stroke the traditional British position that dealing with Europe was essentially a matter of getting the right coalition behind the right agenda to maximize the UK's influence. Bruges gave birth to a nightmare that still dominates Conservative speeches today – the imminent arrival of the superstate. National sovereignty was praised; socialism crushed underfoot. It was potent stuff, given more potency still by aggressive media spinning afterwards. The rapid obsolence of its main argument requires the quotation of the three passages that Thatcher singles out for particular mention herself in her memoirs, by which time (they were published in 1993) it should have been obvious even to its author how out of date this proposition was.

Thatcher began by reminding her audience that the European Community and its member states were not the only manifestation of Europe's identity. To the east, other proud nations were struggling for their independence. We in the west of the continent had much to learn from their experience: 'It is ironic that just when those countries, such as the Soviet Union, which have tried to run everything from the centre, are learning that success depends on dispersing power and decisions away from the centre, some in the Community seem to want to move in the opposite direction. We have not successfully rolled back the frontiers of the state in Britain only to see them reimposed at a European level, with a European superstate exercising a new dominance from Brussels.'

She continued, 'Willing and active cooperation between independent sovereign states is the best way to build a successful European Community . . . Europe will be stronger precisely because it has France as France, Spain as Spain, Britain as Britain, each with its own customs, traditions and identity. It would be folly to try to fit them into some form of identikit European personality.' She began her closing peroration declaring uncontroversially, 'Let Europe be a family of nations, understanding each other better, appreciating each other more, doing more together, but relishing our national identity no less than our Common European endeavour.'

Well, most of the countries that Margaret Thatcher praised and helped (I exclude Russia and several of the former members of the Soviet Union) have given their answer. In Warsaw, Prague and Budapest, they praised her support for their struggle for their own national identity and national sovereignty. And what did they do as soon as they had acquired that sovereignty? They applied to become members of the EU. Did they believe that they were giving up their identity as Poles, Hungarians, Czechs, Slovaks, Estonians, Latvians, Lithuanians, Slovenes to be fitted into a European identikit? Do they believe that they have exchanged commissars in Moscow for commissars in Brussels? Europe is a family of nations – indeed, our continent has more nation states within its geographical borders than ever before – and as I shall argue in a later chapter, the nation state remains the main focus of communal loyalty and affection. What does this family of nation states have in common? Almost every member is already a member of the EU or wishes to become one. The enlargement of the Union in May 2004 was the most forceful rebuff to the Bruges argument, but is also a reason (with further enlargement to come) why the horrors predicted by Margaret Thatcher will not happen. Nation states are pooling or sharing their sovereignty in unique and unprecedented ways without giving up their national identity. They recognize that 'closer political union', as Winston Churchill said to the Congress of Europe in 1948, 'involves some sacrifice or merger of national sovereignty'. They believe that this sacrifice might be viewed, as he went on to say, as 'the gradual assumption by all the nations concerned of that larger sovereignty which can alone protect their diverse and distinctive customs and characteristics of their national traditions'.

The Bruges speech marked the beginning of the last act of the Thatcher era. It was followed by her tumultuous arguments with her colleagues about whether or not Britain should join the Exchange Rate Mechanism (ERM). Most had favoured this course when it was first discussed in the mid-1980s, including the Party Chairman Norman Tebbit, who later became a sceptic of the most overwrought variety. Then came the rows over German reunification – a once sovereign nation bound together again. Shortly after this came the agreement at the Rome Summit of 1990 on monetary union, derided by Margaret Thatcher as 'being taken for a ride' to 'cloud cuckoo land'. But at least her critics could console themselves that three weeks earlier Margaret Thatcher had finally agreed (of course, too late and at a worryingly uncompetitive exchange rate) to Britain's entry into the ERM. Then disaster struck. Having returned from Rome, Margaret Thatcher went to the House of Commons to report on what had happened, and denounced Europe and all its works and pomps. 'No . . . No . . . No,' she yelled, noisily enough to provoke the long-suffering Howe's resignation from the Cabinet. (He was particularly disturbed by her assertion in Rome that Britain would *never* adopt the single currency.) An election challenge followed from Michael Heseltine; Margaret Thatcher failed to see him off conclusively in the first ballot and the trapdoor opened. For the record, I voted for her on the first round. When the Cabinet was summoned one by one to advise her what to do after this setback, I told her that her position was unsustainable; that even if she were to squeak home in the next ballot (which was by no means certain), the result would be a humiliation; that I thought she should resign with dignity. I concluded that if nevertheless she pressed ahead, I would not be able to support her the next time round, not least because for her to run again would split the party. She listened politely but said little. I believe that Kenneth Clarke told her much the same.

Not only was the elevation of national sovereignty and the vilification of sovereignty-sharing curiously ill-timed given what was happening elsewhere in Europe, but it also seems in retrospect particularly paradoxical given what we know has happened across the globe in the years since. When Frederick the Great of Prussia saw the portrait of a man for whom he had very little time hanging on a wall, he is said to have declared, '*Niedriger hängen*' ('Hang it lower'). That would appear good advice to Conservatives and others when considering national sovereignty in a period when interdependence seems more obligatory than ever. The 1990s saw an upsurge in the manifestations and consequences of what we call globalization – an even bigger opening up of markets than occurred a century before, with the results augmented and expedited by technology. In the last two decades of the twentieth century, turnover on the world's foreign exchange markets rose fifty-fold. In the last fifteen years of the century foreign direct investment increased sixteen-fold. In their book on globalization, *A Future Perfect*, John Micklethwait and Adrian Wooldridge note that 'by 1998, the world boasted 60,000 transnational companies with 500,000 affiliates, compared with 37,000 transnationals and 170,000 affiliates in 1990'. Money, goods, tourists and technology flatten borders. I will return later to this point; it is enough here to note that prosperity and security – the things people care about most – can only be secured though international cooperation. Even an island nation state like Britain finds that its borders are porous when it comes to combating drugs, crime, environmental threats, illegal migration, epidemic disease and terrorism. That is why interdependence through sovereignty-sharing makes sense, and it is why others from Asia to Latin America to Africa have taken careful note of the sorts of cooperation we have pioneered in Europe, and are starting to copy them. Whatever else you say about the nation state – and I have already conceded its preponderant ability to attract loyalty and affection – it is difficult to conclude that its inviolate virtues constitute the basis of sensible domestic or international policies at the beginning of the twenty-first century.

Why did these arguments cut so little ice with Conservatives over the last dozen or so years? Why did the Conservative Party sign up to a view of Europe that contradicted its history and desolated its future? Why did Conservatives deny the logical outcome of the policies embraced under Thatcher: the erosion of state sovereignty and the building of a borderless world through free trade, open economies and competition? Why did they fear the consequences in Europe of their own economic liberalism? Why did Conservatives work so sedulously from 1992–97 to make themselves unelectable, and then insist on playing the same lousy hand again and again? We have to return to the defenestration of Margaret Thatcher, for it is that act above all else that explains the dramatic disintegration of Conservatism as a credible electoral force, and until we Conservatives can exorcize it we shall continue to suffer electorally. One of Margaret Thatcher's friends and disciples, Jock Bruce-Gardyne, a clever MP from Scotland (though not, of course, in her days an MP with a Scottish seat), once opined that she would save the country but destroy the Conservative Party. He went on to note that both the country and the party would deserve what was coming to them. It is about time that Conservatives defied his predictions.

The removal of Margaret Thatcher, the Prime Minister in office, by a part of her own party in the House of Commons because they did not believe they could win an election under her stewardship and thought she was becoming increasingly and damagingly erratic in her behaviour, did not seem at the time quite such a calamitous act of regicide as it has subsequently appeared. I do not myself believe we could have won another election under her. But should we have suffered defeat anyway, reckoning on an early return to office? This was not decisive for me personally. I had thought since the previous election in 1987 that I was likely to be a 'goner' next time and had turned down approaches to move to another much safer seat, an act that I regarded as distasteful carpetbagging. Yet whatever my personal circumstances, I do not see how anyone can happily build a strategy on the likelihood of electoral failure. It is never wise to be too smart in politics, and plotting a victory at the next election but one through defeat in the meantime is plain silly. So it was not surprising that the tribe turned on its leader.

But this was a leader with a difference. Margaret Thatcher had been the first party leader from the right of the party for as long as anyone could remember. Moreover, she had given the Right the confidence to believe that their own prejudices and opinions ran with the grain of the nation's character and interests. Not for her the task of reining in their instincts; she loosened the reins and gave them their heads. Second, she had also attracted a praetorian guard of fellow-thinking ideologues in the media, several of whom were converts from the left and felt a loyalty to her but not to the Conservative Party itself. Third, she used a good deal of her political capital in the late 1980s, at Bruges and afterwards, to drag the party into a more critical posture on Europe. This issue helped to bring her down, but her fall left behind supporters for whom any mutiny over Europe was in effect a gesture of pious loyalty to her own blessed memory.

The election of John Major brought to Number 10 the candidate who was thought to come closest to wearing her colours. Maybe he was. I had worked for and supported the election of Douglas Hurd, a man whose wisdom and intelligence I have always admired. I am not sure how much his heart was in the brief campaign. He was uncomfortable with some of the vulgarities of the enterprise: one of the reasons I appreciated him so much. Anyway, John stormed home – the representative, it appeared, both of continuity and change.

Major had never been a Thatcher acolyte. In our days together as young backbenchers I cannot remember disagreeing with him about anything very much. He was a moderate Tory, tough on economic issues, generous on social, and very, very competent – the best of our political generation. Presumably one thing that particularly pleased Thatcher about him was that he was not a smooth man; the product of a public school, then Oxbridge; a member of Brooks's or White's; a man whose opinions may have been rendered suspiciously malleable by a mixture of privilege, guilt and ambition – today a Thatcherite, tomorrow an apostate. I doubt whether she knew him very well. But what she did know was that he had done everything she had asked him to do very effectively, and he had the great advantage of not being anyone else – Heseltine, say, or Howe.

John Major was not Margaret Thatcher either. Two in a row might have been terminally exhausting. Where she had driven her government over potholed roads and around hairpin bends at breakneck pace, he returned to a more traditional and measured style of government. Strangely, what had to some extent held together driven at a lick started to fall to pieces when the pace slowed. Major was Prime Minister for seven years; they were (at least from 1992 onwards) unhappy years for him and they ended with a terrible defeat, after a period (latterly) of very successful economic management. It is reasonable to ask how much he can be blamed for the Conservative Party's misfortunes.

John Major is a nice man, a point that is sometimes made as though it were a criticism. But just as do-gooding has always struck me as preferable to do-badding, so being nice is better than being nasty. To be absolutely accurate, John Major is certainly one of the nicest men I have ever met and arguably the nicest prime minister in my political life. What do I mean by nice? He is honest, generous, kind-hearted and inclined to think too well of others. Machiavelli would disapprove but I quite like political leaders to be nice. Major is also a clever man, much cleverer than he thinks, much cleverer than others assume can possibly be the case of someone touched by so little formal education. When he was Chief Secretary of the Treasury, departmental ministers used to have to negotiate their annual budget settlements with him. It was always a pretty intimidating meeting, which tested among other things a minister's grasp of his own responsibilities. Major would always ask politely whether you would prefer to dispense with civil service advisers and negotiate with him face-to-face. Waiting for such a meeting, in an anteroom surrounded by photographs of all his predecessors, I asked a senior Treasury mandarin, 'Who has been the best of them?' He replied, 'That one,' gesturing at Major's door. The lack of much by way of secondary education, and nothing by way of university education, had not made Major less clever, only less confident about his intellectual authority and social skills. He was sensitive about patronizing criticism, and sufficiently self-knowing to understand that he should not be. A thicker skin, a bit more ruthlessness and the willingness to trade on the tough background from which he had shot to political stardom would together have made him a happier man and probably a more successful prime minister. But I would not have liked him so much.

John Major loved the Conservative Party, or at least his rather romantic idea of the party. It had been a home for him as well as a ladder – a ladder that had taken him from Brixton, garden gnomes and clerical jobs to Downing Street and becoming the youngest prime minister since the Liberal Lord Rosebery in the nineteenth century. He believed it was imperative to hold the Conservative Party together; to avoid divisions and splits; to achieve success through unity (whereas Michael Heseltine had been said by his supporters to offer unity through success). The trouble was not that Major tried to hold the party together, but that it did not want to be held together, and fate dealt him an election result in 1992 that gave mutineers and troublemakers the Westminster arithmetic most favourable to their mischief.

As I have already noted, Major managed the Maastricht negotiations with great skill. Those were still the days when he rather enjoyed meetings in Europe. They were a showcase for his skills – greater mastery of detail than others in the room; courteous but firm argument; a perhaps excessive belief in his ability to read body language; and a clear sense of what he wanted and what he could get. An objective secured at Maastricht was to come back to haunt him. He negotiated an opt-out for Britain from the so-called social chapter, on the insistence of Michael Howard and others that it would be a ball and chain around the ankle of competitive British industry. This argument was probably exaggerated. Having opted back in to the social chapter in 1997, we do not appear to have hindered British economic progress in any significant way (though we occasionally had to fight, as over the Working Time Directive, to retain a sensible measure of flexibility in our labour market arrangements). But the social chapter was anathema to the Eurosceptics in the Conservative Right, and to more mainstream Conservatives too, and it had to be thrown overboard.

During the 1992 election campaign, Europe (to quote from the regular Nuffield election study) 'which a few months earlier, in the days of Mrs Thatcher and of Maastricht, had seemed so important, attracted little notice. Once it was over, nothing attracted more.' With the Government's slim majority of twenty-one, Conservative anti-Europeans, deploying all the sovereigntist arguments of the superstate and the loss of Britain's birthright, could achieve real and damaging leverage, and they did so straightaway against the bill to ratify the Treaty of Maastricht. We had originally thought that we could perhaps get this legislation through Parliament before the spring general election, but Major and I (as Party Chairman) had concluded that to try to do so might constrain our election timing options. When the bill was put to the Commons in the summer, opponents seized on the Danish negative vote in their own referendum on the treaty to insist that parliamentary scrutiny should be delayed. Fatally they were heeded, and by the time parliamentary debate was resumed, Britain had suffered the September humiliation of ejection from the Exchange Rate Mechanism. In retrospect it is easy to see what had gone wrong with the ERM. We went in too late; we entered at an uncompetitive rate; that rate became ever more uncompetitive as the costs of German reunification were borne by the whole system; any possibility of realignment within the system was denied by clumsy financial diplomacy on the British side and insensitive intransigence on the German. Shortly afterwards, the Germans bailed out the French, who were themselves in difficulty, having failed to do the same for the UK. It took little encouragement for most of his Cabinet colleagues at the time to denounce the Chancellor Norman Lamont's handling of this and other issues. But I doubt whether any Conservative Chancellor would have been able to avoid the deluge, which swept away the Government's reputation for competent economic management. The most valuable attribute that any government has is the benefit of the doubt. The Major Government lost it with the ERM debacle, and its subsequent splits and rows ensured that it never recovered this vital ingredient of success.

'Black Wednesday's' chaotic financial crisis emboldened the anti-Europeans, who made hay as the Maastricht legislation stumbled from one parliamentary crisis to another. In the early 1970s, Edward

Heath had been able to call on bipartisan support to get the legislation on the terms of our accession agreement through Parliament. Roy Jenkins had led a group of pro-European Labour members into the government lobbies whenever it was crucial to do so. No such support came from Labour pro-Europeans this time. Taking as a reason, or pretext, the opt-out from the social chapter, they worked to maximize the Government's embarrassment. Conservative rebels plotted with Labour whips to damage the Government at every opportunity. With the bill eventually concluded, there was no collective sigh of relief and a determination to return to normal. With the Conservative Government in retreat, the rebels (like the Party's future leader, Iain Duncan Smith) continued in hot pursuit, hounding ministers and driving policy in an ever more Eurosceptic direction. The descent into shambles continued to the election and overwhelming defeat.

Several factors fuelled the journey downhill. The Conservative Party in Parliament is not on the whole terribly interested in policy, and it was probably a mistake to think that the majority could be saved for sanity by encouraging an open debate on Europe. The normal stabilizing influence of the majority – the common-sense bottom of the party in Parliament – was largely lost in the ERM disaster. It made it look as though the anti-European argument might be correct across the board. Moreover, the newspapers that MPs and party activists read urged them on to ever greater anti-European excess. In pursuing pro-European policies in the 1970s and early 1980s, Labour moderates had done so with the backing of much of the media. Conservative pro-European moderates found themselves fighting against the tide of much media opinion. The Conservative Party, both then and since, suffered from the consequences of democratization in a contracting party. As party membership has declined and got older, so it has also increasingly reflected the views of the leader writers of the right-wing newspapers that these Conservatives read. The exchange of right-wing prejudices has become circular. More anti-European and right-wing views mean fewer party activists, and fewer party activists mean more anti-European and right-wing views. By the mid-to-late 1990s, it was tough being a moderate pro-European Tory MP in any constituency, and well-nigh impossible for anyone with such declared views to get selected as a parliamentary candidate.

The management of the party in these circumstances has been criticized. Things would not have got so bad, it is said, if Major and his colleagues had been tougher with their critics. Such a course of action would not have been easy. Dissent was driven by the mad, the bad and those beyond ambition. There were the long-time anti-Europeans. There was a group of new young members – the so-called 'Thatcher's Children' – who were regularly encouraged in private by their political matron to demonstrate their principles by voting against the Government. There were those who had failed as ministers and discovered their own consciences in dismissal from office. There were those who felt they had gained no advancement after thirteen years in office; dissidence had grown from disillusionment. Any party after a long period in office builds up such a residue of the disenchanted. It is not easy to manage. Major was always concerned lest he should push too hard and risk splitting the party like Peel. He did not want to be remembered for bringing down his own government.

The trouble is that once you start bargaining with extremists, once you start accommodating and playing for time, the slope opens up steeply in front of you. Margaret Thatcher might have offered from her handbag the slip of paper on which were written lines from another of her favourite Kipling poems:

> . . . we've proved it again and again,
> That if once you have paid him the Dane-geld
> You never get rid of the Dane.

Major promoted his opponents, 'the bastards' as he accurately called them; they behaved like even bigger bastards, leaking and plotting against him. He tossed out concessions on policy, until our posture on Europe turned into an ineffective and even embarrassing parody of Thatcherism. We blocked the nomination of the Belgian Prime Minister Jean-Luc Dehaene as President of the Commission, and got instead a Luxembourger, who was less able and arguably more federalist than the wily Belgian. We tied ourselves in knots over voting rights and enlargement. We courted humiliation over mad cow disease, with British beef the hero of the hour in the land of the chicken tikka (provided it did not kill you). We conceded a referendum on the euro, with no discernible impact in stemming the tide of voter desertion. We sent the Foreign Secretary Malcolm Rifkind – a clever and wonderfully articulate Scot – around Europe to lecture our fellow member states on the sort of Europe they really wanted if only they woke up and realized it. And this is the real point. Conservative sceptics, anti-Europeans, obsessives have no idea what to put in place of the arrangements against which they rail, except the argument that we really know what is best for the rest of Europe but cannot quite describe it for the time being.

Do the most outspoken Conservative sceptics really want to stay in the Union at all? Some say they want no more than a free trade area. But we tried that and found it wanting. And why should we be able to achieve a negotiated disengagement from Europe tailor-made for all our priorities and presumably downgrading everyone else's? Some advocate that we should join Norway, Iceland and Lichtenstein in the European Economic Area, or Switzerland, which has negotiated its own bilateral commercial arrangements with the EU. So we should preserve our sovereignty and give up any chance of leading Europe, by opting for life as a sort of Switzerland with the bomb.

In my job as a European commissioner I was responsible for relations with Norway, Switzerland and the rest. My conclusion was clear. They enjoyed all the enhanced sovereignty that comes with staying at home while the decisions that intimately affect their own economic life are made by their neighbours in Brussels. We put a diplomatic gloss on it of course. But to enjoy our market, they have to follow our rules: rules that they do not make or share in making. Norway, for example, applies all the single market rules in order to export to the Union. It also makes as great a budgetary contribution to Brussels as Denmark, without receiving any financial support in return. When we enlarged the Union, these outer-ring countries had to pay into the funds that we make available to help the poorer new members. I remember a Swiss negotiator telephoning me to plead that this subscription should be presented as a voluntary donation for development in the deprived parts of Europe, not an additional fee for access to a larger market. I was happy to oblige. But we both knew what the truth was. De facto sovereignty or de jure?

There are also some Conservatives who really want us out of Europe altogether. Their position is no different from that of the United

Kingdom Independence Party (UKIP). Some of them drifted in and out of Jimmy Goldsmith's populist Referendum Party, and they dwell permanently in the xenophobic twilight, hating Europe and not much liking the United States either. They will continue to obstruct any efforts to drag the Conservative Party back into a more sensible and comprehensible European posture.

These Conservatives have hawked their attachment to national sovereignty, a vociferous commitment to the continuation of a millennium of glorious independence, and a hostility to the ambitions of the nightmarish superstate. Theirs has been a programme whose main achievement was to exclude from all hope of the party leadership the man – Kenneth Clarke, the successful architect of Britain's economic recovery in the 1990s – most likely to be able to restore the party's fortunes in the wilderness years from 1997 to 2005. Others with similar views to his were driven to the outer fringes of Conservatism, to watch with dismay the continued infatuation of the party they loved with a ruinous fantasy. It was such a pity, not to understand the new plot.

Fallen into the hands of the deepest-dyed Eurosceptics, the Conservative Party also became the play-thing of its right-wing, where Euroscepticism finds its most enthusiastic disciples. This led to election strategies in 2001 and 2005 that proved disastrous. Mr Blair had moved his government if not his party activists to the right, onto the political middle ground whose topography had largely been shaped by Conservatism in the 1980s and 90s. The phrase 'middle ground' does not signify much more than the prevailing political consensus, with which unsurprisingly most voters feel comfortable. This majority is not left or right in the sense of supporting a sharply defined ideological agenda. Ideology may have infused part of every voter's political thinking. Yet by and large, common sense suggests that simple, dogmatic answers rarely explain everything. Moderation rules most heads as well as hearts.

The consensus of course can change. The social welfarism launched by Labour in the 1940s and accepted by Conservatives in the 1950s was smashed by union abuse and by Margaret Thatcher's convictions in government. Mr Blair's political genius has been to lay plausible claim to the capture of this Conservative territory. He is the proud father of Blaircherism. It orignally comprised fiscal prudence, now alas abandoned; the embrace of market economics (often confused by Mr Blair with cosying up to millionaires); public section reform; labour market flexibility; and a strange transatlantic alliance. While some of these ideas have been pursued only haphazardly by a Prime Minister who dazzles us oxymoronically with his profound superficiality, he at least deserves credit for recognising the wisdom of sending some of his party's sacred cows to the abbatoir: New-ish Labour indeed. How did Conservatives react? Mr Blair's shift to his right encouraged Conservatives after 1997 to turn to their own right. Mr Blair moved on to Conservative ground where he reaped popularity; Conservatives found themselves gathering unpopularity, embracing policies that appealed mainly to existing hardcore supporters. It takes a certain genius to win the political argument but to lose elections by a street. The Conservatives managed this in style and, in 2005, refined the strategy into what became known as the dog-whistle tactics; the Conservative leader, Michael Howard, blew and blew his whistle on issues like immigration and crime and summoned to his heel hard-core Conservatives of whom, alas, there were insufficient members to avoid electoral defeat. After the election, and Mr Howard's wise withdrawal from the party leadership, where his views had been on all too visible display, the Conservative Party decided to jump a political generation and chose as its new leader David Cameron, fresh of face and pretty fresh of mind, to lead it. While he remains saddled with some rum notions about Europe, which time we must hope will change, on other matters he is smart and bold and has set about hauling the Conservatives back onto the political *terra firma* of moderation, liberality and common sense. He will find as he approaches the next election that nothing too fundamental has changed in the British state that he seeks to govern. Despite the fears of his anti-European supporters the Queen – as Douglas Hurd has noted – is still on her throne, her head is still on our banknotes, the Bank of England still sets our interest rates (rather above European levels), and we still send our young men and women to war at the behest of an American President. Sovereignty lives on, splendid and threadbare.

4

Poodle or Partner?

*Intreat me not to leave thee, or to return
from following after thee;
for whither thou goest, I will go;
and where thou lodgest, I will lodge . . .*

The Old Testament, Ruth 1:16

The most famous speech about post-war British foreign policy was made by an American, Dean Acheson, a former US Secretary of State and one of the founding fathers of the world order shaped under President Truman's leadership. Acheson was, in the words of the British ambassador at the time, David Ormsby-Gore, an 'old and true friend of the United Kingdom'. He was also a strong supporter of European political and economic integration, believing with most of the other paladins of Washington's foreign policy establishment that America needed a genuine partnership of equals with a resurgent western Europe. Acheson's speech in December 1962 to the West Point Military Academy raised questions about Britain's international role that remain unanswered to this day.

'Great Britain,' Acheson noted, 'has lost an empire and not yet found a role. The attempt to play a separate power role – that is, a role apart from Europe, a role based on a "special relationship" with the United States, a role based on being the head of a "commonwealth" which has no political structure, or unity, or strength and enjoys a fragile and precarious economic relationship by means of the sterling area and preferences in the British market – this role is about played out.' The truth, hot and strong, is rarely well received in diplomacy, though in my view one should not conclude from this that the word 'diplomacy' itself is generally a synonym for casuistry and polite obfuscation. Certainly on this occasion, umbrage was taken in large British spoonfuls; the nation's dignity had been outraged. The Prime Minister Harold Macmillan replied in terms with which Margaret Thatcher would have sympathized: 'Insofar as he appeared to denigrate the resolution and will of Britain and the British people, Mr Acheson has fallen into an error which has been made by quite a lot of people in the course of the last four hundred years, including Philip of Spain, Louis the Fourteenth, Napoleon, the Kaiser and Hitler.' Macmillan went on to criticize Acheson for failing to understand the role of the Commonwealth in world affairs.

Within weeks, two decisions were taken that demonstrated both the limits and the potential of the Special Relationship, and also showed the effect of that perceived relationship on others. Britain was still struggling to remain a military nuclear power of sorts. The original choice of the next generation of weaponry, the British Blue Streak, had already been scrapped in favour of a cheaper joint venture with the Americans, Skybolt. Now the Americans decided to cancel Skybolt and Britain was left begging for permission to purchase the American Polaris at a knock-down price. Reluctantly, the Americans agreed – largely, it seemed, because President Kennedy wanted to help Macmillan out of a hole. So Britain stayed in the nuclear club, with a deterrent that was anything but independent, enraging General de Gaulle in the process, confirming his instinctive suspicion that Britain was tied to Washington's apron strings, and provoking his infamous *Non* to our bid for membership of the Common Market. America had helped to abort what she wanted – an unequivocal British commitment to European integration – by allowing what she did not greatly favour – the prolongation of Britain's nuclear role. It was one of the few examples of the Special Relationship being allowed to affect America's judgement about its own national interest.

Like much else in Britain's twentieth-century story, the Special Relationship was largely the creation of Winston Churchill whose mother of course was American. It became a mantra for successive British governments that American presidents are occasionally prevailed upon to mention with appropriate reverence. For Churchill, it incorporated both the sentimental ties that bound together Britain and its most famous former colony – ties forged out of shared Enlightenment values and the bonding of 'kith and kin', tested in battle and expressed in a common language – and a guileful geo-strategic ambition. Initially, Churchill hoped that a close partnership with America would help Britain hang on to some of its empire, or at least its status as a world power. In the former case, his hopes were rapidly dashed; in the latter, Britain managed most of the time to get its bottom on to a seat at the top table.

At its most wholesome, British enthusiasm for the American connection reflected admiration for American vigour and optimism. Churchill himself gave voice to this when, in a 1941 radio broadcast, he quoted Arthur Hugh Clough's famous lines:

> For while the tired waves, vainly breaking,
> Seem here no painful inch to gain,
> Far back, through creeks and inlets making,
> Comes silent, flooding in, the main.
>
> And not by eastern windows only,
> When daylight comes, comes in the light;
> In front, the sun climbs slow, how slowly!
> But westward, look, the land is bright!

'Bright', perhaps, but not always very knowledgeable about the 'old' country. I recall almost twenty years ago the poll taken at Penn State University, shortly before the actor Roy Dotrice performed his one-man show about Winston Churchill there, which showed that only one-third of the students had ever heard of the great man. What would the figures be today?

At its worst, British mush about America has contained a large ration of condescension. During the Bretton Woods negotiations of 1944, when America was firmly putting Britain in its place in the emerging post-war economic world, British negotiators comforted themselves with these lines:

In Washington Lord Halifax,
Once whispered to Lord Keynes:
'It's true *they* have the money bags,
But *we* have all the brains.'

The analogy of a once powerful empire, fallen on hard times, now playing the role of wise if world-weary friend and mentor to its youthful, unsophisticated successor has been a constant theme in Britain's transatlantic relationship since the 1940s, and we can still hear echoes of it today, albeit without Harold Macmillan's mastery of the classical comparisons. Speaking to the Labour politician Richard Crossman in 1944 about America's leadership of the Allies, Macmillan observed: 'We, my dear Crossman, are Greeks in this American empire. You will find the Americans much as the Greeks found the Romans – great big, vulgar, bustling people, more vigorous than we are and also more idle, with more unspoiled virtues but also more corrupt. We must run [Allied forces headquarters] as the Greek slaves ran the operations of the Emperor Claudius.'

It says much for Britain's American friends that they have by and large put up with this sort of maudlin and supercilious nonsense. At least French arrogance comes unvarnished, without the handwringing servility of an Edwardian retainer. David Cannadine has pointed out in his book *In Churchill's Shadow*, that Ian Fleming's James Bond has a similar Greek-to-Roman relationship with the CIA's Felix Leiter. While Bond is notionally subservient to America's secret service, he is the agent who does real damage to the enemies of Western democracy. It is, as Bond explains to Leiter in *Thunderball*, the UK that is most prominent in the front line defending the West. 'Perhaps it's just that in England we don't feel quite as secure as you do in America. The war just doesn't seem to have ended for us. Berlin, Cyprus, Kenya, Suez . . . There always seems to be something building up somewhere.'

Americans occasionally play up to the corniness themselves. 'The Special Relationship,' wrote the American intellectual and former government official Eugene Rostow, 'is not a policy but a fact – a fact of history which reflects not only a shared devotion to Shakespeare and Jane Austen but the congruent interests of Great Britain and the

United States in world politics.' Is this how Mr Average American would see things? It is nice to think of American and British citizens joined culturally at the hip. Where this is so, literature is less likely to be the agent of adhesion than film, popular music or fashion. And 'national interest' is usually of more importance to Americans than anything else. As the former American ambassador in London, Ray Seitz, has argued in his memoir *Over Here*, relations between states are not often advanced by sentimentality. 'Nations pursue their interests, and important interests tend to remain stable,' he writes. 'This is how nations behave.'

During the years of the Special Relationship, a brass plate that Ambassador Seitz declined to polish, America has rightly and invariably pursued its own national interest, and Britain has invariably, and not always rightly, assumed that its own national interest was to line up dutifully behind America. This is called 'being an Atlanticist' and a 'believer' in the transatlantic relationship. The idea that occasional disagreement might make that relationship stronger does not appear to be worth serious consideration. Defining Atlanticism entirely in terms of unqualified support for whatever America says at one time or another is in her national interest, is to twist the concept into a shape that leaves no place for partnership. Good friends should give each other the benefit of the doubt. They should eschew rivalry; but one should not demand or expect subordination from the other.

America fought beside us in two world wars, understandably coming late to the slaughterhouse each time but hugely welcome and essential as an ally in the struggle to overcome the worst effects of European nationalism. It took the Japanese attack on Pearl Harbor and Hitler's declaration of war on America to bring her into the Second World War. Polls showed that as late as October 1941 only 17 per cent of Americans favoured fighting Germany. Americans, including their president, feared that Britain would use its most powerful ally to help it hang on to its empire. The editors of *Life* magazine wrote an open letter 'to the people of England' in October 1942 in which they said: 'One thing we are sure we are not fighting for is to hold the British Empire together. We don't like to put the matter so bluntly, but we don't want you to have any illusions.' Gandhi had told President Roosevelt in 1942 that, 'If India becomes free, the rest will follow,' and the President had no interest whatsoever in helping Britain and the other colonial powers to retain 'the archaic, medieval Empire idea'. Scolding Churchill for the suspicions he harboured about Stalin, Roosevelt said: 'You have four hundred years of acquisitive instinct in your blood and you just don't understand how a country might not want to acquire land somewhere if they can get it.' Roosevelt even tried to get the British to give up Hong Kong to the Chinese as a gesture of goodwill at the end of the war. The Americans did not hit the bullseye in that case, but elsewhere they were more successful in helping to speed the exit from empire by the colonial powers, while not always liking (as in Indo-China) the consequences.

Before the war's end, the future institutions of global governance had been planned – the United Nations at San Francisco and the International Monetary Fund and the World Bank at Bretton Woods, New Hampshire. Anyone who thinks that sentimentality gets a look-in when America is negotiating about money and commerce should read Robert Skidelsky's biography of John Maynard Keynes, the head of the British delegation at the economic conference. 'The Agreement was shaped,' Skidelsky notes, 'not by Keynes' "General Theory", but by the US desire for an updated gold standard as a means of liberalising trade. If there was an underlying ideology, it was Morgenthau's [the American Treasury Secretary] determination to concentrate financial power in Washington.' Skidelsky goes on to quote the assessment of the *Commercial and Financial Chronicle*: 'The delegates did not reach an "agreement". They merely signed a piece of paper which looked like an agreement.' One Bank of England official called Bretton Woods 'a swindle'; another said it was 'the greatest blow to Britain next to the war'. It certainly ended London's days as *the* financial centre of the world. The empire went, and our position as the premier financial player went as well, although London has established itself again as one of the most important financial marketplaces in the world.

Britain and America worked hand in hand in the construction of the post-war world order. For America, part of the new order was to be a politically and economically integrated western Europe. There was a recognition, in the words of a State Department report in 1943, that 'like the little girl in the nursery rhyme, a European Union, from the point of view of our long-run economic interests, can either be very, very good, or horrid'. But by the Truman presidency, officials had come down heavily on the side of the benefits of European integration. Both President Eisenhower and President Kennedy called explicitly for a partnership of equals, with Eisenhower himself anticipating gains for peace from a 'third force Europe' that he hoped would establish 'an industrial complex comparable to the United States, having, in fact, more skilled labourers than the US'. Pascaline Winand, in her study *Eisenhower, Kennedy and the United States of Europe*, describes a two-part American programme:

First, European energies should be concentrated on building a European political community solidly rooted in economic integration. This would give Europe greater influence in world councils and reduce the attraction of nationalism. Western Europe would therefore become the economic and political equal of the United States. Second, the potential of the European co-equal should be harnessed to that of the United States for two common enterprises – world economic development and military defence.

There was never any doubt in American minds that Britain should be a wholehearted member of this enterprise, committed to its political purposes and not hedging every pro-European gesture with qualifications and caveats. When, for example, Britain refused to participate in discussions about the establishment of the European Coal and Steel Community, there was much grumbling in the US Congress with some members seeking to cut off Marshall aid to Britain if she persisted in opposing membership.

American enthusiasm for British cooperation in Europe rested on a number of considerations. First, there was no sympathy for Britain's delusion that it could retain a great power role based on a few shards of the Empire and the creation of the Commonwealth. Even Harold Macmillan, the most Europhile Cabinet Minister in the early 1950s, declared unequivocally, 'The Empire must always have first preference. Europe must come second.' What was involved was both mission and status. Anthony Eden explained it like this: 'These are our family ties. That is our life; without it we should be no more than some millions of people, living on an island off the coast of Europe, in which nobody wants to take any particular interest.' But the Empire was melting away, and the family ties were growing weaker. While appeals to Commonwealth solidarity as a reason for resisting European integration still had some resonance in the 1960s, for example when Gaitskell beat the drum, Americans were surely more perceptive in understanding that the days of the Empire were over for Britain – brought to a reasonably successful conclusion by the old imperial power – and that the Commonwealth added little political weight to our status. Governments were never able to transfer to the Commonwealth the public enthusiasm that had been generated by the Empire, and the curtailment of immigration from the Caribbean and south Asia made nonsense of efforts to suggest that the Commonwealth bestowed a common citizenship and common rights on those who had once dwelt under the Union Jack. Even in the 1990s, many Conservatives and much of the British media resisted any idea that we should be moderately generous in the award of citizenship to some of those who had lived in Hong Kong (often directly serving the colonial power), and deserved a guarantee that, if necessary, they could look to Britain for a home after 1997. *Civis Romanus sum* was not to be translated into a modern British obligation. Australia and Canada, both of course Commonwealth countries, were much more generous over the granting of citizenship to Hong Kong residents. They were a lot more maternal than the so-called Mother Country, and have benefited greatly from the Hong Kong migrants that Britain turned away.

Second, Americans undoubtedly felt that Britain would provide the European integration process with the benefits of its experience and good sense. Better, they believed, to have Britain helping to steer in the front seat, rather than simply offering advice and criticism from the back. This sentiment could easily shade into seeing Britain as a potential American Trojan Horse in Europe, able to ensure that western Europe did not embrace policies inimical to American interests. This was what de Gaulle feared; that Britain would get its marching orders from Washington and see every European issue from the American viewpoint. It is not an entirely fair assessment of America's intentions, but there is a bit of truth in it.

Third, Americans believed that the net effect of Britain joining the Common Market would benefit American trade. Britain's growth rate, which then lagged behind that of the six Common Market countries, would be stimulated by membership and this would increase American opportunities for trade and investment.

The fact that America supported British membership was one of the reasons why much of the British political establishment was so lukewarm about the idea. Clearly, it was felt, America wanted to see Britain placed firmly in the second division, a middle-ranking European country not a world-class player. This suspicion was strengthened by the lamentable Suez expedition of 1956; one of several examples in the years since Munich (Iraq being the most recent) of the alleged lessons of that humiliating meeting in 1938 being used to justify a disastrous foreign policy initiative. For Harold Macmillan, at that time Chancellor of the Exchequer, the Egyptian leader Colonel Nasser was 'an Asiatic Mussolini', and Britain and France had to cut him down to size before he destabilized the Middle East. The Americans, it was reckoned in London, would look the other way. 'I know Ike,' said Macmillan, 'he'll lie doggo.' The implicit assumption was that Americans would allow Britain and France to go on acting like imperial powers. Washington would provide cover for their occasional imperial adventures. The miscalculation could not have been greater. The Americans were horrified, not least by the impact of the invasion on opinion in the Arab world. At the UN they demanded British and French withdrawal, and threatened to kick away the props under the pound and the British economy unless Britain complied straightaway with international opinion. There was no choice: the economy was too weak for Britain to defy America, and the sterling area – a last vestige of world-power standing – had to be preserved. Britain backed off, reminded with bruising force of our real status in the world.

While the British Government moved quickly to try to repair the Special Relationship, there is no doubt that it took a heavy hit as a result of the Suez fiasco. Noël Coward spoke for many in Britain when he argued that the Americans had 'behaved vilely'. There had, of course, always been an undertow of anti-Americanism in wartime and post-war Britain, directed initially against those GIs who were 'overpaid, overfed, oversexed and [thank heavens] over here'. Anti-Americanism was to be found on the right, for instance in the novels of Evelyn Waugh, and on the left, in the work of Graham Greene. American 'betrayal' at Suez stoked it up; some shopkeepers put up signs 'No Americans served here'. Macmillan worried that it would increase an isolationalist mood in Britain, which was already directed against Europe. In December 1957, he noted 'the anti-Americanism of many of our supporters, which of course reached its culminating point at Suez but has not yet died down. It is partly based on real apprehension and partly, I am afraid, represents the English form of the great disease from which the French are suffering more than any other people – that is, looking backwards to the nineteenth century instead of looking forwards . . .' Some of the anti-Americanism was cultural. There was a worry that we were being swamped by American values, exemplified above all by Hollywood's domination of the cinema industry. We tried to protect our own film-makers with subsidies, quotas and levies, but despite the efforts of the Ealing film studios, the Californian tide of glamour, sex and violence continued to wash over us. Concerns about the Americanization of the British way of life were at the heart of the debate in the 1950s about the introduction of commercial television.

By the late 1960s anti-Americanism was more associated with the political Left than the Right. Vietnam was the cause, with the young in particular identifying with the poor Asian peasants who withstood whatever tonnage of munitions American B-52s dropped on them. Around the world, America's enemies attained heroic status on the left. This produced some stomach-turning results such as the lionizing of Cuba's wretched dictator Fidel Castro. What began in Vietnam and Cambodia was continued in Chile and Central America. The Sandinista Left became a significant element in British municipal socialism. A Prince Valiant of this movement was David Blunkett, later to become the hammer of civil libertarians in Tony Blair's Labour government. Interviewed in 1983 about the tradition of raising the American flag on the Fourth of July over the city hall in Sheffield (where he presided over a council of comrades), he responded, 'Independence Day. It would be nice if we were independent of the United States, wouldn't it?' Mr Blunkett deserves some sort of recognition for having made the journey from populist left to authoritarian right without being touched by even the shadows of the European liberal tradition.

But the Special Relationship lived on. It survived the British withdrawal from east of Suez in 1967, the biggest military recognition yet of our reduced circumstances. It was battered by Harold Wilson's sensible refusal to commit British troops to the American side in the Vietnam war, and by American snubbing of his piddling efforts to mediate between them and the North Vietnamese. It leapfrogged the Heath years, when that short-lived and ill-starred prime minister declined to reach for the old familiar comfort blanket and made it clear that he was a European prime minister above all, not an American surrogate. But then it came roaring back to life again during the Thatcher years when, despite rows over the American invasion of Grenada, public hostility to the bombing of Libya, American pressure to curtail European dependence on Soviet energy supplies, and concerns in London about President Reagan's flirtation with Mr Gorbachev over nuclear disarmament, the relationship was sprinkled with stardust and put to music. President Reagan and Margaret Thatcher got on conspicuously well; ideological soulmates, they sensed that they were cresting together a wave of anti-Communism and free market economics. Perhaps their joint resolve to stand up to Soviet pressure and to assert the moral superiority of the Western cause, coupled with their recognition that Mr Gorbachev was a different sort of Soviet leader, helped to quicken the collapse of Russia's Communist empire in Europe. Elsewhere the 'special' fruits of the Special Relationship were difficult to spot, though at least the Americans – after considerable initial misgivings and hesitations – provided valuable, indeed at times crucial, intelligence and logistical support as Britain sought (rightly) to preserve the last remnants of the Empire from Argentinian rapacity in the South Atlantic.

Before the Iraq war, conventional wisdom had it that whatever was left of the Special Relationship had largely disappeared with the end of the Cold War and the fundamental shift that this engineered in America's geo-strategic interests. Ambassador Seitz saw the successful coalition politics of the first Gulf War as 'the last hurrah of the old regime'. He regarded disagreements and misunderstandings about

Bosnia in subsequent years as a sign of changed times. Before turning to the most recent manifestation of Britain's understanding of its relationship with America, and America's views on what is required of its junior partner, it is worth reviewing how in practice each side has seen the relationship.

For America, it has been useful to have a dependable ally who never strays far from Washington's pursuit of its own strategic interest. Britain and others are allowed to depart from the script when issues like trade, the environment and economics are concerned. But anything touching on security brings with it a three-line whip. On the whole, America has believed that its interests are best served with Britain on the inside in Europe rather than outside. She is still more interested in European integration than in British sovereignty. British membership of the European Union can complicate the relationship with Washington, often in ways that Washington finds difficult to understand since it still tends to confuse a union, in which sovereignty is shared at a deep and comprehensive level, with an alliance. But while membership can snarl up the relationship, it is vital to it. British withdrawal from the EU, even semi-detachment, would greatly worry most of America's foreign policy establishment. America also feels that it is entitled to intervene in British politics on the Irish issue, and latterly has been encouraged to do so, with the aim both of pushing the peace process forwards and of securing its outcome. I wonder myself how much payback has been received from American investment in Gerry Adams and Sinn Féin. I suspect that Mr Adams has got more out of Washington than London and Dublin have got out of Mr Adams. Maybe I allow myself to be excessively influenced by a personal distaste for those who fudge the distinction between politics, murder and crime.

What counts in the scales on the British side? We persuade ourselves that we can influence our most powerful ally in ways that we presumably deem beneficial to our national interest. Since the days when Churchill's efforts to broker agreements between the USA and the Soviet Union were brushed aside by Washington, the influence has been much exaggerated. Where substance is important to America, the most that Britain can usually do is to affect process. In return for the prospect of influence we provide a sign to the world that America is not unilateralist. Britain is a multilateral emblem to pin in America's lapel. Perhaps our privileged status as friend of first resort underpins our position in NATO and on the Security Council of the UN. We have access to intelligence, particularly through global eavesdropping, which would otherwise be denied us, and who knows what errands we perform in return? This is as valuable as intelligence ever is. The former Cabinet Secretary Lord Butler has said that intelligence is uniquely worthy of scepticism. We are a nuclear power thanks to American largesse. British officials also usually find it easier to deal with their American cousins, though this is not always the case – as any trade negotiator will attest, or as I can myself confirm from my involvement over recent years in negotiating, among other things, issues of transport security with Washington. An exaggerated combination of the sentiments in this paragraph submerges two simple propositions. First, Britain will usually agree with the United States on security issues. Where we and our friends in Europe do not do so, it is sensible and in the interests of Britain, Europe, America (and usually the world) to work to try to reach agreement. But if Britain announces at the outset that whatever America finally decides to do, her eternally subordinate ally will be in her traditional place, then she ceases to serve Britain's national interest and probably in the long run does few favours to America, either. Second, foreign policy should not be a brain-free zone. 'Feel' is no substitute for cerebral activity; hearts and flowers should not take precedence over reason.

As we have seen, it has been a constant theme of American foreign policy for sixty years that Britain should be a part of the process of European integration. It has equally been a constant in British policy that we should be an influential player in both Brussels and Washington; it has even been argued that playing the European game hobbles Britain internationally and as an independent partner of America. We search desperately for an answer to Dean Acheson's question about our international role – an answer that avoids any clear choice. The dilemma is well illustrated in Richard Weight's superb history of post-war Britain, *Patriots*. Drawing on the work of Nick Cull, professor and film historian, Mr Weight takes the popular British film *The Italian Job* as a metaphor for the British problem. In the film, a gang of typical British characters shows what chumps the Continent's 'bloody foreigners' are. The gang plans and carries out successfully a gold bullion robbery in Turin, masterminded by a patriotic convict played by Noël Coward (who, six years before the film was made in 1969, had told the annual dinner of the Battle of Britain veterans that 'England has become a third-rate power . . . we are vulgarized by American values'). The intention is that stealing the bullion will help tackle Britain's balance of payments crisis. The gang makes its escape from Turin in a fleet of Minis, the last mass-market favourites of the British car industry, soon to be as dead as Mr Cleese's parrot. The robbers change from their cars to a coach that, racing through the Alps, takes a bend too fast and only just manages to stop with the front end on the road and the back, containing the stolen gold, hanging over a precipice. Every move towards the gold by the gangsters jeopardizes the delicate balance of the coach. As the credits roll, the gang leader Michael Caine says, 'Er, hang on a minute, lads, I've got a great idea.'

The great idea for Britain has been . . . what? To go it alone? To seek a comfortable berth in Washington's back pocket? To throw in our lot with our European partners? Can we confound those who tiresomely insist, like the late Mr Acheson, that we really have to choose, and show them how Britain can bridge the Atlantic, a solid and dependable link that can carry traffic in both directions? Which brings us rather obviously to Mr Blair, President Bush and Iraq. There is already a rich and angry literature on Mr Blair and the calamitous military invasion of Iraq. It includes some first-class journalistic history and two official reports – an absurd contribution by a former senior judge, Lord Hutton, and a subtle critique of the way Mr Blair conducts his government by former Cabinet Secretary Lord Butler. I do not intend to add much to these pickings, least of all to try to establish – like the author of a country house mystery – who did what to whom, where the bodies are buried, and whether there are any fingerprints on the weapon. My own starting point so far as the Iraq controversy is concerned is the ending of the first Gulf War.

In the last days of February 1991, the fighting was rapidly coming to an end. Iraqi forces were streaming back from Kuwait City to Basra along what was called the 'Highway of Death'. John Major had asked me as Party Chairman to go and have dinner with him alone in his flat in Downing Street to discuss political tactics for the coming months and in particular whether we should listen to the advice to call an early election, taking advantage of his own political honeymoon (he had only been in office a few months) and of the successful prosecution of the war. To his credit, Major made absolutely clear that he had no intention of playing politics with a military triumph that had been supported in any event by the main opposition parties. I agreed with him that it would be a tacky thing to do, and almost certainly bad politics as well. We were sitting after supper on our own in his drawing room surrounded by cricketing memorabilia and copies of Trollope when the telephone rang. It was the duty clerk from his office down-stairs to say that President Bush wanted to speak to him. The gist of the conversation was clear. On the advice of his military commanders, the President wanted to call off the fighting, which had now become a one-sided slaughter. The President and the Prime Minister went through all the main issues, with Major asking tough questions about the consequences of letting Saddam Hussein off the hook. They dis-cussed the terms of the UN resolution that had launched the coalition, the prospect of the coalition fracturing, and the problems associated with pressing on to Baghdad. I recall the President's clinching argu-ment: 'If we chase Saddam all the way to Baghdad, we'll own the place.' Which, it became clear, was the last thing he wanted to do.

The first President Bush spelled this point out in *A World Trans-formed*, the book that he wrote with his National Security Adviser, Brent Scowcroft, in 1998:

Trying to eliminate Saddam . . . would have incurred incalculable human and political costs . . . We would have been forced to occupy Baghdad and, in effect, rule Iraq . . . There was no viable 'exit strategy' we could see, violating another of our principles. Furthermore, we had been self-consciously trying to set a pattern for handling aggression in the post-Cold War world. Going in and occupying Iraq, thus unilaterally exceeding the United Nations' mandate, would have destroyed the precedent of international response to aggression that we hoped to establish.

President Bush also saw the danger that the whole Arab world would be turned against America and that young American soldiers would be condemned 'to fight in what would be an unwinnable urban guer-rilla war'. Writing in the periodical *Foreign Affairs* in 1992, Colin Powell (the Chairman of the Joint Chiefs of Staff in the first Gulf War) noted that occupying Baghdad would involve 'an unpardonable expense in terms of money, lives lost and ruined regional relation-ships'. I may be unimaginative but I have never moved much beyond these arguments.

Part of the collateral damage of the fixation on Iraq was the failure to finish the job that was begun in Afghanistan with the unseating of the Taliban regime there. In order to build a new nation in that desperately poor country, it was essential first to provide the security on which political authority and development depend. That has never been achieved. The military commitment was kept to a minimum throughout 2002, presumably so as not to impinge on the build-up for an invasion of Iraq. European countries found it all too comfortable to shelter behind America's security assessment and keep their own military deployments in the region, principally in the international security force, to a minimum. We all kidded ourselves that we had bought the warlords, whereas it swiftly became apparent that we had only rented them. Poppy-growing and opium production mush-roomed as the American and European troops were discouraged from interdicting the manufacture and trafficking of heroin. With up to 90 per cent of the heroin on the streets of Europe's capitals originating in Afghanistan, we created a particularly malign version of the Common Agricultural Policy. Demand exploded and no serious effort was made to control supply. The warlords profited hugely from the proceeds of a trade that brought together, as in Colombia, terrorism, organized criminality, and the sapping of the authority of the State. At the Tokyo Donors Conference, held in 2003 after the fall of Kabul, I pledged on behalf of the European Commission a minimum contribution to Afghanistan's development of one billion euros over five years. (We have actually been spending more than this – not just committing the money, but in a dangerous environment contracting and spending it as well.) I stretched the elastic of my political authority about as far as it would go in making a pledge from the community budget of this size, and had to withstand a good deal of tiresome criticism from the French delegation at the conference as a result. What became increasingly frustrating through 2002–04 was to see development funds exceeded by the drugs income made by the warlords, and President Karzai's government inhibited from extending its authority and making the maximum use of development assistance because of the dangerous security situation. There were times when it seemed that his government's authority did not run very far outside battered Kabul. We could have started far more rapidly to build a modern nation in Afghanistan – poor but decent. We shall now have our work cut out to avoid the establishment of a narco-state, exporting terrorism as well as drugs.

Sir John Stanley, the former British Conservative defence minister, has observed that the Iraq invasion was the first time that a British government had gone to war 'specifically on the strength of intelligence assessments'. The dossier that collected those assessments together in September 2002 has turned out to be a turkey. As John Kampfner, author of *Blair's Wars*, has noted, none of the nine main conclusions in that report has been proven. Whether or not the Prime Minister connived at squeezing out of the intelligence services the answers he wanted, it is at the very least true that he overstated evidence, which he himself described as 'extensive, detailed and authoritative', and which Lord Butler much more accurately assessed as 'very thin'. It also seems clear that Mr Blair had concluded from the time when he met President Bush at Crawford, Texas, in the spring of 2002 that the Americans were not to be deflected from invading Iraq and that Britain could not leave them to act on their own. Britain went to war because America chose to go to war. Mr Blair told the Cabinet and Parliament, and perhaps convinced himself, that his reasons were other than this: to track down weapons of mass destruction; to prevent their proliferation or use; to strengthen the authority of the UN by insisting on compliance with Security Council resolutions; to get rid of a wicked tyrant and serial abuser of human rights on a massive scale. This is, I suspect, an example of what an unnamed American official called 'rolling rationalization [that] is one of the less attractive features of British foreign policy'. We are now led to believe that Mr Blair had always been preoccupied by the dangers represented by Saddam Hussein, though his interest in Iraq (like that of many American officials) does not seem to go back to the days when Western countries were arming its dictator and looking the other way as he gassed, murdered and tortured Iraqis. In those days the infamous tyrant was on 'our' side: silly, really, that he failed to understand how we play the game of an ethical foreign policy – or perhaps he understood it for most of his career all too well.

I have never myself had to take decisions directly that send young men and women to face danger and perhaps death, though I shared in the collective decisions that the British Cabinet took in 1990 to join the coalition in the first Gulf War. I remember saying to John Major at the time that this sort of decision was particularly difficult for politicians of our generation – the first in Britain who had not had to fight in a war themselves. In that sense we are different from Americans of our age group, though a surprising number of those who are most enthusiastic these days about sending in the Black Hawks and the Humvees had, in Vice President Cheney's apposite phrase, 'other priorities' than military service during the Vietnam War. Awareness of the gravity of the decisions taken about life, death, maiming, war – particularly, I repeat, by those who have never themselves had to go through the fire of armed conflict – makes me reluctant to assign base motives or assume a frivolous lack of moral anxiety on the part of those who reach different conclusions to my own about the necessity of going to war. So what is it about Mr Blair, who is manifestly not a bad man, that enabled him to convince himself that what he was doing was right, and indeed that his real motives were those that he expressed with such power and eloquence?

There is no doubt about Mr Blair's political talents, which were on impressive display in July 2005 when within the same dramatic week he lobbied successfully in Singapore for London to be awarded the 2012 Olympics, chaired the G8 Summit at Gleneagles and coped with the aftermath of the terrorist bombings in London. But there is a heated debate about whether this very able politician has any convictions. 'He is,' Lord Jenkins noted, 'too Manichaean for my perhaps now jaded taste, seeing matters in stark terms of good and evil, black and white, and with a consequent belief that if evil is cut down, good will inevitably follow.' Lord Jenkins concluded that the colour grey seemed to be missing from his political palette. On the other side, there are those who regard Mr Blair as a meretricious chancer, supremely gifted at what the Americans call 'triangulation' (touching all the political bases – yes, no, maybe – at the same time), squaring circles, finding the colour grey and painting it in a brighter hue. Such critics are likely to regard the 'third way', a nebulous all-things-to-all-men political style much associated with Mr Blair and other successful politicians of the centre left, as (in Tony Judt's felicitous description) 'opportunism with a human face'. Mr Blair regards his own early years as a CND anti-European as part of a necessary phase he had to go through in order to become a senior Labour figure able to change his party into a more electable and sensible political vehicle. Most political sophisticates buy this – an example of acceptable careerism justified by such a satisfactory outcome. Perhaps I am too romantic about politics, but I find myself sucking my teeth a bit at this. I warm much more to careers that have a more principled core, though I hesitate to exaggerate the point lest I drift into sanctimoniousness.

My own view is that Mr Blair, a usually likeable man, has convictions to which he holds strongly – while he holds them. His convictions change on issues as disparate as hunting, nuclear weapons, civil liberties, the constitution, the euro and the reasons for going to war, partly to reflect what he believes to be prevailing, convenient opinion. I do not for a moment deny that from time to time Mr Blair has had to show considerable courage in defending a policy he has decided to pursue. Iraq fell squarely into this category, though the Prime Minister and his advisers probably assumed with American officials that an early victory would turn opinion around and that the invasion would be seen as the liberation of a tyrannized people rather than the descent in 2003–04 into a bloody quagmire. But whatever his changing position, Mr Blair and his supporters insist that his actions should be seen to have the seamless and principled continuity that you would expect of 'a regular kind of guy'. This is where he is at his most dangerous. There can be no questioning his integrity. His veracity, decency and dedication to a higher good than vulgar pragmatism have to be explicitly conceded. He has to be accepted as a man of unchallenged honour; it is heresy to suggest that, like most of us in politics, he may occasionally have been a bit of a charlatan. Mr Blair's integrity has to be defended at any cost.

The convictions that drive Mr Blair do not always seem well thought through. Let us take, for example, his Gladstonian instinct to root out wickedness and install good in its stead. I have considerable sympathy for the notion that foreign policy should not be devoid of ethical considerations, and reckon that there is frequently an overlap between expedience and morality. But I am unclear when exactly Mr Blair came to this conviction, and how clearly he has worked out some of its implications. When in 1997 Robin Cook produced his mission statement for the Foreign Office, arguing the case for an ethical foreign policy, I do not recall much echoing enthusiasm from Number 10 Downing Street. Mr Cook, with all his fussiness about arms sales and with his manifest concern for Palestinian human rights, was clearly regarded as rather tiresome. In foreign policy you also have to be a little careful about just how strongly you associate what you are doing with a higher morality. America and Britain have had to assemble a pretty eclectic group of partners to prosecute the cause of democracy and good governance in Afghanistan and Iraq. An embarrassingly large number of them have dubious human rights records, not admittedly as bad as Saddam Hussein's but certainly not up to the minimum standards that would come close to satisfying Amnesty International or Human Rights Watch. The mission, however virtuous, makes the coalition, but the coalition is not always very virtuous. I wonder, too, whether there is not an embarrassing disproportion between the rhetoric of Mr Gladstone and the power that Britain can actually deploy today, which is a fraction of what was available to our Victorian forebears. Even Mr Mugabe, a tinpot tyrant if ever there was one, can snap his fingers at Britain and tell us to go hang. Time was when he would have lasted as long as it took to send in the King's African Rifles.

Mr Blair also has an even stronger belief than most leaders in personal diplomacy and in his ability to shape other leaders' perceptions of their own national interest through the exercise of his considerable charm. I am very doubtful about this general approach, which too often sucks much of the intelligence and consistency out of the conduct of foreign policy, a point that I shall argue later in relation to Mr Chirac and Mr Schröder. Before either of them had taken up with Mr Putin, Mr Blair was all over him; Putin was offered 'best friend' status, a central place in the fellowship of leaders that Mr Blair hopes he can orchestrate to Britain's advantage. Gladstone or no Gladstone, Chechnya and the destruction of Grozny do not seem to have featured much in the early Blair–Putin conversations. What started so propitiously turned sour as Mr Putin went his own way on Iraq, publicly humiliating Mr Blair in Moscow, and joining Mr Chirac and Mr Schröder (whom the Prime Minister also seems to have mis-read) in opposing the Iraq war. Sir Christopher Meyer, Britain's ambassador to Washington during the build-up to this war, has added his own kiss-and-tell gloss to the analysis of Mr Blair's personal diplomacy, arguing that the Prime Minister did not argue his case sufficiently strongly with President Bush and his entourage. I always doubted myself how much bad news he would be happy to impart to President Bush and the American political establishment once he had been given a hero's reception by Congress.

Before turning to some of the substantive consequences of the poli-cies followed, and of the reasons for them, I want to mention one further question of governing style. Before he became Prime Minister, Mr Blair had never been in government. This seems to have exacer-bated his contempt for the existing institutions of government, the traditional approach to decision-making and relations between poli-ticians and civil servants. Power was concentrated in his private office and entourage, who rampaged across Whitehall. Part of the quite astonishing naïveté of the Hutton Report is the assumption that seems to underlie it that the evidence before the judge conveyed the workings of a normal government. It had certainly never been 'normal' before for the head of communications in Downing Street to get involved in the presentation of intelligence. The concentration of power in Number 10 Downing Street completed the destruction of the Cabinet Office as the official conductor and progress chaser of government, a process begun, alas, under Margaret Thatcher. This has reduced the competence of government in Britain, and played a major part in the dismantling of the barriers of discretion and seemliness between politicians and civil servants.

One of the government departments most affected by the accumulation of power in Number 10 has been the Foreign Office. The position of this department today recalls the letter written by Sir Thomas Sanderson, its permanent under-secretary, to Lord Salisbury (who was then Foreign Secretary but absent from the office) at a time when the Prime Minister Arthur Balfour was in temporary charge of it. 'I am now,' wrote Sanderson, 'a sort of standing dish at Arthur Balfour's breakfast. When his attention is divided, as it was this morning, between me and a fresh herring, there are alternately moments of distraction when he is concentrating on the herring, and moments of danger when he is concentrating on foreign affairs.' The appointment of a senior foreign policy adviser to the prime minister is not new; what has been novel is the number of such advisers at Mr Blair's right hand and their direct role in overseeing foreign policy on the key issues. They are not bad officials; indeed they have mostly been outstandingly good – in the case of Sir David Manning, and also Sir Stephen Wall, just about as good and decent as officials can get. This is to Tony Blair's credit; he chose them. But for a prime minister with no previous experience of foreign policy, and with an excessive regard for his own 'feel' for the subject, to take on so much himself is unwise and dangerous. Where is policy on the Middle East made today – in Number 10 or the Foreign Office? Who handles the most sophisticated traffic between London and Washington? There are questions about the role of the Foreign Secretary. Is he to regard himself as the Prime Minister's senior adviser and policy implementer on the big issues of the day? Or should he occupy himself with those issues that do not feature on the Prime Minister's radar screen? It cannot have been helpful in the build-up to the Iraq war and in its aftermath that the Prime Minister was divorced from the informed scepticism that the Foreign Office would have brought to a discussion of the available policy options. Certainly, making policy over the heads of the State Department and the Foreign Office has not been conspicuously successful.

Blair's principal aims in foreign and security policy are admirable. He wants a strong alliance with the United States, the only superpower, which he hopes Britain can influence in the way that it exercises its global leadership. He wishes to see a strengthened United Nations, which can provide legitimacy for international intervention in the affairs of sovereign states in order to protect the human rights of their citizens and to deal with real threats to the security of our own. He would like Britain to take a leading role in the affairs of the European Union, and to lay to rest our ambivalence about membership of the Union. How has the Iraq war advanced these goals?

Mr Blair committed Britain and British soldiers to the American side in Iraq because he believed that it would be perilous for us, indeed for all America's allies, to leave our friend to fight alone. He also felt that we would be able to influence America in Iraq and elsewhere if we were prepared to fight alongside her. With Britain in the bag, America was able to build a 'coalition of the willing' (or 'billing' as one wag called it, pointing to the favours promised to the ragbag collection of allies in the adventure). Without Britain could America have definitely invaded? The answer is that she probably would have done so, but the enterprise would have been more politically hazardous and it is possible that British hesitation would have encouraged doubts in the American establishment. Even if this is an absurd speculation, would we have damaged our own interests or America's by warning the Bush administration exactly what was likely to happen, repeating the warnings of the President's father and his father's senior advisers? Choking off our own grave doubts, the sort that Foreign Secretary Jack Straw evidently put to Mr Blair at the eleventh hour, did Washington no favours. Moreover, did fighting alongside America deepen sentimental attachment to the transatlantic relationship or weaken it? Is it really the role of a good friend to suppress real anxieties rather than express them candidly? Supporting the Bush invasion of Iraq is probably the worst service we have paid America.

What influence did we buy for ourselves by going along with this ill-judged adventure? At the Crawford meeting in the spring of 2002, Mr Blair had given Bush and his senior advisers to understand that, whatever happened, if there was fighting we would be shoulder to shoulder with them. According to Peter Riddell (author of *Hug Them Close*), Lewis 'Scooter' Libby, Vice President Cheney's Chief of Staff, until he was charged by a grand jury with five felonies including obstruction of justice and perjury, and resigned in late 2005, asked a senior British official in the autumn why Mr Blair was so worked up about the UN since he 'is going to be with us anyway'. What influence did we ever exercise over substance as opposed to process – over the prosecution of the war, or the government of Iraq when the war was formally over, with the 'mission accomplished' but the fatalities about to mount?

I visited Baghdad in September 2003 to discuss the assistance Europe could provide for the reconstruction of the country. After an exciting flight into the city, with our RAF plane diving and weaving into its approach like a Welsh wing three-quarter dashing down the touchline, and an equally thrilling helicopter ride to the safe-ish Green Zone via the bombed UN headquarters where my friend Sergio Vieira de Mello had died, we spent forty minutes with the cocky, clever, confident American Paul Bremer. He told us how much the security position was improving – a reassuring message, which was somewhat undermined by the fact that we had been refused permission to stay overnight in Baghdad for reasons that owed nothing to the shortage or expense of hotel accommodation. We then walked twenty yards down a long corridor in what had once been one of Saddam Hussein's palaces to talk to Bremer's deputy, the former British ambassador to the UN, Sir Jeremy Greenstock. He was painstakingly loyal to the official line while delivering it with more subtlety and less unqualified self-assurance. But what influence was this clever diplomat able to bring to the shaping of decisions by Mr Bremer and his bosses in the Pentagon? To what extent was he part of the governance of Iraq? It is revealing that whatever the disastrous mistakes made by the occupying power – the purging of Baathists, the employment of the sort of military overkill tactics used by the Israeli defence forces, the Grozny-ization of Fallujah and other towns – no one has ever pointed the finger of blame at the British. No one holds Britain to account because no one thinks for a nanosecond that Britain is implicated in the decisions. Britain is there as part of the feudal host, not as a serious decision-sharing partner. This point was reinforced by the publication of Mr Bremer's unconvincingly self-justificatory memoirs in 2006 in which he barely mentions America's pro-consular partners, though he does pause to cuff them about the ears for being rightly reluctant to confront the minor Shia cleric Moqtada al-Sadr, whom confrontation turned into a dangerous force.

We have also been assured that we have been influential in persuading Mr Bush and his colleagues to become more involved in pushing forwards the peace process in the Middle East. Conceivably one day this will be true. But in the years when I saw, close up, the process deliberately driven into a lay-by, Britain's principal role was to find excuses for American inaction, not reasons for prodding Washington into doing something. During the Danish presidency of the EU in 2002, we produced a European, not an American, initiative – the first part of the so-called Road Map (every plan in Europe these days is called a road map) aimed at rescuing Israel and Palestine from continuing bloody mayhem. America took some convincing of the merits of this plan, which departed from previous proposals by arguing for parallel actions by both sides rather than sequential progress. In the past, Israel had argued (and still does, in defiance of the central principle of the Road Map) that she would only move on political issues, such as settlements on the West Bank, once the Palestinians had delivered complete security on the ground. Now, in the imaginative Danish draft, we pressed for both sides to take steps at the same time. We discussed the plan in the Quartet – the United States, the UN, the Russian Federation and the EU – and, after a few perfectly reasonable tweaks from the American side, the State Department bought it. But what of the White House, where President Bush had just appointed a well-known Likud-supporting hawk, Elliott Abrams, as his principal Middle East adviser? We went along to see the President and Vice President in late 2002 to discuss the plan. President Bush assured us of his extremely welcome commitment to a Palestinian state, and to what he explicitly called 'a' road map. But he urged us against early publication. The Road Map was put away in the locker. We were eventually 'allowed' to publish it in 2003. Despite numerous meetings and much froth, nothing much happened about it. Some of our moderate Arab friends understandably began to refer to 'the Quartet, *sans trois*'. Moreover, the essential element of the Road Map's approach – the rejection of sequentialism – never seemed to become a part of American policy.

This must have been a grave disappointment to Mr Blair, who had promised in his party conference speech in 2002 that 'final status' talks on the Middle East would start by the end of that year. He presumably continued to nag away at Washington about the Middle East and got his reward when he visited Washington two days after Ariel Sharon in the spring of 2004 to be told that President Bush had bought the Israeli Prime Minister's plan for withdrawal from Gaza, the retention of settlements in the West Bank, and no right of return to Israel for Palestinian refugees. This sharp change in American policy brought no word of disapproval from Mr Blair. We were apparently to welcome the policy shift as a step forwards along the road to peace, entirely consistent with the Road Map. Shortly after the Bush–Blair meeting, there was a weekend European foreign ministers' meeting under the then Irish presidency in the constituency of their Minister for Foreign Affairs Brian Cowen. The Irish had been consistently sensible about the Middle East, refusing to allow anyone to pretend that progress was being made when all that could be charted was continuing murderous failure. We were all a little surprised to hear Jack Straw, poor man, giving us the party line that nothing had really changed in Washington or, if it had, we should welcome it as a breakthrough. Such was the influence exercised through Britain's Very Special Relationship. Mr Blair's views, however forcefully they were expressed (and his forcefulness seems to have been pretty meek), clearly counted for nothing against those of Karl Rove and Elliott Abrams. I often wondered how our British, and European, failure to speak out more eloquently on the Middle East and related issues must have undermined the position of Colin Powell and other sensible moderates in Washington.

Mr Powell, of course, had to contend in Washington with those whom James Naughtie (in his book *Accidental American*) tells us he described as the 'fucking crazies', a description one assumes of the neoconservatives and their assertive nationalist allies such as Vice President Cheney and Donald Rumsfeld. In an interview with Mr Naughtie for his book, Mr Blair surprised the author by declaring, 'I never quite understand what people mean by this neocon thing.' If this really does represent Mr Blair's state of ignorance about the febrile political atmosphere in Washington, then perhaps he also failed to study *The National Security Strategy of the United States of America*, issued by the White House in 2002, which asserts, to quote the great American historian Arthur M. Schlesinger, Jr., 'the revolutionary idea of preventive war as the basis of US foreign policy'. The Iraq war was such an engagement. It did not pre-empt an imminent threat; it prevented a speculative threat. If Mr Blair has signed up to this world view, in which preventive wars are acceptable for America as the global superpower, though for no one else, and in which America can in practice follow its own rules and do whatever it likes, then he has done immeasurable damage to our historical relationship with the United States, to the values on which it is based, and to our previously shared commitment to the international rule of law.

I will come back in later chapters to two other aims of Mr Blair's foreign policy – legitimizing intervention in other states, and securing our position as a leading member of the EU. At this point, for the sake of completeness, I will merely sketch out how the achievement of these hopes has been set back.

Mr Blair is right to argue, as others do, that the Treaty of Westphalia in 1648 no longer provides an adequate basis for international law. That treaty, which brought to an end the Thirty Years War and inaugurated the modern European state system, also concluded that one state should only take up arms against another and intervene in its affairs if it were itself to be attacked by that state. That is plainly no longer sufficient as a central assumption in international law. How does a state deal with threats to it, or attacks on it, by a non-state actor (such as a terrorist group) which are supported by a state? How do states deal with a state whose institutions of government have broken down, with the resultant chaos threatening the stability and security of others? (Both these instances were relevant in the case of Afghanistan.) How do states prevent the manufacture, threatened use and proliferation of weapons of mass destruction? Do states have no obligation to intervene in a state that is abusing the human rights of its citizens? If there is not a right to intervene, is there not at least (as Gareth Evans, former Australian foreign minister, and others have argued) 'a responsibility to protect citizens of other states whose human rights are being abused'? How should we cope with Rwanda and Kosovo? Is it only states that have rights, and not their citizens?

Mr Blair feels strongly that there should be an international consensus, rooted in the practices and principles of the UN, which can legitimize armed intervention in the sorts of cases I have mentioned, where other efforts to prevent a crisis fail. Mr Blair's views on intervention were set out in a speech in Chicago in 1999 entitled 'Doctrine of the International Community', where he laid out five main considerations that could justify our intervention to prevent 'threats to international peace and security'. Were we sure of our case? Had we exhausted all diplomatic options? Were there military options that would be undertaken prudently? Were we prepared to stick things out for the long term? Were our national interests involved? Did Mr Blair think that these tests were met in the case of Iraq? The problem about going to war in a democracy on the sorts of grounds to which the Blair doctrine refers, the attempt to pre-empt danger (for example, stopping a destabilizing flow of refugees that would result from attempted genocide), is that it depends crucially on trust. Electors are asked to give their leaders the benefit of the doubt. They are not faced with an armed intervention across their border, which they have to resist. The danger is less immediate than that. They have to trust the judgement of their democratic leaders. Has Iraq made it more or less likely that when the pre-emptive use of force is required in future, voters in Britain and other democracies will support it? Do voters feel they were told the truth about Iraq? Were they objectively told the truth? Were the judgements on which intervention was justified sensible? Have the invasion and occupation increased the dangers of terrorist attack on free and independent states, or has that danger been abated? One of the principal concerns about Mr Blair's policy on Iraq is that it has made it more difficult in future to put in place a policy of pre-emptive intervention with the backing of international law and of public opinion in democratic societies.

Mr Blair is clearly committed to Britain playing a strong role in Europe. He has worked hard with France (beginning in St Malo in 1998) to develop a more effective European defence capability, which has fluttered the dovecotes in Washington. While Americans want Europe to do more for itself in the field of security, they are reluctant to see the development of capacity leading to any decoupling from a chain of command that they themselves control. Mr Blair is right to worry that at the moment Europe dwells in the worst of all worlds: our pretensions worry the Americans without giving us much additional ability to work with them to make the world safer.

Unfortunately, Mr Blair's European ambitions have been thwarted in Iraq. Maybe he could have been more effective in bridging the Atlantic – representing Europe to America and America to Europe. But it would have taken a clearer and more outspoken determination to speak up for European doubts from time to time. Did Mr Blair ever speak out against populist American attacks on 'the cheese-eating surrender monkeys of Europe' or their 'axis of weasel'? Did he try to explain the strength of public opinion in Europe – far more united in hostility to the Iraq adventure than governments ever were? Did he think twice before confirming Mr Rumsfeld's views about 'old' and 'new' Europe (expressed in an article he co-authored for the *Wall Street Journal*) with other European governments that supported America? Did he protest against the suggestion that the Spanish election result in the wake of the Madrid bombings was the result of cowardice in the face of terrorist atrocities? What did he believe would be the benefits for Britain's European policy of blaming France and its president for the failure to get a second Security Council resolution – an outcome that was never on the cards despite all Britain's efforts – during a week in New York that represented one of the most humiliating episodes in recent British diplomatic history? Is it unfair to single out the British Prime Minister in this way? Is it playing the man rather than the ball? The problem is that in this case the man and the ball were pretty well identical. Even members of his own party clearly doubt whether the British engagement in Iraq would have developed in the same way without him. Would a Brown-led government – whatever Mr Brown may have said loyally on the hustings in 2005 – have gone to war for the same reasons? Now we must hope and work for a peaceful democratic future for Iraq. We can at least support Mr Blair in that. But we cannot forget the journey that brought us here.

Mr Blair flew to Crawford and to Washington. He told Mr Bush that 'whither thou goest, I will go'. He went to Iraq. He drove France and Germany into each other's arms (the reverse of what should be Britain's abiding European strategy). He subordinated Britain's national interest to American interests and raised serious questions about the exercise of Britain's de facto and de jure sovereignty. Politically weakened by Iraq, he surrendered to populist media pressure for a referendum on the Constitutional Treaty. As the 2005 general election campaign showed, he sacrificed the public trust that would have been needed to win that referendum. He weakened his position as well in Europe so that at precisely the time when the referendum votes in France and the Netherlands, the political problems of Mr Chirac and Mr Berlusconi, and the departure of Mr Schröder gave him the chance to seize and shape the European agenda, he had less political authority to do so. A victim of his own interpretation of the Special Relationship, Mr Blair is all too likely to be judged by history as a leader who was braver in defending Mr Bush's agenda in Iraq than he was in standing up for his own, and Britain's, strategic objectives in Europe.

5

From Brussels to Istanbul

The Governor of She asked Confucius about government. The Master said, 'Make the local people happy and attract migrants from afar.'

The Analects, Confucius

Perfect, it is not.

So intense is the hostility to the European Union in Britain that there is a tendency for its champions to cover up its warts while advertising its winsome charms. Moreover, at least some of the odium results from the habit, prevalent in particular in parts of the Brussels establishment, of implying in the first place that the EU stands above criticism, that its genesis and its works exist in a world beyond politics, that those who carp and censor must be motivated by base designs. The European idea may not, unlike the fated Challenger space shuttle, have touched the face of God, but it is certainly deemed to have felt the breeze as the Dove of Peace flew past.

The chords of Beethoven's 'Ode to Joy' can animate a provocative light-headedness about the European project. I recall a colleague in the Commission returning to one of our meetings hotfoot from an intergovernmental conference of presidents, prime ministers and foreign ministers to complain that there was no 'European feeling' in the corridors. No carpet, no chairs – that I could understand; but no European feeling? If this meant anything at all, I suppose it indicated exasperation that the democratically elected leaders of twenty-five nation states were disinclined to put what they perceived to be the interest of their own countries second to some more amorphous caprice. What the idea – if it really is an idea at all – overlooks, is the fact that the original supranational ambition was embraced because it suited national interests, just as supranational agreements do to this day. This does not somehow detract from the value and significance of the agreements themselves.

What European feeling did I detect during years of attending European summits? At these meetings, we were all seated (about forty in my early years, sixty or so by the end) at a hollow square of tables, each bearing the name of the country we represented on inverted V-shaped cards that looked like the expensive chocolate bars at airport duty-free shops. Indeed, when we enlarged from fifteen to twenty-five, I half expected to spot the Prime Minister of Toblerone in a distant corner. In the centre of the tables there would usually be a half-hearted floral display, a few funereal ferns and the occasional dusty begonia. The Swedes once presented us with an exhibition that looked like a tropical rainforest (doubtless there had just been a meeting of environment ministers) and I recall another floral tableau that bore an uncanny resemblance to the topography inhabited by the Teletubbies, complete with big yellow daisies, mock toadstools and dinky green hillocks. Where was Laa-Laa? Where Po?

The behaviour of the distinguished participants distracted attention when interest flagged as, say, the Dutch Prime Minister Mr Balkenende, who really does look like Harry Potter, nagged away (doubtless in a European spirit) at some detailed textual amendment to a draft communiqué on the workings of the internal market, or when the rival merits of the possible sites for some new European agencies were canvassed (not much European feeling there) by their national champions. Observing President Chirac provided hours of innocent entertainment; he is to body language what Shakespeare is to the spoken word. Like President Mitterrand before him, he usually made a point of arriving late, surrounded by saturnine courtiers from the Elysée Palace, moulded from the best clay that the École Nationale d'Administration (ENA) could provide. A uniformed aide-de-camp always hovered by his side carrying a large briefcase. Did it contain the key to the *Force de Frappe* in case the President was minded to launch a pre-emptive nuclear strike against a hereditary foe or was it merely carrying a little extra something for the President's lunch? Perhaps – though not, I reckoned, very probably – this was the man who like the slave in a Roman victor's chariot, muttered '*Memento, homo*' ('Do not forget, you are only mortal') in the capacious presidential ear. President Chirac, whose appetite is legendary, would sit invariably deep in contemplation of a pile of saleroom catalogues for Asian artefacts, his long fingers hovering like birds of prey over the jars of mints and trays of biscuits that were berthed between the bottles of mineral water and pots of coffee. Intervening in debates, the President was part emperor, part ham, carrying all before him – or at least conveying that impression even when his audience had plainly come to a conclusion that completely contradicted his own. In the early years, poor Mr Jospin was locked in cohabitation with him as his socialist prime minister. In the President's company Mr Jospin, a nice and courteous man, always looked as though he was wincing even when good manners dictated otherwise, and bore a look of stoic disapproval. I recall a working dinner in Stockholm when President Chirac, who usually made a clamorous point of drinking the local alcoholic brew, forced a bottle of aquavit on his reluctant prime minister. Mr Jospin passed me a note across the table: 'Have you seen your British film, *Saturday Night and Sunday Morning*?' he enquired, referring to a film that I recalled depicted another particularly stormy cohabitation. Chirac–Jospin was not a marriage made in heaven.

Kant once observed: 'Out of the crooked timber of humanity, no straight thing was ever made.' That is as true of the EU as of every other institution I have come across during my political career. In politics, where aspiration is so exaggerated, the gilt never stays long on the gingerbread. Walking into the chamber of the House of Commons for the first time I was excited and a little misty-eyed; speaking for the first time there, I could smell my own fear, just like it said in the books. Joining the Cabinet, being sworn a member of the Privy Council, were emotional experiences. But it was not long before the romance wore off, and I could detect like others the weaknesses in our system of parliamentary democracy and the trumpery of much that is claimed these days for Cabinet government. The fact that I could see what I thought was wrong did not mean that I concluded that we should throw parliamentary democracy and Cabinet government overboard. Nor does my criticism of the way the EU works mean that I think it is fundamentally flawed and that we should seek a rapid exit. Recognizing the blemishes, I remain convinced that it provides the best forum in which to pursue Britain's national interest and that of its other members. But it does need to change.

As I have noted before, the EU is our continent's response to the bloodiest century in our history. We believe in knocking down barriers to trade because we recall the results of dog-eat-dog protectionism in the interwar years – the slump, the unemployment, the misery, the revolutions. We seek to institutionalize reconciliation because we know that for all our self-puffery about European values we have in the recent past used our creativity to bring technology to the service of mass murder. We believe in accommodation, consensus, co-operation and international rules that apply equally to everyone, because without these things we have suffered and we have caused suffering. When the American polemicist Robert Kagan distinguished between the Mars of America and the Venus of Europe, he touched one or two partial truths. It is fair comment that in Europe these days, we are less comfortable with the use of force to support our view of how the world should be ordered than Americans are – and sometimes we are wrong to be so nervous about the need for armed might to sustain the international rule of law. It is also true that our European preference for non-violent options to the world's problems, and our enthusiasm for any analysis that sustains this sort of choice, is partly a result of our military weakness. If we packed a larger punch, we might well be more prepared to get into fights. But this is to a great extent explained by our past. After all, we once followed Mars and learned some hard lessons. I recall debating in the Presidential Palace in Prague with the leading American neoconservative, Richard Perle, who clearly rather enjoyed the sobriquet 'The Prince of Darkness' (which he had earned through a lifetime's attachment to military options in and out of both government and the better-compensated employment of Conrad Black). As I listened to Perle's sophisticated advocacy of aggression, I wondered how Americans would feel if similar views were being expressed nowadays by a German. Europeans

have learned to be deeply suspicious of the terrible romantic temptations of leather and bayonets.

Creating a peaceful and stable continent has never required the
death of the nation state. I do not deny that there are some who have
always taken a contrary view. For them the nation state is an out-
moded concept, discredited by war. Now they view it as fading away
under pressures of globalization from above and of multiculturalism
and regional revivals from below. While global challenges and threats
and the porous nature of frontiers require nation states to work
together, to share their sovereignty, they do not dispose of the fact
that nations are – despite the pressures on them – the largest units to
which people will willingly accord emotional allegiance. That looks
unlikely to change for the foreseeable future, which is no bad thing.
It is, after all, the differences within Europe – our various histories,
languages, traditions and patterns of thought – that give Europe its
depth and fascination. The EU should not aspire to eliminate those
differences; nor could it do so, even if it wished. What it should be
seeking is a supranational settlement that can combine what is best
about those differences, while overcoming what has been worst about
them: extreme nationalism, xenophobia, mutually destructive trade
and monetary policies, unstable balance of power politics, and above
all war. The EU should seek, in short, to contain nationalism while
retaining and indeed welcoming patriotism.

When you mention the nation states' central invigorating importance in Europe, you are invariably described as a Gaullist in or out
of the closet. But most of us *are* in the strictest sense Gaullist. When
the colonies in North America met in Philadelphia to agree a constitution they were sub-national communities trying to become one
nation. In each of the treaties that provide the legal base for the EU,
and in the latest discussions on the Constitutional Treaty, we have
witnessed ancient nation states laying down the ground rules for
sharing sovereignty. They were not creating another nation or another
state. The proposed but now rejected Constitutional Treaty for Europe
was what it said it was, with the heads of the participating nation
states listed in its preamble putting their names to a treaty on constitutional issues between nation states, not to a constitution for a single
state. The power that is transferred in Europe's laws and treaties flows

NOT QUITE THE DIPLOMAT

from the democratically elected parliaments and governments of the nation states to the institutions established to manage shared sovereignty; it does not flow down from *those* institutions to the nation states. 'What are the pillars on which Europe can be built?' asked General de Gaulle in 1960. He answered correctly, 'In truth they are the states, states that are certainly very different from one another, each having its soul, its history and its language, its glories and ambitions, but states that are the only entities with the right to give orders and the power to be obeyed.'

The political classes spend a great deal of time in Europe discussing the institutions of government and the relationships between them – the European Parliament, Council, Commission and so on. The institutions that we do not consider sufficiently, though they are the ones that matter the most in Europe, are the governments and the parliaments of the member states; that is where democratically mandated power really lies. They are, first, the institutions that do most to shape the EU. Its design has not come down on tablets of Carrara marble from the top of the mountain. It is largely the result of thousands of meetings between the representatives of the member states and tens of thousands of compromises, and those compromises are usually between the strongly held national viewpoints represented in the no longer smoke-filled meeting rooms of Brussels, Strasbourg and Luxembourg. Second, it is the strength or weakness of the governments of the member states that determines the strength or weakness of Europe. Strong national leaders produce a strong sense of direction in Europe; the reverse is also true. Take the 1997 Stability and Growth Pact as an example. It sought to establish a fiscal framework for the Eurozone and to avoid the profligacy of some countries attempting a free ride in the financial markets, paid for by the hair-shirted prudence of their colleagues. The rules that were initially set were tough, reflecting traditional German concern to ensure a strong currency, and to prevent other weaker economies being carried on German coattails. In changed times with a different government, the Germans found the rules too tight for themselves and went along with French pressure to relax them. Let us be clear what happened. Two of the largest member states decided the rules were too tough. So the rules were changed. There was not much sign of a superstate here! It was more a question of two nation states behaving badly, and riding roughshod over the smaller and more fiscally upright ones, a point that contributed to the Dutch No vote. There was little that the European Commission could do to stop it, try as we might to retain the credibility of the system. We had anxious discussions in Commission meetings. Pedro Solbes – the commissioner responsible, and the former and future Spanish finance minister – denounced the backsliding. But member states are the ultimate arbiters of how they run their own economies. There is no question that it would have been better for European economic performance if the Commission had been able to get its own way; democratic reality pointed in another direction.

This raises questions that de Gaulle's answer does not adequately meet. He had gone on in the same speech to say: 'To fancy one can build something effective in action and acceptable to the peoples, outside or above the States, is a chimera.' We have in fact done exactly that, creating institutions – principally the European Commission – to manage pretty effectively the sovereignty that we have agreed to share. But not in a way that is very 'acceptable to the peoples'.

We have shared sovereignty for reasons that are mundane as well as exalted. Of course the creators of the old European Coal and Steel Community wanted an end to war and to the ability of individual European nations to compete in building the instruments of death; they also had an eye to the industrial needs of Alsace-Lorraine and of the Ruhr. To persuade France to join the Common Market enthusiastically, she had to be offered a high external tariff, exchange controls, the association of her colonies and the subsidizing of her farmers through the Common Agricultural Policy. The CAP has eaten up (and still does so) a very large share of the EU's financial resources. It has been right to help poor farmers and rural development. But the policy created for primarily French reasons discriminates against the products of poor, developing countries, burdens European consumers, and causes rows between the member states. This complicated monstrosity squats at the heart of the EU, though reform is eroding its worst features, and its end in its present form may be visible on the far horizon. Like President Chirac, it will not – it is reasonable to assume – be with us forever. We came back again and again to CAP reform in our Commission discussions and put forward on several occasions more liberal and far-ranging reforms than ministers (led by the French) were prepared to accept. One result was continuing unfairness to poor countries, a point that Mr Blair once put very courteously to the French President at a European Council meeting. I had a front-row seat for President Chirac's explosive finger-wagging reaction. It was a case of precision targeting of a very raw nerve. Until the French face up to the impact of their implacable support for an unreformed CAP on poor farmers in poor countries, much of their eloquent concern about development in Africa and elsewhere is heavily sauced with hypocrisy.

Sovereignty-sharing has, therefore, its costs as well as its benefits. How much of it do we want? How much is required by Europe's nation states? How much will their citizens bear? The original Treaty of Rome (1957) committed the member states to work for 'an ever closer union among the peoples of Europe'. Is this a mandate for Brussels gobbling up everything; pushing back the bounds of national sovereignty as far as possible, as often as possible? Does it point the way eventually to a federal Europe, in which powers are transferred from 'we, the people' in the member states to a central political authority, which then passes back powers, as it sees fit, to the governing institutions of those same member states at national or regional level? This would, indeed, be a superstate, a 'United States of Europe' or the country 'Europe'. There are some people who argue for this, and there are some who give the impression that they would like such an outcome to creep up on us without much debate. For example, Jean-Claude Juncker, the long-serving, chain-smoking Prime Minister of Luxembourg, has said, according to The Economist magazine, 'We decide on something, leave it lying around, and wait and see what happens. If no one kicks up a fuss, because most people don't know what has been decided, we continue step by step until there is no turning back.' This is the sort of mission creep that has given Europe and democracy a bad name. It would doubtless be justified by some on the grounds that 'more Europe' must be 'better', even if most Europeans do not see things like that. But the 'better' is not often defined. A paradox about the countries that have usually argued the 'more must be better' line is that they are usually those with the worst record of implementing the policies that have already been accepted as desirable at the European level. Northern European curmudgeons on the subject of mission creep are invariably the first in the queue in implementing European laws.

Bureaucratic momentum has also been at the service of role inflation. The European Commission (with staff about the size of a large British municipal authority) is the motor of the EU. Established as an independent initiator of policy and legislation, it has come to manage too much and has aspired to manage even more. I spent five on the whole happy and interesting years as a member of the Commission, described as a college (like that of Rome's cardinals) to convey both the sense of its independence and of the shared responsibility of its members for the decisions it makes. When we became members each of us took an oath to serve Europe's interests not our own country's, a reasonable requirement given that our countries believed that their individual interests were best served through an effective Union. On the whole, members were surprisingly restrained (or discreet) in defending national positions, with one or two exceptions whose flag-waving diligence usually backfired. Nor was there much ideological dissent, though on economic issues there was a discernible divide between those who took more, and those who took less liberal positions, with the distinctions often bearing only a confusing resemblance to the political labels worn by individual commissioners. Thanks to the friendly, avuncular style of the President of the Commission Romano Prodi, and to his willingness to delegate to colleagues, the Commission was a pretty happy team with little acrimonious bickering or bureaucratic turf warfare.

In terms of individual quality, I would place the Prodi Commission on a par with the British Cabinets in which I served (and with more recent Labour Cabinets), though it is true that we lacked anyone with the rough allure of John Prescott. But there were several commissioners who would have qualified for inclusion in a category I have often used to describe British politicians. Mario Monti (Competition), Frits Bolkestein (Internal Market), Pascal Lamy (Trade), Franz Fischler (Agriculture), Günter Verheugen (Enlargement), Pedro Solbes (Economic and Monetary Affairs), Margot Wallstrom (Environment), and António Vitorino (Justice and Home Affairs) were all 'big beasts in the jungle'. The civil servants who worked for me were as good as those I had encountered as a British minister – some were outstanding. It was probably more difficult to move or sack the inadequate than it would have been in Britain, a consequence of having an international civil service with each member state prepared to fight over appointments to important jobs. Neil Kinnock fought hard to introduce fairer and more meritocratic procedures into personnel policy, against Union opposition and foot-dragging by some of the member states.

During and since my years as a commissioner, I have rarely been able to get into a London taxi without receiving an earful of advice about the European Commission, which seems to provide a cathartic safety valve for the frustrations that taxi drivers and others feel about life as a whole. No subject, save the whims and fancies of the London Mayor Ken Livingstone, so excites their interest. The Commission clearly fulfills the same sort of role in British public life as the United Nations does in America. Very often the 'taxi drivers' appear at dinner parties too. I recall one evening being told by a companion at dinner how corrupt the Commission was. 'I suppose I should remind you that I work for it,' I said. Rather lamely she struggled for a way out. 'How very brave of you,' she concluded. Writing about 'nooks and crannies' in relation to European legislation could, I suppose, slide effortlessly into 'crooks and nannies' when it comes to the Commission. The Commission is everyone's whipping boy. In so far as the facts are likely to change perceptions and prejudices – gentle Irish rain falling on flint, I fear – what do they tell us?

The Commission's overall management performance is not much different from that of the governments of the member states. Indeed, it is probably better than most. The EU's budget for 2004–05 was just over £70 billion, less than that for Britain's Department of Health and about a quarter of total central government spending in the UK. About 6 per cent is spent on administration. The European Commission, with its staff of fewer than 30,000, is responsible for implementing the budget. However, 85 per cent of this budget is spent through member-state governments and regional and sub-regional bodies, and it is this part of the budget whose handling has been regularly criticized. The Commission has to depend on the member states to ensure that the money is spent according to the rules.

Alas, we in Britain can no longer lecture others on issues of governance. The handling of mad cow disease and the foot and mouth epidemic, the design of the poll tax, the management of the social security system, the Child Support Agency, successive computerization initiatives in Whitehall, the administration of immigration and asylum policies, even the Treasury's inability to control (let alone know the costs of) the refurbishment of its own buildings – none of these reflect well on the current standards of public-sector management in Britain. How do the figures for fraud in Brussels and London compare? It is reckoned that 1 per cent (about £700 million) is obtained fraudulently from the EU, most of this in the parts of the budget spent through the member states. There are shortfalls in revenues from taxes, levies and duties and subsidies are paid for crops that are not being grown or for land that is not being cultivated. Much of this money is recovered. What happens in Britain? The Department for Work and Pensions loses 2 billion pounds a year through fraud and errors in payments. That is presumably why its accounts have been qualified by the National Audit Office (NAO) for each of the last thirteen years. The equivalent body in Brussels, the Court of Auditors, is often called in evidence to show how badly the Commission is run because it has failed to give a positive opinion on part of the EU budget for ten years; this largely covers the money distributed by the member states for agriculture and support in the poorer regions. In their 2004 report, the Court noted that 'the consolidated accounts of the European Communities faithfully reflect the revenues and expenditures and the financial situation of the Communities'. They tabled one reservation concerning the treatment of debtors. None of this gives much support to the notion that the Commission is run by the Mafia. But if I was a minister in the British Department for Work and Pensions, I would avoid taxis and dining out.

There *has* been mismanagement and fraud in Brussels. That is totally reprehensible. We should, however, be rather less prejudiced and a little more factual in discussing it. My colleague Neil Kinnock had the demanding job of trying to reform the Commission's management. Any fate that gives one man in his political lifetime the job of reforming both the Labour Party and the European Commission cannot be described as kind. He laboured successfully – changing the accounting methods, for example, from a cash-based to an accruals system, and establishing (as I have noted) a modern promotion and personnel policy. And much thanks he got for it! I passed much of my own period in Brussels trying to turn around our performance in the management of foreign assistance programmes – both conventional development aid to the poor and support for more obviously political purposes like reconstruction in the Balkans. I wanted as much as possible of the aid to be managed out in the field. It was uphill work. After five years we were reckoned (by the Organization for Economic Cooperation and Development and others) to have made significant improvements and were probably managing our funds about as well as the EU average. Not that anyone outside seemed in the event to care very much – in Brussels, more than anywhere else I have ever worked, unacknowledged success came first through the quiet avoidance of disaster.

There was one consequence that was a real downside of tackling mismanagement. Each new incident created new rules and regulations, which made it more difficult to run things competently and to take decisions quickly. The cat's cradle of controls with which we were obliged to cope would have made it impossible in Hong Kong (to take the most obvious example from my own experience) to move as rapidly as we did in implementing policy decisions, not least investments in infrastructure. I had been spoilt in Asia. Too many officials in Brussels, like those in many other bureaucracies, now have to spend too much of their time covering their own backs. But it does not save them from the scourge of the press, especially in Germany and Britain.

By its very nature, the Commission was bound to be greedy for more power unless it were to be deliberately steered in another direction. The founding treaty assigned to the Commission the guardianship of its legal provisions, and this conferred a sense of responsibility for the legacy of Monnet and Schuman. The Commission stands guard over that 'European feeling' rather as the six Vestal Virgins in Rome preserved and protected the sacred flame of Aeneas. The awareness of this solemn duty sanctifies bureaucratic ambition. The Commission already has plenty to do – initiating policy; drafting and implementing legislation; administering vast tracts of Europe-wide programmes. It should pay more regard to Montesquieu's wise remark that unnecessary laws merely enfeeble necessary ones. Bureaucracies often talk about the need to do less; they are rarely as good as their word.

The concept that is supposed to determine what is done at which level of government is called subsidiarity. This is a word barely heard outside the debating chambers of the EU, except by those who study the 1931 papal encyclical, *Quadragesimo Anno*, in which Pius XI sought to maintain Church authority against State encroachment, defining the appropriate roles for each. What it means in the EU is that decisions should be taken at the most appropriate level – Brussels, national government, or regional and local authority. For some, the most appropriate level always seems to be Brussels. I recall a discussion in the Commission on energy efficiency, during which we solemnly agreed to specify how often ten-year-old boilers should be inspected. The great European idea had come to this.

Yet there is a real problem for the Commission in deciding exactly what it should and should not do. The single market, for which (remember) Britain campaigned harder than any other country, is an engine for ever more regulation to iron out national differences that represent barriers to trade; to create the desired if sometimes mythical 'level playing field'. The Commission is endlessly being lent on, by (shall we say) the manufacturers of billiard cue tips. They complain about some example of outrageous national protectionism. By the very logic of its mission, the Commission feels duty-bound to respond. But one man's 'level playing field' is another man's 'nook and cranny' (I use the term the right way round this time) into which Europe infamously pokes its nose. It is genuinely difficult to know where to stop, and the boundary changes with the Zeitgeist. Subsidiarity can never be an exact science. The Commission's essential task is defined in ways that drive it forwards and it cannot easily be faulted for this. It cannot itself define the limits of its mission because logic would carry it all the way to a superstate. As Samuel Butler said: 'Extremes are alone logical, and they are always absurd; the mean is alone practicable and it is always illogical.'

The Commission's difficulty can only be dealt with by creating a countervailing institutional force on the side of leaving well alone and by specifying legal limits on the process of centralization. This is what the much-criticized Constitutional Treaty set out in part to do. It was the result of a novel experiment in European decision-making. The first draft was produced by a representative convention under the magisterial presidency of Valéry Giscard d'Estaing. He was assisted by a wily Scottish diplomat, John Kerr, a very clever and funny man who has not allowed the often necessary cynicism of his trade to destroy his remarkable creativity as a public official. He and Giscard, though similar in intellectual firepower, were otherwise about as alike as Puligny-Montrachet and malt whisky. These two brainy men helped to craft a well-balanced treaty (soon to become the punchbag of everyone in Europe with a grouse about anything at all), which drew all the lines in more or less the right and acceptable places. Their work then went to heads of government and foreign ministers in what is called an intergovernmental conference (IGC) for further manicuring. The draft survived Silvio Berlusconi's eccentric presidency of the EU, which he ended (thanks to the doctors) looking a lot younger than when he began. At the European Council meeting in December 2003 at which it had been hoped the treaty would be agreed, Berlusconi presided over rather desultory conversations. One session began with a long silence that was eventually broken by another of the Italian Prime Minister's flirtations with political incorrectness. 'Well,' he said, 'if no one has anything to say about the treaty, why don't we talk about football or women? You start, Gerhard,' he went on, gesturing to the German Chancellor. 'You know a lot about both.' There was an embarrassed silence. It is fair, I think, to say that there is a sort of Berlusconi line across Europe, south of which he evidently does well but north of which he would not stand much chance of getting elected. It runs pretty close to the Alps.

The Italian presidency was followed by the Irish in the first half of 2004, which brought that country's prime minister, or Taoiseach – to use his correct vernacular name – into the chair. The Irish steered the constitution through the IGC with great skill. Bertie Ahern, their prime minister, is a canny operator whose calculatedly unsophisticated style masks a clear mind, a mastery of detail and tactical wizardry. As often happens when a smaller member state has the task of presiding over the EU's affairs, the Irish were not encumbered by a host of national preoccupations. There was no Dublin wish list that took priority over Europe's agenda. They also had outstanding officials both in their Brussels team and back home in Dublin. Perhaps one result of working in a smaller bureaucracy is that very good civil servants are more likely to be given their heads.

The Constitutional Treaty was widely regarded in the rest of Europe as a triumph for the predominately 'British' view of how the EU should work. I think it is fairer to say that the treaty recognized that we had gone about as far as we could or should in developing supranational policies and institutions. The real world of twenty-five nation states and national parliaments had intervened. The supranational bargains already struck were not to be disparaged, but enough was enough. The treaty made clear that member-state governments, for example, had ultimate control of their budgetary, employment and social security systems; the EU can neither tax nor borrow, which quashes the suggestion that Europe is intent on becoming a superstate. We shall need to be more rigorous in future in defining when value can really be added by running policy at the European level. The debate here has swung strongly against encroachment into what should be member-state domestic policy areas. Jacques Delors, once a leading proponent of a 'Social Europe' (counterbalancing economic integration with social protection in the single market) had come to a different conclusion by 2000: 'I believe that areas like education, health, employment and social security, in short everything that creates social cohesion, must remain within national competence.' There is a simple democratic reason why this is wise. If powers that should be exercised at national and local level are appropriated by the EU, voters are in effect disenfranchised. They are in a sense also disenfranchised, and certainly hoodwinked, if powers that can only effectively be exercised at the European level are retained by local and national politicians. (In Britain, successive national governments have of course been disenfranchising voters for years by destroying local government.)

The paradox of the Constitutional Treaty's rejection by French and Dutch voters – and others would have said No too if given the chance

– is this. The treaty sought rightly to draw a line in the sand so far as further integration is concerned. Yet much of the satisfaction at rejection is on the part of those who have sought precisely the same outcome as that contained in the treaty. There is another irony. The preparation of the treaty through the initial Convention was regarded as the most open attempt to involve the public in the reform of the EU's institutions that had yet been attempted. Yet voters gave it a Wagnerian raspberry partly because they dislike the feeling that Europe is made over their heads. The reasons for rejection in France and the Netherlands were very different, most seeming to have little to do with the treaty itself. However, in both countries and elsewhere in Europe there is clearly a sense that the European project has gone too far, too fast for many of Europe's citizens; there is a sense too that Europe's political leaders have allowed the institutions that they themselves have created to drift away from the citizens whose interests those same institutions are supposed to serve. There is no sufficiently convincing political narrative connecting the institutions to the voters – especially in the older member states where the workforce is encouraged by some populist politicians to take fright at the mythical threat of Polish plumbers, rather than the real competition from Asian workers. It is easy enough to see what we should stop doing: no overreach, no pushing for more power here, there and everywhere. We have to focus on what we need to do to improve the lives of our citizens in a world of competitive challenges and the sort of threats that individual countries cannot face on their own. But how do we make what we are doing more accountable? How do we improve the sense of democratic control in Europe when plainly voters in France and the Netherlands, and other democracies including Britain, do not feel they have much control over what is happening in their own countries let alone in the EU as a whole? We should of course give more powers (as was proposed in the Constitutional Treaty) to national parliaments in order to police European legislation and subsidiarity, though they will need to take the job more seriously than they have in the past. The majority of national parliaments have failed for years even to make the most of their existing powers, ducking the serious job of scrutiny, which they could have performed much better. But unless they discharge their scrutiny functions in relation to European

1. Going home from Hong Kong in style – the taxi queue at Heathrow was still to come.

2. Hail and farewell – Blair arrives, the author departs, Hong Kong hand-over.

3. Democratic accountability – answering questions in the European Parliament. But where's the electorate?

4. Another hard day at the office – waiting for the end of a press conference during the Irish presidency in 2004.

5. Margaret Thatcher and her deputy, Willie Whitelaw, say Yes to Europe in 1975. 'No, No, No' came later.

6. Prime Minister Thatcher and President Reagan – a special relationship sprinkled with stardust and set to music.

7. Joined at the hip – Javier Solana and the author, speaking with one voice for Europe.

8. Wise, charismatic but beleaguered – the U.N.'s Secretary-General, Kofi Annan.

9. Colin Powell – Europe listened but did the White House?

10. Getting the Clinton treatment in the Oval Office.

11. Madeleine Albright – a good partner and friend in the Balkans and beyond.

12. The author with Swedish Foreign Minister Anna Lindh and Palestinian President Yasser Arafat in 2001 – a good woman but not a good man.

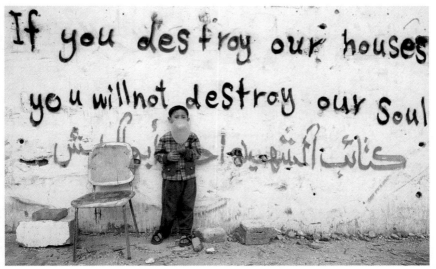

14. The writing on the wall in Gaza.

13. Is it a wall? Is it a barrier? Is it a security fence? Whatever it is, it changed the facts on the ground in the Middle East.

15. Have you heard the one about British food? Old friends Putin, Schröder and Chirac share a joke. Do they share the same values?

16. Whatever you do, don't mention Chechnya.

business more conscientiously, it will continue to be very difficult to bridge the gap between national electorates and European affairs. For the moment, alas, I do not see how much more accountability can be achieved through the democratic machinery we have created at the European level, namely its eponymous Parliament.

There are several reasons for this, only a few of which are the responsibility of the Parliament's members. They always seemed to me rather similar to national parliamentarians. Working in two extraordinary buildings in Brussels and Strasbourg – one resembling a great glass jukebox, the other a modish vacuum cleaner – they contain some very hard-working and knowledgeable politicians, and the usual small minority of idle, expense-collecting layabouts, probably unemployable in any other walk of life. This is just like every other parliament, and is customarily said to be justifiable on the grounds that in a democracy everyone deserves to be represented, including the bums. In my area – external relations – I worked with some real experts in the European Parliament, was subjected to far more scrutiny than would have been the case at Westminster, and was particularly impressed by the mechanisms established to secure budgetary accountability. Fighting for my budget each year gave me the same sort of headaches that would have been experienced by a member of an American administration in Congress. During my years, the Budget Committee was chaired by a wise and experienced Member of the European Parliament, the socialist Terry Wynn. It is no disrespect to him to say that he was probably largely unknown outside the European Parliament; within it, he was as skilful a parliamentarian as I have encountered.

So the Parliament largely does its best and it has real and growing powers. But it cannot avoid giving the impression that it is a virtual parliament, debating in the virtual languages of interpretation, representing a virtual electorate, organized in virtual ideological groups and disconnected from the political world at home. There are some things about which it can do very little. It cannot create a real European electorate; there is none. Europe's demos is fractured. Goods may know no boundaries in Europe, but politics are locked firmly into national cultures, stereotypes, histories and institutions. Attempts to cross frontiers – right, left and centre groupings on a European scale – are pretty superficial. Nor can it probably do very much about the fact that it is an itinerant body, obliged to travel between Brussels and Strasbourg each month in order to meet the terms of a deal done long ago with France (at which Britain, to its eternal shame, connived during the Edinburgh European Council in 1992 in order to secure some assumed benefit elsewhere). Maybe parliamentarians should dig in their heels and make more of a fuss. 'Hell, no, we won't go.' As things stand, moving like a travelling circus every month – lock, stock and filing cabinet – is hardly conducive to the creation of a serious, well-run parliamentary body. If there is little they can do about these things, parliamentarians could at least reorganize their own procedures so that debates are not simply a procession of speakers in an ill-attended chamber. Members do like to pontificate, and like most parliamentarians are never happier than when expending hot air on subjects over which they have absolutely no control.

There should also be more of a political career structure within the Parliament. There is a rapid and large turnover of members, presumably reflecting in part the fact that MEPs do not cut much of a dash in their own countries. Who knows who they are? How many people vote for them? Many of the ambitious ones move to national politics as soon as they can. Even so, service and competence should be more obviously and often rewarded in internal election to important offices. Above all, European parliamentarians have dragged their feet over the reform of their indefensible system of expenses for travel and office costs. This has given them the not undeserved reputation of riding a 'Béarnaise sauce train'. You cannot pose effectively as a guardian of the taxpayers' interest if you are suspected of bending the rules for your bank account's benefit.

I fear, however, that no matter how much the institution is reformed, it will be difficult for it to acquire for some time the democratic credentials needed to diminish popular alienation about Europe and to bridge the accountability gap. G. K. Chesterton once remarked that unity may be as simple as changing ten shillings into a ten-bob note or as absurd as trying to change ten terriers into a bulldog. As problems go, trying to turn twenty-five different political cultures into one parliament and one electorate is at present nearer the bulldog end of the scale than the ten-bob note.

Here is another reason why we need to draw breath before contemplating any further transfer of powers to the centre. There are now twenty-five member states. Other aspirant members hammer on the door. The scale of the enterprise should set limits on the ambitions of the centralizers. There used to be a rather simplistic suggestion that there was a choice between broadening the Union or deepening what it did. In practice we have broadened *and* deepened, but you cannot deepen everywhere. With twenty-five or thirty-five member states the centralizers cannot continue to draw everything to Brussels. Political reality as much as political will have changed the game.

It is about time. Unless we call a halt to the process of vacuuming powers to the centre, we will find people – not only in Britain – questioning their political obligation as well as voting No in referendums. If citizens in democracies (and in other societies) feel they have no say, that policy is being made over their heads and that the law is a scourge rather than a protection, they will eventually revolt. As Edmund Burke said, 'People crushed by law have no hopes but from power. If laws are their enemies, they will be enemies to laws.' Every time a referendum result goes wrong, every time a pro-European result gets home by a whisker, every time a pro-European proposal is rejected at the polling booths, every time turnouts in European elections fall to a new low, too many European politicians behave as though what has happened is an aberration or, worse still, as though the European electorate does not deserve the wise leaders it has. Prime Minister Juncker produced a plum example of this attitude in his response to the French and Dutch referendums. 'I do not believe,' he said, 'that the French and Dutch voters rejected the European constitution.' Moreover, he added, the results 'do not call into question citizens' attachments to the construction of Europe'. This brings to mind Bertold Brecht's observation in his poem 'The Solution':

> After the uprising of the 17th June
> The Secretary of the Writers Union
> Had leaflets distributed in the Stalinallee
> Stating that the people
> Had forfeited the confidence of the government
> And could win it back only

By redoubled efforts. Would it not be easier
In that case for the government
To dissolve the people
And elect another?

If a cricketer asks why he should obey the umpire – by what right he is given out – you can answer by explaining the rules, and even the position of the governing body of the sport, the Marylebone Cricket Club. Beyond that there is nothing to be done but to say, 'You must return to the pavilion because this is a game of cricket.' That is the knock-down argument. You must obey because we are operating within an accepted set of procedures. The growing problem regarding perceptions of Europe in Britain and in several other parts of the Union (and if only cricket were played elsewhere beyond the Netherlands in Europe, the metaphor would be better understood) is that too many people are coming to think it is 'not cricket', in the sense that there is something unfair about what is going on. Cricket, they discover – all right, football if you must – has sprouted all sorts of new rules while they were not looking. They pine for the game they used to play and love, in which their own national political institutions stood proud and unchallenged at the centre of debate and decision-making. But that is like a conservative cosmologist during the Renaissance pining for the medieval model of the universe, which was comfortably geo-centric; when the planets moved in perfect circles; and when there were no loose ends. The game has moved on. We are still building the new model, and we have to be a lot more careful about how we involve our citizens in the task. But there is no going back to the old one.

Europe's great test is not how it configures its governing institutions, but what those institutions do and what they achieve. What are the results? For thirty years after the Second World War, the results in western Europe were spectacular. Democracy rose from the ruins of fascism and authoritarianism, and with it came the freedoms that had been so often lauded in the nineteenth century but so often denied since. Helped by Marshall aid, by growing trade between states that opened their markets to one another, and by the migration of cheap labour from the countryside and from former colonies, the European economy took off. Annual growth in western Europe during 1945–75 ran at 4.5 per cent and gross domestic product (GDP) per head rose at an only slightly lower rate. In 1979 a French economic planner, Jean Fourastié, wrote a book that began by describing two seemingly different villages – one backward, the other developed. They turned out to be the same village, transformed by what he described in the book's title – taking as his analogy the thirty glorious days of the July Revolution of 1830 – *Les Trente Glorieuses ou la Révolution Invisible*. The 'trente glorieuses' gave their name to the modern period.

In his excellent history of modern Europe, *The Struggle for Europe*, the young American historian William Hitchcock notes that 'in narrowly economic terms ... the Marshall Plan did not save western Europe'. But what it did do was enable Europe to follow a path of industrial expansion and investment in heavy industry, 'while at the same time putting into place a costly but essential welfare state'. The $12.3 billion of Marshall aid between 1948 and 1951 helped give Europeans the chance to choose that mix of economic and social policies that proved to be mutually reinforcing. Economic growth paid for social policies, and the social policies helped to underpin the economic progress. The German economy was the engine and the Christian Democrat Ludwig Erhard gave the policy its philosophic raiment, 'the social market economy'. In the years immediately after the war's end, 100 million people in Europe were being fed at a level that seriously damaged their health; even Britain's ascetic Chancellor of the Exchequer Stafford Cripps, during the freezing winter of 1947, thought that things were so bad that 'the best place to be was in bed'. Thirty years later both the quality and the standard of living had been transformed for most citizens in western Europe; their standard of living roughly calculated in terms of GDP per head had risen exponentially and stood at 70 per cent of the American figures. Mae West once said that she used to be Snow White, but she drifted. This was Europe's Snow White period.

The drift began with the two oil shocks of the 1970s. Unemployment and inflation rose; growth rates faltered; public finances deteriorated. Stuttering recovery was set back at the end of the 1980s by a glorious event, the reunification of Germany. Glorious but costly:

transfers from Berlin to the eastern Länder have amounted to 1,250 billion euros since 1991. The 1990s were increasingly dominated by painful efforts to align the costs of the social policies that we had come to take for granted with a desultory economic performance. Preparation for the creation of the Eurozone applied a discipline to the member states concerned to clean up their public finances. While they kept inflation low, unemployment in several countries remained worryingly high, with social costs and rigid labour markets inhibiting job creation.

Europe's economic problems are often exaggerated, just as our economic vitality was in the past oversold by economists like Lester Thurow, who confidently predicted that by now we would be knocking the socks off our American competitors. Comparisons with America are most frequently used to try to demonstrate that Europe is clapped-out. It is true that the US economy has been growing more rapidly than Europe's, but that is largely the result of America's 1 per cent annual population growth. Figures for productivity growth and productivity per head tell a far more confused tale, partly because American statistical methods, in European eyes, overstate performance. In the last few years, GDP per head has arguably risen slightly faster in Europe, and if you measure GDP by the hours worked, Europe and America are level pegging. Moreover, America's far greater size gives it advantages that show up particularly in the whole-sale and retail sectors, which can benefit from expansive physical layout and easier traffic flows. Some studies suggest that 60 per cent of the difference between US and European productivity in the last ten years is explained by the Wal-Mart or Home Depot factor – large shopping sheds on out-of-town greenfield sites. Many Europeans would also question whether America's saving rate – less than 2 per cent of household income – shows a fundamentally stronger economy (or society) than Europe's, which stands at six times that figure. All this said, it remains true that we have not continued to close the gap in the difference between American and European living standards, partly because Europeans take much of our productivity gains in more leisure and shorter working hours. We are more inclined in Europe to take holidays than risks. In addition, where flexible labour markets in America have meant that the impact of new technology has raised levels of inequality while retaining high employment, inflexible markets in Europe have meant that we have lost jobs while not seeing a big inequality gap. Europe's jobless figures would be unacceptable in America; America's inequality figures would be politically intolerable in much of Europe. I shall come back to this point.

Measuring our performance against America is not the biggest economic challenge that Europe faces. We do need to improve our competitiveness in order to raise our growth rate; without that, it will be difficult to pay for the famous social model to which I alluded at the very beginning of this book. European governments in 2000 declared an ambitious objective of turning the EU into the most competitive and dynamic knowledge-based economy in the world by 2010. Dream on. This betrays a characteristic European tendency to prize the enunciation of rights, freedoms and objectives (full employment, a cleaner environment and so on) over more solid but unspectacular achievements. But there are three powerful reasons why we really do need to raise our game economically.

The first is demographic. It seems to be a universal truth that prosperity, female education, and easy, cheap and acceptable access to reliable contraceptives lower fertility rates. That has happened dramatically in Europe. The fertility rate has fallen well below replacement levels in every European country except Albania and Norway, and is still falling. The countries with the lowest birth rates are those – like Italy – which have had the most traditional views of the role of women. Indeed, if you look at fertility rates in the larger Catholic countries – Italy, Spain, Poland – you cannot conclude that the teaching of the Catholic Church is having much impact on family life. So we have followed a baby boom with a baby bust. At the same time, people are living longer and there is no good reason to suppose that this trend is about to peter out for biological or health-care reasons. The result is a rapid change in the dependency ratio, with fewer people in work supporting more people out of work. In the past, as Adair Turner has argued, each generation has been larger than the one before. No longer. Europe's population is likely to fall by almost a fifth by mid-century, while the number in retirement compared with those of working age is predicted to double from 24 per cent to almost 50 per cent over the same period. Unless we act urgently, Europe's shrinking population, and particularly the fall in the working-age population, will result in lower growth rates. We would then find ourselves with slowing economies, higher social costs, and of course a declining share of world output. The policy choices we have to make are pretty clear: more of us need to work; we will have to postpone our retirement; and we will have to accept more flexible working conditions. We will also have to pay more for the social provision we take for granted – health care and pensions, for example. None of this should be impossible, but it will require social disruption in some countries and bold political leadership. It will also provide greater opportunities for many people (to be better educated and trained), above all for women. Surveys in well-off developed countries seem to show that women would like to have more children but are deterred by the difficulty of combining motherhood and a career. Removing these barriers should help women to meet both their maternal and their social and economic aspirations.

The second big challenge that Europe faces – even France – is globalization, and this can be expressed very simply. According to the economic historian Angus Maddison, between 1500 and 1800 the combined economies of China and India accounted for 50 per cent of the world's GDP. As the Industrial Revolution lifted economic performances elsewhere – in Britain, Germany, the US, Japan and so on – India's and China's combined GDP declined by 1950 to about 8.7 per cent of the world figures. Between 1820 and the early 1950s, the Chinese economy was only growing by about 0.2 per cent a year compared with 3.8 per cent in America, and 1.7 per cent in Europe and Japan. The two decades after the middle of the last century saw continuing stagnation in both countries, but since then China and India have been transformed by rapid economic growth. By the century's end, they represented between 15 and 20 per cent of world GDP. With growth rates almost in double figures, and with a combined population of well over two billion, they will rapidly become powerful economic players. Their wealth per head still lags far behind American and European figures, so that while their overall economic size will increase exponentially their citizens will remain poorer than those in western countries. They also face significant challenges that could throw them off course. But if they manage to sustain anything like their present performance, by 2050 the EU could have a GDP just under half that of China and three quarters that of India. But we should not forget that in terms of wealth per head, Europe will still be way ahead of the Asian giants, and it is a lot easier for rich countries to stay rich than for poor countries to become rich. There is an apposite Asian saying – 'it is better to join a short queue than a long one.'

The rise of India and China, and of other Asian economies, is not necessarily a threat to Europe's prosperity. American and Japanese economic success has not taken place at the expense of Europe. On the contrary, it has certainly benefited us. Similarly, Indian and Chinese growth means new clients and new markets for European firms. In recent years, about a third of the increase in the volume of world imports has been accounted for by China. There are, however, two things that we need to bear in mind. First, even today, some of the competition from China and India is in areas where we have assumed that we have a technological advantage. In Hong Kong, the economy was transformed from a low value-added manufacturing base – cheap textiles, toys, plastic flowers – to a sophisticated high value-added competitor in much less than one industrial manager's lifetime. With technology speeding up change, we shall find that competition from India and China affects not only our cheaper service and manufacturing sectors. The growth in the number of Indian and Chinese engineering and information technology students (proportionately a far bigger figure than in America or Europe) also points towards more intense competition for us in the future in areas where we may have assumed we had an unshakeable lead for some time to come. Second, at the very least the EU, with its falling population, and with a share of world output that may almost halve over the first fifty years of this century, is unlikely to maintain the same clout in economic or political matters that it has today. But at least if they work together, European countries will have more influence than if they were to try to manage on their own in glorious isolation.

The third big challenge is that enlargement of the EU also demands an improved economic performance. This would both meet the immediate difficulties of incorporating ten new member states and, in a way, highlight the principal conundrum we have to resolve: how do we cope with the consequences of our attractiveness to our neighbours? The enlargement in May 2004 increased the EU's population by 20 per cent, but only added 5 per cent to our GDP. It led to a drop in output per head of 12.5 per cent. The arrival of new member states in the past – for example, Greece, Spain and Portugal – has brought a sharp pick-up in their growth rates, and a positive impact on the Union-wide economy. The same thing should happen again, and indeed the growth of output and productivity has quickened in all the new member states, whose performance over the last five years has outstripped that of the US as well as the rest of the EU. But the gap in the standard of living between the old and new members will require substantial shifts in resources if we are to establish a real sense of community from the Polish border to the Atlantic. The difference in wealth between east and west Europe is not simply the product of Soviet colonialism, though that greatly exacerbated it. Ever since the eighteenth-century partition of Poland by Austria, Prussia and Russia, central and eastern Europe has been a victim of Great Power politics, and that has carried an economic cost. Per capita incomes in the west were twice the figure of central and eastern Europe as long ago as 1870. The betrayal of Czechoslovakia at Munich in 1938 is part of a sad pattern of behaviour, which also ignored the sacrifices of central and eastern Europe in the two European wars, overlooked their contributions to European civilization and downplayed their aspirations for national independence during years of Soviet occupation. Central and eastern Europeans were far more likely to regard the United States as their faithful friend during the dark decades of Communism than any western European country (although Margaret Thatcher in the 1980s greatly earned their respect). Now we have welcomed central and eastern Europe home and we must not be too niggardly about the benefits they should enjoy as members of Europe's club.

The relative poverty of the new members should not be regarded by those who live in greater comfort as an outrageous advantage. I am sure that most Slovakian or Estonian workers would happily exchange their own weekly payslip for a German, French or British one. Low pay and low corporate taxes in central and eastern Europe will inevitably attract investment from the old member states, and some movement of jobs. The former French Finance Minister Nicolas

Sarkozy (brought back after the French referendum as the Interior Minister), and other western Europeans, have attacked this as unfair, and have called for less financial support for those countries that do not raise their tax rates to the levels that prevail in some western European countries. Cutting tax is described as tax dumping. The same attacks were made in the past on Ireland, which took no notice and grew into the Celtic Tiger as a result. The answer, if a country is worried about the impact of tax cuts elsewhere, is to cut taxes on its own businesses. High tax deters investment and job creation and we should not criticize the new members for discovering and acting on this ancient verity. A better economic performance across the board in Europe would reduce the pressure that produces these sorts of argument. It is not central and eastern European workers who threaten the standard of living of western Europe's workers, but western European politicians who obstruct reform and deny its necessity.

Managing the present phase of enlargement will increase enthusiasm among our neighbours to be part of further phases. The countries of south-east Europe are already either on the train, or at least waiting on the station platform, with Romania, Bulgaria, Croatia and Macedonia negotiating membership, and with all the countries of the West Balkans cherishing what the bureaucrats call 'a membership perspective'. What is happening in the Balkans is a reminder that the most potent instrument in European foreign policy – our most effective instrument of soft power – is the offer of membership of the EU. It is driving reform in that war-torn region; they all want to join the EU. In earlier times it helped to consolidate democracy in Spain, Portugal and Greece when they shook off authoritarian regimes, and it cemented the process of democratization and economic reform in the countries of central and eastern Europe after the collapse of the Soviet empire. The EU has proved itself to be an outstanding agent and sustainer of regime change, rather more effective than America for all its flamboyant attachment to the notion. So we have stabilized our neighbourhood and exported democracy and markets. But when does this process reach its limit? Jacques Delors believed that there was something that was not quite membership, which could be offered to countries like Finland, Sweden and Austria. He thought then that every further increase in EU membership would dissipate the political and economic coherence of the EU. But the ambitions of those countries were not to be satisfied by a table in Europe's anteroom. They were not prepared to be bound by rules over which their citizens were denied a say. The democratic logic for their membership was inexorable.

The most worrying aspect of the No votes in the French and Dutch referendums was the evidence of opposition to the recent enlargement of the EU, and of even greater antipathy to any future enlargement. We have a lot of explaining to do if we are to carry public opinion with us on this issue. We cannot simply ride roughshod over public sentiments. But nor can we throw in the towel. The issue is far too important. In the western Balkans, delivering on the promises we have made – to Croatia, Bosnia, Albania, Serbia and Montenegro, Macedonia and Kosovo, that if they reform, if they meet our standards, they will be welcome to join the European Union – could ultimately make the difference between war and peace in that region. And this is not a matter of soft-headed do-gooding; it's as much a matter of hard-headed security. Conflict in the Balkans – or elsewhere on our periphery – means refugees on the streets of our cities, and it is likely to result in the need for costly and risky military intervention. Political leadership at its strongest in democracies seeks to mobilize opinion behind policies that voters may initially regard with suspicion or downright hostility. So, if we can persuade our citizens that enlargement should continue, where do we tell them that it should stop? Do we simply continue adding rings of friends and neighbours until we get to the Caspian Sea or the Pacific? What do we say when Israel, Iraq or Azerbaijan come knocking on the door?

Plainly there has to be an end to the process somewhere, and we have tried to put it firmly in place with a so-called Neighbourhood Policy. This seeks to establish a series of neighbourhood agreements with the countries around the southern and eastern littoral of the Mediterranean and the countries to the east of Europe – Ukraine, Moldova, Georgia, Armenia and Azerbaijan. Russia stands out on its own – too big and grand to negotiate such a deal, though erratically enthusiastic about some sort of special relationship with the EU. These agreements offer the countries that are parties to them a share in our market and in some of our policies (research, the environment and so on) in return for implementing democratic and economic reforms. But membership of the EU is not on the table. Our partners are welcome to set up their stall in the marketplace, but not to set foot in the town hall.

It is an imaginative try, but two events will make it difficult to hold the line, demonstrating that politics is as much an arbiter of decisions on this issue as principle: first, the agreement in 2004 that Turkey can begin to negotiate membership of the EU; and second, the Orange Revolution in Ukraine. At my first ever meeting with a foreign minister from Ukraine in 1999, he asked me – doubtless knowing my support even then for Turkey's membership – why I regarded Turkey as a European country but not Ukraine. What, he asked, was so special about Turkey's European vocation and so deficient about Ukraine's? I stumbled through an unconvincing answer, one that convinced me even less in retrospect when I discovered that two of my officials present at the meeting had parents who had been born and worked in what is now Ukraine, but which then had different borders.

The question of the further enlargement of the EU arrives at the most important question of Europe's identity, of what Europe is to become, of what Europe is to represent in the world. Certainly, we cannot enlarge forever. But I do not believe we can stop yet. It has often been said of the EU that managing it is rather like riding a bicycle; you have to go on adding to its tasks, peddling like fury, otherwise the bicycle will come to a halt and you will fall off. As metaphors go, it is far from perfect. After all, you *can* stop a bicycle without falling off. People do it every day. On my new snazzy two-wheeled roadster in Oxford, complete with basket and bell, I even manage it myself. Moreover, as I have said, the aggregation of power in Brussels has necessarily come to a halt. But I believe we have to make progress in another sense, and that it is administratively possible to do so. The narrative of the EU – its *raison d'être* – was to end war in Europe. We have done that on the whole (though we have been shamed by recent ethnic cleansing in the Balkans). We have also ended Europe's divisions; the barbed wire, the barricades and the bunkers have had their day. No one of my daughters' age – from their mid twenties to early thirties – can be blamed for taking all that for granted. 'That's great, Dad. We haven't had a world war for sixty years. So what's next?' There has to be a 'next' – a difficult 'next', which will define our Europe, secure its stability and confirm our place in the world as a post-Christian society with Christian roots, a secular society that takes its values for granted. The 'next' task will do more than anything else we could attempt to prevent that 'clash of civilizations' predicted by Samuel Huntington and devoutly hoped for by extremists, especially (but not solely) Islamic ones. The reconciliation of France and Germany was the necessary and admirable European accomplishment of the twentieth century; reconciling the West and the Islamic world, with Europe acting as a hinge between the two, is a major task for the twenty-first.

The Turkish application for membership of the EU rouses deep passions and turns up the heat under some of the most sensitive issues in European politics – for example, immigration and the need to build tolerant multi-religious communities in our cities. Valéry Giscard d'Estaing argues that the entry of Turkey would mean the end of Europe. But which Europe does he mean? He is far too intelligent and cultivated to believe that Europe can be properly depicted only as a Christian club, barring the advance of Islam into what the Polish historian Oscar Halecki called 'nothing but a peninsula of Asia', just like the besieged citizens of Vienna in 1683. What is this Europe that Pope Benedict XVI, when a cardinal, identified almost exclusively with the Christian faith? The doctor in Chaucer's *Canterbury Tales* was learned in the works of scientists from Greece, Rome and the medieval Islamic world. Mathematics, astronomy, chemistry and scientific experimentations were some of the things that Christian Europe brought back from its raids on Islamic civilization and that Moslem occupation seeded in Spain and elsewhere. Our identity as Europeans absorbed the heritage and influence of the ancient Greek and Roman worlds, and of Islam too. The beginnings of Christianity were rooted in Asia and Africa as well as Europe. Byzantium was as lineal a descendant of the Roman Empire as western Europe. How should we seek to explain to the Metropolitan of the Syrian Orthodox Church and the Patriarchs of the Armenian Orthodox Church that they are outside the Christian Club? Do we write the

Orthodox Churches out of Europe's history alongside the Moslems, and how do we pass over the extraordinary Jewish contribution – out of all proportion to their beleaguered, often vilified numbers – to what we call European civilization? The proposition that Europe can be defined by religion is not only false but dangerous. In many ways, the EU is a reaction against the idea that we can define ourselves by ethnicity or religion, and thus define others as beyond consideration.

Whether or not Turkey should be a member of the EU surely depends on three things. First, is Turkey European? If we were simply to allow aspiration to be our guide, the answer would have to be a resounding Yes. Turkey has resolutely steered a European course ever since Atatürk decreed the end of the Ottoman Sultanate in 1922. The feeling runs deep and has been promoted with unrelenting vigour by successive Turkish governments. The legacy of Atatürk, born in Thessaloniki and convinced – despite the condescension of the European powers of the day – that his country's future lay to the west, is ever present. And his presence is sometimes more than historical – any meeting in any Turkish government office takes place under the cool gaze of the Ghazi, immaculate in determinedly Western suit and tie. Does Turkey respect our principles – of democracy, liberty, respect for human rights and fundamental freedoms, the rule of law and so on? This is where substantial doubts have properly been raised in the past by the treatment of minorities and by the role of the military in politics. Those questions were very much more pertinent in 1963 when the then President of the European Commission signed the Ankara Association Agreement with Turkey, declaring, 'Turkey is part of Europe. This is the deepest possible meaning of this operation which brings, in the most appropriate way conceivable in our time, the confirmation of a geographical reality as well as a historical truism that has been valid for several centuries.' Many Turkish observers would be astonished if that was deemed to be less true now, under a government that has carried on and even redoubled a programme of constitutional reform designed to entrench democracy, promote the protection of minorities and limit the area of the military in government. This helps make them as reluctant as were Austrians, Finns and Swedes to accept some status that denies them full membership of the

Union. In their eyes, Turkey has grappled with its existential question, against a background of economic uncertainty and terrorist activity, and has unequivocally chosen the European course. How, they ask, can some Europeans fail to recognize that?

America does not always make it easy to convince European doubters about Turkey's embrace of democratic values. It is aggravating that American presidents regularly offer Turkey EU membership, as though it was for them to bestow this gift, and that the diplomatic pressure from Washington – both in public and in private – on Turkey's behalf is so relentless. But the real damage is done when it seems as though America's only interest is not democracy in Turkey, or the enhancement of the EU's role, but Washington's own security agenda. When, for example, Turkey's parliament in the run-up to the invasion of Iraq refused to accede to America's request to launch operations from southern Turkey, the then American Deputy Secretary of Defense Paul Wolfowitz was dispatched to Ankara, where he scolded Turkey's military command for not taking a tougher line with their democratic leaders. Mr Wolfowitz is too clever a fellow to think that this is the way democracies behave, and he presumably does not believe that the EU could welcome as a member a country where the generals told the elected government what to do. Democracy should be respected, even when it is inconvenient for the Pentagon. It was a particular surprise that Mr Wolfowitz should have undertaken this mission, since he is one of those neoconservatives associated with the argument that the Iraq war was the foundation stone of a broader strategy to spread democracy throughout the region.

The second issue to consider is that Turkey lies on the cusp between the current EU and the Islamic world. Throughout its history, Istanbul – Constantinople as it was – has been a bridge between worlds. At one time, and particularly when western Europe itself was a more savage place, Turks and Turkey were admittedly the very incarnation of the threatening outsider. But that was when 'Europe' and 'Christendom' were (however imperfect and inaccurately) synonymous. Are we to return to that exclusive and warped idea of who and what we are? Today, there is a simple geopolitical question to answer. Can we afford to ignore the continuing importance of Turkey as a bridge between worlds? What message do we send out to the world beyond the bridge if we now shun a neighbour who has demonstrated the falsity of the case that Islam and democracy do not mix? Turkey has done pretty well all that we ask of the Islamic world on our borders (much of which has been done already by our Islamic friends in southern and south-eastern Asia). What are the consequences for those countries around the Mediterranean, what effects will there be on the moderate activists for democracy and reform, if we make it clear that regardless of our promises since 1963, and regardless of its own efforts – if they succeed – to become a pluralist democracy under the rule of law, Turkey is not welcome in our club because it is Islamic? We should make no mistake. However we were to couch the message of rejection, that is how it would look – and if we are honest, that is how it would in reality be.

Third, there is the question of Islam within our own borders. There are at least 12 million Muslims living in western Europe: approaching 4 million in France, 2.5 million in Germany, and 1.75 million in the UK. Their religion is the fastest growing in the world. In some of our countries, Islamic religious observance outstrips that in the traditional Christian Churches. I doubt whether this number is likely to be mass-ively increased by immigration, and if Turkey were to join the EU their terms of membership in ten or twenty years would doubtless include some constraints on the speed with which they could exercise complete freedom of movement within our borders. Immigration to Europe raises questions about how much assistance we give our neigh-bours to grow and prosper, but above all it calls attention to what we can and are doing to encourage better community relations. I have no trouble with the argument that we should have tight border controls. Europe is far smaller than the United States and the pressure on available space is more intense, as anyone who lives in south-east England will attest. (The population density of the five most densely populated north-eastern states in the USA is 40 per cent of England's.) We should encourage immigration for particular labour market requirements, but we should not kid ourselves that immigration could solve our demographic problems. The number of migrants required to improve significantly the age dependency ratios in Europe would be so large as to be unmanageable in political, environmental, social and economic terms. But a firm hand on future immigration, and a generous approach to the economic requirements of our southern neighbours, is entirely consistent with our imaginative support for what Soheib Bencheikh El Hocine, Grand Mufti of Marseilles, has called 'active cohabitation, not just a juxtaposition of closed communities'.

Fear of the Islamic communities within the EU has been exacerbated by September 11th and the events following it – for example, the discovery of 'sleeper cells' of al Qaeda in cities like Hamburg and the bombings in London. In the Netherlands, France and Denmark, and to some extent Britain too, we have also seen assaults, not on the Christian nature of our European societies, but on something that has not always been synonymous with Christianity – the tolerance that we prize above almost all else. It is the same tolerance that welcomes different ethnic, religious and cultural groups to Europe and allows them to practise their own rites and customs provided they do not assault the broader tolerance we prize and incorporate in our rule of law. This tolerance helps delineate our pluralism. But that very pluralism can be difficult to sustain when, as in the controversy over the Danish cartoons depicting the prophet Mohammed, our traditional freedoms come into conflict with the values of another civilization or religion. While this debate was hijacked by some authoritarian regimes in the Middle East for their own purposes, and while a few extremists in Europe seized the headlines, the reaction of most Muslims was strongly felt but moderately expressed. The majority of Muslims do not wish to be dominated by an extremist minority. To convince the doubters in the Muslim community, to win the argument on the streets, in the homes and in the mosques, we not only have to make the right economic and social policy choices in deprived areas, we also have to show that the standards we cherish, and on whose acceptance we insist, inform our relations with those outside as well as inside our frontiers. We will not win the battle for tolerance in Amsterdam or Paris or Manchester, if we show signs of double standards in the way we deal with Islamic neighbours. There is a tendency for some American commentators, when they witness tensions between the majority and minority Islamic communities in Europe – rows about headscarves, or freedom of speech, for example – to react with a sort of 'told you so' reproach. Now, they suggest, you see what we Americans are trying to do in the Middle East. But, damn it, this is our neighbourhood that is being talked about; our neighbourhood in which we have been painstakingly pursuing a reform agenda for years (as I will argue in a later chapter). What is geo-strategically important for the US is rather more simply and directly our own backyard. Throw petrol around there (excuse the appropriateness of the metaphor) and we in Europe are the first to get caught in the flames.

My plea then is for Europe to define itself as a symbol of tolerance – democratic, prosperous and free – able to bridge civilizations, to prevent division (geographical and cultural) between the West and the Near East, and to demonstrate the way in which what we stand for can transform societies with very different histories and cultures. Turkish accession should be seized as an opportunity to give the EU a new dynamism and purpose. But this will be a tough argument to get across; politicians cannot hope that the argument will look after itself.

We know that globalization destroys boundaries, and in the process raises fears – fears about the loss of our cultural anchors and identity. With the blurring of the geographical boundaries of nation states, what else can continue to bind us together as citizens at ease with the identity of the community in which we live? Can we turn the tolerance of diversity in an open society into a bond far tighter than cultural introversion and the exclusion of difference? Can we make tolerance the element that defines our European community, our 'European feeling'? This is Europe's challenge in the next few years, bigger, more important and far, far more difficult than spelling out competences and delineating institutional boundaries in a constitutional treaty. We can haggle and barter in Brussels, but it may be that it is in Istanbul that we shall write the next chapter in our European story.

6

Strong Nouns, Weak Verbs

And on the issue of their charm depended
A land laid waste, with all its young men slain,
Its women weeping, and its towns in terror.

'Embassy' in *Sonnets from China*,
W. H. Auden

Travelling home to Worcestershire on the train in the 1930s, Prime Minister Stanley Baldwin's study of *The Times* was interrupted by a question from a fellow traveller. 'Weren't you at Harrow in the eighties?' he was asked. 'Yes,' replied Baldwin. 'Thought so. So was I,' said his Harrovian contemporary. 'So what have you been doing with yourself since then?' It is a story with which I identify. When I returned to London from over five years of incessantly circumnavigating the globe as Europe's Commissioner for External Relations, I found that my years of service in the cause of 'CFSP' were not uppermost in many people's recollections: 'The C-What?' 'Didn't you used to be Chris Patten?' was admittedly only said to me once, but it did catch the flavour of the moment. For most people, I had been last seen departing from Hong Kong. Since then, there was hardly anywhere from which I had not departed – from Moscow to Montevideo – and sometimes my departure followed all too rapidly my arrival. I recall a crazy visit to Rio de Janeiro for a morning meeting to negotiate (unsuccessfully as it turned out) a deal with four Latin American foreign ministers. One night there, south; the next night, north. No wonder I have a bad back. One year my diary princess – a young

Welsh woman whose calm and boundless competence included a creative mastery of the world's air routes – calculated that I had got on and off over one hundred and eighty aeroplanes. 'Cabin crew – cross check, doors to manual' were the words I had heard far more frequently for five years than 'Welcome home'!

For what purpose and to what end were these Odyssean travels made? Was Europe or the world better off? What did the acronym, for which I had consumed so many airline cashew nuts, mean – and what impact might it have had on the lives of British or European citizens?

By the mid-1990s, European governments had concluded that Europe had to aspire to a status greater than that of a glorified and successful customs union. That hope had in fact long been in the script. As one of the two most powerful economic and trade blocs in the world, European leaders had begun in the 1980s to discuss more honestly and seriously the gulf between the European Union's economic and political strength. We described ourselves in the self-lacerating cliché of the time as an economic giant but a political pigmy. This was not wholly true. Individual member states still counted for something in the world. Four of them, after all, were members of the G7/G8 and two – France and Britain – had nuclear weapons and were permanent members of the United Nations Security Council. Several were major aid donors and regular contributors of their armed forces to UN peacekeeping efforts. Most were members of NATO, whose battle-free triumph over Soviet imperialism was imminent. In different corners of the world, the clout of individual members mattered – Spain in Latin America, Belgium in central Africa and so on. But there was no distinctive EU voice or presence at the world's conference tables, nor specifically European contributions to crisis prevention and the resolution of conflicts. If European countries were able to act together, the argument went, we would be able to do more than individual countries acting on their own; we could draw on our varied resources, and our different experiences and histories, to promote solutions to global problems.

British politicians, including those on the right like Margaret Thatcher and Michael Portillo, urged Europeans to do more to share America's security burdens, and it had always been an American hope that an integrated Europe would help it to discharge its global role. Throughout the 1980s, ambitions were stirred but nothing much was achieved. The name for the wannabe European foreign policy was 'European Political Cooperation'. EPC meant that no major subject on the international political agenda could avoid discussion by Europe's foreign ministers and their diplomats. There was no hiding place from Brussels' attention. Europe had an opinion on everything, though life being what it is, clever textual compromises between the different positions of sovereign states sometimes rendered these opinions bland and even feeble. Europe's policies were declared in the conclusions of the General Affairs and External Relations Council that brought foreign ministers together each month. Looking through these conclusions today, one is struck by the contrast between the strong adjectives and nouns, and the weak verbs. Europe talked a passable game, but no one got their shorts muddy. We did not do too much harm (except in the Balkans), and we did not do much good.

Aspiration was transformed into action of a sort by a number of events – world-changing, conscience-arousing, bloody and embarrassing. First, there was the collapse of Russia's Communist empire in Europe and the immediate consequences of that historic event. Europe could no longer define itself as freedom's vanguard against Marxist tyranny. All the old certainties provided by the barbarians at the gate melted away. We now had to cope with the results of the ending of Europe's division. We found a policy to support the emergence of open markets and democracy in central and eastern Europe – the enlargement of the EU. This has been the most successful foreign policy pursued by Europe.

It was not only the swift collapse of Communism that pushed Europe into going beyond a foreign policy composed of communiqués. In one outpost of the Communist world, though not a Soviet colony, the 1990s brought the sort of chaos that Europe believed had been laid to rest in our history books. Yugoslavia after Tito and Marxism reverted to that state recalled by Rebecca West as inseparable from her earliest memories of liberalism. Leafing through piles of dusty Liberal pamphlets in second-hand bookshops, the subject of the Balkans would regularly recur. 'Violence', she wrote in 1941, in *Black Lamb and Grey Falcon*, was 'all I knew of the Balkans'. 'Balkan', she went on to note, was a term of abuse in France, suggesting a type of barbarism. The descent in the 1990s into bloody war – primitive brutality, siege, ethnic cleansing, burning families from their homes and inside their homes – suggested that the French slang was all too accurate. All this was happening on the EU's doorstep, in a country to which Europeans could drive in a matter of hours. Dubrovnik under siege, bombarded from the heights above by Serbian mortars and artillery, was where Europeans had browned themselves in the sun not long before. The massacres were not kept under wraps, only to be discovered well after the event by intrepid journalists. They were shown nightly on our televisions.

The hatreds that consumed Yugoslavia were cousins of the xenophobic nationalism that the EU had in part come into existence to prevent. Here was a chance for Europe to exert itself, to show what it had become, to export and if necessary impose its values on another European country where their overthrow was so hideously destructive. We should not have needed America to give a lead, and anyway for Washington this was a faraway country of which it knew little and wanted to know even less. Secretary of State James Baker did not believe America had 'a dog in this fight' and his successor, Lawrence Eagleburger, opined in 1992, that 'until the Bosnians, Serbs and Croats decide to stop killing each other, there is nothing the outside world can do about it'. So we were on our own and rather gloried in it. This was Europe's hour, as one foreign minister memorably observed: Europe's hour and Europe's humiliation.

What should we Europeans have done in the Balkans? Should we have tried to prevent the dismemberment of Yugoslavia, or sought to guide that process without conflict? Should we, we wondered, get involved or turn our backs, lest intervention suck us into military commitments, casualties and expense? Should we work to resolve this latest posing of the Eastern Question by another Congress of Berlin, negotiating new internal borders – a proposal made by the Dutch in 1991, but not taken up? We sent emissaries. They made recommendations. We ignored them. We rained communiqués down on the heads of Milosevic and Tudjman and the war criminals who marauded across the country. We placed those of our forces who were deployed to protect civilians in the intolerable moral position of being silent witnesses to rape and murder. In Bosnia alone perhaps 220,000 people died. The concentration camp made a return visit to the continent that had invented it, or at least had borrowed the idea in a horribly big way from Britain's Boer War experience.

Because our foreign policy was solely declaratory – like the Pope, we had no divisions – even sensible proposals had no traction. The fact that the US was sitting on its hands was more important in the region than the EU's puny efforts. US inactivity was decisive; EU activity was irrelevant. And ironically, the most damning critics of EU incapacity were the strongest opponents of European integration. Out of this debacle came one thing at least: the determination that Europe should not find itself in the same position again, a determination so far only tested at the margins and certainly not yet proven.

The meetings of European leaders in Maastricht in 1991 and Amsterdam in 1997 agreed to establish a Common Foreign and Security Policy (the aforementioned CFSP). By the second of these meetings the Balkans was much in everyone's mind, as were the horrors of Rwanda and Somalia where, again, we had stood aside with others while crises turned predictably and savagely into disasters. The Amsterdam Council made the CFSP more actionable, with the decision to appoint a High Representative for the policy, together with his own secretariat.

The fact that the policy to be pursued should be common, and not (like the currency) single, and that the Council of Foreign Ministers should be in the driving seat, said something fundamental about the nature both of foreign policy and of the EU. Foreign and security policy goes right to the heart of what it means to be a nation state. It raises different issues from, say, trade policy. If foreign policy goes wrong, it may lead to decisions about the use of force. Diplomacy can be the only alternative to death, as was pointed out by W. H. Auden in the poem quoted at the head of this chapter. It should be inscribed over the door of every foreign ministry. In Auden's poem, diplomats in 'a conversation of the highly trained' seek to avert crisis:

> Far off, no matter what good they intended,
> The armies waited for a verbal error
> With all the instruments for causing pain . . .

When it comes to using those instruments, the governments of Europe's nation states make the key decisions and stand over the consequences. Trade policy, monetary policy, even (controversial though it is) the issue of a country's banknotes, do not touch on the core of a nation's sense of community in the same way as a policy that can lead to men and women being asked to risk their lives. Parents would not be happy to allow their sons or daughters to risk injury or death on the say-so of a commissioner in Brussels. Europe is not a country.

On the other hand, countries in Europe may conclude that their national interests are best served by acting together; that way, they have more influence, make more impact, achieve more. So they aim to work in common. To have a single policy, not a common one, would imply either a denial of the bonds that create a national sense of community or the fraying of those bonds and their replacement by a wider sense of loyalty and attachment. This may be a nice idea but there is not much sign of it happening yet. For the foreseeable future, Europe will have twenty-five foreign ministers and twenty-five foreign ministries committed to trying to work together, but not trying to do themselves out of a job.

Two officials were responsible for implementing the common foreign policy: the EU High Representative for the CFSP, Javier Solana (former Spanish Foreign Affairs Minister and NATO Secretary General) and myself, the Commissioner for External Relations. Solana was the representative of all the foreign ministers; I had charge of the Commission's external services – development and cooperation programmes, and the coordination of all the activities that had a major bearing on other countries. As far as I was concerned, Solana occupied the front office and I was in charge of the back office of European foreign policy. Some of my staff did not like this analogy. They would have preferred me to have made a grab for foreign policy, trying to bring as much of it as possible into the orbit of the Commission. This always seemed to me to be wrong in principle and likely to be counterproductive in practice. Foreign policy should not in my view, as I have just argued, be treated on a par with the single market. It is inherently different. To attempt to grab foreign policy for the

Commission would have courted humiliating rebuffs from ministers in the Council. If they were obliged to choose between backing Javier Solana or me, there was only one possible outcome. In any event, playing entirely within the rules, the Commission was in an extremely strong position. We were 'associated' with the conduct and formation of the common policy, and we managed many of the instruments that sustained it and gave it teeth. The more sensibly and competently we did these jobs, the more influence we would have in making policy: we were responsible for trade and economic cooperation and for environment policy; we managed large development programmes both for the poorest countries and those where Europe had big political interests, for instance in the Balkans and the Middle East. Increasingly, the EU was trying to act jointly to deter organized crime, drug trafficking and illegal immigration; we managed complex relationships with other countries covering regulatory convergence, transport, customs cooperation, research and education agreements, health and consumer safety rules. All these matters represent the detailed and sometimes prosaic, but important, business that makes up external relations today. It was not always very sexy. But at least in the back office, the levers were connected to machinery; pull them and something normally happened, if sometimes too slowly.

Moreover, the back office often provided most of the content of a policy – or, at least, most of the content that worked. For years, since the mid-1990s, Europe had been attempting through what was called the Barcelona Process to create a free market around the Mediterranean, and to promote political and economic reform in the region. The policy was based on a network of partnership agreements between the EU and individual countries, from the Maghreb to the Mashraq. We spent over three billion euros a year on this policy in the form of grants and loans (for economic and social development, training, infrastructure and the promotion of good governance). The policy was led and managed by the Commission. It supported the policy positions taken by member states in our relations with the Arab League. What else were we doing that mattered as much in the region as this? In Palestine, we drove the process of reform in the Palestinian Authority. Without our help the Authority would probably have collapsed, and would certainly have retained all the corrupt practices associated with President Arafat and his court of cronies. We talked a lot about the Middle East. We attended meetings. We flew hither and yon. I am not sure that in five years we could count many achievements for all that effort, beyond the fact that the makings of a government for a Palestinian state still existed. But without the EU's assistance, anarchy in the West Bank and Gaza would have had no rival. (I will return to this subject in the next chapter.) The back office also provided the bones of our strategy in the Balkans – the so-called Stabilization and Association Process (clearly not a name invented by an advertising agency copywriter) that sought to buttress the commitment to reform in the region with the prospect of membership of the EU for those who lasted the course of this policy. In short, the Commission had and has plenty to do, and should not feel sidelined in foreign policy.

There were inevitably tensions between the institutions that served front and back offices. The secretariats that worked for the Council of Ministers and its High Representative for the CFSP resented the Commission's access to useful things like money. Some of its members would have liked to take over bits of the Commission's responsibilities whenever it suited them – money here, the negotiation of an agreement there – and move on as the world's headlines changed, leaving bureaucratic confusion and policy discontinuity in their wake. Early in my time as a commissioner, I produced a note for my colleagues in the Commission on the difficulties we had playing our part in foreign and security policy. The note was distinguished by the elegant and witty clarity of my *chef de cabinet*'s prose style. Elegance, wit and clarity were not usually the hallmarks of Commission documents. The result was foreseeable. The document was leaked and gave offence for correctly noting, among other things, that foreign policy was about more than photo opportunities, and that the Commission was always likely to be treated like a maid, expected to serve the meal and then clear up the dirty dishes when the guests had departed.

The institutional architecture for the CFSP was plainly, to use Brussels language, suboptimal. To make it work required the High Representative and the Commissioner for External Relations to get on well together. Javier Solana and I are not totally lacking in *amour propre* though I suspect that the fires of political ambition in both our breasts had burned low by the time we were thrown together. We genuinely liked each other – Spanish Socialist and British Tory – and simply made things work, despite the advice and attentions of some of the institutional warriors in both camps. In over five years, and thousands of media reports, no one was able to point to a single occasion when one of us had contradicted the other – a tribute, I believe, to our common sense. It did sometimes require saintly behaviour by both of us, for which I hope that our reward will one day come, if not in this world then perhaps in the CFSP-free next. Solana is ubiquitous and charming, an intelligent and well-read networker of prodigious energy.

The EU Constitutional Treaty proposed dealing with the institutional disjuncture by merging the jobs of High Representative and Commissioner for External Relations. This is called double-hatting; to sound a little theological, it is proposed that two functions should reside in one person. The High Representative would also be the Vice-President of the Commission. He would chair the Council, overseeing foreign and security policy and would at the same time take responsibility for coordinating the Commission's services that bolster Europe's external role. He would stand at the confluence of two streams of activity: the first, political and security, which would remain in the hands of the member states; the second, those functions which the member states have already assigned to the Commission. This Even Higher Representative would be extremely busy, though presumably he would be provided with deputies covering both sorts of function. It is not a perfect piece of institutional engineering, an uneasy compromise between the minority in the convention that drew up the draft treaty and some member states (who wanted to go further in giving foreign policy a distinctively European personality and management) and the majority keen to preserve the previous division in responsibilities. Despite the dumping of the draft treaty, some arrangement like this is likely one day to emerge.

How would a double-hatted foreign policy chief – the word bipetasic has not yet been used, but it can only be a matter of time – relate to and deal with foreign ministers? This is the most problematic area of all. He or, since there are now so many women foreign ministers, sooner or later she, would preside over the Council that makes policy.

I am not sure this is wise; to be responsible both for chairing meetings and for providing their main input would create some scratchiness. Looking around the table at twenty-five other foreign ministers, would the High Representative be their boss – or just their representative? What would they think the answer is in the Quai d'Orsay or in Britain's Foreign Office? Many years ago Henry Kissinger asked his famous question: 'If I want to find out what Europe thinks, whose telephone number do I call?' Ironically, there have been plenty of times in recent years when Europeans could have asked the same question about America. Should we telephone the State Department, the Pentagon, or the National Security Council in the White House? And when we got through, would anyone know the answer? During the first Bush administration, for example, Kremlinology had been replaced by Washingtonology. Who owned this or that piece of policy turf? But so far as Europe is concerned, is the number to ring in future going to be the High Representative's? What will the German, British or French foreign ministers think of that? Take the recent European negotiations with Iran over constraining any nuclear ambitions it might have. The earliest European overtures to Iran were made by Solana, myself and successive foreign ministers in the presidency of the Council. We visited Tehran to have Machiavelli quoted approvingly at us by President Khatami and to be asked by Foreign Minister Kharrazi whether we would like to conduct meetings with him and his colleagues in English or French. When the issue got bigger and more significant in 2003, the 'Big Three' foreign ministers took over – 'the three tenors' we called them – not even bothering to take Solana or a representative of the country in the presidency of the Council with them to Tehran (though Solana is now fully involved in the policy). Will this instinctive reaction in London, Paris and Berlin change if double-hatting occurs? An American Secretary of State will continue to have to make several telephone calls. What matters most is not whether there are several telephone numbers but whether there is a similar response or message from whoever is on the line.

The dominance of the Big Three goes to the heart of the question of the effectiveness of European efforts to make foreign and security policy. I mean no disrespect to the twenty-two other member states, but there is no European policy on a big issue unless France, Germany and Britain are on side. Unless *they* work together, nothing else will work. It is as clear and simple as that. Of course, others can make important contributions, and the addition of new members constantly adds to the insights that can be offered about parts of the world with which the other member states may be unfamiliar. But without the 'big three', there is no policy.

That was most evident over Iraq, which also exposed some of the weaknesses of the present system of trying to make European foreign policy. The subject of Iraq was scarcely debated in the Council: as the arguments hotted up elsewhere – at the UN in New York, on the telephone lines between London, Paris and Berlin – we pretended in Brussels that there was nothing amiss. The great Iraqi elephant sat in the corner of the room, and we edged nervously past it pretending it was not there. 'Elephant? What elephant?' There was a sort of code that was usually observed, which dictated that no foreign minister should say anything too direct or blunt that might embarrass a colleague. To their credit, one or two ministers (for example, Finland's and Ireland's) occasionally broke the unwritten rule and raised a contentious issue. It was a little like committing some physical indecorum in a great aunt's drawing room – maybe excusable but not very nice. All this made for a very friendly atmosphere, but meetings were not always as useful as they should have been. Sometimes they happened principally because it was that time of the month. Maybe making foreign policy is always like this, with the cut and thrust of debate confined to smoothly clever diplomats and kept away from ministers. Maybe (and this much is certainly true) it is early days. After all, the EU was in a sense created as an alternative to foreign policy. Our policy for years had been to biff our neighbours; now, we were in bed with them all. And maybe – the biggest 'maybe' of all – making foreign policy with fifteen or twenty-five is such a public activity that it is bound to involve more genteel play-acting than real-life, kitchen-sink drama.

Meetings of the Council were certainly large. The ministers accompanied by a senior adviser sat at the table; the ranks of Tuscany milled behind, not raising a cheer but conducting their own diplomatic activities directly with one another – amending a text here, negotiating a compromise there – or by mobile telephone. (Some telephones had distinctive calls; Joschka Fischer, for instance, was summoned by an American cookhouse bugler, presumably not a paid-up member of the Green Party.) Gradually over the years, the number present was cut down so that instead of having, say, 150 or more in the room, there were only 50 or 60. It was an improvement, and conducive to doing rather more serious business. The size of the gathering meant that the most sensitive business was usually done at lunch, at which only the ministers themselves were present. Their diplomatic advisers hung about in the corridor outside, hoping that their minister would keep a good note of what was going on. I was very bad at this myself. My own officials usually had to make do with the official record, and my occasional anecdotes. I often recalled a colleague from the 1980s whose manuscript note of such a meeting simply read 'Mr X spoke well for Britain'.

Restricted meetings, at which only ministers are supposed to be present, can lead to bizarre ruses. At the Maastricht meeting, with a session at which only presidents and prime ministers were in the room, John Kerr (then Britain's ambassador to the EU) managed to position himself at one crucial moment under John Major's table. The nearest thing I saw to this occurred at a meeting between European and Asian ministers. On that occasion, ministers were dining at an inner table, with one official per delegation seated behind. At one point, the Japanese minister – a feisty woman – began reading from a script that bore no relationship to the subject under discussion. Her official crept across the carpet from his place to hers, holding the appropriate brief (not, admittedly, Labrador-like in his teeth) and, having arrived under his minister's table, placed the relevant speaking note on top of the one she was reading before reversing on all fours to his seat.

One result of so much of the sensitive and interesting business at Council meetings being done at lunch was that some ministers were barely present for any other part of the proceedings. They would arrive in the late morning and depart in early afternoon. This meant in effect that foreign ministers, perhaps inadvertently, gave up control of the overall coordination of the European agenda. In the 1980s, foreign ministers had been given the responsibility for resolving single-market blockages in other Councils because only they had the clout to do it. By the 2000s they had lost that clout, and had even lost the primitive urge to fight for it. This reflects the extent to which traditional, high 'foreign policy' has been sucked into the offices of presidents and prime ministers, while European policy is no longer regarded as 'foreign'.

Consistency and continuity in foreign policy are difficult when a new calamity can always knock you off course; another day's headline can impose short-term decisions that threaten long-term objectives. The imminence of high-level meetings can also drive decision-making in a manner that is unhelpful or precipitate. As a manifestation of its arrival on the world stage, the EU had put in place a calendar of summits and bilateral meetings at senior level. We had summits with America, Canada, China, India, Russia, Japan – sometimes twice a year. There were regular meetings with our Mediterranean Arab and Israeli friends, Latin Americans, the Gulf Cooperation Council, the African Union, Australia, New Zealand, the lot. The more senior the level of the meeting, the greater the pressure that we should take some gift to the table to confirm the pretence that we were having a good and useful meeting. Russia was particularly adept at understanding how to play this game against our own interests.

Summits, meetings, visits – much of the routine for foreign policy practitioners involves a stately progress from one airport VIP lounge to another. The issues covered by a minister's brief can be fascinating, and when you get the occasional opportunity to do a real negotiation it pumps up the adrenalin. But too often, the interesting business has been done before the arrival of the so-called principals. Officials have conjured 'deliverables' from the mush of unresolved business between the parties – something for you, something for me – to advertise success and a further 'thickening up' of the relationship. There will probably also have been days and nights of haggling over a communiqué, so that nothing contentious has to be resolved when ministers arrive with their entourages of advisers, secretaries and spokesmen. The infinitives are already split; the qualifying clauses appended; the clichés added to taste. Meetings can easily degenerate into the reading of speaking notes to people who are not listening, with occasional allegedly informal exchanges of view that turn too easily into *café du commerce*, a slightly superior cab driver's world view – '. . . and another thing'. But travelling the world, albeit at a frenetic pace, seeing at least something of other places from the window of a speeding car, is a more inherently interesting and privileged activity for a politician (though not necessarily more valuable) than trying to manage social security or immigration policy. And you find yourself sitting on the sofa with more celebrities, famous and infamous, than can be claimed by even the usual run of chat-show hosts. My first experience of this came when I was Britain's Minister for Overseas Development, on my initial visit to Islamabad. Pakistan's then military dictator, General Zia, gave me an hour of his time a couple of years before his aeroplane was mysteriously blown out of the sky in 1988. The General, whose moustache and gap-toothed smile bore an uncanny resemblance to the British actor Terry-Thomas, was seeking to make a point to me about Pakistani politics. He began his comment, 'As I said to the late Mr Bhutto.' With a chill down the back of my neck, I recalled that the General had not long before hanged Prime Minister Bhutto, whom he had overthrown. Fascinating as many one-to-one meetings have been, nothing since has given me the same frisson as that first outing.

How do you get any consistency when policy is made by twenty-five ministers all busy flying around the world? I tried to approach the question crab-wise by encouraging them to discuss our budget – the resources that we had to support our policy – and to check whether our spending priorities matched our political ones. Robin Cook was keen on the idea but otherwise I did not make much progress; foreign ministers are not very interested in budgets, which is one reason why they get pushed around so much by finance ministers who see foreign ministry resources as an easy target for cost-cutting. This has led in Britain to the development of an obsession in the Foreign Office with management, in order presumably to demonstrate to the Treasury that every penny is well spent. This is pretty pointless. The Treasury is a bad manager of its own resources, as the House of Commons Committee of Public Accounts would attest. Moreover, no manifestations of spreadsheet culture will ever convince the Treasury that diplomats do anything more useful than nibble canapés and drink one another's Sancerre. It is sad to see experienced diplomats, trained to draft brief and lucid telegrams about the latest political development in Serbia or Suriname, terrorized into filling in questionnaires from management consultants by the yard. In the days of the Heath Government, *Private Eye* used to run a strip cartoon called 'Heath-Co', satirizing the Prime Minister's alleged obsession with management mumbo-jumbo; there were long discussions about the operation of the automatic beaker disposal unit. It is sad to see the Foreign Office going the same way. Its best minds are required these days to pursue change management for a changing world, narrowly avoiding as they do so cascading objectives (how painful if you get hit by one of those), and seeking to find their way through their strategic resource accounting matrix. To make it all worse, diplomats are expected, under Orwellian pressure, to evince enthusiasm for this work. It brings to mind Wellington's letter, while he was trying to drive Napoleon out of Spain, in which he admitted to 'hideous confusion' about how to deal with raspberry jam in his accounts. Ambassadors should stand and fight, but I fear all may be lost already. I was recently invited to a Foreign Office 'breakout session'; I had previously thought it was the Home Office's Prisons Department that did breakouts.

We were consistent about one thing at least in Brussels. When we did not have a policy, we would go on a visit, or send Javier Solana, or both him and me, or the so-called Troika. Troikas had, not surprisingly, usually come in threes. They had consisted of the foreign minister currently presiding (for six months) over the Council, his predecessor and his successor. They came to mean the presiding foreign minister, Solana and myself – with perhaps one or two others thrown in. I once spent an interesting week flying around the Congo and its neighbouring states with the Belgian and Spanish foreign ministers, the EU's Special Representative for the African Great Lakes and Javier Solana. So the number was flexible, but the purpose usually the same. An active presence on the ground was too often an alternative to having anything very useful to say or do once we had got there. This is what I had meant by foreign policy as photo opportunity. If we succeeded in getting as far as the conference table, the European interest was apparently served.

Despite all these problems, the positive aspects of our attempts to launch a European policy far outweighed the negative, especially when one considered the complexity of the whole business. We were trying to make policy with, and for, fifteen and then twenty-five member states. What is surprising is not how much we did not achieve, but how much we did – though in my judgement there was one big failure, Israel and Palestine, and one less justifiable missed opportunity, Russia. The overall balance sheet is positive, an outcome that was not inevitable and owed much to a growing sense that Europe did have a distinctive contribution to make in international affairs.

The EU's contribution to international affairs has been especially evident in the part of Europe that saw our terrible humiliation in the 1990s, the Balkans. By the end of the decade, we had developed a clear strategy for the region and by and large we managed to stick to it. Taking as our model the way we had related to the newly liberated countries of central and eastern Europe a few years before, we offered the countries of the former Yugoslavia, plus Albania, the prospect of becoming members of the Union. If they started to put their countries in order, politically and economically, we would enter into agreements with them, similar to the Europe Agreements that had performed the same function when our ten new member states were candidate countries. The successful conclusion of these agreements would un-lock the door to the commencement of negotiations for membership of the EU. We would assist their post-conflict stabilization through associating them with us, and the more closely their governance and economy resembled our own, the faster we would move to bring them into the EU.

We embarked on this policy in the wake of the death of the national-ist leader in Croatia, Franjo Tudjman – even with Milosevic still pre-siding over his gang of criminals and hard-line generals in Belgrade. The Kosovo war had just ended and our first task, partly in order to show that the campaign had been justified, was to begin the task of reconstruction there, working with and through the UN mission that was charged with administering the territory.

My first visit to the capital, Pristina, in the autumn of 1999, revealed the scale of the task. Kosovo had been badly knocked about by the fighting; everywhere there were burned-out houses and farm build-ings, bombed churches and mosques, wrecked military vehicles. On top of the war damage, there was overwhelming evidence of years of neglect and underinvestment. Kosovo might have been regarded by the Serbs as the Albanian jewel in their crown, but clearly they had not cared very much about how well it was governed and cared for. One of our earliest tasks was to attempt to provide a few hours of electricity every day. I have toured all too many power stations during my career, from Khartoum to central India. Most of them appear much the same to a history graduate: but not Kosovo's two plants. They looked as though they had been assembled using the larger bits from a car boot sale. The blackened boilers grunted and squealed in grimy cavernous halls. We were shown around by a regiment of electricity workers, plainly a recently recruited cash nexus of Albanians replacing Serbs on a welfare payroll. Outside the power stations' main buildings, in between piles of junk, a few end of season Iceberg roses struggled to remind us that there were nicer and better things in the world than clapped-out power plants. (A couple of years later, I saw a similar contrast in the shadow of the grim nuclear plants at Chernobyl in the Ukraine. A wild bitch played with nine beautiful puppies in the brambles and scrub surrounding that dreadful, murderous place.)

We were the main donors in Kosovo, and faced an early problem. How could we spend our assistance rapidly and reasonably well? Not a week passed without Madeleine Albright (then American Secretary of State) or her Balkans frontman, Jim Dobbins, telephoning to find out how we were translating promises into contracts, plans and real-time spending. Our past performance did not give them much confidence. This was the first big test of our ability to run things competently, and we passed it – speeding up delivery by cutting corners where we could, setting up the European Agency for Reconstruction, and giving the excellent officials sent out to manage it delegated authority and political cover. We did about as much as we could to restore infrastructure, rebuild homes and provide a skeleton government. But the unresolved question of Kosovo's long-term status – the tensions between the majority Albanian and minority Serbian communities, and the hold of organized criminals over much of what there was of commercial life – deterred the inward investment that the territory still needs if it is to have any chance of picking itself up.

Kosovo provided a paradigm of the problems we were to face elsewhere, and will continue to face, in trying to rebuild a failed state after conflict or after internal breakdown. First, how do you turn donors' pledges of support into real and useful investment? The end of a war these days (Kosovo, Afghanistan, Iraq) or the launch of a peace process (Palestine, Sri Lanka) is followed by a donors' conference at which well-wishers flap cheque books at one another in rival displays of generosity. Unpicking the offers is the first problem – grants are mixed up with loans, old money with new, multi-year promises with single year. The objective of these conferences is never to get an accurate figure for real donor commitments but to tot up the largest figure possible. Then comes the task of turning that figure into spending on the ground. In the time lag between pledge, contract and expenditure, history packs its bags and moves on to the next political disaster and the next donors' conference. The UN – particularly through its Development Programme (UNDP) – should keep a close, public tally on what is promised and when it is actually spent. Those who regularly promise but do not spend should be identified.

When this first wall of spending hits a decrepit economy, it can have a hugely distorting effect, not least as local employees are recruited to work for well-meaning, incoming agencies at external salaries. Schoolteachers suddenly discover that it pays better to drive the car for an aid official than to teach children. This problem is exacerbated by the swarm of new non-governmental organizations (NGOs) that arrive in the wake of conflict to join those brave ones already on the scene. I have always been a great supporter of NGOs; when I was a development minister, I switched part of Britain's aid budget into their programmes. They can be brave groundbreakers and represent part of the core of civil society. But they are not beyond criticism (some of their lobbying can be extremely damaging, as Sebastian Mallaby has pointed out in his recent book on the World Bank). Given the numbers that pour into post-conflict zones they can be a menace as much as a benefit. They need to regulate their own affairs with greater self-discipline, and also to work with the UN to demarcate more clearly the humanitarian space between NGO activity and civil/military work. As military planners have come to appreciate more clearly the relationship between security and reconstruction, they have fudged the distinction between the work of soldiers and the work of NGOs. This puts aid workers at risk.

Successful reconstruction in a place like Kosovo requires security, and we are not yet at all good at managing the transition from decisive military intervention to heavy-duty policing. As we have seen more recently in Afghanistan and Iraq, it is much easier to put military personnel into the field than paramilitary or regular police officers, judges, prosecutors and prison warders. We are trying to remedy this deficiency; it is uphill work. You do not require a degree in criminology to know what is required to clean up places like Kosovo. First, you need to be able to identify and catch criminals; then to hold them securely; then to protect witnesses; then to organize a proper trial; then to have an honest judge, paid enough or independent enough to hand down a correct verdict; then to be able to hold the guilty in secure prisons. Putting in place the various stages in this chain is very difficult, as Paddy Ashdown found in his heroic efforts to forge one in Bosnia-Herzegovina.

Kosovo also showed the importance of building up governing institutions at the local level; democracy takes root there better than at the top. Functioning and responsible local democracy (alongside security and job prospects) is crucial to dealing with one particular problem throughout former Yugoslavia – the return of refugees. The international community established a right of return in the Balkans that Britain would never have attempted in Northern Ireland. There, a Protestant family hounded out of a house in Catholic West Belfast would have been resettled in a Protestant community. In the Balkans, from Croatia to Macedonia, we have insisted that Catholic Croats, Orthodox Serbs, Moslem Albanians or Bosnians, should be able to return to homes from which they were driven. It is an admirable policy, showing our opposition to ethnic cleansing and ethnic clearance, but putting it into practice is tough work. Governments in Balkan countries will promise their support for the policy at the centre; it only works satisfactorily if local communities are committed to it as well. It is gratifying that, though the task of returning refugees to their homes has not been completed by any means, so many refugees have already gone back to houses and villages from which they fled in fear not long ago.

My saddest experience in Kosovo was returning in the spring of 2004, just after Albanian Kosovo gangs had turned on their Serbian neighbours in a brief orgy of burning and killing. There was a nasty Balkan symmetry to this violence. We had intervened in Kosovo to protect Albanians from Serbs, and now Serbs were being persecuted in their turn. It was not only apologists for the Albanians who said that the violence was the result of frustration at the failure to resolve the question of Kosovo's final status and to confirm that Kosovo was liberated from any prospect of return to rule from Belgrade. The violence certainly cast doubt on our previous policy of insisting that Kosovo would have to show that it lived up to civilized standards before we could consider its status. We cannot walk away from our insistence that decent standards should be observed there – above all, the protection of minority rights – but we need to deal with the status question at the same time as we insist on higher standards, not afterwards. Whatever happens as a result of the UN-brokered shuttle diplomacy now launched between Belgrade and Pristina we cannot allow Kosovo to turn into a barbarous bandits' haven on the edge of the EU.

The fall of Milosevic gave the people of Serbia the chance to escape their history, an opportunity that they have had some difficulty seizing in recent years. I like to think the EU contributed to the dramatic events that toppled him. We gave financial support to NGOs in Serbia and, more important, to the independent media. We arranged exemptions to the oil regime in force against Milosevic's government and also ran oil into the democratically controlled municipalities in Serbia, to which Milosevic had denied oil supplies for homes and public buildings. This project – named Energy for Democracy – strained our rules of financial accountability, but we managed somehow to stay within them and got the fuel to the parts of Serbia that comprised the heartland of opposition to the old regime. It was a bold but imaginative policy, the brainchild of the current Serbian Deputy Prime Minister Labus and his group of opposition economists. Milosevic tried to stop the deliveries but they got through, to the delight of people in Nis and other opposition cities, and helped the opposition – literally – to keep the home fires burning through a harsh Balkan winter. The following autumn in 2000, Milosevic was overthrown.

No policy in the Balkans will be entirely successful unless we can persuade Serbia to embrace wholeheartedly the need for political and economic change. It is the largest piece in the old Yugoslavian jigsaw, previously the centre of economic life there. The assassination of the post-Milosevic Prime Minister Zoran Djindjic, a complicated, clever, sinuous young man, showed that the tentacles of organized crime were still wrapped around some of the institutions of the state. There were plenty of good, competent political managers in Serbia – the economic ministries were usually in professional hands – but progress was held back by a refusal to shake off the past. The main national-ist leader Vojislav Kostunica, a decent enough man, exemplifies the problem, resisting a policy of full cooperation with the Yugoslav war-crimes tribunal in The Hague (although in 2005 a number of high-profile indictees have at last been sent to the tribunal) and giving sustenance to wholly unrealistic aspirations to take back Kosovo, or at least play the main part in determining its destiny. The cause of reform in Serbia may well have been retarded as well by our insistence that Serbia and her sister republic, Montenegro, should try to make a success of their existence as two parts of the same federal state. Montenegro is a small country that runs down from the mountains (the site of its capital Podgorica, a monument to the worst of 1960s brutalist socialist architecture) to a beautiful coastline. In the closing years of Milosevic, we gave Montenegro support as an outpost of opposition to his regime. Montenegro has one industry – an alu-minium plant bought by the Russians – and another rather more lucrative activity: smuggling (mostly duty-free cigarettes). Alarmingly, Russian investors have started to show an interest in Montenegro. I doubt whether they are the sort of investors who would get a seal of approval from Transparency International.

We insisted on the Serbia–Montenegro marriage for defensible reasons, worrying that without it Kosovo's status might be raised prematurely, and that other territorial boundaries in the region would come under scrutiny. I now doubt whether allowing Montenegro to go its own way would have much effect elsewhere. It would free Serbian politicians to concentrate on the reform agenda that really matters for their European destiny, and would also enable us to focus rather more energy on pushing reforms in Montenegro, whose future should consist of more than boosting European morbidity figures by lowering the price of smoking to the continent's nicotine addicts.

The organized crime that has corrupted political life in Serbia is probably – apart from the need to escape from history – the greatest problem facing the whole region. The Balkan countries pretend to us that they are tackling it energetically; and we sometimes pretend that we believe them. We don't. The problem is particularly bad in Albania, where criminal gangs seem to have evolved naturally out of the old clan system. The years of Stone Age Communist isolation have been followed by an explosion of entrepreneurial activity: international crime. Albanian gangs are the most feared in Europe and, now, in America. They run the drugs, illegal immigration and prostitution rackets in a number of European countries. Albanian gangs have taken over the crime in several American cities. They are a threat to the stability as well as the prosperity of their own country and of some of its neighbours. Our efforts to build the capacity in Albania to fight crime have had only partial success. I recall a dinner with one Albanian prime minister in Tirana, at which he tried to persuade me that he and his government were doing everything they could to crack down on crime, a point that I found difficult to accept given that every time good and conscientious officials were appointed in Albania to senior positions (for example, the head of the customs service) they were, soon afterwards, removed. While we were having dinner together in a private room in our hotel, one of my officials was in the hotel's bar observing the prime minister's bodyguard negotiating his gambling debts with a bunch of heavies in dark glasses from Greece.

The fallacy that distorts much diplomatic discussion about the Balkans holds that, if only we could change a few of the national boundaries in the region, all would be well – swap the area north of Mitrovica in Kosovo for the area in the south of the Presevo Valley in Serbia, tinker with the northern reaches of Macedonia around Tetovo, carve up Bosnia-Herzegovina again, and so on. I said earlier that before Yugoslavia was dismembered by force, it might have been possible to arrive at a neat solution – straight out of nineteenth-century Great Power diplomacy – to the Eastern Question. But it would have been a long shot. Today, it is difficult to see how boundary tinkering could lead to anything except calamity.

Bosnia and Herzegovina is the best example of the sort of trouble that would be likely to explode. This country, whose geographical and political identity was carefully crafted under hands-on American tutelage at Dayton in 1995, is an uneasy amalgam of Bosnians, Croats and Serbs. If it were to break apart, the fall-out for the whole region would be catastrophic. Bosnia and Herzegovina was the stage for the worst atrocities of the Balkan wars – above all, the massacre at Srebrenica, where some 8,000 Bosnians were slaughtered by Serb forces. Sarajevo itself, scene of the assassination by a Bosnian Serb of the Archduke Franz Ferdinand and his beloved wife Sophie on St Vitus's Day in June 1914, still bears the many scars of its siege and bombardment by later Serb killers. We are committed to making Bosnia and Herzegovina work as a country, even while its two highly autonomous entities shy away from the creation of the national institutions (in policing or defence, for example, or the tax system and customs service) that are required. The slowness of the progress is only bearable when one recalls the bloody pit out of which the journey began. Paddy Ashdown presided from 2002–2005 over Europe's and the international community's efforts to nudge and shove the country in the right direction. He is a natural for such a task. It is a pity that we do not still have an empire for someone with his decent instincts and extraordinary, youthful energy to help run. There is a paradox when someone with this sort of flair takes on such a job. It is desirable to develop local political talent with the courageous determination to take and own the most awkward political decisions. Ashdown inevitably filled most of the available political space. Which local leaders will come after him? Nevertheless, under his overlordship Bosnia and Herzegovina made real progress, not least in seeing the return of refugees to their original communities and the establishment of a working system of law and order, a major achievement. The EU has mounted its first major military operation there, which may be a model for future European security activities outside NATO.

We came closest to a return to ethnic conflict in Macedonia, or – as we had to call it to massage Greek sensitivities – the Former Yugoslav Republic of Macedonia, FYROM for short. Tensions between the majority community and the Albanian minority boiled over in 2000–01 as the government went half-heartedly through the motions of addressing minority grievances. There was fighting in and around the main Albanian town in Macedonia, Tetovo, and the government (led by a politician devious even by Balkan standards) began buying weapons it could not afford from Ukraine, which of course assured us that it was not selling them. The Secretary General of NATO George Robertson, Javier Solana and I flew backwards and forwards to Skopje nagging, coaxing, bullying those political leaders prepared to listen into calming the atmosphere, accepting a small NATO security presence, and reaching a wide-ranging framework agreement named after Lake Ohrid where it was signed, which dealt with Albanian grievances over issues such as language, public sector employment and university education. We were helped by a decent president with a lot of courage, if little political power. President Trajkovski was, rather improbably, a Macedonian Methodist and frequent attendee of prayer breakfasts worldwide. He was a great bear of a man, much given to hugging and tears. I remember one particularly stressful night with Javier Solana and I encouraging him to act as boldly as his instincts told him was required, while a mob of extremists bayed outside the small presidential palace for our blood. Occasional sounds of gunfire were not terribly good for morale. I suppose that if we had been shot we would have made an inside page of a few broadsheets. President Trajkovski, alas, died in an aircraft accident after the crisis was over, in great part thanks to his own courage. The coordination between NATO and the various arms of the EU was exemplary, and resulted for once in a successful act of conflict prevention. NATO's muscle and Europe's political influence and money averted disaster. Macedonia (FYROM in Athens) has now lodged its own application to join the EU, though its journey will be quite a long one.

That should not be the case in Croatia, in many ways the star pupil of the region. Part of that expression would not find favour with the Croatians themselves: they do not like to think of themselves as Balkan at all, and when you read their history, visit Zagreb or Dubrovnik, or look at their gross domestic product per head figures, you do understand their point. The Croats played their own, often discreditable, part in the violent break-up of Yugoslavia, and though a Catholic I cannot say that I much admired the role of the Church both in Croatia itself and in the surrounding countries. It became a focus for and

protector of intransigent nationalism, cultural identity and irreden-
tism. In Mostar in Bosnia and Herzegovina, the shelling of whose
fifteenth-century Turkish bridge by Croat forces became for many a
symbol of the communal animosities that launched the Balkan wars,
the divisions between Catholic and Moslem citizens are advertised by
the huge crucifix raised on the Catholic side of the city, looming in a
show of less than Christian triumphalism over the ruined streets
below. I wonder whether the bishop and his local clergy have ever
asked themselves what Jesus would have thought of the raising up of
this giant representation of His torture and death. He died for the salvation of *all* mankind, including Bosnian Moslems. After Tudjman's
death, the Croats moved fast to install an open democracy. They have
held fair elections at which power has been transferred from one party
to another. They have a good and professional civil service, which has
implemented the reforms pressed on them by the EU rapidly and well.
Successive governments have faced down extremist opponents. But
the government has to demonstrate its continuing and unremitting
commitment to the work of the Yugoslav war-crimes tribunal in The
Hague, and the pace of refugee returns, though much improved, has
been slower than was desirable. But Croatia works as a country. It is
determined to gain EU membership. Now that, with the arrest of the
indicted war criminal General Gotorina, it has complied fully with
the Hague tribunal, it has begun membership negotiations.

In the Balkans our 'push-me-pull-you' policy that impelled countries
along the path to reform, with a lot of financial support and the
prospect of one day joining the EU, worked pretty well. I will deal in
the next chapter with the two areas where I think our policies were
less successful. As for other countries and continents, it would be
wearisome to tour the world, describing visits here, there and everywhere, recounting small victories and whitewashing small defeats.
When I was a speechwriter, there was a particular sort of speech that
I always tried to avoid drafting – the *tour d'horizon* of domestic or
international policy. Any paragraph that began 'And now I turn to
agriculture . . .' or 'Moving on to the Ivory Coast . . .' was plainly part
of a speech that no one should want to deliver, and no one would
want to hear. Denis Healey had his own phrase for orations like this,

a 'tour de gloss'. I will therefore avoid trying to spin a rambling tale that would seek to incorporate Singapore, Wellington, São Paulo and a cross-section of all the other places to which I travelled and which deserved my attention during five years globetrotting.

However, there was one bizarre visit in May 2001 to Pyongyang to see the North Korean leader Kim Jong-il, which reminded me that the EU should not get too big for its boots. Europe is not a significant political player on the Korean peninsular, though we have delivered in less than a decade more than 500 million euros in humanitarian assistance and in support for the development of alternative power supplies to their nuclear plants. We went to North Korea largely as a political favour to President Kim Dae-jung of South Korea. He had made a visit to Washington in the early days of the Bush adminis- tration to confirm that it would continue to support his Sunshine Policy of reconciliation with the North. Despite reassuring noises from Colin Powell and the State Department, he was cold-shouldered at the White House. His policy seemed to be in ruins and he turned to Europe for a gesture of support. The Swedish government (then in the EU presidency) were rightly happy to see if there was anything we could do to give some more encouragement to the reconciliation policy. It was agreed that Prime Minister Persson, Javier Solana and I should fly to Pyongyang to try to persuade Kim Jong-il to resume the dialogue and contacts he had begun to make with Seoul.

We flew into Pyongyang to the airport with the longest and largest number of runways that I have ever seen, presumably because their principal purpose was other than civil, and were greeted by a crowd in traditional costumes waving what looked like gaudily coloured feather dusters. We were driven to the despot-sized state guesthouse (it had the largest bedrooms and the smallest bars of soap I have ever seen), where we awaited the 'Dear Leader'. Over two days we saw him for more than six hours. Each meeting was a surprise. We would get a sudden order to be on parade in a salon or corridor, and Kim would appear through a door or from behind a wall-hanging like a character in pantomime or a Feydeau farce: now you see him, now you don't. I half expected him to appear at any moment through a trapdoor in the floor, and perhaps that is what he was doing. He looks extraordinary – a bouffant hairstyle all his own in which each hair seems to have been individually seeded in his scalp, built-up Cuban heels and shiny gabardine boiler suits. He would usually see us with just an interpreter and one other official. He struck us all as highly intelligent and spoke frequently without any briefing notes. Kim's tyranny is unfathomable to the outsider, and presumably to most insiders as well. Pyongyang itself looked like a gloomy stage set; it was impossible to know what went on behind the façade of the buildings that we passed in our motorcade. Unlike every other city I have ever visited, there was no sign of any commercial activity whatsoever. We banqueted with Kim and a group of grumpy old men, with faces like Christmas walnuts, in heavily bemedalled uniforms. We were served much better Burgundy than we would have drunk in Brussels. Outside, the people starved.

Since then, the nuclear crisis in North Korea has turned into a front-page story. Others may be able to help solve it, especially the Chinese, South Koreans and Japanese. But it is only really the Americans who matter, a point which we rapidly came to understand on our own visit. There we were, visiting peacemakers from Europe, and all that this tiny tyrant wanted to talk about was ... America. Why did policy seem to have changed from Clinton to Bush? Why were the Americans so rude about him, calling him awful names? Why were the Americans able to manipulate the South Koreans? Who did they think they were, threatening his poor country? Why did they have so many weapons threatening him from the South? Apart from that, all he wished to raise was whether he might be able to make an official visit to Sweden, a point on which Mr Persson ducked and weaved with consummate political skill. Anyway, there it was. We went as European peace emissaries, accomplished nothing despite our best efforts and intentions, and we spent all our time discussing what American policy might be.

America is a superpower, partly because it is the only country whose will and intentions matter everywhere, and are everywhere decisive to the settlement of the world's biggest problems. Europe can help to solve those problems, but there are only some parts of the world – like the Balkans – where our role (while not necessarily crucial) is as important as, or more important than, that of China in the case of North Korea. I turn at the beginning of the next chapter to one of the places on our doorstep where that is true.

7

Neighbourhood Watch

Neighbours, everybody needs good neighbours,
But here's a friendly word of warning,
Just be careful what you say . . .
Neighbours, you pick your friends but not your neighbours,
Just a slight misunderstanding
And the mayhem never ends.
Neighbours, interfering with each other,
Be sure that that's where the friendship ends.

Words sung to the theme tune for the
TV soap 'Neighbours'

All politics, we are told, is local; diplomacy too starts close to home. Priority is sensibly given by foreign ministers to securing a stable neighbourhood for their countries. In the case of Europe, we have seen how this bolstered the case for offering the liberated countries of the Soviet empire in central and eastern Europe membership of the European Union. What better way could there have been of treating a neighbour than inviting him into our home? Since, as I remarked previously, that process cannot go on indefinitely, and since not every neighbour will want to become an EU member state, other policies are required. Framing them is not easy, especially given that our neighbourhood poses large and different problems.

To the east, the Russian Federation gripes about its loss of empire and watches suspiciously as its one-time colonies join the EU and NATO, or aspire to do so. Putting its faith, as before in its history, in a strong man rather than strong institutions, it resiles from any serious commitment to establishing pluralist democracy. Europe should clearly work for a comprehensive partnership with Russia, but at the moment it is nonsense to suggest that this will be based on shared values. Later in this chapter, I will come back to our difficulties in putting together a consistent and coherent policy on Russia, and to some of the results of this failure.

To the south, beyond Shelley's 'blue Mediterranean', lie the troubled lands of some of the Arab League states from the Maghreb to the Mashraq, countries that share the southern littoral of the sea that has both brought Europe and the Islamic world together, and kept us apart. Here, crowded together, are some of the most intractable problems facing the world today: poverty, protectionism, political alienation, religious extremism, authoritarianism, abuse of human rights, gender discrimination and violence. In some countries, democracy begins to stir: in all of them, the remnants of ancient cultures remind us of better and happier days. Across the whole region, the dispute between Israel and Palestine poisons politics, aborts progress and nurtures conspiracies and suicide bombings.

These are countries with which most European countries have ties of history, culture, politics and commerce. We have colonized them; killed their inhabitants and been killed by them; stolen their wealth; bought their products; borrowed from their civilizations; suppressed their aspirations; corrupted their systems of government; and recently and fitfully tried to show them better ways of governing themselves. We know one another well, and now many of their former citizens dwell in our own countries. Many more will do so – the majority perhaps illegally, if we mishandle our relationship with them in the future. This is part of the intimacy of our relationship. For America these countries comprise an immensely important geo-strategic relationship, given a particular depth by America's emotional ties to Israel and its concerns about energy supply. For Europe, it is rather different; these are our next-door neighbours.

Nothing matters more to Europe than the way we handle our relationship with this sharp edge of the Islamic world. Get it wrong, politically and economically, and our borders will be subjected to unmanageable migratory pressures; the tensions in Arab countries will spill over into our own societies; and our tolerance will be tested to breaking point. We are seeing this already, as civil liberties in some European countries are curbed because of fears about the violent problems we may import. As I shall argue, I do not believe that there is a war on terrorism in any conventional sense, nor that we can realistically look forward to a day when the threat of terrorism has been totally eliminated. But I do think that a successful partnership with the Arab world could go far to limit terrorism's threat.

The relationship between the Arab lands and Europe will either bring closer the future predicted by the American political scientist Samuel Huntington, or else consign it to the university library shelves. His essay in *Foreign Affairs* in the summer of 1993, subsequently lengthened into a book, foresaw a 'clash of civilizations' that we sometimes seem in recent years to have been sedulously promoting. Some of the global problems that we shall face in this century – for example, whether China can make a smooth accommodation between economic licence and political authority – are probably matters for the consideration of a circumscribed few, in this case a small cadre of bureaucratic politicians in Beijing. Others – for example, environmental disasters – have already been set in train by greed and ecological pillage, and we (particularly America) appear reluctant to try to mitigate the consequences. But a clash between the world that likes to think of itself as being primarily made in the mould of the New Testament, and the Islamic world of the Koran raises issues for all of us. Yet we could still avoid such a clash, though there is a real danger that we will trigger catastrophe through acts both of omission and commission. How can things have come to this?

Let us for a moment revisit Samuel Huntington's thesis. Hot on the heels of liberalism's triumph in the 1980s and 90s – the breaching of the Berlin Wall; the fall of Europe's last empire; the opening of markets by technology and international agreement – Huntington warns against the easy assumption that we can now relax, the Cold War having been won without the use of any of those engines of death stockpiled in silos from Utah to the Ukraine. Conflict is not, after all, a subject for the history books. 'The most important conflicts of the future,' he writes, 'will occur along cultural fault lines separating civilizations from each other.' The differences between civilizations are more fundamental than those between political ideologies, and the more the world shrinks through the use of technology, the more we become aware of them. Globalization has weakened local and national identities, and the gap has been filled by religion, with non-Western civilizations returning to their roots – re-Islamizing, for example, the Middle East. Moreover, cultural – or as Huntington largely argues it, religious – characteristics are less likely to change than those that are political or economic. 'Conflict,' he notes, 'along the fault line between Western and Islamic civilizations has been going on for 1300 years . . .' He also comments that on both sides 'the interaction between Islam and the West is seen as a clash of civilizations'. Popular in some academic circles in the West, his theories are also extensively quoted on jihadist websites in the Arab world.

There are other civilization clashes as well to which Huntington draws attention. But his arguments have never convinced me. I spent a good deal of time during my years in Hong Kong pointing out that there was not some cultural divide between the West and the so-called Confucian world ('so-called' usually by those who have never read Confucius and tend to confuse him with Lee Kuan Yew), which strips Asians of their civil liberties and denies them democracy. Sun Yat-sen had apparently never existed. Many of us argued that human rights were universally valid, and that democracy under the rule of law was the best system of government everywhere. And with the Asian financial crash and the discrediting of the Asian model of crony capitalism and authoritarian politics, the controversy seemed over. The clash of civilizations could have been regarded as the stuff of provocative academic seminars. Then the planes slammed into the Twin Towers, and the world changed.

Well, of course, it was not quite that simple. The pretexts, the causes, the narrative of atrocity began much earlier than 2001. And we had scholarly guides to point us down the right exploratory tracks. Oh, to have been the publisher of Professor Bernard Lewis, sage of Princeton and scholar-almost-in-residence to Vice President Cheney and his Washington tough guys. I admit to a personal debt to Professor Lewis's scholarship. I have enjoyed, and I hope learned from, a number of his books. But I started to worry as I moved on from reading *What Went Wrong?* to *The Crisis of Islam* that I was being carefully pointed in a particular direction, lined up before the fingerprints, the cosh, the swag bag and the rest of the evidence. 'Most Muslims,' Lewis tells us in *The Crisis of Islam*, 'are not fundamentalists, and most fundamentalists are not terrorists, but most present-day terrorists are Muslims and proudly identify themselves as such.' Well, yes – and it's a sentence that resonates (as I have suggested) in parts of the policy-making community in Washington. But what if I had tried a similar formulation on some of these same policy makers back in 1983, just after the IRA bombed Harrods in London? 'Most Catholics are not extremist Irish Republicans, and most extremist Irish Republicans are not terrorists, but most terrorists in Britain today are Catholic and proudly identify themselves as such.' I suspect that it is not a sentence that would have increased my circle of admirers in America – not because it is wrong, but because it is so loaded with an agenda. Anyway, what we have been taught is that there is a rage in the Islamic world – in part, the result of history and humiliation – which fuels hostility to America and to Europe too, home of past crusaders and present infidel feudatories of the Great Satan. Clash go the civilizations.

However we address the Islamic world, it is important to avoid sounding like Silvio Berlusconi and those other politicians and church leaders who suggest that we dwell on a higher moral plane in Europe, custodians of a superior set of moral values and attitudes – conveniently managing to file and forget gas chambers, gulags, and our Christian heritage of flagrant or more discreet anti-Semitism and Islamophobia. Our prejudices may be rock solid but our pulpits are made of straw. What of this Islamic world that allegedly confronts our own civilization? Sometimes we forget that three quarters of its 1.2 billion citizens live beyond the countries of the Arab League, in, for example, the democracies of Malaysia, Indonesia, the Philippines and India. Asian Moslem societies have their share of problems, not least dealing with pockets of extremism, but it makes no sense to generalize about an Islamic anger allegedly engulfing countries from the Atlantic seaboard to the Pacific shores.

If we focus on a narrower range of Arab countries – North Africa, Egypt, the Levant, the Gulf, the countries in the cockpit of current struggle and dissent – what do we find? In 2002, the Arab Thought Foundation commissioned a survey by Zogby International of attitudes in eight countries: Egypt, Israel, Jordan, Lebanon, Kuwait, Morocco, the United Arab Emirates and Saudi Arabia. Their survey confirmed other similar, if not identical, surveys (for example, by the Pew Research Center). From the results it is clear that, like Americans or Europeans, Arabs are most concerned about matters of personal security, fulfilment and satisfaction. Perhaps it is a surprise that they do not appear to hate our Western values and their cultural emanations: democracy freedom, education, movies, television. Sad to say, the favourite programme on Arab television is 'Who Wants to be a Millionaire?' Other survey evidence underlines this point about the most significant values. The second Arab Human Development Report, published in 2003 by the United Nations Development Programme, quotes from the World Values Survey, which shows that Arabs top the world in believing that democracy is the best form of government. They are way ahead of Europeans and Americans, and three times as likely to hold this view as East Asians.

There is not much sign of a clash of values here. The problem seems to be rather simpler. The Arab world does not mind what began as American and European values, but it cannot stand American policies and, by extension, the same policies when embraced or tolerated by Europeans. As the American Director of National Intelligence John Negroponte said explicitly, in hearings in the Senate in early 2005, 'Our policies in the Middle East feed Islamic resentment.' So the Arab world holds very negative opinions of the United States and the United Kingdom (even while holding, according to the World Values Survey, positive views about American freedom and democracy). Why is the UK in this pit of unpopularity alongside the USA? Partly, I suppose, because of what we are seen to do, and partly because of what we are silent about. Who knows how widely St Thomas More is read in Arab lands? But his tag *qui tacet consentire videtur* ('silence is seen as agreement') is true everywhere. Perhaps it cheers us in Britain to discover that France comes out best in these surveys, scoring very positive ratings, as do Japan, Germany and Canada.

What sort of policies feed Islamic resentment, and particularly the hostility in Arab countries? The invasion of Iraq obviously features high on the list. But in 2002 the issue that stood out from the Zogby survey was, hardly surprisingly, the absence of peace in the Middle East. The survey's authors write that 'after more than three generations of conflicts, and the betrayal and denial of Palestinian rights, this issue appears to have become a defining one of general Arab concern. It is not a foreign policy issue . . . rather . . . the situation of the Palestinians appears to have become a personal matter'. As the recent work of, for example, Richard Perle and David Frum has shown, this apparently incontestable point is, for a particular school of American thought, a deliberate and alarming blind spot.

Terrorism has given a savage twist to the debates about values in the Middle East and about the best way to abate hostility to America and to some European countries. American attitudes to terrorism were inevitably shaped by the terrible events of 11 September 2001. Initially, the atrocities drew Europe and America more closely together. For example, I flew straight away to America with Javier Solana and the Belgian Minister for Foreign Affairs Louis Michel (who was in the EU presidency) to discuss immediate assistance for America in the counterterrorism campaign. Among the issues we discussed with Colin Powell was the provision of support for Pakistan to encourage it to fight terrorism, and within days we visited Islamabad. But as the months passed, and the war on Iraq was advocated and planned, we drew apart, with Europe not always fully appreciating the extent of America's trauma – the sense of violation, and the shock at discovering that to be invincible was not the same as to be invulnerable. The subsequent 'war on terrorism' has been understood in Europe as a metaphor: a phrase to describe the myriad responses required of the civilized world to address problems that do not admit of definitive solutions, let alone of military ones. America, by contrast, has really felt itself to be at war; it is a war that ratchets up patriotic sentiments to an unparalleled potency. The election in November 2004 was won by a president at war – Kabul and Baghdad under his belt, and with more citadels to storm, more heights to seize.

Terrorism is abhorred in Europe. We have every reason to hate it, from Spain to Ireland, from the United Kingdom to Italy, from Germany to Greece. The Spanish, for example, have shown extraordinary resolve in standing up to ETA's Basque activists, and it was deplorable to characterize their voting behaviour after the Madrid bombings as a sign of national cowardice. I have already noted my own resentment at the past indulgence shown by some Americans towards the champions of Irish terrorism and its paymasters on the other side of the Atlantic. So, we all hate terrorism. But we in Europe are also uncomfortable with the one-dimensional nature of the debate in some American quarters; the unwillingness to accept that terrorists might on occasion use abhorrent means to pursue ends that we may or may not agree with, but which are susceptible to reason and whose causes can be addressed without going to war. It is as if any discussion of the causes of alienation and hatred was evidence of appeasement. The idea of a world divided between good and evil – between us and them – sits uncomfortably with most Europeans. Throughout recorded time, asymmetric threats have been the weapon of the weak against the strong. We find them sanctioned by history when the cause is just, the means proportionate and the outcome good. The morality is not always very clear. History, after all, is written by, or largely about, the victors, including England's national hero of the fifteenth century, Henry V, who murdered his prisoners before the victory at Agincourt. As Sir John Harington wrote in the early seventeenth century:

> Treason doth never prosper, what's the reason?
> For if it prosper, none dare call it treason.

Our history, from Kenya to Israel to Ireland to South Africa, is peppered with examples of terrorism, which events have elided into politics.

Terrorism sometimes has precise political causes and objectives – the Mau Mau, the Stern Gang, the Irish Republican Army, the African National Congress. Sometimes it has had less focused aims – for example, Errico Malatesta's *'propaganda dei fatti'* ('propaganda by the deed'), which tried to draw attention to injustice and destroy the nerve of ruling elites by murdering presidents and princes, tsars and kings. Today's terrorism by Islamic groups, able through the advance of technology to shatter civilized order through terrible acts of destruction, seems closer to the anarchists than to the gun-toting politicians such as the Irish ones I myself know best (who were notorious for their ability to carry both a ballot box and an ArmaLite). The ideas that sustain Osama Bin Laden and those who think like him, not all of them the members of a spectacularly sophisticated network of evil but nonetheless fellow believers in a loose confederation of dark prejudices, can hardly be dignified with the description of a polished political manifesto. They do not travel far beyond the old graffiti 'Yankee, Go Home'. But they do represent a form of political, social and cultural alienation, which we should seek to comprehend. Joseph Conrad investigated these dark corners in *The Secret Agent*. He described one of his fictional terrorists like this:

He was no man of action; he was not even an orator of torrential eloquence, sweeping the masses along in the rushing noise and foam of a great enthusiasm. With a more subtle intention, he took the part of an insolent and venomous evoker of sinister impulses which lurk in the blind envy and ... misery of poverty, in all the hopeful and noble illusions of righteous anger, pity, and revolt.

Conrad knew that 'The way of even the most justifiable revolutions is prepared by personal impulses disguised into creeds.' It is not normal for men and women to want to get up in the morning and strap bombs to themselves or to their children and set out to kill and maim. How does a sense of injustice, which so often inspires surrender to religious simplicity, come to trigger evil? Why does our own notion of the spread of freedom, capitalism, and democracy, look to some others like licentiousness, greed and a new colonialism? We should surely try to fathom the answers to these questions, and understand that we can make it either easier or more difficult to solve the problems they pose. Is it really a surrender to organized evil to assert that there are some policies that would demobilize the recruiting sergeants of terrorism? No one should seek to excuse or explain away the outrages of 11 September 2001. The cause was horribly unjust; the means abominable. But the reasons for what happened cannot be placed beyond rational discussion. Nor, in my view, can terrorism ever be eradicated from the face of the earth. Complete elimination of the threat could only be achieved in a global Orwellian police state that denied freedom to everyone. That would negate the values for which America and Europe stand. Paradoxically, it would also demand of good men the sort of just resistance – and potentially violent resistance – that we are seeking to stamp out.

Americans and Europeans are now agreed on a positive agenda (as well as a fist of security options) for combating terrorism and its causes. Americans have come rather late to the issue, albeit with muscular enthusiasm. But their credentials are suspect and their application of principles is prone to a pretty blatant display of double standards. Europeans have been labouring in the vineyards for a decade but with too little conviction, energy and tough-mindedness. Indeed, so low-key have been our efforts that most Americans (including many otherwise well-informed policy makers, academics and journalists) had no idea what we were doing. What is this 'hit the jackpot' issue? Simple, really. Or at least, simple to describe: the promotion of democracy, good governance and open markets throughout the Arab world. If there was only one area of policy where we really should try to make the Atlantic Alliance work more successfully, this would be it. We have the ideas, the money and the need. There will be no excuse if we turn these ideas into a shambles.

In 2002, the UNDP produced its first report (the predecessor to the one I mentioned earlier) on the Arab League countries. *Time* magazine called it the most important publication of the year. It unleashed a tidal wave of debate across Arab countries about the reasons for the region's comparative backwardness and inadequate performance. Well over a million copies of the report were downloaded from the Internet, many in Arab countries. Why did a scholarly survey have such an impact?

The first reason is that its authorship caused surprise and endowed credibility. It was written by Arab scholars and policy makers, not well-meaning outsiders. Second, its analysis was captivatingly honest and politically bold: too bold for some. When I raised it with a group of Arab League foreign ministers, there was a lot of averting of eyes and shuffling of papers. They were anxious to move on to to the next agenda item. How could it be that in terms of economic performance in the last quarter of the twentieth century, the only region that did worse than the Arab countries was sub-Saharan Africa? Why had personal incomes stagnated through these years? Why had wealth per head in this region fallen from a fifth to a seventh of the Organization for Economic Cooperation and Development (OECD) average? Why were productivity, investment efficiency and foreign direct investment so low? How could the combined gross domestic product of all Arab countries be lower than that of a single European country, Spain?

The answer came in the prescription summarized by the UNDP's Arab regional director. Arab countries needed to embark on rebuilding their societies on the basis of:

1. full respect for human rights and human freedoms as the cornerstones of good governance, leading to human development;
2. the complete empowerment of Arab women, taking advantage of all opportunities to build their capabilities and to enable them to exercise those capabilities to the full;
3. the consolidation of knowledge acquisition and its effective utilization.

Governance, gender, education – this is the Arab world's own formula for improvement and modernization, and a formula too that European partners on the other side of the Mediterranean have been trying gently, too gently, to promote through the Barcelona Process for almost a decade. We have been attempting to establish a free trade area around our shared sea (the aim is to complete it by 2010); to encourage more trade between Arab countries; and to assist those (like Morocco and Jordan) who are themselves committed to modernization, democratic reform and the nurturing of a more lively civil society. The more I worked on this policy with its ambitious objective, the more I began to fear that Europe was more concerned about a free trade *area* than about free *trade*, at least in the sort of agricultural products grown in southern European countries.

There is a strong link between better government and better economic performance, and between the accomplishment of both those objectives and greater stability. Authoritarian governments are less likely to be good economic managers; they shelter corruption and suppress the sorts of pluralism – a free press, for example – which bring transparency to economic governance. The result of authoritarianism in the region is twofold. First, lower economic growth fails to create the jobs that demographic pressures constantly demand in the Arab world. Young men without jobs, without the dignity of work, and without cash in their pockets, are easily attracted to other causes than the relatively innocent occupation of making money. Second, the denial of civil liberties itself causes resentment, driving debate off the streets and out of the coffee shops into the cellars. Bad economic performance, especially when associated with large wealth and income differences, combines with the suppression of dissent to breed trouble – big trouble.

How should the West, how should the Arab world's European neighbours, support a process of modernization that is so greatly in our own interest – lowering the pressures from illegal immigration; opening new and expanding markets; exporting stability to our near neighbourhood? I do not for a moment accept that it is none of our business, since successful and stable neighbours are very much in our own interest. Nor do I buy the argument that encouraging democracy in the Arab world only creates trouble, with the risk that we will replace more or less compliant authoritarian friends with rabid fundamentalist regimes, established on the basis of 'one man, one vote, once'. I have never been convinced by the argument that free politics is inherently more unstable than command politics. Is Saudi Arabia more stable because it knows only the first fragile green shoots of democracy? Has it in the past inadvertently exported young terrorists, and not so inadvertently financed extremist activity, because it is too free? Which offers the best prospect of stability in Egypt – continuing the past policies of President Mubarak or allowing the political openings cautiously advocated by his son? Does oil wealth across the region bring democracy-lite stability, or simply postpone a violent democratic shock? We would already have done much more to promote modernization, better economic management and improved government if we had been more committed to reducing our dependence on environmentally deadly fossil fuels. Cash-rich oil producers have been able to buy off the need for reform. Every gas-guzzling sports utility vehicle, lumbering through urban traffic on the school run, is a symbol of some of the worst environmental and economic practices sustaining some of the worst political ones.

There are some clear ground rules that outside well-wishers should follow. We are talking about other people's lives and countries, not our own. 'Better,' as T. E. Lawrence argued, 'to let them do it imperfectly than to do it perfectly yourself, for it is their country, their way, and your time is short.' It is imperative that the agenda of modernization – in education, in the rule of law, in participatory government, in opportunities for women, in nourishing civil society – should be owned by Arab countries themselves. Recognition that this will all take time, and that you need to prepare for the long haul, is not code for procrastination. Developing democracy is not like making instant coffee. Arab ownership of both the process of democratization and the end result requires Arab commitment and energy. It is not enough, for example, for Arab intellectuals to say what they want and then hunt for excuses to do no more about it. Authoritarian governments in the Middle East have been adept at using the Israel– Palestine issue to legitimate their rule and to provide an excuse for avoiding reform. Too many Arab modernizers have gone along with this, burying the democratic cause in the wider issue of a struggle for Arab dignity.

We also have to be careful in supporting better government and democracy, not to preach nor to offer – as we have in such grotesque profusion – evidence of double standards. We should expect the same of everyone, regardless of how pliable some authoritarian countries may be when our transient strategic interests throw up new short-term imperatives. If democratic modernization looks like a Western tactic for securing our own interests, we risk discrediting the ideas in which we believe and turning our Arab friends who share the same ideas into seeming stooges. Above all, as we have very painfully discovered, it is difficult to impose a free society through invasion and military might, spreading democracy through the region in the tracks, as it were, of Jeffersonian tanks. Some suggest that the elections in Iraq administered a sharp democratic jolt to the region. This may in part be true, and the bravery and determination of those who voted in Iraq were certainly impressive. But the jolt came at a very high cost, for the Iraqis themselves and for the reputation of America and its allies.

The argument for democracy in the region began, as we have seen, well before the Iraq invasion. Moreover, the invasion was not justified on the grounds that, after thousands of innocent casualties, we would be able to hold an election and thereby demonstrate to others in the region the benefits of democracy. The allies stumbled on the case for democracy when their other justifications for the war crumbled in their hands. That we now have to make the best of what has happened (forgetting the costs and focusing on the exit of Saddam and his murderous cronies), while abundantly true, is not the same as saying that the war – its pretexts, conduct and aftermath – was warranted all along. The invasion certainly emboldened and recruited terrorists, and may well have caused some of the modernizers in Iraq's neighbours, for example Iran, to question whether the price paid for democracy in terms of death, injury, instability and societal breakdown was too high. For conservatives in those countries the sight of democracy being, as it were, imposed by force may have confirmed their view that it is an assault, a secular Western abomination. In addition, you cannot make war on another country every time you want to give democracy a boost. So, we want to see democracy in Syria next: does the Pentagon have the battle plan ready yet? Whatever else we may have learned in Iraq, the lesson spelled out by Winston Churchill in *My Early Life* comes bleakly to mind:

Never, never, never believe any war will be smooth or easy, or that anyone who embarks on the strange voyage can measure the tides and hurricanes he will encounter. The statesman who yields to war fever must realize that once the signal is given, he is no longer the master of policy but the slave of unforeseeable and uncontrollable events.

There are better ways than war of spreading democracy and the rule of law. The strategy that Europe has pursued, though with insufficient ardour, is our Euro-Mediterranean partnership. It is based on a series of trade and cooperation agreements between the EU and individual countries in the Euro-Mediterranean basin. They have taken a long time to negotiate and almost as long, on the European side, to ratify. It was sometimes difficult to explain to our Arab co-negotiators how it was that agreements, to which we allegedly gave so much priority, spent years rambling up and down the legislative corridors of Europe's parliamentary democracy. When I became a commissioner, the EU had negotiated agreements with Tunisia, Morocco, Israel and the Palestinian Authority. During my tenure, we completed negotiations with Algeria, Egypt and Lebanon and came close to doing so with

Syria. We opened our markets a bit to our southern neighbours – with the promise of more progress on sensitive agricultural products and services – and they opened their markets a bit to us. We committed about 1 billion euros a year in grants to support Arab development, and about twice that in loans from the European Investment Bank.

The agreements were supposed to encourage economic and political liberalization, so that the creation of a free market would be accompanied by a growing approximation of systems of governance, laws and regulations. We also wished to promote greater cooperation in areas like policing and immigration control. Any ambitions to promote security cooperation were thwarted by the Israel–Palestine strife. The performance of our partners varied enormously. Jordan and Morocco won most of our gold stars, combining some political modernization with sensible economic management. The Tunisians were good economic performers and were progressive on gender issues but had a human rights record that was the source of frequent angry debate in the European Parliament. The Egyptians were subtle, charming and difficult to help, with one or two ministerial holdovers from the days of Nasserite socialism slowing down our development programmes. (It is instructive that Egyptians seem to be so successful entrepreneurially everywhere else except in Egypt.) The most difficult of our partners were the Syrians. Dealing with them made the task of Sisyphus with his boulder seem straightforward. No one can visit Damascus without seeing what a formidable country Syria could be, both culturally and intellectually. (I remember a passionate discussion on Margaret Atwood's novels with the president's and foreign minister's hard-line female interpreter and adviser.) But Syria is caged by history, corruption and authoritarianism, with its young president unable to move the country out of the shadow of his late father and of his father's brutal cronies. At my first meeting with Bashar Assad – a young ophthalmologist who had studied in London – I thought him a charming, open, rather geeky young man. He said most of the right things. Unhappily, delivery proved more difficult. Syria has been bogged down, until forced to quit, in its colonial adventure in luckless Lebanon and ensnared in a not wholly paranoid fear of Israel. Our economic negotiations threatened the cartels operated by the military and Baathist lackeys, and it was clear that the successful conclusion of this part of our talks represented a hard-won success for the president and his young advisers. With its security services almost certainly out of control, Syria will need tough but constructive handling.

Late in the day in the Syrian talks, we were obliged to insert into the text of the proposed agreement a clause on the proliferation of weapons of mass destruction, in addition to a clause on terrorism. Importing other policy objectives into the drafting of agreements has become a feature of EU diplomacy that hobbles our negotiating and reduces our flexibility. The process had begun with the attachment of human rights clauses to all our agreements, not only in this region. This would be laudable if the agreements were then policed fairly rigorously. They are not. In one of the more unsavoury twists of Western diplomacy, we Europeans were concluding negotiations covering human rights with countries to whom our American allies were shipping terrorist suspects to be tortured as part of the process known as 'extraordinary rendition'. This took outsourcing to unimagined lengths. A human rights clause was one of the more difficult nuts to crack in our trade negotiations with Saudi Arabia and the Gulf countries. I remember a long night's discussion in Brussels on human rights with a group of Gulf foreign ministers, after which I felt that all of us on the European side of the table might be expected to show that we understood the error of our ways by driving down to the Grand' Place to search out a few adulteresses to stone.

There are two better options that are both honest and practical. First, any conditions applied to an agreement should be made positive not negative (a point that I will shortly describe); you should reward good behaviour not threaten to penalize bad. Second, if you think that an issue is sufficiently important – terrorism, proliferation – you should not even start to negotiate an agreement with a country that is not equally serious about the matter. It devalues the currency to draft clauses with painstaking solicitude that you know are likely to be honoured mainly in the breach. Winking at electrodes, as it were, makes for wretched diplomacy. Few authoritarian governments go weak at the knees at the prospect of a European *démarche*.

Europe is now trying to turn the existing Mediterranean agreements into a tighter and more generous neighbourhood policy, and this will obviously be the main vehicle for our contribution to the drive for reform and modernization in the region. There are three problems. First, the offers we make to our partners are insufficiently generous. We are still far too cautious about agricultural liberalization. The southern European countries that are most insistent on the political importance of the Mediterranean are usually the most resistant to concessions on importing products from Arab countries – olives, tomatoes, fish, cut flowers, soft fruit and so on. There is a simple trade-off. If we do not take their tomatoes, we will be on the receiving end of shiploads of their illegal migrants. Moreover, we will reduce employment prospects for the young, making it all the more likely that some of them will become radicalized. We also need to speed up the harmonization of standards – of good safety, public health and so on – to deal with one of the main non-tariff barriers to trade.

Second, we should offer more development assistance, in addition to greater generosity on trade, but this is where my argument about positive discrimination bites. If we want to help drive reform, we should set aside a larger share of our budget to support those who commit themselves to it. We were starting to try this at the margins with the programmes run by the European Commission; I hope these efforts will survive. In my experience it is very unusual for European governments to agree to cut back programmes because of, say, a bad human rights performance in a particular country. There will always be a European president or a prime minister, with a particular client or friend in the region, prepared to intervene on the client's behalf even when that partner's government has been reneging on its promises of economic reform, or hanging dissidents up from the rafters by their thumbs. President Chirac, for example, had a soft spot for the Tunisian regime. So a more effective European contribution to better governance in the region should combine greater generosity with more tough-mindedness about its recipients.

Third, we need to be much more active in promoting trade and investment within the region. The countries of the southern Mediterranean want to trade more with Europe and America, but they hardly trade with one another. Perhaps 5 per cent of their trade is with their Arab neighbours. In too many countries there is still an autarchic reflex – a belief in economic self-sufficiency. But they are too backward and usually too socialist to manage on their own. They lose out on all the economies of scale, all the opportunities for shared investment and manufacturing that regional integration would provide. Outsiders put their money elsewhere, further afield. With all the arguments about outsourcing in Europe, and all the debate about offshore manufacturing, no one ever points a finger of blame at the Arab world. The money stays away; it goes to Asia; so the unemployment grows. There have been belated efforts by some Arab countries – Tunisia, Morocco, Jordan, Egypt – to create something closer to a common market; it is called the Agadir Process. When it was finally launched after years of discussion, one of the foreign ministers responsible for it said to me, 'We have saddled the camel.' Maybe, but it plods rather slowly up the first dune. America and Europe should increase their efforts to promote free trade around the Mediterranean, and between the Mediterranean countries and those Arab countries to the east, the members of the Gulf Cooperation Council, Iran, Iraq and Yemen. Trade, investment, growth, jobs: these are a large part of the answer to the growth of extremism and the spawning of terrorism.

In Europe, we did not spend very much time discussing these issues, on which we could make a considerable difference, preferring instead to wring our hands and rend our garments over Palestine and Israel. It was a tribute to the resilience of the Barcelona Process that it survived with Israel, rightly, a full participating member. It provided the only forum where Israelis and Arabs regularly met, debating political as well as economic issues. But so long as the bloody dispute over the future of a Palestinian state persists, it will be impossible to incorporate regional security into the partnership.

It would not be an exaggeration to say that European foreign ministers discussed Palestine and Israel virtually every month (usually at the lunches I have already described) and at larger occasional informal meetings as well. Sometimes a minister had just been to the region and had something to report back, which from time to time could even be interesting. Sometimes someone was sent to do the usual round of visits. Sometimes there was about to be, or had just been, a formal meeting with the Quartet – the US, the UN, Russia and the EU – or with our partners in the Barcelona Process. Nothing ever changed very much, certainly not for the better. After the first rela-

17. The human cost of ethnic conflict and political failure in the Balkans, 1999. Today we're doing better.

18. Supporting Turkey in the European Parliament. The future of Europe may lie in Istanbul.

19. Entente Cordiale – the then French Foreign Minister (now Prime Minister) Dominique de Villepin in cahoots with Jack Straw, Britain's Foreign Secretary.

20. A hot reception in Colombo in 2003 for the author's attempts at peace making in Sri Lanka.

21. Another Pakistani President from the officers' mess – General Musharraf, ally of the West in Afghanistan.

22. Democracy in Iraq – will it bring more freedom for women and more stability for all Iraqis?

23. Welcome to the twenty-first century – the mass murderer as hero. So how do we change their minds?

24. Guantanamo – a legal and every other sort of black hole.

25. And the President's reply? 'Get Lost'.

26. The Quartet – all six of us – discuss the Middle East with President Bush, Vice-President Cheney and the White House Press Corps.

27. Poodle or partner? Tony Blair stepping out with the Commander-in-Chief.

28. Another crackpot tyrant who has ruined his country.

29. We are better at delivering humanitarian assistance in Africa than making it unnecessary in the first place.

30. The author with Swedish Prime Minister Goran Persson and North Korea's bouffant-haired 'Dear Leader' Kim Jong-il – 'Why don't the Americans like me?'

31. Afternoon tea with China's President Jiang Zemin – the rehabilitation of a 'sinner condemned for a thousand generations'.

32. China's growing might – more missiles, more economic muscle, and much more demand for energy.

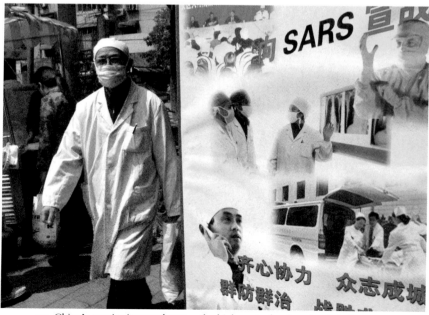

33. China's continuing weakness – the high cost of a closed political system.

tively hopeful period in 2000–01 with talks at Camp David and then later at Taba, everything went downhill – faster and more disastrously than anyone had anticipated – from Ariel Sharon's walk on Holy Mount, to Ehud Barak's political destruction and then Yasser Arafat's at best ambiguous attitude to the employment of the most horrendous violence against Israeli targets. The massacres of the innocent, the reprisals, the house demolitions, the blockades, the building of the security barrier, clocked up ever more dreadful statistics of hopeless horror.

We all meant well and worked hard. Javier Solana in particular worked himself into the ground. But what did we achieve? Maybe we could never have achieved anything on our own. What was certain was that a Pavlovian rejection of any course of action that might distance us from the Americans was the main determinant of our political behaviour. It was in a way absurd. We had, at least in theory, the same objectives as the Americans. But declaring those aims too strongly, along with proposals for trying to achieve them, risked opening up some clear water between us and Washington. While we were prepared to do this from time to time, for example over the Israeli fence, on the whole we preferred to delude ourselves that Washington was as committed to an end to settlements, and to an agreement based on the 1967 borders, as we were ourselves. It may be that with the 2004 presidential election safely in the bag, Washington's policy and Europe's will coalesce. What is clear is that unless we make better progress in resolving the conflict, it will continue to embitter the West's relations with the whole Islamic world. Washington's engagement is certainly essential to a solution, but Europe could legitimately be more independent in setting out its own views. This would raise the political cost of America hanging back from active engagement. Meanwhile, we have spent five years talking, visiting and drafting communiqués, while the two communities of Israel and Palestine were locked into a downward spiral of death and destruction, each seemingly intent on causing pain to the other, with one side plotting revenge and the other exacting a terrible retribution against the last ghoulish act of vengeance.

I should stand back for a moment and offer a confession that will attract criticism by the bucketload. I believe that, in the Middle East, there are two legitimate howls of rage, two storylines not one. I also share with Israel's former Foreign Minister Shlomo Ben-Ami, a wise and intelligent man, the view that, in his words: 'The Holocaust . . . should not give the Jews and Israel any moral immunity from criticism, nor is it proper for Israelis to conveniently dismiss all and every attack against their reproachable policies as anti-Semitism.' I regard the anti-Semitism that was part and parcel of Christianity for centuries as a dark stain on my religion. The behaviour of the leadership of my own Catholic Church in the terrible Holocaust years was deplorable. Anti-Semitism is a malevolent sentiment that I find difficult to comprehend. I hope some at least will understand how much deep offence they cause when they ascribe to anti-Semitism any criticism of Mr Sharon or the policies of the Likud Party. Of course, hostility to Mr Sharon's policies and the practices of the Israeli defence forces *can* drift into anti-Semitism. But it is unfair always to conflate the two.

On one of my early visits to Washington as a commissioner, a senator said to me, 'You'd better understand. We are all members of the Likud Party now.' Well, I was not. The people I most admired were those like Yossi Beilin and the other leaders of the Israeli peace movement, whose activities demonstrated that however great the security problems in Israel, it remained a free society. There was far more debate in its media about Israel's strengths and weaknesses, about the successes and failures of policy, than is evident in the way the American press and television cover these issues. B'Tselem and other human rights organizations point out the human and civil liberties costs of the occupation of Palestinian lands. Judges rule against the government, insisting that even in dealing with security issues there is a price that a free society has to pay to retain its moral core. Israel is a plural, free society, and it should not be treated like an illegitimate pariah.

Ending the bloodshed does not await the discovery of a hitherto secret diplomatic formula. The ingredients of a peace settlement are well known. They were at the heart of the discussions at Camp David and Taba in 2000 and 2001. The Mitchell Commission Report covered them in 2001. The Quartet's Road Map gave the international community's endorsement to a political gazetteer for putting them in place in 2002. The Geneva Initiative in 2003 demonstrated that there were still courageous men and women in Israel and Palestine who could find the path to peace and to a way in which the two states could live harmoniously side by side in what, with shame if not irony, we still call the Holy Land. We know that a two-state solution will require cast-iron guarantees to Israel about its security; the normalization of Israel's relations with its Arab neighbours; borders between the two states based on those that existed in 1967 with negotiated territorial swaps; the sharing of Jerusalem as the capital of the two states; the end of Jewish settlement activity; and an agreed curtailment of the right of Palestinian refugees to return to what is now Israel. We know how the violence should end, but will it?

The international community's policy in the last few years was based on three propositions. First, that Mr Sharon and his government genuinely believed in the creation of a viable Palestinian state. Second, that the Palestinian political leaders would be able and had the will, to convince their community that that goal would only be achieved if they give up violence, even against what they saw as an illegal and aggressive occupation of their own land. Third, that Mr Sharon and his government would take action (for example, on the dismantling of settlements), which would help the Palestinian leaders to accomplish the leadership tasks assigned to them. It took gymnastic leaps of faith to believe over the last few years that these propositions remained true. Now we face the real test, in circumstances made more propitious by the arrival in 2004 of 'time's wingèd chariot', and its departure with Mr Arafat on board.

Throughout the first Bush administration, we were told in Europe that Arafat himself was 'the' problem. I heard Dr Rice say it over and over again. She would brook no disagreement. Most of us found no difficulty in recognizing that he was 'a' problem, and a very big, bad one indeed. But 'the' problem? Whether with a definite or an indefinite article, the problem is in any case no longer there, so progress should be a lot easier, and in a second Bush term there will presumably be fewer political constraints on heavier involvement in the region. If, that is, there were any at all before. Mr Sharon's decision to quit Gaza was welcome, provided it was a step on the road towards creating a viable Palestinian state – not a collection of different scraps of territory, divided by concrete, soldiers and barbed wire. No state that resembles a Swiss cheese can be regarded as viable. No sustainable solution can be found in establishing a mixed bag of Palestinian Bantustans with the symbols of sovereign statehood, but the reality of fragmented and impoverished dependence. Should we have any doubts at all about the outcome that Mr Sharon (cut down and incapacitated in late 2005 by a massive stroke) and those in Washington who have supported unquestioningly this 'man of peace' would like to see? If the building and expansion of settlements is a guide, scepticism is, alas, justified. While the Oslo Peace Process rolled on, building confidence it was said, Israelis continued to build settlements around Jerusalem and on the hillsides of the West Bank. Settlement activity – creating new facts on the ground – continues to this day. Settlements housing a few are closed down in Gaza; settlements housing many are constructed on the West Bank. Tear down here, build up there. When Mr Sharon's senior adviser Dov Weisglass said in late 2004 that the plan to disengage from Gaza in effect froze the peace process (that it was so much 'formaldehyde'), and that the Americans agreed to Israel retaining large settlements on the West Bank with many being dismantled only when 'the Palestinians turn into Finns', his remarks had a pretty authentic ring.

Europeans should be tough with the Palestinians over security, much tougher than we were able to be when Arafat still survived in the rubble of his office, his baleful influence far greater than his governing authority. We should press for far tighter monitoring of Palestinian security activities. The help we give the Palestinian authority should continue to be dependent on Palestinian fulfilment of strict conditions. (The institutional arrangements in Palestine that everyone now accepts as a suitable channel for assisting the would-be state are largely the result of the pressure we in Europe exerted in recent years.) However, we will not secure the long-term changes necessary in Palestine unless there is clear evidence of an equivalent Israeli response, and the dismantling of settlements is the best measure of Israel's commitment to a sustainable solution.

Palestine saw President Bush's commitment to democracy in the Middle East sorely tested. He was right to believe that the democratic tide that had risen in Europe, Latin America and even parts of Africa in the last two decades of the twentieth century should not be held back with America's connivance in the Middle East. Whatever the reasons for the apparent transformation of American policy in the region – and cynicism about them is not wholly justified – it came as a bracing tonic when his Secretary of State, Condoleeza Rice, announced in the summer of 2005 that America had learned its lesson after spending sixty years backing stability rather than democracy in the region and fetching up with neither. She even rapped President Mubarak's knuckles when he arrested the Egyptian opposition leader Ayman Nour. The sceptics noted that in Iraq, the January 2005 elections took place because of the insistence of Grand Ayatollah Ali al-Sistani, who argued powerfully against several American attempts to postpone them or water them down. But to the credit of the Iraqi people the elections did take place, and further elections followed later in the year. Maybe the commitment to democracy in the Middle East promised a bumpy ride, but it seemed genuine.

Now we shall see. In an Islamic world divided roughly between missionary elements, jihadists and political activists, the electoral process brings on the activists, especially where authoritarianism has previously quelled dissent. So in Egypt, when the controls on political activity were released, out sprang the Muslim Brotherhood. At which point President Mubarak clamped down again, cancelling planned local elections. He received in return, not another scolding by Dr Rice, but an increase in American military aid. Wherever elections are likely to take place in Arab countries, it looks as though the winners will be very unwilling conscripts to President Bush's view of the world, nowhere more so than in Palestine where the victory of Hamas in the elections advocated by America and Europe owed much to the corruption and political incompetence of the Fatah party, but much as well to previous Israeli, American and perhaps even European policies in the country. What next? Are the results to be respected or do we now all collude publicly in a policy to isolate Hamas and bring down their government as soon as possible? There is a real difficulty here. Hamas remains committed to violence, even though it has recently observed a ceasefire with Israel, a state which, provocatively and absurdly, it does not recognize. We cannot pour development assistance into the Palestinian treasury if it is controlled by Hamas, until the party abjures violence. On the other hand, we should neither wish to hurt further the Palestinian people nor to drive Palestinian politics into a cul-de-sac of guns and suicide bombers. At least we may be able to go on channelling humanitarian assistance through UN and NGO channels. The promotion of democracy in the Middle East is going to be a messy business, as past policies and their present consequences unravel in political environments made more volatile than they would anyway be by the Palestinian question.

A peace settlement between Israel and Palestine would help transform the prospects for the relationship between the West and the Arab Near East, and indeed between the West and the whole of the Islamic world. It would be absurd to suggest that Islamic terrorism has been driven above all by compassion for the Palestinian people, whose condition does indeed deserve the greatest sympathy. But the terrorists exploit the Palestinian issue: and it fertilizes terrorism's breeding grounds. Television footage of Israeli helicopter gunships rocketing Palestinian refugee camps alongside similar pictures of American assaults on Iraqi Sunni heartlands inevitably result in more or less complete identification in Arab minds of the Israeli and American causes. This does not help America, or Europe, or the moderates and reformers in the Arab world. Nothing matters more in President Bush's second term than peace between Israel and Palestine.

Mr Sharon exploited very cleverly the American fear of terrorism, and the understandable determination of the American people and administration to root it out, in his handling of the Palestinian intifada. Similarly, President Putin has sought to identify his own war in Chechnya with the global campaign against terrorism. This is not a wholly unreasonable point. The Chechen rebels are wicked and brutal. If one were, however, to take the comparison entirely on the Russian president's terms, the conclusions would be pretty depressing. The Chechnya war grinds horribly on, contaminating the northern and southern Caucasus, an indictment of Russian incompetence and corruption. If the overall effort to contain and reduce terrorism goes as badly elsewhere, then we all face a miserable and very dangerous future.

It is easy to understand how we in Europe could find it so difficult to put together an effective and coherent position on the Middle East and on Iraq. But it is more puzzling to fathom why we had so much of a problem in managing sensibly our relations with Russia. It should be an important aim of European policy to promote the growth of prosperity, stability and freedom in Russia as in our other neighbouring countries. Indeed, the task in Russia should be given priority because Russia is so large, with a history of superpower status, a hugely influential cultural heritage, and energy supplies that Europe needs. You do not have to warm to the angst-ridden Russian soul or enthuse about all those dripping birch forests to recognize how much western Europe owes culturally to our great Slavic neighbour; how much we created problems for ourselves by cutting Lenin's Russia off from the rest of Europe (which, admittedly, it wanted to consume in the flames of revolution); and how much the resistance to the post-war threat of nuclear-armed Communist tyranny helped to define the nature of west European democracy. We should sympathize with Russia's efforts to recover from the crude early effort to embrace democracy and capitalism without property rights, the enforcement of contracts and the rule of law. This produced chaos, robbery, inequality and lawlessness. We should also be understanding about the bruised sensitivities caused by loss of empire. Many of us have experienced that. But sympathy and understanding can only stretch so far. When I hear some Russian spokesmen on this theme, I wonder how much Britain's partners would have commiserated with us in the 1940s and 50s if our world view had sounded like the self-pitying rant of a member of the League of Empire Loyalists.

After seventy years of isolation, the Russian economy remains small – perhaps 1 per cent of world output – with low investment, a decaying infrastructure, large and distorting subsidies to housing and electricity, little by way of a small-business sector, and doubts about private property rights. The economy floats on the success of the energy sector – oil and gas – and has benefited from cautious management in the last five years as well as institutional and legal reforms, some of which have even been properly implemented. Yet when Russia becomes a member of the World Trade Organization (WTO), I doubt whether we should expect the profile of Russian exports to Europe and the rest of the world to change much. Energy and commodities predominate; it will be a long time before 'Made in Russia' is a label that attracts customers. Russia receives little foreign direct investment given its size, and the Yukos affair – the looting of a private company whose owner's political ambitions riled President Putin – will reduce the flow even further. Capital flight from Russia and the laundering of cash through Cyprus and other offshore banking centres suggest that many members of the Russian entrepreneurial class (both within and outside the law) see better prospects of earning a fast rouble abroad than at home.

The demographic prospects in Russia are grim. The population shrank in the decade after the collapse of the Soviet Union by 5 million; it has the highest mortality rate in Europe and one of the lowest birth rates. Russia's own estimates suggest that the population will contract by over 30 per cent to 101 million by mid-century, but statisticians concede that it could be lower. At the moment the death rate exceeds the birth rate by 70 per cent. There is an epidemic of public health problems – drugs, alcohol, tobacco and sexually transmitted diseases – and the war in Chechnya has helped to spread TB. Russia has a skilled and educated workforce, and a strong community of scientists, but public health and demographic problems continue to affect the size and quality of the workforce and, if President Putin is to be believed, national security as well. In his first state of the nation address in July 2000, he warned, 'We are facing the serious threat of turning into a decaying nation.'

I imagine that it is often tough in Russia to distinguish between legitimate business and organized crime. A friend of mine tells the story of a next-door neighbour in his block of flats – quiet, from the northern Caucasus – who kept to himself. Once a week a large car stopped outside the block; two bodyguards got out, covering the street with concealed weapons; one then entered the flats ahead of a third man carrying a bag full of money. The neighbour took delivery. It was all very matter-of-fact – 'Neighbours', Russian-style. The consequences of corruption are equally evident. Where the Yeltsin family and their hangers-on blazed the trail, the former secret policemen who now surround President Putin follow close behind. When we were negotiating WTO access with the Russians, the last two sticking points were awkward precisely because they touched on corrupt private interests: the overflight charges that European airlines have to pay to fly over Siberia, and the liberalization of telecommunications.

President Putin's regime rests on pillars that would have been familiar to the last tsar before the revolution – the army, the secret service, the Kremlin bureaucracy and nationalism. 'Our partner' and 'our friend', as President Chirac and Chancellor Schröder call him, has tightened the grip of his security apparatchiks over political life in Russia. Taking the wicked massacre of children by terrorists at a Beslan school in 2004 as an excuse, President Putin has continued the squeeze on such Russian pluralism as had begun to flower. His government now controls the audiovisual news media; print journalists are browbeaten and even poisoned; provincial governors are handpicked by the Kremlin rather than elected; and the security services have greater powers to silence opposition. For all those who have seen strong signs of nascent Russian pluralism – as I did at the so-called Moscow School (a training course for democratic activists) – the Kremlin's reversal of policy on modernization and reform is doubly depressing.

I first met President Putin in late 1999. We were in Helsinki for the EU–Russia Summit. At the last moment, President Yeltsin was indisposed, not a rare occurrence during his presidency. He sent acting Prime Minister Putin to represent him. Putin is a slight, fit-looking man, sharp witted, very cold-eyed, with a good line in rather hectoring argument, seizing on alleged double standards to deflect criticism. He is well briefed and holds particularly strong opinions about Moslems (he turned away questions on Chechnya from one journalist at a press conference with an unsavoury reference to the brotherhood of the circumcised), about terrorism, about the Baltic States and their attitude to their Russian-speaking minority, and about the strategic importance of oil and gas. That first encounter was on a day when the news agencies were reporting explosions and great loss of life at a market in Grozny. We asked him about the reports. He claimed to be uninformed but said he would check on them. He came back to us to say that it was what counterterrorist experts call 'an own goal'. The Chechen rebels ran a weapons bazaar and some of their own explosives had detonated. At lunch he sat between Javier Solana and me. We quizzed him about this response. He looked us in the eye and repeated the story. It was odd. I had never been so blatantly lied to at a meeting like this before. Normally, mendacity comes in better disguise. The damage had, of course, been done by Russian forces, which were soon to reduce Grozny to a ruin similar to Beirut or Kabul. We knew that Putin was lying. He knew that we knew he was lying. He did not give a damn, and we all let him get away with it – on that occasion, and again and again.

At first we used to raise Chechnya at meetings. At the heads of government meeting a few weeks after that first encounter in Helsinki, with the media in a frenzy of concern about Russian abuse of human rights in Chechnya and the disproportionate use of force against the rebels there, Chancellor Schröder supported by President Chirac suggested that we should put on hold the provisions of our long-standing cooperation agreement with the Russians. This was a meaningless gesture, and I said so, questioning exactly how I was to describe the results of our decision if pressed by the media or even by our own officials. The President loftily responded that this was a matter of bureaucratic detail, and that the Commission should leave the big political issues to leaders. This was the high-water mark of President Chirac's insignificant stand for human rights in Russia. Within weeks he was cosying up to Putin and he never looked back. And also within weeks my officials and I at the European Commission were being hectored for being uncooperative with Russia.

The whole Chechnya story continued to be depressing. Critics of Russian policy could not fool themselves that there was an easy way out of the murderous crisis. The state that was created after the first Chechnya war in the mid-1990s was a terrorist haven. It was never going to be easy to find a political accommodation, and while Russia exaggerated the threat that Chechnya posed to her territorial integrity, she could legitimately expect the international community to give this integrity unqualified support. We could also have provided more practical support for fighting terrorism in Chechnya and for reconstructing the economy of the territory. But there was never a realistic Russian political strategy; the Russian armed forces were brutal, corrupt and incompetent; and our efforts to help – for example, through the provision of humanitarian assistance – were treated with derision. Russian officials – President Putin, prime ministers, foreign ministers – obfuscated and lied. They ignored our letters. They denied that we had raised concerns about specific issues with them – for example, access for humanitarian workers to the UN's secure radio network. Naturally, they got away with it.

As I said, in the early years we would raise Chechnya with Russia at meetings. This usually happened when the presidency was in the hands of the smaller, northern member states – Denmark, Ireland, Sweden. But increasingly Chechnya was regarded as a rather tiresome obsession of the European Commission. At a summit in Moscow under the Spanish presidency, José María Aznar – who had flown to Moscow in Mr Putin's private jet – brushed the issue aside as being of little consequence. Prime Minister Berlusconi went a step further and acted, in his own words, as President Putin's defence attorney at a toe-curlingly embarrassing press conference, giving him extravagant cover on Chechnya, the Yukos affair and media freedom. Meanwhile Russian and Chechen casualties in the northern Caucasus mounted. Some estimates suggest that in the wars fought by Presidents Yeltsin and Putin, 250,000 Chechens have died and the population of the territory has fallen from 1.5 million to 500,000 at the most. Our ally, friend and partner in the fight against terrorist barbarity does not appear at first blush to have much to teach us.

The effect of our feebleness in handling Russia is as bad for Russia itself as it is for us. Negotiations are endless and do not get very far. In every discussion the Russians try to 'cherry-pick', focusing on the issues that concern them and ignoring the ones that bother Europe. Because we are not consistent and firm, we do less business than we would like and so do the Russians. In five and a half years, we did three significant deals with Russia. We had a more or less satisfactory negotiation on WTO access, despite the efforts of some member states to push us into unnecessary and disadvantageous concessions. We also concluded a difficult agreement with Russia about Kaliningrad. A third agreement in 2004 extended the trade and cooperation agreement negotiated with Russia by the original fifteen member states to the ten new members. I had responsibility for these two latter sets of talks. Negotiations on Kaliningrad were particularly troublesome because Mrs Putin herself came from Kaliningrad, and because the key issue of access through Lithuania to this part of Russia (now girdled by the EU) meant that all the President's and the Duma's dislike of the Baltic states, once part of the Soviet Union, bubbled to the surface. Despite the behaviour of some of our member states, we got an agreement on Kaliningrad during a Danish presidency, with the tough, no-nonsense Prime Minister Anders Fogh Rasmussen in the chair on our side of the table. In the case of the extension of our Russian agreement to the new members, we were helped above all by them. The arrival in the EU of the former Soviet satrapies, now proud and independent states with a certain experience of dealing with Moscow, firmed up our policy. An ounce of their experience was worth several tons of humbug from Paris, London, Berlin and Rome.

Why did the bigger member states – France and Germany in particular – find it so difficult to develop a sensible, principled strategy on Russia? In Germany's case, maybe Chancellor Schröder was affected by Mr Putin's fluency in German, though it is odd to like someone for an attribute acquired in order to function as a spy in your own country. Whatever the reason for Schröder's regard, it was handsomely rewarded when, within weeks of stepping down from the chancellorship, he was made chairman of the company that will build a pipeline under the Baltic, supplying Germany with energy direct from Russia, without the need to transit other Eastern European countries. The company, domiciled in a Swiss tax haven (useful for exercising social democratic principles) reeks of the good old days when fraternal relations between Berlin and Moscow were kept in good shape by the Stasi and the KGB. I imagine there were three main reasons for the Chirac-Schröder approach. First, President Putin was seen as a useful occasional ally against the United States (for example, during the Iraq war); and the notion of Europe as a counterpoise to Washington might have been given a little more credibility if Russia were to be added to the European mix. Second, President Chirac in particular sees diplomacy in terms of great men, the leaders of great countries, talking together in mirrored, marbled halls. Cast detail to the winds; history is made by those who understand the grander picture, and who can summarize its most salient features in a portentous platitude. Third, some Europeans assume that Russia's energy resources give Moscow a hold over us. In truth, Russia needs our market just as much as we need Russia's product, and if we were smarter we would strengthen our negotiating hand by doing more to increase the flow of oil and gas to Europe from the rich fields of central Asia and Azerbaijan.

The main victims of our failure to develop a better and more balanced relationship with Russia are its neighbours. Again, here we fool ourselves. I began this chapter by saying that Europe wants stable, well-off neighbours. This is not Russia's aim. Russia wants weak neighbours and a sphere of influence inhabited by dependent suppli-cants. So we make no progress in solving the disputes that enfeeble Russia's neighbours: Moldova's problems with the breakaway, bandit territory of Transdnistria; the dispute between Armenia and Azerbai-jan over Nagorno-Karabakh; the weakening of Georgia through Rus-sian support of South Ossetia and Abkhazia. 'Where can you still see the Soviet Union these days?' I once asked. 'In the Russian Foreign Ministry,' was the reply. Actually, the ministry's DNA has older origins. Russian foreign policy around its borders is tsarist in intent: post-imperialism as practised (in Georgia's and Moldova's case) under the protection of corrupt Russian troops involved in the smuggling of drugs, weapons, fuel and alcohol. As Professor William Wallace has observed, there is something dangerously absurd about a policy that bitterly resists any autonomy in Chechnya in the northern Caucasus while supporting the secession of non-viable parts of Georgia in the southern Caucasus.

Perhaps we should take some recent comfort from Russia's decision not to intervene in the last triumphant stages of the Orange Revolution in Ukraine – whatever Russia had been conspiring to do earlier. It will take vigilance to ensure that Ukraine is not now bullied off the democratic path it has chosen, either by political threats or by Russia's manipulation of Ukraine's energy requirements. At the beginning of 2006, for example, Russia's natural gas monopoly, Gazprom, briefly shut off supplies to Ukraine in order to press more forcefully its demands for a four-fold price increase. Any notion that this was simply a commercial dispute was swiftly spiked by President Putin's top economic adviser, Andrei Illarionov, who had recently resigned in protest at the authoritarian drift of policy in the Kremlin. He noted that Gazprom had agreed to charge Ukraine a low price for its gas in 2004 in order to help the candidate it was backing in the presidential

election. With its favoured candidate defeated and President Yushch-
enko in office and facing tough parliamentary elections in 2006, the
price that was supposed to last until 2009 had been sharply increased.
Gazprom, Russia's largest company, was clearly a crude instrument
of Russia's foreign and security policy, which was aiming in this
case at the destabilisation of Ukraine. One lesson drawn by many
Europeans, even while – as chairman of the G8 countries – Mr Putin
highlighted the importance of energy security, was that European
countries should reduce their dependence on Russian oil and gas.
Another lesson should be the importance of doing more to sustain
pluralism and market economics in Ukraine.

But the survival of a democratic prospect in Kiev does not tell us
much about what will happen in her bigger encircling neighbour.
Russia has been one of the great survivors of history. With luck she
will resume her erratic journey towards democracy and pluralism. We
are not, however, doing much to encourage this process, conniving
rather at policies and attitudes that will create a more dangerous
neighbourhood for us all. Russia needs a strong and outspoken partner
in Europe, not a mealy-mouthed pushover. If we want Russia to share
our values, a good place to start standing up for them is in Russia
itself.

8

Happy Families

Forget Europe wholly, your veins throb with blood.
To which the dull current in hers is but mud . . .
O my friends, thank your God, if you have one, that He
'Twixt the old world and you set the gulf of a sea.

James Russell Lowell

It is, I suppose, what Donald Rumsfeld might call a 'known known'. Even while we are pelting one another with genetically modified tomatoes, we do know really that there is more that unites the transatlantic community – North America and Europe – than divides us. The speech that asserts this proposition, so regularly made and sometimes even heeded, comes easily: 'The new republic formed from the human, cultural and political stock of old Europe . . . the shared attachment to Enlightenment values . . . participative democratic government under the rule of law . . . the common sacrifice in war . . . the joint post-war commitment to new forms of global economic and political governance . . . the struggle to repel Communism's advance . . . the vision of a world, prosperous, democratic and free . . . hands across the ocean . . . "westward, look, the land is bright" . . . to "the indispensable nation" add "the indispensable partnership".' And so on. Both sides of the ocean can do this stuff in their sleep.

Like many known knowns, it is broadly true, but it is not of course the whole story. Moreover, a known *un*known is that we cannot be entirely sure what is going to happen to the partnership in the coming years. To raise this question, to suggest that change may be in the air, to strip away some of the myths that obfuscate the story of the alliance – the myth that it has always been plain sailing, or the myth that it has only been in recent times that the alliance has hit roughish water – is to court disapproval. In *Henry IV, Part II*, Shakespeare noted:

> Yet the first bringer of unwelcome news
> Hath but a losing office . . .

Unless, however, we discuss these issues free of cloying cliché and political prejudice, we may find it too tough to manage our relationship as it changes in the years ahead, to our mutual benefit and to that of the rest of the world. We will also set back the prospect of the values that we publicly esteem, and sometimes uphold, gaining sway in other continents as the century advances.

At the beginning of the 1890s, America might have been described as a free-rider in a world made pretty safe by Britain's imperial reach and naval might. The British navy had 33 coaling stations and 11 bases in the seas around America, which – while claiming by then the status of the world's greatest industrial power – possessed no battleships and had only 25,000 men under arms. For years America had successfully pursued its revolutionary foreign policy, offering friendship to all but concluding alliances with none. In a world of empires, America the republic had chosen another path. That all changed with the Spanish-American War of 1898. America annexed Hawaii, Guam, Wake Island and the Philippines, where 200,000 civilians died between 1898 and 1902. The republic's innocence was lost, but not its aspiration to avoid foreign entanglements, wherever possible. Though persuaded reluctantly to come to the aid of Britain and France late in the First World War, America was not keen to become enmeshed in the problems of war, peace and economic depression with which others wrestled unsuccessfully in the 1920s and 1930s. Neville Chamberlain was not alone in thinking that, 'It is always best and safest to count on nothing from the Americans but words.' That changed with the Second World War and its aftermath. Now America, the planet's mightiest military and economic power, faced a world in which the world's oldest empires were disintegrating. Only the new Soviet empire in Europe remained, threatening the rest of the continent with subjugation to tyranny. America embraced, with becoming reluctance, a new role of global leader, in command of a virtual empire of commercial and cultural predominance and of more or less willing dependent feudatories. 'We have got to understand,' said Dean Acheson, 'that all our lives the danger, the uncertainty, the need for alertness, for effort, for discipline, will be upon us. This is new to us. It will be hard for us.' And so it was, though the task was handled with extraordinary dexterity and commendable commitment.

Even for a great power, diplomacy is not easy, and America had to cope regularly with the assumption that it was throwing its weight around, even when it was doing no such thing. It also had to deal with three other problems. First, there was the resentment of those who had been saved, militarily and economically. In *The Analects*, Confucius noted the colleague who was cross with him even though, as Confucius pointed out, he had done him no favours. Second, there was condescension masquerading as sophistication. Third, there was resistance to what was seen as the Americanization of indigenous cultures and ways of life: we dressed like Americans, listened to their music, watched their films, and drank their carbonated drinks – even while we rejected some of what they seemed to stand for, particularly in the miserable years of the McCarthyite inquisition and during the failed efforts to bring what Senator William Fulbright called 'little pissant' Vietnam to heel.

It is plain wrong to see anti-Americanism as a phenomenon of recent years, the reaction to an assertive, nationalist president, whom we in Europe do not understand and with whom we assuredly fail to empathize. In the most creative, generous-spirited and comradely years of American leadership there were still those in Europe who carped and bitched. Sometimes there was at least a shred of justification for the resentment – at America entering the war so late, and at the ill-disguised relish with which Americans read the last rites over the British Empire. But more frequently the European antagonism was reprehensible. Unsure whether it should take greater exception to the help it was offered, or to the prospect that it might not receive all the assistance it wanted, France took the lead, displaying what the historian Robert Gildea describes as 'a kind of petulant ingratitude'. *Le Monde*, founded in 1944 after the liberation of France, supported an armed and neutral Europe standing between the US and USSR. The arrival of the new NATO commander in Europe in 1952 was greeted by French riots. Those political fatheads, Simone de Beauvoir and Jean-Paul Sartre, were in the thick of the troublemaking. As early as 1946, de Beauvoir was complaining that America's attitude to Europe and France was one of 'arrogant condescension'. The American soldiers who had once been 'our liberty' were now 'our dependence and a mortal threat'. Later she was to opine that '*our* victory had been stolen from us', though the use of 'our' in this sentence begged a few questions. But as the early victories in the battle to keep Coca-Cola out of France were reversed by the French courts, it became clear that no corner of France was safe from the incoming American tide.

The British had their own special brand of patronizing contempt, which was not anti-American, old boy. It is just, said Harold Nicolson to an American acquaintance, that Europeans were 'frightened that the destinies of the world should be in the hands of a giant with the limbs of an undergraduate, the emotions of a spinster, and the brain of a peahen'. You find the finest literary flowering of these sentiments in the novels of Graham Greene, particularly *The Quiet American*. Greene was prescient about what was to become the bloody quagmire of Vietnam, but even so the depth of his hostility to America is pretty shocking. Again and again, he puts the boot in. The young American idealist Alden Pyle 'was determined to do good, not to any individual person but to a country, a continent, a world . . . He was in his element now with the whole universe to improve.' Most famously Greene notes (and he is clearly talking about all Americans, not just Pyle): 'I never knew a man who had better motives for all the trouble he caused.' In the frontispiece to the novel (published in 1955) he quotes Byron:

> This is the patent age of new inventions
> For killing bodies, and for saving souls,
> All propagated with the best intentions.

So it was not only the boulevard Bolsheviks, the frequently traduced French intellectuals, who seethed and scorned. Within a few years of American-led military victory, the foundation of the United Nations and the launch of the Marshall Plan, here was old Europe showing its appreciation. As Randy Newman once sang:

We give them money – but are they grateful?
No, they're spiteful and they're hateful . . .

There was never a golden age in transatlantic relations when all Europeans doffed their hats to the superpower that defended our freedom. We were always a bit tiresome, and sometimes – as I have said – there was a good reason for it.

For all the talk about family, Europeans and Americans are at once cousins and strangers. We are more different than we like to admit, and are surprisingly ignorant about one another. Europeans note with surprise how many Americans have never travelled outside their own country and how some politicians even make a virtue out of not possessing a passport. More tellingly, Studs Terkel notes how the taxi drivers in his home city of Chicago, who come from every part of the world, regularly express to him their astonishment at how little their American passengers know about the cabbies' countries of origin. I guess this casual disregard of the world outside has much to do with being a superpower. Some days you can scour in vain even quality American newspapers to find a story about Europe. This reflects, in part, where most of the significant political action is. In any newspaper in any other part of the world, there is page after page of news about America – its politics, its business, its popular culture. So we really should know more about Americans than they know about us.

I doubt if that is true; and our own assumption that America is much like us only bigger, faster and richer, is constantly upended. It is a more regular experience if you are a native English speaker. Shared language creates a presumption of similarity that does not long survive a brush with reality. I remember the shock on my first visit as a student when I realized that I felt more at home in Athens, Greece, with few English speakers, than in Athens, Ohio. The sense of cultural alienation varies from one part of the country to another. I recall a long visit of speaking engagements to the West Coast of the United States, when I was Governor of Hong Kong. My visit began in Orange County, south of Los Angeles. It might as well have been the moon. I dined off that legendary rubber chicken, with a limp salad, iced water and weak coffee, and then tried to answer questions from an audience that clearly regarded me as a quaint even exotic creature, with curious views way off any recognizable political map. We moved north to Los Angeles and then on to San Francisco and Seattle (one of my favourite cities anywhere in the world). As we struck north, I felt increasingly comfortable, though San Francisco is sometimes politically a little piquant even for my own tastes. But Seattle felt like home: a lovely city whose inhabitants, I suspect, fib about the climate in order to keep outsiders away. As one might expect, Seattle has one of the greatest bookshops you could ever hope to find, the Elliott Bay.

The surprising realization that you are very foreign in many parts of the United States comes hand in hand with the shock of discovering how difficult it is to generalize, and that in a way is what makes me doubt how accurate is the endlessly parrotted observation that we are all, Europeans and Americans, much the same, and share basically the same values. Which Americans are we talking about? Do we mean Americans who are more obese than any people I have seen anywhere in the world, or Americans who live a life governed by ascetic fitness regimes with carefully controlled diets of vitamin supplements and steamed broccoli? Do we compare ourselves to evangelical Christians, who wait expectantly for Armageddon and a rather dramatic end to the Middle East Peace Process, or to those for whom religion is an intolerant gospel of political correctness that puts many of the values of the Age of Enlightenment to the sword – seeking, for example, to hound from office the president of one of the world's greatest universities for speculating aloud about the sources of gender differences? Do we identify with Americans who preach a gospel of rugged, individual capitalism, scattering its riches widely to the benefit of all, or Americans who appear to stack the cards in favour of those who have plenty and who ignore those who have little or nothing? Which America shares European values?

In so far as these things bother him (after all, he has been elected for a second term, and this time without the judicial intervention of the Supreme Court), President Bush's problem with much European opinion is that he stands at the heart of several of these puzzling questions about how much we Europeans really *do* have in common with our American partners. The European identity itself is admittedly complex. What does an Andalusian peasant have in common with a

Swedish lumberjack, a Catholic priest in Trieste with a Lutheran pastor in Tallinn? There are certainly differences in Europe. But on the issues of religion, patriotism, political conservatism and inequality, Europeans are clearly much closer to one another than they are to Americans – and all these issues have become increasingly important to the way America is seen and behaves around the world.

Alexis de Tocqueville wrote that 'peoples always feel the effects of their origins'. We should not therefore be too surprised that America today asserts its religiosity with such selective and self-centred force. The Puritan Founding Father, John Winthrop, argued that the early colonists were creating 'a City upon a Hill, the eyes of all people are upon us'. The colonists were doing the Almighty's work. 'Thus stands the cause between God and us,' said Winthrop. 'We are entered into Covenant with Him for this work.' From the very beginning then, Americans saw themselves in Herman Melville's words as:

... the peculiar, chosen people – the Israel of our time; we bear the ark of the liberties of the world ... God has given to us, for a future inheritance, the broad domains of the political pagans, that shall yet come and lie down under the shade of our ark, without bloody hands being lifted. God has predestined, mankind expects, great things from our race; and great things we feel in our souls.

Some of those who lay down 'under the shade of our ark' needed some persuasion. True, America is predominantly the home of old Europeans who fled west to escape political persecution or economic hardship, or who emigrated simply out of the hope of a better life. Most of them found one, not least the relations of my Irish forebears (nine out of my stepfather's ten West of Ireland uncles emigrated to North America), who followed 'the tenement trail' from slums to suburbs. But there were others who had the choice made for them – the native Americans (W. H. Auden's 'cudgelled people') and the African victims of the slave trade.

The concept of 'a chosen people' can be attractive when its leaders summon their fellow citizens to a generous and whole-hearted commitment to the ideals of a religion that boasts charity (in the case of Christianity) as the greatest of its three theological virtues. Martin Luther King's crusade for justice for black Americans, couched in biblical language, gave many non-Americans the vision of a city *being built* on a hill. It was work in progress. When black Americans were 'free at last', we sensed that there was a chance for more people in other countries to be free as well. The example was catching. Yet too often the chosen people seem to have assumed possession of a golden share in God. They are unique among His creatures, like many of Queen Victoria's subjects, practising and aspiring to standards that no one else can attain; yet because of their uniqueness they are able to impose their own way of doing things on all the lesser people of God's largely unfavoured earth. Might is clothed in holy orders – and the 'orders' embrace both meanings of the word. A former Archbishop of Canterbury, Robert Runcie, setting out the limits of Christian patriotism in an admirable sermon (though much disliked by Margaret Thatcher and the tabloids) at the thanksgiving service to mark the end of the Falklands War in 1982, argued that, 'Those who dare to interpret God's will must never claim Him as an asset for one nation or group rather than another.' It was true of Britain then, and it is true of America now. The American theologian Reinhold Niebuhr went much further, exploring the irony of a country full of committed Christians tempted in the post-war years to play God with the world, helped by nuclear weapons and the Central Intelligence Agency. Today President Bush's rhetoric is packed with references to the concordance between God's will and America's mission in the world. 'The liberty we prize,' the President says modestly, 'is not America's gift to the world, it is God's gift to humanity.' But it is for America to define both the liberty – God not being immediately available to do the job Himself – and the best way to secure it. In this sense, when the President was deemed after 11 September 2001 to have misspoken his launching of a crusade against Islamic terrorism, because of unfortunate medieval parallels, he was really enunciating a profound truth. He is seen by many of his supporters as playing a quasi-sacerdotal role: God's instrument to accomplish His will on earth, and by direct identification the will of His chosen people too.

The prominence of religiosity in American political language, electoral rhetoric and policy-making, is another reminder of how wrong the experts were who predicted, not long ago, that religion would play a declining role in international politics. Our late Polish Pope

John Paul II helped to redraw the boundaries of freedom in Europe, though he does not seem to have had much impact on the family behaviour of Europeans. Islamism grows in intensity – and, in some of its manifestations, toxicity. How influential (and benign) is American religion? Clearly the importance of evangelical Christians has been strengthened by their alliance with right-wing Catholics (over abortion, stem cell research, sex education and gay issues) and with right-wing Jews (over the Middle East). Although, if I were Jewish, I would think twice about throwing in my lot with those Christians who foretell an imminent last battle between Good and Evil in the Holy Land and the conversion of the Jewish race to Christianity. Many Europeans, including those like me who are practising Christians, are uncomfortable with the messages, behaviour and beliefs of America's fundamentalist Christians, just as we are with fundamentalism elsewhere. We have suffered from fundamentalism in Europe ourselves. I used to muse, when we were condemning the Taliban's desecration of Buddhist carved figures in Afghanistan, about Oliver Cromwell's troops riding from one English cathedral to another to smash the heads off the Christian statuary. We are still not entirely free from religious fundamentalist bigotry; Northern Ireland comes to mind. But on the whole, this is part of our history, and the Christian message is usually today conveyed in moderate tones that do not deny past crimes done in God's name nor the existence of the modern world.

One reason why 'Come to Jesus' oratory may grate is that, while Europeans have not wholly turned their backs on religion, it seems to matter less to us than to Americans. According to the Pew Research Center, 59 per cent of Americans say that religion is very important to them, compared to only 27 per cent of Italians, 21 per cent of Germans and 11 per cent of the French. America remains, in G. K. Chesterton's phrase, a nation 'with the soul of a church', a church moreover with some surprisingly traditionalist views, for reasons that may not be wholly dissimilar to the reasons for Islamic fundamentalism. In its seeming destruction of familiar landmarks and signposts, globalization perhaps encourages a reversion to what we take to be simple, ancient truths and customs. The church, mosque or temple provides an oasis of certainty, order and beauty from the assault of alien ideas and temptations. In his book *The European Dream*, Jeremy

Rifkin sets out some of the statistical evidence of religious belief in America, where 46 per cent of the population describe themselves as born-again Christians in what has been called the fourth great religious revival to sweep America in the last three centuries. Over two-thirds of Americans believe in the Devil (the figure is the same for college graduates). A third of all Americans believe that every word in the Bible is God's and a quarter think that the teaching of creationism should be mandatory in publicly funded schools. A recent Gallup Poll showed that almost half of Americans believe in creation-ism and just over a quarter in evolution. Four out of ten Americans believe that the world will end with an Armageddon battle between Jesus and the Antichrist, and 47 per cent think that the Antichrist is on earth already. (There are no figures for those who believe he is camped out on New York's UN Plaza.)

Does all this actually matter? Rifkin notes that according to the World Values Survey, most Europeans, Canadians and Japanese reckon that there can never be absolutely clear guidelines about what is good and evil; circumstance plays a part in determining the dis-tinction. Most Americans, on the other hand, believe that the guide-lines about what is good and evil are clear and apply to everyone regardless of circumstances. If you are trying to form a common trans-atlantic view of what sort of world we want to live in and how we can achieve it, it is hard to believe that these differences are of little consequence. Perhaps they will matter most in those areas likely to have the greatest impact on the human condition, where science pro-vides the evidence and the goad for international policy: for example, concerning the environment (to which I will return in the last chapter). Does Jesus have a view on gas-guzzling, four-wheel drive vehicles? I do not spurn religion's role in public debate, but recall Einstein's observation, 'Science without religion is lame, religion without science is blind.'

As one might expect, Americans – the 'chosen people' – are more nationalistic than those who are all too aware of their own imperfec-tions. The visitor to the United States is struck by the public evidence of this. Drive through American suburbs and you see so many flagpoles with the Stars and Stripes fluttering over the front lawns. In Britain, it takes an international football tournament, or the very occasional commemoration of a wartime victory, or a rite of passage in the House of Windsor to get the British to fly the flag, led by the regiment of patriotic cab drivers. For a party to mark the fifth anniversary of my departure from Hong Kong, I hung the old governor's Union Jack from a first-floor window at home. My neighbours thought I had gone mad. Britain's Prime Minister-in-waiting (not for long, he hopes), Gordon Brown, will have his work cut out trying to get the British to take his advice and run the Union colours up their domestic flag poles to show their patriotism. One also gets the impression that American visitors to Washington's tourist sights are doing more than spending a jolly family holiday in the capital. They are like Catholics visiting Rome, solemnly trooping around the shrines of a religion. In a National Opinion Research Center Poll, the United States came first of 23 countries in its citizens' sense of national pride. Seventy-two per cent of Americans said they were very proud of their country. Less than half the sample in the main Western democracies – including Britain, Denmark, France, Italy and the Netherlands – said the same. It may surprise Americans to learn that the Pew Research Center found that only one out of every three Frenchmen believed that their culture was superior to others. The figure for Americans was about twice as many. What on earth has got into the cheese-eating brigade? Has 'defeatism' joined 'surrenderism'? While generally kind and welcoming to visitors, Americans have long resented – even more than most others – any criticism of their country. Tocqueville called this 'irritable patriotism'; it is not new but it can be unsettling.

As a British, indeed as a European, Conservative, I believe among other things in markets, individual enterprise, limiting government's role, participative pluralism, personal responsibility, the importance of the family and the rule of law. I am a Catholic and a patriot. So far, I suppose, I am describing someone who could be part of the fast-growing American Right. Dig a little deeper and the comparison starts to look a bit tattered. Capitalism does not for me supersede democracy, nor guarantee it. Nor is it synonymous with the very rich bosses of large corporations making ever more out of a system rigged to their benefit. Capitalism is not a form of religion. Those who play casino capitalism should not be what Tom Wolfe described as

'Masters of the Universe', they should be subject to the same laws, and ethical values as the rest of us. Capitalism should operate within the law, not the law within capitalism. It is offensive that senior figures in political life find it so easy to confuse making their own private fortune with the public good; the names of Vice President Cheney and Halliburton come to mind without much intellectual strain. And it is surely laughable when the highest awards are showered on those who promote the most gimcrack schemes to make themselves rich, at least for a while. The geniuses who invented the pyramid of derivatives at Long-Term Capital Management were awarded the Nobel Prize for their cleverness, not long before the whole edifice came crashing down with the financial community digging deep into its pockets to prevent too much collateral damage. To every excess, there comes a reaction. Failure to insist on high corporate standards, and on a sense of responsibility to something broader and more important than the maximization of reward for senior executives, strips away part of the essential protection of and justification for what remains the best system for increasing the prosperity of a community.

It is curious that the apologists for the most rampant and uncontrolled forms of capitalism are invariably the greatest critics of government, even though they usually seek to suborn government and the public purse for their purposes. They seek handouts and tax breaks, government contracts and commercial sponsorship. The lobbyists of corporate America crowd around the policy makers and legislators of Washington, helping to make its environs one of the most prosperous parts of the country. Government spending, not least at the Pentagon, helps promote industrial development and the fabulously endowed research programmes on university campuses. Just as the first telegraph line was built by the federal authorities, so at the heart of what used to be called the New Economy lies technology that owes most to government. 'Both the basic science and the technology of the Internet,' writes Godfrey Hodgson in *More Equal Than Others*, 'were largely the product of research and development done under the impetus of the Cold War.' What sense can it make to believe that wealthy corporations should be able to lean on government but that everyone else should stand on their own feet?

As a European Conservative, I believe strongly that the State should not do too much. For most members of the Left and Right in Europe, this debate about the State is a matter of degree. I would like to see the State doing rather less, and individuals doing rather more for themselves. I do not think it makes sense for conservatives to trade promises with the Left about greater public spending on state services. Conservatives should offer lower taxes, better management of the public sector and the use of market instruments for enhancing the quality of public provision and the resources available to it. I think there is room for greater private provision in health care, education and pensions. I am happy to define a centre-right domestic agenda in these terms, and to be attacked and described as an expenditure cutter as a result. I know of no sensible definition of conservatism that includes the belief in a Big State and writes its manifestos on open cheques for public services.

But I *do* believe in good public services for those who require them. Slash and burn is not a conservative approach to government. Government is not inherently suspect, to be treated as an enemy of a conservative society. Since, as a Conservative, I believe in stability and order under the rule of law, I want government that is responsive, respected and properly endowed to carry out its many functions.

I am also sufficiently conservative to believe in balancing the government's books. I do not like deficits – either when they are run up by governments or by households. As a Conservative in America, I would be appalled at the size of the structural budget deficit and the trade deficit – both now standing at 5 per cent or more of gross domestic product – and at the debts carried by ordinary families. Are these things signs of a vigorous family-oriented Conservative society? America has to attract more than $2 billion a day – weekends included – just to finance its current account deficit. More than 4 dollars out of every 10 of American Treasury bonds, bills and notes are presently held by foreigners. In 2004, America attracted 80 per cent of global savings. In this mad world, the savings of poor Chinese peasants purchase American Treasury securities to help keep interest rates in the US lower and the financing of the deficit more secure. The trade-off for the Chinese and other Asians for investing in this mountain of paper is that it eases the pressures on them over the exchange rate of their own currencies and over the size of their surpluses with America.

They fund US debt so that Americans will continue to buy their products. But how would I view this as a Conservative with European values living in America? I would surely be unhappy about my country borrowing so much from the rest of the world in order to purchase whatever the rest of the world is making. What an old-fashioned Conservative I have clearly become!

I would also be uncomfortable at the scale of household borrowing. Is this a sign of sustainable prosperity or is it a bubble? Americans now save less than 2 per cent of their disposable income. The savings rate in the euro area is about 12 per cent. Total household debt in the US represents 84 per cent of GDP; it is 50 per cent in the euro area. American debt represents 120 per cent of personal disposable income. The euro area figure is 80 per cent. Real increases in wealth come from technological progress or productivity increases, not from asset inflation.

Indebtedness does not feature in my own list of family values, nor do I like the idea of the State abandoning families financially while condoning interference in their private lives. When we talk about the European social model, we are often referring to policies that vary a good deal from country to country, that do not always work particularly well any more, and that certainly require reform. But these policies have one underlying characteristic. We do not believe that extremes of inequality make for social stability, a proposition that also used to find favour in America. Indeed, Tocqueville begins *Democracy in America* with this sentence: 'Among the novel objects that attracted my attention during my stay in the United States, nothing struck me more forcibly than the general equality of condition among the people.' He could not write the same sentence today. There is greater inequality of wages in America than there was, with corporate chief executive officers earning 107 times as much as average workers, double the ratio in 1989 and 5 times the figure of 40 years ago. There are similar figures for income and wealth: the incomes of the richest grew three times as fast as those of the average family in the 1990s, and during the same period the very rich also increased their share of national wealth. Theodore Roosevelt, a Republican, argued that 'this country will not be a permanently good place for any of us to live in unless we make it a reasonably good place for all of us to live in'. Presumably growing inequality is regarded by most voters as an acceptable condition since the issue does not overturn administrations in the way that it would anywhere in Europe (where inequality has also been growing in some regions, though with much less extreme results).

Europeans use state and public funding to support families in a way that would presumably appal an American Conservative, who believes that most social ills can be alleviated by economic trickle-down (from the bank accounts of the rich to the small wage packets of the poor) or by voluntary action by charitable organizations, for example church groups. Failing social improvement, there is always policing and the penitentiary. In Europe there are 87 prisoners per 100,000 population; in America 685. In Europe more or less free health care and education are at the heart of family policy. Partly as a result, we live longer than Americans and have a much lower infant mortality rate. The health statistics in urban Washington bring to mind those in a developing country. America spends more than anyone else on health care but comes 37th in quality of service. Standards of literacy and numeracy among American school children are poor in comparison with their European and Asian peer groups, but American higher education is the best in the world, partly because of government funding of research but also because of generous support by alumni much encouraged by the tax system.

For many Europeans the greatest difference in values comes in attitudes to human life. It would be dishonest to pretend that Europeans are uniformally opposed to capital punishment. They are not, even if their governments are. But there is far more public opposition to the State taking life than exists in America, and I do not believe that any European country even under the threat of terrorist violence would today restore capital sentences for the most wicked crimes. The greatest difference in attitudes lies elsewhere. I am writing this sentence on a morning when the newspapers have been full of reports of the case of Terri Schiavo, a brain-damaged Florida woman. Congress has rushed through an unprecedented bill to try to encourage the courts to save the life of someone said to be in a permanent vegetative state, a condition from which the American Academy of Neurology says that no one has ever recovered. The President has sacrificed his holiday to return to the White House to sign the bill into law in the middle of the night. Mrs Schiavo's husband and legal guardian wants to withdraw her feeding tube; her parents want to keep her alive; judges have found in the husband's favour; politicians manoeuvre; the Republican Party's supporters on the religious right bang their Bibles down on the table.

As I write, the morning news has come on leading with the story of another teenage boy who has ran amok with guns killing several schoolmates and members of his family. What chance of Congress passing laws to restrict gun sales and gun ownership, to prevent any more of these sadly too frequent childhood slaughters? There is occasionally evil and insanity, even among children, everywhere. But what sort of family values turn a blind eye to the access that minors have to weapons in America? Worse still, what family code raises its voice against doing anything serious and effective to prevent further teenage atrocities? What would we be told by the right-to-lifers who worked through the night to 'save' Terri Schiavo about the incontinent use of firearms? The usual argument is that it is not the guns that are the problem, it is the people who use them. Extend the argument. It is not the crack cocaine that is the problem, it is the people who use it. It is not the missiles that are the problem, it is the North Koreans who may fire them. Sometimes you extend an argument to absurd lengths to demonstrate its inherent weakness and folly. But this argument begins stupid and ends in small coffins. As it happens, I have always voted in favour of more legal restrictions on abortion and against capital punishment. I think there is some consistency between the positions. But I deplore excessive political interference in right-to-life issues, especially when it is so hypocritical.

Let me reprise my positions as a conservative European. I am a fiscally conservative, free-market believing, family-supporting internationalist, who thinks as a Catholic that my Church goes too far in what it preaches on the family and sexuality. Reading the 2004 study of American conservatism by John Micklethwait and Adrian Wooldridge, *The Right Nation: Why America is Different*, I think that I have found someone with whom I could sympathize. He supported civil rights, a higher minimum wage and larger immigration quotas. He favoured higher tax when necessary to pay for education and for the nation's science and defence bills. He was a member of Planned Parenthood and a friend of Estelle Griswold, whose legal challenges helped to enshrine the right of sexual privacy in American law. He co-sponsored the bill that set up the Peace Corps. He hated McCarthyites and scorned partisanship. According to the authors, 'his hostility to the radical right was as much aesthetic as intellectual'. His name was Senator Prescott Bush, the present president's grandfather.

Micklethwait and Wooldridge argue that his sort of conservatism is now only for students of history. The new right, they argue, is the new establishment, whose rise (to paraphrase Tocqueville) has been 'so inevitable, and yet so completely unforeseen'. Perhaps they are correct, although a country's centre of gravity shifts from time to time, and I am more persuaded by those who argue that President Bush was re-elected as a war president than by those who contend that he succeeded principally because he articulates the new Conservative values of a growing majority. Yet certainly for the moment, it looks as though the divisions in attitude between Europe and America may grow, or that, at the very least, they will not dissolve, and that previous assumptions of unity across the Atlantic may come to appear as the unnatural consequences of the Cold War. One of the main criticisms of this thesis of a swelling conservative majority comes from those who argue that because of immigration, America will become more Hispanic and Asian over the coming years. But this should not bring too much comfort to Europeans looking for evidence of shared values. The main source of immigration to America in the past has been Europe. Even as late as the 1950s more than two-thirds of those admitted for settlement to America came from Europe and Canada. By the 1990s, fewer than one in five of new immigrants set out from Europe, almost half were from Latin America and one in five from Asia. It has been estimated that by the middle of the century half the total American population will be Hispanic. Who can tell what the consequences will be for American attitudes and values?

That America is in many respects so different from Europe is a proposition more likely to be opposed than the statement that the country is a mighty superpower economically, culturally and militarily. As an economic powerhouse, America is little bigger than Europe – each economy represents about 30 per cent of world GDP, with Europe exporting rather more. What is striking is that whatever the cultural and attitudinal differences, the economic ties are intimate and growing, and appear to survive unscathed despite occasional political turbulence. The figures assembled by Dan Hamilton and Joseph Quinlan, in *Partners in Prosperity* for the Center for Transatlantic Relations at Johns Hopkins University, are compelling. Despite the North America Free Trade Agreement (NAFTA), the rise of Asia and emerging markets elsewhere, the US and Europe remain by a long way each other's most important commercial partners. The transatlantic economy generates roughly $2.5 trillion in total commercial sales each year. Most American and European investments flow to each other rather than to lower-wage developing nations. Despite all the rows over Iraq in 2003, corporate America invested nearly $87 billion in Europe in that year, with $7 billion in Germany, and $2.3 billion in France, a 10 per cent increase on the previous year. (This was the year of the American car bumper stickers proclaming 'Iraq Now, France Next'.) American investments in the Netherlands in that year were almost as great as in the whole of Asia. Over the past decade US firms have put ten times as much capital into the Netherlands as into China, and twice as much as into Mexico. Total European investment in the US exceeds $1 trillion, this accounts for nearly three-quarters of all foreign investment in America. American companies make half their annual foreign profits in Europe, and many European multinationals regard America as their most important market. It would take an awful lot of uneaten French fries and boycotted bottles of Pomerol to equal the value of the growth each year in European sales to the American market.

There are, periodically, suggestions that we should try to stimulate further transatlantic economic integration by working to create a free trade area around our ocean. This would be a vast political undertaking, and I have doubts about how much it would accomplish and how long it would take to achieve results. Most of the barriers to even greater trade and investment across the Atlantic are not old-fashioned tariffs but complex issues of harmonizing our financial and other regulations. Negotiating improvements here would be a marathon, with twenty-five countries on one side and America's quasi-independent regulatory agencies on the other, buffeted as they are by protectionist industrial lobbying. It will, for example, take a painfully long time to negotiate an open skies agreement between America and Europe that would bring so many benefits to air passengers. Security concerns add a troublesome dimension. As a European commissioner I shared responsibility with my Dutch colleague, Fritz Bolkestein, for negotiating with the Americans on their right to have access to the details of passengers travelling to the United States. American concerns were wholly understandable; the way they went about expressing them was rather less so. With Bolkestein I had a wretchedly complicated job trying to squeeze concessions on their original impossible conditions out of Americans, and then sell the same concessions to the European Parliament. The Americans thought the two of us were unreasonable; the Parliament thought we were Washington's patsies.

American officials have a tendency to declare their policy and negotiate about it afterwards, having created all sorts of problems for their partner, in this case over our data protection legislation. I guess this is the sort of behaviour that you expect from a superpower. But is it imperial? Are we all dealing today, like it or lump it, with the new Rome to whom as outlying feudatories we must pay homage and our dues. America's military might, and the way it is deployed, provide the evidence that some seek in order to make this charge. America spends on defence more than Europe, Russia and China combined – indeed, probably as much as the rest of the world put together. Through the last decade defence spending has amounted to about 4 per cent of America's GDP. America could knock over any government in the world if it wanted to do so. It has the technology to destroy with greater precision than a military machine has ever had before, though as many Iraqi and Afghan casualties testify the precision is far from perfect. It can spy on us all, friend or foe, its satellites reporting back what we say and photographing everything we do, though there is here a second caveat. As both Colin Powell and the UN Security Council retrospectively discovered after the Iraq war, the interpretation of photographic evidence can sometimes mislead. Like a Shakespearean monarch giving orders to his baronial followers – Essex to Warwick, Pembroke to Carlisle – an American president can say 'Go' and his tanks and guns will be embarked on carriers or be deployed from aeroplanes and helicopters to whatever land he wishes, however inhospitable the terrain. America's military might is truly awesome and its field commanders – the C-in-Cs responsible for all this coiled and sometimes deployed power – travel the world like the proconsuls of old. With their own planes, diplomatic advisers, technology, telecommunications and legions, they are more potent by far than any ambassador or assistant secretary from the State Department.

So this may look like an empire – an 'unofficial' empire as I said at the outset – but is it a *real* empire? The existence of so much military power on its own does not make it so. In any event, as Professor Joseph Nye has argued, the US defence burden in the 1990s was lighter than it had been in the 1950s. While the American economy has grown, military spending has declined steeply in relative terms from an average of 10 per cent of GDP in that earlier period to 4 per cent today. Past empires spent much higher proportions of their wealth on military power than the United States. Nor is there much sign of an imperial impulse to take up 'The White Man's Burden', to use the racist title of Rudyard Kipling's poem, written in 1899. In his excellent biography of Kipling, *The Long Recessional*, David Gilmour notes that it was addressed to the American people, exhorting them to annex the Philippines. He writes:

The message to the Americans was close to the justification Kipling habitually gave for British rule in India. After the rulers have taken possession, they remain to toil and to serve, to prevent famine and to cure sickness, to dedicate their lives and even to die for the sake of the 'new-caught, sullen peoples'. It is literally a thankless task: no pomp, no material reward, 'no tawdry rule of kings' – just the blame and hate of the people 'ye better'.

This was, indeed, the best justification for nineteenth-century imperialism, but to their credit it never had much appeal for Americans in the twentieth century, and I cannot imagine many Americans choosing this path of duty, sacrifice and dominion today. American universities do not train an imperial caste; Americans do not on the whole seek territory – though they are concerned about military bases and secure oil supplies. They import people rather than export them – most Americans resident abroad are in rich countries making or saving their money, not settling and seeking to govern or exploit poor nations. The historian Niall Ferguson, who would rather like the Americans to take on the role of a liberal empire, notes that even American officials would prefer to stay at home rather than go off somewhere abroad to learn Arabic. He quotes one CIA case officer: 'Operations that include diarrhoea as a way of life don't happen.' There are too few Alden Pyles to run a real empire, something I have heard bemoaned by a few Europeans. I recall sitting one glorious July evening in the open air at a dinner at Stanford's North Californian campus, listening to the once very left-wing, now very right-wing, British polemicist, Paul Johnson, lecturing the assembled rather conservative throng on the need for them to take on the burdens of empire. Again, in Kipling's words, the injunction to Americans was:

> Go bind your sons to exile
> To serve your captives' need;
> To wait in heavy harness,
> On fluttered folk and wild . . .

Generously, he offered that Britain would be there alongside, 'searching [our] manhood/Through all the thankless years'. The audience, polite if puzzled, heard him out, got into their Cadillacs and Mercedes and drove back to their homes in Palo Alto to prepare for another busy and profitable day at the office. Americans are not by nature imperialists: hallelujah!

There have, as I noted earlier, been lapses. The Spanish-American war of 1898 was one such. 'The taste of Empire is in the mouth of the people,' wrote *The Washington Post*, 'even as the taste of blood in the jungle.' Albert Beveridge, soon to be Senator from Indiana, proclaimed the Americans 'a conquering race . . . we must obey our blood and occupy new markets and if necessary new lands', taking them from 'debased civilizations and decaying races'. He poured scorn on anti-imperialist arguments: 'Cuba not contiguous? Porto Rico not contiguous? Hawaii and the Philippines not contiguous? [We shall] *make* them contiguous . . . and American speed, American guns, American heart and brain and nerve will keep them contiguous forever!' Mark Twain was called a traitor for opposing this. 'Shall we go on,' he asked, 'conferring our Civilization upon the peoples that sit in darkness, or shall we give those poor things a rest? Shall we bang right ahead in our old-time, loud, pious way, and commit the new century to the game; or shall we sober up and sit down and think it out first?'

For much of the twentieth century, America seemed to heed Mark Twain. Her greatness was measured not in territorial acquisition or in military or political domination, but in her exemplification of the benefits of liberal democracy, human rights, individual free- dom and material progress. But is that how things are still seen around the world today? Even if American attitudes have not changed fundamentally, even if America has not explicitly set its sights on donning the imperial mantle, has the longevity of American predomi- nance and the way it is today expressed symbolically, diplomatically, politically and militarily shifted sentiment decisively against American leadership?

I noted at the beginning of this chapter that transatlantic rows are not new. There were disagreements over America's growing commitment in Vietnam in the 1960s and the associated radicalization of a genera- tion that detested American militarism. There was the removal of NATO from France and of France from NATO. Then came Henry Kissinger's 'Year of Europe' in 1974, when both sides of the Atlantic were reeling from the after-effects of the oil shock and looking for a better way to understand each other's decisions. So concerned were Europe's foreign ministers that they held an emergency and informal meeting at a German castle called Gymnich, which has given its name to the now regular, informal meetings that these ministers still hold twice a year. Five years later, Helmut Schmidt set off years of demon- strations with his brave decision to allow the United States to station a new generation of nuclear weapons – medium-range cruise and Pershing missiles – on German soil. When President Reagan spoke to the Bundestag in 1982, 400,000 protestors took to the streets. Has anything really changed? Have we not merely witnessed a spasm of rage before, during and since the Iraq war – in Europe and beyond – much like the occasional brouhahas of earlier years?

I am not sure that it is as simple as that. Even before the Iraq campaign, surveys of international opinion – for example, those carried out by the excellent Pew Research Center – showed growing disenchantment with America. Its image has been on the skids, even in countries like Britain, Poland and Turkey, whose populations had previously taken extremely favourable views of the United States. As the *Financial Times* reported in discussing a 2003 Pew survey: 'Views of America are becoming more contradictory and ambivalent: some remain positive but ... uneasiness or outright hostility to America's position as sole superpower and global hegemon is creating more negative perceptions.' The newspaper went on to argue that these were rubbing off on the market attractions of some of the most popular American consumer brands. Maybe the professional skills of President Bush's former spokesperson Karen Hughes, who has been drafted into the State Department to overhaul and improve its public diplomacy, will transform attitudes to and impressions of America.

The problem is in part the cumulative aggregation of images. Even for a senior foreign official dealing with the US administration, you are aware of your role as a tributary: however courteous your hosts, you come as a subordinate bearing goodwill and hoping to depart with a blessing on your endeavours. Some of this may be the result of security, to some extent understandable, though it is a pity that these necessary controls (not only in the US) seem so frequently to be in the hands of men and women who have suffered a charm and initiative bypass. In the interests of that humble leadership to which President Bush rightly aspires, it would be useful for some of his aides to try to get in to their own offices for a meeting with themselves some time! Attending any conference abroad, American Cabinet officers arrive with the sort of entourage that would have done Darius proud. Hotels are commandeered; cities are brought to a halt; innocent bystanders are barged into corners by thick-necked men with bits of plastic hanging out of their ears. It is not a spectacle that wins hearts and minds. The avoidance of calamity cannot surely demand such public relations fiascos. The *Newsweek* columnist Fareed Zakaria noted, shortly after the war on Iraq: 'Having travelled around the world and met with senior government officials in dozens of countries over the past year, I can report that with the exception of Britain and Israel, every country the administration has dealt with feels humiliated by us.' Ms Hughes – more power to her elbow – might spare a moment or two to look at what the impact of American hegemony feels like close up.

How much is President Bush himself the problem? It is true that his is a brand that does not travel well. From Dayton to Delhi, President Clinton could make himself loved with behaviour, words and body language so accurately described by Joe Klein in his novel *Primary Colors* and in his book on the Clinton presidency, *The Natural*. No one could say that Bill Clinton's appeal outside America was because he did not seem American. He is a man of his place and his times, more gifted than anyone I have met in politics at moving a conversation seamlessly from interesting anecdote to principle to policy wonkery. First he would tell you a story about a village he had visited in India where someone had just acquired a computer; then he would muse on the extent to which technological progress could easily increase the divide between rich countries and poor; finally, there would be some credible scheme for bridging this divide. He talked and talked until he felt he could do no more to make himself loved by everyone in the room. His charm lasered in on everyone in his company. Until he thought that he had won you over, or could do nothing else to accomplish this objective, a meeting with him would run on and on. He was a scheduler's nightmare. I have met some people in politics whose choice of career has surprised me: they clearly do not like people very much. But there was no questioning why Bill Clinton was a politician: he loved us all to bits, all God's children. Big, beefy, brainy – he could not get enough of people.

Whatever may be the personal skills with which President Clinton woos and wows non-Americans, it is plainly the case that his successor has much more difficulty charming Europeans, and others. In some ways this is not very fair. In person, he comes over as a likeable man, friendly, courteous, direct. The head slightly on one side, he draws you with a smile and a kind word into his circle for a moment or two, deploying the magnetic force that comes with being the world's Number One. The last time I met him, in Ireland in the summer of 2004, he greeted me with a cheery, 'Dad says to say "Hi".' Oh yes?

But the effort was more natural than calculating. The President's walk is the most curious thing about him: the arms swing loose from the shoulder; the wrists face forwards. Is this the way my physiotherapist wants me to rearrange my shoulder-slumping posture?

It may not be the man himself who rubs Europeans up the wrong way, but the reputation with which he arrived in office and the policies he has pursued there. President Bush came in with the reputation of a dim cowboy at best intellectually lazy, given to tripping over even the simplest words in the language that he spoke in his odd jerky drawl. Much of this was patronizing and wrong. It was not as if, when he came to Sweden for his first summit with Europe's leaders in 2001, he was sitting down at the table with a group of philosopher kings, though one or two of them clearly saw themselves as such in his company. When we had our first restricted session with him – half a dozen on each side – he seemed well briefed, articulate, amusing and comfortable to delegate issues to his colleagues. He had no need to show that he was the boss – he obviously was. At subsequent meetings, I never found myself disliking the man, however much I disagreed with what he was saying. It is usually easier in politics if you dislike the person as well as the words, so I guess I feel more comfortable with Vice President Cheney.

My surprise at observing Bush the Younger was how little he could be described as a chip off the old block. His father was more East Coast, more low key, even as president somehow less noticeable. I remember a reception at Buckingham Palace in 1991 when Britain was chairing the G7. We were milling about, sipping warm champagne, when I heard a tall gentleman with an American accent behind me responding to the pleas from the lady next to him about the state of the National Health Service. 'I'm so sorry, Ma'am, but I can't help you. My name is George Bush, I'm President of the United States.' No one would have made that sort of mistake with his Texan son. But perhaps, anyway, the father and the son were distanced by the younger president's experiences – from hell-raising, money-losing and booze to born-again Christianity. When Bob Woodward asked President Bush the Younger whether he consulted his father on the Iraq war, he replied, 'He is the wrong father to appeal to in terms of strength. There is a higher power I appeal to.' It does sound a bit unsettling to a European. 'We don't do God,' Mr Blair's media Rottweiler, Alastair Campbell, told a journalist who sought to lead a not wholly reluctant prime minister down the aisle. But the fact that Europeans 'don't do God' is not a reason for heaping ridicule on a politician who does.

Style is not at all the issue with Bush's vice president. Mr Cheney does not do style. He is two fingers to style. He is what and who he is, and sees no reason to disguise it or pretend to be anything else. If he was not averse to even the most distant reflections of transparency, this 'I don't give a damn what you all think of me' attitude might command a certain reluctant admiration. As it is, he is an implacable presence – conservative if not reactionary – low tax for the very rich, make as much of it as you can, aggressively nationalist, conspiratorial, the patron of the Washington branch of the Likud party. I too am a conservative, but feel that Mr Cheney's conservatism is cut from timber from a very different part of the forest.

Behind all these matters of touch, feel, impression and image lies a far more substantive question. Henry Kissinger drew attention to America's awesome power in a book published in 2001, *Does America need a Foreign Policy?* He wrote: 'At the dawn of the new millennium, the United States is enjoying a pre-eminence unrivalled by even the greatest empires of the past. From weaponry to entrepreneurship, from science to technology, from higher education to popular culture, America exercises an unparalleled ascendancy around the globe.' But that, he concedes, is not enough. It does indeed create its own set of problems. You can be almost too powerful, or be seen to be too powerful, for your own good. His sentiment was foreshadowed by Edmund Burke who, near the height of Britain's imperial pomp, had commented:

I dread our own power and our own ambition: I dread our being too much dreaded . . . We may say that we shall not abuse this astonishing and hitherto unheard of power. But every other nation will think we shall abuse it. It is impossible but that, sooner or later, this state of things must produce a combination against us which may end in our ruin.

Dr Kissinger the historian knows this as well as anyone, and indeed in the dying sentences of the book from which I have already quoted, he notes that the challenge facing the United States is 'to transform power into consensus so that the international order is based on agreement rather than reluctant acquiescence'. It is not an impossible trick to take. For so long the world's verdict was that America stood for very much that was good. It had given the rest of us the post-war international order. It was plainly a land of opportunity and individual freedom. The real source of its greatness was not its unrivalled power, but the fact that the world bought into its dream, recognized its intellectual and scientific supremacy, and acknowledged the strength of its economic and political model. How on earth can America regain that global image? How can it rebuild international order based on agreement, and how can Europe help?

9

Invincible but Vulnerable

*At some point we may be the only ones left. That's okay with
me. We are America.*

President George W. Bush, 2002

In Europe we spent the first months of the Bush administration trying
to get a fix on the new team. We had known more or less where
we stood with the Clinton administration. They were familiar faces,
pursuing familiar policies, embroiling us from time to time in familiar
rows. They were heavily involved in the Middle East. They were
pursuing a strategy of tough engagement with North Korea. Following
initial hesitation, they had settled for a cooperative policy with China.
After India went nuclear, they had slowly rebuilt a relationship with
Delhi. They worked closely with us in the Balkans. They seemed to
understand what we were becoming in Europe. They argued with
us on trade but seemed to share our sentiments on development
assistance. They disagreed with us on the outcome of a variety of
multilateral negotiations – for example, banning landmines, and
binding the international community to act in combating climate
change – but differences of opinion rarely degenerated into sterile
slanging matches. Madeleine Albright was regularly on the telephone
inducing us to deliver what we had promised and complimenting
us when we did. When you went to see her or Sandy Berger, the
National Security Advisor at the White House, you had the impression
that they were genuinely interested in what you had to say. I remember
a visit that Albright and I paid to Bosnia, during which we agreed on

a timetable for the changes that local politicians needed to make. We met political leaders in Sarajevo together and took turns to bang the table. The French made a mild and silly fuss about it in Brussels. What was all this hobnobbing with the Americans? In the Commission, we took no notice.

Not everything in those days was sweetness and light in our relations with Washington. There had been serious quarrels, for example, about the conduct of the war in Kosovo, and we might recall Ambassador Seitz's feeling at an even earlier stage that the two Atlantic partners were slowly drifting apart. But no one then was talking about marital breakdown; the focus – when our relationship was discussed at all – was on mediation or counselling.

Whatever else we anticipated from the Bush presidency, we certainly did not expect that everything would continue as before. There were rumours that the acronym chosen to describe policy was ABC – Anything But Clinton. Yet any changes that might be taking place (and I will come shortly to three of them) were delivered to us gift-wrapped by a new Secretary of State, who initially calmed incipient anxiety just as later on he aroused puzzled sympathy. Colin Powell is a marvellously reassuring figure, knowledgeable, articulate and charming. It is, I imagine, a coincidence that the three public officials I have met who best combine natural grace and authority are all black: Nelson Mandela, Kofi Annan and Colin Powell. Powell was as calming an influence on Europeans as other members of the administration and some of its hangers-on were irritants. If America wanted to look like Gary Cooper in *High Noon*, send in Colin Powell; if it wanted to appear like Charles Bronson in *Death Wish*, then deploy the public talents of Vice-President Cheney, Donald Rumsfeld or one of the neocons like Richard Perle. I had personal reason to be grateful to Powell. Once or twice when I expressed concerns about the drift of American policy – on, for example, the 'Axis of Evil' speech and Guantánamo Bay – his public responses were pretty friendly and gentle by the standards that were to become all too common. On a trip to Washington on one occasion, I was outraged by two columns in *The Post* denouncing Europeans as anti-Semites, and suggesting that, having failed to complete the 'Final Solution' in Europe, we were now trying to make good that failure by promoting it in the

Middle East. I wrote an angry rebuttal, denouncing anti-Semitism but distinguishing between that hateful prejudice and criticism of the policies of Mr Sharon and the Likud Party. A couple of days later, in Madrid for a meeting, I had a call on my mobile from Washington. It was Colin Powell to congratulate me on the article.

The three policies that made us a little nervous were first, the Middle East; second, the Korean Peninsula; and third, the abrogation of the 1972 Anti-Ballistic Missiles (ABM) Treaty, which had sought to forestall the development of long-range nuclear missiles through limiting the defensive systems against them. The Bush team was plainly not minded to continue the Clinton level of engagement with Israel and Palestine. The reason given was simple. Clinton had tried so hard at Camp David and Taba (2000–01). Because of Yasser Arafat he had failed. It had been a humiliating rebuff and even Clinton himself could not have gone on like that. Progress was extremely unlikely so long as Arafat was in business. So the Bush team stood aside, the politics drifted and the violence grew.

On Korea, even before North Korean breaches of past promises on nuclear weapons became public, President Bush appeared to turn his back on the reconciliation policy pursued by the government in Seoul. Colin Powell had initially endorsed it. Hence, the surreal visit we paid to Pyongyang. On the ABM Treaty, the Americans made it clear that this was a matter between them and the Russians; and if the Russians could be pushed into accepting what was in effect a *fait accompli*, then there was no place for the rest of us to grumble around the table. The ABM Treaty had to go so that America could resurrect the Star Wars defensive shield so beloved of President Reagan and many defence industry manufacturers. With Anna Lindh, Sweden's foreign minister, boldly in the lead, we raised the issue at a meeting with Dr Condoleezza Rice, then the National Security Advisor at the White House, in her cramped office. We got a sharp dressing-down. It was not for us to question America's identification of threats to her security and her assessment of the best way of tackling them. If Washington perceived a security threat then the administration would be derelict in its duty if it did not deal with it. The ABM Treaty was scrapped; Star Wars tests were conducted, without providing much positive evidence of the effectiveness of the system; tragically, a few months later America was attacked with less sophisticated technology but with devastating effect.

There was one issue, above all, that went well beyond the usual foreign policy agenda. This issue really turned off European opinion and underlined that things had changed. It was President Bush's brutally direct rubbishing in 2001 of the 1997 Kyoto Protocol on global warming. We were not stupid. We knew that any American administration would have great difficulty getting binding commitments to the reduction of greenhouse gas emissions through Congress. But the President's rejection of the treaty – he said it was 'flawed' and 'unrealistic' – went well beyond a statement of the prevailing political reality in Washington. It was like the Pope denouncing Galileo. This is Washington here, ex cathedra, and we tell you that the sun goes around the earth. World, get stuffed. Even Colin Powell could not sell this one, try though he might and indeed always did, rarely allowing even a hint of body language to indicate disagreement with the ill-judged orders he often had to follow.

As the months passed, a political grouping with members both inside the administration and among the ranks of its cheerleaders outside began to make itself and its opinions increasingly well known. The assault on America in September 2001 gave these ideologues greater prominence and their ideas more resonance. They were the so-called neoconservatives, who gave a spurious intellectual dressing to the muscular assertive nationalism that guided Washington's policy in the wake of al-Qaeda's murderous assault. I am not convinced that it makes much sense in practice to attempt an elaborate dissection of the differences between, say, Mr Rumsfeld and his former deputy, Mr Wolfowitz. While the example I give is a world away from their own positions, perhaps there is the same sort of distinction as exists between a Marxist–Leninist who has a system in which he believes and which explains everything, and a Stalinist who simply wishes to exercise power without constraint. Neoconservatives certainly possess a body of received opinion and an unhealthy enthusiasm for conspiracy, which betrays perhaps how many of them have journeyed from the far left to their present political home. Assertive nationalists, on the other hand, simply want to do whatever they believe to be in

America's immediate interest, with no hand-wringing appeal to allies or debate with Nervous Nellies and Doubting Thomases.

The one thing that neoconservative does not mean is conservative. As is often the case, 'neo' means not 'new' but simply 'not'. Neo-liberals are not usually liberals; neo-intellectuals rarely open books; neoconservatives are definitely not conservatives. After all, conservatives want to conserve things, especially if they are working pretty well, recognizing with the Sicilian prince in Lampedusa's great novel, *The Leopard*, that things must occasionally change in order to stay the same. But a world made by America, largely in America's image, in which America has done so well, is not (in the neoconservative opinion) to be preserved, with change coming only where necessary to maintain order and stability. The present world order must not merely be changed. It must be overthrown, overturned, with Afghanistan and Iraq becoming the Normandy beaches in the next World War. What is required in this neo-world is permanent revolution, or at least permanent war. This is Mao, not Madison. A prominent neoconservative, Max Boot, told readers of *The Wall Street Journal* that he looked forward to 'a new era where America, like the British Empire, will always be fighting some war, somewhere, against someone'.

Many of the neoconservatives cut their teeth thirty years ago with the late Senator 'Scoop' Jackson of Washington State; socially a liberal, and a strong environmentalist, Jackson opposed détente with the Soviet Union and supported the Vietnam War. He championed Soviet Jewry and gave strong backing to Israel's policies in the Middle East. Some of these acolytes went on to serve in the first President Bush's administration, but thought too many of its policies, particularly the failure to topple Saddam Hussein, anaemic and deficient in chutzpah. They strongly supported Benjamin Netanyahu and the Likud Party in the 1990s, opposed the Oslo confidence-building process in the Middle East, and pressed President Clinton to return to the first President Bush's unfinished business in Iraq. For them, the events of 11 September 2001 provided a justification for war on Iraq. For all the relevance this had to stamping hard on al-Qaeda, it could presumably just as well have been war on Egypt, Saudi Arabia or Syria.

It is a characteristic of neoconservatives that the world is divided into good and evil; the faithful judge political character according to the willingness to use force and believe that the main factor in determining the relationship between one nation and another is military power. Islam is seen as a threat to America's interests and in many of its guises plainly belongs to the Manichaean dark regions. Israel and its history appear to be seen literally through the chapters of the Old Testament books of Joshua and Judges, where Jericho and Ai are torched – the latter 'an heap for ever, even a desolation unto this day', where the enemy kings of the Amorites are hanged from five trees, where the children of Israel are delivered into the hands of the Philistines for forty years, and the blind Samson takes revenge for his two eyes as he pulls down the pillars and buries his enemies in the rubble. I find this biblical approach to politics as chilling as is occasionally the case with the use of the Old Testament on war memorials. There is a plaque at Hyde Park Corner in London commemorating the role of the Machine Gun Corps in the First World War. It reads 'Saul has slain his thousands, and David his ten thousands', a biblical tribute to the technology of mass killing. Fire and sword, shock and awe: this is the world of the neoconservatives, dangerous to us all because in Edmund Burke's famous phrase 'a great empire and little minds go ill together'.

Yet as I have argued, the world against which American neoconservatives and nationalists rail and roar was largely made by their own countrymen. The draper from Missouri, President Truman, with the help of an extraordinary generation of public servants, used the might of America to remake the world in the spirit of Woodrow Wilson's dream after the First World War. The undertaking in the 1940s was extraordinary. Dean Acheson later wrote:

The enormity of the task . . . only slowly revealed itself. As it did so, it began to appear just a bit less formidable than that described in the first chapter of Genesis. That was to create a world out of chaos; ours, to create half a world, a free half, out of the same material without blowing the whole to bits in the process.

President Truman, Secretary of State Marshall, and their colleagues created the institutions of global governance – political and economic – that shaped and arbitrated our times. They actively promoted the winding up of Europe's empires through self-determination. They created the military alliance that contained the last 'evil' empire – Russia's colonization of central and eastern Europe. They encouraged the opening of markets and invested hugely to help put continents back on their feet. The formula worked in Europe and it worked in East Asia.

This is the world in which I grew up. It was not a time when everything went right. Vietnam demonstrated the limits of rationalism and metaphor in the conduct of foreign affairs – a point to remember whenever dominoes are called in evidence in discussing some alleged security imperative. We also discovered in the jungles and paddyfields of south-east Asia that technology and wealth are insufficient to fight and defeat an idea. In addition, our tendency throughout the Cold War to divide the world between good countries that supported us and bad ones that flirted with the Soviet bloc, distorted policy, often laid up problems for the future, and from time to time corrupted values. You could be very bad indeed but provided you were on our side – taking our money, our weapons and our whip – your sins would be forgiven.

Yet overall, the American post-war settlement was a spectacular triumph. By the century's end, America's President was able to claim, and did so regularly, that for the first time in history more people lived in democracies than in tyrannies. Moreover, in fifty years we saw a six-fold increase in world output accompanied by a twenty-fold increase in trade in goods; we were producing the same amount of goods and services every three years that it had taken the whole of the previous century to produce. Pax Americana was good for the world.

You can pick up the threads of America's strategy in the speeches of George Marshall, not least his famous Harvard Commencement address in 1947, which announced his aid plan for Europe. Marshall argued at Harvard:

Our policy is directed not against any country or doctrine but against hunger, poverty, desperation and chaos. Its purpose should be the revival of a working economy in the world so as to permit the emergence of political and social conditions in which free institutions can exist.

Elsewhere he took this point further. On a visit to Oslo in 1953 to accept the Nobel Peace Prize, he said:

Democratic principles 'do not flourish on empty stomachs . . . people turn to false promises of dictators because they are hopeless and anything promises something better than the miserable existence that they endure.

All of which convinced this soldier and statesman that he should vigorously oppose – again in his words – 'the tragic misunderstanding that a security policy is a war policy'. It was on the basis of this philosophy that America helped to create a world richer and more stable than any would have imagined possible at the outset of the enterprise. But however fabulous American power, she still had to work with others, by and large legitimizing her leadership through her acceptance of the rules that she more than any other had created. Another soldier turned politician, President Dwight Eisenhower, made the point in the same year, in his 'Chance for Peace' speech: 'No nation's security and well-being can be lastingly achieved in isolation but only in effective cooperation with fellow-nations.'

The world has changed, partly because of some of our successes. But there is never a moment when the task of keeping the peace is finished, when liberal democracy is secured for ever. The first volume of Karl Popper's thrilling defence of the open society, written during the Second World War, ends with a reminder that we have to go on carrying our cross, fighting for humaneness, reason and responsibility, planning for both security and freedom. The struggle never ends. The beginning of a new century has brought new dangers, though not in my judgement a better way of tackling them than the cooperative, consensus-building, example-rich approach we have taken over most of the last sixty years, with America in the lead.

The first group of threats that confronts us today emerges from, and survives among, the detritus of empires from the Balkans to the Gulf, to much of Africa, to the central Asian republics, to Kashmir, and even in a sense to the Korean peninsula. We have to add to these other flashpoints, like Taiwan, that have been left behind as history has rolled forwards. In several of these cases, the prevention of conflict is made both more necessary and more difficult by the weaknesses in the international agreements we have negotiated to prevent the manufacture and proliferation of nuclear, chemical and biological weapons.

Secondly, on every continent, failed or failing states spawn problems. In the past, developed countries perhaps kidded themselves that they could insulate themselves from the problems of the world. If a country collapsed into penury and civil war, that was sad for its people. We might offer them loans and assistance. We might lecture them about the benefits of open trade, good government and so on. But ultimately it was their problem, if they could not dig themselves out of their hole. Today we see that we cannot wall ourselves off from the misery around us. There is, for a start, the so-called CNN effect. The availability of 24-hour network news makes it harder to inure ourselves to starvation and genocide when we witness it in our homes. But, even if we could, there is the problem that failed states become the breeding ground for terror. Once, our concern was with state-sponsored terrorism. Today we are equally concerned by terrorist-sponsored states of the kind that existed in Afghanistan. A US official rightly remarked, when America's *National Security Strategy* was published in 2002, that the threats in today's world are more often from failing states than from conquering ones.

Then there are three horizontal groups of problems, all in some ways connected. There is the revolt of the alienated, to which I have referred already. Traditional communities and cultures are undermined by urbanization and modern science, which constitute a threat to existing beliefs. Literal interpretations of Genesis are challenged by Darwin; ancestral orthodoxies about gender are confronted by social, economic and political changes; television invades domestic lives where even books were hitherto only rarely seen. Reversion to religious fundamentalism is a very human reaction to what is seen in many societies as the worst of Western culture and values, and as brash imperialism. The issue is not just a question of Islamic fundamentalism. It occurs in other religious traditions. And it exists within cultures as much as between them: just look at the messages spelled out on some of the Christian fundamentalist websites. It is not easy to adapt to new ideas, new science and new influences that challenge traditional authority and received opinion. This resistance to the new and the global does not necessarily turn into a threat. But religious fundamentalism does sometimes find expression in political radicalism and hatred of alien, often Western and specifically American influences. Radicalism may be eminently justified by the brutality, greed and inefficiency of a great many governments in the world. The current, widely prevalent hatred of America is *not* justified. But nor will it be eliminated by dropping bombs on those who hate all things American.

Closely allied to the revolt of the alienated is the revolt of the dispossessed. The simple fact is that much of the world is desperately poor. And with modern communications and the aggressive marketing of Western culture, the poor are now much better informed about how the other half lives. It is hardly surprising that there is widespread hostility to globalization seen as a Western conspiracy designed to benefit primarily the aggressive advocates. I have little doubt that globalization – the combination of technology, capitalism and the opening of markets – has made most people better off. But over a billion have been left behind to subsist on less than a dollar a day. So there is a risk of the case for globalization choking on its own inequities. That argues strongly for more generous flows of development assistance – more generous and better managed. While we should not exaggerate the past failures of development aid, nor delude ourselves about the extent of our generosity (a particular problem in America), we have too often – to borrow from the title of William Easterly's book on the subject – found the quest for growth in poorer countries elusive. How *can* we better convert good intentions and large cheques into less global inequity, especially in some countries where the concept of the nation has carried little force, and where development has had less impact among elites as a governing philosophy than staying in power and amassing wealth?

I was a development minister in the 1980s spending a good deal of time in Africa. I lived for five years in Asia in the 1990s and then began visiting Africa again in the next few years. The comparison was a depressing experience. There is still much poverty in Asia, but there is also rising prosperity, greater stability, and hope. The greatest development problems accumulate in Africa, where in too many countries violence, tyranny and corruption incubate misery and disease.

We have frequently aided and abetted the process of turning bad polities into kleptocracies through ill-directed development assistance, instead of providing the right incentives for recipients. It is all very well hunting for excuses, and admittedly there are plenty – the long-term consequences of colonialism in some cases (though not by any means all); the impact of geography which, while not destiny, can create prodigious natural difficulties in that belt of countries either side of the Equator; unfair global commercial arrangements and inadequate external support. All this explains some of the problems faced by Africa, but we are perhaps too prissy, too nervous about political correctness, in pointing to some equally pertinent reasons for endemic failure – wickedness, greed, murder, bad government, pillage. A great American journalist, Keith Richburg, spent years as *The Washington Post*'s Africa correspondent, in the era of genocide in Rwanda and civil war in Somalia. Richburg is black and wrote a brave book, *Out of America*, about his pride in identifying himself as an American, and his inability to feel a similar sense of identity with what he witnessed in Africa. So for him, the description '*African* American' was not a bit how he felt.

I have too many memories of the horrors of African decline, not least a long visit in 2001 to the shambles of the Democratic Republic of Congo and its neighbouring states, which have spent the last few years robbing the Congo of its natural resources (blood diamonds, for example) and fighting their proxy civil and tribal wars across its vast impoverished spaces. The capital, Kinshasa, is a wreck of a city. The poor Congolese: to have endured (read Conrad) the worst of colonialist exploitation and then the worst of post-colonial misrule. I visited Harare on the same trip, for an awful encounter with President Mugabe whose army, doubtless commanded by some of the best officers that Sandhurst could train, has been the worst of the looters in the Congo. I had visited Mugabe last in the mid-1980s, when he was frequently cited as a model of African magnanimity. No more. He had turned into a crackpot tyrant, with a gang of thuggish cronies who are together ruining their beautiful country. The two-hour discussion with him largely focused on Western mendacity, wicked colonialism, the pleasures of doing business with the wise Margaret Thatcher, and the serpentine behaviour of Mr Blair's allegedly homosexual clique. I am quite sure that neither prime minister would have recognized the picture that he painted.

Mugabe looked and sounded deranged. When Lord Carrington was doing business with him negotiating the relegitimizing of Rhodesia in the early 1980s, he used to muse on the pleasant Lancastrian ring to the pronunciation of his name backwards 'E-ba-gum'. Just over twenty years on, President Mugabe has moved far beyond humour. Yet when he addressed the United Nations General Assembly in 2001 in the wake of explicit evidence of vote-rigging, the use of violence against his opponents and the growing impoverishment and starvation of his people, he was cheered to the rafters by most of the African delegates present. For me, this said all too much about what is wrong with Africa. Until the African Union, and the continent's regional organizations – led by South Africa and Nigeria above all – are prepared to take a tougher line on bad government, corruption and the destruction of democracy, we are not likely to be able to make much difference in tackling the continent's woes even if we spend more money (as we should) on development assistance. Countries can recover from disaster, as Mozambique has recently shown. But without political stability, too many problems fester and deteriorate with results from which we in the West cannot insulate ourselves.

Throughout my years as a European commissioner, we were intermittently involved in efforts to bring peace to Sudan, where one conflict succeeded another. As we witnessed the latest killing in Darfur I had a grisly sense of *déjà vu*. War in that country seemed without end. Back in late 1988, I had made my third visit in a year to Ethiopia, this time to visit the camps on the Nile River plain in the south-west of the country, which were accommodating refugees from the brutal war between the government in Khartoum and the Sudan People's Liberation Army in the south of the country. I had long discussions with some of the younger Sudanese inhabitants in the camps about their experiences. Most of them had similar stories. They had spent three or four months escaping from Sudan, trekking backwards and forwards across the country to get away from marauding gangs of hostile tribesmen or detachments of the Sudanese army. About half of those who started off on the journey actually got through. One group of young boys – led by teenagers about the same age as my older daughters – told me of their long march; seventy began the journey; forty eventually completed the march sustained over three months by a diet of berries, roots and leaves. I asked one of the sixteen-year-old leaders how they had found their way to the Ethiopian border. He replied matter-of-factly that it was very easy; they had simply followed the trail of corpses.

At the end of my visit, I was asked if I would address the school that had been set up for the 12,500 camp children, 60 per cent of whom were, in the euphemism of the aid workers there, 'unaccompanied', by which they meant orphaned. After I had spoken, they asked if they could sing to me. They sang the Lord's Prayer in their language, Dinka, and then a text from Isaiah, which I assumed to be the verses about beating swords into ploughshares. I was wrong. Lying in my bed that night in the British ambassador's comfortable bungalow on the hillside above Addis Ababa, as the old fan whirred above my head, I spotted a Gideon Bible on the table and looked up the reference they had given me. What they had actually been singing under the hammering African sun was a text familiar from carol services at home: 'The people that walked in darkness have seen a great light: they that dwelt in the land of the shadow of death, upon them hath the light shined.' Too many in Africa still dwell in that land of the shadow of death, with little prospect of the light shining on them unless we can combine better government with more generous assistance.

There are other lessons about poverty and development. Compare an earlier period of globalization almost as remarkable in its effects, at the end of the nineteenth and the beginning of the twentieth centuries. The results were memorably described in Keynes's *The Economic Consequences of the Peace* in 1919. In those years, the gates were open to trade in agricultural products as well as in goods, to the movement of people as well as that of money. At the very least, we have to ensure that the international trade talks that began in 2001 in Doha result in fairer rules and greater access to our markets for the things that poor countries produce, especially food. It is indefensible for rich countries to spend almost seven times as much on subsidizing their agriculture as they do on aid.

Finally, there are the problems thrown up by increasing globalization, which require a coordinated international policy response. Globalization offers tremendous opportunities; look today at Asia's advances and the fall in the number of people living in poverty in China and India. But Dr Jekyll is stalked by Mr Hyde. As well as the benefits of modern science, machines and communications, and the prosperity that may be derived from freer trade, there is also the dark side of globalization, from environmental degradation to the drugs trade, from terrorism and the proliferation of weapons to transnational crime and communicable diseases like Aids. What does it require for us to move from an intellectual understanding of these problems to a more determined attempt to turn comprehension into policy and effective agreements? Perhaps the threat of avian flu hanging over Asia and the rest of us will do the educational trick – though only, I fear, when we find ourselves dealing with its dreadful consequences rather than, in the first place, preventing it turning into a pandemic. All these problems should remind us that stability and prosperity – a goal of foreign policy in each separate nation – can only be achieved if nation states act together in pursuit of interests that transcend their boundaries.

Put all the present-day horrors together – failed states, alienation, poverty, the global reach of terrorist violence – and what do you get? One consequence for sure was the atrocity of 11 September 2001, which so shocked America and rather improbably gave the neoconservatives the chance to shape policy in the image of their own fears and dreams. America's horrified surprise at its own vulnerability confirmed neoconservatives in their view that their country should not allow herself to be a buried piece on the global chessboard, a queen hemmed in by pawns. As the pre-eminent world power, America believes it has the strength to insist that it should exercise power unencumbered as far as possible by entanglements of international law or by allies – rather than obedient followers – with ideas of their own. It is not just a question of whether America *can* behave like this. There is a persuasive, sometimes dominant school of thought in America that argues that it *should*. One American sovereigntist, Jeremy Rabkin, has described recognizing that your first duty is to protect your own democracy and the rights of your people as a 'dictate of the law of nature'. Another prominent neoconservative, John Bolton – promoted in 2005 to be US Ambassador to the UN in a gesture that indicated the Bush administration was not without a rather macabre sense of humour – has indicated on a number of occasions how this definition should be seen in practice. For example, at a UN conference in 2001 to discuss controls over the deadly trade in small arms when he was Under Secretary of State for Arms Control and International Security, Mr Bolton asserted frankly, 'The United States will not join consensus on a final document that contains measures abrogating the Constitutional right to bear arms.' Armed thugs in Sierra Leone and Sudan, dependent on the small arms trade for their killing power, could take comfort from the mantle of protection apparently thrown over their activities by the American Constitution.

We should pause here and give due deference to Mr Bolton's role and reputation. Much is made in the description of this unusual diplomat of his moustache, and it is indeed a magnificent creation, a more benign addition to his upper lip than those other more abbreviated moustaches that achieved such notoriety in the twentieth century. With the publicity attendant on Security Council meetings, it will soon be a world star, fêted across continents. But I think if I was concerned about America's public diplomacy, I would be more worried about the words that will issue from the lips beneath. *Cave*, Karen Hughes.

Mr Bolton is the Pavarotti of neoconservatism; his views have taken the roof off chancelleries around the globe. For him there is no *United* Nations, there is only one nation that counts, America. Cooperation is for sissies. Some apologists in Europe for the Bush administration claim that his appointment to the UN did not represent a blow to multilateralism, but was a shrewd way of advancing support in America for a reformed UN, at the same time getting him out of policy-making in Washington. Representing the superpower at the UN is not like hiding your lantern under a bushel. We will assuredly hear more from Mr Bolton. The last time I saw him, I opined that we needed to use sticks and carrots to deal with Iran. 'I don't do carrots,' he replied. No, indeed, but the rest of the world may soon do a good line in raspberries.

For neoconservatives like Mr Bolton, unilateralism is not just a reflection of US power, but a positive virtue. America's hegemony is benevolent, and such is the primacy of American values and institutions that it is no bad thing if others must adapt themselves to US preferences. I can see why that view is so attractive. There is something dismally repellent about philanthropy and international do-goodery divorced from real human relations: well-meaning and well-dressed peripatetic internationalists talking interminably about poverty in a variety of the world's more expensive capitals; the endless fudge; the dreary, unreadable declarations; the maelstrom of self-interested humbug masquerading as high principle. At one such meeting, I happened to be reading Charles Dickens's *Bleak House*, and wondered whether Mrs Jellyby might have slipped unnoticed into the conference hall with her concern about 'cultivating coffee and educating the natives of Borrioboola-Gha on the left bank of the Niger' rather than her own neglected children. Better, surely, than this the honest pursuit of profit and national interest. Did we learn nothing from Adam Smith?

While understanding this point of view, I cannot share it. On the contrary, the instinct to return to a narrow definition of the national interest – to assert the primacy of US concerns, and especially economic interests, over any outside authority – constitutes a threat not just to the developing international order, but to the US itself. As I have argued, for the best part of fifty years, the United States, almost above all other nations, has been internationalist – and a tremendous force for good in the world. Has the system of global governance created after the Second World War now outlived its usefulness? Is conventional multilateralism now outdated because of the imbalance between American power and that of all others? Has technology unleashed forces that overwhelm the borders and conventional governing institutions of nation states, so that traditional modes of cooperation between them inevitably fail? Has the liberal dream of an international community been shown up for a sham by the selfishness of rich and powerful countries ruthlessly focused on the protection and enhancement of their own interests? Answer Yes to all those questions and you are left with a pretty bleak outlook, a Hobbesian world in which capitalist democracy defends its wealth and values from the random violence of the angry and the poor – like the 'gated communities' in rich suburbs. Is that how the world has to be?

It is not obvious to me that the Taliban and Al Qaeda, Palestine and Pyongyang, heroin and Aids, the Pentagon's precision-guided munitions and the spasmodic acceptance of the UN's authority – to name a few salient features of our times – demonstrate that the Truman-Marshall approach no longer works. On the contrary, it seems clear that we need more of it not less. But it is equally clear that unless the United States is prepared to lead a rejuvenation of multilateralism, it is not going to happen. So how do we persuade Washington of this?

First, it is important to recognize that the task is not impossible. Opinion surveys (for example those undertaken by the Chicago Council on Foreign Relations and the German Marshall Fund) demonstrate that many of the views of Main Street America on international affairs have not changed all that much, whatever the mood within the Washington Beltway and whatever the growth in conservative and Christian fundamentalist sentiment. American voters still believe strongly in international cooperation; indeed, large majorities even appear to favour signing the Kyoto Protocol and supporting the International Criminal Court. They also, rather sensibly, believe that America should try to share its global role with Europe, even when Washington sometimes disagrees with European governments. Why should a sensible American citizen want his own country to bear the heaviest burden in order to defend civilized countries against so many threats to their security and well-being?

The biggest doubt is not whether most Americans would like Europe to help carry the world, but whether they think we really will. In Europe, we huff and we puff; how much breath does that leave to do anything serious? We know the nature of the task of advocacy that we have to perform. We need to persuade Americans that the concept of a nation whole unto itself is anachronistic; that the 'national interest' implies *inter*national cooperation and *inter*national obligations; that the things Americans want – jobs, prosperity, peace – can only be secured if the United States works with others; that the problems I identified as the dark side of globalization can only be tackled by unprecedented levels of international cooperation; that the threat or use of military might is not always the only or the right way to keep the world safe. But in order to perform this last task, we in Europe have to be prepared to face the question that force *is* sometimes required to uphold the international rule of law, and be able to provide some of that force ourselves. Overall, to make Americans believe in multilateralism we have to do more to sustain it ourselves.

Neither the task of persuasion, nor the demonstration of increased European capacity to make multilateralism work, will be easy. As we have seen, there is today a much more aggressive strain of nationalism in America's attitude towards the rest of the world. Watch Fox News and get the taste of this piping hot. Explaining the difference between American and international news coverage of the build-up to the war in Iraq, the channel's star, Bill O'Reilly, asserted, 'Well, everywhere else in the world lies.' America can set its own course, ignoring the doubters and the liars, because if it needs to do so, it can destroy any enemy just like that. And this military certainty comes apparelled in moral conviction. Anatol Lieven reminds us in his book *America Right or Wrong*, published in 2005, that the Vice President's wife Lynne Cheney writes in her A to Z 'patriotic primer' for school-children: 'Z is the end of the alphabet, but not of America's story. Strong and free, we will continue to be an inspiration to the world.' I hope this becomes true again. But the book brings rather alarmingly to mind the Victorian alphabet called *Babes of the Empire*, which included this classic quatrain:

> D for the Dervish in sunny Sudan.
> Oh see him perform his eccentric can-can!
> But now he has joined us – the pride of our nation;
> He dances from frenzy to civilisation.

Perhaps no one was listening when Mr Blair, in his fine speech to both houses of Congress in 2003, said (greatly daring), 'All predominant power seems for a time invincible, but, in fact, it is transient.'

The notion of belligerent self-sufficiency infused the Republicans' presidential campaign in 2004. Admittedly, no one expects election campaigns to have much in common with a Socratic dialogue. Hyperbole rules with the assistance of a smidgeon of mendacity. Nevertheless, even by the customary standards, the outpouring of hostility against foreigners and their multilateral entanglements came as a surprise. To suggest the need to consult allies was apparently to advocate the outsourcing of foreign policy to Paris and Berlin. All seemed to take their lead from President Bush himself, who had said in his second State of the Union address in 2003, 'Yet the course of this nation does not depend on the decisions of others.' A successful election campaign behind him, and with his former National Security Advisor, Dr Rice, installed as Secretary of State, the President set out to mend fences with the treacherous Europeans. But was he using real planks and nails? Had there been a conversion, on the flight to Brussels, to the need for allies, who might be expected to have their own opinions and to wish to express them occasionally?

Evidence of a change from neo-conservatism to what was dubbed neo-realism (which presumably means a return to a more traditional diplomacy) was squeezed out of every potentially propitious sign. Mr Wolfowitz went off to be President of the World Bank, an institution in whose activities he had not taken a very obvious interest though he did tell me and a group of colleagues in 2005 that he would be the first President who had lived in a developing country. This was literally true – although being Ambassador in Indonesia is not quite like working on poverty's front line. Mr Bolton had gone north – as noted earlier – to the UN to ply his prejudices there. Others of their political faith had moved on as well. As frequently mentioned as these personnel changes was the decision in February 2005 to drop American opposition to a UN resolution seeking to refer potential war criminals in Sudan to the International Criminal Court, a body whose existence had hitherto been long and noisily opposed by Washington. In addition, a rather higher level of engagement in the Middle East on the part of Dr Rice, an apparent preparedness to work with Europe on Iran, and the American administration's eleventh hour agreement at a conference in Montreal not to bring crashing down negotiations on the future of international efforts to abate global warming and climate change, were given as further welcome signs of a switch. Nudges and nuances, we are assured, are once again back in fashion; partners are encouraged to speak and not just wait to be spoken to; the recent past is in the past. Perhaps all this is bankable, but it would be unwise for Europeans to count our chickens and our blessings too quickly. There is still, in America – in newspaper columns, think tanks, academia, congress and the administration – an intellectual battle to be won. Even the Iraq debacle has not permanently silenced all the sovereigntists and neo-conservatives.

There will be several difficult tests of whether there has been any real and substantive post-election shift. But since a current and perhaps understandable strand in European thinking is that, if we can, we must avoid any impression of damage to or change in the transatlantic relationship, there will be a reluctance to ask any of the questions that may produce the wrong answers. So no one, for example, will raise the issue of one of the central tenets in the Bush administration's national security strategy, namely the new doctrine of pre-emption of threats, which roughly translated into Rumsfeldian means this: since we in Washington don't know a lot of things that we don't know, we should reserve the right (being bigger and more powerful than anyone else) to attack others before we are attacked ourselves. Two of the greatest living historians in Europe and America have given their verdict on this assertion of *droit de grand seigneur*. Sir Michael Howard regards it as 'one of the most important documents in the history of America', which 'seemed to be demolishing the whole structure of international law as it had developed since the seventeenth century'. He could have cited President Eisenhower's view: 'We cannot consider that the armed invasion and occupation of another country are peaceful means or proper means to achieve justice and conformity with international law.' For Arthur Schlesinger, the strategy represented a fundamental shift from a foreign policy based on containment and deterrence through multilateral agencies to hitting your enemy (if necessary on your own) first. As the strategy asserts, 'The best defence is a good offence.' Successive presidents, he has noted, have rejected this approach, which he believes dwells on the very edge of legality. In the most controversial application of this principle in Iraq, Professor Schlesinger argued that the Americans went beyond pre-emption and that President Bush chose to fight a preventive war. In his book *War and the American Presidency*, Schlesinger wrote in 2004: 'The entire case for preventive war rests on the assumption that we have accurate and reliable intelligence about the enemy's intentions and military capability – accurate and reliable enough to send our young men and women to kill and die.' We now know that the information on Iraq – and this is the mildest criticism one can make – was neither accurate nor reliable. So what price prevention, pre-emption and wars of choice today? What is the status of a strategy that reminds us of President Truman's dictum, 'You don't "prevent" anything by war, except peace.'

Our best bet in Europe is probably to act in ways that make it less likely that the strategy of preventive war will be tried out again, and more likely that the United States will return to more familiar, popular and successful ways of dealing with the world and of exercising global leadership. This requires that we should define more clearly what Europe wants to do and can do in international affairs and then narrow the gap between aspiration and delivery. There should be, first, no question of us trying to be another superpower. We cannot be and we should not try. There is presently only one superpower, and it is our task to live alongside it and help it to carry out its responsibilities effectively. Second, there is nothing to be said for Europe in effect assuming a role as unfriendly neutrals, captious critics of what America does but incapable of doing much ourselves to make the world more as we would like it to be. Third, I am not attracted by the idea of aspiring to be America's global adjutant, obedient acolytes who do more or less what we are told, like it or lump it. The sensible role that we should want to play is as a capable partner, respected for our advice and our ability to act on our own when necessary, defining ourselves not in contradistinction to America but as ourselves – allies with minds of our own.

This requires of Europe at least four things. First, we need to make greater progress in developing and upholding common positions on foreign and security policy. The problems in doing this are overwhelm-ingly political rather than institutional. Does Prime Minister Blair want to carry other Europeans with him when seeking to play the part of friend at court in Washington? Does Chancellor Schröder have any clear idea at all of how to develop Germany's role, balancing its Atlanticist sympathies against its traditional role of helping to define and lead the European debate? He always gives the impression that the very short term is for him very long indeed. Does it matter much what Prime Ministers Berlusconi or Balkenende think outside Italy and the Netherlands? Is there any consistency or meaning to President Chirac's practice of French exceptionalism? Even when they are right, the French can be infuriatingly perverse or incomprehensible. Having scolded the Americans for bullying the world, in 2002–03 President Chirac then tried to bully Europe's new member states for having the cheek to disagree with him. There was more than a hint of Napoleon, and more than a wisp of inherited glory, about his biographer, the silky smooth and amiable Dominique de Villepin (then French foreign minister and now prime minister) when he spoke in the UN Security Council against America's Iraq policy. 'France,' he said, 'has always stood upright in the face of history before mankind'. Does this mean anything at all? Obviously it sounds much better in French. It echoes General de Gaulle's words, carved on the pedestal of his statue on the Champs Elysées: 'There exists an immemorial covenant between the grandeur of France and the freedom of the world'. Change the name of the country and an American Republican neocon could not put it any better.

Secondly, Europeans have to do more to shake off the reputation that we are non-paying passengers in America's chariot. We are too inclined to criticize America while depending on her security shield; too prone to advocate multilateralism while knowing that if a multilateral solution requires force nothing much is likely to happen unless America is involved. We are now starting to develop the capacity to act with and even without NATO support in peacekeeping roles; we have done this in the Balkans and in Africa. Whenever there is heavy work to do, as in the air war over Kosovo in 1999, we have to call on American firepower. We should be able to do more for ourselves, and Americans are right to scold us for not having the capacity. Yet when we try to develop it, many of them detect a dagger at the heart of NATO.

It is depressing that most surveys of public opinion suggest that Europeans want their countries to do more together on the world stage, provided it does not cost taxpayers more money. This disingenuous self-deception should be challenged by those political leaders who bang the European drum. France and Britain both spend about the same proportion of their gross domestic product on defence – 2.6 per cent and 2.4 per cent respectively. They are the most serious military powers in the European Union. Italy spends 1.9 per cent, the Netherlands 1.6 per cent, Germany 1.4 per cent and Spain 1.2 per cent. Procurement and research budgets are correspondingly low. The story might not be quite so gloomy if Europeans spent their existing budgets better with improved standardization and interoperability of equipment. We regularly set goals for improving our capabilities, which we subsequently miss. It should not be as bad as this. Even though Europe spends much less than America, we still have in aggregate the second largest defence budget in the world and have on paper 1.5 million troops. On paper. In fact we have difficulty meeting the target of a force of 60,000 for rapid deployment. We require for this purpose three rotations a year; that requires 180,000 troops and the ability to move them a long way at short notice. We can just about manage the deployment, provided we can lease transport aircraft from Ukraine, Russia or America. Plans to construct our own military transport began in 1984 and stretch ahead to 2020 – that's if we are lucky.

There have been other deficiencies, which reflect the fact that we were moderately well prepared to fight a war against a Soviet threat across the central German plain thirty years ago, but rather less capable of dealing with today's security problems. For example, it was evident from our experience in the Balkans that we had not invested enough to protect our communications against modern interception. Serbian and Croatian intelligence were able to monitor our electronic communications during operations in Bosnia in the last few years. To be fair, we have done slightly better at developing the capacity to undertake the sort of civilian jobs that are required during and after military deployments – the provision of police, lawyers, judges, prosecutors, experts in civil administration and civil protection teams. But the overall picture is far from good enough to satisfy inquisitive American friends. Even a modest improvement would enhance our credibility as a partner.

'Military power by itself is never enough to sustain your predominance,' Mr Rumsfeld was told by a panel he set up to consider the global pressures on America's military machine. This brings us to the third task for Europe, to show that we understand the relationship that George Marshall highlighted between security and economic development. We have to do more to reduce poverty, promote sustainable development and build governing institutions in poor countries. I have already noted some of the difficulties here, and also stressed the importance of the work. It is work where the European contribution outstrips the American; we should not crow but, since it is easier to persuade European taxpayers to give more for development assistance than for defence, we should further increase the work we are prepared to do here.

Joseph Roth, who chronicled the last days of the Austro-Hungarian Empire, wrote in one of his short stories: 'Towards the end of the nineteenth century, the people of my native place were of two sorts: they were either very poor or very rich. To put it another way, there were masters and servants.' That empire did not last. Extremes of affluence and poverty threaten today's global stability for similar reasons. The international community is committed to reducing these huge disparities with the target of meeting a series of so-called Millennium Development Goals, set out by the UN in 2000 and endorsed at a conference in Monterey in 2002. The targets include halving the proportion of people whose income is less than one dollar a day between 1990 and 2015, reducing over the same period by two-thirds the mortality rate for children under five, and meeting a host of other objectives in education, health and the environment. To achieve these goals there will need to be a big increase in aid from developed countries, whose performance in this respect worsened through the 1990s. In the late 1980s total development assistance from the rich countries as a percentage of their income was about 0.33 per cent; today it stands at 0.25 per cent. There is still an accepted target that this figure should be increased to 0.7 per cent. A few countries, all of them European (Norway, Denmark, Luxembourg, the Netherlands and Sweden), keep this pledge. To put these percentages into absolute figures, the rich countries have pledged to double the amount they were spending in 2002 to about $100 billion per year in 2010. Another $50 billion per year would be required to meet the goals they have accepted. These figures are not outlandishly high when set against the $900 billion per year that the world spends on armaments, and the figure of more than $300 billion per year that we spend on subsidies to farmers in rich countries.

Europe has set about meeting the targets set for budgetary increases in a way that is far more sensible than in the past, when everyone endorsed the 0.7 per cent figure and then most countries forgot about it. We have agreed that over a succession of target periods those EU member states that spend less than the average percentage of gross national income allocated by the whole of the Union should raise their budgets to at least that figure. Each time that happens, the average will rise, the target will increase, and aid budgets will be ratcheted up towards the UN figure, at least for the better-off, older member states. All of the fifteen older EU member states have now pledged to get to 0.7 per cent by 2015. Europe's performance is not great, but it is getting better.

America's contribution to development has become a fraction larger in recent years starting from a much lower base. Jeffrey Sachs has pointed out that since 2001 defence spending in America has gone up by 1.7 per cent of gross national income, tax resources have declined by 3.3 per cent, and development aid has grown by 0.04 per cent. Surveys suggest that Americans think they give about thirty times more in development aid than is in fact the case. Nor is it true that private giving by Americans makes up for public parsimony. The figures given to make this point erroneously include as development assistance private workers' remittances to their families back home. Despite President Bush's admirable commitment to global programmes for combating Aids, America's contribution to poor countries is at the bottom of the league table published by the Organization for Economic Cooperation and Development: even Italy's miserable 0.17 per cent beats America's 0.15 per cent. The gap between America and the rest of us looks set to continue to grow. That may well be part of the price we pay in Europe for demonstrating that when it comes to meeting broader multilateral targets, we are not paper tigers.

The fourth task for Europe is to do all we can to persuade Americans that the best way of applying what the UN has called 'the glue of common interest', is by working to strengthen that global institution in whose creation the United States played the decisive role. For Europeans to prevail upon Americans to love the UN may be as tough an assignment as for Americans to induce the British to love the European Commission. Both institutions play the role of symbolic bad guy in national debates, partly because of the things they get wrong (exaggerated though these failings may sometimes be), partly because of the way (perhaps inevitably because of the behaviour of their members) they come to personify the gap between human aspiration and all-too-human delivery. A day at the UN does bring into especially sharp focus the lavish dollops of fudge to which I referred earlier in this chapter. But for every hypocrite and scoundrel at the UN, there are dozens of men and women working for it in miserable places around the world, putting their lives on the line and often losing them – more UN civilian workers have been killed in recent years than peacekeeping soldiers. The UN represents what we should want the world to be, and the fact that it falls so far short of the ideal is our fault, not that of the ideal itself and of those who try to serve it.

Scandal and mismanagement eat away at confidence in the institution and we are more merciless about it because it is an international body, staffed by people with diplomatic status, than we would be about the same failures at home in national institutions. While American critics hammered away at the UN's serious mishandling of the oil for food programme in Iraq – much of it the fault of the member states themselves – the surprising and expensive role played by Halliburton in Iraq's redevelopment seemed to pass by equivalent public scrutiny and attack. In the spring of 2005, Kofi Annan put on the table a comprehensive set of proposals for managing the UN better, for restoring some of its moral authority, for improving its effectiveness in dealing with threats like terrorism, for reasserting its functions in legitimizing the use of force in international disputes, for enhancing its ability to build democratic institutions in countries torn apart by strife, for preserving human rights everywhere, and for giving it greater clout in tackling economic, social and environmental dangers. Some of the Secretary-General's ideas, such as the establishment of a Peacebuilding Commission, survived a UN summit in the autumn of 2005; others, for example on non-proliferation, ran into opposition from what police officers might call 'the usual suspects' among whom Ambassador Bolton was prominent. They gave the impression that in their view the UN is inherently unreformable. The UN is only unreformable if we choose not to reform it.

Reform is in the interest of small and weak states. But it is even more in the interest of the large and the powerful, and above all it is in the interest of the US. This is one of the reasons the UN was created in the first place. America needs a strong and credible UN; it needs the UN to do some of the dirty work to prevent conflict and to clear up afterwards, as in East Timor, Kosovo and Afghanistan. It needs the UN to shield its might from the world's resentment and to communicate its purposes to the rest of the world. It does not diminish itself by accepting the UN's authority, something it should and often does want others to do. American power requires an agent of legitimization in order to ensure that America does not lose the authority that has come with its historic commitment to the rule of law. Machiavelli was wrong: it is not better to be feared than loved. It is even worse to be neither feared nor loved.

European governments have to say these things politely but firmly to our American partners. Europe should accept the UN reform proposals and campaign for them aggressively together as one, and singly as twenty-five member states. We should tell the US that we want it to be what it was when it helped rescue Europe from the dark: the world's leader, acting through working institutions of global governance, the world's moral and political exemplar at home and abroad. America can continue to change the world for the better – not simply because of what it can do to other countries, but because of what it can persuade those other countries to become.

IO

Meanwhile, Asia Rises

Two separate reports from *The Wall Street Journal*, Monday
13 June 2005:

1. Kamal Nath, India's Minister of Commerce and Industry –
'China may win the sprint, but India will win the marathon.'

2. Bo Xilai, China's Minister of Commerce – 'Chinese people
have a saying: "If you respect me by an inch, I'll respect you
by a foot." '

Once upon a time the muzak of China, blaring out in railway stations
and from the megaphones on government buildings and street corners,
was the old Communist Party anthem 'The East is Red'. It isn't red
any more. In China, Maoist command economics has given way to
. . . what exactly? Let's call it for the moment 'market Leninism.' And
in the Asian continent's second great land power, India, a gentler,
more benign but not much more successful brand of socialism is
gradually, too gradually, being replaced by more open and liberal
economic management. And the result? The number living in poverty
in both countries plummets; two great countries begin to resume their
place as world leaders; and the rest of the world either ignores what
is happening or ponders nervously the consequences of these transfor-
mations for all our futures.

I have been a more direct witness of events in China, though as
Minister for Overseas Development I visited India frequently in the
1980s because Britain's largest aid programme was there, and I have
seen close up the changes in that country as well. My initial sighting

of China was in 1979. I had gone to Hong Kong during my first summer vacation at Westminster, with a small group of MPs. During our week in the colony (or territory, as it was usually euphemistically called), we were taken up to see the border with China between the main crossing at Lo Wu and the next crossing to the east at Wen Jindu. From police posts, we peered over the barbed wire at the village of Shenzhen, the meadows, the paddy fields and the slow-moving sailing barges on the waterways. This was where several Hong Kong policemen had been killed just over a decade earlier by Red Guards during the Cultural Revolution, whose atrocities spilled over into bombings and violent demonstrations in the colony. But the scene we saw that day in 1979 had the timeless and gentle innocence of the pictures on blue and white porcelain. So this was willow-pattern China, stretching unknown and unknowable back into a history from which it could not break free, and away to the distant mountains, deserts and mighty rivers that criss-cross its vast spaces.

As Governor of Hong Kong, I returned to this border frequently to show visitors what now lay on the other side of the boundary fence, and to inspect the work of the police patrols who attempted to prevent immigrants crossing illegally into Hong Kong to find out for themselves whether its roads were really paved with gold. By now the village of Shenzhen had become a bustling Special Economic Zone, turned into a sort of suburb of Hong Kong by China's embrace of capitalism. The porcelain pictures were shattered. Now there were skyscrapers, shopping malls, discotheques, businessmen, crooks, factory workers and prostitutes – and traffic jams, too. I remember one night-time inspection visit to the border, looking across close to midnight at the blazing headlights of the traffic in Shenzhen's busy streets. It was raw, frontier capitalism – Adam Smith stir-fried by Gradgrind and Fagin.

For many China watchers, it is the transformation of Shanghai that provides the yardstick for measuring change. This is hardly a rigorous test. Periodic visits to Shanghai tell even less of China's overall development than occasional snapshots of New York or Los Angeles would tell of America's. Nevertheless, Shanghai does provide dramatic evidence of change. When I first used to visit the city in the 1980s it was difficult to recognize in the drab urban surroundings the louche, glitzy, international city of the pre-war years. It would be an exaggeration, but not much of one, to say that after 8 or 9 p.m. you could count one by one the dim electric lights in the streets. On the famous Bund, Shanghai's waterside esplanade, only the Peace Hotel and its ageing jazz band recalled the vivid past. It was never clear how these vintage musicians along with the elderly quicksteppers, the dusty worn carpets and the cut-glass whisky tumblers, had survived the Gang of Four, including Jiang Qing (Madame Mao), who had made Shanghai the stronghold of their political madness during the Cultural Revolution. Today, the city has recaptured the razzle-dazzle of the past. On a recent visit to make a programme for the BBC, we sat after dinner, Australian Cabernet Sauvignon in hand, on the roof-level terrace of our restaurant on that same Bund bathed in neon, looking across at the skyscrapers on the other side of the river in the area called Pudong. Shanghai has elbowed its confident way into the new century.

Where Shanghai blazed ahead, others now follow. In the 2000s gazing out of your hotel room in other Chinese cities, you see a sight familiar from Shanghai or my old home, Hong Kong: everywhere you look, there are cranes. On an official visit in 2001 to Xian, the city that stands at the gateway to the poor western provinces, we finished our banquet with the deputy governor of the province early, and went for a walk in the old, Moslem quarter of the city. We strolled along the broad medieval city walls, but hearing the sound of dance music from a park below, climbed down to see what was going on. In a corner of the park, with fairy lights in the trees, there was a large public dance floor, and two or three hundred Chinese kids line-dancing. The clothing labels were the same – whether or not the garments were pirated copies – as they would have been from Tokyo to Toronto: Nike trainers, Ralph Lauren polo shirts, Pepe jeans. It's less than half a lifetime since Mao suits and disciplined drudgery. At least today, even if you cannot practise politics freely in China, you have the liberty more or less to escape from politics. As Deng Xiaoping might have said, it is indeed glorious to get rich – and far, far better to line-dance than to starve.

And China *is* getting rich, though not with the inevitable accumulation of rewards assumed by so many foreigners, and by Chinese investors like my interpreter in Xian. I noticed as we drove from meeting to meeting (and from terracotta warriors to museums of magnificent Han dynasty artefacts) that he spent most of his time making calls on his mobile phone. 'What are you doing?' I asked. 'Talking to my stockbrokers,' he replied, using the plural. 'I make more money playing the market than working for the government.' 'But what happens,' I asked, 'when the market falls and you lose money.' 'You never lose money,' he replied confidently, 'investing on the stock market in China.' I hope the day never comes when he discovers this is not true. China, with its present political structure, would have great difficulty coping with a feel-good factor that turned suddenly and nastily sour.

But so far, so good for most Chinese. The number living in extreme poverty fell by 220 million in the last two decades of the twentieth century. This is substantial progress from what amounted to a ground-zero start. Less than forty years ago, 38 million Chinese died in Mao's great famine; hundreds of millions struggled to survive on a daily calorie count (itself probably exaggerated by Mao propagandists like Han Suyin) that was below the level deemed just about sufficient to sustain human life in Auschwitz. While the people starved, grain and other foodstuffs were sold abroad to buy armaments and the equipment for Mao's crackpot heavy industry projects. Resources were misallocated in what were horrendously large quantities for a poor country – in order, for example, to shift industries from their original locations to what were deemed by Mao to be more strategically defensible inland sites. He wished as much as possible of China's industrial infrastructure to survive the nuclear war that he coolly contemplated. '*Mercacciones innumeras*' ('an incalculable amount of trade'), Christopher Columbus had noted in the margins of his copy of Marco Polo's *Travels*. This has always been China's condition. It took the malign genius of Mao Tse-tung, who was probably responsible, according to the brilliant biography of him by Jung Chang and Jon Halliday (*Mao: The Unknown Story*), for over 70 million deaths, to add yet more impoverishment to the ruin caused by the civil wars of the 1930s and 40s and by the Sino-Japanese war. The full measure of Mao's wicked years of power is the speed and scale of the recovery since his own death and the beginning of the reforms boldly launched by Deng Xiaoping. When you bounce back from hell, the recovery looks all the more impressive. For some economists, the big question is not why China has done so well in the last quarter century, but why it has not done even better.

For eighteen of the last twenty centuries, China's economy has been – so far as one can make these measurements – the biggest in the world. Later in this century, it will be again, which should not come as too great a surprise given that its population is about one fifth of the world's. This growth is admirable: it has been managed without regional or global disruption; it does not look as though it is about to end; it is manifestly good for China and the rest of us; it is not something to fear but something we should hope can be sustained. As I was writing this book through the winter and spring of 2004–05, it looked as though China and the US were responsible for about half the world's recent growth – China as a result of making and selling things, the US largely as a result of borrowing (particularly from China) to buy the things that others (again particularly the Chinese) manufactured. Wal-Mart had become a larger trade partner of China than Russia or Australia. China makes two-thirds of all our photo-copiers, microwave ovens, DVD players and shoes, half of our digital cameras and two-fifths of our personal computers. The new workshop of the world, China has become the third largest exporter, and within a decade is likely to be the world's largest exporter and importer too. When I became Governor of Hong Kong in 1992, China's average tariffs stood at 41 per cent; after China joined the World Trade Organization in 2001, they fell to 6 per cent, the lowest level for any developing country. China's own market is increasingly important for its neighbours – many of its factories assemble the components it imports from other Asian countries – as well as for the rest of the world. China's economy surges ahead, leaving a clutter of superlatives in its wake, with even the starchy economists in the International Monetary Fund predicting that she will be able to continue growing at a scaled-back 7.5 per cent a year into the indefinite future, drawing on an almost unlimited supply of cheap labour and the benefits of a gradual shift in investment from the inefficient public sector to the far more dynamic private sector. Too good to be true? As usual there are those who tumble over the dividing line from rational to irrational exuberance.

This has always been the case. The potential riches of trading with China have invariably unhinged Westerners. They have been seduced by statistics that would have been impressive even without the old Chinese tradition of exaggerating them. In their book on the Sino-Japanese conflict in the 1930s, *Journey to a War*, W. H. Auden and Christopher Isherwood recorded that 'the daily news bulletin was read by Mr T. T. Li: "Of seven planes brought down by Chinese ground forces, fifteen were destroyed by infantry."' The tradition lives on. But when it comes to economic discussion, it is no longer really necessary because the story is sufficiently impressive without hype. Nevertheless, the Chinese dream is always oversold and comes smothered in snake oil. I do not particularly blame the Chinese for this, or at least I share out the criticism in equal portions. A Chinese official once explained to Jonathan Mirsky, the distinguished American journalist and sinologist, why Mao's China in the 1970s was so enthusiastically and so incorrectly misreported in the West. 'We wanted to deceive you,' he said, 'but you wanted to be deceived.'

The best account of the results of mindless China frenzy is *The China Dream* by Joe Studwell, the editor of the *China Economic Quarterly*. He notes how many of the great warlords of Western capitalism made fools of themselves and sometimes lost the collars and sleeves of their shirts by leaving their usual commercial criteria and commonsense at home when they set out, great corporate visionaries, to take China by storm. McDonnell Douglas, General Motors, Daimler-Benz, General Electric and AT&T, are a few of the giants who bear the scars associated with being a sino-visionary. Studwell is particularly good at picking apart the meagre commercial results of the 'showbiz' tours to China made by Western political leaders with ever-growing regiments of businessmen. In Hong Kong I usually saw their entry to or exit from China. I counted them in and I counted them out, along with the huge figures they claimed for new business. Germans, French, Canadians, British, Americans – they came and went with presidents, prime ministers and trade ministers leading the pack. Very few people – a few tiresome journalists on *The Asian Wall Street Journal* and commentators like Mr Studwell – ever asked what happened to all these alleged deals. The answer was – not much. Studwell concludes: 'Even with state-supported exports at fire-sale prices, it is unlikely that a quarter of the $40 billion of deals signed on government-to-government trade missions in the mid 1990s ever went ahead.' The most significant sales on a commercial basis were aircraft, which the Chinese bought because they needed them not because they were doing political favours to anyone. However, they still made as much as they could out of playing off Boeing purchases against those of the European Airbus. None of the major deals allegedly agreed in $12 billion of memoranda signed by American missions to China at this time ever came to anything. On his first 'showbiz' trip to China, American Commerce Secretary Ron Brown claimed to have netted $6 billion of business. An official at the American Embassy in China told Studwell that the actual business resulting from this visit added up to about $10 million.

The main British business delegations to China, while I was Governor of Hong Kong, were led by the Trade and Industry Minister, or President of the Board of Trade, to give him his full Churchillian title, Michael Heseltine. I am a big fan of 'Hezza', as the tabloids call him. His career is a justification for having politicians running things rather than civil servants; he makes a difference and gets things to happen. He is a man for the big gesture, and is much more often right than wrong. His commitment to urban renewal in Liverpool and elsewhere after the city riots of the Thatcher years was morally right and politically effective. There is an unashamed dash and even, when necessary, corniness about him that makes him a formidable political performer, and any squeamishness about his showmanship is relieved by the sense he conveys that he, like you, knows it is all a bit of an act. I always admired three other things about him. First, he is as brave as a lion. Second, he has an enviable ability to master a great department of state without getting bogged down by the work. He followed me in 1990 for his second stint as environment secretary. I had found it a grindingly tough job, regularly doing four or five hours of paperwork after returning from the House of Commons or an official dinner as late as ten o'clock at night. Most weekends brought about ten hours of departmental paper with them. Michael Heseltine ran the department extremely well, without ever taking home more than the odd piece of paper. He mastered the big issues and despatched business without any apparent effort. Third, he has what was used to describe the outside cultural interests of politicians like Roy Jenkins and Denis Healey, a hinterland. He knows a great deal about horticulture, especially trees, and is a birdwatcher, every bit as avid as Kenneth Clarke.

Just about the only issue on which we have ever been in disagreement was Hong Kong and China. The difference of view was not acrimonious; he was open and above board about his opinions. He thought what I was doing in Hong Kong was wrong and was bad for British business prospects in China, though as I pointed out in *East and West* there was no objective evidence of this. Our trade with China increased during my governorship. Anyway, in 1996 Michael Heseltine led his second trade mission to China and announced that he and his wife would depart through Hong Kong where he would spend a weekend with the governor and his family. He arrived radiant with sino-frenzy, and I spent the whole of an otherwise delightful weekend, during which we walked in the New Territories, identified exotic trees and shrubs, spotted birds and bought antiques, dreading the moment when Michael would give me a piece of his mind. Nothing happened until Sunday evening. After dinner he said to me, 'Do you think we could have a quiet word tomorrow morning?' 'Sure,' I agreed, and was duly taken aside by him after breakfast. 'Let's go outside,' he said to me, leading me out on to a terrace that proudly displayed a collection of ancient bonsai trees. 'Look,' he said, 'I hope you won't take this personally, but there's one thing I've got to say to you as a friend.' I waited nervously. 'You're not,' he said, gesticulating towards them, 'pruning those bonsais properly.'

Will the China boom continue? There are plenty of reasons for caution. Corruption exacts its own tax, consuming – according to some estimates – between 10 and 20 per cent of the country's gross domestic product. Misgovernment is widespread, with environmental degradation (for example, desertification) and public protests over municipal housing, the loss of jobs and arbitrary local taxes. Failed and failing state enterprises gobble up investment, leading to the politicization of credit and an incipient banking crisis. There is a huge overhang of bad debts. Regulation is non-existent or haphazard, with rampant fraud, counterfeiting, and smuggling. How in these circumstances can e-commerce or credit cards be developed? There is widespread tax evasion and capital flight. Overseas investors, who pour their money into China, extract only the same returns from these huge commitments as they receive in aggregate from much smaller investments in South Korea and Taiwan. Investing in China is not like winning the lottery. And for all the spectacular growth figures, China remains much poorer than the West in terms of income per head, even when you base the calculations on the lower costs of the services that people sell one another domestically, such as haircuts, transport fares or restaurant meals.

Despite all this, the Chinese economy keeps thundering away, and there is plenty of good news on the other side of the balance sheet. With 60 per cent of the population still living in the countryside, China has access to much more cheap labour whenever she needs it. As the state sector shrinks, the private sector, which is growing about twice as fast as the rest of the economy, will be able to attract more of the resources available for investment. The more efficient allocation of capital should boost productivity. China's economy is more open to trade and investment than most others, with exports and imports making up 75 per cent of GDP against an average of 30 per cent for comparable countries. *The Economist* magazine calculates that if China grows at about 8 per cent a year, and income distribution remains the same, by 2020 the top 100 million households in China will have an average income equivalent to the current average in Europe. This will represent a huge middle-class market for the sort of consumer goods made in Europe and America, though increasingly Asians design, make and sell these products themselves. In Singapore I recently saw a brand of Asian malt whisky called 'Matisse'. Whisky, not cognac. Branding in this case clearly demonstrates the sort of cross-cultural myopia that would encourage Samuel Huntington to reach for his laptop.

At the end of his book on Western advisers in China, *The China Helpers*, which takes us from the Jesuit missionaries of the seventeenth century to the Soviet military advisers who gave early assistance to China's nuclear ambitions, Jonathan Spence argues that for China the time for turning to outsiders for help is over. He concludes: 'Chinese advisers have begun to compete in many areas with advisers from the West, seeking to provide the validity of a Chinese world view through the sophistication of Chinese expertise. The battle has been joined. China, which once surpassed the West, then almost succumbed to it now offers to the world her own solutions.' The book was first published in 1969, and it did look then to some observers as if China, even in the middle of the Cultural Revolution, had a new model of austere socialism to offer the world. We now know what this amounted to and the suffering and hardship it produced. So what happened? For all the talk about Chinese characteristics and socialist trappings, China bought into capitalism – into all its virtues and all its vices – so that the Communist regime could survive, but also (to be fair) so that the people could prosper and make the most of their formidable energies and aptitudes. A Confucian society that had espoused one Western ideology, dreamed up by a German Jew in Europe, now turned to another that we in the West like to claim as our own, even though its principles are everywhere valid and its practices everywhere more benign than any known alternative. How should we now react to China's capitalist conversion and its results?

There is a Chinese saying for every eventuality. As I left Hong Kong in 1997 in the pouring rain, I heard my smartest diplomatic adviser telling a group of Western journalists that there was an old Chinese adage: 'When a great man leaves, the heavens weep.' Challenged by me to admit that he had made it up, he stood his ground but looked sheepish about it. My own preferred approach in present circumstances would go far beyond another – real – Chinese saying: 'What you can't avoid, welcome.' China's economic progress is good, not bad, for America, Europe and the rest of the world. It has lowered the price we have to pay for many of the goods we buy (look at the 30 per cent reduction in real terms over 10 years in the cost of clothing and shoes in the US); it has created a bigger market for our own goods; it has provided a motor for regional and global growth. The only present economic threat China poses is to low-paid uncompetitive jobs in the West. Why do so many Western politicians seek to preserve badly paid jobs for other people, rather than vote for the funds to retrain them for much better paid jobs? No politician that I have ever met wants to work in a badly paid job himself.

Recent protectionist squawks in the West have been directed at the surge in China's textile exports following the end of the global quota regimes at the beginning of 2005, and these protests have also been linked to grumbles about the unfair advantages Chinese exports enjoy because of her undervalued currency. We always knew that the end of quotas would lead to a surge in Chinese clothing exports; we prepared gingerly for this outcome, dismantling protection too late and too slowly. We have not given China a good lesson in the virtues of free trade. As for the currency, it is worth recalling that China's maintenance of currency stability during the East Asian financial crisis of 1997–98 helped to abate the effects of that crash and to assist the recovery from it. I doubt whether any likely revaluation of China's currency will make much difference to the economy's competitiveness in global markets.

Overall, China's economic recovery has not disrupted the world's economic progress but enhanced it. Would we have preferred it if China had continued poor and backward? Where problems arise they should be dealt with not by trying to contain or harry China, but by seeking to involve her constructively in global economic management. Russia (which would not have qualified on economic grounds) was added to the G7 as a sop for wounded nationalist pride and as a reward for abandoning totalitarianism for an abbreviated form of democracy. Russia will even chair the G8 in 2006. Frankly, Russia – despite her energy riches – is not going to make much difference to our economic futures. But China will. Even if we wish to retain the democratic credentials for membership of the rich countries' G8 club, we should be looking for ways to involve China (and perhaps India, Brazil and South Africa) more formally in its economic discussions.

Some of China's neighbours regard her rise nervously as a real or at best a potential threat. They worry that like nineteenth-century Germany, she may be just too big and powerful for her own continent. Japan has watched the Chinese economy grow from one twentieth the size of her own in 1980 to a quarter of the size today. She observes nervously the development of China's navy, and China's ambitions to explore for oil in seas where Japan, too, feels it has proprietary interests. For its part, Russia notes that while its own Far East territories lose people and industry, neighbouring Chinese regions boom and prosper. Is China a threat to its neighbours, and to the only global superpower, the United States?

Nothing will prevent China having a huge impact on the coming century. Whether or not that is for good or ill will partly depend on how the rest of us handle her and help shape her global role. We will have to do a lot better than the superpowers of the past. Russia manipulated Chinese politics and conflicts with the primary intention of containing Japan and installing a puppet regime in China. The puppet outgrew and outlasted the string pullers in Moscow. The US followed messy involvement in China's civil war with containment of the country she was accused by McCarthyites of losing from the ranks of the free world. Nixon and Kissinger wisely restored relations, although the degree of their infatuation with Mao Tse-tung and his subaltern in tyranny, Chou En-lai, was as unnecessary as it was abject.

An unhealthy growth of belligerent nationalism – seen most notably in the anti-Japanese riots that were tolerated, and even encouraged, in 2005 – is probably the main reason for concern about China. This nationalism is partly a result of the historic distrust and animosity between China and Japan. China's criticism of Japan is understandable, as anyone who has visited the memorial in Nanjing to the Chinese civilians slaughtered by Japan in 1937 would surely agree. Japan's apology for its war record in Asia has never been as generous and wholehearted as Germany's in Europe, and some Japanese diplomats still question whether criticism of their behaviour in China is wholly justified. For the record, it is. Japan's nationalist Foreign Minister, Taro Aso, has argued that 'it is extremely difficult to have the same kind of understanding of history'. The difficulty is indeed extreme when some of a country's politicians are in denial about its past. But China should beware allowing in her own country the growth of the sort of aggressive nationalism that set Japan off on its own militaristic path in the pre-war years. That nationalist sentiment also endangers cool thinking in China about how to handle Taiwan. America and Europe have to discourage Taiwan from provoking the mainland, for internal domestic reasons, through flirtations with the symbols of sovereign independence. On her side, China had better understand that, while it may not be a point that can be explicitly conceded, Taiwan's political reunion with the mainland (following on the deepening of economic relations) will have to await political change in China. Chinese leaders should not fool themselves that better equipped armed forces and (by 2020) the possession of more than one hundred long-range missiles will bring the happy fulfilment of their national dream.

The best way of encouraging China to behave responsibly, and of discouraging the deliberate stoking-up of nationalist sentiment as an alternative to the sort of quasi-moral fervour that Communism used to inspire, is to treat China as a responsible partner and to draw her into multilateral relationships and the growing network of inter-national rules and regulations. This is exactly what we did with the negotiation of Chinese accession to the World Trade Organization. We shall need to treat China (and India) in a similar way if, as I shall argue in the final chapter, we are to defuse one of the continent's greatest security challenges – North Korea – and deal with the broader issue of which Pyongyang's behaviour is merely the most strident example, as well as tackling other global problems.

My own relationship with China and Chinese officials when I was Governor of Hong Kong was the subject of much comment and indeed some amusement as a result of the imaginative use of the riches of the Chinese language to denounce me. Much of this invective was presumably motivated by the old Chinese strategem of killing the chicken to frighten the monkeys. But the chicken was neither killed nor spit-roasted, and emerged two years after my departure from Hong Kong as the European commissioner responsible for external relations, including those with China. From that moment on, Chinese officials behaved impeccably towards me, giving me considerable 'face' as they would say, rolling out red carpets and generally showing their most generous and genial side. I have inevitably mused about the reasons for this, trying not to kid myself that there had been an instantaneous conversion to my virtues, nor believing – since I went on saying much the same things – that Chinese courtesy had bought me off when it came to talking about democracy or human rights. First, Chinese behaviour was very professional; their senior officials are invariably much more sensible than the advice they get, for instance, from business supporters. They were more likely to serve their own interests by trying to get along with me than by ostracizing me. The Chinese take a long and practised view. In Hong Kong I had been doing my job. They knew exactly where they stood with me, even if they did not like what I did and the way I did it. On the other hand, I suspect that when I left they concluded that they had not been very well advised on what I was up to and on how to handle me. Hong Kong was stable and rich. We had not looted the colony before our departure nor sailed off in *Britannia* with the silver teaspoons. They assumed sovereignty over a splendidly successful city. Second, I think they recognized that whatever my views on democracy and human rights (which they knew well and were to get to know even better) I had an almost obsessive interest in their country, believed it would shape all our futures, and wanted my own country and Europe to have the best possible relationship with China. The first time that I met a senior Chinese official after I became a European commissioner, he said to me in English, 'Pang Ting-hong' – my Cantonese name – 'this time we should cooperate.' 'Agreed,' I replied, 'but that is what I would like to have been able to do last time!'

My semi-formal pardon for past crimes came a few months after I arrived in Brussels. The then Chinese Foreign Minister Tang Jiaxuan came to see me. Like his successor Li Zhaoxing, he was a cheerful and experienced diplomat. He sat down at the large table in my office and looked up at a line of photographs of my daughters on the wall. 'How come,' he enquired, 'such beautiful daughters have such an ugly father?' 'The Minister is telling a joke,' the Chinese ambassador said quickly. Minister Tang went on from his opening crack to tell me that senior leaders – he read this sentence out carefully from his brief – had concluded that I was 'an element of concord not of discord'. So there it was: not just remission but a pardon. While I was a commissioner, I saw President Jiang Zemin several times (after one of these meetings, his interpreter asked if I would sign a copy of my book *East and West* for him) and met his successor, Hu Jintao.

I was lucky to be dealing with China at a time when Europe's relationship with her was developing strongly. This partly reflected the fact that continuing European integration – the launch of the single currency, the broadening of the single market, enlargement – fitted into China's world view, in which there are several poles of influence not simply one hegemon: not a very surprising idea if you represent over a fifth of humanity. I sometimes felt when I met Chinese visitors that they seemed to believe more strongly in Europe's world role than we did ourselves. They certainly took resolutions from the European Parliament almost as seriously as the European Parliament did. We produced two sensible strategy documents during my years as a commissioner. They drew cordial and thoughtful responses from the Chinese side. We became increasingly important trade and investment partners, and developed close working contacts in many other areas – the environment, education, research, economic regulation, transport, satellite development, combating illegal immigration and so on. We worked assiduously – particularly Trade Commissioner Pascal Lamy – to secure China's entry into the WTO. An annual summit with Chinese leaders kept an eye on the progress of this burgeoning relationship. I recall a state guesthouse meeting in Beijing with Jiang Zemin that had been planned for rather too close to the hour at which my colleagues arrived on an overnight flight. I was fortunate to have flown in the day before. We sat in the usual horseshoe-shaped arrangement of white antimacassar-covered chairs, the lidded mugs of tea on the small tables beside each of us constantly replenished from large vacuum flasks. The room was hot; the night flight had been long; and I suddenly realized that I was the only member of the European party who was awake. Jiang Zemin and I had an interesting discussion about Shakespeare. I recommended that he should read the history plays, which underlined the importance of political stability. He nodded with interest.

Not everything was harmonious. We had strong disagreements about human rights, and it often fell to me at our regular meetings with the Chinese government to set out our criticisms of China's record. We had agreed with the Chinese that we should have a separate dialogue between experts on human rights, which we supported with programmes for training judges, developing democracy at the village level, and funding some civil society NGO activities, for instance on the environment. The dialogue was courteous enough but it did not really make much progress, a point that we would raise from time to time with our Chinese colleagues. The exchanges could become quite boisterous, especially with any of the Chinese leaders who were prepared to depart from their script. After a meeting in Copenhagen at which the formidably impressive Chinese Premier Zhu Rongji led the

NOT QUITE THE DIPLOMAT

Chinese team, we had a vigorous debate about capital punishment. The Premier and I traded the sort of arguments that I have not heard since I used to discuss such questions with my constituents in Bath.

I usually got the job as well – though it was really a matter for the member states – to set out the EU's views on the continued relevance of the arms embargo that had been first imposed after the Tiananmen killings in 1989. This did not come up at every meeting, but when it did, the Chinese position was always the same, expressed firmly though not with table-banging passion. It went as follows. We had different interpretations of Tiananmen. In any event, things had moved on since then. China had changed: a new generation of leaders was coming to the top. China did not want the embargo relaxed in order to make huge new arms purchases; it wanted this so as to end a humiliating situation in which it was placed in the same category as Burma and Sudan. This was an affront to China's dignity. When I replied, my line was usually to say that we understood the Chinese position; that even if we were to drop the embargo, there was still a code of conduct on arms sales that would restrict them; and that, while we were not suggesting that there was any linkage, it would help us to persuade opinion formers in Europe that we should look at this situation again, if China were to ratify the UN International Covenant on Civil and Political Rights and take other measures that we had been pressing on them in the human rights field, such as allowing Red Cross visits to China's prisons. Then we would move on. I think I am sufficiently experienced in negotiating with Chinese officials to know the difference between an issue on which they feel strongly and one that will help determine the whole relationship. Arms sales fell into the former category; attitudes to Taiwan into the latter. When I opened a strictly commercial office in Taiwan to deal with some of the problems associated with their entry to the WTO, as well as to handle our commercial interests in what was Europe's third-largest Asian market, I took elaborate care to explain this position very carefully to Chinese officials, and there was no protest.

So that was the situation on this issue at the end of 2003, until the Schröder-Chirac duo sought – initially successfully – to railroad through the Council of Ministers a change in policy. On a commercial visit to China, during which he was heavily promoting German exports, Chancellor Schröder announced that in his view the arms embargo was out of date and should be dropped. At the European Council meeting of heads of state or government shortly afterwards, President Chirac raised the issue himself – after initially trying to get Romano Prodi to do so. Since the whole Council had voted to take a common position to impose the embargo, it required a decision in Council to drop it. Chirac wanted an early decision that he could announce during the state visit that President Hu Jintao was to make to France at the end of January 2004. He was unable to get the quick announcement he wanted, but other governments – including the British – seemed prepared to go along with dropping the embargo, provided we could point to a more transparent and effective code of conduct restricting the sale of arms where they might, for instance, be used for internal repression or could contribute to regional instability. Greater transparency about arms sales did not attract as much enthusiasm from the French as dropping the embargo.

As the months rolled past, as we gave a good working demonstration of how not to conduct a European foreign policy, and as meetings of experts went round and round the same old arguments, it became increasingly clear that, while dropping the embargo might lead to a modest further warming of the relationship with China, it was likely to lead to a sharp deterioration in Europe's relationship with America (a much bigger market for arms sales than China) and in particular our relationship with Congress, where Europe seemed to be living up to its reputation for cynical shopkeeper diplomacy. In addition, European arms production is heavily dependent on America as most defence companies are now transnational (and mainly US) conglomerates. Europe is especially dependent on the import of high-tech components whose flow to us would be threatened if the US believed that they would make their way to China.

America's hands on this whole issue are not entirely clean. According to calculations made by the Friedrich Ebert Foundation, 6.7 per cent of China's arms imports come at present from America as against only 2.7 per cent from Europe. Moreover, American Humvees – the armed troop carriers familiar from news footage from Iraq – are actually made in China for the People's Liberation Army. But to be fair to America, the worry was not about low-tech equipment.

Washington was more concerned about the sort of high-tech exports that could assist in the digital warfare of the future. Here there was another issue, however, that America seemed to be ignoring. The second largest arms seller to China (after Russia) is Israel, which reverse engineers the technology it gets from America (for example, in fighter planes and helicopters) and sells it on to its clients, who include China, Cambodia and Burma. When an American surveillance plane was forced down by F8 fighters over China in 2001, photographs of the incident showed they were carrying Israeli-built Python 3 missiles under their wings. China itself has a profitable arms trade – for example, selling missiles and launchers to Iran. America will presumably wish to take a more comprehensive look at the issue of arms sales than simply to stamp its feet in response to Europe. After all, this is a good area for international agreements.

Nevertheless, the European position did appear irresponsible and short-sighted, not only to America but also to other Asian countries, like Japan and Taiwan, especially when China maladroitly passed legislation authorizing the use of force to counter any Taiwanese assertion of independent sovereign statehood. It is America, not Europe, that guarantees stability in Asia, and America therefore deserves to be properly consulted about any policy change. The arguments adduced publicly for the new policy were confused and even absurd. On the one hand, it was said the policy shift would not lead to any increase in arms sales; it might even lead to a reduction. Yet according to French Defence Minister Michele Alliot-Marie, if Europe sold arms to China, this would avoid China manufacturing arms herself. This argument could, I suppose, be used to justify selling nuclear technology and missiles to North Korea. European references to the need to respond to China's hurt dignity were clearly a weaker motive for the policy than the assumption that going along with China on this would lead to more European exports, starting with Airbus. There is no evidence that China does business on a basis any different from everyone else; it seeks the best product at the best price. The fact that it goes on hinting that friendship and compliance with Chinese positions can lead to big, fat contracts is a tribute to Western (including American) gullibility. We cannot blame the Chinese for this. If we *so* regularly behave like suckers, why shouldn't they treat us like suckers?

During the course of 2005 this whole wretched arms embargo saga slipped and slithered into European attempts to backtrack on to more defensible ground, returning with such dignity as we could muster to the position to which we had adhered before the Schröder-Chirac initiative. To drop the embargo, it is now said once more, will require a significant Chinese gesture in the human rights field and agreement on a transparent code of conduct. We came full circle, back to where we had started. In the course of this policy ramble, Europe has lost face with China, America and Asia. Europe cannot conduct its relationship with China on the basis of ill-judged commercial aspirations. We need to talk to America about China, and to China about America, and to encourage these great countries to talk to each other. It is important to work at convincing Washington that China should not be regarded as a strategic threat, but as a crucial partner. If the arms embargo rumpus has damaged our credibility on China in America, we will have done her no favours.

The greatest peril we face is not how we can cope with China's continuing success, but what we do if China gets into difficulties. The most troubling prospect is the mismanagement of the political change that will at some time inevitably follow the sweeping economic and social changes in the country. Some still argue that it is misguided to think that China can become democratic and pluralist. But history does not suggest that Confucianism is inherently hostile to freedom, any more than it supports the notion that Christianity always favours it. For much of the first half of the last century, following Sun Yat-sen's democratic revolution, China debated and even from time to time practised democracy before Mao slammed the door shut on it. He did this because he was a tyrant, not because he was Confucian. Taiwan today is Chinese, Confucian and noisily democratic. An even more pessimistic argument asserts that recent Chinese experience – division, warlordism, civil war – has left the Chinese twisting and turning between the alternatives of stability with servility on the one hand, or instability plain and simple on the other. So it is said that China needs an emperor with a strong hand, even if having one makes it more difficult for China to join the modern world. Reports today of wide-spread rural and urban protest against social inequity and arbitrary misrule do not lead one to believe that China (under its modern emperor) is very stable, but at the very least suggest that China's condition is one of stable unrest. Moreover, where technology was once thought to entrench totalitarian rule, today it liberates the individual. Over 250 million Chinese have mobile phones and more than 70 million are regular Internet users. Even blocking some of the most politically sensitive websites, and inveigling the owners of search engines like Google and Yahoo (to their shame) to practise self-censorship, cannot give the government the total control over access to information that it once enjoyed. The handling of the SARS virus epidemic was one indicator of the incapacity of even an authoritarian state to write its own story and to cope with modern menaces without greater transparency, so too was the exposure of the lies and cover-ups surrounding the spill of toxic benzene that poisoned the water supply in the city of Harbin.

China – like other authoritarian regimes in recent years in Asia – shows that it is possible to develop an economy without democracy. But I doubt whether you can sustain a modern economy for long without democracy and its principal fixtures and fittings – pluralism and the rule of law. A tightly controlled and inflexible political system does not create an environment conducive to innovation and creativity. It is to our own academic and commercial benefit in the West that so many of China's brightest scientists and entrepreneurs come to America and Europe to study, work and register companies. For all China's professed interest in creating a legal system that will be regarded as fair and predictable by foreign investors and companies, it is well-nigh impossible to do this so long as the law is still regarded as one of the Communist Party's main instruments of control. The authority of the government still depends in part on public anxiety about exactly where the limits of an admittedly enhanced personal freedom lie. How much can the individual write, or think, or say without overstepping an invisible line? This is the phenomenon described by the American sinologist Perry Link as 'the anaconda in the chandelier'.

On a visit to China in 2002, I was invited to speak to the Central Party School. 'What would you like me to speak about?' I enquired. The reply came back that the cadres (whose then school president is now China's president, Hu Jintao) would like me to give my thoughts on politics in a post-ideological age. This seemed rather a Blairite, New Labour-ish sort of subject, but I nevertheless sought to oblige. I tried to argue, with perhaps an excess of subtlety, that globalization was one of the factors that was breaking down the old divisions between the politics of the individual and the politics of the State, between choice and the market rather than command economics, between pluralism and authoritarianism, between right and left. But at the same time, as it narrowed the ground over which the political battle was customarily waged, it also asserted its own tested orthodoxies about what was most likely to sustain economic development and to guarantee stability. We were slowly but surely – East and West – moving towards similar approaches to good governance. By my own standards, I was cautious and even tortuous, but I think I must have got across what I was trying to say, because the first question was about how greater government openness could help deal with corruption and money-laundering.

Chinese leaders are wholly correct when they say in response to criticism that life has got far better for their citizens and that they do enjoy more freedom than was even recently the case. They also point at Western failings and double standards. But none of this remotely justifies the continuing widespread abuse of human rights – the imprisonment of dissidents, the incontinent use of capital punishment, the persecution of religious groups and sects, the treatment of Tibet. The real threat to the regime from Falun Gong was not its beliefs, which appear to embrace traditional Chinese views on breathing exercises and pretty harmless generalizations about the condition of humanity. What worried China's leaders was waking up one morning to find thousands of the sect's followers sat outside the leadership compound, without anyone in that leadership knowing in advance that it was going to happen or understanding how it could possibly have happened. Where were the security services and the police? How could this sect mushroom and organize without the State's knowledge? At a meeting with European leaders, when we quizzed Prime Minister Zhu Rongji about his government's handling of the Falun Gong, he expressed his frustration at trying to deal with them. He said that he had taken the trouble (the political risk as well, probably, given the story of Zhao Ziyang's visit to the student demonstrators in Tiananmen) to go out and try to talk to some of the crowd. They were not open to reason, he said. But what sort of reason is it that tries to deny individuals the right to believe what they want? And what is the alternative belief system offered by the Communist Party in China today? Whatever else it may be, it is not Communism. Its main philosophical refrain is little more profound than the old soldiers' ditty: 'We're here, because we're here, because we're here, because we're here.'

How much do China's leaders understand the need to change? Is change something they can manage smoothly, or will they face – as Tocqueville noted of the *ancien régime* before the French Revolution – the maximum danger of instability at precisely the moment that they try to loosen the screws? Can they simply manage their way through a continuing period of controlled turbulence, juggling so many awful problems at the same time without anything clattering to the ground, thanks to a continuing, growth-induced feel-good factor?

There is undoubtedly a good deal of debate in today's China about how change might be managed – building, for example, on the experiments in democratic village governance and in extending the choice offered among party candidates for official positions. Early hopes, however, that President Hu Jintao might prove a closet reformer have borne no fruit, perhaps not wholly surprising given his stint as party secretary in Tibet in the late 1980s, which concluded with the imposition of martial law in Lhasa. To be fair he has on the whole been judicious in his decisions on foreign policy and has shown a commendable concern about rural poverty and the environment. But he has also cracked down on the media, religion, the Internet and all forms of dissent. The view of party leaders appears at best to assume that China can change the way the system works without changing the system itself. This is almost certainly impossible. Until attempts are made to change not only the way the way the system works but the system itself, there is a continuing and growing danger that when change inevitably comes it will be massively disruptive.

India is the world's largest and in some respects greatest democracy. It does not appear to face the sort of seismic shift that threatens China.

India is poorer than China – enjoying only half China's national income per head at the beginning of the century – and her growth rate is lower. Her population on the other hand is growing faster than China's and she will outstrip China in size during the course of this century. India's economic performance – what has been called the sluggish Hindu rate of growth – is sometimes deemed to be a consequence of her pluralism. It is said to be the price that India pays for its majestic democracy.

That is unfair and underrates just what Indian democracy has managed to achieve. Since the bloody days of the transition to independence on the subcontinent, India's political progress has been remarkable. Democracy has helped to ensure that ethnic and religious tensions have not blown the country apart. Moreover, as Professor Amartya Sen has observed, it has helped to preserve India from calamity. There has been no man-made famine such as killed tens of millions in China. There has been no cultural revolution. There has been no bamboo gulag. There has been no Mao, though there are a lot of Indian Communists who unlike their Chinese cousins appear still to believe in Communism. The problem in India has come not principally from pluralism and participative government, though admittedly the Indian political system sometimes has difficulty bringing to a decision-making end the discussions that lie at the heart of any democratic society. But the real brake on progress has been the economic policies that were for too long pursued, with socialism written into India's independence constitution.

Change began slowly under Rajiv Gandhi in the 1980s and then moved ahead more rapidly in response to a foreign exchange crisis in the 1990s. With Manmohan Singh as finance minister (he is now, thanks to Sonia Gandhi's statesmanship, prime minister), India took the first steps to abandon what was called the 'licence raj' scrapping over-regulation and controls and opening up the economy. This liberalization has further to go and India still suffers from too many of the relics of a centralized socialist economy. There is insufficient investment in the infrastructure and in telecommunications. The manufacturing sector is too weak. But growth has picked up; real incomes per head rose by about 50 per cent in the 1990s; there was a fall in the number of the very poor; and the middle class – described as the 'consuming class' by Indian statisticians and numbered at about 150 million – is growing fast. India is moving from the bullock cart to the motorbike to the car.

The Indian economy has not been held back by democracy but by fiscal mismanagement, corruption and a history of overprotection. Where India has been able to get over these impediments – for example, in information technology, software and services – it is doing extremely well. Bangalore is home to over 300 software companies and 150 high-tech multinationals. One hundred and thirty of the Fortune 500 companies have offices in the state of Karnataka, India's science capital. Yet India remains worried about China's relatively better performance measured, for example, by the amount of foreign investment both countries attract. It is still true that many Western businessmen overfly India on their way to invest in China. The figures that suggest a twelve-fold Chinese advantage exaggerate the position, largely ignoring the investments in India by her diaspora and including the 'round-tripping' through Hong Kong by Chinese investors. India has not, however, yet triggered anything like the enthusiastic interest engendered by China's performance. Greater economic liberalization should in time focus more international attention on the advantages of investing money in a democracy under the rule of law where there are institutional safety valves to cope with crises and where that famous playing field really is flat.

The Indian Defence Minister George Fernandes suggested in 1998 that his country's development of its own nuclear weapons was not prompted by worries about Pakistan, with the Kashmir dispute still proving a drain on both countries' resources, but by concern about China. India has certainly had a difficult relationship with China, with a sharp military defeat in the border dispute more than forty years ago, and with the worry today that India is being encircled by Chinese influence in Bangladesh, Pakistan, Nepal, Burma and even Sri Lanka. For everyone else's peace of mind, and in their own political and economic interest, it is important that India and China establish a harmonious relationship. They should be dynamo economies in the twenty-first century, and major players in regional and global governance.

*

India and China are inevitably much cited in the debate about the relationship between political and economic freedom. I recall the wise remark of Margaret Thatcher when she was once asked during a visit to China which came first, political liberty or economic freedom. She replied that it did not necessarily matter which one you started with, since you would inescapably finish up with both. There is, however, one Chinese community where there is no democracy but a free economy, and indeed a broader liberty that goes well beyond the ability to make money doing whatever you wish within the law. That community is Hong Kong, the only place I have ever been able to identify that is liberal but not (alas) democratic.

The modest democratic progress made, albeit far too late in the day, in response to the promises to Hong Kong's citizens in the Joint Declaration signed by Britain and China, were partly and predictably rolled back after 1997. Apart from that, a continuing adamantine refusal to countenance greater democracy, and one or two cack-handed interventions in the legal and political affairs of the community, China appears to have resisted the temptation to meddle constantly in Hong Kong's affairs – at least until recently. Hong Kong has not been politically lobotomized; its high degree of autonomy has been clipped but not suppressed. Hong Kong remains one of the freest cities in Asia, with a resilient economy that has survived and recovered from the Asian crash, and an equally resilient citizenry.

Nearly a decade after the handover, no one can dispute that Hong Kong also retains its sense of citizenship; it is the only Chinese city to have one, sustained by a vigorous civil society, strong professions and clean and efficient public services. Chinese leaders seem reluctant to relax and to recognize that they have nothing to fear from Hong Kong's moderate political ambitions. If China's leaders were to learn to trust Hong Kong, it would be an important step on the road towards managing with wisdom, sophistication and the prospect of a successful outcome the political transition that China herself will one day surely have to make. We all have a stake in the smooth attainment of that venture. As in political so in economic matters, we will all benefit from a China that succeeds and be damaged by a China that fails.

11

An Education to the World

'I don't know what you're talking about, about international law. I've got to consult my lawyer.'

Interview with President George W. Bush, 2003

Back to the beginning.

At school with the Benedictines in leafy suburban London, most of the clever boys were pushed into the classics stream: Latin, Greek and ancient history, at least until Ordinary Level examinations at the age of fifteen. We were taught the history of the classical world by a Cambridge graduate with a West Country burr, a penchant for turning every subject into a tripartite list (pretexts, causes, results), and a passion for Thucydides. So we, of course, had to read his great history of the thirty-year Peloponnesian war, the fracticidal struggle between Greek city states that began with the Athenian empire ruling the seas and ended with its terrible defeat by grim Sparta.

The war exemplified what Thucydides at the time, and Plato and Aristotle in the long, sad aftermath, regarded as the central evil of politics – namely the abuse of public power. A key and disastrous event on Athens' road to defeat was the sack of Melos. The Athenians attempted to bully the Melians into switching sides from Sparta to them; the Melians declined to do so; they were besieged and captured, the men slaughtered, the women and children sold into slavery. Thucydides records in detail the dialogue between the Athenian envoys and the Melians that took place before the atrocity. The representatives of mighty Athens, flexing their muscles, tell those of weak

Melos to recognize reality. First, they should understand a dictate of
nature:

Our opinion of the gods and our knowledge of men lead us to conclude that
it is a general and necessary law of nature to rule whatever one can. This is
not a law that we made ourselves, nor were we the first to act upon it when
it was made. We found it already in existence, and we shall leave it to exist
for ever among those who come after us. We are merely acting in accordance
with it, and we know that you or anybody else with the same power as ours
would be acting in precisely the same way.

Second, the Athenians give the Melians a sharp lesson in the meaning
of justice:

We recommend that you should try to get what it is possible for you to get,
taking into consideration what we both really do think; since you know as
well as we do that, when these matters are discussed by practical people, the
standard of justice depends on the equality of power to compel and that in
fact the strong do what they have the power to do and the weak accept what
they have to accept.

Until recently, America has not acted like the Athenians. Indeed,
American global authority for almost a century has been rooted in an
understanding of the lessons of that dialogue and of its consequences,
which explains why the rest of the world has on the whole accepted
that in the American age there is a difference between ascendancy and
intimidation. America has not stamped its foot and expected the rest
of the world to tremble. The ideas of President Wilson, and the actions
of Presidents Roosevelt, Truman and their successors, have shaped an
international order largely in America's image. It has been marked by
three developments. First, there has been the end of colonial empires
and the triumph of self-determination. At the Paris Peace Conference
in 1919, a young Vietnamese kitchen worker at the Ritz hotel sent a
petition to Wilson asking for self-determination for his country. Half
a century later, having defeated the French colonial power and the
American superpower, Ho Chi Minh got what he wanted, though
he interpreted the 'self' in self-determination rather too literally for
democratic tastes. Overall, however, we did see – as the second decisive theme of the twentieth century – the progress on every continent

of democracy and a greater respect for human rights. 'The world,' Wilson said, 'must be made safe for democracy.' To which G. K. Chesterton responded, 'The world cannot be made safe for democracy, it is a dangerous trade.' So it has proved, in the Congo for example, and in Chile, yet the advance of democracy has by and large brought the benefits of better government, greater prosperity and order to most countries. America has intervened directly again and again to promote democratic progress. Just looking back over the past two decades, the US played a big part in bringing democracy to Taiwan, South Korea, the countries of central and eastern Europe, and of the Balkans, exerted economic and diplomatic pressures on repressive regimes like South Africa, and in the 1980s alone stopped military coups in Bolivia, Peru, El Salvador, Honduras and the Philippines.

From the end of the Second World War, America tried to alchemize its own sense of constitutionalism, due process and civil liberties into a rule book for the whole world. Eleanor Roosevelt, the president's widow, led the efforts to agree the Universal Declaration of Human Rights, which in 1948 promoted the values enshrined in the US Constitution. 'We wanted as many nations as possible,' she said, 'to accept the fact that men, for one reason or another, were born free and equal in dignity and rights, that they were endowed with reason and conscience and should act towards one another in a spirit of Brotherhood.'

Third, the last half-century saw the victory of capitalism and the opening of national markets under rules that most obeyed. So the twentieth century ended as it had begun, with surging trade – albeit with too many unfair restrictions on the economic activities of today's Melians, the poorer, weaker countries.

US military power has been deployed to secure freedom and, in much of the world, stability. In western Europe, American missiles and soldiers guarded the democracies against Soviet advance. In east Asia, where the absence of the sort of reconciliation between Japan and China that Europe witnessed between Germany and France has denied the continent an equivalent geopolitical stability, the American fleet has helped to keep the peace. But just as important for the superpower has been the sense in other parts of the world that its awesome might was a force for good. Resentment, envy and anger at what America represents and what it does have usually been overwhelmed by a stronger sense that, for all its mistakes and imperfections, America really is 'the city on a hill', to whose standards most aspire and whose values most admire. This is at the heart of what is called 'soft power', America's weapon of mass attraction.

Soft power has many components – economic, cultural, political, military and educational. The last of these is hugely influential and (if public spending priorities are any guide) equally greatly underrated in Europe. America is not only the city on a hill, it has most of the campuses on the hill. Look at any league table of the world's greatest research universities and it is dominated by America with Europe a poor second, threatened with being overtaken by Asia and Australia in the next couple of decades. This is largely a matter of money. America spends twice as much on research and development as Europe, both on campuses and through industrial laboratories. American universities have far higher private endowments than European ones. Only two European universities – Oxford and Cambridge – would get into the list of the top 150 American universities in terms of private benefactions, and the American taxpayers have also been more generous to research and universities than their European counterparts. One result is that American universities act like a magnet to many of the brightest and best students from around the world. This should give the US a great opportunity to inculcate its values in the next generation of academics, business leaders and politicians around the world, except of course that so many foreign-born graduates stay in America when they have finished their courses, adding to America's economic, educational, scientific and cultural wealth.

Much of this can be welcomed by Europeans. Scholarship knows no boundaries, and universities from Harvard to Stanford probably have a much more benign effect on all our futures than the Pentagon (though it does admittedly pour dollars generously into many of their research programmes). European concern should not be about what Americans do well, but about what Europeans are now doing so badly. What does our underfunding of universities and research tell us about ourselves with all our pretensions to sit around and safeguard the cradle of Western civilization? We lose some of our best minds at the moment in their academic lives when they are likely to embark on the sort of research that will win for some the accolade of a Nobel prize. Ten years ago half the European students on doctoral programmes returned home after completing them; today the figure is only a quarter. We beat our chests about our aspirations to have a more competitive economy that draws strength from pushing back the frontiers of knowledge. But we still have a European budget that favours yesterday over tomorrow, subsidies to farmers who contribute a dwindling share of our gross domestic product rather than investment in scholarship and technology. Above all, what does our collective meanness about research and universities say about us as a society? Self-confident societies invest in their futures and leave an intellectual legacy to future generations. What will *we* leave? It is possible to dig up passable excuses for the extent to which America outspends us on armaments and military power. But what possible excuse is there for the huge discrepancy in the investment in knowledge? America, Mars: Europe, Venus? Add Athena to Mars, and if you are European feel thoroughly ashamed.

A central feature of American soft power has been that the US has usually accepted that its hard power – its ability to get its own way if it wanted by virtue of its size and strength – should be constrained by a network of rules and agreements. The rules that it wished others to follow, it would follow too. Naturally, if it wanted to it could ride roughshod over the rest of us. But that is not the path America has customarily chosen. It has followed the advice of Thomas Jefferson in the Declaration of Independence, and shown 'a decent respect to the opinions of mankind'. Doing that, it has respected its own better self, and secured its own better interests, another example of where doing right is also to do the right thing.

It should not come as a surprise that the globalization of economic activities, of the prospects for betterment, and of the threats of calamity, has led to a broadening and deepening of the structure of agreements that America played the major part in assembling in the first place. The environment, the theft of other people's bright ideas, the security of investment, the opening of markets, the proliferation of weapons, the laundering of illegally acquired money – all these issues and many more have brought a growing web of rules and agreements. It is called the international rule of law. It is what protects us from the other sort of law, which would otherwise fill the growing space that globalization creates, the law of the jungle. It protects the Melians and allows the Athenians to hold on to their power without being hated for having it. It does not threaten the identity of the nation state, but it allows nation states to get on with one another, in a more harmonious and civilized way. Like domestic law, international law conserves order. Big, strong conservatives should be its greatest admirers and advocates.

Some Americans suggest that there is no need to sign up to a nebulous international rule of law to show their better face to the world; their crusading commitment to democracy should suffice to achieve this goal. But the point about the rule of law is that it applies everywhere; the fight for democracy tends, for old-fashioned reasons of realpolitik, to vary in enthusiasm and consistency from region to region and country to country. The cause itself can therefore be discredited by the perception that it is only being pursued selectively.

No one doubts that Washington today wishes to see democracy unroll across that part of western Asia that we call the Middle East. But what happens when we reach the Silk Route countries to the north of Afghanistan – Tamburlaine's stamping grounds – or Pakistan to the south? Pakistan provides a high-octane example of double standards. Democracy has had a hard time of it there. Government has tended to move, turn and turn about from Punjabi soldiers to often corrupt but elected Sindhi landowners, both ruling castes dependent on usually excellent civil servants. General Musharraf represents the latest military turn of the wheel. The streets of his capital, Islamabad, bear the names of all the appurtenances of a pluralist constitution, but the real constitution is down the road at the military cantonment in Rawalpindi. Musharraf is an impressive soldier – courteous, bright, voluble (not least when telling you things you know are not true about weapons proliferation or terrorist attacks on Kashmir). One can quite see why the American administration and many in Europe regard him as a reliable buttress against the dangers of Islamic extremism in his country. 'Après lui, le déluge.' He has supported efforts to weed out the Taliban and al-Qaeda in Afghanistan, and while we cannot overlook the fact that Pakistani military security helped to plant them there in the first place, we can perhaps allow them the excuse that at least initially they were acting as surrogates in America's efforts to tie down the Soviet Union in Afghanistan and then expel it from the country. When great powers sow bramble patches, they do not always remember that plants grow.

But whatever you say about General Musharraf, he is not a democrat. He installed himself in a military coup; under his leadership the military has infiltrated swathes of commerical life and civil society; he has flirted with elections but the nearest he has come to the real thing is to rig a referendum in his own interests. There may well be arguments for turning a blind eye to all this, as well as to the continuing disgraceful treatment of women and the inadequate efforts to replace the schools run by Islamic extremists with state-managed or controlled institutions (donors should be more helpful in this sector). But Musharraf will not last forever. A strong man will not save Pakistan from extremism, unless he is encouraged to develop strong institutions to underpin his rule. It would be better to talk to President Musharraf about participative democracy rather than sell him American F-16 fighter jets. F-16s are not going to safeguard Pakistan, however attractive the roar of their engines in the officers' mess in Rawalpindi.

Travel north and double standards become more blatant still. The central Asian republics are not an alarming accident waiting to happen but an accident that has begun to happen. They have remembered more than they have forgotten from their decades as Soviet colonies. Political repression, corruption and command economics hold them back and gnaw at their foundations. Kazakhstan is probably the most secure thanks to its huge energy resources. Elsewhere oil and gas reserves ensure Chinese and Russian support, but that is not going to defy reality. Cotton production has created terrible environmental problems, depleting the Aral Sea. In Turkmenistan, Tajikistan and Uzbekistan it has enriched small cartels of traders favoured by the government and reliant on cheap – including child – labour. Turkmenistan suffers under one of the world's most oppressive regimes, its economy mired in corruption and criminality (with evidence of official involvement in drug-trafficking) and its political system in thrall to a president whose stamp on affairs runs as far as banning gold teeth, though not gold statues of himself. Kyrgyzstan has already witnessed the overthrow of one regime, though we await evidence that its successor will be a significant improvement. Impoverished Tajikistan has recovered from a bloody civil war in 1997 but still lives uneasily with the tensions generated by the rivalries of warlords.

Uzbekistan – with a population of 25 million – is cause for the greatest worry. To the romantic names of Tashkent, Samarkand and Bukhara, we must now add the less well-known name of Andijon, the city in the east of the country where in May 2005 up to 750 mostly unarmed Uzbeks, including many children, were gunned down to end what the government mendaciously claimed was a revolt by Islamist extremists. President Islam Karimov is an unreconstructed Soviet toughie. It is quite difficult to pinpoint a redeeming feature. At a two-hour meeting with him in the spring of 2004, he did not give an inch on any of the concerns I raised with him: torture did not happen in his country; his opponents were dangerous jihadists; the economy was doing fine. Uzbekistan is what the World Bank rather coyly calls a 'low-income country under stress', which is a diplomatic way of saying that it is a failing state that could implode at any moment. Official figures seek to cover up a miserable economic performance that has seen widespread social discontent and high unemployment among the young. Opponents and critics of the regime are harassed, locked up and routinely tortured. Karimov's government drives moderate Islamists into the hands of extremists and, sadly, the West – especially America – is associated with it. These points were all made trenchantly by the last British ambassador in Uzbekistan, Craig Murray, who – whether or not it is connected – is no longer a member of the diplomatic service. Why do we take such a feeble position regarding a repressive government that plays the role of recruiting sergeant in such a dangerous part of the world? During a visit to Tashkent in February 2004, Donald Rumsfeld spelled out the reasons: 'The USA recognizes Uzbekistan as a key initiator as regards maintaining peace and stability in central Asia and all the region as a whole. It supports the country's clear-cut efforts in this direction. Relations between the two countries are aimed at achieving exactly these goals.' So Uzbekistan can go its own miserable way because it is a useful base for fighting extremism in Afghanistan. In due course, will we be using bases in Afghanistan to fight extremism in Uzbekistan?

A researcher in Bukhara cited by the International Crisis Group in one of its reports on the country, reported an Uzbek schoolteacher who told him: 'I had heard a lot about American democracy. I thought that the appearance of American troops here would change the situation for the better. Now I see that the regime has only been strengthened, and arrests and abuses only increased.' America's $300 million assistance to the government in 2002–03 largely supported a security relationship that threatens to produce long-term insecurity. Surely America should look again at its strategy in this region, alongside its European partners, who have cooperation agreements and modest assistance programmes here that achieve at present very little, though there are many meetings at which Europe tut-tuts about human rights and the lack of economic reform.

America's status as a superpower is not going to be rivalled by Europe. But Europe, if it is encouraged to act effectively, if it has the political will to do so, and if it is prepared to invest the money often required to play this role effectively, should be able to help America to act as a global leader in ways that enhance a system of global governance that suits market democracies, great and small. We have not got much time if we want to put our own stamp on this process. I wrote earlier of the re-emergence of China and India as substantial economic players in the world; their economic significance will have political consequences. They will not simply accept the West's agenda in finance, trade, the environment or security policy. What are we in Europe to do? Side with them against America, or with America against them? Or should we try to persuade both America and Asia, but first and most important our Atlantic partners, to accept a development of the multilateral system and the rule of law that will enable the older re-emerging powers to live peacefully and prosperously side by side with the more recently established powers of the West?

In most of the key areas that will determine our future safety, prosperity and well-being, China is crucial, beginning with the environment. China's economic growth has been one of the reasons for the recent rise in oil and other commodity prices, forced up by escalating demand. Today, China uses over 8 per cent of the world's oil – replacing Japan as the world's second largest consumer – and has been responsible for two-fifths of the increase in global consumption since 2000. Its oil demand has doubled in the past decade, and energy (as well as the need for other natural resources) has started to shape China's foreign and security policy. China deployed 4,000 troops in Sudan to protect an oil pipeline that it had helped to build there, and was notably reluctant to support UN sanctions against that country in response to the Darfur atrocities. China's basic manufacturing industries guzzle energy, burning today 40 per cent of all the coal burned in the world. What does all this economic development and energy use mean for the environment? At the beginning of the century, China was the second biggest emitter of carbon (according to the Pew Research Center), responsible for 14.8 per cent as against 20.6 per cent for America, 14 per cent for Europe, and 5.5 per cent for India. The emissions grow, and simple extrapolation can easily cause nightmares, even perhaps for a Texan oilman like President Bush. Take car ownership. At the moment only one Chinese citizen in every seventy has a car, compared to one in two in America. What happens as this gap is closed? How many Chinese sports utility vehicles would we be happy to see on east Asia's roads?

Together, China and India have a combined population of over 2.25 billion. As their economies surge ahead, they burn ever more fossil fuel. If we want them to do something to ensure that their *future* growth is more environmentally friendly than was the developed world's *past* growth, how can we persuade them to act differently? Is the best way of doing this for America, the world's greatest emitter of damaging gases, to tell them 'don't do as we do, but do as we say'? Or does Washington contend that the problem does not really exist, or that it is exaggerated? Is the American administration in denial? America is by a very long way the biggest emitter of greenhouse gases – per head of population as well as absolutely. The average American produces each year about 12,000 pounds of CO_2 emissions. These American emissions contribute mightily to what the UK's chief scientific adviser, Sir David King, has called a bigger threat to the world than terrorism. While a tiny minority of scientists deny the evidence, there is an overwhelming consensus – backed by a number of the main private energy companies – that the phenomenon first observed in the early nineteenth century of gases in the environment trapping heat close to the earth, has grown steadily with industrialization, and is changing our climate and threatening the survival of some communities.

The United Nations Environment Programme and the World Meteorological Organization established in 1988 the Intergovern-mental Panel on Climate Change to assess the evidence of what was happening. Their work led directly to the drafting of a convention on climate change agreed at the world's Earth Summit in Rio de Janeiro in 1992 and signed by the first President Bush. That led in turn to the negotiation of the 1997 Kyoto Protocol that committed developed countries, which have after all created most of the problems, to limit or reduce greenhouse gas emissions in a first period for 2008–12 to at least 5 per cent below the 1990 levels. During this stage of the agree-ment, developing countries are not expected to make cuts in carbon emissions, but in later stages (which still have to be negotiated) they will have to play a part in combating what is, after all, a global threat.

The threat is real and immediate. In my own city, London, the evidence grows each year. Before 1990 the barrier across the Thames below Greenwich, which prevents serious flooding of the city, used to be raised once or twice a year. The average has now risen to four times a year and is predicted to rise to thirty times a year by 2030. Indeed, it is predicted that later in the century the barrier will fail altogether. This would put Westminster under six feet of water and presumably be bad for property prices except for those living in Hampstead and Highgate. We are not unaccustomed to rain in London, but freak weather conditions (as predicted by the inter-governmental panel), brought the storms in 2004 that caused flooding and the killing of thousands of fish as 600,000 tonnes of raw sewage were discharged into the Thames. So even in my own country, global warming has started to exact a toll, with more flooding and coastal erosion forecast by the government's experts. The problems in poorer, developing countries are far greater, with warnings about health risks, the sabotaging of economic development and the extinction of species.

President Bush's broadside against the Kyoto Protocol in 2001 appeared to be based on three arguments. First, America faced an energy crisis. What crisis? Presumably the President was not referring to the badly botched deregulation of the power industry in California. If there actually is a crisis, or the makings of one, it is surely the result of America's incontinent consumption of oil. This should argue for using the price mechanism to reduce demand for a product that more than ever America has to import. It is still cheaper to fill up the tank in America than anywhere else; bottled water costs more than cans of petrol. America is a vast country; many Americans live in suburbs; public transport is bad; the car is king. So no American politician wants to make an enemy of motorists. But should not leadership consist in trying, even at the margins, to get people to be more responsible about their use of energy? And if as a conservative you believe in markets, is there any better way of doing this than through more realistic pricing? Is it now impossible for any American politician to get elected on a policy that would serve his or her country's strategic, economic and environmental interests?

Second, the President argued that if America was to reduce its emissions too sharply, growth would be cut back and the whole world would suffer. The immediate impact of Kyoto compliance on economic growth is exaggerated, but most of the rest of us have in any case started to discuss growth in terms of its sustainability. It may be that a greater present-day threat to sustainable growth in America is the heavy dependence of its economy on the savings of Chinese peasants; but a longer-term and growing threat is surely excessive dependence on fossil fuels.

Third, like other American politicians – and indeed like the government in Australia, a country that is itself a big and irresponsible energy guzzler – President Bush declined to sign up to an agreement that for the time being let developing countries off the hook. This is both curious and worrying. The notion of common but differentiated responsibilities was enshrined in the 1992 Rio treaty and passed unanimously by the American Senate. It is that principle that Kyoto repeats. We face a common threat; the developed countries have done the most to create it; the rich should bear initially the largest share of responsibility for tackling it. In time, we shall need developing countries to join the effort. That will require persuasion. How do rich countries persuade poor ones to act, if the richest country of all refuses to budge?

At this point relative politeness is strained beyond breaking point. US policy is not only selfish but foolish and self-destructive. Higher energy taxes reduce dependency on the Middle East; encourage people to start insulating their houses and businesses; promote more exploration; and help to fill the alarming revenue gap that has opened up since the Clinton era. US industry claims that there would be dire economic and employment consequences. That has not been the European experience (though we have made a good job of driving up unemployment and depressing our economies in many other ways – notably through labour market inflexibilities).

The irony is that we have had in the past to negotiate deals between developed and developing countries on the environment, which have recognized the difference in responsibilities. With America's forceful leadership we reached in the past a wholly successful conclusion. In the 1970s and 1980s, America was active and creative in environmental diplomacy. President Nixon supported the creation of an environment programme in the UN, and himself proposed the World Heritage Convention to protect areas of unique worth worldwide. In succeeding years, America was active in negotiating agreements on oceans, fisheries and endangered species. I was able myself to witness the most successful example of America's work for the environment when, as I mentioned earlier, I chaired in 1990 the London Conference that extended the provisions of the 1987 Montreal Protocol. This imposed constraints on the production and use of substances such as hairspray propellants and the chemicals in refrigerators, which were depleting the ozone layer above the earth's atmosphere. America had pressed for action and, despite scepticism and foot-dragging by several European countries, a series of tough and effective measures were demanded and taken.

The Reagan administration got Europeans to accept the so-called 'precautionary principle'. This involved action to prevent what could be serious threats – in this case hazardous rays piercing the thinned ozone layer – even when the science was not totally proven. There was, however, a problem. It was very expensive for developing countries to comply with the terms of the protocol. They needed to invest in new technologies and to buy new products. They thought it unfair that they would be penalized economically for a problem that other richer countries had been primarily responsible for creating. The Indian and Chinese ministers at our conference in London made it clear that, while recognizing that the threat we were discussing had global causes and global effects, they had no mandate to assume new burdens that would, for instance, make it more expensive for their own citizens to have a refrigerator. With America using charm, creativity, money and muscle, we drafted new rules giving India and China a period of ten years' grace to meet the targets for banning the production and use of chlorofluorocarbons and halons. We helped India and China with technology transfer and with financial assistance to enable them to comply with the protocol. It was a model of how, through sensible persuasion and generosity, to broker a global environmental agreement. No one – specifically, no Australian minister over whose country the most prominent hole in the ozone layer loomed – grumbled that the Indians and Chinese were being allowed to postpone their commitments. No American official suggested that others should combine to save the ozone layer but not them. No one argued that the world could meet its obligations through voluntary action – which is today's dangerous pitch by the Americans and Australians to India and China. No one argued that the 'precautionary principle' was too expensive, and that we should await a few hundred thousand more cases of skin cancer before we could be sure of the case for acting. What has happened to persuade America that this approach to environmental hazard is wrong?

Several American states are trying to take action on greenhouse gas emissions themselves. There are also bipartisan efforts, for example by Senators Lieberman and McCain, to build a coalition for a much stronger policy. Senator Lieberman clearly hopes that evangelical Christians may be encouraged to pray for a presidential conversion on this question. He notes wryly that, 'The earth is, after all, a faith-based initiative.' We all need a Bush conversion on the road to Delhi and Beijing. In his State of the Union speech in 2006, the President at least noted that America was too dependent on imported oil and promised greater spending on research into sustainable technologies (even while existing programmes were being cut). This was a step in the right direction, albeit a very small one. Unless America is prepared to accept its environmental responsibilities for the future, it is difficult to see how we will ever get India and China to do so.

The energy demands of India and China raise political as well as environmental issues. When I visited Kazakhstan in 2004 all the talk was about Chinese enthusiasm for building oil and gas pipelines eastwards from central Asia. The year before, in our gloomy hotel in Tehran, there were groups of visitors from India and China who were there to talk about oil and gas. Both countries have invested heavily in Iranian energy production, with the main Chinese oil and gas company – Sinopec – particularly prominent. So far as we know neither country has been sharing its nuclear military secrets with potential nuclear powers, though the Americans are suspicious about the activities in the field of weapons proliferation of some of Sinopec's subsidiaries. But there has been no suggestion of the existence of a Chinese or Indian illicit network to rival that of the Pakistani nuclear scientist Dr Abdul Qadeer Khan.

Khan's activities demonstrated one of the most important threats the world faces, requiring greater and tighter cooperation. It will of necessity heavily involve China and India. It has already been possible, as the head of the International Atomic Energy Agency (IAEA), Mohamed ElBaradei, has argued, to design nuclear components in one country, manufacture them in another, ship them through a third, and assemble them in a fourth, with the prospect of eventual turnkey use in a fifth. This threatens to destabilize our so far reasonably successful efforts to control the spread of nuclear weapons. There are three dangers ahead. First, there is the chance of a terrorist organization getting hold of a nuclear weapon; second, it is likely that other countries will develop the capacity to enrich uranium or reproduce plutonium so that they could move fast, if they wished, towards becoming military nuclear powers; third, we should aim to prevent any more countries taking this route and joining the nuclear club of eight – America, Britain, France, Russia, China, Pakistan, India and Israel. China and India will be crucial to the accomplishment of these aims, not least because of the relationship they both have with Iran, and the fraught relationship that China has with North Korea, which claims that it already has nuclear weapons and could probably set itself up quite quickly as a weapons production line for others.

For thirty years the main instrument for dealing with this problem has been the Nuclear Non-Proliferation Treaty (NPT), which came into force in 1970 and provides the global framework for preventing the spread of nuclear weapons, for stopping the development of nuclear energy for the purpose of producing weapons, and for promoting nuclear disarmament. The NPT, along with the strategic stand-off between the West and the Soviet Union, helped to avoid the worst predictions about proliferation coming true. For example, President Kennedy feared that by 1975 there could be between fifteen and twenty-five countries with nuclear weapons. We stopped that happening and, indeed, when some countries tried in the 1980s and 1990s to develop weapons in secret, intelligence, verification and diplomacy exposed their activities, and in the case of Libya and Iraq halted them in their tracks. Libya abandoned its efforts voluntarily and Iraq's programme was in effect dismantled by the IAEA in the 1990s – as their inspectors would probably have been able to confirm if given a little more time before the invasion of the country in 2003. That leaves Iran and North Korea, but forty other countries probably possess the intellectual and technical capacity to produce nuclear weapons. We depend heavily on their goodwill not to do so.

The seriousness of this issue is beyond dispute. It recalls Albert Einstein's observation: 'Since the advent of the nuclear age, everything has changed save our modes of thinking and we thus drift towards unparalleled catastrophe.' To avoid that, we need tougher international rules with more effective political backup and sanctions. It is not obvious that there is any better way of doing this than through the UN – principally the Security Council – and its specialized arm, the IAEA. We need a system that makes tough verification, to prevent clandestine activity, mandatory for every country that signs the NPT, with sanctions against non-compliance or withdrawal from the treaty. We require tighter controls over the export of sensitive material and technology. There should be limits on the production of new nuclear material through reprocessing and enrichment. We have to agree on how we can share the international responsibility for the management and disposal of spent nuclear fuel. We must get rid of the weapon-usable nuclear material that is already in existence, and we must help countries to halt the use of weapon-usable material in their civilian nuclear programmes.

Strengthening the NPT in this way would make the world a lot safer, but it also represents what much of the world regards as an unfair bargain. So long as there are as many nuclear weapons in store as there are, threats to our safety clearly remain. Moreover, the non-nuclear countries question a bargain that is framed, so far as they are concerned, almost entirely in the interests of the existing nuclear club, the N8. Why should others – Brazil, South Africa, not to mention Iran – sign up to a treaty in which all the 'give' is on their side of the table, and all the 'take' on the other? They refuse to accept that it is morally acceptable for some countries to have nuclear weapons, while others are regarded as outlaws if they wish to retain the capacity to join that club. This will not be solved by pressing for a ban on all nuclear weapons and the destruction of all stockpiles. That will simply not happen before the the the dawning of that, alas, improbable day when we base the world's security structure on our shared humanity. But the existing nuclear powers, led by America, must make *some* gestures to the others. They must be more open about the weapons they already have. They must get rid of many of them. They must verify and bring into force the Comprehensive Test Ban Treaty. They must abandon any further research and development to produce yet more advanced nuclear weapons. This last requirement is principally a matter for the United States. If we are going to draw the line more firmly and clearly around the existing possession of nuclear weapons, then the line cannot wobble and wiggle when it comes to the obligations of the N8.

It is difficult to see how the present dispute over Iran's evident determination to complete the fuel cycle and become a civil nuclear power (with, many believe, ambitions to move on to develop a military capability) can be resolved without opening up this broader issue of the overall scope of the NPT. If one wisely rules out the use of force to prevent Iran going nuclear, then the only alternative – unless we can break out of the box of present policies – is the attempt to install a sanctions regime on the basis of UN Security Council authority. It seems doubtful whether this could be made to stick with so many countries believing that the big nuclear powers are behaving unreasonably. To contain proliferation, not least in Iran, the provisions of the NPT need to be looked at again.

American interest in the rise of India and China has grown and will grow exponentially as their weight of numbers and economic size constrain America's ability as the only superpower to do what she wants, when she wants, simply by an exercise of will. There are other and better ways of asserting the primacy of the values in which America has always believed than ultimate dependence on exceptionalism: doing whatever America wishes to do because she can get away with it. As we have seen, international agreements and the rule of law offer more effective ways of guiding the international community and protecting America's interest. This is presumably what Mr Rumsfeld meant, at least in part, when he hoped and prayed that 'China enters the civilized world.' It is a slightly odd turn of phrase given what has happened in China over the last three thousand or so years. A millennium before the Periclean Golden Age in Athens preceding the Peloponnesian War, which laid that city state low, the Chinese were casting in bronze and weaving silk. I have a beautiful figure of a small sleeping dog of about that period, carved out of jade. Most of us would think that a country that could do those things was already an impressive civilization. We must assume that the American Secretary of Defense had other things in mind: the transformation of the last huge totalitarian state into a pluralist democracy; obeying the norms of what we associate with civilized behaviour at home; acting responsibly within an infrastructure of global rules and institutions abroad. How do we best secure such a transformation?

Here we arrive at the worrying consequence of current American behaviour. Around the world, America is seen more and more to contravene the principles that it enjoins others to follow. It appears too often to abjure its own ethos, to repudiate its own history. Time was when piazzas and parks, boulevards and buildings, were named after American presidents and public officials. Looking through the London street map, the A to Z Gazetteer, I can see a Roosevelt Way in Dagenham, a Truman Close in Edgware, an Eisenhower Drive in the East End and Kennedy Courts, Closes, Gardens and Houses all over the city. The same is true in other cities and other lands. Will we one day name our squares and streets after Bush, Cheney, Rumsfeld and Rice?

America was founded on the rule of law; the heart of Britain's first Atlantic empire, it broke loose from the shackles of a dynastic state partly because of what it deemed to be the illegal actions of King George III and his ministers. America's Constitution and Bill of Rights removed from the new nation state's government those features of the old world that were deemed to be unjustifiable in the new. In more recent years, as we have noted, America has been a pioneer of international agreements and the rule of law. America pressed, for example, for the establishment of war crimes tribunals in Nuremburg and Tokyo, and then supported the establishment of the tribunals to deal with the atrocities committed in Yugoslavia and Rwanda. In the countries of former Yugoslavia, America linked the provision of assistance to explicit compliance with the Hague Tribunal, and regularly pressed me and others to take an equally firm line as far as Europe was concerned. Why then has America been so hostile and obstructive towards the creation of the International Criminal Court (ICC), an institution almost fifty years in the making?

American negotiators participated in the drafting of the statute that establishes a court to deal with war crimes, genocide, crimes against humanity and gross violations of human rights. The final outcome met some, though not all, of America's concerns: the ICC will only act if national authorities have failed to do so themselves; there are safeguards to prevent rogue prosecutions. But America did not secure the right of permanent members of the UN Security Council to veto investigations. This was a curious aim for America to assert given that it has always criticized the scope within the ICC for politicizing international justice, a point which also sits oddly with the politicization of judicial appointments in America. The Bush administration has not only refused to have anything to do with the court, (with the exception, as we have noted, of the agreement not to veto sending Sudanese war criminals to it), but has campaigned actively to obstruct its establishment and undermine its ability to operate. In particular, the United States has pressed other countries to sign what amount to bilateral immunity agreements, under which these countries undertake not to surrender any American national to the court without American approval. Many of those who decline to endorse such agreements lose military aid as a result.

This issue triggered some of the most heated arguments between America and Europe during my years at the European Commission. In the summer of 2002, one of the German commissioners, Günter Verheugen (responsible for our enlargement negotiations), and I heard that Washington was putting great pressure on the candidate countries – for example, Poland and the Baltic States – as well as the putative candidates in the Balkans to sign immunity agreements. This was unacceptable to us. The EU had been a strong supporter of the establishment of the ICC; we had worked for years to achieve its creation; we helped to fund organizations that themselves acted as advocates for the court. Europe had adopted a common position on this. Countries that wanted to join us should recognize that we had a clear policy and should not be bullied into taking a line hostile to that of organizations of which they hoped to become a member in 2004. Romania – a candidate for later EU membership in 2007 – had buckled to American pressure by the time we heard what was going on. But we set out clearly for other countries exactly what the EU line was, and undertook to give them detailed legal advice on what sort of deals they could negotiate on this issue with America without in our view being in breach of the agreement they had all signed to set up the ICC and prescribe its jurisdiction. We just managed to hold the line, but not without some bruising telephone conversations with normally more affable colleagues in the State Department, who must have been under strong pressure from elsewhere in Washington. I recall setting off on holiday in July, and getting three calls from Washington on this subject within the space of the drive from Brussels to Charles de Gaulle airport in Paris. It was one of many occasions when I have cursed the existence of mobile phones.

Of course, it is legitimate for the world's superpower, so often called on to stand in the front line to keep the peace, to prevent vexatious legal actions launched for political reasons against its soldiers, diplomats and leaders. The statute that establishes the court appears to others to provide such guarantees. They are sufficient to satisfy Britain and France, for example. The court does not have jurisdiction over wars of aggression, which is an issue left to be decided on the day, probably just this side of the Greek Kalends, when a common definition of aggression can be agreed. There is also more than a hint of double standards – indeed, they parade in dress uniform, bands playing and flags flying – about pressing international jurisdiction on Serbs and Croats but denying its legitimacy, even theoretically, for Americans.

This really is all about being able to get away with it, and to most of the world it does not look as though America wants to do this because it is different from and better than others, but because it is all too similar to the rest of fallen humanity. That is the heavy price that America pays for Guantánamo Bay, Abu Ghraib, equivocation over torture, and exporting suspects in secret so that others can torture them. There was a time when America might have been excused for saying, 'We won't sign up to all these international norms because we don't need to. The rest of you do; so sign on the dotted line.' No longer. It is not that America behaves worse than others in similar circumstances. Look at the record of Britain and France, as colonial powers. Recent allegations of British abuse of human rights in colonial pre-independence Kenya during the Mau Mau emergency reminds us that our own colonial record has a seamy, unsavoury side. Torture and murder during the last years of French colonial rule in Algeria divided France then and still do today. The violence, the murder and the abuse of human rights extended to the streets of Paris with, for example, the savage repression of demonstrators there in 1961–62. So we in Europe even in the post-war years could ourselves say with Thomas Jefferson, 'I tremble for my country when I reflect that God is just.' But the public discovery that such scorching self-criticism has recently been so relevant to America's behaviour too does not buttress the case that America should be above the international rule of law.

What have we witnessed? There was the deliberate creation of a legal black hole down which 650 terrorist suspects were dropped in Guantánamo Bay. For how long will this legal outrage continue and how will it be ended? It has been condemned by human rights organizations, international jurists and the Secretary-General of the UN; more circumspectly, a generous word in the circumstances, Mr Blair has said 'it's an anomaly and sooner or later has got to be dealt with'. Meanwhile, the anomalous cells in no-man's land remain occupied. On top of this, were the awful degrading pictures from Abu Ghraib revealing porno-sadistic practices for which no one could be held responsible above the lowest ranks of the lumpen military. There was the logic-chopping, morality-mincing debate about what constitutes torture and how America could evade the explicit provisions of the Geneva Convention. Was it really torture to keep a suspect's head under water or to slip needles beneath his nails? Could hooding, the denial of painkillers to the injured, beatings and sleep deprivation not be justified? Was not the president in his role as commander-in-chief of America's military entitled to place himself above the quaint prohib-itions of international law? Surely if an interrogator's primary purpose was trying to obtain information, not to cause pain, he could apply the pincers wherever he wanted? For me, it was this cool, bureaucratic argument about an issue that has been at the heart of almost every human rights agreement that caused most offence and, to be frank, surprise. I simply did not believe that America could behave like this – the America to whose lawyers, human rights organizations and politicians I tried to justify the investigative methods, transparency and conclusions of my police enquiry in Northern Ireland. We fought terrorism in the UK. Spain fought terrorism in Madrid and Bilbao. We knew that our democracies had to fight terrorism with one hand tied behind our backs, because that was the only way in the long run we would win, because to act otherwise was to obliterate the moral gap between the state and the terrorists, because to behave like the terrorists was to deny all that we thought we were and wished to be. And who stood for that most resolutely, proudly, persuasively, openly in the world? America. But perhaps that was then.

America surely wants to help create a world again where her embassies do not all have to be replicas of Fort Apache. She must want to shrink the distance between the Statue of Liberty and how she behaves around the world. She should want the whole world as her friend and not much of it as a sullen vassal. She should be reminded to put her faith again in the sort of global order that she created over fifty years ago and will only abandon to her lasting cost – and to our cost as well, in Europe as in other continents. For it remains the case, in the words of General John Shalikashvili (former chairman of the Joint Chiefs of Staff) that without American leadership 'things still don't get put together right'. If Europe can only forget its prejudices and introverted preoccupations, it should see the importance of working to help America put things together in the right way. That sort of partnership should help restore American faith in her better self, in international cooperation and in the rule of law for all of us.

In 1994, the Bodleian Library in Oxford published a pamphlet first issued by the United States War Department in 1942. It had been prepared for the American servicemen who were going to Britain to prepare for the invasion of occupied Europe. As the librarian of Rhodes House (where the original copy is held) has written, it is a ' "snapshot" of wartime Britain, as seen by a sympathetic outsider'. I was particularly struck by the good sense of some of the important do's and don'ts that the pamphlet lists:

Be friendly – but don't intrude anywhere it seems you are not wanted . . . Don't show off or brag or bluster – 'swank' as the British say. If somebody looks in your direction and says 'He's chucking his weight about' you can be pretty sure you're off base. That's the time to pull in your ears . . . By your conduct you have great power to bring about a better understanding between the two countries . . .

It puts me in mind of the history book with which I began this chapter. Some time before Thucydides records the debate between the overbearing Athenian envoys and the Melians, he reports the famous funeral oration that Pericles gave at the end of the first year in that long war, which was to destroy the supremacy both of Athens and of those virtues with which Pericles was identified. The speech probably reflects what Thucydides thought Pericles should have said and would have meant rather than what he actually declaimed. It is trenchant, powerful, eloquent and relevant – to Athens then and to today's great power. Once the bones of the Athenian dead had been laid in their burial place, on the most beautiful approach to the walls of the city, Pericles mounted a high platform and addressed the mourners proclaiming the virtues of his city, a democracy in which he argued that everyone was equal before the law. Athens was a model for others to follow, he claimed. 'I declare that our city is an education to Greece.'

For so much of my lifetime America has been an education to the world – to every nation, every continent and every civilization. It has been a living lesson, a paradigm to which others could aspire, an example for others to follow. I hope that Europe can help America to be that again. When it is, it will not be America that triumphs but the ideas that, until recently, America has unequivocally represented. Then the century ahead would not be America's as was the last one. It would belong to mankind. It would be a century dominated by the values that American history enshrines and that American leadership at its best embodies and defends without bragging or blustering: democracy, pluralism, enterprise and the rule of law.

Index

United States of America, The
(White House) 112–13, 246
NATO: *see* North Atlantic Treaty
Organisation (NATO)
Naughtie, James 112
Naumann, Michael 40
Negroponte, John 184
Neighbourhood Policy 144–5
neo-realism 256
neoconservatives 241–3, 252–3
Netherlands 33, 131–2, 135, 141, 221,
228, 261
New York 9–10
New Zealand 47
Newman, Randy 214–15
Nicholson, Harold 214
Niebuhr, Reinhold 218
Nigeria 249
Nixon, Richard 276, 302
Nobel Prize 54
non-governmental organizations
(NGOs), aid programmes 169–70
North American Free Trade Agreement
(NAFTA) 228
North Atlantic Treaty Organisation
(NATO) 29, 64, 99, 153, 175, 232,
259
North Korea 177–8, 240, 304–5, 305
North Sea 19–20
Northern Ireland 12–13, 72, 98, 170,
219, 311
Norway 84, 139, 261
Nour, Ayman 201
Nuclear Non-Proliferation Treaty
(NPT) 305–7
nuclear weapons 97, 304–7
Nye, Joseph 230

Oakeshott, Michael 41, 58, 70
Oates, Captain Lawrence Edward
Grace 39
oil 190, 208–9, 298–9
Olympic Games, 2012 104
O'Reilly, Bill 255
Organization for Economic
Cooperation and Development
(OECD) 128, 262
organized crime 158, 173

Ormsby-Gore, David 87
Orwell, George 38
Osborne, John 46
Oslo Peace Process 200
Out of America (Richburg) 248
Over Here (Seitz) 91
ozone depletion 302–3

Pakistan 185, 288, 295–6
Palestine 167, 180, 185, 191, 192,
196–202
Palestinian Authority, the 158–9
Paris Peace Conference, 1919 291
Partners in Prosperity (Hamilton and
Quinlan) 228
Patriots (Weight) 99–100
Patten, Chris: in Addis Ababa 38–9; at
Balliol College 6–8; birth 2; as
candidate for EU presidency 26–7;
Catholicism 4; as Chairman of
Independent Commission on Policing
in Northern Ireland 12, 13;
childhood 3–4; conservative beliefs
221–4, 226; as Conservative Party
Chairman 22–3; Coolidge
scholarship American tour 8–10; as
Director of Conservative Research
Department 16; early European
influences 5–6; early political views
7–8; education 290; enthusiasm for
American empire 2; as Environment
Secretary 11, 18–20, 21, 271; Euro-
Mediterranean partnership
negotiations 192–5; as European
commissioner 23–4, 31, 84, 126,
128, 133, 229, 279–80; as European
commissioner for External Relations
152–3, 157–8, 159–60, 161, 166,
175; family background 2–3; family
holidays 6; family life 5–6; first
experience of working in Brussels
17–18; foreign policy note 159; and
France 52; as Governor of Hong
Kong 14, 58–60, 266, 272, 274,
277–8; infected with politics 9–10;
joins Conservative Research
Department 10–11; and the Kennedy
assassination 7; loses parliamentary

325

PENGUIN HISTORY

THE NEW PENGUIN HISTORY OF THE WORLD
J. M. ROBERTS

A book of breathtaking range by the pre-eminent giant-scale historian of our age. One of the most extraordinary history bestsellers on the Penguin list, John Roberts's book has now been completely updated to the end of the last century and revised throughout to make sure it keeps its amazing appeal to a new generation of readers. The entire text has been overhauled to take account of the great range of discoveries that have changed our views on early civilizations and to bring it fully up-to-date. The book has also been completely redesigned and reset. The result is a book that is both an essential work of reference for anyone with the slightest historical interest and a great reading experience.

'A stupendous achievement – the unrivalled World History for our day. It extends over all ages and all continents. It covers the forgotten experiences of ordinary people as well as chronicling the acts of those in power. It is unbelievably accurate in its facts and almost incontestable in its judgements'
A. J. P. Taylor, *Observer*

'A work of outstanding breadth of scholarship and penetrating judgements. There is nothing better of its kind' Jonathan Sumption, *Sunday Telegraph*

'This is a book I would like to put into the hands of anyone interested in the past' Alan Bullock

'Anyone who wants an outline grasp of history, the core of all subjects, can grasp it here' *Economist*

PENGUIN POLITICS

GLOBALIZATION AND ITS DISCONTENTS
JOSEPH STIGLITZ

'A massively important political as well as economic document … we should listen to him urgently' Will Hutton, *Guardian*

Our world is changing. Globalization is not working. It is hurting those it was meant to help. And now, the tide is turning …

Explosive and shocking, *Globalization and Its Discontents* is the bestselling exposé of the all-powerful organizations that control our lives – from the man who has seen them at work first hand.

As Chief Economist at the World Bank, Nobel Prize-winner Joseph Stiglitz had a unique insider's view into the management of globalization. Now he speaks out against it: how the IMF and WTO preach fair trade yet impose crippling economic policies on developing nations; how free market 'shock therapy' made millions in East Asia and Russia worse off than they were before; and how the West has driven the global agenda to further its own financial interests.

Globalization *can* still be a force for good, Stiglitz argues. But the balance of power has to change. Here he offers real, tough solutions for the future.

'Compelling … This book is everyone's guide to the misgovernment of globalization' J. K. Galbraith

'Stiglitz is a rare breed, an heretical economist who has ruffled the self-satisfied global establishment that once fed him. *Globalization and Its Discontents* declares war on the entire Washington financial and economic establishment' Ian Fraser, *Sunday Tribune*

'Gripping … this landmark book … shows him to be a worthy successor to Keynes' Robin Blackburn, *Independent*

PENGUIN POLITICS

FREE WORLD: WHY A CRISIS OF THE WEST REVEALS THE OPPORTUNITY OF OUR TIME
TIMOTHY GARTON ASH

'A compelling manifesto for the enlargement of freedom and a new era of world politics' Vaclav Havel

At the beginning of the twenty-first century, the world plunged into crisis. What began as an attack on the West by Osama bin Laden soon became a dramatic confrontation between Europe and America.

Britain has found itself painfully split, because it stands with one foot across the Atlantic and the other across the Channel. The English, in particular, are divided politically between a Right that argues our place is with America, not Europe, and a Left that claims the opposite. This is today's English civil war. Both sides tell us we must choose. In this powerful new work, Timothy Garton Ash, one of our leading political writers, explains why we cannot, need not and must not choose between Europe and America.

Drawing on an extraordinary range of sources, from unique conversations with leaders such as Bush, Blair and Schröder, to encounters with farmers in Kansas and soldiers in Aldershot, from history, memoir and opinion polls to personal observations based on a quarter-century of travelling in Europe and the US, he demolishes the popular claim that Americans are from Mars and Europeans are from Venus. He shows why Washington can never rule the world on its own, why the new, enlarged Europe can only realise its aspirations in a larger, transatlantic community, and why the torments of the Middle East and the developing world can only be addressed by working together. To remain true to itself, the West must go beyond itself.

In fact, this crisis reveals a historic opportunity for free people everywhere to advance together from the cold war West to a new international order of liberty. Defying conventional wisdom and eschewing easy answers, this timely, provocative book should be read not just by those who purport to lead and inform us, but by anyone who wishes to be a citizen of a free world.

PENGUIN HISTORY

**THE PRESIDENTS: THE TRANSFORMATION OF THE AMERICAN
PRESIDENCY FROM THEODORE ROOSEVELT TO GEORGE W. BUSH**
STEPHEN GRAUBARD

The Presidents is a magnificent history of the men who have held the world's
most powerful elective office over the twentieth century – their personalities,
administrations, achievements, crises and legacies.

Stephen Graubard gives a candid assessment of each president, ranging from
brilliant reformer Franklin D. Roosevelt to JFK and the myth of Camelot; from
duplicitous 'Tricky Dick' Nixon to populist anti-communist warrior Reagan; from
the charismatic Clinton to neo-imperialist George W. Bush. Examining each one
in turn, Graubard asks: what political capital did they bring to the White House,
and how was it used? How did they cope with crises, both domestic and foreign?
What innovations was each responsible for? What was their legislative
achievement? How were they perceived when they were in power, and how are
they viewed today? His answers are informed, convincing and often surprising,
revealing each president in a sharp new light.

The Presidents also explores how the role of the presidential office itself was
transformed in the course of the century – through military force, the influence of
money and media, the increase in bureaucracy and espionage – and asks: has the
presidency now become too powerful? But Graubard also argues why in thinking
about these leaders we must avoid both uncritical praise and the search for evil
that characterizes so much contemporary writing about American politics.

This book is essential reading for anyone seeking to understand the transformation
of American power in the twentieth century, and how it arrived at the
overwhelmingly dominant position it occupies today.

PENGUIN HISTORY

DARK CONTINENT: EUROPE'S TWENTIETH CENTURY
MARK MAZOWER

'Brilliant but disturbing ... his controversial thesis is bound to stir debate ... this superb book is a frightening reminder of how fragile democracy has been' Orlando Figes, *The Times*

'Mazower has comprehended the whole of European history in this century, suggested a convincing explanation of its evolution, and constructed a text every undergraduate will find on his reading list well into the next ... He also leaves us, in this wonderful book, with an account of our century that anyone who takes an interest in Europe's present and future will enlarge their mind by reading' John Keegan, *Daily Telegraph*

'They are few who can walk with A J P Taylor. One is Mark Mazower. *Dark Continent* is *The Struggle for Mastery in Europe* for a new generation ... a tour de force' Alex Danchev, *TES*

'Combines narrative verve with wise and humane analysis. For anyone who wants to know how Europe came to be the way it is in the years since 1900, this is the work to provide the answers' David Cannadine, *Observer*, Books of the Year

PENGUIN HISTORY

**THE GERMAN TRAUMA: EXPERIENCES AND REFLECTIONS
1938–2001**
GITTA SERENY

'Uniquely searching, vivid and judicious ... a better book on its subject can
scarcely be imagined' Ben Rogers, *Financial Times*

'Unputdownable ... Sereny herself leaps from the page as thoughtful, non-
judgemental and courageous' Mary Wesley, *Daily Telegraph*, Books of the Year

As a schoolgirl, Gitta Sereny was captivated by the theatrical spectacle of a
Nuremberg Rally. Later, when the Nazis marched into Vienna, the spell was
quickly broken when she saw an eminent Jewish doctor forced to scrub the
pavement by Nazi thugs. The war years forged Sereny's lifelong fascination with
Hitler's Germany and the indelible mark it made on the twentieth century. In this
book of 'experiences and reflections' she threads fragments of her own life into
her larger quest to understand what it is 'that leads human beings so often and so
readily to embrace violence and amorality'.

'The book plunges us into a dark and unpromising jungle of war criminals,
hoaxers, deniers and Nazi sympathizers ... She is a marvellous combination of
historian, investigator and priest ... [with] the energy and commitment to keep on
in the face of denial, excavating layer upon layer of self-deception and evasion'
Mark Mazower, *The Times*

'She never absolves evildoers, but lets us hear them ...The rewards of her
sleuthing include revealing interviews with the former Austrian president Kurt
Waldheim, and with the propagandist film-maker Leni Riefenstahl. There is an
intriguing new twist to the Hitler diaries scam. Most haunting of all is her prison-
cell profile of Franz Stangl, commandant of the Treblinka death camp'
William Cook, *New Statesman*

'Sereny is, surely, our stellar investigative journalist' George Steiner, *Observer*

PENGUIN POLITICS

THE RIGHT NATION: WHY AMERICA IS DIFFERENT
JOHN MICKLETHWAIT & ADRIAN WOOLDRIDGE

'Conservatism's 40-year climb to dominance receives an examination worthy of its complexity in *The Right Nation*, the best political book in years' George Will, *Washington Post*

What makes America seem so different from the rest of the world? *The Right Nation* **is the definitive portrait of a United States that few outsiders understand: the nation that votes for George Bush, that supports the death penalty and gun rights, that believes in minimal government and long prison sentences, that pulled out of the Kyoto Protocol.**

America, argue John Micklethwait and Adrian Wooldridge, award-winning journalists at the *Economist*, has always been a conservative country; but over the past fifty years it has built up a radical conservative movement unlike any other. The authors examine how these right-wing radicals took over the Republican Party, and deconstruct the Bush White House, examining its many influences from neo-conservatism to sun-belt entrepreneurialism. Their quest to understand the mindset of the overlooked and often disdained, but crucial, Middle America takes them from young churchgoers in Colorado Springs to gay gun clubs in Massachusetts to black supporters of school vouchers in Milwaukee.

The Right Nation drives to the heart of a question that is relevant to us all: why is America – increasingly, and often frighteningly – different, and what does this mean for the world?

'A remarkable achievement … *The Right Nation* is authoritative, entertaining and astonishing in its breadth and objectivity. It can perhaps make claim to an extraordinary boast as the best book on modern America in print'
Graham Stewart, *Spectator*

PENGUIN HISTORY

REFORMATION: EUROPE'S HOUSE DIVIDED
DIARMAID MacCULLOCH

Winner of the Wolfson History Prize and the British Academy Book Prize

'Magisterial and eloquent' David Starkey

'Monumental … *Reformation* is set to become a landmark' Lisa Jardine, *Observer*

'A triumph of human sympathy' Blair Worden, *Sunday Telegraph*

'From politics to witchcraft, from the liturgy to sex; the sweep of European history covered here is breathtakingly panoramic. This is a model work of history' Noel Malcolm, *Sunday Telegraph*, Books of the Year

At a time when men and women were prepared to kill – and be killed – for their faith, the reformation tore the western world apart. Acclaimed as the definitive account of these epochal events, Diarmaid MacCulloch's history brilliantly re-creates the religious battles of priests, monarchs, scholars and politicians, from the zealous Luther to the radical Loyola, from the tortured Cranmer to the ambitious Philip II.

Weaving together the many strands of reformation and counter-reformation, ranging widely across Europe and even to the New World, MacCulloch also reveals as never before how these upheavals affected everyday lives – overturning ideas of love, sex, death and the supernatural, and shaping the modern age.

'A masterpiece of readable scholarship … In its field it is the best book ever written' David L. Edwards, *Guardian*

'A historical *tour de force*… breathtaking' Daniel Johnson, *Daily Telegraph*